PASSION, INTRIGUE, TRIUMPH!

Beginning at the close of a tumultuous century of rebellion, and surging forward through the magnificent reign of Victoria, FAUNA is the enthralling epic of three generations of women that sweeps from Jamaican slaver's coves to dazzling London ballrooms and private royal chambers.

It is the story of a woman with a past—Fauna, whose beauty was beyond words, whose life was sold below the deck of a slaveship, and whose love reached across time to touch her child and grandchild . . . but could not save them from the family legacy that began so long ago in the jungles of the dark continent.

Other Avon Books by
Denise Robins

FAUNA

DENISE ROBINS

AVON
PUBLISHERS OF BARD, CAMELOT AND DISCUS BOOKS

AVON BOOKS
A division of
The Hearst Corporation
959 Eighth Avenue
New York, New York 10019

Published by arrangement with the author.
Library of Congress Catalog Card Number: 78-56423
ISBN: 0-380-37580-X

First Avon Printing, July, 1978

Printed in the U.S.A.

CONTENTS

BOOK ONE

Gold for the Gay Masters

PART I

Chapter One

Captain Humbleby of *The Nauticas* was drunk, very drunk. He had need to be. He had entered the tavern known as The Three Spaniards just before midday when his ship docked at Jamaica. The hell-ship. "The devil-ship" thus designated by the Master himself, groaning under its load of fearful human freight—a batch of new slaves from Africa.

From midday until now, eight o'clock at night, Captain Humbleby had consumed vast quantities of liquor. In the mucky, foetid atmosphere of The Three Spaniards on the quayside, he had tried to shut out the devils that danced in his imagination; the horrid thought that seventy-five per cent of his appalling human cargo had died before *The Nauticas* ever reached the West Indies.

The sweet, heavy wine that Captain Humbleby had poured down his throat had for the first hour or two made him a cheerful and rollicking figure whom none would recognize as the tough gentleman who terrorized his crew and kept law and order with the whip lash or a pair of cocked pistols. A man who walked perpetually with the stench of death in his nostrils and in his ears the unholy music composed of the groans and screams of the tortured slaves. A merry gentleman for a time this Samuel Humbleby with his rollicking laugh, a wench under each arm, and a huge appetite which a half-Spanish, half-native landlord had willingly satisfied. These seafaring men who put in at the West Indies had money to burn and it burned merrily and with many an obscene jest inside the four walls of The Three Spaniards this day.

But by nightfall Captain Humbleby was not so merry. He had thrust the half-naked wenches from him and lapsed into sullen silence. He had one blind eye. The good one, fierce and yellow with jaundice, glared so malevolently at those who endeavoured to rouse him from his stupor that he had been left severely alone.

The trouble was that Humbleby had a conscience. Only a small one but there were moments when it jabbed at him and reminded him that there was a Life Hereafter and an Almighty to be reckoned with. Someone who might not approve of Captain Samuel Humbleby's methods of moneymaking. Fortunately for him that conscience only awoke when he was very drunk indeed. The owner of *The Nauticas* and of several other trading vessels was a millionaire. For fifteen years Captain Humbleby had sailed ships for that very exclusive company. During those years over one hundred thousand Negroes had been exported from Africa and brought in *The Nauticas* alone to the West Indies.

As a younger man, Humbleby had disliked the methods of procuring these slaves, although with the years he had toughened and paid small heed to the cruelty and suffering. The pay was excellent. Mr. Rufus Panjaw, ship owner of Bristol, was to be relied upon. Captain Humbleby had had no need to complain of his treatment while he was with the firm.

But things were not like they were, and just now Captain Humbleby regarded his profession somewhat uneasily. Back in England, six years ago in fact, ever since Mr. Wilberforce introduced the Bill to put an end to the importation of slaves, there had been a growing feeling against slave trading in the country. There was Mr. Fox with his precious party of Whigs, labouring for the Bill even now. Captain Humbleby did not like it. He did not like it at all. And most of all he disliked the conditions under which he had been forced to sail when he brought this last load to Jamaica from the African coast.

He could ease his conscience by the fact that he had told Mr. Panjaw that the "damned black creatures" had no stamina and they could not stand the hellish heat in the holds. The long weeks of the sweltering confinement. The sickness and the misery. And Panjaw's orders were "Carry on." What could Samuel Humbleby do but obey his employer?

Nevertheless the animal noises issuing from the bowels

of *The Nauticas* had begun to unnerve Captain Humbleby and *this time*, horrid fact—seventy-five per cent of the wretches had died.

Captain Humbleby staggered along the quayside. His straight greasy locks hung, like a Mexican's, in strands to his neck. He was indescribably dirty, his uniform stained with spilt drink and food. He held his tricorn hat under his arm, and he swore and growled under his breath as he made his way back to his ship on this hot humid night.

Through the vapours, the stars looked down upon Captain Humbleby like large reproachful eyes and he avoided looking back at them. He was suffering from lumbago. And he had had a tussle with one of those yellow-skinned saucy wenches which had caused a lot of laughter in the tavern, but increased Captain Humbleby's physical discomforts. To the devil with women! He would give up wenching. He would give up the sea and slave trading. He would return to Bristol and live quietly with Emily, his wife. A good woman Emily. Albeit she had a sharp tongue and was scarce the kind a man craved to tumble in his bed.

Captain Humbleby endeavoured to raise his drooping spirits by singing:

"*God Save Our Gracious King. . . .*"

Alas, poor King George III—tainted with madness. A terrible thing, madness, reflected Captain Humbleby. He had visited one of the houses where they confined the dismal wretches and heard their screaming and squawking.

Fearfully, his good eye made out a blurred outline of ships. He listened a moment to the yelling of a group of half-naked seamen hanging around a pile of timber waiting to be shipped to England. Maybe *he* would go mad, he reflected, if he continued with this poisonous trading of black men and this drinking.

He sniffed and spat. A nauseous odour drifted from the docks. A beautiful, poisonous place, Jamaica. He hated it. The sea was a dark purple. The coco palms were pencilled black against the sky. The miasma in Captain Humbleby's brain cleared a little and he fell to thinking of something strange—very strange—that had just happened on *The Nauticas*. A discovery made by one of the officers serving under him shortly before they sighted land this morning.

The First Mate was an Irishman and a Papist. Captain Humbleby was not partial to Papists, but Larry O'Sullivan was good at his job and loyal, and a man was in need of loyalty in these days of threatened mutiny.

Up to the Captain's cabin had come O'Sullivan with his eyes popping out of his head, saying:

"By all that's holy, Captain, these two blue eyes have just witnessed that which Larry O'Sullivan never expected to see on this devil-ship or any other ship that sails the ocean waves."

"And what might that be, dammit?" Captain Humbleby had asked.

O'Sullivan had taken him along to his cabin. There crouching on the bunk was a sight which the Master of *The Nauticas* had found astonishing, albeit he had long since thought himself incapable of being surprised.

There in the stuffy cabin on dirty blankets sat a child. A girl of ten or eleven years old maybe, very small and thin, and wearing a yard or two of blue cotton material swathed like a cummerbund about her. It revealed a good deal of her slender immaturity; her long fine legs and arms, her naked shoulders. But what staggered Captain Humbleby was the face of this apparition. For although it was streaked with tears and dirty, with curls in a wild tangle and verminous, the face was of such fabulous beauty that even he who had no great appreciation of such things, could not fail to be impressed. Her eyes were enormous—native eyes black, with immensely long lashes and full of that melancholy that Captain Humbleby had seen a thousand times before in the faces of most of the female slaves from Africa. Eyes full of suffering and sorrow, mutely appealing against the indignities imposed upon ebony flesh by white traders who broke up their villages and pillaged their homes for the sake of gold. The kind of eyes that haunted Captain Humbleby when he was in a state of intoxication.

But at this moment when O'Sullivan took him to see this extraordinary and unexpected passenger, Captain Humbleby was quite sober. His one jaundiced eye stared, flabbergasted, at the little girl—flabbergasted because her skin was not black as one would have expected with such eyes but ivory pale. *And the hair was fair.* Those filthy tangled curls were a bright red-gold. Her wrists and ankles were as delicate and fine as those belonging to any lady whom Captain Humbleby had ever seen back home in England.

He uttered an oath:

"Who the devil is she? Where did she come from?" he demanded.

O'Sullivan—a huge man yellow-haired and bearded and a man of religion, despite the fact that he was one of a crew on a vessel bound on barbarous trade—crossed himself.

"The Holy Mother knows I only came upon her by chance less than an hour ago."

"Explain!" roared Captain Humbleby.

Hurriedly O'Sullivan told his tale. Soon after sighting land, and when he had been making a round in the hold with one of the sentries who guarded the gang of slaves, he had come upon an old dying man. A fine-looking Negro of aristocratic mien, with iron-grey curls. O'Sullivan was not quite sure how so old a fellow came to be included among the hundreds of stronger and younger ones that they had taken on board at Freetown. Perhaps because he spoke English which they had thought might increase his value. And because he had with him what appeared to be his grandson—a boy with a flute-like voice whom the old man had begged to be allowed to bring with him.

"Sell him along with me, Massa," he had appealed when he was first brought aboard. The tears had rolled down his cheeks. He seemed devoted to the little boy and anxious not to be parted from him.

O'Sullivan had taken notice. A small boy with a singing voice might fetch a high price and make a pretty slave for some fine lady. Here in the Colonies or in England, small black slave boys had recently become the rage. Ladies of wealth and fashion paid a high price for them.

"I left the two chained together and thought nothing of it, Captain, sir," continued O'Sullivan.

Humbleby interrupted, bawling at him:

"What has a black boy to do with *this*?" pointing to the apparition on the bunk.

The girl crouched in the corner in an attitude of abject

terror, showing the whites of her eyes which she rolled between the two fierce-looking men. She shook like a small jelly, and had a cold and forlorn air about her.

O'Sullivan hurried on with his tale. The Captain would remember how many slaves had taken ill and died and been chucked overboard. Well, the Negro grandfather himself fell sick forty-eight hours ago. Fever and starvation—the barbarous treatment handed out to the unhappy captives on this or any other slave ship sailing the high seas in the year 1797—had finished him. He had suffered appallingly at the hands of those directly attending to him, but something about O'Sullivan had won his confidence. Just before he died he had pushed the weeping little black "boy" into O'Sullivan's arms and bidden him take care of *her*.

The boy was a girl. The old man, fearing that she might come to harm because of her sex, had hidden the fact—keeping "him" clothed as a male slave, and never allowing "him" out of sight. But now the truth had to be told.

"But hell take it, this child is *white*!" roared the Captain.

O'Sullivan scratched his head.

" 'Tis true," he said. "The cunning old man stained the little girl's skin with an unguent before we sailed."

That was one of the troubles, he added. The child was a quadroon. And now the history which the old man had confided to the First Mate, unique and absorbing, was repeated to Captain Humbleby. The old Negro was headman of a good tribe and had been like a king in his own village. Thirty years back this village had been visited by a missionary. The missionary had had an Italian wife. After the sudden death from smallpox of her husband, this Italian woman decided to remain in Freetown. She became wife to the head tribesman. Of that marriage sprang a daughter—a beautiful half-caste—who in turn was married to a renegade Irishman who came from County Donegal (O'Sullivan's own county). The Irishman had been of decent birth (but the dying Negro had been unable to remember his son-in-law's name) he had dropped this name years back and "gone native," and lived in the African village until ten years ago when his daughter had been born. In giving birth, the mother had died. Almost immediately after, the Irishman, who had always been a heavy drinker, drank himself to death.

This quadroon girl was the strange result of that unattractive union. Half Irish, quarter Italian, quarter African. A "throw-back" to the father's race, with those red-gold curls, to the grandmother's maybe with that pale fine skin and those delicate limbs. Only her magnificent eyes and lashes were a legacy from her grandfather—a reminder of the dark blood that flowed in her veins.

"God's teeth!" muttered Captain Humbleby and stared at the little quadroon. In all his twenty years on the sea he had never seen the like. It was just one of those things that did not happen. And he listened while his First Mate told how the old grandfather had turned up his toes and been thrown to the sharks with the rest of them, and how he, O'Sullivan, had put the child, screaming and protesting, into a bath and with water and soap exposed the little one for what she was—a girl child who might pass anywhere for a European.

"If her eyes had been blue she would have been a true Irish beauty," O'Sullivan concluded and wiped his nose with the back of his hand: "Begorra, I have seen the spit of her in County Donegal, with hair of flame and a skin like milk, Captain Humbleby, sir."

Such poetical allusions coming from the coarse lips of his First Mate reduced Captain Humbleby to bawdy laughter, but the laughter broke off abruptly. He advanced farther upon the shivering little figure swathed in the folds of blue cotton which were nothing more than rags.

At once she screamed and put up both her hands to cover her face. Well-formed little hands with slender fingers. Humbleby put out a hand to touch her and then drew it back. He sweated. Never before did he remember hesitating to touch female flesh. Wherefore now had he become squeamish? Maybe because this was such white flesh, and this girl was a child. Captain Humbleby had children of his own. All the same, the quadroon was a female, and her strange beauty held a definite menace on board a ship full of women-hungry men. Men with less conscience or humanity than O'Sullivan.

Humbleby scowled and drew back from the trembling captive. There was only one thing to do.

"Blacken her face and put her back in boy's garments," he said. "I do not care if you haven't any. Sew her up in something and keep her in it until we get to Bristol. Confine that hair in a cap and sew *that* up too. Keep her with you and see that she comes to no harm."

O'Sullivan stared.

"Holy Saints," he began to stutter.

"Argue and I'll break every bone in your body," roared the Captain.

"Aye aye, sir," muttered O'Sullivan and pulled his beard and glowered out of the corners of his eyes at the little girl. She was sobbing under her breath. She looked pathetic enough, but O'Sullivan had had a taste of the spirit that lived in that thin fragile young body. Washing her in his locked cabin, away from prying eyes, he had treated her with a rough kindliness such as he would have meted out to one of his own children, for he, like the Captain, was a family man. But she had bitten his hand through so fiercely as to draw blood. He had had to smack her hard to stop her fighting. To be saddled with *that* for the rest of the long voyage back to England held small appeal for O'Sullivan. Nevertheless, he saw the sagacity of the Captain's suggestion.

He did not mean to leave her here in Jamaica the Captain added, he could get a better price for her in Bristol. In fact, he would hand her personally over to Mr. Panjaw. She was the ship's prize. The thing to do was to feed her up, fatten her, and teach her a few words of English. At this point Mr. O'Sullivan as proudly as though he were the adoptive parent of his discovery announced that the quadroon could already speak English. The old headman, her grandfather, had taught it to her, proud of the fact that she was three-quarters white.

The Captain smacked his lips. Better and better. She might fetch a very fine price indeed. True, there was little or no slavery at home. Well enough did the Captain remember that in the year 1772 when his lordship, the great Mansfield, was in office, he had stated that "*as soon as a slave sets foot on English soil, it shall be free.*" But there were a great many (and Mr. Panjaw among them) who took little notice of that dictum. Anyhow Mr. Fox had not yet carried through the Anti-Slave Bill. The quadroon with the red-gold hair would sell—by God she would!

"Has she a name?" he rapped out at O'Sullivan.

The First Mate pulled his beard and looked embarrassed.

"Holy Saints, but 'tis a strange one. So far the little imp has not spoken except to snarl at me, but the grandfather called her *Fauna*."

The Captain spat.

"That is no name."

"All the same—it is hers."

"Spell it!"

"F.A.U.N.A."

"What manner of name is it?"

O'Sullivan shrugged his shoulders.

"Something to do with the Italian. I have not learned the Latin tongue, but the old nigger had instruction from the missionaries, Captain, sir. He mumbled to me that the name was of Latin origin."

The Captain brooded upon it. *Fauna*. Strange . . . not unbeautiful. But ungodly. He turned on his heel.

"Forget it. It is a boy for the rest of the voyage and damn my eyes see to it, or you'll swing before you ever look at the goodly sight of Bristol harbour again."

"Aye, aye, sir," said O'Sullivan.

"Look well after her—*him*," added Captain Humbleby. "Keep 'him' locked in here whensoever you leave your cabin. Nobody else must get at 'him,' understand?"

"Aye aye, sir."

Then Captain Humbleby had left the quadroon with the First Mate. Standing outside the cabin door to light a cheroot, he had heard O'Sullivan's voice cajoling but firm.

"Now, my pretty—now then, come along. No nonsense. You're going to be given a black face again my pretty dear, and if you're good I'll treat you daicently and feed you well. Come along now, or I'll beat the liver out of you——"

Then the sound of tears and a hoarse young voice repeating:

"Grandfather . . . my grandfather . . . *my grandfather*!"

It was that cry that Captain Humbleby remembered tonight as he staggered blindly back to his ship.

Before God, finding this girl Fauna had been like finding a jewel amid the black dust on *The Nauticas*. And he was going to get a pretty price from Panjaw in addition to what had already been paid him. He'd see to that. But the girl was white. Like his own little Martha, except for those native eyes. Dammit—it would be like selling a brat of one's own nationality. All the more reason for him to give up this hell's job of sailing a trade ship and of finishing with the whole nauseous trade.

Chapter Two

On 15th June *The Nauticas* floated down the brown swollen waters of the river and docked in Bristol Harbour.

It had been raining. High on Brandon Hill low-lying mists obscured the stone-built houses. Samuel Humbleby, sober as a judge this morning, brought his ship in with loving care for the timbers, dropped anchor, and the gang-plank went down.

A crowd, including women and children waving ker-chiefs to the men who were returning to them, lent some colour to an otherwise grey day. A warm summer's day. The sun straining to break through those banks of cloud under which the fields and trees looked very green to the eyes of the sailors who had been at sea for long tedious months.

A soberly but fashionably dressed man, about forty-five, peruked and wearing long soft leather boots, was the first to go aboard. The people of Bristol who recognized him fell back respectfully. He was well known, Mr. Rufus Pan-jaw, one of the wealthiest ship owners in the city.

Behind the respectful salutations and curtseys of the fisherwomen, the townsfolk, and the half-naked sweating dockers lay a certain antagonism, for Mr. Panjaw was not popular. He was as mean as he was rich, and the poorer and more godly the people, the less they liked Mr. Panjaw, well aware that his fortune was obtained from slave trad-ing. But with his Russian leather portfolio under one arm and a cane under the other, his pale narrow face disdainful like his hooked Jewish nose, Mr. Panjaw walked stiffly aboard *The Nauticas* to be greeted by the First Mate and taken direct to the Captain's quarters.

Just before this, in O'Sullivan's cabin, the quadroon girl, Fauna, stood peering out of the porthole with eyes growing bigger every moment with astonishment as she looked for the first time upon Bristol.

To her, the busy port presented a bewildering spectacle. The smoke pouring out of tall factory chimneys must come, in her childish imagination, from a Devil's cauldron. And all these people in their queer clothes were devils, bustling and shouting and streaming along the quayside. She saw the big Shire horses straining under the lash of a driver's whip to pull loads too heavy for them. The sight of their rolling eyes and streaming flanks and the sound of the cracking whips mingling with the oaths and curses of the men, reminded Fauna all too painfully of the day when she and her grandfather had been torn from their home. Not so long ago, although it seemed to her that it had been in another life and that she now existed alone and defenceless in a new world. A terrible world which brought to her new fears and new cause for sorrow with every dawn that had broken since they sailed from the African coast.

The continuous crack of whips sent shudders through Fauna. In such a way the whip had curled around the shoulders of her grandfather and his proud ebony body had strained and flinched like the bodies of those horses. In such a way he and she had been driven on to the ghastly slave ship, chained together. Grandfather had not uttered one sound, for he was too proud, but the younger captives had howled and moaned, the women had torn their hair and beaten their breasts with loud lamentations.

The little girl dreamed almost nightly of that fearful morning just before daybreak when the slave traders had rounded them up, burnt down their kraals, not sparing even grandfather's more civilized dwelling which was built of wood like a hut, and had been furnished crudely by her Irish father.

Fauna, motherless from birth, did not remember much of her father, although in the dim recess of memory she recalled herself at the age of three being hoisted on to the shoulder of a red-headed man who danced drunkenly with her round a native fire then seated her upon his knee and wept maudlin tears over her until she slept. But that was very long ago. Her more recent and most vivid memories were of grandfather, and of his third wife, Nunu—a young ebony-skinned woman with shining white teeth and woolly pate of amiable disposition, who had taken care of Fauna's bodily needs, and treated her like a little princess. She had been the princess to them all out there in Africa. Her nostalgia was for those dark primeval forests, for the jungles, the animals, the chanting songs of the African tribesmen, the feasting, the hunting, and the long hot languorous days under a baking sun.

It was grandfather who had ordained that Fauna should be set apart from the rest of the tribe and given great due because of her white blood—blood of a great civilized people—that ran in her veins. The Italian strain he had fostered because it had belonged to Flora, his beautiful half-caste daughter; the Irish blood because it came from his red-headed son-in-law who although he drank heavily and had been banished from his own land as a ne'er-do-well—had been an educated man. Born of good parents; sole issue of an elderly father, who had in his time been a scholar—a professor of entomology. It was the Irishman who had ordered that his baby daughter should be called "Fauna." Swaying beside the grave of the woman whom he had married in Freetown and lost so soon, he had raised his infant daughter aloft and said: "She shall be *Fauna*—child of *Flora*. From the Latin *Favore*, which means the bestower of fruitfulness. My father, your Irish grandfather, studied the fauna and loved it till he died. Fauna, my child, you shall be."

Grandfather had told her that story many times. Every day he read to her from the only two English books that had not fallen to pieces rotted by the damp heat, or eaten by insects. Her maternal grandmother's Bible and a volume of Irish folk tales which her father had kept in an old trunk among the relics of his past.

By the time she was nine, Fauna was able to read a little. She spoke English slowly, carefully. Only in the native tongue was she really fluent, and from Nunu she had learned of spells and incantations and witch-doctoring. With childish nimble fingers she could weave a mat and thread beads into crude yet cunning designs. She had grown to love violent colours and was used to the violent, savage customs of grandfather's tribe. She looked upon birth and marriage and death with indifference, accepting these mysteries as she accepted food and drink; all part of the pattern of living. Like the other children of her age, she knew of the existence of sex and accepted that, also, without fear. In her step-mother's tribe, virginity was important and to be preserved by a young maiden for her marriage day. If Fauna had continued to live out there in Africa, it might have been difficult to find a suitable husband for her because of the pale skin and red-gold hair which kept her apart from the others. No man had ever dared cast an eye in her direction. She had been regarded as sacred. In any case a marriage would not have been considered for her for at least another two years. And if she had ever thought about it, it was only with faint curiosity, with a childish knowledge of animal life and of the coupling of beasts which was a daily occurrence. Part of the native ritual with which she had grown up. But she herself remained quite innocent.

Much of that innocence had been sadly troubled since the ghastly change wrought in her young life after the murder and rapine perpetrated by those who looted her village. While she remained physically intact, her grandfather had repeatedly warned her against the brutish assaults that might be made on her by these men who had so fearfully disillusioned him. Men of the great race of English, of whose blood he had been so proud. Now that very blood, mingling in the blood of his grand-daughter, cried aloud to Heaven for vengeance.

"Protect yourself with tooth and nail; fight always for your honour, my grand-daughter," he had besought her even as he died, "and may the God of your father and your mother grant that you may be permitted to avenge me and my people."

On the missionary's old Bible and on the more crude emblem of one of grandfather's old gods—for he had never really embraced the Christian faith—the child had sworn it.

Now every instinct in her bade her beware of the white men and their clutching hands and the grotesque manner in which they behaved when they drank the liquid fire of their distilling.

She had had no cause for anxiety in the care of the First Mate, O'Sullivan. The huge bearded man had proved gentle enough despite the fact that he had beaten her twice for biting his flesh. She had only bitten him because she was afraid—like a wild thing when it is first captured.

But he had fed her well, with faithful obedience to the Captain's orders, and given her sweetmeats which he had found in his locker—French bon-bons coloured and deliciously flavoured such as Fauna had never before tasted. They fascinated her. She ate them greedily, every one, which fact had made O'Sullivan guffaw with laughter.

"Begorra, the little varmint, but she knows what she likes!"

He had not beaten her again and she had learned that it was wise to behave with a certain docility, and that if she did so, he would not touch her. The man whom he called "Captain" she did not like so much. That one yellow inflamed eye of his, goggling at her, filled her with loathing and disgust. But he had only come to see her once or twice since they sailed from the West Indies, and then she had been glad that the bearded man had blackened her face and kept her covered from head to foot so that none could see her body. She need not fear another shameful exposure such as she had endured when she was first stripped and bathed.

For most of the voyage Fauna had lain prostrate, seasick and sorry for herself. She had, indeed, been seasick ever since they left Jamaica and ran into poor weather. She had no stomach for the sea. She had almost died down there in the stinking, suffocating hold of the ship. It had been a living horror to her to see her grandfather's body thrown without ceremony into the deep blue waters. But day after day, all the way from Jamaica to Bristol, she fretted alone here in her prison—for it was still prison even though luxurious compared with that hell below. She had fretted, and even when she felt less nauseated, and could eat, the good food had not put much flesh on her fragile bones. Her face grew pinched and whiter than ever with the lack of air and exercise. She missed the sunshine, the freedom of her former surroundings, the air scented with musk and frangipani flowers, the date-palms, the blue skies, and the innocent amusements indulged in by her grandfather's tribe. At night in O'Sullivan's stifling cabin she slept badly on her bundle of sacks, forced to listen to the heavy snores of the bearded First Mate who nearly always came to bed in a state of inebriation and no more spoke to or looked at her, than he would have done if she had been a small dog. And for fear she leaped out, the porthole was permanently fixed.

By the time they reached Bristol, Fauna was itching, alive with vermin again, and at times shaking with fever. Particularly when *The Nauticas* ran into home waters and heat gave place to cold and rain. It had been a wet summer all over England so far that year. This morning she had been given water, soap, and a towel and told to bathe, and this time left to do it for herself. She had found it quite amusing to use the soap and rub the black juices from her face which she could see in the cracked mirror which hung on the cabin wall. A relief to scrub away the filth and the bugs. Her hair had grown longer and hung in silken ringlets down to her shoulder. And now the miserable neglected little girl became aware, with all her feminine instincts stirring in her, of her potentialities. She was shy, suddenly ashamed of her nakedness. To cover her childish limbs she seized a coloured blue quilt from the First Mate's bunk and wound it around herself under the arms over the immature bosom, tucking one end in like a native sarong into the waist and bringing the other over her shoulder. She had seen her grandfather's third wife do this with yards of cotton material. Poor Nunu who had not been brought aboard the slave ship, and Fauna had not seen her since she first rushed out of her burning home with the traders in pursuit. Grandfather said they had murdered her and had never mentioned her name again.

Now Fauna stared out of the porthole and asked herself in fear and trembling what fate she might expect in this strange place. It was England—so much she knew. O'Sullivan, when he was sober and in a good mood, talked to her of London and of life in the rich, gay capital. But once or twice there had fallen from his lips sinister warnings that the child had been left to brood over. The word "slave" always seemed to come into it. She must learn to be obedient, for she was to be sold as a slave, he said.

"Holy Mary protect you and may the dear Lord Jesus have mercy on my immortal soul for the part I am playing, but you must be sold, my pretty dear," he had sighed over her one evening. "In a slave ship you have come to England and a slave you are, my pretty dear. Black, even if you are white, if you see my meaning."

Fauna did not see it. She did not try. But she did know too well what it meant to be a slave. She had suffered enough to last her for a lifetime. Was she to be chained in the bottom of a ship again, like grandfather, and starved and beaten until she died? Fauna began to shiver—feeling not for the first time today the cold damp air on the bareness of her skin. These grey skies and the low temperature depressed her, accustomed as she was to the warmth and brilliance of the country in which she had been born.

Her full red lips pouted. She turned and looked back at the cabin. She was thankful the ground was at least steady under her feet. There was scarcely a movement of the tide this morning. She had had enough of the creaking and groaning and rocking while *The Nauticas* was at sea.

The cabin was not very clean. In a cracked bowl on the table was milk which the obliging O'Sullivan had brought her earlier in the morning. A fly had settled in it. Gloomily Fauna stuck one small finger in, pulled out the fly and flicked it on to the floor where it lay sodden and moribund in the dirt. Then she drank the milk with no sense of repugnance, swallowing it, rolling it over her tongue delicately like a kitten. O'Sullivan had also brought her ship's biscuits, butter and fruit. The butter was rancid, and she left it, but she ate the fruit.

Her attention was caught suddenly by the sound of women screaming. She ran to the porthole and looked out. On the quayside two sturdy sun-tanned young women wearing striped petticoats and looped skirts—vendors from the fish market—had begun to fight. A tall merry-faced boy in blue pantaloons and a striped vest, and with a black straw hat as worn by naval men of the period perched on his yellow curls, stood on his bare brown feet watching. He laughed as one of the girls bore the other down to the ground and fell upon her, clawing and ripping her blouse until her throat and breasts were exposed. The sailor laughed louder. A crowd gathered. The struggling bundles of female flesh were then hidden from Fauna's gaze. She was both startled and bewildered by what she had seen. It was horrid yet it was an amusement, and she had thought the fair-haired sun-burned sailor goodly to look upon. Much nicer than Mr. O'Sullivan with his matted beard and his snores which kept her awake. *Or* the one-eyed sinister Captain.

Fauna did not realize it, but it was the first time in her young life that she learned to judge a man by his looks and to be intrigued by the sight of a laughing handsome boy.

She watched eagerly, hoping to catch another sight of him. But the fight was over now, the crowd dispersed, and the sailor moved away. The victor was congratulated by her friends and the vanquished attempted to stop her nose from bleeding while she sobbed and gathered together her torn shift, covering her shoulders from the jeering audience.

It was all very confusing to Fauna. Then a much more exciting thing happened. A yellow and blue curricle drawn by a spanking chestnut drove along the docks. The smart coachman pulled up alongside *The Nauticas* at a vantage point so that Fauna could see the gentleman who stepped from the curricle and kissed the hand of the lady he left within it. He walked towards the gang plank that led on to *The Nauticas*. But it was at the young woman in the curricle that the little girl stared, fascinated. The first lady of fashion Fauna had ever seen in her life. Her eyes goggling, she noted the lady's elegant cocked hat which was tied under her chin; the powdered curls falling to her neck, her handsome, velvet mantle, cherry coloured like the hat. Her face was indistinct, but the gay expensive attire of the young lady went to Fauna's feminine head like wine. She was intoxicated by the sight. Vanity awakened in her and she ran to Mr. O'Sullivan's cracked mirror and looked at herself. Oh, if she could only be dressed like that lady when she grew up, and ride in a fine carriage! What utter bliss!

Hanging on a nail in a corner of the cabin was an old beaver hat with a low crown which Mr. O'Sullivan used when he was ashore and out of uniform. The child took it down and stuck it on the side of her head. Then with a piece of string she tied back her curls and pulled them around until they lay over one small naked shoulder. She giggled at her reflection and held out her hand with an affected air as she had seen the lady in the curricle holding hers.

Without knowing it, the child had all the potentialities of a good actress and excellent mimic. She had by no means become indifferent to her unhappy state on the slave ship, but she had a natural sensuality and desire for gaiety which conquered grief. She hovered, like the infant she was, between tears and laughter.

It was at this point that the cabin door was unlocked and three men came into the room. Three men who towered above Fauna and seemed to her frightening and monstrous in the way they filled the small cabin and overwhelmed her.

Two of them she knew; Captain Humbleby and Mr. O'Sullivan. The other was a stranger. A fine gentleman dressed in grey holding a cocked hat and cane under one arm and a leather portfolio under the other. The gentleman whom she had just seen stepping from the blue and yellow curricle.

She was so aghast at being found like this in Mr. O'Sullivan's hat, that she remained immovable like a small statue, her magnificent eyes staring at all three men in turn.

They stared back. O'Sullivan's lips twitched.

"Holy Mary, what is going on here?" he muttered. "The saucy young varmint."

Captain Humbleby turned his one mean eye slyly upon his employer.

"There you are, Mr. Panjaw, sir, that is the female. Very unusual, I might say, unique—is she not, sir?"

Mr. Panjaw laid down his folio, cane, and hat. From one of the huge flat pockets in his cut-away coat he pulled a lace-edged handkerchief and passed it across his nose. His pale sneering face puckered with disgust.

"Pugh! The place smells, Captain Humbleby, it smells!"

Humbleby's eye glared at his First Mate. Mr. O'Sullivan went red about the gills and started to stutter.

"The child has been locked in here, sir, and not allowed out, and if Nature calls, Mr. Panjaw, sir——"

"Enough!" broke in Mr. Panjaw. "Throw the window more widely, I beg of you. *Animals*," he added the last word *sotto voce*. But when his ruthless gaze had first fallen upon the child standing there with the beaver hat so rakishly set on the side of her gleaming head, and noted her beauty, the length of her lashes, the delicacy of her pale skin, he had felt that he had not wasted his time by coming on board today. She was all and more than the Captain had described.

Mr. O'Sullivan was opening the porthole. Now Fauna's nostrils quivered as the tang of the keen salt air cut through the foul atmosphere to which she had grown accustomed in her misery.

Then she panicked. She took off Mr. O'Sullivan's beaver hat. She looked from side to side as though to try to find an exit, to escape the eyes of these men. She stumbled over her long cotton sarong and would have fallen. It was Mr. Panjaw who caught her. His long thin fingers, which had sharp polished nails, fastened around one of her delicate wrists like a vice. They shook her until her teeth rattled.

"Stand up. Look at me. Untie that hair. Remove your garment. *Sing*. These gentlemen tell me that you have knowledge of African songs. Let me hear them!"

Fauna was by this time so frightened and confused that she could not take in any one of the questions the fine English gentleman shot at her. She only knew instinctively that the milk of human kindness did not flow in the veins of Mr. Panjaw. He had a cruel face, his fingers hurt her, and that there was no justification for the anger he showed. She had done nothing wrong.

Mr. Panjaw repeated his questions. He continued to shake her until her cheeks were crimson and she gasped for breath. Now she began to cry.

"Stop crying!" Mr. Panjaw said between his teeth. "Not another tear, or you shall be beaten, *do you hear*? Wretched little girl, you are my property. A slave—daughter of a slave."

"Grand-daughter, Mr. Panjaw, sir," broke in the Captain uneasily, "and worth a biggish price, sir. Look at her skin and her shape. When she is older, sir——"

"Silence!" broke in Mr. Panjaw in his grating voice. He turned the baleful gaze of his cold pale eyes once more upon the wretched child. She made no sound now, but her little bosom heaved with gasping breaths, and her huge velvet eyes stared up at her captor as though he held for her a horrid fascination. Tears trembled on the exquisite lashes and rolled down her cheeks.

In the background, the First Mate hastily crossed himself, *by all the saints he would burn in hell for the part he played in this,* he reflected, *it was unchristian thus to terrorize so small a female, whether she had black blood in her veins or not.* In his peculiar simple way, Mr. O'Sullivan had grown quite attached to Fauna. He wished that he himself had enough money with which to buy her, then grimaced at the thought of what his good wife would say if he returned to County Donegal with *that* under his arm.

Captain Humbleby said:

"You disappoint me, Mr. Panjaw, sir, if you see no great worth in the female."

Panjaw released Fauna's wrist. She nursed it with one small hand, patting its redness, and watched with that fascinated terror while Mr. Panjaw drew a gilt snuff box from his pocket, and with his thumb applied snuff to each of his nostrils, then sneezed loudly.

"The stench in here overpowers me," he muttered. "Bring the girl into your cabin, Captain Humbleby."

The First Mate advanced upon Fauna and spoke to her in a voice that was meant to be wheedling.

"Go along, my pretty dear, do as the gentleman says. It will be better for you."

Suddenly the child's mind recognized the fact that she was about to be torn from the side of the only friend she had in the world. She did not much like Mr. O'Sullivan, but at least he had fed her and refrained from beating her, and he had grown familiar in this unfamiliar frightening world into which fate had so heartlessly flung her.

With a scream she stumbled towards Mr. O'Sullivan.

"Fauna stay with you. Not go with them!" she gasped in the curiously clipped English which she spoke with just a suspicion of an accent.

Mr. O'Sullivan coughed with embarrassment and glanced over the child's head at the other two. The Captain was swearing under his breath. Mr. Panjaw's gaze narrowed. Then he walked back into the cabin slowly. With a sudden savage movement, he seized a bunch of Fauna's red-gold curls and tweaked them.

"Miserable girl, learn to obey those who own you body and soul," he said in an icy voice.

She began to shriek and struggle, but the grip on her hair did not loosen and it was most painful having it pulled from her scalp. So with a return to her savage habits, half out of her mind with fear and loathing of this new man, she bent and sank her teeth into his thumb.

Mr. Panjaw uttered an exclamation. He went white, then red with fury. Speedily he wound a handkerchief around the thumb. Mr. O'Sullivan held his breath. There were tales circulating through Bristol city about Mr. Panjaw's tempers. There had been a scandalous affair not long back when he had killed a manservant in his employ because the fellow had upset wine accidentally on Mr. Panjaw's new flowered satin coat.

The First Mate crossed himself again and felt a shame such as he had not known since his boyhood, while Mr. Panjaw reacted to Fauna's infantile display of rage. With his long pointed fingers Panjaw ripped the child's cotton sarong from top to bottom revealing the slender naked limbs. Then he seized his cane and beat her across her back until red weals sprang up on the magnolia whiteness of that delicate flesh and she began to scream. Mr. O'Sullivan put his hands to his ears. Even Samuel Humbleby looked with more gloom than pleasure upon this sadistic performance. The cabin was filled with the sound of the cane whistling through the air and the child's screams. Mad with fright and pain, Fauna twisted and turned, trying to avoid the punishment. Then after a few seconds it was as though Mr. Panjaw grew weary of the sport. His feelings were relieved. He flung the cane into the corner, brushed an imaginary speck of dust from his embroidered cuffs, wiped away the sweat that had pearled on his forehead and straightened his peruke.

"So—my little tiger-cat—you will learn not to bite like the wild animal you are," he said softly. "Now, get up and follow me."

He turned to the door.

Captain Humbleby led the way to his quarters indulging in the melancholy reflection that the great ship owner was in a nasty mood and that he, Humbleby, might not get as much money for the quadroon as he had anticipated.

Fauna lay face downwards on the floor, hysterical with grief, pitiful in her bewilderment and broken pride. O'Sullivan, cursing Mr. Panjaw, picked the little girl up, wound her tightly in the cotton sarong until it was as though she were in a cocoon, and carried her out of his cabin. Much as he deplored this affair, he knew that it would be better for *her* not to cross Rufus Panjaw further.

Fauna lay in the First Mate's arms with the reek of his garlic-laden breath on her cheeks and fought against the desire to be sick. She reverted to the old desolate cry:

"Grandfather! . . . my *grandfather*!"

Chapter Three

In the Captain's cabin where there was a rug, a mahogany locker and chairs and some small claim to comfort, Samuel Humbleby poured a glass of wine out for his employer. Mr. Panjaw tossed it down. He had wasted enough time on this quadroon brat and been bitten through the thumb for his pains. And the young woman whom he had left in the curricle—his mistress of the moment—was waiting for him. He had no objection to keeping her waiting except they had been on their way to a cock fight which he wished to see. But when *The Nauticas* docked he had had to postpone it and pay this visit in order to find out exactly what the slave trader had achieved this voyage. Captain Humbleby's announcement that seventy-five per cent of the cargo had perished before reaching the West Indies was responsible for the unpleasantness of Mr. Panjaw's present mood. He said:

"Why did so many die?"

The Captain cleared his throat.

"Conditions in the hold, Mr. Panjaw, sir. As I told you, sir, they should be bettered, for neither man nor animal can live like that in the heat. And there was not sufficient food. I did my best, sir, but 'tis a wonder that twenty-five per cent reached Jamaica still breathing."

"If things go on like this," said Mr. Panjaw, locking his fingers behind his back, "I shall be ruined."

Captain Humbleby gave a discreet cough. Mr. Rufus Panjaw was not likely to be ruined. His coffers were full to overflowing and *The Nauticas* was not the only slave trader in his possession. The Captain muttered:

"And what of the young female? Three-quarters *white*, Mr. Panjaw, sir. You disappoint me, sir, if you do not find her most marketable."

Rufus Panjaw put his tongue in his cheek. His eyes were slits as they watched the First Mate deposit Fauna in a tight bundle in the Captain's chair. She had stopped crying. But she still trembled violently and she had grown very pale. Mr. Panjaw's gaze travelled over her. He was not going to let this old reprobate of a captain know just how valuable a prize he had secured. Besides which, the girl was not Humbleby's to sell; anything on this ship belonged to Mr. Panjaw. On the other hand, slaving was not popular in England just now. Mr. Fox was receiving a great deal of support, too much so for Panjaw's liking. It might not do if the Church, for instance, learned that a child with so much white blood in her veins, and one who could read the Bible, was being sold into bondage. He must, therefore, placate Captain Humbleby by offering him a certain bonus. But Mr. Panjaw's mind seethed with private plans for the little girl's future. Egad! he was far from disappointed and having satisfied his sadistic rage, he was now ready to admire what he saw. In truth, in another three years Fauna would be a fabulously lovely young woman. He had seldom seen a skin more marvellous; it had the creamy hue of a camellia, and her complexion was dazzling. As for those enormous black eyes, they were most remarkable contrasting with the fiery gold of her curls. The little devil! What a spirit she had. Now when she was ten years old it must be beaten out of her. Later subdued in a more amorous fashion. Then Mr. Panjaw, who had a lewd mind, began to chuckle to himself evilly.

Fauna stared at him in sullen misery. He turned from her to the Captain.

"I think," he said in a smooth way, "I know of someone who might give a very fair price for the quadroon girl, Captain Humbleby. He happens to be paying a visit to Bristol this very evening—to his aunt, the Duchess of Perithorpe, it so happens."

Captain Humbleby licked his lips.

"Nephew of a Duchess—and who might that exalted personage be, Mr. Panjaw, sir?"

"A certain Lord Pumphret, a connoisseur of art, Mr. Humbleby, with a lady wife who would appreciate this addition to her husband's treasures. It was mentioned to me that if I had a suitable small boy for sale, Lady

Pumphret would be interested. But a quadroon girl of some beauty with red hair, too, might be even more amusing for her ladyship. You will bring this child to my house tonight—let us say at eight o'clock," said Mr. Panjaw. "You will have her scrubbed before you bring her. I want no vermin in my abode."

Captain Humbleby's yellow eye flickered sullenly.

"She has been scrubbed already, Mr. Panjaw, sir."

"Repeat the process," said Mr. Panjaw, rose to his feet and applied snuff to his nostrils with a disdainful gesture.

"And the price, Mr. Panjaw, the bonus?" the Captain ventured, his lips working.

Mr. Panjaw walked to the porthole. He looked out upon the misty outline of Bristol, and at the distant figure of his mistress in the blue and yellow curricle. He was impatient to be off. A certain Mr. Brennin was holding one of the cock fights of the season and Mr. Panjaw had a financial interest in one of the birds which had been bred by the famous Gilliver of Derby. Besides, Sophia would be in a fine temper if he kept her sitting out there in the damp waiting much longer. Sophia was a plump golden-haired Austrian with an exceedingly fine figure; wife of a certain Admiral who was at present at sea. She was a sensuous beauty with four small children in whom she had little interest. She enjoyed the embraces of Mr. Panjaw, whose ruthlessness added for her a certain spice to his amorous approach. And since he enjoyed making a cuckold of the Admiral—the alliance was—for the moment—attractive to them both.

Mr. Panjaw considered the possible amount that Milord Pumphret might pay for this extraordinary little creature whom they called Fauna. Then he turned back to the master of *The Nauticas*.

"All in good time, Captain Humbleby. After I have seen his Lordship and learned his wishes, you shall receive your reward."

The two men bowed to each other. Fauna's dark frightened gaze had scarcely left Mr. Panjaw's face. Her back was sore and every bone in her fragile body ached from the beating she had received. She remained in the chair a little bundle of misery and terror until the terrible men left.

Then Mr. O'Sullivan came back and she held out her hands to him with an anguished cry.

"Do not send me away with *him*. Oh, save me!" she babbled the words in an extremity of terror.

The First Mate uttered an obscene oath which was directed very violently against Mr. Panjaw. Rough man though he was, brutalized by his trade, O'Sullivan found it difficult to resist the appeal of the little quadroon. He picked her up in his great arms and nursed her as he would have done one of his own children. Fauna with her arms around his neck, wept and moaned and shrank every time he touched her tender back. Then Captain Humbleby returned and glared at them.

"Get on with the scrubbing, didn't you hear Mr. Panjaw's orders?" he bawled.

O'Sullivan, red and more perturbed than he cared to own, growled back:

"It ain't right, Captain Humbleby, sir, it ain't right. She is but an infant and——"

Captain Humbleby cut him short. If he agreed with his First Mate he was not prepared to admit it and he was in a rage because he fancied that his cold-blooded and remorseless employer was seeking to do him out of the bonus due to him on account of this human prize. On the other hand, he was afraid of Mr. Panjaw. And he had his living to earn. He yelled at O'Sullivan.

"Death and damnation, are you becoming squeamish, like a female, Mr. O'Sullivan? Take the little varmint and see that she has no vermin left on her or when we take her ashore tonight Mr. Panjaw will have us all flogged. Do you hear me?"

Mr. O'Sullivan heard. He carried the moaning child out of the Captain's cabin back to his own. Laying her on his bunk, he pulled a bottle of liquor out of a cupboard and gulped the fiery liquid. Squeamish like a female, *to hell* with the whole lot of them, he reflected. And a good thing he would be off this devil-ship tonight and back in Co. Donegal soon among respectable people.

When he was drunk enough, he shut an ear to the unfortunate Fauna's feelings, forced the red-gold curls into soap and water and scrubbed her until she became convulsed with tears again, howling with pain when the soap ran into her eyes. By the time the First Mate had finished, she had no strength left to protest, and lay motionless on his bunk. She had been sick, she was very white. There was no spirit left in her when, later on, they wrapped her in a cloak and carried her ashore through the grey twilight.

She was indifferent to her fate as she found herself in Mr. Panjaw's study in his small elegant residence built a decade ago, and commanding a fine view of the harbour.

Fauna might ordinarily have been interested in the strange and unaccustomed sight of an English home—of this room with its fine thick carpet, velvet curtains, and the candles burning in silver sconces against the panelled walls. But she was too paralysed with fright now because she was in the presence of Rufus Panjaw again, although he paid little attention to her. She lay on a couch still wrapped in the cloak, looking like a small mummy, and so pale that even Captain Humbleby had muttered to his First Mate:

"A pest on it—the girl looks sickly. It will drop the price. A pity Mr. Panjaw ever gave her that thrashing."

What Mr. O'Sullivan said in answer was not fit to record. And never to his dying day was he to forget the speechless misery with which the little quadroon girl looked at him when he bade her farewell—never to see her again. He went straight down to the Golden Cock Tavern and drank himself into a state of insensibility. From that hour on he was a changed man, so subdued when he reached home that his wife thought he had contracted some strange disease from foreign parts, and rushed to physic him.

Mr. Panjaw, whose game cock had won the fight, was in an affable mood. He had on the way home called at a silversmith and bought his Sophia a bracelet. Wine was served and cheroots lighted. He seated himself at his desk and took a few notes of certain things that Captain Humbleby had to tell him about the recent voyage. He still confessed himself angered at losing so many slaves in *The Nauticas*. But he made no further comment. At a quarter past eight, the double doors were thrown open and a manservant announced unctuously:

"Lord Pumphret."

The girl on the couch turned her gaze upon the tall man

who entered the room. Her lashes quivered. She did not know whether she experienced fear or curiosity, but never in her whole life had she seen a man like this. Lord Pumphret was plainly but elegantly dressed in bottle green. He wore a bob wig. He exhibited a flowered satin waistcoat, and had handsome buckles on his shoes. In his late thirties, Lord Pumphret was a good-looking man with a long aristocratic nose and big blue eyes, heavily lidded. He was very stupid and came of a long line of stupid men. The Pumphrets had ever been noted for looks rather than intelligence. It was the Pumphret women who had the brains. The men nearly always chose wives more intelligent and alert than themselves, as though they needed the stimulation.

Lord Pumphret was exceedingly wealthy and in his fashion kindly and good tempered, but weak; his weakness was for pretty females. The ruling passion of his life was his own capricious wife, Henrietta—one of the most spoiled beauties who had ever appeared at the Court of his Majesty, King George III. To please her, there was little Lord Pumphret would not do. Entirely to win her approbation, indeed, he had left his aunt's house tonight and come here to the house of Mr. Panjaw (whom he cordially disliked) in order to buy a new "toy" for her ladyship.

To the dazed and brow-beaten child on the sofa, Lord Pumphret, however, presented a heartening sight. She responded at once to the gentleness and humour that marked him. He advanced to the couch, scrutinized curiously what he could see of the little creature—the exquisite face and the aureol of shining hair, and the eyes, so big and black as to give one almost a shock—then he gave an exclamation!

"Mercy on us! 'Tis a doll, it cannot be real," and he burst out laughing heartily.

Mr. Panjaw and the Master of *The Nauticas* exchanged glances. Mr. Panjaw said in the servile voice he reserved for his patrons:

"Beautiful—is she not, milord?"

"The face is angelic of a certainty. Quadroon, eh? Quarter black blood. Yes, in those eyes, but by my faith, in all other respects she might be European; even her nails have no trace of her native blood——" and Pumphret picked up one of the small hands and examined it closely, adding:

"Well-shaped oval nails—slender. She has breeding. What is her history?"

Mr. Panjaw repeated it. Lord Pumphret, sipping the wine that had been offered him continued to stare at Fauna and to receive the full glance of those fabulous eyes. Then Mr. Panjaw moved forward and unwrapped her cloak. The verminous cotton sarong had been forcefully removed from her by the reluctant Mr. O'Sullivan and by the Captain's orders. Lord Pumphret now ceased to sip his wine and looked upon what might well have been a small alabaster statue. It was of such perfection of symmetry and grace that it momentarily robbed him of speech. Then his healthy face flushed and he quickly threw the cloak over her again. He was not squeamish but he had an innate sense of decorum which forbade him to treat this pale bud of womanhood as he might have done a black-skinned slave. Gazing upon Fauna it was hard to believe that she had ever sprung from a half-caste mother and that her grandfather had been an African Negro. Pumphret's cheeks retained their flush as he saw the pitiful way the child clutched the cloak about her, and how her own small face had changed to an angry crimson as she shrank from Mr. Panjaw's fingers.

Said Pumphret:

"How much?"

There followed some bargaining, out of which Mr. Panjaw, as usual, emerged the victor. Lord Pumphret would not pay the first and ridiculous price that was asked for the quadroon girl, but he agreed to a compromise. He admitted, he said, that her ladyship would be vastly entertained to number this unique specimen of a slave girl in her personal retinue. Henrietta had been badgering him to buy a little black boy because her great friend, the Marchioness of Rustingthorpe, had a beturbaned and bejewelled little monster; who followed her about the house like a dog and held the candles for her while she bathed. Henrietta had envied this possession.

"Of course, he is laughable, but Rustingthorpe tells me he has a particular odour that issues from black skins," added his lordship. "I dislike the idea. But there is no such odour from this girl. I return to London next week. The quadroon is thin and pale. See that she is well fed and better clothed. See also that she is ready for my return journey—next Sunday morning. I will call for her with my travelling carriage after breakfast."

Panjaw rubbed his hands. His narrow eyes gleamed. Sophia should have something more than the bracelet tomorrow. Milord Pumphret had paid a pretty price for the slave. Before Pumphret left, he asked the name of his purchase, and when he was told, and it was said that Fauna's grandfather had been a professor of entomology, he burst out laughing again.

"Fauna! 'Tis laughable. Is she then a little animal?—an insect? However, we will retain it. It has an unusual sound, and some charm."

Suddenly, to the astonishment of the three men, Fauna wriggled off the couch, and in the effort to reach the tall gentleman in bottle green with the kindly face, tripped and fell headlong at his feet. He picked her up.

"Come, come, Insect, what would you?"

Now she clung to his boots and raised those enormous eyes streaming with tears. The small beautiful face was convulsed.

"Do not leave me with *him* . . . ," she gibbered, and pointed at Rufus Panjaw. "Oh, do not. Let me go with you!"

Pumphret raised her in his arms, marvelling at the lightness of her weight. Her red-gold curls brushed his chin. He examined the extraordinary length of her lashes and the sweet lifting curve of her upper lip which already gave promise of voluptuousness. Her teeth were like pearls. All within George Pumphret that loved beautiful things, stirred —as did, indeed, the sight of her tears. He glanced at the two men who were watching, uncertain of what might be the consequences of this display on Fauna's part.

"It seems that the Insect does not care for you gentlemen," he murmured and laughed.

Captain Humbleby winked his eye ferociously. Mr. Panjaw bowed.

"No doubt she finds her—er—present conditions strange after her barbarous upbringing."

"Not so barbarous," said Milord, "considering how prettily she speaks our language. This Insect is an extraordinary phenomenon, my dear Panjaw."

"Shall I relieve you of her, Milord?"

And Panjaw made as though to take the child who suddenly awakened to passionate fear and rage combined, sat up and spat at him over his lordship's shoulder, like a little tiger cat.

"No—no—*no*!" and she clung wildly to Pumphret, disarranging the Geneva linen band at his throat.

It struck Lord Pumphret then and there that he did not wish to leave this beautiful and pitiful little object with the man who obviously frightened her and, perhaps, used her ill. Quickly he bethought himself of a certain female in the employ of his aunt, the Duchess, to whom he might entrust Fauna for a few days, and who would feed and clothe her properly, and so prepare her a little for introduction into his own London house.

"There—cease your weeping, Insect," he murmured and touched the red-gold curls with careless fingers, "I will take you with me. I have bought you, my pretty little slave girl. So I will wrap you up and take my purchase away with me this very moment, eh?"

Mr. Panjaw shrugged his shoulders. He preferred to be rid of the girl. Captain Humbleby turned his eye upon the packet of notes that his lordship had just flung on the desk. But Fauna pressed her tear-stained cheek against Pumphret, and sniffed delightedly the odour of pomade that clung to him. She liked it and she liked him. Between sobs, she murmured something in a native language which he did not understand. But he knew it was very friendly. And the satin-smooth texture of that tear-stained cheek against his brought the colour back to his own face. Faith, but the little thing had a way with her—a strange seductiveness even at her age, he thought.

He carried her out to the sedan-chair that waited for him.

Fauna had been sold into bondage—victim of man's infamy. But she had emerged from the mire of that hell-ship, virgin and triumphant with Lord Pumphret as first conquest of a beauty and strange fascination that was in future years to become every man's desire.

Chapter Four

The Lady Henrietta Pumphret, daughter of an earl, wife of a baron and mother of two cherubic little daughters—lay on her chaise-longue in her famous Chinese boudoir and listened to the chatter of her friend Clarissa, Marchioness of Rustingthorpe.

Lady Henrietta, who had just stepped from her bath, wore a red silk embroidered bed gown that exposed her snowy neck and most of her bosom. Her hair fell across the gold-satin cushions in raven-dark ringlets, but in a few moments Abigail, her well-trained maid, would be dealing with those curls, pomatuming and powdering them into one of the high showy confections which were all the rage.

Henrietta had just shown her friend the *ensemble* she was wearing for her dinner-party tonight. It had been made by a French dressmaker who had escaped from Paris during the Revolution and settled in London. He was reputed to have made well over a hundred exquisite confections for the ill-fated Austrian Marie-Antoinette. This gentleman now attended to the wardrobe of many titled ladies in England and Henrietta Pumphret was one of his enthusiastic supporters.

The young Marchioness looked a trifle enviously at Henrietta's transparent airy dress. It shimmered gauzily like a butterfly's wing—and at the watered silk petticoats sewn with silver butterflies, and the dark violet velvet mantle she was to wear over all. A silver net, too, waiting to float from Henrietta's head-dress. All very engaging and expensive. Clarissa's William was richer than Pumphret but not so forthcoming with the money for his wife's toilette, Clarissa sighed. Nobody in their set was as lucky or extravagant as Henrietta. George spoiled her disgracefully. And at times—la! la! how she ranted and stormed at him.

Darling Henrietta had *such* a temper. Nobody who had ever seen her in one of her rages would believe she was the mother of those two little cherubs, Harriet, aged five, and baby Arabella, aged two. The Lady Pumphret who presented to the world such a touching picture of a virtuous and gentle matron. Poor George! Clarissa sighed—always a little affected by the thought of handsome easygoing George. He was truly more amiable and easy to manage than her William. And naughty Henrietta did not want more children and George must needs have a son and heir, so there were such tantrums and weepings from Henrietta and such bleatings, reproachings and cajolings from George. And only Clarissa, the favoured family friend who saw behind the scenes in the Pumphret's big establishment in Fitzroy Square, knew more about these things.

But she loved Henrietta. So sweet—when she was in a good mood. And vastly entertaining. With a fund of saucy stories; and Beau Brummell for one of her friends. Henrietta's drawing-rooms when Beau appeared in one of his newest attires were treats not to be missed by the rest of London Society.

The Lady Henrietta, in turn, suffered the pretty little Clarissa rather more gladly than any other of her so-called friends. Clarissa had a sweet babe—a four-year-old son, drat it—who played with baby Harriet and Arabella. Clarissa was younger than Henrietta who had reached the great age of twenty-four (and in her opinion was ageing far too rapidly). Henrietta liked Clarissa who was timid and seldom argued. She was a devoted and most admiring friend. Henrietta lapped up devotion and admiration—as a cat laps cream. And like a cat she had particularly nasty claws to use when she felt like scratching.

Other women—with the exception of Clarissa—were afraid of her and cautious in her presence. But men found her raven curls, her almond-shaped agate-bright eyes and that brilliant complexion and ravishing form—most inspiring. It was a pity, Henrietta often reflected when looking in her mirror, that Gainsborough had died—just too soon. He would have been at her feet and eager to immortalize her dark beauty. That full-length portrait down below in the withdrawing-room, which was of George's grandmother, had been executed by the great and much lamented Gainsborough.

Clarissa in her flute-like voice was recounting a naughty story about an acquaintance of theirs—a certain Lady L—— whose lover, one of the gentlemen-at-waiting to the Prince, had recently been found hiding in a cedarwood press in her bedroom by the lady's irate husband who set his lackeys on the unfortunate young man and then flung him outside in the street for all to see, clad only in his underwear.

The two ladies laughed until they cried at the thought of this edifying spectacle. Then, said Clarissa, looking at Henrietta with her vacuous blue eyes:

"Have you heard, my dear soul, that Mr. Brummell expects to be made a captain in His Majesty's own regiment, next year?"

"Alas, yes, and he will be busy with his duties and no longer able to grace my gatherings—our dear, *arbiter elegantiarum.*"

Clarissa sighed.

"How clever you are, dearest Henrietta, the way you speak Latin. I do not know what you mean but I am sure it is beautiful."

Henrietta yawned. Clarissa had begun to bore her, for she had seen and admired everything new that George had recently purchased for Henrietta and when there was no more for Clarissa to envy—Henrietta always lost interest. To be envied was the breath of life to her. To be forced to envy another—purgatory, itself.

She continued to yawn delicately, glancing around her boudoir with her bright acquisitive eyes. She was growing tired of that Chinese wallpaper with its fantastic design of birds, trees, and pagodas. Perhaps she would have it altered —panelled in satin, hand painted with sylvan scenes of shepherds and shepherdesses—little amorous classical episodes. Henrietta enjoyed posing as a woman of learning. Thus, she had studied both Latin and French and played the spinet quite brilliantly. And she adored making expensive alterations to the house.

Over the carved fruitwood mantelpiece hung a delicious nude painted in oils, in an Italian frame. A brightly plumaged macaw hung in a gilded cage in front of one of three big windows—overlooking the quiet elegant square. Now and again the bird rocked on his perch and screamed malevolently. He was a new acquisition, and had been bought to replace Jacko, the baby monkey who had died of bronchial pneumonia, neglected by his mistress during a cold spell last spring. As a rule Henrietta kept a suffocating heat in here, but she had gone away on a visit with her husband and left Jacko behind. The housekeeper, who had hated the animal for his dirty habits, had not bothered with him, so he had died of exposure and starvation. Henrietta had stormed at the woman and threatened her with instant dismissal—then forgotten it. Mrs. Clack was too good and too reliable a controller of her kitchens and staff to lose; besides which Henrietta was up one moment, sky-high, and down the next, indifferent to all that had previously disturbed her. She had no great heart. No truly fond affections. Her passion for George, whose good looks, fortune and title had attracted her, had long since petered out. She liked her babes because they were of her flesh and blood although she had at first hated them for not being boys. Now they amused her because they were pretty and engaging. Her real passion at this period was for a certain young gentleman named Anthony Lennox; related to Lady Caroline Lennox, mother of Mr. Fox, the Whig leader. Anthony was only twenty—four years younger than Henrietta—extremely handsome, a bit of a rake, and a budding politician like his distinguished uncle; more exciting than her poor dear George. Anthony was madly in love with Henrietta, too. As yet she had not succumbed. She was keeping her head and wondering how long he would keep his. But it certainly made life thrilling.

Her yawns became prodigious. She had a late night ahead of her and it would take her two to three hours to perfect her coiffure and to dress. The dinner was to welcome George home from Bristol. Anthony was invited, of course, among other distinguished guests. The evening promised to be amusing and George always brought her home a present when he had been away. Suddenly Henrietta narrowed her gaze and smiled significantly at her friend.

"Maybe when I see you again, Clarissa my pet, I shall

have a little black monster to do my bidding—like your creature, Zobbo."

Clarissa bridled slightly. Zobbo, her ebony dwarf of a slave, was one of the few treasures she personally possessed at Rustingthorpe House that naughty Henrietta desired. It would not be so much fun to own Zobbo if Henrietta managed to get a replica.

"But dearest, no more slaves are to be imported," she began.

Henrietta interrupted:

"The Bill is not yet passed. Anthony tells me they are fighting it in the House tomorrow. Anyhow George went to Bristol to see Aunt Louisa and it is there he knows a gentleman who owns a fleet of slave traders. He promised faithfully to buy me a Zobbo—if he could."

Clarissa pouted. Rising, she patted a fair curl into place and drew on her high bonnet on which nodded handsome jade green feathers. The June afternoon was close. The sun had gone in—hidden behind a bank of grey cloud. London was stifling. Clarissa was thankful that tomorrow they were all moving down to Caddlestonhaugh, William's house in Brighthelmstone. She was weary of town and a ceaseless round of parties, and William spending so much time playing faro at the club. Weary even of her dear Henrietta's company. Henrietta never would allow her any little triumphs. She managed somehow always to make her feel she had nothing—nothing *enviable*.

Zobbo with his huge rolling eyes and ebony face and comic personality used to make Henrietta laugh, and over and over again she said that she wished Zobbo were hers. Now she was going to have a Zobbo of her own—alas!

But Clarissa kissed Henrietta's smooth cheek tenderly.

"Till tomorrow, my dear soul. Pray give my respects to dearest George. . . ."

"Au revoir, my dearest Clarissa," murmured Henrietta returning the kiss.

Clarissa, her green silk mantle rustling, passed through the boudoir doors and was conducted by a footman to her waiting sedan-chair. Rustingthorpe House was only a few steps away from the Pumphret's residence in Fitzroy Square.

Left alone, Henrietta sighed for relief, twiddled her bare

toes and gave herself up to pleasurable dreams of what Anthony might do to her if she allowed him the privilege.

Presently she rang her bell for Abigail to come with brush and combs, pads and false curls, tongs and ribbons, and start the gargantuan task of dressing milady's hair.

Chapter Five

Darkness had fallen by the time Fauna was lifted into the arms of his lordship and carried into Pumphret House. Two lackeys hearing the clatter of the vehicle and the clip-clop of the horses racing around the square had hastened to throw open the doors of the big mansion. Fauna blinked as she saw the bright beams of light slanting from the hall and the lanthorns held aloft by the men servants.

She cuddled closer to the man who had bought her as a slave to satisfy his wife's whim.

On the whole, Fauna felt drowsily content. Ever since she had escaped from the slave ship and the clutches of Mr. Panjaw she had been introduced to a more kindly world. Pumphret's aunt, the Duchess, had never laid eyes on her (she would have been shocked so to do) but the little girl had been well fed and looked after by a female servant in the household whom his lordship bribed, not only with a golden guinea but with an embrace for which any serving women would give her soul, from the handsome laconic nobleman.

"It was not fitting," the good creature had told his lordship, "that a bought slave with black blood in her veins should be dressed like a lady." So hastily a sewing woman had fashioned for Fauna a frock of coarse, home-spun material which concealed her delicate limbs. It was of a hideous shade of saffron yellow which would have destroyed any beauty but Fauna's, and this triumphed over the worst attire. Clean, and with well-combed shining curls, a little brown fustian mantle and a bonnet with ruched rim, she now looked like the child of poor but respectable people. Fauna's normal personality was hidden, but she presented an extraordinarily English, demure aspect which made his lordship laugh when he saw her. He took note of her little clogs and mittens, and it was his private opinion that the woman had done her best to dim the child's almost shocking good looks. But once Henrietta got hold of Fauna, she would soon alter *that*. Henrietta had a *penchant* for the bizarre.

Fauna felt uncomfortable in this attire and chafed by her coarse cotton underwear, and she hated her hat and her clogs. Never before had her small perfect feet been thus imprisoned. But she suffered it because George Pumphret had told her that she could no longer look like the little savage that she was. With idle generosity, he tossed her sweetmeats and cake and fed her until she was sick twice on that long journey from Bristol to London which lasted two whole days.

Fauna had conceived a passionate love for the tall handsome nobleman who, in turn, was amused by the spaniel-like worship with which she regarded him. All the same, as he drew nearer to London he became a little uncertain as to how Henrietta would receive this phenomenon which he had bought from Panjaw at so high a price.

Fauna could not say that she really enjoyed the journey. She was frightened by the swaying movement of the big "flying coach" drawn by four powerful horses; and by the strangeness of the countryside through which they passed. Mile upon mile of green deserted pasture—dark woods, up-hill and down-dale, through small rustic villages. The coachmen brawled and shouted incessantly among themselves and got drunk when they changed horses at Newbury. They stayed the night there. Lord Pumphret was well received by mine host of the Saracen's Head. For the first time in her life, Fauna slept in a real bed which was in the servants' quarters and only a truckle one, and she had to share it with a flea-ridden coarse young scullery maid. She found it most uncomfortable. But worn out with excitement, she was soon fast asleep. Then early in the bright June morning, they pressed on towards London, passing the Bristol Mail which, Lord Pumphret informed her, had been held up and robbed on this very road only the other day.

"The country is going to the dogs, Insect," he informed her—retaining his amusing nickname for her, "it is an outrage that in the year 1797 respectable people cannot take a journey without fear of highwaymen."

He did not explain further and Fauna had not asked. She was more interested in a certain gentleman who had entered the flying coach at Newbury—a young musician on his way to join an orchestra in the court of the royal prince.

He produced a flute and played upon it prettily to beguile the tedium of the long journey, and also to keep himself in practice. Fauna, deeply interested, started to move hands and feet, and hum in time to the melodies he played. So enchantingly did she make these gestures and such aptitude did she show for singing—as though her ear had been trained—both men listened and watched, entranced. Milord gave his great laugh.

"Faith I have bought my lady a Fauna who will trill like a lark and dance like a nymph," he said. "Bravo, Insect. You show much talent."

She laughed with the men, delighted because she was admired. Much of her fear of the white men was vanishing and with every hour that she spent with Pumphret she was growing more conscious of her own ability to charm. So for forty-eight hours she lived in a world that seemed to her much more rosy than that about which her poor old tortured grandfather had made such gloomy prophesy. Almost she forgot the terrible days and nights she had spent dressed as a boy, after being driven from Africa on board *The Nauticas* and chained in the hold to her grandfather. Her true awakening was yet to come.

She was half asleep as the coach rattled over the cobbled streets on the outskirts of London. Milord shook her, anxious that the little savage should see the capital. He wished to watch the effect upon her. He saw her huge eyes widen at the sight of the tall narrow houses, the lamps, the brightly lit taverns outside which on this summer's night crowds were gathered singing, dancing and drinking. That they were coarse low-born people and that the gutters were choked with slime, and that it was not safe for any gently born person to be out at night, Fauna could not know. She thought it all very festive—people dancing and singing as they did in the kraals in far-off Africa. She was astonished by the size of some of the buildings and clung to his lordship's arm, gasping, when she first looked upon the size and splendour of the great buildings. She goggled at the busy river so crowded with ships and barges, at the parks and the better-class residences of the rich. It was a staggering sight for a child brought up in a primitive African village.

Once and once only, his lordship had a difficult few moments with her. That was when they passed a place of public execution. A miserable bundle of bones swung from the gibbet. Carrion crows sat, pecking the eyes from the almost fleshless face of the dead criminal. Fauna could see it all clearly for the coach slowed down at that point. A thrill of revulsion and horror went through her. She screamed.

"Drat—'twas a pity she saw it," muttered Pumphret and patted the child's curls until her sobs subsided. "What a sensitive Insect it is! Dry your tears, little one. You must learn that life is not all sweetmeats and petting and that there is much wrong-doing and violence. Also, that crime is punishable by death. No doubt that poor wretch you saw swinging, stole a joint of beef for his family and so paid the price of robbing an innocent butcher."

Fauna did not understand. Stealing among her grandfather's tribe was punishable, too, but not by death. To pay with one's life for a hunk of meat—that seemed a terrible punishment. The sight subdued and haunted her and she was still in a state when she was carried into the house in which she was to live during the next six years of her young life.

Dazed she looked upon the big entrance hall of the palatial house, at the panelled walls hung with the ancestral portraits of the Pumphrets, the musician's gallery, the great banks of hot-house flowers, the hundreds of wax candles burning in vast crystal chandeliers which swung from the ceiling. Her tired overwrought mind could hardly take in so much magnificence—all in such direct contrast to the only dwelling she had ever known. The place seemed to be thronging with people. Gentlemen wearing powdered wigs, velvet, or brocade coats, and breeches, magnificent waistcoats and diamond-buckled shoes. Ladies looking like a variety of butterflies in their multi-coloured gowns—with their high head-dresses—gold and silver nets, flowers and a blaze of valuable jewels. Music was being played softly by the orchestra in the gallery. Up and down the wide staircase couples were moving. Two flunkeys in the gold and chestnut livery of the Pumphrets had just thrown open the double carved doors that led into the dining hall where supper was now being served.

"Zounds," muttered Pumphret, "My lady has a party and I shall be chivied for my tardiness."

Which he was! For Lady Henrietta came sweeping down the staircase tapping a painted fan on one thumb nail, looking exquisite in her gossamer French toilette, looped with pearls. There were pink rosebuds in her powdered hair, but a very angry twist to her painted mouth.

"In truth, my lord, you have chosen a pretty hour to return from your journeys! You promised to come early. I have had to receive our guests without you. And here you are, travel-stained and not properly dressed. I am most displeased——"

"Your pardon, my dear love," Pumphret bowed from the waist. He rarely lost his temper with his beautiful and *exigeante* spouse, "but we were unavoidably detained. Just before entering Newbury on the turnpike road, we found a chalk waggon stuck across in our way and it took time for the men to remove it. We——"

"What *have* you got in your arms," broke in her ladyship.

Pumphret, looking a trifle sheepish, set Fauna down on her feet.

" 'Tis what I promised my sweet lady."

"What you promised me?" repeated Harriet and stared—blinking amazedly at the little girl in her sober bonnet and cloak. "Have you lost your mind, Pumphret?"

He pulled the lobe of his ear. Several of the guests gathered round and peered curiously at Fauna. Then with some defiance, Pumphret added in her ear:

"There was a slave ship in at Bristol. You asked for a creature like Clarissa's Zobbo but I thought this would be vastly more to your liking, my dear. She is a quadroon and yours to command."

Henrietta gulped. Lord Pumphret leaned down, unclasped Fauna's cloak and drew off her hat. The child half dead now with fright, began to tremble. But the winking lights from the candles turned the colour of her ringlets to fiery gold and sparkled in her huge velvety eyes. In her nervousness she seized a fold of her coarse gown and lifted it, showing slender little legs and beautiful ankles. There rose a chorus of admiration from guests of both sexes.

"But she is quite *white*."

"A red-headed quadroon—lud!"

"Such magnificent eyes and eyelashes. . . ."

"Such a skin. What is she . . . a fairy thing? Surely not human!"

Milord stood by, smiling foolishly, glancing down at his purchase.

Then Henrietta said in a level voice:

"Bring her upstairs."

Fauna understood those words. Immediately she lifted her arms up to Pumphret. Her heart was beginning to beat fast with confusion, with the old fear of the unknown.

"Fauna stay with you . . ." she whimpered.

Milady heard those words and froze.

"Who and *what* is 'Fauna'?"

" 'Tis her name, my love," explained his lordship, "F-a-u-n-a. Her Irish grandfather being in his day a professor of entomology. I call her 'Insect'," and he laughed sheepishly.

My lady put on her fiercest voice.

"Insects are made to crush under one's heel, Pumphret."

She said the words more to be perverse than anything, for she did not think it diplomatic to show too much pleasure at any of the gifts George purchased for her. Privately she was altogether fascinated by the sight of the little slave. A quadroon . . . and of a most remarkable beauty . . . that would be one up on dear Clarissa, and any of their other acquaintances who employed coal-black pages.

She excused herself to her guests.

"Go into supper my dear souls, I pray you," she bade them. "My lord and I will join you presently."

And she kissed the tips of her fingers which glittered with diamond rings, to those left standing in the crowded hall. In particular she cast a languishing glance towards Anthony Lennox. He was a slim young man wearing grey flowered satin. A debonair youngster with a pair of wicked eyes that sent a brazen message of love back to the Lady Henrietta. He wished privately that my lord had never returned from Bristol. He had hoped, at least, that my lord would be many hours late. He had hoped great things of his Henrietta tonight—his not altogether—but whom he fully intended to make his mistress before the season was out. A pest on this quaint-looking quadroon child in whom Henrietta seemed so interested.

In my lady's boudoir, Pumphret once more set the tired child on her feet and murmured that perhaps it would be best to send for Mrs. Clack, the housekeeper, and get her to bed.

"One moment," said Henrietta imperiously, "she speaks English. I heard her address you. How can this be?"

Pumphret sketched a brief outline of Fauna's history as given to him by Rufus Panjaw. Fauna, swaying with fatigue, looked dazedly around the scented elegant room. She was on the verge of tears. Life had jostled her too rapidly from one point to another. Her young untrained mind could not deal with it. She felt miserable and insecure and had taken instantly a dislike to the beautiful lady with the ornate headdress, who spoke to her with the same cold unkindness dealt her by Mr. Panjaw.

She yawned and battled against her tears and fatigue. She was also feeling sick again, for Pumphret, meaning to be kind, had stuffed her with sweetmeats in the coach. Henrietta said:

"So! A full-blooded Negro for a grandfather and a half-caste mother and—this is the result."

"Is it not pleasing to you, my love?"

My lady reflected, her keen scheming mind working fast.

"She has looks and is not coarse and the voice is pleasant."

"She can both sing and dance, my dear."

Henrietta tapped the fan on her thumb nail again, her almond eyes narrowing.

"But a girl . . . there may be trouble later on."

Secretly George Pumphret agreed with this. Trouble, forsooth! Plenty if the Insect developed into the gorgeous butterfly of which she gave promise. Butterfly, perhaps was the wrong symbol, he told himself wryly, for all the time he had spent with her he had become conscious of her extreme femininity. Veritable flesh and blood and neither *fauna* nor *flora*. Born with natural allure for men—happily or *un*happily. Who could tell?

"There may be trouble," repeated Henrietta.

"Pshaw!" he muttered, "you can look to that. Mrs. Clack will keep her in order as she does all your serving wenches."

"How shall I use her?" murmured Henrietta, her mind racing on. To outshine all the other hostesses in London—to give the most amusing parties—to be *envied*, and particularly by Clarissa, Marchioness of Rustingthorpe, that was Henrietta's most burning ambition. Well, to her most certain knowledge nobody, not even Beau Brummell (or Queen Charlotte herself) had a quadroon for slave.

To produce a beautiful little girl as her personal attendant—her toy—her whim—would be bound to cause a great deal of chatter and attention in London. She—Henrietta—would be *envied*—oh, undoubtedly! Everybody knew how difficult it was nowadays to buy a slave. Henrietta gave her husband a sly look.

"Is it not unlawful to retain this creature in slavery?"

He made a deprecating gesture.

"Oh, I think we can get over that, my love. It can be said that she is an orphan to whom we have given shelter. The word *slave* can be modified—used with discretion and my Henrietta knows so well how to be discreet."

My lady's colour rose. She liked to be flattered. And she was planning how she would dress the little girl. One day as a little Turk—with a yashmak . . . how fascinating those eyes would be over a yashmak . . . or one day as a shepherdess with a crook, and with a live lamb perhaps to follow her. Abigail had poor sight, her red-rimmed eyes were beginning to affect my lady unpleasantly. This *Fauna* (not a bad name) should be trained by Abigail to attend to my lady's nails and toes and perform many other personal services for her. Fauna would have to do exactly what she was told. She was no free orphan but a creature with black blood, to be used as such. Clarissa stood no nonsense from her Zobbo. Henrietta would have no nonsense from the girl.

"Well, my love?" asked Pumphret anxiously.

"Go, George, and attend to your dressing," said Henrietta, "I will use your extraordinary present. She shall amuse me."

Pumphret's brow cleared. He was a simple man and judged all women, and particularly his Henrietta, by the most simple signs. When she called him "Pumphret" she was displeased. When she used his Christian name, he could know he was in favour. Sighing with relief, he bent over the tapering hand which she held out to him, and kissed it. Now Fauna saw the nobleman turn away. In her world of confusion and change, he—like the rough O'Sullivan on board *The Nauticas*—had become familiar and she could be sure of kindness from him. She gave a wail and followed him.

"Do not leave me," she began.

"Come back here *at once!*" exclaimed Henrietta.

She was going to have no nonsense. George started to appease the child but my lady got rid of him, then pulled at the tapestry bell, and sent Abigail for Mrs. Clack. Fauna began to struggle and weep. Henrietta's fingers nipped her delicate flesh and one of her rings became entangled in a red-gold curl and tore at it mercilessly.

"Be quiet—how dare you try to follow his lordship. You are *mine*—you belong to *me* now, do you hear?"

Fauna heard but did not care. Once more she was in a paroxysm of fright. Henrietta was aghast. Her own two little darlings had their moments of temper but she never dealt with them. She left them on such occasions to their nurses and attendants. My lady rarely had the energy to soothe their childish griefs. She preferred to show them off to her friends when they were in good humour. Never before had she had a small female creature struggling and carrying on in this outlandish manner. Her quick temper rose. With her fan she struck the child smartly across each cheek.

"No time like the present to teach you a lesson, my girl," she muttered.

Fauna stopped crying. With a convulsive intake of breath, her little chest heaving, she stared up at my lady's painted furious face. The perfumed room reeled around her. Her sickness returned. My lady said:

"Get this into your head, girl, *that you are my slave*, and that you do what you are told without demur, and that if you dare to defy me or those I place over you, you shall be thrashed and locked in a garret without food until you beg for mercy."

It was not that the lady Henrietta was always cruel. She could be most kind and generous and her tempers were soon appeased. But when her anger was roused, she could be a fiend. It went to her head a little to know that she possessed a real live slave . . . a creature whom she could treat as she had treated Jacko the monkey, or one of her dogs, and that none dared criticize or question her right of action. Having hissed what words came into her head at the unfortunate quadroon, she then calmed down and was prepared to be more gracious. But unfortunately at that moment, Fauna chose to be sick—very sick—over the white silky rug on which she stood, and only narrowly escaped soiling my lady's frock.

Then Henrietta screamed and fell backwards in hysterics. The horrible, loathsome child! Oh—what a beginning to their association! With *what* sort of Infant Monster had Pumphret presented her? My lady shrieked. Some of the female staff came running in. Abigail sent for vinegar and burnt feathers. My lord, half dressed, rushed in, hastily donning a bath gown, without his wig. He saw Fauna standing there trembling, deathly white, sobbing under her breath. His lady's jewelled finger pointed at the floor.

"Look! She has been sick—*on my carpet*—it is *infamous!* Take her away. Take her away, Mrs. Clack, and teach her how to behave when she enters my boudoir. Keep her out of my sight until she has learned control of her abominable stomach. *Take her away*, I say!"

Fauna's dazed and swollen eyes had a confused vision of Pumphret kissing my lady's hand, as he endeavoured to soothe her, and of two scandalized young maids bringing in water and perfume and cloths to clean up the mess. She did not realize the enormity of her crime. Fauna did not know what she was expected to do now. Her torture was only just beginning—that misery which her grandfather had prognosticated, and from which he would have spared her if he could.

Chapter Six

A large formidable woman wearing a black silk gown and with a frilled cap tied neatly under her several chins, advanced upon Fauna, seized her by the hand and dragged her out of the room. When she would have drawn back, she received a stinging clout on the ear which made her reel and cry out with pain. She was soon to see that she need expect no mercy in this quarter. Dora Clack was a most excellent housekeeper. She ran the Pumphret house with a skill and attention to detail and an iron hand over the subordinates which allowed for no mistakes, and made her invaluable to her ladyship. Certainly she had no time for the sensitiveness of a ten-year-old girl with black blood in her veins. For Mrs. Clack, like the rest of the staff, had become acquainted with the fact that his lordship had bought a quadroon from a slave ship recently returned from the West Indies, and that this creature, by name "Fauna," had entered her ladyship's service as a slave.

Now Mrs. Clack had never been married but she had taken upon herself the personality of a widow and having invented a Mr. Clack (including his profession of tax collector and his unfortunate death from pneumonia), had almost convinced herself that this gentleman had existed.

She was a thwarted spinster and of supreme ugliness; a martyr to warts and obesity. She looked, indeed, somewhat like one of the mangel-wurzels on the arable farm on which she had spent her childhood. Under the simpering docile manner and servility which she employed when in attendance on her employers lay a coarse and cruel nature. A bitter hatred for young and lovely females who had had better fortune with gentlemen than herself. Her unappeased longings for sex had had a brutalizing effect upon her and could find vent only in the spiteful bullying of those beneath her—some fifty or sixty serving men or women in the service of the Pumphrets.

If there was great dissatisfaction below stairs in the Pumphret household, it never reached the notice of his lordship or my lady—both of whom were too lazy and self-indulgent to trouble to find out what happened to their servants so long as the house appeared to run smoothly—which it did under Mrs. Clack's direction.

A housekeeper in such times as these was a formidable person occupying a powerful position. Not a serving wench or scullion dared defy Dora Clack. They trembled before her anger and toadied for her favours. She had even invented a system of small fines on the young and thoughtless should they forget some small task allotted to them. These fines—coppers which could be ill-spared from the few shillings they earned—found their way into Mrs. Clack's pocket and were finally transposed into a bottle of gin. She and Mrs. Golightly, the cook—a most excellent chef, even fatter than the housekeeper, though of less venomous disposition for she was given to bawdy laughter—were friends. They often sat together sozzling in the housekeeper's private quarters—gossiping over their liquor. Because of her fondness for victuals, Mrs. Clack kept some of her fawning and wheedling for her dear Louisa Golightly.

It was into the care of this terrible woman that the young Fauna was entrusted. The very thought of the *black blood* made Mrs. Clack's spine bristle and her pig's eyes sink more deeply into their several folds of crêpy flesh. As she said afterwards, over the gin, to her dear Louisa:

"It is not for us, my dear soul, to criticize our blue-blooded employers, but there are goings on in the gentry, and we *know* of it. Milady's conduct when his lordship is absent cannot be said to be above reproach. However, this is going *too* far—to import a black girl and ask that she should be taught poor Abigail's trade. Abigail is a sleek cat and a spy but at least she is one of *us*. But a *black* girl, Louisa. Oh, yes—her skin is white but she is coloured. It disgusts me to touch her. And she is defiant, Louisa. I shall have to use the whip. My lady has asked me not to let the girl be seen above stairs again until she has learned that she is no more than a miserable little slave. A creature that has been *bought*, Louisa! An abomination!"

These things were said in the cosy privacy of Mrs. Clack's sitting-room where the two women sat with their feet on the table, their caps off and their stays unlaced—a hideous spectacle.

Previously—to a dim little garret up ten flights of steep back stairs, at the very top of the house, the housekeeper had dragged the reluctant Fauna.

Still feeling ill and frightened, Fauna was given no time to examine her surroundings thoroughly. She could just see a dirty skylight, a scrubbed wooden floor without mats—a straw palliasse in the corner such as might be offered a soldier on campaign, upon which lay a couple of blankets of inferior quality, and a pillow in a coarse cotton slip. The flickering light of a candle lighted by Mrs. Clack, cast huge shadows on a ceiling that was discoloured and peeling; it had been leaking since the last heavy downpour of rain.

The room smelt musty. There clung to it the odour of the unwashed and of stale clothing. Dead beetles and flies had settled on the skylight. On this warm summer's night, the little attic was nauseous and stifling. The room had been recently occupied by an unfortunate scullery maid who, at the age of fourteen, had been worked to death by Mrs. Clack and hustled away to her unfortunate parents before she could inconvenience her noble employers by dying under their roof. She had expired in her mother's cottage with scarcely an ounce of flesh left on her bones; a particular victim of Mrs. Clack's because the child had been pretty and attracted the attention of Mr. Milligan, the butler—on whom Mrs. Clack had cast a lascivious eye without success.

Into this lonely and gloomy bedroom which had certainly never been seen by Lady Henrietta, herself, came Fauna. It was better, certainly, than the hold of the hell-ship of the slave trader, *The Nauticas*. Yet even there she had been in the company of her devoted grandparent and other kidnapped members of their tribe. She had listened to their lamentations but she had also heard their songs and felt their tears and kisses on the little hand of their "princess." But this drear unappetizing bedroom spelt a terrifying and unaccustomed loneliness to the child. With her small hands pressed against her mouth, she looked around her, her breast still heaving with the sobs she had not been able to control since she left her ladyship's bedroom.

Mrs. Clack folded her arms across her huge bosom. She regarded Fauna as she might do a beetle crawling across the boards.

"Nigger!" she hissed.

Without understanding, Fauna's great velvety eyes looked up at Dora Clack's face. It was like that of an infant monster puckered under its frilled cap.

"Nigger! I said," repeated Mrs. Clack. "How dared you be sick on her ladyship's carpet—defiling it?"

Fauna neither answered or moved. She went on staring at the woman in petrified silence.

"Do you know my name?" demanded her tormentor.

The child shook her head. Then the woman leaned forward and shook her.

"Learn it. It is Mrs. Clack. And you will call me 'Ma'am.' You will say *'Yes, Ma'am,'* and *'No, Ma'am'* when I speak to you. You will do exactly what you are told *when* you are told. Do you hear me?"

Fauna heard but her dazed and overwrought mind could ill fathom the meaning of all these things that were being said to her.

"Do you hear me?" thundered the woman.

"Yes," whispered Fauna.

"Yes—what?"

"I do not know."

A resounding slap across Fauna's face. It sent her reeling across the garret. She dropped on to the floor and then picked herself up and like a little scared beaten animal rushed into a corner and stood with her back to it, her enormous eyes like pools of black terror gleaming in the candlelight.

"Come here, *Nigger,*" spat Mrs. Clack.

Fauna shook her head. It was more from a maze of fear and confusion than a wish to defy. But the lack of immediate obedience sent Mrs. Clack into a tantrum. She had no time to waste on training a nigger girl, she told herself, and just to satisfy a whim of her ladyship. And she was not going to have her task made harder by a display of rebellion such as one might *expect* and suffer from those two little nobly born cherubs now sleeping innocently in their frilled cots in the sweet-scented night-nursery downstairs.

That Fauna was only a child and had been used to a free untrammelled existence—first lady of her grandfather's tribe—accustomed to giving royal commands and receiving instant ceding to her wishes—to sunlight, to plenty, to happiness—would never enter the housekeeper's head. And if it had, she would still have treated Fauna in the same way. For here was something she could worry and ill-treat to her heart's content. The scullery maid who had died had caused Mrs. Clack one or two uneasy moments, for the girl had been English born, of honest labouring people. But this *Fauna* . . . wretched heathen name thought Mrs. Clack . . . was only a bought slave. Nothing delighted her more than the idea that she could act on the principle that a black slave must be *treated* as a black slave; never mind her white skin or her red hair. The little girl's remarkable beauty only further incensed Mrs. Clack's desire to crush her.

During the few moments that followed it seemed to Fauna that all hell was let loose and that she had been flung into a lunatic world. She was dragged from her corner. The clothes which the more kindly woman in Bristol had sewn for her were torn from her body. Flung on the palliasse, there she was thrashed with a belt unclasped from Mrs. Clack's gargantuan waist, until that unfeeling woman's breath failed and her arm ached. The attic which had been filled with the sound of a terrified child's screaming, grew suddenly quiet. Dora Clack, the mists of rage clearing from her eyes, looked down and saw what she had done. The little girl did not move or cry out. The white exquisite back was criss-crossed with weals. Turning her over, the housekeeper looked upon an unconscious form. Fauna had passed into oblivion.

The woman saw no tragedy in the defencelessness of that lovely uncovered childish form or of the long lashes sweeping the white little face, but she did not want a repetition of the scullery maid's end, here and now. Fauna had been brought here by his lordship so must not be allowed to die. Mrs. Clack realized that she had gone too far in her insensate desire to make the little slave girl obey her.

Hastily she covered Fauna with a blanket, opened the skylight to allow in some air, then, muttering to herself, trundled down the steep dark stairs, candle in hand. Once in her sitting-room she sent for Amelia, the new scullery maid, a child of thirteen. Amelia had only been in domestic service a few weeks and wore a new cotton frock and starched apron, with her hair, which Mrs. Clack had cut short, well tucked under her mob cap. She was a country girl brought up in poor circumstances and spoke with a strong Sussex dialect; raw-boned, rough, but kindly. She had learned already to be mortally afraid of the housekeeper and bobbed, as she had been taught, as soon as she came into that formidable woman's presence.

Mrs. Clack, fanning herself after her exertions, commanded Amelia to go upstairs with milk and bread and butter for the newcomer, and to apply vinegar to her temples.

"She has had the impertinence to lose her senses," said Mrs. Clack sniffing loudly. "Wretched nigger girl! Bring her back to her senses Amelia, and see that she is fed. In the morning you will take her what victuals Mrs. Golightly may apportion her. And you will see that she does not leave that room. Lock the door when you leave and bring me the key. If she escapes, *you* will answer to her ladyship *and to me.*"

Amelia quaked—she gasped: *"Yes, Ma'am,"* bobbed and fled as for her life.

She, like the rest of the domestic staff had been discussing with the juniors the arrival of the little mulatto slave. She took the milk and the bread and butter up to the garret, her dull mentality grasping only the fact that this slave whom they called Fauna must be no more than a little animal, to be treated as they treated her ladyship's monkey who had died—or one of the dogs or cats.

Amelia was therefore vastly astonished when she entered the attic and saw, in the candlelight, the fair skin and red-gold hair of the child who had now recovered consciousness and was moaning pitifully—in great pain.

"Mercy on us!" gasped Amelia and almost dropped the candle, burning her hand with the falling wax.

The next moment she was kneeling beside the palliasse

bathing Fauna's lacerated back with a rough tenderness. Amelia was slow-witted and ignorant but she would not have done less for Fauna than she would do for an injured animal on the farm where her father laboured. Before long she had somewhat pacified and reassured her and helped her to sit up and partake of some of the simple repast.

But when Fauna clung to this new friend, streaming with tears, begging her not to go, the little scullery maid scratched her head and looked awkward.

"I mun do wot Mrs. Clack, 'er say," she mumbled, "I mun go, me ducky."

Fauna did not understand. She only knew that she was to be left once more to her world of tears, of terrors, of physical discomfort and mental despair. But Amelia promised to come and see her again when she could slip away from work. Meanwhile she cautioned the child to be obedient and do all that Mrs. Clack bade her.

Fauna was left now without the candle, in darkness. She sobbed herself into a fever and lay shivering and sweating in turn, until, at dawn, she fell into an uneasy slumber.

Amelia went down to tell those of the staff prepared to listen to her that the "nigger girl" was "white as milk and beautiful" and that Mrs. Clack had whipped her into a coma.

A certain amount of sympathy was then expressed for this queer newcomer to the household, but it was not expressed very loudly. And it was Mrs. Clack's orders that nobody went to see Fauna nor attend her except the scullery maid who could be relied upon to do exactly what she was told.

So, for a week, Fauna, day and night remained locked in that attic and once or twice was subjected to visits from Mrs. Clack herself. The housekeeper managed each time to reduce Fauna to a state of abject fear, but did not physically ill-treat her. She was frightened that her ladyship would notice those marks on the childish back, and object. She gave Amelia ointment to apply to the weals. But Mrs. Clack was quite satisfied that she now held the girl in the hollow of her hand and that Fauna would do as she was told in future. Fortunately for Mrs. Clack her ladyship did not worry her head about the new toy for a week or so, as she was too busy with Court Balls and State functions at which my Lord Pumphret was in attendance upon the Prince.

It was nearly three weeks, therefore, before Fauna emerged—pale, silent and completely subdued—from that prison at the top of the house, and was conducted once again into the presence of Lady Henrietta.

Chapter Seven

About a month after this—towards the end of July—his lordship announced that if her ladyship were so willing, he would prefer that the household moved into the country to occupy the Pumphrets' country seat which was close to Hampton Court. Henrietta was willing, because baby Arabella had been ailing of late and needed the country air. Besides, Pumphret Park was a charming residence built in the eighteenth-century style—with a fine garden and ornamental lake, and my lady could give some pretty out-of-doors parties there in good weather.

The whole household, therefore, was packed up and made ready to depart from Fitzroy Square.

One afternoon before the closing down of the great domicile, Henrietta lay on her chaise-longue in her boudoir looking very handsome in an India muslin-gown, threaded with cherry-coloured ribbons and with her dark hair unpowdered curling to her bare shoulders, and flirted outrageously with her newest passion.

Anthony Lennox, seated on a foot stool beside my lady, imprisoned one of the snowy hands which he kissed repeatedly and read to her a poem which he had written extolling her matchless beauty. Now and again he sighed. It was a blow to him that his dearest Henrietta must leave London, even for a month or two. His political activities would keep him in the capital, although of course he had sworn to ride to Hampton to see his mistress whenever possible. And his mistress, Henrietta, had, indeed, become, soon after the party given to welcome George back from Bristol. Here, in her airy-fairy, gilded, flower-filled bower, Henrietta had surrendered more than her red lips to the eager and handsome young man. He was, of course, not by any means the first lover she had taken during this somewhat lascivious period, when most titled ladies indulged in amorous pastimes, and morals were extremely lax. But for Anthony Lennox it was the first time he had enjoyed such bounty in the arms of any but the light-o'-loves about whom one did not speak in the presence of delicately nurtured ladies.

When he had finished reading the verses to Henrietta and basked in the compliments she paid him, he spent a little time caressing her, after which she transferred a languid hand to his bright hair. She liked him like this, without peruke or bobwig. She wished the fashion for wigs would go out. But of course it could not while His Majesty and the Prince chose to maintain it.

"It will be a little boring at Hampton Court but I shall live for your visits, my sweet Tony," she murmured.

"One so beautiful and desirable as you should not have to suffer boredom," he said, and added, "what of your new fancy—the little Fauna?"

Henrietta's expression changed. A slightly uneasy look came into her almond eyes. She pouted and ceased to ruffle her Anthony's hair.

"George's 'Insect' (for that is what he calls her)—oh, I do not know, Tony. There are moments when I wish he had never bought her for me."

"Then sell her again," said the young man yawning.

"Oh, no. Clarissa Rustingthorpe is all too mad to possess her."

Anthony laughed, amused by the unfailing desire which his mistress displayed, to arouse the fair Clarissa's jealousy.

"So her whim is not to be satisfied?"

"No," said Henrietta sharply, and examined her pointed nails.

She had had quite a little scene with dear Clarissa after the *soirée* given by the Marquis and Marchioness in their London home in order to introduce a new and excellent violinist to Society. There was a great craze for Mozart and *musicales* at the moment. While the concert was being given, that hateful little Zobbo, wearing a green turban flashing with a real ruby, had held aloft a silver candelabra to shed the light upon the music for the soloist. On the other side had stood another small figure holding a second candelabra. Fauna, the quadroon, whom Henrietta had lent to her dear Clarissa for the occasion. Henrietta had especially designed Fauna's costume for the occasion. As a little Turkish girl in full satin trousers, emerald to match Zobbo's turban, and wearing a yashmak—just as Henrietta had fancied—over which the girl's eyes had gleamed most entrancingly. A little round velvet hat on the side of the red-gold head completed the fascinating outfit. Much of a size the two had been—Fauna, who was only ten and Zobbo who was sixteen and a dwarf. The effect had been original and stunning. All London had chattered afterwards about it. But whereas nobody cared for Zobbo who was mischievous and ugly with his great leathery lips and black oily skin—everybody had gone crazy about Fauna. It was the first time Henrietta had exhibited her in a *Drawing-room*. The ladies had exclaimed with delight, and one and all had envied Henrietta. The gentlemen had murmured:

"She is a miniature *houri* and in a few years' time—*la! la!*"

Not that that had particularly pleased my lady. Fauna as a child was a charming toy, and the excellent Mrs. Clack had done her job well—when Fauna re-appeared nobody could be more obedient and docile. And for one so young, she had learned quickly and intelligently the tasks she was asked to perform for my lady. Her greatest asset to my lady's mind was that she hardly ever opened her mouth. She was silent and sad. But the sadness became her. And as George had promised his lady, Fauna could sing—and did sing when commanded—strange little songs in the African tongue which my lady found soothing, and were for her friends a rare entertainment. But her sex and her attraction definitely were drawbacks.

It was all right as long as Fauna was attending her lady when alone. Young though she was, her fingers were so nimble and delicate and her touch so soothing that she had quite taken Abigail's place as a masseuse, and worked charms when my lady had aches or pains—for Henrietta was a little given to rheumatism in the rainy weather. Abigail was also—reluctantly (but not daring to protest) training Fauna to dress milady's hair into ringlets, and used the tongs with dexterity. And she polished both finger and toe nails until they gleamed. She had tricks, too, learned in her native country, for cleaning and rubbing gems until they shone with added lustre, and when one of my lady's strings of pearls broke, nobody in the house could re-string them with such astonishing speed and professional knowledge as Fauna. Useful, and ornamental at the parties when standing behind my lady while she ate her food, or seated on a stool beside her, holding her fan, or her posy, or a wrap—running countless little errands; riding with her in the park or walking behind her on a shopping expedition with a pretty golden basket in which to carry the packages.

Always, wherever they went, people stared and gaped, or uttered little cries of admiration for the child's fabulous beauty. Henrietta pandered to this and dressed Fauna in all kinds of fanciful clothes. Oriental veils and turbans. Elizabethan farthingales. Scottish tartans. Satins, silks and laces—dressing her up like a doll, with hats and feathers; sometimes making of her an absurdity; sometimes something classical and nymph-like in Greek drapery; or again as a native, staining her skin with betel-nut, and ill-concealing her childish limbs, wearing only a few bead embroideries which she, herself, had threaded. But after donning one of these, standing all day behind my lady at a garden party when the wind grew chill, Fauna had caught a cold and been in a fever for a week. So Henrietta, afraid of losing her, had seen to it that she was more warmly clad in future.

All very amusing—especially when great painters of the day asked too be allowed to portray the quadroon on canvas, and one of the leading caricaturists of the day had featured her in a book. Henrietta had always been in the public eye as a reigning Society hostess before Fauna came. But now she was talked of and written about so much that George Pumphret found it embarrassing, especially when at the Club, bawdy suggestions about Fauna's parents were made, and jests that he had had to repudiate and laugh down. But to Henrietta it was all the breath of life. Until it was reported to my lady that Mr. Milligan, of her household, had been found attempting to break into the lovely child's bedroom one night. He had been soundly belaboured by Mrs. Clack who had been watching. She hinted to her lady (born of her hatred for Fauna) that the quadroon had the makings of a harlot—even at the tender age of ten she had encouraged Mr. Milligan. Which Henrietta only half believed although she had seen Fauna's velvety eyes turn in George's direction, and deplored George's reactions. And one night there was trouble because George had spoken kindly to Fauna and the little girl's eyes had filled with tears, so he had called her to his side and not having seen her since he brought her to the house, asked her how she fared. She had cast a terrified look at Henrietta who tossed her head haughtily, whereupon Fauna had remained stricken dumb as though afraid to utter a word. Then George had actually put an arm around the little creature's shoulders and called her his "poor pretty Insect" and asked why she had such a melancholy air. Then she had begun to weep, so Henrietta had ordered her from the room. George had uttered a mild protest and asked if Henrietta was sure that the girl was well treated, because he fancied that she had grown much thinner and strangely lachrymose. Henrietta had flown at him in one of her rages.

Did she not shower gifts of beautiful clothes on the miserable slave? Was she not permitted to spend most of her time in luxury following wherever Henrietta went? How dared his lordship suggest that the girl was unhappy? Or *thin* . . . for Mrs. Clack said that she ate like a horse and had been most difficult to train, with no sense of propriety or decorum, no gratitude for all the kindness shown her.

Lord Pumphret, who greatly disliked Mrs. Clack, albeit he appreciated the smooth way in which his house was run, wondered if the girl had so much to be grateful for. But he dared not interfere. Rightly or wrongly he had bought Fauna and given her to Henrietta and she was Henrietta's possession. He had learned that it did not please her ladyship for him to speak too often or too good-humouredly to her "toy." But though he was not an imaginative man, it was obvious to him that although Henrietta found it amusing to dress Fauna up and exhibit her and bully her, the wretched little quadroon found it most wearisome and, at times, humiliating.

Henrietta after this forbade Fauna ever to speak to his

lordship or to any of the gentlemen unless she was given permission to do so.

No, thought Henrietta this afternoon, as she passed an amorous hour or two with her young lover, it would never do to keep Fauna once she was adolescent. Her beauty and her obvious appeal to the opposite sex held far too great a menace.

There were other tribulations that "poor Henrietta" had suffered since Fauna's arrival. She used at times to take the quadroon with her when Henrietta had light refreshment with Clarissa. Clarissa, in turn, came regularly to Pumphret House. At such times there was always trouble with Fauna because she had conceived a violent antipathy for Clarissa's Zobbo, while he, the wretched little Negro, slavered and rolled his eyes in the most disgusting manner whenever he came near her. He had made Clarissa and her friend scream with laughter by openly professing a burning passion for the red-headed quadroon. One of the more coarse-minded of the ladies had suggested that when Fauna was older she might be wedded to the little Nubian, at which Zobbo had squeaked approval. But when this was explained to Fauna, the child had gone milk-white and changed in a remarkable way from the apathetic "doll" Henrietta tried to make her into something approaching an outraged woman.

She had stamped her foot, crimson-cheeked, flashing-eyed, glaring at Zobbo.

"Do not touch me. Get away. I will *never* marry you!" she had cried, and added in a fierce little voice some words in the African language which Zobbo understood if nobody else did. For he immediately began to blubber, and falling at Clarissa's knees, whispered that he had been grossly insulted, and that the quadroon had said that she came of a finer and cleaner race than his, and that if they had been in Africa, her grandfather's tribe would have drowned him. This had all been very amusing to the audience which was composed both of Henrietta's and Clarissa's dearest friends, but it had started trouble between the two ladies. Clarissa championed her Zobbo and demanded an apology from Fauna who refused to give it. Henrietta had boxed her ears but to no avail. Fauna was willing, apparently, to accept docilely the cruelties practised upon her by Mrs. Clack, the jealousies and the sneers of the rest of the staff (and particularly of Abigail) and she was even willing to be beaten. But she would not when she was older, she said, be mated with Zobbo.

Henrietta had repeated the story to George. He had been indiscreet enough to take his "Insect's" part.

"You go too far, my dear, with such a suggestion. The child has English blood and a mating between her and that little monster of Clarissa's is not to be considered."

Then the wilful Henrietta had asked to know why. Was Fauna also not from the coast of Africa? Who would he wish her to mate with—if not Zobbo, or one of his kind?

"I do not know who will mate with her and for the moment she is too young for mating," was Pumphret's reply. "But if I have anything to do with it, I shall not see her thrown to the mercy of a misshapen nigger," and he had spoken quite tartly for him.

She had made him pay for that by banishing him from her couch for at least a fortnight, and during that fortnight she had shown Fauna no favours but out of sheer spite told Mrs. Clack to keep the girl occupied in the kitchen. She had too swollen a head, my lady maintained.

For those few days, Fauna, in disgrace, wore none of the pretty perfumed clothes which in one way she despised and in another liked—but rough servant's attire, like Amelia's, and was kept through the long close days peeling hundreds of potatoes or performing the most menial of tasks. All of which delighted Mrs. Clack, and Abigail in particular, who never failed to give her a sly pinch or kick. Abigail was bitterly envious every time my lady rang for Fauna to attend her.

Eventually Henrietta climbed down and agreed with George that there could be no question of a mating between Clarissa's Zobbo and her Fauna. Then Clarissa slyly suggested that it might be a good thing if Henrietta sent Fauna to *her* domain in order that Fauna should become better acquainted with Zobbo. Henrietta flatly refused. She knew perfectly well what lay at the back of Clarissa's cunning little mind. She was still trying to get Fauna for herself. Aware of this, Henrietta restored Fauna to favour and thought out new tasks for her and new methods of producing her in public which would draw attention to Henrietta herself.

But, as she lay there, allowing her favourite to stroke her hand and whisper of his undying devotion, Henrietta thought rather uneasily of that last big party a week ago which had been far from a *succés fou* for her.

Chapter Eight

It was a long time before London stopped talking about that night in Henrietta's great drawing-room—the famous, satin-panelled salon, which was so full of Pumphret treasures. At midnight Henrietta had beckoned her guests into a circle around a long polished table on the centre of which two footmen placed an enormous glittering sugar-covered cake on a silver platter. All lights in the room were then extinguished save those burning on the table shedding soft lustre on the low-cut gleaming dresses and the jewels worn by the ladies present.

Most of the gentlemen were in a state of intoxication. The host, himself, bored by his wife's party, had dissociated himself from it and sat in a corner playing chess with Sir Harry Roddney. He was much annoyed when, about to make a daring move, the room was plunged into darkness.

"*Now* what is my Henrietta concocting?" he whispered to the young baronet opposite him.

He was soon to know, for Henrietta beckoned to the handsome young Roddney.

"Come, you have a sword," she said, beaming upon him, "you shall cut the cake. Gently—where you note that line of sugared almonds—and carefully—neither to the right nor to the left of the line."

Sir Harry sauntered to the table. The others made way for him. He was popular in a certain circle, a noted rake and a close associate of Beau Brummell; one of the more dissolute young men of the day who wasted his time and substance upon gambling, drinking and women. Like Mr. Brummell, he paid immense attention to dress. He was magnificent tonight in claret-coloured satin with exaggerated cuffs sewn with solid gold buttons. He wore a closely curled wig over his own hair which was a deep chestnut. His eyes were a strange hue—bright and green under level black brows, and as thickly lashed as a woman's. His was a delicately cut face and pale. He did not colour or flush easily. He was of such good looks that he might almost have been called effeminate, except for the strength of the square cut chin and firm boyish lips. He was also remarkable for being one of the finest swordsmen in the country. Few of his generation cared to duel with Harry Roddney even when he was drunk.

The unmarried girls in his set both admired and feared him. The older men envied his success with females and his swordsmanship, and some of the more steady ones deplored the wildness of his ways. Indeed it was rumoured that his maternal uncle, Sir Arthur Fayre, ex-Governor of Gibraltar, to whom Harry was heir (his parents being dead) had threatened to cut him out if he did not mend his ways. The Society matrons, safe in their strongholds, vied for his favours, pretending delicious terrors, and found him difficult to conquer. He seemed, on the whole, happier in the company of men, playing faro till all hours, or taking his toll of kisses from the red lips in the bawdy houses, than when in the company of fine ladies.

Nevertheless he was an asset at any party and, drunk or sober, had a keen wit coupled with an insolent tongue and those fabulous looks which few women could resist. Pumphret had little use for the young undisciplined rake except that he managed to play a monstrously good game of chess.

Tonight, Sir Harry was not particularly drunk—but he was particularly bored. He was not even enjoying his chess with George Pumphret as much as usual. This morning, while still in his bed-gown, in his handsome apartments near St. James's Palace, he had been bombarded by a visitation of his creditors; tailors, wig-makers, bootmakers, a variety of shopkeepers anxious to give handsome Harry Roddney credit, but wishful also to lay their hands on a few golden guineas. What a disorder it had been—and with pretty Polly Teddington seen through an open doorway, still in Sir Harry's bed, screaming a little, drawing the bed clothes around her although she did not bother to hide her lovely dissolute face, or a portion of white bosom, from admiring eyes. Sir Harry's scandalized valet had stood by, wringing his hands.

Harry's clothes and Polly's lay all over the floor. In the adjoining room, his mahogany brass-bound writing desk was crammed high with those damned bills. So Harry was forced to make quips and jests with the insolent visitors while he struggled into grass-green breeches and coat, and green top boots. Over a lacquer screen, he watched them walk around, handling his *objets d'art* as though they were at a sale. The silver and the tortoiseshell boxes, the ivories and the *bonbonnières*. The decanters and glasses and ormolu clocks and candlesticks. One of the men even had the impertinence to dangle Sir Harry's big gold watch and seal as though to judge their weight. What a to-do—having to pacify them—to fill them up with wine, then, once again, dispose of them all by a faithful promise to pay his bills before the end of the month. And with his limitless charm which Harry could display on all occasions, his glib tongue, his swearing that his uncle would settle every account—Harry eventually got rid of them all.

Then he had to rid himself of Polly, too. Her artless chatter and sensual charm were repulsive when his temples throbbed and his mind was set on his financial troubles. Disrobing again, he plunged into a cold bath and asked himself how best to wheedle Uncle Arthur. It would not be easy because the last time they had met, the old boy had told Harry that unless he quit this extravagant and licentious manner of living, and got down to some work, he should not receive another pennypiece.

Harry had sweated the drink and dissatisfaction out of himself by hard riding, followed by a Turkish bath. Then he presented himself at my Lady Pumphret's drawing-room this evening. He was not over-fond of the almond-eyed Henrietta. She and her kind were too artificial for him. At a dance, at a party, he could pass an hour or two pleasantly with the pretty perfumed Society pets. But he despised their laziness, their dishonesty, their marital infidelities. Like many another man who, himself, leads a debauched life, he found such habits repellent in the other sex, unless a woman was an honest harlot, and he craved to find a woman as good as she was beautiful which seemed as difficult to discover in London in the year of our Lord 1797 as to reach the snow-crested peaks of the Himalayas.

Harry had of course heard much about the little slave-girl whom George Pumphret had brought his wife from Bristol. He had not yet seen her except from a distance on one or two occasions seated in a carriage, wearing a bizarre costume, beside the elegant Henrietta, riding down Piccadilly. He presumed he would find her here tonight. But so far she had not materialized and he was not sure he would wait. His head ached, unusual for Harry who had superb health despite his attempts to undermine it by the long nights of debauchery.

Dabbing a lace-edged handkerchief against his lips, smiling lazily, and sword in hand, he advanced towards my lady's table. With the point he pierced a layer of the sugar. He fancied he heard a muffled cry and turned to his hostess.

"Egad! There is a living creature within the cake!" he exclaimed.

Henrietta smiled brilliantly at the handsome young baronet.

"Cut where the row of almonds dissects the sugar, Sir Harry, and see what you shall see."

Everybody was silent. All eyes turned to the monumental cake. The atmosphere became tense with expectancy. Harry shrugged his shoulders and now plunged the blade right into the cake—along the line of almonds. Whereupon to the amazement and delight of all present, there rose from the hollow depths of that cunning concoction, a little figure that had already grown familiar to most of Henrietta's friends and acquaintances.

Her name rippled through the crowd.

"Fauna! 'Tis Fauna!"

Harry stood gaping. His cheeks had paled rather than flushed. To himself he muttered:

"Great God, 'tis a child and I might have run her through!"

He had a quick temper and he turned suddenly upon Henrietta who was triumphantly receiving the congratulations of her guests.

"Madam, would it have seemed so laughable to you had I inflicted a fatal wound upon this unfortunate girl?"

Henrietta's smile faded. There was a dead silence. During that silence the child who had been hidden in the cake—curled it was true, into a position of no great danger, well away from the row of almonds—stood motionless and silent. Harry Roddney's green brilliant eyes took in every detail of her. Angry though he was, he was filled with an instinctive admiration for the unusual and breathtaking loveliness of the quadroon. Thus, he thought, might Psyche have risen from the foam—this Fauna—emerging from the sugared depths of her cake, clad only in a diaphanous gauzy garment, arms and legs naked and garlanded with ivy. Her long red-gold curls fell in silken profusion across her immature breasts. That sad meek look which had lately marked her was very apparent to her beholders. Her tiny hands were folded, the wrists bound together with a little chain of gold giving to her an even more submissive air. In the soft candlelight her large dark eyes, thought the young man, were incredibly beautiful. Yet, although she was of such tender age, full of a melancholy that struck at his heart.

"The little slave girl chained inside a cake—what a sweet allegory," murmured one of the ladies with a loud titter.

"Bravo, Henrietta," said another, and Anthony Lennox rushed forward, caught one of Henrietta's hands and kissed it.

"*Brilliant!* So original. A miracle of workmanship on the part of your pastry-cook, sweet lady."

A loud chorus of approval, agreeing with Lennox's speech followed.

Henrietta, piqued by the way Harry had spoken to her, tossed her head with its jewelled and feathered head-dress, but pretended that she had not noticed his reproach. Approaching him, shé handed him a tiny silken purse.

"Therein, Harry, you shall find the key to the lock that confines the wrists of my little slave. You shall unfasten it, then she shall sing and dance for you. You will be charmed."

No answering smile on Harry's face. But he took the key, drew near to the child and unfastened the lock. Taking both chain and key, he tossed them on to the table. Then in a cold voice he addressed his lovely hostess:

"I like to play the part of freeing your slave, if freedom

it means, but I am still unnerved by the thought that I might have caused her death or an injury. I do not find it amusing. Your pardon, if I finish the game of chess with milord, then take my leave."

Like drops of ice these words cut through the hot smoky atmosphere of the brilliant crowded drawing-room. Several people gasped. There was a muffled laugh—hastily concealed. Henrietta in a paroxysm of rage, glanced at the direction whence it came, and fancied that it was her dear Clarissa who had just giggled. *Clarissa* whom she had meant to impress. Henrietta had been so pleased with herself for conceiving this idea of serving Fauna up in a cake. And cut in the way she had directed, the sword point could not have hurt the girl. It was monstrous of Harry to try and spoil her triumph and humiliate her before such a distinguished gathering.

Her lover, Lennox, saved her face. He lifted Fauna from the cake set her on the table and handed her a goblet of wine.

"The song bird shall drink this, then trill to us all and it shall be a song in tribute to the gracious lady to whom she owes so much."

The audience broke into applause. Fauna obediently sipped some of the wine. Tension relaxed. Henrietta breathed again, and felt in better humour when Clarissa ran forward and lisped:

"Now *why* didn't I think of putting Zobbo in a cake—a chocolate one?"

Everybody laughed, but Fauna's eyes followed the claret-coloured figure of the tall young man whose green wonderful eyes had looked at her with pity rather than curiosity, and whose fine strong fingers had unchained her wrists just now—touching her with a peculiar tenderness. Once more he was seated in the shadows, bending over the chess board opposite George Pumphret. Fauna's gaze continued to seek him out. It was as though she wished to imprint every detail of his face on her mind so that she would never forget it, just as she would never forget that he had been shocked and distressed, because he might have touched her with his sword. Indeed she had not been able to restrain that cry of fear when he first pierced the sugar-coating. Her little heart had beaten in wild panic, knowing that the moment had come for the cake to be cut. Oh, it had been terrible when Mrs. Clack and Mrs. Golightly had first taken her by the head and ankles and swung her forcibly into the crater of that cake, with her wrists bound by the chain which her mistress had had wrought especially for the occasion. With what dire threats had they induced her to remain rigid—half suffocated—and in that claustrophobic darkness, after Mrs. Golightly sealed down the upper tier of sugar. They had made only a few holes for air . . . just enough to allow her to breathe for the short interval that she was to be thus imprisoned.

Amelia, the scullery maid, and her only friend in the household, had dared run forward and whisper a word of comfort and sympathy. Even *her* dull mind had grasped the fact that this might strike terror at the child's very soul. Perhaps if Lady Henrietta had thought more deeply about it all she would not have condemned the little slave to such a fate. But she had planned the performance just as she planned everything else for little Fauna—callously and with supreme indifference to everything except the dramatic effect and the applause she coveted.

Fauna as Henrietta Pumphret's plaything, was gradually being deprived of all individual life and, indeed, was losing all individuality. At first she had been entranced by the luxury and beauty with which her ladyship surrounded herself and in a few of the pleasures in which Fauna participated. Anything was better than being locked in her beetle-infested garret, or condemned to the slavery she had to endure in the kitchen. But she was generally too weary and heart-sick to enjoy Henrietta's long-drawn-out parties in the way the less sensitive and coarser-grained Zobbo enjoyed them. Fauna seemed to exist in a constant daze and never to know whether she was about to receive a caress from her ladyship's hand and have a bon-bon thrown at her, or be slapped by that same jewelled hand, or tormented by the pinching fingers of Abigail. She had even had to submit to one or two severe beatings from the sadistic Mrs. Clack—but only when the housekeeper was quite certain the marks would not show and that she would not be taken to task for the cruelties she practised.

Sometimes Fauna had enough to eat—sometimes too much, as when she was present at one of the banquets where everybody pressed rich food and wine on her, and made her sick. At other times there were the long days when my lady had no use for her and she was then kept below stairs and half starved. At night she was robbed of the sleep a child of her years needed, kept up until the morning hours in attendance of Henrietta who allowed Abigail to go to bed but ordered Fauna to wait up for her. When my lady was overtired and had grossly overeaten or drunk, nobody could send her to sleep so well as Fauna, using those magical soothing fingers of hers on my lady's temples and feet.

Then, and then only, Fauna would be allowed to go and stagger up to her little garret to snatch a few hours sleep, only to waken early in order to attend Mrs. Clack who was amused to ape her employer's habits. Nothing filled the little girl with greater disgust than to be forced to brush Mrs. Clack's hateful greasy locks, or touch that jelly-bag, wart-covered face. She preferred the lowest, the most menial task of scrubbing stone floors in the basement. Mrs. Clack's flesh disgusted her. But she had learned never to complain to her lady for fear of another of those terrible beatings. Just as she had learned to subdue her proud spirit and accept humbly her position in this great household as a slave. *Nigger* she was called by those who wished to humiliate and mock her. So in her childish mind, there had gradually evolved a fear and hatred of her black blood—an antipathy for full-blooded blacks like Zobbo and a passionate hopeless longing to be wholly white—and free, even, like the plain, down-trodden scullery maid.

Fauna grew to loathe even her own beauty, and wish that she might change the blackness of those huge eyes that betrayed her heredity for an English blue. She no longer thought with sorrow or affection of the grandfather who had brought her up, nor with nostalgia for the African shores where she had once lived so happily. All that became part of a past that she had been tortured into believing shameful. She brooded much and forgot little. And she had developed one poignant desire: to be freed from bondage and find herself in a position of power (oh fantastic and forlorn hope) and in turn be able to place her foot upon the writhing body of one of these white people who now tormented and enslaved her.

Because she thought so continually and suffered so often, she grew thin and pale and very silent. Now as she stood upon the table where Anthony Lennox had placed her—her mind, as so often these days, was bemused, seeking only to do as she was told and so avoid further pain. But she could not withdraw her gaze from the figure and face of the man they called Harry Roddney. She sang her little African song, as commanded by her mistress, but she sang it for *him* alone. And her whole heart, bruised and aching though it was, flooded with an emotion so fierce that it could never have been experienced by a European child of her age. A mature and savage passion—bred in her by the African jungle and her grandfather's race. She was child no more tonight—but all woman—she who had only just gained her eleventh year (in her grandfather's kraals at the age of twelve they were already marriageable) and the song she sang in the native tongue was of sad nostalgic beauty, an intense yearning directed towards Harry Roddney. This night, the seeds had been sown in Fauna of what was to be the greatest passion of her life. But if Harry heard it he did not recognize its meaning. The melancholy chanting little voice merely disturbed him just as the sight of her budding beauty and her defencelessness had done. Suddenly his fingers, so strong although so slender, closed over his ivory queen, and off his guard, he moved it to a place of danger. Immediately Pumphret seized the queen and tossed her into the box.

"That lost you the game, Harry. What has come over you tonight?" he asked.

Roddney did not answer but rose and with a short bow and a muttered excuse, turned and left the room. He did not even glance in the direction of the little quadroon girl. But the haunting sound of her voice followed him most disturbingly as he walked out of Pumphret House into the night.

PART II

Chapter One

One dark raw morning in February in the year 1803, Fauna opened her eyes and with that terrible effort which she always had to make to rouse herself from sleep, sat up and lit the candle on the floor beside her.

For a moment she sat hunched, shivering in the coarse calico bed-gown tied by a tape around her slender neck, and cupped her hands around the tiny flame of the candle, trying to extract a little warmth from it.

The air struck deadly cold. An icy draught whistled down upon the girl through the skylight. When at last she slid from the rough blankets and walked, yawning, to the one small window from which she could look down upon the back garden, she saw that earth and rooftops were white with snow. London was blanketed. At this early hour of half past five, a pale winter moon was still shining. Dawn had not yet broken. With all speed, the young slave girl put on her underwear, stays and petticoat, then a dark brown woollen gown which was looped at the back, and a little black shawl crossed over her small but beautifully rounded breasts.

After breaking the ice in the jug she sluiced her face in water, ran a comb through her long gleaming hair, then pinned it up, tucking it into a muslin cap.

Fauna had reached her sixteenth year; she had no notion when her actual birthday might be, but because of information imparted originally to Mr. Panjaw (who had passed it on to Lord Pumphret) she was roughly aware of her age, and of the fact that she had left childhood long behind her.

For nearly five and a half years now she had lived under this roof—and known no other home except when she had accompanied the family to my lord's country seat.

They had been five and a half revealing years for Fauna; and the things which had been revealed to her had brought her little save misery.

For five and a half years she had learnt what it means to belong body and soul to her purchasers and to be without status. She had learnt under threat of the lash, of being incessantly driven by such heartless bullies as Mrs. Clack, or such cruelly thoughtless ones as the Lady Henrietta—to suffer in silence. To bear with the tyranny and the cruelty and obey with meekness, make no attempt to rebel. For she had neither kith nor kin; no friend of importance save Lord Pumphret himself and Henrietta saw to it that he rarely came in contact with Fauna. She had no friend even in the domestic staff. The rough kindly Amelia had left the establishment two years ago, having found a gateway to her own liberty and happiness and returned home to marry a farm labourer. No doubt she would eventually die of overwork and incessant child bearing, but she was in her fashion fulfilling her destiny and had departed cheerfully to it.

Fauna wept bitterly to lose her one and only champion in this great house where she was despised because of her black blood.

As a small girl, terror and misery had been her constant companions; but only because she feared punishment. Now as she grew older—carrying out all previous promise of beauty—growing taller, more graceful, more unusual with every year that passed—she grew aware of far greater dangers and pitfalls.

From her fourteenth year onward, these dangers became obvious. She could see how men looked at her, even the lowest-born scullion or pantry boy or tradesman seemed to regard her with that lasciviousness which she was beginning to dread. The butler, Milligan, who had formerly attempted to enter her bedroom had left. The younger one who replaced him, often made his own furtive efforts to waylay the beautiful young quadroon in some dark corridor, in scullery or stillroom, but each time Fauna managed to elude him, and at least in this respect Mrs. Clack was on her side. Nothing infuriated that good woman more than when one of the male members of her staff cast a desirous eye upon Fauna. Her spite was directed then not only at the girl but at the men themselves.

It would have been better for Fauna had she been like Carrie—the uncomely, plump, and pimpled scullery maid who had replaced Amelia. Carrie was the same age as Fauna. She shared Fauna's garret. She never washed unless she was forced to and it was most repugnant to Fauna who had fastidious nostrils, to be shut in that tiny room with her. Besides which Carrie was ignorant, foolish and sly and she spied upon Fauna for Mrs. Clack. Fauna despised her but recognized her as an adversary to be reckoned with. It was all, of course, a matter of jealousy. Carrie was bitterly envious of her room-mate's astounding beauty, and nothing pleased her more than to get Fauna into a row with the others. Or to taunt her because she was a quadroon. It mattered not to Carrie that Fauna had a fine intelligence and that in these five and a half years she had learnt to speak as though she were a well-bred lady, and had a natural dignity and pride which rarely forsook her. Carrie was the one who stayed in bed until six o'clock. It was Fauna who brought the early morning tea up to Mrs. Clack's bedroom—then, because Mrs. Clack knew it was a humiliation for the young quadroon—was forced to take a mug of tea to the rough lazy scullery maid.

All these petty acts of spite which were directed against Fauna, continued through the long years. But under the air of calm submission with which she accepted them, there burned a white hot flame of resentment. A fierce pride; a deathless desire for liberty. She would not, could not, live the rest of her life like this. Without love, without tenderness, without comradeship; without any of the happiness for which her young heart craved.

Perhaps nobody knew it—nor cared—but the young Fauna in her sixteenth year had tremendous potentialities. Whatever they did or said to her here in this house she was made for love and laughter. *And she knew it.* There were moments when she longed frantically to change places with one of the fine ladies who came to see her mistress and upon whom Fauna often waited. While she curtsied submissively to them and kept her lids modestly lowered, she looked at them through her wonderful lashes and wondered why *they* should have been born to liberty and destined for joy, and she only for slavery and sorrow.

If there were any truth, honesty or goodness left in Fauna at all, it was because these things were an intrinsic part of her nature. For she had grown up to witness a manner of life both confusing and incomprehensible; packed with contradictions. Convention and discipline on one side—and a shocking laxity of morals on the other. This house was a place in which most of the servants were disgracefully overworked and bullied, while their mistress lived in complete luxury, extravagance and licentiousness. Fauna could learn nothing of fidelity or truth from her wealthy employers. Even George Pumphret who had been to her, from the first, a godly paragon, had proved the reverse. She who waited personally upon the family, was well aware that Pumphret had his mistresses, and that his wife had her lovers; and that scandal and amorous intrigues whirled around the heads of half the splendid ladies and gentlemen of the Court who were visitors to Pumphret House.

One lesson, Fauna had learned absolutely. That there must never be a relaxation of morals for *her*, for they would kill her—or send her to a bawdy-house where she would lead a far more terrible existence, and die perhaps a victim of depravity and disease. These things Mrs. Clack had seen fit to impress upon the unfortunate girl as soon as she became adolescent. For that reason alone, Fauna lived in terror of her own loveliness, and the effect it had upon men. What chance she would ever be given to find even the humble married happiness to which Amelia had gone, seemed unlikely. My lady, in particular, during recent years had made it plain to Fauna that love and marriage were not for *her*. On several occasions, when some gentleman waiting upon my lady had been indiscreet enough to admire her beautiful serving maid, my lady had afterwards gone into a tantrum and banished Fauna as though she had committed a crime. And Fauna was recalled to my lady's luxurious bedchamber only because she had become invaluable. Henrietta had developed fearful *migraines* and declared that all the physicians' physicking or blood-letting could not ease the pain like the magical touch of Fauna's fingers upon her temples or her back. Added to which,

Abigail had left her ladyship's service and Fauna had largely taken her place. Fauna now cared for my lady's clothes, the decorating of her face, the dressing and powdering of her hair.

Unfortunately for Fauna, she had also proved herself to be exceptionally clever with her needle. Under the direction of a certain French lady whom Henrietta had employed for the purpose, she had learned to embroider exquisitely. Often when my lady was seized with a sudden whim for designs or initials to be added to a scarf or a kerchief or bedcover, Fauna would have to stay up late at night sewing, although half dead with fatigue. Her large eyes frequently suffered from excess of this close work, added to lack of sleep. But it was more than she dared do to complain or attempt to ease the burdens placed on her. She was fenced in on all sides and when she was not attempting to satisfy the exacting Henrietta, she suffered under the spiteful domination of Mrs. Clack.

Thus far, therefore, had Fauna's destiny proceeded. But on this ice-cold February morning, while she opened up the huge kitchens, shivering with disgust to see the cockroaches slither over the stone floors at her approach, she was particularly troubled.

A new menace confronted her. She reflected upon it as she filled an immense copper kettle with water and placed it over the fire which she had just poked into a blaze.

Long past were the days when her mistress used to treat her as a doll and dress her up for theatrical effect, or use her as a page-in-waiting—as the Lady Clarissa used Zobbo. Fauna nowadays occupied a position in the household purely as a servant. And the Fauna of today was in an invidious position. In the old days, Lady Pumphret had alternated between bullying Fauna and pampering her. Nowadays there was no pampering. And although Fauna hardly dared believe it possible, she felt that her ladyship was remotely but definitely *jealous of her*; yes, envious of those marvellous good looks which had become Fauna's enemy.

"Hide your hair, vain girl," Henrietta had screamed at Fauna the other day when a truant lock had escaped from the muslin cap. Or ordered her to lower the hem of her skirt because she showed too much ankle; or widen her fichu as she showed a curve of swelling bosom. Or cut the filbert nails shorter. And once, in a temper, she had even threatened to cut Fauna's sweeping lashes. It was milord who had on that occasion saved the weeping girl. He rarely interfered with his Henrietta, although he had never ceased privately to regret bringing Fauna here. He tried not to think about it but he knew well, the atrocious existence the young girl was forced to lead. He also knew better than to befriend her openly since it only made Henrietta more spiteful. But he would not have Fauna's eyelashes cut off, and for once he showed his wife that he was master. After this Henrietta, herself, regretted the cruel threat, and did no more about it. But worse had befallen poor Fauna yesterday.

My lady's fancies were no longer upon young Anthony Lennox. She had taken into her silken toils a certain wealthy young nobleman named Lord Hamton, who was equerry to the young Prince. The good-looking peer belonged to the circle in which Beau Brummell moved—and Harry Roddney.

Fauna had been ordered to take my lady tea and cakes at five o'clock yesterday. Henrietta lay on her couch in front of a huge cherry-wood fire in her hot-house, candle-lit boudoir. Edward Hamton was seated beside her. She lay on her cushions wrapped in a fur-trimmed velvet négligé, looking remarkably well and pleased with herself. There had been two men in her life since Tony Lennox, but Edward was by far quite the most amusing and Clarissa *envied* her his "friendship." Edward was an inveterate gossip and always had a store of mischievous naughty anecdotes, often bearing the most libellous reference to one or another of their mutual associates.

Henrietta was growing plump. Self-indulgence showed in the increase of weight—the double chin and matronly curves of bust and hip. Nevertheless she was still very handsome, and a great many young men in town angled for her favours.

As Fauna entered the room—the perfumed heat of it almost overpowered her, used as she was to the cold and draughts in her own quarters—she hardly dared look in the visitor's direction. She placed a silver tray on a lace-covered table beside her lady. The Lady Henrietta had just been laughing hilariously over a questionable tale recounted to her by Lord Hamton, and she was gazing at him, enraptured. She adored his choice in clothes. That dark green velvet became him vastly with his curly brown hair and girlishly handsome face. That he was a little plump and dissolute looking she did not mind. He was so entertaining. In good humour, she turned towards the young slave and bade her go through to the bedroom and lay out the clothes which her ladyship intended to wear for this evening's entertainment.

Fauna, with that extraordinary grace and dignified movement which set her apart from other girls, walked silently through the boudoir. Edward Hamton glanced quickly at the peerless form, the exquisite young face which was so pale and worn, and raised his brows. It was only about the second time that he had seen the famous quadroon at close quarters. He had not attended Henrietta's drawing-rooms during those days when she had been showing the child, Fauna, off to her friends in various disguises. But one of his gossips had told him about the famous night when Harry Roddney had cut the cake, discovered the hidden child, and reproached Henrietta openly, then walked out of the house for ever. Mr. Brummell had mentioned it too. The famous dandy had not spoken kindly about my lady. Oh, yes, there had been many stories about the quadroon who came from the far-off shores of Africa. But dash it! the young peer reflected this February afternoon, Henrietta kept the girl well hidden away. She was a jewel—she should be exhibited, forsooth. But he knew his mistress too well to dare comment on the poor young wench's extraordinary beauty.

Suddenly he said:

"You know, I presume, my sweet Etta, that Harry Roddney's uncle has remarried?"

Henrietta, sipping tea, yawned and answered:

"Yes, but I have little interest in Harry Roddney. He behaved most abominably in my house."

"All the same," said Edward nibbling a cake, " 'tis vastly amusing. Sir Arthur hopes for an heir, and if the fair Lady Angela, his new wife, gives him one—poor Harry will be ruined. He has lived on credit for so long, believing himself to be old Fayre's heir. From time to time the old General has settled all Harry's debts. He disapproves of the boy's gaming and his mistresses. But he is fond of him and only at Christmas cleared his more outstanding bills. But I have heard since that. . . ."

There followed much that Edward had heard about the situation between Harry and his uncle and of Angela, the young girl whom Sir Arthur had so unexpectedly taken to wife.

In the adjoining room Fauna stood still, one of her mistress's gorgeous brocade dresses in her arms. She had heard—for the door was open—every word that Lord Hamton had spoken. And her heart began to beat as it rarely did these days. She was generally too fatigued or depressed to feel much emotion. But the very name *Harry Roddney* uplifted her. It was as though a sudden flame glowed in the Stygian gloom within her soul's recess. Never, *never* forgotten that night when she, the frightened child, had been lifted by him from the mock cake on to the table, and looked upon with such deep compassion. How he had defended her, horrified that his sword might have pierced her flesh! And how he had dared to reproach my lady in *her* defence. Oh, never forgotten, his handsome features, his strange compassionate green eyes and the touch of his firm boyish hands.

All these years Fauna had grown up with the thought of Harry Roddney locked at the back of her mind. She had longed to know what had become of him. But she had never heard his name mentioned in this house again until now.

So he had mistresses still . . . and debts! she reflected. Well, that seemed natural for many a young rake today. But that he was perchance to be ruined because of his old uncle's marriage—that was a tragedy. Fauna was seized with the longing to know more of Harry. Usually so patient and humble there sprang within her the sudden incredible longing to find out where he was. *She might run to him.* Yes, she might break away from this hated house, throw herself before him, and beg *him* to take her as his slave. With what joy she would serve *him.* With what willingness she would perform the more menial task for *him.* If only it could be!

She put her hand up to one burning cheek then closed her eyes.

Mad foolish thoughts! Never before had she even contemplated breaking away from her shameful bondage—from my lady—or from the brutal Mrs. Clack who made her life such hell.

She finished what she had to do in her ladyship's fire-warmed bedroom then returned to the boudoir to collect the tea tray and take it downstairs. She found Henrietta gone. The young peer was still there standing in front of the fire, legs apart, hands behind his back. As soon as he saw the young slave girl now that they were alone, he eyed her boldly.

"Your mistress will be back in a moment, child," he began to drawl.

Fauna bobbed and seized the tray. She was troubled by the most painful yearning to speak to him—only to ask him for more news about Sir Harry Roddney. But no words came. Dumbly, afraid of the plump handsome gentleman (as she was of all men) she started to move away. Hamton glanced at the door. Henrietta had left him on a visit to the nurseries, at the request of the head nurse. Young Harriet, who was now eleven, had contracted a chill and the nurse had dared to interrupt my lady's session with her visitor only because the little girl was feverish and asking for her mother. At any moment, my lady would return which Edward realized. So he had to work fast if he wanted to satisfy a sudden sensual urge towards the quadroon. A slave girl was a rare addition to any household in these times. And jove! he reflected, what a pair of eyes the child had to be sure! Black blood or not, she *looked* white, and the grace of her, the voluptuousness of that youthful figure that no ugly clothes could conceal, went to Edward's foolish head like wine. He was mad to see her hair. And suddenly he advanced and with mischievous fingers pulled off her cap. He gasped as the red-gold curls tumbled almost to her waist.

"I'faith," he exclaimed, "you have a glory that should not be hidden! Come—how about giving me a kiss?"

She shrank away from him, terrified. The slim hands holding the tray trembled so that the cups rattled.

"Milord, please," she began in a suffocated voice.

But he, on fire for her—caught her and planted a passionate kiss on the red richly curving mouth. The tray fell from Fauna's hands. The tea spilled on to the priceless rug beside the couch. Fauna gave a low cry of horror and distress. Edward stepped back, laughing a trifle sheepishly.

"A pest on it," he muttered, "What have I done?"

What indeed! for at that moment, Henrietta swept back into the boudoir. She had been annoyed to be called from her tête-à-tête with her lover, and put out because young Harriet was ill, but what she saw when she entered her boudoir sent her into one of those passions which she was never able to control. *Fauna*, her slave, without her cap, with all her hair flowing down her back, and being embraced by Edward. Then the shattered china, the mess on milady's white and rose tapestry rug which had recently come from Paris.

My lady screamed. Edward pulled the lobe of his ear and wondered how to get out of this fix, and Fauna stood trembling, ivory white, her large dark eyes staring at her mistress as though Satan, himself, confronted her.

Chapter Two

George Pumphret had just entered the house in Fitzroy Square when he heard the sound of a woman screaming. The long-drawn out pitiful cries of one whose pain grows beyond endurance. Milord stood rigid, appalled. He looked up towards the rooms beyond the musician's gallery. It being five o'clock, candles were burning in the crystal chandeliers and in the great entrance hall a log fire burned in the open carved stone fireplace. The house was warm and brilliant after the twilit streets on that frozen February day.

Pumphret had just been enjoying a game of chess in the house of a particular friend of his, and afterwards a glass of wine and a discussion of the Despard case. The famous Colonel Despard had been arrested in November of last year after his attempts to organize a society for the subversion of what he called the tyranny of present ministers. Despard had with six of his associates been condemned to death this morning. Pumphret did not altogether approve of the verdict. He had some sympathy with those who desired constitutional independence for Ireland. He thought the finding of the court too harsh. All London was discussing it—and—in lighter vein—Sir Arthur Fayre's marriage to a young girl who might produce a son and thus disinherit young Harry to whom Sir Arthur was leaving all his worldly goods. Without Henrietta's knowledge, George still enjoyed the odd game with Harry Roddney whom she, of course, had struck from her visiting list; albeit George agreed utterly with the reasons of Harry's behaviour under his roof. George, himself, had been horrified to find Fauna in that monstrous cake.

"What next," he had asked his wife indignantly, "will you do to satisfy your craving for notoriety?"

Much water had rolled under the bridge since he had bought the child-slave for Henrietta. For years now he had grown to accept lethargically the fact that Fauna was a nonentity and considered the lowest of the servants in his employ. Alas, his poor beautiful "Insect"! He had hoped to give her a happy home—believed he had done her a good turn in buying her from the infamous Panjaw. But sometimes now he doubted it.

This evening, as he heard the awful screaming, Pumphret's good-natured face changed colour. He flung down cocked hat and stick and with wig awry rushed up the stairs and into the room whence came that distressing sound—his wife's boudoir.

He flung open the door and saw Fauna stripped to the waist, wrists bound behind her, bent over the couch. Her red-gold hair streamed to the floor. Mrs. Clack with a buckled strap was belabouring her—her fat hairy face perspiring, her pig's eyes alight with malicious pleasure. She grunted with each blow she delivered. Beside them, stood Henrietta, pale as ivory, eyes narrowed to slits, in such a rage as even Pumphret had never before witnessed. For unhappy though their marriage had been for some time now, the separate and immoral existence they each led had long been a weight on this weak but kindly gentleman's conscience.

However, it had been his policy not to interfere with Henrietta. He found the personal affection he craved outside his home in other white arms and on more willing lips. So he was—perhaps stupidly—unaware of half that went on in his own household. He had no notion that Fauna was being so maltreated—even if he imagined at times that she was plagued and over-worked, and given no opportunity whatsoever to develop the charming talents God had given her.

He was positively aghast by what he saw taking place this moment in his wife's perfumed bower. That place which should have been the setting for a softer more feminine and less disgraceful scene of cruelty and sadism.

He let out a cry:

"Stop. Stop this—*at once!*"

Mrs. Clack let drop the belt and at once bobbed a curtsey before his lordship. Henrietta swung round, colouring as she saw her husband's scandalized face. She had not anticipated that Pumphret would be home so soon. Less than half an hour ago, she had ordered her lover from the house—for daring to shame her so as to embrace her own "coloured-slave." He had made a hasty exit, the shrill voice of his mistress following him; ranting hysterically. How dared he kiss a nigger with lips that had touched hers, Henrietta's, she had screamed. Never would she receive him again. Never more should he enjoy her embraces. Scoundrel, pig, brute that he was! And thus—until he had left the house and shut the door on the sound of her vituperative voice.

A hackney chair then took Edward Hamton to one of the fashionable clubs in Piccadilly. There, fanning his claret-coloured face and panting, he had recounted the tale to his cronies, stifling his lewd laughter. It was soon to spread through London and reach the delighted ears of Clarissa Rustingthorpe. Henrietta Pumphret had caught her lover in the act of kissing the beautiful quadroon. What a humiliation for the haughty Henrietta! And Edward said that one touch of the slave-girl's beautiful lips had amply rewarded him for the loss of Lady Henrietta's kisses.

After his going, Henrietta had flown like a mad woman at the unfortunate Fauna, clawing at her face, tearing at those beautiful red-gold curls which she accused her of "wantonly revealing in order to ensnare his lordship." She listened to no explanations—accepted no excuses. Fauna was given no chance to tell how Edward Hamton had snatched that embrace and knocked the tray from her hands. She was at the mercy of a hysterical woman who lusted to avenge herself on the young lovely helpless girl who had dared to attract Edward.

Every vile epithet Henrietta could think up had rattled like hailstones from her lips, flailing the shrinking Fauna, who was reminded of her childhood and those two coarse fisher-girls whom she had watched sparring on the docks at Bristol. Then, the degrading sight had excited yet frightened the small ignorant quadroon. Today she, herself, was the victim of a similar violence in the luxurious gilded bower of a great lady.

But worse was to follow. Henrietta forced Fauna to her

knees—her cheeks stained with tears and blood, torn by the long pointed nails—then rang for Mrs. Clack.

The housekeeper was only too charmed to bring her belt and administer to Fauna the thrashing ordered by her irate ladyship.

"I have hinted many a time that this wretched nigger is unworthy to be in your service, and that she only causes trouble my lady," she had said.

"She shall cause no more trouble here," were her ladyship's words, spat through clenched teeth. *"She shall be sold to the highest bidder*. In his lordship's absence, you shall fix this, Mrs. Clack. Get her out of my sight do you hear? And the sooner the better."

But first, Henrietta must see Fauna beaten. Beaten until there was little grace or beauty or vitality left in that slim young body with which to draw the attention of men—especially one whom her ladyship desired for herself.

It was in the midst of this fearful thrashing that Lord Pumphret appeared. He ordered the housekeeper from the room.

"Vile woman—get out of my house—never to return," he said hoarsely.

Mrs. Clack started to snivel and Henrietta to protest. But George Pumphret was now determined to be master in his own home. He lost his temper—most rare occurrence—and raised his cane threateningly to both the women. Mrs. Clack hurried out of the room. Henrietta subsided and burst into a passion of sobbing, trying to make out the story that she had discovered the girl flagrantly attempting to seduce young Edward Hamton and that she deserved chastisement.

George listened without looking at his wife. His gaze, appalled, rested on Fauna who had slumped to the ground half conscious and lay there moaning. The sight of the naked white lacerated back and the pitiful marks left by Henrietta's raking nails on the soft childish cheeks, made him feel sick with anger—and with shame for the woman who was his wife and mother of his children. Oh, Henrietta's abominable temper! That—and her craving for publicity—would one day be her ruin.

George made a brief answer to her garbled accusations against Fauna, few of which he credited.

"There would have been no need for the child to attempt the seduction of Edward Hamton. Rather would I believe that that contemptible young fop and gossip made the effort to seduce *her*."

Henrietta winced.

"How dare you, sir——?"

He made no reply but stooping, lifted Fauna up in his arms and laid her on his wife's bed. He ignored Henrietta's screaming protests. But as she followed him, he glared at her over one shoulder.

"Fetch cordial, and cloths and ointment for her back. Woman—if this child succumbs to your cruelty, I shall bid the lackeys throw you into the snow—and your daughters after you."

Henrietta squeaked and put a hand to her lips. Never had she seen George look at her—or speak to her thus. His face was a purplish hue. His large blue eyes were inflamed. She feared he had been drinking. She also feared *him* when he was like this. And, as ever, when her violent and insensate rages subsided, she began to feel ashamed of what she had done. She obeyed his instructions and brought cognac and warm perfumed water in a silver bowl. She even volunteered, herself, to sponge Fauna's back and bind her wounds, then hold the cordial to the pale lips until Fauna revived.

The slave-girl came out of that swirl of agony and despair, to find herself being supported by George Pumphret's arm, while with one hand, as gentle as a woman's, he stroked her glorious hair.

"Poor Insect—poor, crushed child," he whispered.

She essayed a smile, while her torn face like her back burned and smarted. She had not heard that foolish nickname for long years. The tears rolled desolately down her thinned face. In an anguish of longing for human contact and affection she caught the hand that smoothed her hair and bathed it in her tears, Henrietta stood by now like a figure of silent wrath and sullenly applied smelling salts to her own nostrils. Never would she recover from the slight administered by her Edward—or this subsequent hour. But she dared not annoy her husband further. Later, she reflected, she would cajole him into getting rid of Fauna. The girl had definitely become a menace.

Henrietta knew her George. Not only did she fear his anger and disapproval but he held the reins—the money bags. But he was not as yet blind to her opulent charms and in his arms, tonight, she would appeal for his pardon. She would say:

"Take the slave away. I would have done with her."

He would consent, pleased to be in her bed again. Then tomorrow, she would send for Edward. She would pardon him, maybe, and he would be pleased to be restored to her favours. She knew Edward's sly wagging tongue—he was better as a friend and lover than an enemy. She would be especially sweet and beguile him into forgetting the wretched quadroon, and his misdemeanour of today.

Thus thinking, the Lady Henrietta began to work her way back into George's good graces by murmuring gentle words to the suffering girl—ordering food and fresh clothing for her—and even having her carried to a guest room—there to be nursed and left to recover. When Pumphret asked Fauna if she would like this, she gave that touching smile and nodded.

" 'Twould be paradise, my lord."

Still sick with shame for what had happened, he handed her over to Henrietta but with a warning.

"You have shown a poor disposition and most unchristian cruelty to this unfortunate child, madam," he said. "I shall visit her regularly to ensure that she has your goodwill and that retribution is being done. Later, we will discuss her future."

Once more Henrietta was forced, sulkily, to assent.

Thus for the first time in her young life, Fauna, daughter of the half-caste Flora, and of an Irish gentleman, found herself wearing a silk embroidered bed-gown (graciously chosen from her ladyship's own collection) lying between soft linen sheets in a four-poster bed, be-curtained, and under a mound of blankets. She had been given a prettily appointed bedroom overlooking the square. Outside, the wind howled and the snow came blinding down. It was one of the worst nights of the winter. But Fauna, soothed and in deep wonder, lay in great comfort despite her injuries, and gazed awhile at a flickering fire which a scandalized and envying Carrie had been ordered to light for her former room-mate. Fauna was further warmed and comforted by a dish of eggs, new bread, and creamy butter followed by fruit—sent up by Mrs. Golightly. The latter had discussed the affair in horror with her friend Dora Clack. Both ladies were somewhat dispirited and troubled lest they found themselves disgraced and dismissed by his lordship. What they said of Fauna passes description. But Henrietta persuaded George to allow Mrs. Clack to remain with her on condition she never entered Fauna's presence again.

The quadroon slave passed from a glorious drowsy contentment into a deep sleep of exhaustion, following the third, worst and last thrashing she was ever to receive. For that strange night with its mixture of pain and pleasure heralded a new and more important phase in Fauna's life. First, a week while her wounds healed and her mind healed, too, and strength and hope returned to her.

Then George Pumphret, having made up his mind to remove the quadroon from his wife's vicious and unkind superveillance and grant her her freedom, and find a better home for her—was suddenly struck down by an apoplexy to which he was subject.

The snow was thawing that night. London streets were filthy with brown slush. Evil-smelling puddles lay in roadways and gutters. Fauna was still in the delightful prison of that magically comfortable guest-room—being well fed and cared for by a newly appointed French maid to her ladyship who understood nothing of what had happened, and was told to care for the beautiful red-haired girl as though she were an honoured guest.

Henrietta had her plans. George had returned to her embraces only too willing, poor fellow, to believe that she was truly repentant and anxious to make amends not only to him but to the quadroon. But Henrietta had done more than recall her husband to her bed. She had had a touching reconciliation with dear Edward who in his turn was pleased to participate in it—for Henrietta's drawing-rooms and Henrietta's parties were far too fashionable and amusing to be missed. Besides, he had had enough fun at her expense. And he was too displomatic to ask what had become of the miserable Fauna whom he had, in his careless way, so deeply hurt.

Henrietta was waiting her time . . . waiting for an opportunity to dispose of Fauna. She had forced herself to visit the girl daily and showed her false sympathy and contrition. But she hated her now—with a deep, vicious hatred.

Fate seemed to be on Henrietta's side. For soon she had no need to fear George's displeasure, George most conveniently threw a fit and passed from unconsciousness into death. On that nasty drizzling February night, his flunkeys picked up the twisted and fallen body of his lordship soon after he returned home from playing faro in the company of other gentlemen.

"I will see you tomorrow, my Lord Pumphret," one friend had said as George departed.

But neither he nor any man would see George Pumphret again save as a corpse. Later that night poor George lay on his bier with death candles at his head and feet, and only the muffled sound of weeping breaking the silence in the bereaved house. Henrietta, with her wailing daughters and her dearest friend, Clarissa, weeping beside her, lay on her bed in hysterics—frightened (if relieved) by this sudden snatching away of her lord and master.

But almost as soon as the physician left with the old women who came to lay the body out, Henrietta remembered the unwanted presence of Fauna in the house. She exulted because she was mistress here now. Her word would henceforth be law. In her new fearful dignity of widowhood she summoned Mrs. Clack. A few whispered words and the delighted housekeeper marched into the guest-room where the poor young girl sat up in bed drinking soup which the new maid had just brought to her.

At once Fauna's expression altered. During the week she had lain here she had actually put on a little flesh. The hollowed cheeks had filled out. She had more colour. She looked extraordinarily beautiful with a lace wool shawl over her slender shoulders and her gleaming curls neatly arranged. But the moment she surveyed the dreaded and familiar spectacle of Mrs. Clack's vast bulk, which cast a monstrous shadow on the ceiling, Fauna dropped her spoon. Every nerve in her body jumped.

Lord Pumphret had promised that she should never set eyes on Mrs. Clack again. What was this? Then Mrs. Clack advanced to the bedside and said in a terrible voice:

"Get up."

Fauna's large dark eyes stared.

"Yes, Ma'am. . . ." Five years of hard training brought those familiar words to her lips although her very flesh crept as she saw the malevolence in Mrs. Clack's small eyes and those hairy hideous chins. "But why—what——?" she added a stuttered question.

Mrs. Clack took much pleasure in explaining.

"His poor lordship has dropped down dead of a fit. My lady wants you out of the house. You have done enough harm with your ogling, and a'trying for to win kisses from the gentlemen and the rest of it. His lordship spoiled you but you'll be given no more chances to wink at men or spill tea on my lady's carpet. You are finished, you slut! Up, and quick about it."

Fauna put her hands to her cheeks. She went on staring at the woman. Her heart sank. Sorrow and fear crept once more to her side and clamped their remorseless fingers upon her shrinking spirit. One week of rest—of peace—of plenty. One week of dreaming about a bright and happier life. Then *this*. . . . Alas! Alack! Her kind and noble master *dead*. Now Fauna began to understand the meaning of the commotion, the faint cries of lamentation that she had heard outside her room. The reason why his lordship had not visited her as usual.

Never again to feel his gentle hand on her hair—to benefit by his weak but kindly attempts to uphold her cause—or to hear him call her by that name which had always managed to bring her childish comfort, even some little merriment. *"Insect!"* Oh, alas!

"God rest your soul, my lord. . . ." She murmured the words aloud remembering the Christian prayers she had been taught, while the tears dripped through her fingers and her body shook with sobs.

But Mrs. Clack had no time to waste, and no respect for what she called "Nigger's grief." The sooner she got the quadroon slave out of the house the better. She stripped the clothes off the girl and clutched at a fold of the silken bed-gown.

"Wearing my lady's apparel? Off with it and into your own things."

Under her arm she had brought the bundle of the coarse

garments Fauna used to wear. She flung them at the girl who rose and with trembling fingers dressed herself. Sobs choked her as she fumbled with tapes and buttons, remembering the poor deceased gentleman. Mrs. Clack added a few vitriolic words to the effect that his lordship might not have expired had Fauna not caused trouble between his lordship and her ladyship, all due to Fauna's disgraceful conduct which had had an impoverishing effect on my lord's health.

Fauna was too stunned by the shock of the news that had been imparted to her to take in everything that the housekeeper said. Within a few moments she was clothed and her wonderful hair once more wound around her head and concealed under the little cap. Much as she hated Mrs. Clack, she made an appeal to her now, driven by a great longing.

"Pray, ma'am, be so kind as to let me say one prayer beside his lordship's body, for I loved him well."

Mrs. Clack sneered.

"A nigger has no right to love a white gentleman. On no account shall you sully the death chamber with your presence, *slut*."

All that was spirited and proud in the girl rebelled against that word and for the first time she dared to defy the woman.

"As God is my judge, I am no slut and have done no ill!" she cried. "I have the right to pray for my master's soul, and none shall stop me."

And, so saying, she rushed past the scandalized housekeeper and out into the corridor. The woman followed, but her fat bulk and short legs would not let her catch up in time to prevent the defiant girl from having her way.

Fauna knew where his lordship's bedchamber was situated and in a whirl of grief she opened the door and glanced in. For an instant she paused. How sombre, how huge was the bedchamber—magnificently appointed as it should be for a nobleman—but what dread it struck within her. It was dim save for the light from four huge Roman candles burning in tall sconces at the head and foot of the great tester bed. Under the high-fringed canopy, Pumphret's body lay, stiff and statue-like. The face did not seem to Fauna at all like the kindly smiling familiar visage of her master. So suddenly struck down in a fit, poor George Pumphret's features were swollen and unbeautiful. Two death-watchers knelt with folded hands on either side of the bed. The young girl looked dazedly at them and made as though to move towards the bed. She could, at least, she thought, kiss one of his lordship's hands and whisper a prayer.

Then she felt the grip of fingers on her shoulder. Merciless fingers. She swung round believing that Mrs. Clack had caught up with her. But she saw the Lady Henrietta who had come to pay a visit to the funeral chamber and found Fauna there.

The sight infuriated the widow who had long since ceased to regard the quadroon girl as a pet, or even as a useful maid. She was a menace whose youth and beauty had come between Henrietta and her admirers. One whom she had been forced by George to mollycoddle during this last humiliating week. But now George was gone. Henrietta ruled in the House of Pumphret supreme. She pulled Fauna into the corridor and closed the door, shutting out the sight of that rigid and terrifying corpse in front of which she hardly dared maltreat his protégée.

"How dare you come here?" she hissed.

Fauna recognized the fact that she was to be subjected to the old hatred and tyranny, even from her mistress. She bowed her head, her tears continuing to fall thickly.

"You wish me to leave, my lady? Where shall I go?" she asked.

Mrs. Clack had overtaken them now and stood at a respectable distance. Henrietta shivered in the big draughty corridor. Ugh! How hateful was this house of death, and what a good thing it would be when they could lay George Pumphret among his ancestors in the vault of the chapel adjoining their country house. Once that was over, and the time of mourning expired, she might pass an admirable summer in the guise of a melancholy widow. Not that black became her with her raven locks. She must change it soon for a violet hue, she had already decided, and thought with tenderness of the exquisite bouquet which had just reached her from dear Edward, sent with a suitable message of sympathy. She might do worse than take Edward for her second husband. He was very rich and as Lady

Hamton, she would have something that even Clarissa could not boast . . . a husband nearly ten years younger than herself. That would be an improvement on old Rustingthorpe, even though he *was* a marquis! A jealous old scoundrel, William Rustingthorpe—poor Clarissa was forced to live in an unfortunate odour of sanctity. She dared not even take a flirt.

Meanwhile Henrietta must pass a few days and nights heavily garbed in black *crêpe* and Edward must not come here. But to one thing Henrietta had made up her mind—when Edward came again he would not find the quadroon under this roof.

This morning, when Clarissa came to mingle her tears with those of her dearest friend, those tears had dried like magic because Henrietta . . . poor, sweet bereaved Henrietta . . . had told Clarissa that she must retrench her expenditure and the first thing she would do would be to rid herself of the quadroon slave who was barely worth her keep. The Marchioness had wanted Fauna from the start for her own. So Henrietta had sold Fauna to Clarissa—*for Zobbo.* And she told the girl so now, taking infinite pleasure in watching the effect of this appalling piece of news upon the young quadroon. Fauna's face blanched to a milky whiteness. Her eyes filled with a horror and despair which quite made up to my lady for the jealousy she had suffered through this wretched girl.

Fauna gasped:

"No, no, *no*! Oh, my dear life, not *that*!"

A vile chuckle from the background where the housekeeper was standing. Henrietta's ice-cold voice continued to embroider details for her victim. She did not speak violently but in cool, cruel measures so that Fauna should understand very well what she was saying. Zobbo needed a wife. He had grown melancholy of late and was too much alone, since there was no suitable mate for him among the white servants at Rustingthorpe. What better than that a girl of nigger blood should be taken by him as wife? The Lady Clarissa consented most generously to give Zobbo a purse for the wedding and even to stage the ceremony in her own home; and all should be asked. Then as Zobbo's wife, Fauna could remain to serve the Marchioness. Zobbo would look after her and make quite sure no white gentleman would ever again look at her with amorous intent. And these last words were uttered by Henrietta in freezing accents.

Fauna listened until the end. She was shaking so that her legs would scarcely support her. In spite of her week's rest in warmth and comfort she was still only able to endure so much and no more. This was just the one drop too much. Her whole being revolted. Wild with fear and disgust she contemplated being forced into a marriage with the African manikin. Why, she had grown a full head taller than Zobbo and besides, she was *white*. Here in this house they called her "nigger" but she was *white*. A mating with an ebony black slave who was no more than an animal was not to be tolerated. She would kill herself rather than endure it.

Fauna fell at my lady's feet and began to plead for mercy. Henrietta looked down and noted that the muslin cap was awry, allowing a silken lock of bright hair to escape. If any pity stirred in Henrietta's soul for this orphaned and helpless girl who was only five years older than her own daughter—it vanished at the sight of that wayward curl. For it brought back the memory of Fauna's streaming locks when she had been found in Edward's arms.

Henrietta bent down, unclasped Fauna's hands from her black velvet mantle, and walked away. Fauna saw Mrs. Clack approaching. Then a wildness seized her. A terror greater than any she had ever experienced before. On the wings of it came a strength of purpose not to be defeated.

She jumped up and fled down the corridor. Mrs. Clack's voice followed, croaking, ordering her to stop. But Fauna's extreme fear lent her speed. She fled down the wide noble staircase. The handsome smirking faces of former Pumphrets looked on with blank stupid eyes from their great gilt frames. Down, down to the front hall went Fauna and out of the front doors which crashed and reverberated behind her. When Mrs. Clack arrived panting, and stood on the steps, looking into the dark wet night, she saw nothing. Fauna had gone. Night—and London—had swallowed her up.

Chapter Three

Sir Harry Roddney knocked on the door of the narrow but elegant house in which he lived. The bell from St. James's Palace tolled the hour of midnight. Usually at such a time the night's entertainment would only just be beginning for Harry Roddney and his friends. But he had spent, what were for him, two or three unusually serious hours this evening in the house of a certain Mr. Wilberson, a director of the East India Company. This was the most powerful business organization in England today. And Sir Harry had a mind to become a member of that most excellent concern. To do, in fact, what General Sir Arthur Fayre had been endeavouring for years to talk him into. *Work*. Work and put an end to the lazy, dissolute, and purposeless life which the young rake had been leading since he left Oxford.

For far too long Harry had lived on his wits as well as the allowance his uncle made him. But this new marriage that General Fayre had contracted with a young healthy woman who might so easily bear a son and disinherit Harry, had forced the young man to change his views—or go to perdition. In truth, also, he was growing weary of too much philandering, and in particular of that type of frivolous young woman with whom he was accustomed to associate. There was no paramour in Harry's life at the moment. The attractive Polly had left him when she thought his fortunes descended to a level on which she could no longer expect a jewel or even a bouquet. It had given Harry some cynical amusement to discover who his friends really were during this winter of his threatened downfall.

Then had come two strokes of luck to awaken hope again. First, extraordinary good fortune which had pursued him every night for a week playing at faro. He had made a pile with the gambling recently. Even now his pockets were stuffed with gold pieces and there were more in his coffers at home. Secondly, the return of James Wilberson from India. It was with Wilberson that he had just dined. He had told Harry that the British hold on India was strengthening and it mattered not that my Lord Pelham had informed Parliament that another war was possible with France. Napoleon's insolent conduct was causing not so much alarm as a determination on the part of Great Britain to reject the great soldier who had become a megalomaniac. There was bound to be trouble between France and England but, Mr. Wilberson had assured Harry, one by one the great territories in India were falling into English hands and business was flourishing.

Harry, who had idled so much of his youth away, had nevertheless never failed to read—to study the affairs of state and his country which he found intriguing. Once while his own uncle was Governor of Gibraltar it had been broached that Harry should take up a career in the Foreign Office.

James Wilberson had suggested that young Roddney should join with him now. He knew that the boy had an intellect behind that façade of idle dandy, it was a brain too good to waste on the crowd encircling such gentlemen as Beau Brummell and his associates. Harry had charm combined with tact and courage. He was a fine swordsman and if he chose to preserve it, he had splendid vitality.

"Come daily to my offices and I will see that you receive some instruction in business matters, then perhaps at the close of the year you might sail with me to Delhi and earn an honest living—that is if you wish it."

Harry was not yet certain if he wished it but he was willing to consider the offer. The kindly and successful business gentleman had opened this field to him because he owed a debt to Harry. Some two years back, Wilberson's own son, Esmond, who had none of his father's staunch character or will to work, had been embroiled in a fight with low ruffians who had accosted him on the high road passing through Chiswick. It so happened that Harry Roddney had been riding that way and seen the lad fighting hopelessly against three assailants. In a twinkling Harry had leapt to Esmond's side and with a flourish of sword, ran through two of the ruffians and wounded a third. He had then driven the fainting and repentant young man to his father's dwelling—a large country mansion on the outskirts of London.

Wilberson had thanked him and, much moved by the knowledge that Harry had saved his son's life, sworn that he would never forget it and that one day he would seek to repay him for his courage and audacity.

The boy, Esmond, had since died abroad of the plague. Wilberson was now a childless widower, and lived in seclusion when he was not in the Far East. But he had never forgotten young Harry Roddney. He had, of course, heard of the young nobleman's profligate habits but that concerned him not. When it came to his ears that Roddney was almost ruined, he made it his job to seek the young man out and approached him with his handsome offer which they had discussed this evening.

Harry, after leaving him, had avoided the company of his usual gay companions in the gaming houses, and returned to his own dwelling.

As his manservant opened the front door and took the rain-spattered cocked hat which Harry handed him, the fellow said:

"A young woman awaits you within, sir."

Harry unclasped his great-coat which was also soaked by the rain, closed the door against the icy wind that whistled down St. James's Street, and frowned at his man.

"I thought I told you, Vincent, I wanted no more of wenches."

"It is not Mistress Polly, sir, nor begging your pardon, sir, any young woman I have seen before. This one seems in sore distress. She is very young, sir, and begged with tears that she might be allowed to await you. I had not the heart to reject her, sir, and trust I did no wrong."

"A very young girl," repeated Harry, and put a hand up to his bob-wig and patted it. He frowned harder then shrugged his shoulders.

"I have not the faintest idea who she might be," he said and walked into his drawing-room.

Candles burned in brackets against the oak panelled walls. A pleasant fire crackled in the grate. The room was warm and odorous from the leather of many books, leather-seated chairs and the fragrance of smoke from the fresh pine logs that Vincent had piled on his master's fire.

On a table by the velvet curtained windows stood a tray bearing cut glass decanters of wine and brandy, and a platter of sandwiches. The good Vincent always made sure that his young master had victuals left in case he came home late and in need of refreshment. Faithful Vincent who, although most of Harry's valuables had long since been removed from these rooms, and been sold to keep Harry "in the swim," had stayed on in his service without payment. He adored his master.

Harry Roddney stood still on the threshold.

The figure of the girl who had been seated on a stool crouched in front of the fire rose to greet him and he was filled with amazement. For a moment he did not recognize Fauna but saw a slim and graceful child whom he judged to be of some fourteen or fifteen years, wearing neither cloak nor hat but the indoor garments of a serving-wench. Her dress was looped at the back showing a striped petticoat, her hair concealed under a muslin cap, and she had a little fringed shawl across her bosom. But it was not her clothes that held his attention. It was her face. A white delicate face which bore signs of recent weeping, and her enormous velvety eyes of a most unusual darkness, with lashes marvellously long.

She looked at him nervously and spoke in a low faltering voice.

"Sir Harry, sir—pray forgive me. I have come to throw myself on your mercy. I have no other friend now that his lordship is dead!" She uttered the last words on a sob, then bent her knee in front of the astonished young man and bowed her head.

Harry closed the door behind him and stared down at her.

"Who is dead? Of whom do you speak? Whence do you come?" he demanded.

"Do you not remember me," she asked sadly and lifted her face. "I am Fauna—slave of the Lady Henrietta Pumphret."

Harry's jaw dropped in his astonishment. *The slave.* Dear heavens! Of course he remembered, with a swift flash-back of mind to that night—it must be six years ago—when he had first seen the little quadroon. He had pulled her from the cake, and thought her both hapless and beautiful. She, whom he might have pierced with his sword! Since that night he had not set eyes on the Lady Henrietta but he had often talked with George Pumphret. Poor George who had so suddenly departed to a better life.

"I am Fauna," the young girl repeated in a tragic voice.

With an exclamation Harry lifted her to her feet.

"Do not kneel to me," he said abruptly. "I am not your master neither do I recognize slavery. There are men in Parliament, my child, who labour to forbid such monstrous trading, and to restore to all human beings, black or white, the liberty that is their right."

Fauna made no answer. Her heart was beating very quickly. Red blood mantled her cheeks. With a candid innocent delight she looked up into the face of the handsome winning young man whose features had so firmly imprinted themselves upon her childish mind when she had first encountered him. Some of the terror, the wild despair which had driven her into the night, fell away from her at the mere sight of that face and sound of his low rich voice. She said humbly:

"If you would buy me, sir, I would serve you with my life."

His cheeks flushed.

"Buy you!" he repeated aghast. "I tell you I do not recognize slavery."

Her big dark eyes looked at him with bewilderment.

"Then do not abandon me to my fate," she implored.

He saw her trembling. He said:

"To what fate do you refer? Why are you here? Who sent you?"

Explanations tumbled from her quivering lips. She told him what had happened to her from the moment of that scene in my lady's boudoir when Edward Hamton attempted to embrace her. Of my lady's rage and the fearful beating she had received, and to which my lord had put an end. Then of the week's respite which had followed, and finally of my lord's death and my lady's intention to hand her over to Rustingthorpe.

"It is not that I would have minded serving the Lady

Clarissa," she ended, "but to be mated with Zobbo . . . oh, sir, you know, do you not, the dwarf who follows my Lady Clarissa. A full-blooded African who bears no resemblance to me, sir. My mother had part African blood but looked like a white woman and my father was wholly Irish. Oh, sir, *sir*, I am no African. I could not endure to be forced into marriage with Zobbo."

And Fauna fell once more at Sir Harry's knees, sobbing as though her heart would break.

He stood a moment looking down at her, a look of intense horror in his handsome eyes. He had lost colour. He had to muse awhile to piece together all that she had told him. Gradually a profound disgust overwhelmed him. *God forgive me*, he reflected, *I have committed many sins and broken many Commandments. I have mis-spent my youth and led a dissolute life. But I have not committed a crime like this . . . to sell so gentle and lovely a child and pass her, body and soul, into the hands of a black dwarf!*

He considered this frightful thing that Henrietta Pumphret would have done to Fauna, seconded by Clarissa Rustingthorpe, and felt that he would spew in a corner if he allowed his imagination to run further. He knew many of the elegant ladies of the Court; their weaknesses, their immoralities, their avarice. But he had never suspected that two well-born gentlewomen could sink so low as to stand by and watch a sixteen-year-old helpless child consigned to such a doom.

"It is not to be endured," he said aloud. *"It shall not be."*

Fauna lifted her big streaming eyes.

"Oh, then you will save me!" she exclaimed.

"Who knows that you are here? How came you to seek me out?" he asked and once more lifted her from that abject posture and led her gently to the couch. He fetched her a glass of wine.

"Sip a little of this, my poor child," he added.

She drank it gratefully while she answered his question. She had run away before Mrs. Clack could prevent her, she said. She had rushed through the streets, crazily, without much covering for such a night. For once more a north wind had sprung up and hardened the slush until it became crusted with ice again. A fresh fall of snow was threatening London.

Twice Fauna had met drunken men who would have caught and detained her but she escaped. She had remembered hearing Lady Henrietta speak many times of a certain club in Piccadilly wherein my Lord Pumphret used to encounter his friends and play a game of cards, or chess or picquet. She had remembered also hearing that *he*, Sir Harry Roddney, frequented this same club. She had never forgotten his kindness. She staked all on finding him and securing his help. It might so happen that she would never have reached him nor gained his protection, but in the extremity of her fear she had used what wits she had and hoped for the best. She stopped a passing hackney chair and demanded that the owner should take her to the club.

"He demanded money but I told him the gentleman would pay," Fauna finished her story, adding in that humble voice which Harry found so pathetic, "I crave your pardon, sir, for the impudence but I had no alternative."

"Go on," he said, nodding, watching her, and thought: *How well she speaks. She has breeding and a strange sweet accent. She is not without education which raises her far above the head of any serving wench in England. It is strange and most intriguing. Her eyes are the most brilliant and beautiful I have ever seen.*

Fauna finished her tale. She had persuaded the man who brought her here in the hackney chair, to take her to the club. A manservant had informed them that Sir Harry was not there but offered his address. So she had been carried here through St. James's Street, and the kindly Vincent to whom she had fervently appealed, had settled her fare and allowed her to sit by the fire until his master had returned.

"He shall be well rewarded for this night's work," muttered Harry.

Fauna eyed him anxiously.

"You will not let them find me, sir?"

Harry ruminated; seated beside her now, he loosened his coat, and removed his wig. Astonished and delighted, the girl examined his close-cropped head. His hair was such a dark chestnut in colour as to seem black, but when he moved, the candlelight caught the reddish glow of it. Like her own, she thought shyly. Oh, how handsome a gentleman he was! and in kindness he somewhat resembled her old master who lay stiff and stark on his bier in that terrible house from which she had escaped. She was just beginning to breathe again—to feel that she had been allowed to emerge from a bottomless pit of raving hell into the daylight, and a spring of purest happiness. Yet it was not altogether peace for Fauna, for she was of a naturally strong passionate temperament and her maiden heart was shaken by a strange tempest of emotion towards this charming young man. His eyes were not sleepy and lazy like her former master's had been. They were brilliant, restless, almost mesmeric. As they gazed thoughtfully into her own, it was as though they probed her very soul and drew her magnetically towards him.

Suddenly Harry rose and began to pace the room.

"I know not what to do," he muttered. "It is an invidious position. You have run away from Pumphret House and if I keep you I shall be culpable in the eyes of the law. If they find you here, perchance, I shall be accused of abducting you."

She did not understand. But she, too, got up and made fresh appeal to him.

"Oh, sir, do not abandon me. Do not let them sell me to my Lady Clarissa—for *Zobbo*."

She uttered the African dwarf's name with repugnance as though she mentioned a crawling toad. And, indeed, thought Harry, Zobbo resembled a black toad. He had often seen the fellow in the wake of the pretty silly Clarissa. On one occasion she had taken Zobbo walking in the park for all to see and laugh at—dressed like a monkey, jabbering behind her, led by a golden chain, begging from passers-by who fed him with sweetmeats and nuts. A horror of a manikin. And as husband to *this* lovely child? Harry shuddered. No. But his mind was not yet made up as how best to keep her. He pursed his lips.

" 'Tis sheer folly if I keep you here, little Fauna," he said with a sigh. "What's to do about it? Heaven knows—for I do not."

Then she fell to sobbing again, pulling with slender frantic fingers at his arm. He stared at the fingers, so exquisitely fashioned and at the fine filbert nails. He had noticed them when she was but a child. He would not have been true man had he not been stirred by the delicacy of the contours of her face—her long swan-like neck; the perfection of her form, and that quivering rose-red mouth. Never had he seen such an upper-lip, curved, showing a glint of pearl-white teeth; the lower one fuller and cleft, like the small chin. She was thin and her cheekbones jutted out. She would be better for gaining weight, he decided, for he liked a rounded woman. But, dear heaven, her skin was flawless and of a magnolia pallor, and those great dark tormented eyes haunted his imagination. She wept to him:

"Sir, sir, do not condemn me to Zobbo."

"No—never that," he said quickly. "Never while I draw breath."

"Keep me here then. Bid me to serve you, sir."

"Child, I cannot. I have caused scandal enough in London but the wenches who have visited me here have cared not for loss of reputation. But you——"

He paused abruptly. Why should he imagine that Fauna, a quadroon slave, should either have a good reputation or be permitted to retain one? What was this peculiar notion he entertained that she was pure and must be treated as such?

Fauna's eyes great eyes searched his face wildly.

"Pray, sir, reassure me that I need not be returned to my lady or to Mrs. Clack."

"What can I do——" he muttered.

She put a hand to her lips, and imagined for an instant that he regretted his kindness and meant to hand her back to her tormentors. She sprang towards the door.

"Where are you going?" he asked.

"Anywhere—to the river—to kill myself," she sobbed wildly. "Death would be better than—than Zobbo." And she laid a hand on the door-knob. But he wrenched it from her.

"Little fool—come back."

"I do not wish to live if you will not permit me to stay with you as your slave," she said in a voice of profound despair.

The young man could no longer bear her terror and her pain. He pulled her roughly into his arms.

"There, there, my poor girl," he said as he would have

soothed a child. "Do not look thus . . . I will not let Zobbo have you."

She fell against his shoulder, weeping. Her cap was loosened. Gently he removed it. Now the beautiful hair, like molten gold with ruddy lights gleaming in the long silky curls, tumbled down her back. The serving wench was transformed into a young woman of such beauty, of such voluptuousness, that Harry Roddney held his breath. Fascinated he stared at her. Her lids were closed; the thick black lashes swept her tear-stained cheeks. The lovely passionate mouth was half opened, mutely imploring for tenderness. He felt the softness of her young breast and suddenly, his senses reeling, cupped it with his hand and set his lips to that young, exciting mouth.

It was not the first kiss of passion that Fauna had received. Edward Hamton, only yesterday, had thieved its sweetness. But then she had broken away, repelled. Now, as Harry Roddney kissed her, an undreamed-of ecstasy shot through the young girl. Instinctively her slim rounded arms went round his neck. With one hand she drew the man's chestnut head closer. Her lips moved with answering passion beneath his. He gave a stifled cry and held her more fiercely, kissing her thus until neither had breath left and must needs break away. Then Harry Roddney untied her fichu, and kissed the exquisite alabaster throat until the red blood flamed and stayed thus a seal set by his lips. She responded—with a grave acceptance of passion—showing a natural delight in it.

Now, at last, Fauna knew what it meant to love. She loved Harry Roddney, the hero of her unforgotten tortured childhood. To her—love must mean to give. She was all his for the taking in that moment, warm, yielding, infinitely desirable.

But a knock on the door sent Harry reeling away from her. She stood still, head downcast, face one burning blush, velvety eyes pursuing him as he straightened his coat and rearranged the creased white bands at his neck. Then he opened the door. Vincent, his man, stood there.

"Will you want me more, sir, or require further food or wine?"

"No," said Harry, clearing his throat. "No more. You may retire."

Vincent cast a discreet glance at the girl, noting her bright streaming hair and disordered gown. He coughed. Harry said:

"The—the young lady may stay here on my couch. I will find her a rug and a pillow. Bring coffee for two in the morning."

"Yes, sir," said Vincent and departed as quietly as he had come. He was not astonished. It was not by any means the first time he had entered these rooms and found a painted bold young harlot in his master's bed. But this red-haired young thing—she was not like the rest. She seemed quiet and ladylike—even demure. You can never tell, Vincent reflected, as he trundled back to his kitchen to damp down the fires for the night.

Harry walked across to the table, poured out wine and tossed it down feverishly. Then he wiped his lips with a fine cambric lace-edged handkerchief which he tossed aside. After this he felt the crazy throbbing of his body calm down. He looked once more towards the girl who stood there so still, so silent, clothed in the beauty of her wondrous hair.

"Fauna," he said abruptly. "You see why I should not keep you here."

"Why?" she asked.

He coloured and made a gesture of impatience.

"Come—you must know—must realize. You are a very attractive young female and I——"

"Yes, sir?"

"Stop calling me 'Sir' so meekly," he muttered. "Let us not be master and maid tonight. Let us speak together as friends. Call me Harry."

"Harry," she repeated the name with delight. He was charmed by the slow caress she gave to it. Assuredly, this quadroon slave of Henrietta Pumphret's had a beguiling way which she could not have learned. It was natural—inherited, perchance from her ancestors—her Irish father—her Italian, half-caste mother. Whatever it was—she attracted him with an astounding potency as no other woman had ever done. Only when he was partially intoxicated used Harry Roddney to seek the embraces of the light-o'-loves from tavern or stage. And no greedy bejewelled lady of the Court, nor one of their simpering daughters, had so far managed to ensnare him. But this little slave-girl he found irresistible. He passed from compassion and the decent wish to befriend her to an overwhelming longing to possess her utterly. Yet he tried to resist the temptation.

"Listen," he said with roughness. "You came here because you had trust in me. You ran away from those who used you vilely. How then should I use you in the same way and square my conscience?"

She only half understood. She whispered:

"How could *you* use me vilely? You are too kind."

"Yes, I would indeed be too kind," he said with irony. "Child, it would be best for you to leave."

"No, no," she said in terror. "You told the man I could stay."

"For one night, maybe, while I decide what to do."

"Tomorrow they may find me here and take me away and give me to Zobbo."

He put a hand against his burning brow.

"That—*never*. I have sworn it."

"Then buy me—buy me for your slave, oh, I beg of you."

"Even if I wanted to, I could not afford it, I am almost impecunious. They would ask an impossible price to strike their iniquitous bargain."

Fauna clasped her hands together and looked this way and that like a hunted creature.

"Then take me away under cover of night. Sir . . . Harry . . . find me a hiding place so that they cannot torment me further," she begged.

He breathed hard. His mind darted like hers, from pillar to post, seeking a way out. Allow Henrietta to sell the girl to the Rustingthorpes—he would not. But neither dared he keep her here.

The old, audacious Harry who feared neither God nor man suddenly asserted itself. He had done many a mad thing in his time—with and without the fair sex—and taken many a crazy gamble and won. Why not now? Why not act as Fauna suggested and spirit her away through the darkness before her enemies could seek her out?

He would rouse Vincent and send him for a carriage. Then give him a message to deliver tomorrow to Mr. Wilberson at East India House, telling him that urgent personal business might detain him for the next few days but that he would in due course meet him to discuss this idea of his working for the great company.

Now, to spend some of that gold he had so fortunately won during the last week of wild and successful gambling. He had meant to settle his debts but the creditors must wait. Harry had it firmly rooted in his mind that first and foremost he must help this friendless child. He even felt that the spirit of the dead George Pumphret was present—urging him on.

Later on, under cover of night, and with only the trusted Vincent in possession of the facts, he would drive Fauna to a certain small country house which Sir Arthur Fayre had bought when he returned from Gibraltar as a retired army officer. This place, designed and built some twenty years ago, faced a small lake not far from Epping Forest; reached through Blackfriars and Aldgate. Sir Arthur used to stay there with gentlemen, who, like himself were fond of going out at dawn in search of duck, wild fowl, or heron. Of late, struck down by severe gout, the General had had to give up his shooting. The little white house with its Ionic pillars and curved windows, overlooking the lovely lake—and with miles of rough woodland surrounding it—now stood empty. It would make a fine hide-out.

It was within Harry's knowledge that Pillars (for such was the name of the estate) was about to be sold but that so far no purchase had been contracted. The house was in the care of a simple lodge-keeper who kept the place dry; caretaker until such time as Sir Arthur disposed of the place. On the last occasion when Harry had seen his uncle—it had been at that fatal wedding to the smug-faced girl whom Harry had now, unhappily, to address as "Aunt Angela"—Sir Arthur had stated definitely that never more would he pay a visit to the Pillars. His shooting days were over. He intended to remain in retirement with his young wife on the Fayre estate—Porrington Abbey—near Richmond.

At this time of year, with snow on the ground and when the lake was crusted over with ice, there was little chance of anybody visiting Pillars. It struck Harry that he could take Fauna and keep her there in safety until the hue and cry for her died down. Every three months his uncle's bailiff visited the place. But to Harry's certain knowledge, the bailiff had already made his quarterly inspection, and paid the caretaker. He would not be due there again until March. The old caretaker and his wife could soon be bribed into secrecy and silence; or if not willing to accept a bribe, threatened with instant dismissal if they mentioned Harry's arrival. In any case, Harry was fairly sure of obtaining all the help that he needed from old Snelling who had taught him to shoot when he was a lad; in days when Sir Arthur's parties had been regular events.

The young man turned to Fauna. He saw her great troubled eyes watching him. Her lips begged mutely for help. (And for kisses he told himself wryly. But he must stamp out the desire to seduce her. It would scarce be a gentlemanly act in the face of her extreme helplessness.)

Abruptly he said:

"Dress yourself and do exactly as I tell you and I will if I can give you my protection."

She listened, her face clearing and her eyes shining as he rapidly told her his plan.

He added:

"Later, when those who would harm you have settled down to the belief that you are lost for ever, I will think out some further arrangement for your future."

She nodded but she cared nothing for the future. Only for the present, with *him*. Most of her pain, her terror and her loneliness had dropped from her like a sinister cloak. She stood bathed in the radiance with which Harry Roddney showered her. She was secure—immensely happy—she loved him with all her famished heart and her young passionate body. If she could not live with him, she would gladly die for him, she thought. And her lips murmured the name he had taught her to use while she put on her fichu and bound up her hair.

"Harry . . ." she whispered. "Harry . . . *Harry!*"

Chapter Four

The countryside lay white and frozen and uncannily still with neither man nor beast in sight, as the carriage, bearing Harry Roddney and Fauna, turned through the gates of Pillars, and rattled over the stones, stopping before the portico in that cold grey dawn.

Fauna was wrapped in Harry's greatcoat. Warm and snug in the curve of his arm, the young girl felt deliciously happy all the while they made the bumpy uncomfortable journey. She cared nothing for the fact that it had taken so long, nor felt the young man's impatience. It had not even seemed to her aggravating when the wheels stuck in a rut and Harry had to step out and give the driver a shoulder before they could free the wheels. The ghostly journey through east London and along to the lonely marshbound road towards Epping might well for Fauna have been on a route strewn with flowers. She was in a daze of ecstasy. The most wonderful, the most handsome gentleman in the world was helping her escape from those who owned her and wanted to sell her into a shameful bondage. She was with *him*.

And he, glancing now and then down at the young pale face of his companion, dimly visible in the dark of the musty-smelling vehicle, felt renewed tenderness and pity for her.

Now and again he had stroked the soft cheek. And once when he saw that she had fallen asleep exhausted by the long day and her terror, he lifted one of her small delicate hands which all her hard work had not coarsened, and gently kissed it.

There was something very attractive about this girl to Harry. That she had black blood in her veins was of no account. She was more refined and cultured, more exquisitely fashioned than many of the wenches he had tumbled in his time. Remembering his last mistress, Polly Teddington, her coarse wit and boldness, her greed for money and gems, he felt faintly ashamed that he had ever enjoyed her embraces. But the thing that amazed him most was the remembrance of his boyish ideals—the wish he had entertained before he commenced his career of mad extravagance and even of depravity—to find a pure and perfect love. This extraordinary girl, who had been Henrietta Pumphret's slave, had most mysteriously stepped into the niche awaiting the incarnation of that very ideal. Nothing now on God's earth would have induced Harry to give her back into Henrietta's hands.

Fauna watched while he got out of the carriage and hammered on the door. She shivered in the raw cold of the dawn. The coachman climbed down from his seat and stood stamping his feet and clapping his numbed hands together, his breath steaming. He was muttering to himself. The fine gentleman should pay a goodly fare for this long and perilous drive over the snow-caked roads. All for wenching too! The devil take him and his woman whoever she was. She was so muffled he could only just see her face. The gentleman, too, was masked and unbeknown to him. He had no idea whom he had driven here all the way from St. James's.

Dogs barked. A rooster crowed from a distant farm. Dawn pierced the cloud-banked skies with red angry streaks. Then light showed in a downstairs window. Bolts were drawn, chains unlocked, and a grey-bearded man wearing a coat over his nightshirt and a tasselled bed cap flung open the door. A lanthorn swung from his hand. He gaped at Harry and then exclaimed:

"Why, 'tis *you*, Sir Harry, sir!"

"Yes. It is I, Snelling. Rouse your wife, my good fellow, get fires lit in two of the bedrooms and beds warmed and made. And hot spiced wine," added Harry.

The man nodded, yawning, scratching his tousled head, in a bit of a daze after being woken up thus, so suddenly and so unexpectedly. He hastened away calling after him a fierce-looking mongrel dog who had come out to bay at the intruders.

Fauna looked wonderingly about her. She was not unused to country dwelling, having spent five summers on the Pumphret estate near Hampton Court. But this was quite different. She shivered a little as she walked with Harry through the oak panelled hall. Everything was on a miniature scale here. The house was one of the smallest built in that period, it bore faint resemblance to the palatial residences in which Fauna had so far spent years of bitter servitude. Long empty, Pillars smelt musty and was wickedly cold. But within a few minutes, Martha Snelling, the plump good-natured wife of the caretaker, had clothed herself, bustled in and got fires crackling in the grates of the two best bedrooms which adjoined and overlooked the lake.

She was a rough Essex woman, ignorant and humble. She had been told nothing by her husband save that the nephew of their master had arrived and brought a lady with him. Who the lady might be, Mrs. Snelling knew not, but imagined Fauna must *be* a lady. Tongue-tied with confusion and shyness she bobbed a curtsy before Fauna and began to make up a large four-poster bed with clean linen sheets taken from the lavender-scented press. It was quite exciting for her to receive guests here, for Sir Arthur had not visited his shooting lodge for many years. From one winter to another now, the Snellings saw few human beings save neighbours on the farm two miles away.

For Fauna it was also an experience to have nothing to do while a servant waited on her and called her "My lady." First of all it embarrassed her. Then it grew amusing. With a little enigmatic smile, she perched on the edge of a chair and spread her hands out to the blaze that was leaping bravely for the wood was dry and ready to burn.

Harry had paid off the driver and carried in a case which contained food and drink, hurriedly packed by Vincent. The manservant was under orders to keep this visit absolutely secret, and to drive to Pillars later in the week with a fresh supply of victuals for his master.

Harry Roddney stayed downstairs a moment while Snelling stripped some of the chairs of their ghostly dust-sheets and lit candles. He seemed pleased to see his young gentleman whom he had known from boyhood, inquired after the health of Sir Arthur and Sir Arthur's new lady, and assured Sir Harry that it would not take his good wife and himself more than an hour to get the place in order and have breakfast for them when required. Then, in a respectful voice, he added:

"Might I ask, Sir Harry, sir, if the lady who has come with you is your newly wedded wife?"

Harry laughed. Cold and stiff after the uncomfortable journey he now felt much refreshed, having drunk several glasses of spiced hot wine. He felt more mellow, in good humour, and rather maliciously pleased that he had outwitted Henrietta Pumphret. He could imagine how the widow, tomorrow, would set up a hue and cry after her slave girl. But nobody would find her. Fauna had assured him that even the manservant at the club from whom she had gained Harry's address, had not seen her face, nor her telltale hair.

Harry clapped the caretaker over his shoulder.

"No, the lady is not my wedded wife, my good Snelling. I am not married, nor likely to be. Kisses are cheap. Why then should a man pay for them at the price of his liberty?"

The old family retainer was privileged to chuckle with his young gentleman over this jest but, as Harry walked up the stairs, he found himself slightly ashamed of his own words. The right kind of kisses were not, after all, so cheaply bought, as he had bought Polly's; or as Edward Hamton bought Henrietta's. *The right kind were not bought at all.* They were given for dear love's sake, and for love alone.

Harry stretched his arms and yawned, as he walked up the cold staircase.

"I grow sentimental. It is unlike me," he thought with a wry smile.

And how fared his Fauna? His newly discovered protégée whose youth and beauty and helplessness so intrigued him that he had done this thing for her. Now that he thought about it he could see that this would mean days of imprisonment for himself—he would not dare to stir from Pillars nor show his face in London society. Vincent had orders to tell Beau and other of his friends at Court that his master lay ill in bed of an infectious fever and must not be visited. Well, the fashionable Mr. Brummell and those other companions on whom Harry had wasted his time and money, were not like to risk their health by coming near a fever they thought catching.

Mrs. Snelling met Sir Harry at the top of the stairs, bobbed quickly and stuttered that his own bedchamber was ready.

"I have taken my lady coffee and hot water. What more do you desire, my gentle sir?"

"Sleep, my good creature. That is all. And goodnight to you," said Harry in the kindly voice he always used to his inferiors.

She bobbed again and scuttled down the stairs to tell her husband that she had just seen my lady's hair unbound and that it was magical, like a cloak of purest gold with the sunset red in it almost touching her knees.

"But she is not finely clad and I wonder——" she began.

Her husband interrupted roughly. It was not for her to consider what fine gentlemen and ladies did, only to get on with her job and keep her mouth shut. And she had best busy herself milking one of the cows, make butter and bake loaves for the morning meal, while he cut down a home-cured ham and collected eggs.

Fauna was standing by the fire feeling warm and secure when she heard a knock on the door.

"Pray come in," she said, timidly.

Harry entered. She looked at him. He was travel stained and a little weary, the buttons of his long dove-grey coat with its huge pockets undone, revealing a gay yellow-flowered waistcoat. He was without his wig and once more she was struck by his boyishness seen thus with his own dark chestnut-coloured hair. Her enormous eyes regarded him with an expression of impassioned worship. But she said nothing, only stood there meekly with hands folded before her. She was still wearing her homespun robe and with her hair falling about her shoulders. She had taken off her clogs and rough woollen stockings, and he saw for the first time her naked feet—white and perfect and with the smallest ankles imaginable.

The blood began to hammer in his throat and temples again. His pale fatigued young face flushed as he came towards her.

"Have you everything you want?" he asked.

"Yes—Harry," she said.

He liked to hear her use that name. He liked her to speak to him as though she were his equal. And he liked to be with her alone in this room full of firelight, with the candles glowing on the oak dressing chest, and beside the curtained bed. It was warm in here and smelled of lavender. He had slept in this very room when he was a boy, staying with his uncle. Through the open door he could see his uncle's own room prepared now for *him*, grandly furnished, with blue velvet curtains, and fine rugs on the polished wood floor. In there also was firelight and gleaming candles. Outside, the wind had freshened. They could hear it howling down the chimney, rattling the windowpane. It had started to snow again while Harry paid the driver and sent him round to Snelling's quarters for a draught of beer and some sleep before he returned to London. He was a rough fellow and knew neither the name of the place to which he had come nor anything of the gentleman who had been his fare, so it was not to be feared that he would carry information back to London.

It was beginning to impress itself upon Harry that life with Fauna might be good in this lonely house—strangely good—peaceful and most intriguing.

She gave him a touching little smile. "Thank you," she added, "for bringing me here. It is so tranquil and so heavenly—after—Pumphret House."

"Try to think no more of that life, child," he said huskily and turned from the lovely sight of her, walked through the communicating door and closed it, as though glad to put a solid wood structure between him and this mysterious girl who had become the woman of his desire.

Fauna gave a brief sigh. She neither expected him to stay with her—nor wished him to go. She felt curiously detached—negative—this was a strange hiatus in her life. The wind continued to howl down the chimney. The flames leaped more fiercely and the room grew warmer. She blew out all the candles save the one in a silver candlestick standing on the walnut table by her bed—which had been warmed by a copper pan. Then, having no bed-robe, she slid in between the sheets and pulled a pile of snowy blankets and a feather-filled silken coverlet over her. For a moment she lay thus—her great eyes staring with drowsy contentment at the shadows. She felt very warm now. That good creature, Martha Snelling, had made her drink some hastily brewed coffee, with plenty of milk and sugar in it, before leaving her for the night.

Fauna thought of many things ere sleep overcame her, and beyond the thick prune-coloured curtains dawn lightened into a bitter morning. She heard the sad cry of a heron skimming across the ice-encrusted lake. After her life in the huge ever-busy house in London, and the equally crowded manor in Hampton Court—this little place, Pillars, seemed incredibly and beautifully quiet. She felt much comforted. Through that door her beloved saviour lay sleeping, she reflected. No harm could come to her here. But like dark phantoms, gradually growing more distant, the memories of the past chased through her mind . . . spoiling her peace. That noisome cabin of O'Sullivan's on the slave ship. That terrible voyage when Grandfather died and was cast into the shark-infested waters. The one-eyed Captain. Mr. Panjaw and his cruel mouth. Good kind Lord Pumphret—not purple, bloated in death as she had seen him last, but alive—debonair, smiling, bidding her sing while they drove from Bristol in the swaying coach.

"My pretty Insect!" he had said.

Fauna's lips curved into a tender smile of reminiscence. She turned over and pressed her cheek to the downy smooth pillow and shut her eyes. She slept. But almost at once her reveries grew darker and her whole being was beset by violence, the memory of fearful beatings, the hideous malevolence of Mrs. Clack's hairy face and the remorseless cruelty in Henrietta Pumphret's eyes. And then. . . . *Oh heavens!* The monstrous figure of Zobbo came toward her with his long simian arms and thick rubbery lips. Someone from behind her was pushing her, *pushing her* towards the disgusting African dwarf.

Fauna awoke screaming, bathed in a cold sweat.

In the next room, Harry, only half asleep and restless, all too conscious of the temptation so close to him, woke fully at the sound of the scream and sprang out of bed. He lit a candle and walked into Fauna's room, holding the light aloft clutching his thick bed-gown to his chest.

"What is it? What ails you?" he asked.

She did not reply. He came close to the bed and pulled aside the curtains which she had half drawn. The fire which was still burning merrily illuminated the gilded cloud of hair that fell about her shoulders. He could see the reflection of his candle gleam in her big eyes, and the terror written on her soft childish face and quivering lips.

"What ails you?" he repeated. "Did someone come in?"

She shook her head, struggling with the tears.

"No one. I—I had a—bad dream, sir. Pray forgive me for disturbing you," she stammered.

"Sir? Still *'Sir'* to you?" he asked, smiling, laid the candle down and took both her hands. They were very cold. He pressed them and added: "Poor child. Bad dreams, yes, no doubt there is much of suffering and fear to haunt you even in your sleep."

She hung her head as though she had done wrong. Harry's green bright eyes wandered with a quickening excitement and interest over her bare shoulders. Remembering the honey he had tasted on her lips tonight. No—yesterday he mentally corrected himself. For it was already another day.

He felt her tremble under his touch. She bent forward as though to hide her blushing face suddenly aware of her nakedness. As she bent, he saw with horror and an intake of his breath, the scars on her back. Faint red lines, the legacies of that thrashing which Henrietta Pumphret in her mad jealous rage had ordered Mrs. Clack to administer to Fauna.

"God in heaven!" said Harry. "Your back—your lovely back!"

"It is nothing," whispered Fauna and raised her face and smiled at him. "Now all my pain is forgotten, since you are with me, Harry."

He began to shake—temptation seizing him, for he was so completely alone with her. She was his to take. His, unbeknown to the rest of the world here in this quiet lakeside dwelling.

He said:

"Would you like that I should stay with you?"

Fauna's breath quickened.

"Oh, yes," she whispered back. "If it would please you. Yes."

Her great velvety eyes were star-bright under the sweep of lashes. She leaned towards him. He caught a handful of her wonderful hair and wound it about his throat, then with a stifled exclamation, pressed her back on the pillow. His lips came down on hers crushing them with a mad passion that must now be satisfied. He had endeavoured to resist but he was no hero, he thought ironically; he was Harry Roddney who took what he wanted—when he wanted it. Why, then, grow suddenly quixotic over a quadroon slave? But it was with a lover's hands that he drew that yielding and exquisite body into his arms.

The wood fire in the grate burned to a pale hot ash. The candle dripped wax and gutted. The morning light crept through a chink in the curtains. Grey flakes of snow whirled crazily against the rimmed window-panes and from a snow-covered byre in the distance there came the sad lowing of cold and hungry cattle.

In the big kitchens below, the Snellings chopped wood, lighted more fires and prepared food. So a new busy day began.

But upstairs in Fauna's room, hidden now by curtains drawn around the poster-bed snug and warm from the chilly draughts, sheer exhaustion claimed Harry. He had fallen in a deep sleep, one arm still imprisoning the girl with unconscious possessiveness. She, too, slept now—lovely and flushed, infinitely content for the first time in her whole life.

Midday came and still the Snellings waited for the bell to ring as summons for the morning repast. And the snow went on falling—burying the grounds of Pillars—tree, bush, and grass—under a shroud of purest white.

Nothing seemed to stir. No sound of horses' hoofs or carriage wheels. By this time, little doubt, the road to London would be blocked by snow-drifts, and impassable.

Chapter Five

A church clock, some two or three miles distant, was chiming the hour of one o'clock in the afternoon when at length these predestined lovers were to be found seated before the fire eating breakfast at a table brought in and spread by the amiable Mrs. Snelling. She waited upon them hardly able to restrain her giggles. It was not for her simple and uncouth mind to judge what highborn ladies and gentlemen chose to do, but certainly, to eat breakfast when others were thinking about lunching, was a matter of amazement and some speculation. And despite her husband's caution to her to wait upon Sir Harry in blind obedience to his wishes, the good woman could not resist glancing at the left hand of the beautiful young girl, and raising her brows a little as she saw no gleam of wedding ring.

They were a strange couple. Harry was in excellent humour, still wearing his tasselled night-cap and a fur-lined dressing robe of a green velvet which Fauna declared almost matched his eyes. She was so dizzy with delight and so madly in love she could not take her eyes from him, although with healthy appetite she devoured ham and eggs and drank the good strong coffee. Harry set upon mutton chops and a mug of ale which the estimable Vincent had not forgotten to pack for him.

Martha had relit the fire. The room was splendidly warm. But outside the world was blanched and frozen. Once again the snow had ceased to fall and—Harry said that it was an omen of good—there had come a rift in the eastern sky. A sudden shaft of sunlight pierced the grey clouds. Now everything in the small formal garden of Pillars sparkled. It was as though tree and bush and clipped yew hedge blazed with a layer of diamonds.

A few moments ago, Fauna, wrapped in one of Harry's

velvet mantles, had stood looking out of the window, exclaiming at the beauty of the landscape. But then everything seemed to her beautiful this morning, and most of all, Harry, her dear love in whom she had found such infinite pleasure and to whom she now was forever dedicated body and soul.

While Harry breakfasted, he watched Fauna, himself much in love and never ceasing to find delight in her beauty. He would not allow her to bind the rippling shining hair. It floated to her waist. He, himself, had fastened the clasp of one of his own warm mantles around her throat and tucked her under a rug in the big winged chair by the fire. Once he rose from the table, came to her side, pulled her up into his arms and started to kiss her again as though he could not stop.

When he returned to his chair, his handsome face was flushed and a trifle pinkish. He shook his head at her, laughing.

"In faith, Harry Roddney is not himself. He is a changed mortal."

For he who had ever deemed himself proof against woman's beguiling had at last been pierced by cupid's arrow. And it had been shot at the bequest of this slip of a girl.

"Oh, Harry!" Fauna exclaimed. "I cannot believe my good fortune. For I am only a woefully ignorant female who is fit only to be your slave, and greatly honoured by your passion."

"Not true—'tis I who should be honoured. For, my little heart," he added in a low and tender voice, "I am first with you and I know it."

"And you shall be last with me!" she whispered her face burning.

"Well spoken," he smiled and threw her a kiss.

It was a light gay hour, the morning meal shared by them in the firelit room. Fauna—being a woman—extracted every ounce of the sweetness from the present, shutting her mind to the horrors of the past. Only the man, more practical, turned his attention to the future and found it full of problems. One thing at least last night had taught him. He did not regret that he had yielded to the temptation of Fauna's loveliness. It was a shared experience, as unique in its way for him, as for her. For never had Harry Roddney loved before as he had loved this girl last night. It mattered not one inkling that she was once Henrietta Pumphret's bought slave, and that her grandfather had been an African native. Harry knew only that he loved her with a tenderness which had had no counterpart in any of his other passionate encounters. He knew also that she was fundamentally good as well as capable of being an enchanting mistress. And he would not allow that she was "ignorant." For, as they talked together, he learned a little of what lay in her mind. He was enchanted when, their breakfast finished, she sat on a stool at his feet and with her bright head leaning against his knees, sang him some of the songs she had learned in her childhood. She was all grace and fire and poetry, he thought. She had not a mind set upon baubles and worldly gain, like Polly Teddington, or Henrietta and her kind. She was a child of nature having an almost pagan simplicity of heart. But she also possessed a thirst for knowledge, and showed that talent for music and mimicry which George Pumphret had noticed in her years ago.

She had absorbed much of the culture which now and again it had been her good fortune to discover during the days when she used to accompany the Lady Henrietta to social gatherings. Her quick receptive mind had retained a small but significant knowledge of art and literature and even of politics and what went on in the Court of his present Majesty, King George III. She was less interested, Harry discovered, in follies or the gossip which was so dear to the heart of high-born ladies, than in serious matters. It was astonishing to him to find, while he picked her brains, the extent of her learning and retention of it, gained almost entirely by listening to others. She had kept all her knowledge locked behind a submissive silent façade. She had built for herself an ivory tower of pride and dignity, and shut herself in it, even while she had seemed to submit to degradation and cruelty. She had lived, like the lowest serving wench, consigned to an atmosphere of evil, of licentiousness. But she had remained aloof—curiously impervious to it. As though her purity, her sense of beauty and of truth were things fashioned of steel, both brilliant and inflexible.

Half her charm for Harry Roddney lay in this unique and jewel-like nature which shone through the exterior Fauna presented to the world. Nobody save he and, possibly, George Pumphret in a more careless fashion—had troubled before to recognize her individuality. Henrietta had been too busy endeavouring to mould the girl into what fantastic shape she wished. But now with an ever-increasing sense of security, and happiness, Fauna expanded like a flower before Harry's very sight. She grew talkative. She laughed—and it was as though she had never wanted to laugh before. But always when he asked her what she really desired of life, her answer was:

"To serve *you.*"

With another woman, he might have found it cloying to be thus worshipped. But with Fauna it was an ever-growing delight. A lifting of his own spirit. For he felt the better for her company. A unique satisfaction that, today, he could find the woman he had loved the night before still desirable. He could not imagine himself tiring of her—as he had done of the *others.*

But Harry was exceedingly troubled. *For what was he going to do with Fauna?* He was nearly ruined. It was essential that he should join Mr. Wilberson at East India House as soon as possible. And he could not keep Fauna for ever hidden. How, then, was he to shape her destiny? For now he felt wholly responsible for her and by every right of love she belonged to him.

Besides which, these were troublesome times, he reflected. The gay dissolute Court of the young Prince of Wales danced heedlessly on in unimagined luxury (indeed, had he not danced likewise, himself), while the poor stayed crushed under a terrible load of taxation. Every mortal thing was being taxed these days. Then there was war impending with France and Holland and insurrection in Ireland. And His Majesty's physicians feared a return of King George's old malady, which if it continued meant that the Prince might become Regent. Whigs and Tories were at each other's throats. The situation at home and abroad was far from propitious to any but men of wealth.

For the first time in his life, Harry found himself regretting his mis-spent youth and wasted gold; regretting, too, his fall from favour in the eyes of his uncle who had been everything to him since his parents left him an orphan. Had he not so greatly displeased Sir Arthur, the old man might never have taken to himself a wife and sought to produce an heir.

With moody eyes, Harry gazed at the young and lovely face of the girl who had shot like a star into his firmament at what was probably the worst moment of his career.

She smiled so enchantingly at him that he tried to chase these grave reflections from his mind. He smiled back at her and said:

"If the snow keeps off, my love, I must drive into the nearest town to buy you suitable garments. You cannot remain in mine, and I will not have you in a servant's attire."

She caught one of his hands and held it against her cheek, turning to kiss it, with one of those charming gestures which seemed to come so naturally to Fauna.

"I do not mind what I wear, or what befalls me, so long as I can stay with you," she said.

He sighed, picking up a strand of her hair, looked at the living gold of it, then sighed again.

"God forgive me if I should ever forsake you now," he said.

"Have you a wish to forsake me?"

"None at all, my sweet Fauna."

"If you should leave me, I would not wish to live."

"Child, people do not die so easily, and you must learn that there is something more important than living or dying. It is the courage with which you do either of these things."

He felt her shiver.

"I have tried always to have courage even when they beat me. But to be banished now from your sight and to return to the old slavery instead of remaining in the paradise which I have entered with you—that would be beyond enduring."

The man suddenly put a hand to his eyes.

"Dear God, what a responsibility is mine," he muttered.

She swung round to face him, her great velvety eyes suddenly clouding and her lips a-quiver.

"You do not contemplate leaving me, surely, Harry? I have not in any way disappointed you."

"Do not look like that," he said abruptly and drew her fiercely against his breast. "You have in no way caused me disappointment. On the contrary. But you must realize, my dearest little one, that this house belongs to my uncle and not to me. If he knew that I was here with you like this—he might be angered and well—there is also the question of finance. But these things do not concern you," he added somewhat gloomily. "Females are so improvident and so much more concerned with personal emotions."

"Tell me how I can change, so as to please you."

Now he drew her on to his lap and cradled her, pressing his lips to her rich sweet-smelling hair.

"I would not have you changed, dear heart. You please me enough—too much for my own soul's good. A man has a life of his own, sweet Fauna and, at last, Harry Roddney must face harsh reality. He must needs cease his gambling and wenching and go forth to earn an honest penny."

She did not understand, but safe and happy once more in his arms, twined her slender fingers about his neck. He kept her thus close to him, forbearing to talk of the things that distressed her, but struggling at the back of his own mind for a right and proper solution to the riddles that beset him, and so spoiled for him what was for *her*, perfection.

So the day wore on. Martha came to clear the table. Harry dressed and went out to inspect the estate. He left Fauna to enjoy a gloriously hot bath. Martha had struggled upstairs with a large hot copper urn which she filled for "My lady"—Fauna was further astonished and delighted by the perfumed soap and soft warmed towels that Martha held for her. She thanked the good woman with such touching gratitude that Mrs. Snelling was quite overcome. She curtsied repeatedly, saying:

"Oh, *thank* you, my lady, 'tis a pleasure to wait on you, my lady."

For the first time in her life, a sad and cynical thought passed through the mind of the young quadroon. While she sat by the fire drying the long fine hair which she had also washed, she thought:

"What would this good creature say if she knew who and what I really am!"

After Martha had departed, Fauna walked to the window, looked down and saw the figure of Sir Harry. In his green coat and white breeches—top-boots—and cocked hat on bewigged head, he rode a chestnut mare, followed by two hounds. The mare clip-clopped over the snow, breaking the crust delicately with her hoofs. Fauna's heart beat madly as she saw her lover sitting thus in his saddle, so straight, so fine, so handsome. Then he gazed up at the window and noticed her. He blew her a kiss. She blew kisses back to him, her body bathed in a glow of contentment, of sweet pride. And Fauna would not have changed places then with any fine lady on the face of the earth.

But unbeknown to these two, snugly imprisoned in their solitary lakeside hiding-place, Fate was already moving in a grim sinister fashion to overtake and destroy them.

At Pumphret House, ever since Fauna had escaped, there had been trouble. Dire trouble for Mrs. Clack for ever having allowed Fauna to get away. After my lady had finished with hysterics, she had ranted at the trembling housekeeper and sworn that *she* should be dismissed without a character unless she found Fauna—and before many more moons rose over Pumphret House.

The Marchioness of Rustingthorpe also arrived and added her tears and tantrums to those of Henrietta. Clarissa had looked forward with enormous excitement to possessing the quadroon girl for whom she had paid a handsome price. Dear William had paid it for her not because he was interested in buying a wife for Zobbo—for he despised the little monster—but Clarissa had greatly pleased her William by announcing that she was once more pregnant. He had long since desired another child, so he had asked her what favour she would most enjoy and when she had said the purchase of Fauna for Zobbo, he had shrugged his shoulders and consented. Women were silly frivolous creatures to be sure, but just now he was prepared to smile benevolently upon his Clarissa.

"I shall never get over it if I cannot have Fauna for my poor Zobbo. He has lain in his bed ill with disappointment ever since I informed the poor wretch of her disappearance!" Clarissa wailed to her friend.

Henrietta, more concerned about this matter than the funeral of her late lord and master, applied smelling salts both to her nostrils and Clarissa's. She nodded her head.

"Fauna shall be found. I have my spies everywhere. The police, too, are on the look out for a runaway red-headed serving-wench. There are even those who are combing the bawdy houses, lest she should have strayed into one. A pest on it! I did not think the creature had it in her to dare run away."

Clarissa dabbed her big blue eyes with a lace handkerchief, and sighed:

"I must not be too much harried or, to be sure, I will have a miscarriage and that will set my William against me."

Henrietta brooded. She had small interest in Clarissa's pregnancy. Tomorrow Pumphret was to be buried. It would not be pleasant having to move down to Pumphret Park, in this bitter February weather, she reflected. Thank heaven, her dear Edward was stealing into the house to console her tonight when the servants were abed, otherwise she would die of ennui and depression. The fate of the innocent girl whom she had used so cruelly and driven into the night concerned her only because she had no wish to hand back the money Clarissa had paid. Nor to lose the spiteful pleasure of forcing Fauna into marriage with Zobbo. *Where* could the wretched girl have gone. Somebody must have befriended her, if not she would, in due course, be found dead of starvation and exposure.

Mrs. Clack, meanwhile, breathless and racked with the pain of rheumatism and dropsy, spent the bitter February day in search of Fauna.

Her fingers itched to get hold of the girl and make her pay for all this trouble. Find her she *must*, for Mrs. Clack valued her position in the household of her lady. She did not intend to lose it. In her cunning way, she went about the quest of the slave girl methodically. She called from tavern to tavern, and at many questionable lodging houses in the neighbourhoods beyond the high-class reaches of Fitzroy Square. She had a notion that the quadroon beauty might have been picked up by some men who would think her useful to detain for immoral purposes. But when the dark wintry afternoon drew to a close and Mrs. Clack was still without news, she returned crestfallen to seek consolation from her friend Mrs. Golightly. They drank gallons of tea, while tears of chagrin and fatigue rolled down Mrs. Clack's fat hairy cheeks.

"This will be my death," she moaned. "Oh, if I could but lay my hands on that wretch!"

There were fresh reasons, too, why she wished to find Fauna. She was quite ready and willing to betray my lady's trust—for she had malicious intent towards the Lady Henrietta who had forced her to make this search and caused her such discomfort. If and when she found Fauna she could use her to her own ends. *And my lady would never know*. So far as she was concerned, Fauna could remain missing. But Mrs. Clack had met a certain gentleman who had a mind to hold a secret auction of the beautiful and famous slave—if she could be delivered to him. Gentlemen who attended the auction could be pledged to secrecy, for it was illegal. So high a price might be obtained that it would be worth Mrs. Clack's while to become a partner in the conspiracy and receive a half share. It would feather her nest for the day when she could no longer work either for Lady Henrietta, or anybody else.

This gentleman, who held one of the worst reputations in the east end of London, was a half-caste with Spanish blood in him; by the name of Miguel Lopez. He lived in a small dwelling in Aldgate. He had committed many crimes but so far escaped detection. He was, among other things, a nefarious money-lender and there were several well-known young rakes upon his private list.

To find Fauna, to be able to hand her over to Lopez would cause Mrs. Clack immense satisfaction, for it was perfectly certain that no good would come of it for the girl. It might seem a pity to miss the evil delight of watching her forced to take Zobbo for a husband. But that would mean no money for Mrs. Clack. Her avariciousness overrode her gluttony and the cruelty of her bestial nature.

On the day that Lord Pumphret was laid to rest among his ancestors, Mrs. Clack, in London, continued her search. At least, the weather had changed for the better. Blue skies appeared. The snow thawed—and snowdrops lifted their gentle winsome heads in parks and gardens. With miraculous rapidity a shivering England was transformed by the breath of spring.

It was on the fifth day of her search that Mrs. Clack

found a clue. A most valuable and exciting clue. It came from the person of a certain hackney carriage driver who happened to take Mrs. Clack from Fitzroy Square to Covent Garden where she was set to make further inquiries.

In garrulous fashion, driver and fare started an amicable conversation. And, as Mrs. Clack had been doing to all and sundry for days, she mentioned to this man the name of the girl she was seeking. She asked if he had seen a young serving wench who vanished on the night of 4th February.

The driver scratched his head, pursed his bearded lips and fell to thinking. No, at length he said, he had noticed no stray wench with golden-red locks such as was described. Then suddenly, scowling, he added:

"But it minds me of a strange fare I drove—almost to Epping Forest—in a snowstorm on that very night."

Mrs. Clack looked eager.

It was a bright morning. There was a din and bustle going on in Covent Garden market. Horses straining to pull heavy loads of fruit and vegetables, vendors screaming, the streets running with slime, the air noisome with the smell of rotting food and human filth flung from nearby houses. Ragged children swarmed in the gutter picking up what they could find to eat. The odour of newly arrived fish mingled with the other unpleasant scents. Vendors set up their stalls. It was a typical scene in Covent Garden in the year 1803. But the Londoners were jolly and in good spirits—thankful for the sudden favourable change of weather. The past winter had been long and hard.

Mrs. Clack had eyes and ears only for what the driver was telling her while he patted the flanks of his steaming, stamping horses.

She extracted from him every detail of that "strange fare" he mentioned on the night of the snowstorm. And the more she heard, the more she wondered. . . . *A young handsome gentleman (masked) and a young girl wrapped in a cloak, with her hair pushed out of sight under a cap. A face which even the rough ignorant driver described as being of exceptional beauty.*

It was no real evidence, but to Mrs. Clack it was an *idea* which fastened on her fancy and did not let go.

"Could you find the place again if you had a mind to?" she persisted.

He laughed and spat.

"That I would! Never to be forgotten, ma'am. And a curse I said at the time, on the young gentleman, for a'wenching at such an hour and on such a night, and driving to such an outlandish spot."

"I wonder who the gentleman was," muttered Mrs. Clack. Then she had a bright idea.

She pulled some coins from her purse. The driver saw gold, and his eyes gleamed. Mrs. Clack forced her bloated features into a hideous smile intended to be coy.

"Could you take a lady, much fatigued, on to the house in St. James's from whence you commenced that nocturnal journey, sir?"

Stimulated by the sight of the guineas, he nodded. In a few moments he had whipped up his horses, and Mrs. Clack was driven in style to the wider and more fashionable neighbourhood of St. James's. A beautiful sight this morning with the sun shining on the snow-crusted towers and turrets of the palace. Finely attired gentlemen, with befurred and be-jewelled ladies beside them, drove in gaily coloured curricles, or walked arm in arm up and down the street.

Mrs. Clack was delivered safely at the door of a certain high-class apartment house. She applied the bright brass knocker with a resounding clap. When a whiskered and soberly clad serving man opened the door, she asked if this was the dwelling of a certain young gentleman (to whom she gave a fictitious name).

The serving man shook his head. Mrs. Clack said:

"Dearie me—but are you *sure* 'tis not the dwelling of Mr. Pettigrew, the advocate?"

Her ruse succeeded. Vincent—for it was he—fell into the trap.

"No, 'tis not," he answered irritably. " 'Tis the dwelling of my master, Sir Harry Roddney."

Mrs. Clack's heart almost failed her. Her face grew scarlet with hope and excitement. *Sir Harry Roddney*. Then it was *he* who had driven a young and beautiful girl to the outskirts of Epping. *He*—that very one who, years ago, had incurred my lady's displeasure by speaking in defence of Fauna, on the night they had concealed her in Mrs. Golightly's cake. So, Dora Clack's fancy was right! She was practically sure now that she was on the track of the girl. Somehow or other, Fauna must have discovered where Sir Harry lived and fled to him for protection.

So cunning was she, that the housekeeper did not raise suspicion in the serving man by asking further questions about Sir Harry, but humbly apologized and withdrew.

As she climbed into the carriage, her small eyes glinting with unholy joy, she said:

" 'Tis possible that you may be called upon to drive me to this house near Epping. Meanwhile, I have a mind to call on a friend, a Mr. Lopez, in Aldgate. I will direct you. Go—go—as quickly as you can!"

Chapter Six

Fate played into the hands of the abominable Mrs. Clack on that fine day of early March when she and her confederate, the Spaniard, drove out of London towards Epping.

So mild it was, the snow was running away in rivulets; the sky was a pale blue flecked with fleecy white clouds, the feeble sun warmed the brown earth that had so long been frozen. And despite the fact that the wheels of the carriage employed by Mr. Lopez stuck on several occasions, once on the outskirts of Whitechapel a couple of hostlers from a nearby inn had to help the driver dig them out, Mrs. Clack had never enjoyed a journey more. She was panting, red, breathless with vicious excitement, for she was quite sure she was on the track of Fauna.

Lopez was equally sure. He had a keen sense of business and from what Mrs. Clack had told him, added to what he had heard about the famous slave's fabulous looks, he anticipated that he would make a lot of money once he got hold of her. There were not many slaves in this country. An auction, held in secret, would be a fine amusement for some of his wealthy and more degenerate patrons.

Mr. Lopez was fortunate enough to live in a society that was, at this period of history, lamentably pervaded by vice. The gentlemen who came to him by no means confined their extravagance to gaming. They often squandered their money on fantastic cruel and profligate amusements. The more absurd or unmoral the pastime—to be found—the better. Lopez felt his fingertips itch with longing to lay hands on the quadroon girl. To Mrs. Clack he had already described in his oily and smooth fashion how he would deal with her, and where the auction would be held. Not in his own dwelling; that would be too dangerous right in the heart of London. But in a certain low gaming house in which there was one large room more often than not reserved for gambling, not far from Aldgate. It was run by another Lopez—named Juan, first cousin to Miguel. There was little doubt that a great many wealthy customers would bid high for the girl, especially as Mrs. Clack had stressed Fauna's innocence, and even though the spoils must be divided, the profit would be handsome.

Mrs. Clack folded her hands over her fat stomach and shook with laughter over the whole idea. Not only did she enjoy being instrumental in organizing the auction of the hated slave—but she liked the thought of outwitting the Lady Henrietta. When my lady returned from the country, Mrs. Clack would be able to snap her sausage-like fingers in her face, should she find herself dismissed because Fauna had not been found. *Fauna must never be found.* For this auction would be secret and it would be impressed on the gentleman who purchased her that he would have to dye that tell-tale flame-coloured hair and keep the girl well guarded, otherwise there might be trouble not only with the Lady Henrietta, but the disappointed Marchioness of Rustingthorpe.

It was imperative that they should make their inquiries most carefully once they reached the house wherein Mrs. Clack fully expected to find Fauna hidden. Lopez was a crack shot and he carried two pistols. He felt well able to look after himself if he had to face young Sir Harry Roddney, for all the fact that he was a famous swordsman.

"Leave everything to me, my good woman," Lopez kept telling Mrs. Clack.

She was content to do so. Mr. Lopez looked the part of an elegant foreign gentleman. He wore fine clothes. Today he had favoured a respectable black with white bands at the neck, well-cut breeches, boots and a black cocked hat with silver ornaments. His pistols were well hidden under the great flapping pockets of his coat. To be sure, he had a narrow crafty face, close-set eyes and a mean mouth. But if one did not look too closely, Miguel Lopez might quite well pass for a sober and respectable gentleman from the Continent.

That there was a certain danger attached to this game did not depress Mr. Lopez. All his life he had played with danger, broken the law and enjoyed hoodwinking the authorities. He would not stop at murder nor had he the smallest grain of kindliness in his nature. The soul, the well-being of the slave, Fauna, was of no account to him. His ruling passion was money and for money he was willing to damn his immortal soul not once but several times over. But he fully realized that the game he was playing required a certain amount of cunning.

Now Miguel Lopez had arranged that evening that his own carriage and trusted servants should bring him here. The driver of the original hackney carriage, and their guide, once having directed them, was amply rewarded and sent back to London. Mrs. Clack was to stay hidden in the Lopez's conveyance just outside the gates of the grounds and await events while Lopez called at the house. It so happened that Sir Harry was just returning from the other side of the lake when the strangers arrived. He had gone thither with his fowling-piece to look for wild birds, and obtain some fresh air and exercise on such an exquisite morning.

Harry felt a tremor of misgiving when he first saw the strange carriage pull up at the entrance of his uncle's estate. He was always uneasy lest Fauna's hiding-place should be discovered. *Who were these visitors?* The young man stood a moment, frowning. He had his fowling-piece under one arm and a brace of birds slung over the other. He was looking exceedingly well and feeling it; had never felt better after nearly a week of this peaceful country life and extreme happiness in lieu of the late nights and dissipation to which he was accustomed. And, with every passing day in Fauna's company, he had grown more and more certain that what he felt for her was no idle infatuation. She had made an extraordinary mark on his life and his sentiments.

Mrs. Clack whispered excitedly to Mr. Lopez that this was young Harry Roddney. Now she said she was proved right. Roddney must have abducted the girl and brought her here.

The small black eyes of the Spaniard narrowed. He climbed from the carriage and approached the young nobleman, one hand fingering the butt of his pistol through the flapping pocket. Then he swept a bow. With a sardonic smile, he said:

"Do I address Sir Harry Roddney?"

Harry inclined his head.

"You do, sir," he answered haughtily; but with growing suspicion glanced out of the corner of his eyes at the foam-flecked horses and mud-spattered vehicle. He did not like the look of it, nor of the fellows holding the bridles. His heart sank a little. This might be Henrietta Pumphret's creatures on the trail. His whole being revolted against the prospect of Fauna being forced back to a life of degradation and slavery. She, who was so young and tender and who had become his dearest love.

His worst fears were realized when Lopez spoke again.

"You are, sir, I believe, sir, in possession of a certain female slave belonging to her ladyship of Pumphret. You have brought the said female to this hiding-place, have you not, sir?"

So, Harry reflected, while his blood turned to ice in his veins, they were discovered. *Ah! Fauna, Fauna, I shall not let them take you from me.* And he instinctively dropped the birds and raised his gun. But the Spaniard was too quick for him. A shot rang out through the clear quiet countryside. Harry Roddney, without a sound, fell to the ground, the blood welling from a wound in his head.

Lopez put the smoking pistol back in its holster and called to his men. They were Portuguese, black-browed, pock-marked fellows of saturnine and unpleasing countenance. They had been in the pay of Lopez for many years and could be relied upon. Lopez ordered them to take Sir Harry's body and throw it in the bushes. At the same time, he drew a signet ring from the wounded man's finger—a large square-cut onyx bearing the Roddney crest. This he put in his pocket. Mrs. Clack leaned out of the carriage window.

"Mercy on us, Mr. Lopez, is it *murder*?" she breathed.

Lopez made a quick examination of Harry, fashioned a pad from a linen handkerchief which he found in Harry's pocket, placed it against the wound, then bound it with a scarf which the young man had been wearing.

"It is not a fatal wound, but it will keep him quiet for some hours. Now we must be quick," he said, stepped into the carriage and bade the man drive up to the front door.

Mrs. Clack fanned her perspiring face, her eyes a trifle scared.

"I trust you have not gone too far," she began.

"Leave all to me," he interrupted tersely and in a few words outlined his plan of action.

From the library window, Fauna saw the carriage with the dashing horses pull up at the front door. She had heard the shot and fondly imagined it was her lover aiming at wild-duck. She looked at the vehicle, however, with consternation. Like Harry she sensed danger. This was the first strange carriage to make an appearance at Pillars since Fauna's arrival here six days ago.

She had just been singing, and practising at the spinet. She was often to be heard singing now for she was gloriously content and spent many evenings of music with her Harry. He was teaching her some airs from Mozart. They were like a newly married pair—wrapped up in each other.

How could such love be sin? This was a question Fauna had asked her Harry only last night. During the week that she had spent here along with him she had learned the fullest meaning of life and of love. She had lost all sense of fear and grown radiant and strong both in body and mind; her past terror forgotten. She found Harry a fine companion as well as an ideal lover. He was the teacher, she the pupil. And he told her not once but many times that she made him a most enchanting mistress.

This affair, commenced in difficulty and doubt, had become an idyll; a period of purest happiness for them both. They were the complement of each other. There seemed no ending to the new joys they discovered in one another, shut away in their solitary retreat, wandering through the grounds, talking, or reading during the day-time; close together in passionate and ever new discovery of each other by night. But although Fauna accepted it all as being heaven-sent and could look no farther than the golden moment—Harry had now and then confessed himself troubled.

"Such love as you and I have found may not be sin, my sweet child, if we live by pagan standards alone," he had said. "But there is religion. Even you have learned that from your people in far-off Africa. And I was reared as a good Christian. Never before have I had a mind for marriage. Yet there are moments when I look at you and wonder if I would not make you my lawful wedded wife."

That had brought excruciating happiness to Fauna. She had flung herself into his arms, pressing her ripe red lips to his, but shaken her head.

"Marriage is not for Fauna the slave," she had said.

But he had clipped her fast and whispered through the veil of her silken hair:

"You are, in truth, love's slave, my most exquisite Fauna. Yet you are strangely my equal, I will not think of you in shameful bondage."

And he had fallen to worrying yet again about her future and how best to act for both her sake and his own. The faithful Vincent who brought food and clothing to them had informed his master that London was seething with gossip about the runaway slave. He spoke of Lady Clarissa's chagrin, and of the Lady Henrietta's wrath. There had also come a letter from Mr. Wilberson begging Harry to make haste and reach some decision about accompanying him to India. The threat of war with France was drawing nearer. Prices were rising and England was preparing her fleet. While the youth of the country was being squandered in dissipated living, there was every reason for more serious-minded men to walk a more sober path. And, indeed, as Harry told his mistress, living with her—loving her—had not turned him from his new desire to fasten his mind on business and politics. On the contrary, in some strange way, she had increased his ambition. His former passions and vices used to deplete him. But he arose from Fauna's arms with his physical and mental vigour ever renewed.

Fauna thought of Harry with the utmost tenderness while she sang her songs and waited for his return this March morning. There were several hours to dream away before he returned. But her face paled as Snelling opened the door and Lopez, removing his cocked hat, walked into Fauna's presence.

She looked at him questioningly. His evil heart leaped. *This must be she.* She was dressed like a fine lady in apparel bought for her by Harry—in a sapphire-coloured gown the wide sleeves trimmed with fur. Harry did not like her to powder her hair. Her gleaming curls were natural, tied back with a blue ribbon. She looked well and beautiful. Her only ornament was a rope of pearls; pearls that had belonged to Harry's own mother and which he had bidden Vincent bring him from the coffer in his rooms. They were dear to Fauna not for their value or their lustre, but for the fact that he allowed her to wear his own mother's necklace.

It was her red hair, as well as the singular grace and the great black eyes of the girl which confirmed her identity for Mr. Lopez.

As Snelling shut the door, he said:

"I come from Sir Harry, I am a friend of his."

Fauna put a hand to her throat and fingered her pearls. A friend of Harry's—this strange black-clad gentleman who spoke with an accent? A slight tremor shook her voice as she said:

"From Sir Harry, sir? But have you seen him? Did you meet him on the way, for he has been out all morning."

Lopez smiled.

"I did meet him. He did in fact send a message to me to approach you. He wished to be out when I arrived; that was the purpose of his going a-fowling."

She stared, confusedly.

"I do not understand, sir."

Lopez continued to smile while his penetrating gaze travelled over her, noting with satisfaction the exquisite grace of her form and her unique colouring. Why, she should be worth a *fortune*. She had the dignity and breeding of a fine lady to enhance her value.

Now he said:

"You are the slave, Fauna."

At that, every vestige of colour drained from her face leaving her milky white. Like a wild creature she scented acute danger. She let forth a cry:

"Harry!"

Lopez held up his hand.

"It is of no use to call for him, my dear," he said with a familiarity that appalled her. "He is not here, I tell you it is he who sent me to fetch you."

"To fetch me," she echoed the words through pale lips, her terror increasing.

His cruel gaze raked her.

"Did you think that your foolish romance would last for ever?"

"Oh! What are you talking about?" she stammered.

"Look," he said. "You have been much mistaken in supposing that a fine gentleman like Sir Harry Roddney would be content to remain shut away with a quadroon slave for more than a few days of amusement. He tells me that you demanded his protection and he gave it—*while* he was so inclined. Now he has had his pleasure and is returning to London. He did not fancy a scene, and I, as his friend—Senor Lopez at your service"—Miguel gave a mock bow—"volunteered to represent him. As I have little time to waste, I would ask you to fetch your cloak and accompany me. You can remain here no longer."

Fauna's great eyes stared at him. Every word he said struck like a knife through her very soul. It was incredible. Only a few short hours ago, Harry had held her in his arms and whispered:

"Till tonight. Then we shall exchange a thousand kisses to make up for those we must forswear while I am gone."

How could it be true that he no longer wanted her? Oh, God in Heaven, had he truly brought her here merely for his *amusement*—had all his protestations of love been the idle words of a man who was a hypocrite—and a base deceiver? But he had assured her that to him she was no common slave but an equal. *He who had told her that the only thing that mattered was the courage a human being brings both to the manner of their living and dying.* And he was such a coward that he dared not inform her of his altered feelings, but must needs send a "friend" to say that "the idyll" was at an end?

The Spaniard had come to conduct her back to London. *To what?* She uttered a little cry.

"Where is Sir Harry? Let me see him. Oh, heavens, I will not believe he is doing this to me. It cannot be true."

"I fear that you have a too-exalted opinion of yourself," said Lopez showing his teeth in a humourless smile. "Sir Harry did you honour to waste even six days upon you. But he has rightly regretted his foolishness. He owes a duty to the society to which he belongs. And a certain Mrs. Clack has accompanied me in order to see that you be taken to the rightful place."

At the mention of that awful name, the hair seemed to rise upon Fauna's scalp. She swayed and almost fell.

"*Mrs. Clack!*" she repeated in extreme horror.

"Come," said Lopez impatiently. "Hurry! You are wasting my time."

The girl shrank back. Her world had shattered about her feet. The bubble of happiness that had seemed to glow for her with such iridescence, such heavenly brightness since she became Harry Roddney's mistress, had broken. The ivory tower of warmth, of security, of joy that had been built up about her collapsed. She was flung back into the old abyss of horror and despair. And the most terrible part was the agony of her disillusionment in *him*; the Harry whom she had loved with all her soul.

A fresh protest broke from her quivering lips.

"Oh, it cannot be true. He would not have condemned me to *Mrs. Clack*. Even if he grew tired of me, he would not have betrayed me to her. He was too kind and good. You have come to steal me from him. You are his enemy. I will not go with you. . . ."

And she picked up her skirts, turned and was about to rush away when the man caught her wrist and detained her. Lifting Harry's signet ring from his pocket, he thrust it in front of her sight.

"Sir Harry warned me that you might behave like this which was why he chose to avoid your tantrums, miss. Here is his own ring. Do you recognize it? Yes! Well—will you believe me now when I tell you that he has sent me to bid you leave this dwelling and, to add that he regrets your abduction."

Her eyes, clouded with pain, recognized that signet-ring all too well. Last night, while Harry caressed her, the sharp corner of the onyx had become entangled with her hair. She had cried out, and he had freed the lock, then kissed her most tenderly with his warm lips atoning for that infinitesimal pain. *Oh God!—Oh God!* she thought, *if only I could have died before this hour; died while I still believed that you loved me and would never give me up to my sworn enemies!*

She could not bear the thought that he had held her in such slight regard, that having seduced her, he could fling her back to those who had so cruelly misused her in the past.

Lopez, smiling like a fox, replaced the ring in his pocket. "You had better come," he said.

Suddenly her tension relaxed. It was as though she was utterly deflated. If this was true (and it seemed that it must be so, for how else could Mr. Lopez have known so much?) she cared no longer what happened to her. She felt sick to the bottom of her soul. But in a low voice, she addressed this man who called himself Harry's friend.

"The ring convinces me. But I do ask you one thing, sir: that I may not be forced back into the monstrous toils of Mrs. Clack."

Now this was precisely what Lopez had been playing for and he seized his chance. He laid what was meant to be a kindly hand on Fauna's shoulder.

"I will do all I can. You do not like Mrs. Clack?"

Dumbly she shook her head. She was in a maze and daze of anguish. Her lips kept forming the name: Harry, *Harry*. While she wondered how he could have behaved with such cowardly ingratitude to one who had given him her whole heart's pure devotion.

It was still too much of a mystery to be comprehended, although the ugly facts asserted themselves and were not to be denied. That ring seemed to be living proof. But truly she did not care what fate befell her; yet her flesh crept at the idea of being either returned to Mrs. Clack or—worse still—forced into the company of the dwarf, Zobbo.

Now as the name "Zobbo" danced before her, she caught her breath and clutched the arm of the man who had just delivered a death blow.

"Sir, whoever you are—whatever you are—I beseech you keep me in your own employ—do whatever you so wish, but swear you will not send me back to the Lady Henrietta nor to the Marchioness of Rustingthorpe."

Excellent, thought Lopez. Things were, indeed, going his way. She would go with him now willingly to Aldgate. But he must be prompt, before one of the servants found young Harry Roddney's body. If he were to die, it might look as though he had shot himself with his own fowling-piece. At any rate, he, Lopez, was a stranger to Harry Roddney, so he could not identify him as the man who had found

Fauna here—even if the young nobleman recovered. Harry would never discover where the girl had been taken—or by whom. Lopez said:

"Very well. Put your trust in me and do as I tell you and you shall not be given to either of these ladies."

If it was within the poor girl to feel relief, she felt it now. She thanked the man, then, her tears beginning to flow, unclasped the pearls that were around her neck. They seemed to her to be the price of her betrayal. And Harry was so great a traitor that he was no longer worth a tear. She placed the pearls on the table. In due course he would find them there. She did not wish to take them with her. She asked permission to leave a message with the servants, but Lopez denied her this. He had urgent business in London, he said, and must remove Fauna immediately.

"The servants have their orders from Sir Harry," he said. "They understand what is happening."

Fauna had no fight left; she stayed silent while Lopez himself called to Martha to fetch her cloak. Both the ignorant Snellings looked on without questioning, although with some perplexity; as they saw their young mistress drive away. Martha, scratching her head, said to her husband:

"Wherefore has she left us like this, and what will Sir Harry have to say when he returns?"

Snelling did not know. Neither he nor his wife had heard the cry of despair that was choked on Fauna's lips once Lopez helped her into the carriage, and out of the dimness emerged the bloated triumphant visage of the unspeakable Mrs. Clack.

Chapter Seven

It was the baying of a dog that first warned the Snellings that something was wrong. That and the fact that the master had not returned from his shooting. Martha had grown uneasy. In fact ever since the strange Spanish gentleman had driven the young lady away—the poor young lady who had looked pale and distressed and quite unlike herself—she had suspected trouble.

The continual howling of the dog got on Martha's nerves. She begged her husband to go out and investigate. The good man found the wolf-hound seated on his haunches, muzzle raised to the sky as he uttered those chilling howls—then the man's horrified gaze lit on a pair of boots sticking out of the bushes. He paled and, being a good Catholic, crossed himself.

"Mother of God!" he exclaimed. In a trice he parted the bushes and so disclosed the body of his master. For a moment he stared at Sir Harry's blanched face, with the blood-stained scarf about his temples, in consternation and horror. Then he looked at the fowling-piece which lay beside him. The simple man decided that there must have been an accident. He did not pause to conjecture as to whether it were possible for a man to make such an injury himself—for that neat round wound in the temples had certainly not been fired at close range. Neither did he so much as contemplate the idea that it might be a case of suicide. He took it for granted that it was purely an accident—stupidly ignoring the fact that Harry could not have bound up his own head wound. Going down on his knees, Snelling unbuttoned his master's coat and waistcoat and placed his ear against the heart. *The Saints be praised,* he thought, that noble heart was still beating, although faintly. But Sir Harry was not dead.

The man got up and rushed into the house. A moment later his wife was with him and they staggered into the house bearing the unconscious form between them. They laid Sir Harry on the sofa and fetched cordial. But though they moistened the pale lips, he neither stirred nor spoke nor unclosed his eyes. He was in a deep swoon and his face bore the pallor of approaching death. It terrified the simple servants. Snelling rose to his feet.

"This is a black day, wife," he said. "An accident has befallen our beloved young master and when he awakens it will be to find his lady gone. Woe is me!"

"Go quickly, saddle one of the horses and fetch a leech," said his more practical wife. "Meantime I will stay beside him and sponge the blood away."

When Snelling returned an hour later with an elderly physician from the nearest village, Harry had not yet moved or spoken. Dr. Angus Knox was Scots born and Edinburgh trained—twice Sir Harry's age. He had in the past attended Sir Arthur Fayre for his gout.

The first thing Knox had to do was to extract the bullet, which must be done immediately. It was fortunate, he told the frightened and weeping servants, that it had not penetrated the brain, but Sir Harry was certainly in danger of his life. His uncle at Porrington must be told.

The March day wore on to its close. The fleeting sunshine had departed. Once again clouds banked over the little house and the formal gardens wherein Fauna and Harry had been so happy. But there was no happiness here now. Fauna, with her rich beauty and her genius for loving and laughing, had gone. Harry lay insensible in the big four-poster bed wherein he had once tasted all the sweets of Love's perfection.

The doctor had performed the operation skilfully. There had been much loss of blood during the three hours that the young man had lain out there in the bushes. But he had an iron constitution; the strength and vigour of extreme youth and a sound heart. Although he could not tell what had befallen him and had not so much as stirred or groaned while Dr. Knox operated, his heart continued to beat. The pulse was slow and it seemed that all strength had been drained from him. The handsome winning face that Fauna's lips had kissed inch by inch was marble and statue-like—as pallid as the bandages the doctor had wound around his skull. Yet he breathed. The good doctor informed the Snellings that there was a chance that he would yet vanquish the angel of death.

All night, Dr. Knox stayed there. The intelligent and educated gentleman was certain that this was no accident and that there had been foul play. His inquiries brought forth little from the Snellings beyond the fact that "My lady had hastily left the house with strangers a few hours before the howling dog had led us to the scene of the accident."

But who could have fired that shot and why? These were questions the good doctor could not answer. As for the hasty departure of a lady whom they described as being of marvellous beauty, and whom Sir Harry had called "Fauna," that conveyed nothing to Dr. Knox, either. He awaited the arrival of the young man's uncle. Word had already been sent to the General's home at Porrington.

At dawn Harry Roddney unclosed his eyes and uttered a low groan. Immediately the doctor bent over him.

"I am here, my boy—what can I do for you? Tell me what happened to you."

Harry moved his lips. His fingers twitched in the doctor's hand. It was as though he struggled to say something and could not; as though he fought with a dark phantasmagoria in his mind. Then he gave it up, closed his eyes again and sank back into unconsciousness.

The doctor shrugged his shoulders but the patient's pulse beat a little more evenly and strongly which was all that mattered to him for the moment.

It was noon on the following day when General Sir Arthur Fayre, accompanied by his newly wedded wife, both heavily wrapped in furs, driving in a high yellow and black travelling carriage with two liveried postillions and two outriders, reached Pillars.

The General, tall, gaunt, wearing a peruke, and with his gouty foot swathed, entered the house leaning on the arms of his young wife and a valet. He looked fierce and displeased as he sank into a chair before the library fire. Snelling and Martha stood at a respectful distance and told their story to which the doctor added his.

"It is my good fortune that I managed to arrive in time

to minister to your nephew," Knox added, "and can announce now that his condition is grave but no longer critical."

The General grunted. His wife, a pretty silly-looking little woman with vacuous eyes and powdered curls, untied her fur-lined bonnet, and poured out a glass of cordial for her ageing husband.

"Do not distress yourself, my dear love," she said soothingly.

Sir Arthur brushed aside the wine. His gouty foot was throbbing and burning and he was in poor temper. The last thing he had wanted to do on this cold March day was to take a long and uncomfortable journey over poor roads, but he had thought he received a summons to his nephew's death-bed. Now he was slightly resentful. He had been brought here under false pretences. The boy was not like to die. For the last three or four years, Sir Arthur had wearied of young Harry's mad extravagances, his incessant appeals for more money, and his succession of mistresses. Again and again the General had called him to task, lecturing him on the crime of incurring debts which he could not liquidate, beseeching him to give up the reckless crowd in which he moved, take to himself a good wife, and lead a more sober and godly life. But Harry had not listened. He was the son of a noted baronet—Sir Gregory Roddney—like Sir Arthur a distinguished soldier. When Gregory died, Arthur had gladly taken the boy and brought him up as his own. He had loved Harry because of his charm and character, and there was much good in him. And, up to a year ago, the General would not have thought of leaving his fortune to anyone else.

But, weary at last of Harry's follies, and having met Angela, a young maiden lady whose parents owned the neighbouring estate to Porrington Abbey, he had suddenly proposed to her and been accepted. His dearest wish was that she should give him a son of his own. He had finished with his wild libertine of a nephew for ever.

And now *this*. The General growled, scratched his bald pate under the peruke, and ascertained a few more details. All that he was told amazed him. To begin with, he had not known that Harry was at Pillars. As for the red-headed beauty with him—she was no wife, he grunted at Dr. Knox, but a mistress. Harry had plenty of those.

"Damme!" exploded Sir Arthur. "What right had the young scoundrel to bring one of his wenches here to my respectable house? I can see what happened. She couldn't get enough money from him so went off with another admirer."

The Snellings exchanged glances. This theory did not strike them as being at all correct but they dared not argue with the master.

As for the mystery of the shooting—it little mattered, Sir Arthur said, whether Harry had shot himself or been shot. The thing had occurred. It was only to be expected after the life he had been leading. He was bound to come to this end.

Then the doctor politely reminded Sir Arthur that young Harry's end was not yet come. Sir Arthur settled down to the fact that he had better stay at Pillars for a few more days. He quite liked the little place and if his gout had not been so infernally bad, he might have volunteered to take a fowling-piece out on the lake before breakfast tomorrow. But his loving Angela assured her Arthur that this was not possible.

"Well—well—we will bide here," he said, "until such time as my nephew can speak to me. Then I shall arrange for his future. He must be sent abroad. I will have no more to do with him, even though he is my flesh and blood."

But it was two more days and nights before Harry opened his mouth. It seemed as though that shot, although not fatal, had in some way paralysed his brain. His young aunt-by-marriage, who volunteered, prettily, to help nurse the redoubtable young man, thought him very handsome and tragic and would not be cross with him. Being a female, and romantically inclined—Angela had married the General only because her father insisted on account of his great wealth; but she could not love him. His embraces repelled her. However, as she sat by Harry's bed and lightly smoothed the chestnut hair back from the sculptured forehead, her heart beat quite fast. Truly, he had the most wonderful beauty, she decided, and she wondered who his mistress had been—the one with red hair whom

Mrs. Snelling described as being of wondrous beauty. And, *why* had she run away. Angela would not have run away from such a man!

On the third morning, Harry unclosed his eyes. He looked without recognition at the vapid and unfamiliar face of his aunt-by-marriage. She rushed away to fetch her husband. The General limped into the room looking more gaunt and plain than usual without his peruke. He sank heavily into a chair by Harry's bedside. Then Harry said in a voice scarcely above a whisper:

"I seem to know you, sir."

"Damme!" exploded the General. "You should do. I am your uncle, sir."

Harry reached up a hand and touched his bandaged head.

"My uncle? And I——?"

"My nephew, sir. Most unfortunately, of my flesh and blood."

Lady Fayre hovered in the background and cast an anxious glance at the young man in the bed. She blushed prettily as he gravely returned her scrutiny.

"And I am your Aunt Angela," she ventured.

Within a few moments it became quite apparent to the General that Harry had lost his memory. He would return to health and strength but his mind was a blank so far as his life preceding that shot was concerned. Dr. Knox interfered and remarked that it would not do for them to harry the sick man by over much cross-questioning. Later that day, Harry spoke with his uncle again. He was melancholy in the extreme, and complained of headache. It did not matter to what Sir Arthur referred, Harry confessed himself ignorant of all. He did not even know his own name. But he accepted without argument the facts given to him. He was Sir Harry Roddney—nephew to this fierce-looking old man and his young wife. He had rooms in St. James's Street. He had led a dissolute life among the gentlemen of the Court and was, in particular, a friend of Mr. Beau Brummell, the leader of fashion. All these things were told to him, including the fact that he was heavily in debt and had caused his uncle much grief and trouble. Behind the pain in his head there were shadows, tormenting, juggling, obscured. He was perplexed and confused but must, it would seem, apologize for his misdeeds. As for women in his life—he had nothing to say about these. Nor could he recall that he had been living here with an illicit love—a red-headed wench, they said, who bore the outlandish name of "Fauna."

At length he broke down and sobbed in an unmanly fashion which aroused some of the old affection and tenderness in his uncle. It was obvious that poor Harry was very sick.

"Hush, my boy," he said gruffly but kindly. "You shall be looked after and when you are well enough to travel, shall return with us to Porrington Abbey."

"Oh, yes, indeed," seconded Angela and clapped her hands.

The General scowled at her.

"You may retire, madam," he growled, and decided that he would not, after all, take Harry to Porrington.

As the days went by, the young man grew strong enough to sit up, and finally to dress and go downstairs. He was feeble through loss of blood. But once he started to gain strength made a rapid recovery. He was conscious of continued gloom, and of a strange burden hanging over him which he could neither explain nor banish. He only knew that as he grew better, he grew also bored and wished himself far away from Pillars. It seemed a sinister place. He also wished, earnestly, that he could remember his past. That at least, sounded interesting. But no amount of probing or struggling for recollection was of any avail.

His uncle had meanwhile sent word to Harry's rooms thinking that a visit from Harry's old and valued servant, Vincent, might penetrate the darkness. But the messenger returned from St. James's Street with the shocking news that Vincent had been murdered. Some weeks ago, Harry's apartments had been rifled—the few treasures he had not already sold were gone, and the faithful man was discovered in night-attire with a bullet wound in his throat. It was considered the work of a criminal who had thought to find gold and been surprised by the servant whom he shot in self-defence.

Harry heard this news without being much affected. He

could remember nobody of the name of "Vincent," nor did he mind what had happened to his London dwelling. The past was a blank, painful and impenetrable.

There was nobody who could tell either Harry or Sir Arthur that Vincent had died at the hands of one of Miguel Lopez's hired assassins. Lopez had deemed it wise that Sir Harry's personal servant should be exterminated. He might know too much. Now there was nobody left to tell how the slave, Fauna, had fled to Sir Harry for protection on that night three weeks ago.

It then happened that, going through his pockets, Harry found letters written to him by Mr. Wilberson from East India House. He handed these to his uncle. The General sent word to Mr. Wilberson who made a journey down to Pillars for the express purpose of interviewing Sir Arthur and the young man to whom he had once offered a job. He confessed that he had been surprised that Harry had not got in touch with him before this. He had almost decided that Harry was no longer interested in joining The East India Company.

He was shocked and distressed to find so great a change in the young man who had once been high spirited and so full of vigour and good humour. In his place was a melancholy, dispirited Harry with a brooding look in his sunken eyes. Harry strove to recall something about Mr. Wilberson, but could not. However, when the kindly gentleman renewed his offer to take him abroad almost at once—the young man assented. And the General warmly encouraged the idea. A job of work was what the boy needed. He would deck him out with money and clothes and there could be an end to the past and the beginning of a new life for Harry Roddney.

"You join The East India Company with my blessing," he said, clapping Harry on the shoulder after the three men had held their discussion.

"I thank you both," said Harry with a faint smile. "And believe me, I am not ungrateful."

He left his uncle to talk further, alone with Mr. Wilberson. As Harry passed through the hall, Martha Snelling approached him and bobbed.

"My young master, what am I to do with this?" she asked timidly.

She handed him a string of pearls which, she said, she had found on a table in the library.

"Your young lady unclasped them and left them there before she departed," she said sadly. "I have taken care of them while you were ill, sir."

Harry fingered the pearls, his brows knit.

"Why did she leave them, if they were hers?"

"I think, sir, that they belonged to your mother—she told me so," stammered the woman.

Harry sighed, shrugged his shoulders and slipped the pearls into his pocket. Then he drew a hand across his forehead around which a bandage was still pinned.

"Oh, God," he muttered. "What does it all mean? Who was this girl? Why did she leave me? Why was I shot?"

Martha wiped a tear away with a corner of her gown. It grieved her to see the young master look so pale and drawn, so sadly altered.

"Oh, sir," she said, "the memory of my lady's face when she left us haunts me. She looked afraid, sir, as though forced to depart against her will. Oh, sir, she was so sweet and you were so happy!"

Harry gave a brief laugh.

"Was I? Well, I do not think I shall ever be happy again," he said in a sombre voice. "Everything is a sad mystery. Oft-times I would that I had died, for my life holds nothing now. I am bereft."

Martha wept openly.

"Do you not recall my lady, sir? She was so happy and so beautiful and young. Her hair was like a red-gold cloud. You called her *Fauna*, sir, if I might be so bold as to remind you, sir."

"Fauna!" Harry repeated the name slowly. Somewhere in the recess of his clouded mind there stirred a memory but it vanished as quickly as it came. He was conscious only of headache and depression. He added, " 'Tis a curious name. From the Latin. Insects are *faunae*. How came this girl of such a peculiar and pagan-sounding name?"

"I . . . I . . . do not know, sir," stuttered the woman.

"There, good creature, do not weep for me," went on Harry in a kind voice. "Nor for the fact that I remember not My Lady Fauna. I am not interested in her nor in any other lady."

So saying, he passed out into the garden to breathe the mild March air. His heart was heavy within him.

Two days later, Pillars was closed, shuttered like a tomb. Everybody had gone again except the simple couple whose lives had been for such a short time filled with excitement —and the final tragedy. Now it was the grave of love, of youth's passionate desire.

Sir Arthur and his wife returned to Porrington Abbey. Harry Roddney to London with Mr. Wilberson. There they spent a fortnight in Chiswick and soon afterwards boarded the packet for Holland. Thence on a journey to India which swallowed Harry up for well over two years.

His memory did not return but a new life and new work began for him. It was nearly three years before he returned to England. Then he had somewhat recovered his spirits although he was very much more serious than he had been in the past. There were grey threads to be seen in the chestnut hair under the fashionable wig. He had learned to take fresh interest in life—and more especially in the business and politics of his country which had gone once more to war with France. And he had, within the course of those three years, completely filled the void left by the death of Mr. Wilberson's son. He and the man whom he now called "Uncle James" had become devoted; almost inseparable.

In the year 1806, Harry's aunt-by-marriage, the Lady Angela Fayre, died in a sad effort to give her spouse a son and heir. The old man, disappointed and inconsolable, followed her shortly afterwards into the family vault. And so, after all, Harry found himself no longer a penniless rake but a man of parts—sole possessor of the Fayre fortune and master of Porrington Abbey.

Pillars was not yet sold. All these years it had remained empty, with the Snellings still in charge. Harry did not go near it. For some queer reason he shunned the place. For him, a shadow of tragedy hung over the place and kept him away. But for a reason he could not explain, even to himself, he did not want that lonely lake-side dwelling to pass into strangers' hands.

Once he inherited his uncle's property, he withdrew Pillars from the market.

Chapter Eight

We must return to a March morning during that week following the shooting of Harry Roddney and the abduction of Fauna.

At the window of a grey stone, strongly built house with rounded towers which greatly resembled a miniature castle, and overlooked a creek of the Colne estuary, a man stood looking out to sea.

His hands were locked behind his back. He carried gauntlets and a riding crop. He was dressed as for a journey and with a cape of military design thrown over his shoulders. He was a slight man of medium height. From the distance he looked young on account of his slender build and dark unpowdered hair which he wore tied back with a ribbon. But on closer examination it could be seen his hair was threaded with white and that he was much wrinkled with pouches under eyes which were as grey and profound as the waters of a pool. But not a stagnant pool for they were the eyes of one given to swift, deep thinking, full of infinite knowledge.

Lucien, fifth Marquis of Chartellet, was in his late fifties. Before the Revolution, one of the wealthiest gentlemen of France which country he had left before the guillotine could claim his head. He was one of the minority who had had the foresight to transfer the bulk of his fortune, plus a fabulous collection of books and art treasures, to England.

Lucien de Chartellet had been ever a serious and resourceful man—one much given to study and to accumulating *objets d'art*. He had never idled away his time or his money, neither used he to appear often in the Court of the ill-fated French monarch who had been consigned with his family to such a shameful death. De Chartellet was a man of strong character and a merciless hardness that had made him feared if not avoided. He had married in his youth a young and lovely girl who had died leaving him a daughter. To that daughter he had devoted seventeen years. Then in 1792 she had married against his wishes a certain young gentleman of France who was in personal attendance on the unhappy Marie Antoinette. When the uprising was threatening land and property as well as heads, and just before France fell finally into the convulsions of the Revolution the Marquis had tried to persuade this beloved and only child to leave Paris and accompany him across the water whither his strong presentiment of the gathering storm had led him. She had refused. Later, the Marquis, hearing that she had been arrested, had been about to set sail for France, determined despite all dangers to attempt her rescue, only to receive a message that she and her husband had already paid the price of their allegiance to the Court, and lost their innocent heads.

From that hour onwards, Lucien de Chartellet conceived a bitter hatred of his own country and determined never to return there. Lately he had received a secret envoy from France suggesting that he might return and take his place at the side of Napoleon Bonaparte. He had refused. He had settled in England. He would not leave it now. He spoke English with scarcely a trace of accent. Except for his title and certain mannerisms which he would never lose, he was now, to all intents and purposes, an Englishman.

Sorrow had not sweetened his nature. Intensely cold and reserved at all times, he had become far more so after losing the only two things he had ever loved—his wife and his daughter. He was a man of bitter humour, and with a razor-edge to his tongue which did not make him a favourite with his associates. At the same time, being a widower of great wealth and the fact of owning not only this property but a large and handsome house in London seemed to him acceptance in a society which for the most part he shunned. He was to be seen at times in the fashionable clubs, was a noted expert on cock-fighting. He, himself, had bred some of the finest game-cocks in England. But he never remained long in town. He seemed to prefer his remote castle by the sea. Lucien had that elegant and supreme indifference to flattery which drew women to him like a magnet. But not one of the noted beauties had yet managed to secure the coveted title of its Marquise de Chartellet. The idea of becoming Lucien's mistress held a sinister fascination for many who regarded the interesting and unusual French gentleman as a difficult but rich prize worth securing. And it was known that several highborn English ladies had for a short time been heard boasting that they were the recipients of his favours. But never anyone for long. It would appear that the Marquis soon wearied of his paramours, and returned to the seclusion of his house in Brightlingsea (he was a member of the Cinque Ports) and his books.

That he was harsh, rapacious, and wickedly sarcastic, that he had no belief whatsoever in romantic love—was also a known fact among those who had made his more intimate acquaintance.

A certain famous beauty had been heard to say:

"Lucien de Chartellet is exquisitely courteous but behind the courtesy lies a sadistic brute. *I hate him.* But he has the finest diamonds that ever came out of France!"

And he was not ungenerous—to those who were privileged to be seen at his side on the rare occasions when he graced London's social circles. It was significant, perhaps, that he chose his mistresses from the most experienced and voluptuous of the women he encountered, but that he shunned youth and innocence. Also that he refused to be possessed. The moment a woman became proprietary Lucien was finished with her. Nobody really knew anything about him, which was another of his attractions. Even his mistresses confessed that he remained as chilly and mysterious in his dealings with them as the peaks of Everest. He was that type of man against which a woman has little chance to use her powers—a cold sensualist.

Inevitably endless rumours circulated around his head; often of the wildest kind. He was a fiend. The books and the learning to which he gave so much time, were the works of the Devil. His name should not have been Lucien but *Lucifer.* Any woman who had anything to do with him, or wore one of his fabulous jewels as a mark of his fleeting esteem, would not long survive her triumphs. Those he favoured pined away and expired (this because two of his favourites during the past seven years had died before their time).

All, for the most part, superstitious nonsense, as Lucien de Chartellet knew, and was vastly amused. Meanwhile he lived as he desired and continued to draw the veil of mystery over a life which, if it could be probed, might well be said to have become utterly boring to him. It was as though he had combed every experience—and every emotion. Now he was drained. He had no faith, no illusions, no ambitions. He was utterly blasé.

Once a year Lucien held a fabulously extravagant and glittering ball in his London home which was one of the larger and more fashionable houses facing the Green Park. More often than not, these parties developed into orgies. So much money was spent, so much grandeur exhibited, that it dominated the talk of London for weeks afterwards. But the host remained sober. Maliciously amused, he would walk through the great rooms and gaze with cold disdainful eyes at his guests who sprawled inebriated on couches or rugs. Men who would wake with blinding headaches and scant recollection of their imbecilities; women—great ladies some of them—with wine-stained disordered dresses apt to become conscious in the dawn of some new sin to add to a long line of feverish follies. Lucien de Chartellet was a connoisseur of food and had the finest wines of France in his cellars; but he was never guilty of drunkenness. His chief crime in the eyes of his friends was that he could never be made to lose his head, but was an adept at making them lose *theirs* under that cold mocking scrutiny which earned for him the nickname of "*Satyr.*"

On this particular morning faint sunshine dappled the grey choppy sea, and the first daffodils gilded the walled-in garden of the miniature castle which was Lucien's country home. It had been built in the twelfth century and modernized during the reign of Queen Anne. It used at one time to belong to the chief constables of the seaport. When the Marquis first purchased it he spent a great deal of money on improvements. The domicile was now magnificently appointed inside, and full of treasures shipped from the Chartellets' estate which was near Fontainebleau. At one time called Colne House the little castle had been renamed The Bastille, a name given it with ironic humour by the inhabitants once Lucien came to live there. It looked forbidding enough from the exterior with its grey walls rising steeply from the cliffside, and its narrow prison-like iron-barred windows. And, even after turning it into one of the most gorgeous and sought-after country houses on the English coast—Lucien de Chartellet was amused to keep that name. So, The Bastille it remained.

De Chartellet had no English servants. He had brought his entire staff with him over from France. And he had no women working for him except one who came to wash and iron, and who had to be bribed handsomely to enter this home of *The French Fiend*.

Only during the last twelve months, The Bastille had boasted a resident English employee. A young man named Aubrey Burkett. He was exceedingly erudite and studious and of the utmost integrity. He had at first come here for the purpose of cataloguing the Marquis's world-renowned library. But he had stayed on as a permanent secretary.

Young Aubrey cared nothing for the fantastic reputation of his employer but bowed before the superior knowledge which lay in that ice-cold brain. Being himself of such academic disposition, he was pleased to serve the Marquis. He was the exact right type, for Aubrey Burkett was a silent fellow who could be trusted to discuss none of his employer's private affairs with those curious enough to inquire into them. He was also one who kept his ears and eyes open and could tell his master whatsoever he wished to know; of things that occurred in London during the Marquis's long spells of absence.

If Lucien had a weakness—it was for knowing other people's business while he practised such secretiveness about his own.

The day before yesterday, Aubrey had returned from a visit to town with the news that a certain half-Spanish gentleman, of scandalous repute, was to hold in private the auction of a beautiful slave girl who had only just reached sixteen summers.

Knowledge of this unusual—and illegal auction—was by no means common property. The secretary had gleaned it in confidence from a friend—also a secretary to a nobleman who had recently gambled away half his fortune and received a considerable loan from Miguel Lopez. Lopez had offered to clear this gentleman's debt on condition that he remained discreet, and saw to it that other gentlemen with money to burn, and who could be trusted to keep the secret, attended the sale. The address at which it was being held was in Aldgate. Tomorrow evening shortly before midnight. Nobody would be admitted who could not present the highest credentials. For the quadroon slave who was being sold must be regarded as "stolen property." It was essential that her previous owner should not gain knowledge of the transaction. She remained nameless but it was said that she possessed astounding beauty of both face and form, and was of a high order of intelligence. This information had caused Lucien to think. At first he dismissed the proposition as being of no interest to him, then he found that the idea haunted him. He had purchased most uncommon things. He had not only a unique collection of antique and modern clocks—things of ormolu, of china, of gilt, with exquisite silver chimes—but the most perfect and valuable ivories and fans in Europe, and a formidable array of weapons dating back to earliest Chinese and Egyptian—also an aquarium of valuable and rare ornamental fish. He found it soothing at times to sit in the shadows and watch these tiny multi-coloured glittering denizens of the deep dart ceaselessly through the candle-lit water in their crystal tanks.

He was a man who took up hobbies and as often dropped them again. In recent years he had complained that nothing any more gave him pleasure. Nothing, that was, in this world, and that he had only the unknown mysteries of the next world to look forward to.

Now came *this*—something out of the common—and which he had not so far owned. A young female slave, reputed to be of surpassing loveliness—and with a keen mind to boot; and with only a quarter black blood in her.

De Chartellet turned the thought over in his mind until he became obsessed with the wish to attend the secret auction and outbid every other gentleman of means who hoped to possess the girl.

Now he awaited the arrival of his secretary with the chaise which was to convey him from Brightlingsea to Aldgate. He had previously sent Aubrey to pay his respects to the brothers Lopez and inform them that a gentleman who wished to remain anonymous would come to the auction disguised, promptly at a quarter to midnight, and have pleasure in bidding for the girl for so far as it amused him.

At length there arrived the Marquis's handsome yellow and cream chaise, with two postillions, and an outrider wearing the dark purple livery of the de Chartellets.

He heard the horses stamping into the courtyard around which the semi-circular walls of The Bastille had been built, and went out to meet it.

Despite its sinister prison-like exterior, the courtyard of The Bastille was charming—a variety of old stone vases were gay with spring flowers and dwarf ornamental trees fringed the enclosure. A fountain played into a centre basin. Water gushed from the mouth of a great stone horse, bearing a naked rider who had the body of a girl flung over his shoulder. Her curling tresses, cunningly carved from the stone, dipped into the water. Her expression was one of terror yet delight as though her nature warred between fear of her captor and pleasure in the abduction. It was one of the French treasures which the millionaire Marquis had shipped from Fontainebleau and which had stood on the terrace before his ancestral chateau. He had always liked it and would not leave it behind him even though it took a fantastic number of men and horses to transport the statue to the English coast. But here it was—lending a Continental air to the place. The somewhat warped mind of the Marquis found perpetual delight in the curiously human sensual expression of the magnificently sculptured captive girl.

He watched his secretary descend from the chaise and approach him. Aubrey Burkett was a tall young man of a Saxon fairness—his hair was golden under the fashionable powdered bob-wig which he wore. His skin was as delicate as a girl's and he blushed easily. He had weak short-sighted eyes ruined by overmuch reading of close print in poor light. He had a sober taste in clothes and today wore dark grey with a high-collared grey top-coat, and black cocked hat. He carried a business-like portfolio under one arm. From it he drew several sealed letters which he had brought his employer from their London home. He handed them to him with a deep bow.

"How now, Aubrey?" murmured the Marquis. "Is all ready for our amusement this evening?"

"All is prepared, milord," answered the young man.

"We are expected?"

"Yes, milord. And I have brought you these."

Now he drew a packet from the portfolio. The Marquis opened it and found therein a dark false imperial and a velvet mask.

"If your lordship will wear these—no one will recognize you—even should there be one of your acquaintances there, which I doubt," added the secretary respectfully.

With a sardonic laugh, Lucien de Chartellet turned and walked indoors. He returned a moment later, looking a complete stranger wearing beard and mask. Aubrey gave a cry of approval.

"Not a soul would know you for the Marquis de Chartellet," he said.

"Good. Order the men to change the horses and we will depart."

"Very good, milord."

The young man bowed again and turned to give the waiting grooms the necessary instructions.

Less than half an hour later, Lucien de Chartellet, conscious of a strange excitement which had not stirred his immensely bored spirit for a long time, was being borne in the comfortable padded satin-lined chaise over the main road, away from the seaport and the grey shadow of the little "Bastille" towards the Lopez brothers' gaming house on the outskirts of London.

Chapter Nine

The ugly, narrow house belonging to Juan Lopez, situated in a low, ill-lighted street in the neighbourhood of Aldgate, was the scene of considerable activity on this cold March night.

Several gentlemen, some coming on foot, some by sedan-chair or hackney carriage, presented themselves, knocked upon the door, were examined through a grilled slit of a window and later admitted. The brothers, Juan and Miguel, were both there, and had a list of those whom they knew to be reliable customers—and who were to be allowed to attend the auction of the slave girl either because they were already known to the brothers, or introduced by patrons who could be relied upon not to deliver them up to the law.

There was none to present themselves that memorable night known personally either to Henrietta Pumphret or the Rustingthorpes. The cunning Lopez brothers had taken care of that. And Miguel had taken care, also, that he would not be betrayed by the redoubtable Mrs. Clack. For he had by dint of much persuasion and bribery made that abominable woman resign from the Pumphret household and accept a new post here with his brother in this very house. Food and wine were always prepared and served to those who came here either for gambling or to attend one or the other of the vicious pastimes promoted by the Lopez brothers. Mrs. Clack was excellent as a caterer and manager of staff. They found her useful. She had, of course, been reluctant to leave her dear friend, Louisa Golightly, to say nothing of her former employer's luxurious and respectable home. On the other hand, easy money tempted Mrs. Clack sorely and in any case she knew that by allowing Fauna to get away she had cooked her goose with

Henrietta. And if she were to believe Miguel Lopez, she would make twice as much money working for his brother. After the sale of the quadroon she would, if she so desired, be able to retire and set up an establishment of her own. She fell for the temptation. And thus, poor Fauna after leaving Pillars and that sweet paradise of peace and beauty shared with her true lover—found herself in the hands of that much hated and dreaded tyrant again.

But there were no more beatings or starvation. The Lopez brothers were far too intent upon receiving a spanking sum of money for their prize. They made detailed arrangements for the disgraceful auction of this defenceless human merchandise. Working under their instructions, Mrs. Clack had to see that Fauna was well fed and given ample opportunity to rest and so preserve her health and strength.

Fauna, therefore, had no cause to complain of ill treatment. But from the hour that she was locked within the confines of that house of ill-repute, she entered upon a new term of torture—mental rather than physical suffering this time, almost harder to bear. For Fauna had seen the light —learned to love and feel herself beloved—with passion and without lust. Learned to smile, to sing, received kindness and consideration, and to feel *safe* . . . in Harry Roddney's arms. It was the deprivation of her newly discovered security and the belief that Harry had betrayed her that crushed Fauna so completely. She felt scarcely able to hold up her head. She had neither pride nor faith left. She had received treachery from the one quarter in which she had been sure of loyalty. She had been cast into utter darkness when she had thought to walk for evermore in the blissful sunshine. She had been flung from a brief-lived heaven into the bottomless pit of hell.

Hell, for the present, meant this small bed-chamber in Lopez's nefarious residence. The window overlooked a sooty yard. The room itself was furnished with some degree of comfort, if in a gaudy style which Fauna, whose eye was trained now to more cultured and beautiful surroundings, found disagreeable. She detested the pink frills, the garish wallpaper, the frowsiness of it all. She felt unable to breathe in the over-heated atmosphere which reeked with cheap strong perfume. Her meals consisted of great platefuls of food and mugs of spiced wine which she could neither eat nor drink. So, contrary to the wishes of her captors, she grew thin, pale and heavy-eyed. Mrs. Clack had only to enter her room to reduce her to a state of trembling and nausea and when that lady strove to be amiable and to cajole her, she only felt worse. She suspected fresh treachery. She trusted no one. The Lopez brothers—as alike as twins with their crafty faces and mean close-set eyes—terrified her when they came at intervals to look at her as though she were a strange rare species of animal to be regarded with curiosity. The confinement, lasting over a week, in this gilded, gaudy prison, set her nerves on edge. Nobody would tell her what ultimate fate she might expect. She knew only that Dora Clack was no longer in Lady Henrietta's service and that she, Fauna, need not fear my lady's malice. Also she felt fairly confident that she was not to be handed over to Zobbo. For so much she could be thankful. But for the rest—the mystery and the strange new life in what she felt, rather than knew, to be a house of evil, was a continual nightmare.

Day after day she questioned Mrs. Clack who answered tartly that she must "wait and see." Night after night, Fauna lay in her bed, wide awake, apprehensive, and shuddering with the horror of all the things she imagined might possibly befall her. She was in bad hands and among enemies. It astounded her that Harry could have allowed such a fearful thing to happen. But that he *had* allowed it, seemed indisputable. Lopez had shown her Harry's ring. And neither Lopez nor Mrs. Clack could have found her at Pillars if he had not betrayed her.

At first Fauna brooded and wept so incessantly over her wrongs and her lost love—that it seemed likely she would go into a decline—or starve herself to death.

Miguel Lopez and Mrs. Clack then decided that sterner measures must be taken. Certain powders were secured from an apothecary and mixed in coffee given to the unfortunate girl. After taking this medicine she relaxed and became more docile. She slept all night and was drowsy and listless by day. But she no longer refused her food. She ate and drank what Mrs. Clack served to her. She seemed incapable of making any further decisions or of troubling as to what had happened in the past or might happen in the future. She became wax in the hands of those who were preparing her for the day of her "sale."

She did not even protest when one afternoon they came with strong dye and turned the red-gold glory of her rippling hair to the blackness of ink. Now with that dark, purple-black cloud of hair—the big eyes—the white delicate skin—she looked even more fascinating. Hers was the dark haunting beauty of the East—of Persia—of Araby, or even of ancient Egypt—she had a new heavy-lidded inscrutability.

"The doped air becomes her," Miguel Lopez remarked to his brother after he had paid the final visit to Fauna. "We will get the Clack female to attire her thus—as a harem slave of an almost forgotten era. It is strangely voluptuous and will enhance her value."

When Mrs. Clack brought the garments designed by Juan Lopez, who was in his way an artist, and especially made for Fauna—the girl made no effort to resist. She allowed the woman's fat detestable hands to attire her.

She had had another long day of poppy-dreams—for they were giving her a form of opium—and passed, as usual, from sensual sleep to tired awakening. There was a half smile on her lips; a strange dilation of the pupils which made her eyes look even larger. She had taken to singing to herself—in a low, lilting voice. Now and then she glanced at her reflection in a mirror—and stared without recognition at the slim black-haired stranger who stared back in so melancholy a fashion. But her lips continually formed a name.

"Harry! . . ."

Whenever Mrs. Clack heard it, she sniffed. She had heard news of Harry Roddney. It was now known in London circles that he had been found shot by an unknown assailant in the grounds of his uncle's house in Essex, and that he was lying there ill; but not critically so. Mrs. Clack told Fauna nothing of this. On the contrary she repeatedly informed the girl that her lover had wilfully deserted her. To which Fauna in her present semi-delirious state made no answer. But from hour to hour she whispered that name that had so imprinted itself on her consciousness.

"Harry. Harry!"

The reiteration of it got on Mrs. Clack's nerves. The sooner Fauna was sold and taken away, the better for them all, she decided. And the farther she went—the better pleased Mrs. Clack would be. Evil woman though she was, the whole thing was beginning to cause her some unease.

At a little before midnight, the drugged girl was led from the pink and gilt bed-chamber which had imprisoned her for over ten days now, down to the gaming salon which was below ground. It was a long, low room lit dimly by candles in wall sconces. As a rule there were a number of card tables here and, at one end of the room, a buffet laid with food and liquor. Because of the low ceiling and poor ventilation, the place as the night wore on became unbearably stuffy, and filled with smoke from an evil-smelling stove. There were two or three questionable French prints on the dark-red papered walls; several vulgar caricatures perpetrated by one of the leading caricaturists of the day. It was not an elegant club—if club it could be called. But it rarely lacked clients. The Lopez brothers had a genius for supplying unique entertainment as well as finding money when and where money was needed. At one end of the room there was a roughly fashioned platform across which a heavy red plush curtain was drawn.

Fauna saw nothing—heard little. When the Lopez brothers led her into the middle of this stage she stood there obediently. They had chained her delicate wrists. She had a dim recollection of being so chained years ago when she was a child, and that somebody called Harry had unfastened the padlock and set her free. Her brightly reddened lips formed the name repeatedly.

"Harry!"

The Lopez brothers exchanged glances. Miguel scowled but shrugged his shoulders. The holding of this auction was a daring venture and, like Mrs. Clack, he felt that he would be glad to see an end of it. When he had glanced into the salon just now his eyes had gleamed with satisfaction. This was not the usual crowd. Only twenty men, perhaps, but they were twenty men with a great deal of money in their pockets and few morals. Among them, a duke. They had surrounded Lopez trying to question him, all filled with interest in the viciously attractive sale of this sixteen-year-old slave. Among them was an oldish man who had in fact once run a fleet of slave traders in the West Indies. Now that he was old he felt that it might be amusing to see re-enacted a scene that used to be common enough to him. He had watched the proceedings in many a slave market in his time. All were eager to know what the girl looked like and whence she came. Lopez had smiled and shaken his head. He had nothing to say but that the gentleman to whom the prize fell must take the girl away and keep her hidden for some considerable time.

Most of the gentlemen present wore masks or were disguised unwishful for recognition. An air of excitement prevailed. There was considerable drinking. The silence was broken finally by the sound of a zither being played in the shadows by a Hungarian, a woman in Juan Lopez's employ. Juan was an artist not only of design but dramatic effect. He knew that the faint plaintive music brought an air of mystery and sensual charm to the scene. Finally, a serving man extinguished all the candles. The audience, now in darkness, seated themselves before the small stage. Juan Lopez came forward and said:

"Gentlemen—the sale commences!"

At that moment a door opened and two men walked unnoticed into the room; the figure of the Marquis de Chartellet, followed by his secretary. The masked and disguised Marquis slid quietly into the seat offered him.

As the curtain lifted, there was no sound to be heard but the curiously monotonous and fascinating lilt of the zither.

The little stage was brilliantly lighted with hundreds of candles. Then from the crowd eagerly craning forward rose a chorus of astonishment and approval as they saw the slave-girl for the first time.

Fauna stood in that curiously meek silent pose, as a million slaves before her must have stood in Eastern slave markets in the pagan past. She wore a long skirt of transparent gauze. The small waist was girdled with silver. Lopez had been clever enough not to spoil her natural charms by over-loading her with ornaments. The mantle of long hair rippled to her knees. The long lashes had been touched with kohl, the lips red, otherwise her face bore the pallor of marble. She might have been a statue, she stood so still and with her great eyes staring blankly in front of her.

"Ye gods, what an exquisite creature!" whispered a man's voice excitedly.

"She is all and more than Lopez promised," murmured another.

"I can see that I will ruin myself to buy her," said another.

Lucien de Chartellet sat rigid and silent but his cold penetrating gaze never left that fascinating figure on the platform. He, the connoisseur of beauty, the collector of rare treasures, knew that here was a ruby above price; one of the most beautiful women he had ever seen in his life; and a mere child at that. It was that curious air of defencelessness and fragility clinging to Fauna as she stood there with her chained wrists, exposed to the gaze of all, that excited the Marquis's fullest interest and even compassion. Here was no coarse harlot, no dark-blooded houri, but a pearl of womanhood. The man who had just said that she was "all and more than Lopez had promised" had spoken the truth.

For the first time for years, the blood began to run a little less sluggishly through the veins of the Frenchman. His eyes narrowed. Turning he whispered in his secretary's ear:

"You will bid for her to the uttermost limits. *She is to be mine.*"

Aubrey Burkett said:

"Yes, milord."

He, himself, had never had time for women in his academic career. He was the aesthetic type, with that coldness of brain that had originally drawn him to de Chartellet. He did not indulge in amorous pastimes. He had never known a woman's love. Yet even *he* found his blood kindling at the sight of the young slave girl in all her transcendent loveliness. She was mysterious and tragic; child and woman; she was *every man's desire.*

The auction began.

Lopez said:

"I have a bid for one hundred guineas. An insignificant price. I expect an improvement on that."

"Two hundred," ventured the Duke.

The Marquis sat back, arms folded across this chest, his thinly cut lips smiled. Aubrey called:

"Two hundred and fifty guineas."

"Three hundred," said another voice.

The elderly man who had owned the slave-traders turned and whispered to a friend:

"Beelzebub! I am out of it. I had no idea there would be this big money in it. Of course she is *excessively* fascinating, and would appear to be quite white. Who would guess that she was a quadroon? I have never seen her like!"

Fauna continued to stand motionless in the brilliant candlelight that made agate pools of her wonderful sorrowful eyes. She heard the men's voices, the bidding, but it all meant nothing. With the narcotic dulling her senses, she had no keen realization of the shameful proceedings. If she heard anything clearly—it was only the music from the Hungarian zither. Her bemused mind led her down the labyrinths of time. She was not on this platform now but in a swaying coach. A young man was playing upon a flute. Somebody was laughing greatly because she sang and danced, saying:

"Bravo, Insect! You show much talent!"

It had been George Pumphret bringing her from Bristol to London. He had bought her, not in a public auction, but in private—and not for himself but as a toy for his wife. Fauna laughed aloud. The laugh was lost in a hubbub of voices for now the Lopez's clients one by one gained their feet, drawing nearer, examining Fauna more critically and closely. Their hot eager eyes raked her. Their hands reached out to touch her ankles. The bidding became fast and furious. The price had reached five hundred guineas.

Miguel Lopez standing in the background beside Mrs. Clack grinned at her and the woman grinned back wiping her fat face. She was panting and perspiring. Such a *price*. And she was to share it. What fools men were to waste their gold on a chit of a girl with nigger blood in her, she thought derisively, but she was vastly pleased. She would never need to work again once she got her share for this night's work.

Unmindful of the fact that her future life hung in the balance—that it was only a question of price and of who could bid highest and longest—then she would be knocked down like an inanimate object and given to her purchaser

—Fauna remained in her poppy-stupor—she was pursued by fevered phantasies.

"Harry!" she said.

And she began to sway in time to the music lifting her chained wrists above her head. Miguel whispered to Mrs. Clack:

"She needs no instruction. Look how she dances—*she sells herself!*"

The beauty of Fauna's movements in that strange unsolicited dance—the perfection of the white graceful limbs plainly visible beneath the folds of gauze—drew a roar of approval from the audience. Somebody shouted:

"What is her name? Tell us her name, Lopez."

The Spaniard answered:

"Nay, sir—she is nameless!"

Now, suddenly, as though fatigued, Fauna stopped dancing. Her head drooped and her long hair fell across her breast. Then the Marquis with an exclamation sprang to his feet. Those falling locks—that expression of mingled torture and delight—great God, he thought, *it was the girl on the stone horse*—the carved nymph slung over the shoulder of the sculptured man in the courtyard of The Bastille. *Now he knew that he must have her*, even though he bid the last guinea he owned in the world. His sparse body shook with excitement. He sat down again and clutched Aubrey by the arm.

"Let us have done with this farcical sale. Say that I bid a thousand guineas."

The secretary's eyes widened but he rose to his feet.

"On behalf of my master, I bid one thousand guineas," he called out above the hum of voices.

There was a sudden silence in the smoke-filled salon, all eyes stared in his direction. Juan, his crafty face beaming, said:

"I am glad to see that there is a gentleman who realizes that what I offer is of true value. One thousand guineas is bid. Is there anyone to better it?"

The Duke, very much incognito, glared at Aubrey.

"One thousand one hundred guineas," he snapped.

"I'faith," muttered the man beside Lucien, "one does not have the chance of possessing such an exquisite nymph every day. But one must live, and the costs in this country are rising. I, for one, cannot afford to bid higher."

Only two men were left in the battle now—the unknown duke and the Marquis de Chartellet. The others fell out, muttering, disappointed. De Chartellet waited in the shadows, fixing his gaze again on the form of the girl who appeared now to be overcome with weariness, or drugs. Lucien strongly suspected that she had been doped. He was thinking:

"I shall be much amused to deck her out with jewels and elegant attire more suited to her unusual beauty. Every gesture she makes also suggests that she has music in her blood. She shall be trained to dance and to sing. She will be a new and unique amusement for me during this coming summer."

Aubrey Burkett made a fresh bid. The price had reached one thousand seven hundred guineas. Then the Duke fell out, glaring resentfully at the secretary, wondering whom he represented. He did not recognize the bearded and masked gentleman beside him.

The auction was over. Fauna had been sold to Lucien de Chartellet.

Lopez struck a gong. The red plush curtains fell. Serving men hastened to re-light the candles in the salon. There was a good deal of grumbling, of speculation as to who had so much money to waste, and some good-humoured flattery cast at the Lopez brothers for their entertainment. It had been a singular evening, and it seemed a pity, as one gentleman remarked, that Mr. Fox and my Lord Grenville seemed likely to carry through the Bill prohibiting the exportation of slaves. Not that it was common to find such a girl as this nameless wonder! Perish the fellow who had the wherewithal to purchase her.

Now Lucien de Chartellet said to his secretary:

"You have the money. Pay Lopez. I am going to fetch the girl."

Fauna had by this time succumbed completely to the effects of the drug given her. She lay with closed eyes on a couch in the small ante-room used privately by the Lopez brothers. The Marquis picked up one of the girl's hands and fingered the pulse. It was beating strongly enough. His eyes, cold and sardonic, looked at the mean faces of the

Spaniards, and then at the unspeakable countenance of the gargantuan Mrs. Clack.

"I have no doubt that you have sold me stolen property but I will not inquire into that," he said. "It was agreed. I will keep to my share of the bargain. But there are one or two questions I mean to ask. Is there any among you who can tell me something of this young girl's breeding and origin?"

Mrs. Clack bobbed a curtsey, overawed by the aristocratic bearing of the gentleman with the black beard. She was so entranced by the thought that she had become so rich that she was willing to be amenable.

"I know a little, your lordship," she squeaked.

"See that you make it a little and be careful," Lopez muttered in her ear, "unless you want those who knew the slave to be at our throats."

Lucien saw the fellow whispering and said through his teeth:

"Let the woman speak or I will withdraw my offer."

Lopez bowed and backed away. He was not willing to forgo what was to him a small fortune.

Mrs. Clack then informed the Marquis that the girl had come originally from Jamaica; that she had been born in Africa of an Irish father and a mother with Italian and Negro blood in her and that she had had quite a deal of culture, and was adept with her needle. Also that she could speak good English.

"And I do assure you, my lord," added the terrible woman, her chins wobbling, "the dear soul is as innocent as a new-born babe. She has been well guarded and is worth her price."

Disgusted by the woman, the Marquis turned.

"Carry the girl out to my carriage," he said briefly.

A few moments later all those who had attended the auction had left the Lopez establishment in Aldgate. The house was plunged into darkness and silence. From St. Paul's came the boom of the clock chiming the hour of four. Through the deserted streets, the Marquis's chaise bore him and his secretary and the nameless slave towards his dwelling near Green Park. There they would remain until morning, and after sleep and food return to Brightlingsea.

Fauna slept like a child completely insensible to her surroundings and her fate, her head resting against the Marquis's shoulder. Her perfumed hair touched his cheek. And to his own surprise and consternation he was curiously moved; as he had not been moved since his own young daughter had slept thus in childish fatigue, after a game. And he thought:

"I will see that she comes to no harm. Under my roof she shall be well cared for. *I wonder whence she came!*"

As the horses turned into Piccadilly, their hoofs striking fire against the cobbles, Fauna leaned closer to de Chartellet. In her sleep she murmured the name:

"Harry!"

"And who the devil is Harry?" Lucien de Chartellet said aloud, "I must find out."

Chapter Ten

In the private room of the Lopez brothers, three people sat round a table on which stood a bottle of porter and a candelabra; the candles almost gutted, spluttering, dripping wax, casting monstrous shadows on the ceiling of the unattractive trio who sat there carousing. Now and again Miguel Lopez rattled a chamois leather bag which lay on his lap. The chink of coins made pleasant music. The only other sound in the house this grey ghostly dawn was the gulping of liquor down three dry throats.

Miguel was drunk but alert. Juan gradually becoming comatose. Mrs. Clack, buttons undone, face scarlet, fat short legs thrust out in ungainly fashion, swayed as she lifted her mug to her slobbery mouth. Now and again she mumbled:

"One thousand seven hundred guineas. Ish-a-miracle—all thanks to Dora Clack."

Miguel wiped his mouth on his sleeve, and cast her a malevolent look. His face was waxen and wet, shining vilely in the candlelight.

"Thanks to *me* and my brother you mean, woman!"

"No—to me," she corrected him and hiccoughed.

"Shurrup, begone to bed, the pair of you," put in Juan.

"Not together, brother dear, for pity's sake . . ." cackled Miguel and cast a glance at Mrs. Clack which was scarcely flattering. She got on to her feet, tottering.

"Time to—go—to—bed. Yes, but firsht—my share of t'gold," she muttered.

Juan gave a foolish laugh and slithered suddenly under the table. He stayed there, snoring.

His brother rose, mug in hand. He was not so intoxicated as his confederates. His eyes glittered wickedly at the bag of gold that had been handed over by Aubrey Burkett.

Half of it to this fat sow of a female? No, not if Miguel Lopez knew better.

Slyly, smiling, he slid near her and tucked an arm under one of hers.

"Wouldst care for a little dalliance with me, sweetheart?"

She cackled with laughter. Her hideous flesh kindled. Not many men so much as touched Dora Clack's fingers these days. Behind the alcoholic fumes, her addled mind fought to remember that the most important thing of all was to secure her rightful share of the money paid for Fauna, the girl she had so viciously ill-treated, betrayed and sold. But she was willing to indulge her carnal appetite as well.

"A guineash worth more than a kish," she said with lewd laughter. "But I've no ob-objecshun to some dalliance, Master Miguel."

He made pretence of dropping a kiss on her cheek, but even he, hardened criminal that he was, was revolted by her hairy chin and drew back. He pressed one of her huge bare arms again while she panted and ogled him.

"Firsht—more liquor!" he said, waving aloft his empty mug. "Come, sweetheart—to the cellars—to find a fresh bottle. *One thousand seven hundred guineas, eh?* Worth a celebration before we split the gains—think you?"

Mrs. Clack's pig's eyes, bemused, seeing most things in duplicate, tried to focus on Miguel's smirking waxen face. He clawed at her, and pretending to be more drunk than she, swayed beside her leading her at the same time through the open door to the back of the dwelling. There, an inky blackness and the odour of damp-rot prevailed. The drink-inflamed housekeeper sniffed and hung back.

"Don' like the dark. Look you—my little Spanish gentleman—fesh a candle."

"You don' wan' a candle," he hiccoughed and slyly propelled her forward.

Still the woman hung back as though, in her animal fashion, she sensed danger. The domicile of the Lopez brothers was too quiet and seemed sinister at this hour before daybreak. Besides she did not trust them any more than they trusted her.

"Lesh go back. Don' wan' more drink," she began.

But he had opened a door before her.

"There, sweetheart—get on with you! 'Tis a cellar full of fine liquor. Best in London. You shall choose your own tipple. Wait, if you will—I'll strike a match."

She mumbled a protest, her head fevered, her mind dazed. She saw only darkness, and heard the sound as of water. *What water?* she asked herself fearfully. This place was not on the river. But she could swear some animal, like a rat, had splashed into a pool. She gave a sudden cry and tottered back, panting with fear, leaning against her companion.

"Back," she muttered. "Wanna go back. . . ."

Miguel laughed. The sinister utterly evil quality of that low-pitched laugh froze the blood in the housekeeper's very veins. She made a final desperate effort to turn and break from him, and seek the more agreeable atmosphere of the room they had just vacated. But she was too late. Never to know that he had opened a trap-door and that the thing she had heard, had indeed, been a rat—a-scuttling down the slimy steps that led directly into the sewers that ran beneath this very house.

The next moment, Miguel's merciless arm gave that enormous female bulk of sharp, fierce push that sent the woman reeling, clean off her balance. She gave a frightful scream and fell—down, down—striking her head against the last step. Then the muddy evil-smelling waters closed over her and swept her away, into the noisome tunnel—into the darkness of death.

Miguel shuddered as he heard what he thought to be the echo of Mrs. Clack's appalling cry. Swiftly he shut the trap-door and placed a rug over it. Then he returned to the room in which his brother lay insensible, still snoring. Miguel was sweating, although the March dawn was chill. He picked up the bag of guineas and rattled them, soothed by the chink of the gold piecs.

"*One thousand seven hundred guineas,*" he muttered. "And no half-share for a corpse. The rats will get at *that*. Juan and I alone shall enjoy what we have earned this night. And not a soul will miss Mistress Clack nor mourn for her. *She is no loss.*"

And those words were Dora Clack's epitaph. Her career of greed, of cruelty, of rapaciousness was ended. She had died a fearful death at the hands of a man whose thirst for money exceeded her own. *And she was no loss to anybody in the world.*

Chapter Eleven

For forty-eight hours following her sale by the Lopez brothers to the Marquis de Chartellet, Fauna lived in a world of shadows.

She could walk and talk but drowsily and without making much sense. She laughed and wept and passed from this state back into a coma. A physician hastily summoned to attend her in Lucien's London house diagnosed what the Marquis had already thought. The girl had been strongly dosed with opium. But fortunately there need be no lasting ill-effects. Perhaps it was fortunate for her, he had thought, that she should know so little about what was happening to her at this period of her life.

Mingled with his strange pleasure in his new purchase, was a longing to chase the shadows from the girl's mind, elucidate it, and restore her will-power and control. Then he would make a close study of her; as he had so often studied well-chosen treasures. But the fact that this one was human and of exceptional beauty made the pastime doubly fascinating to the Marquis.

When Fauna first became clear as to what was going on around her, she awakened to a new world. A world far removed from that lived with Henrietta Pumphret—or that paradise which she had so briefly shared with Harry Roddney.

It was a mild March afternoon. She opened her heavy eyes to find herself lying on a couch at right angles to a huge fireplace of carved stone, in which enormous logs crackled merrily in a wrought-iron basket. Slowly her languorous eyes took in every detail, wandering with curiosity and amazement around her. It was all so magnificent. The walls on three sides of the long room were lined with handsome leather-bound books. Facing her was an oriel window framed by looped curtains of deep purple velvet, fringed with gold. Through that window Fauna could see only the cloud-flecked sky. But later, she arose and walked across the room and found she could look down on the glistening rocks over which a grey sea churned and creamed. There were cushioned seats beneath this fine window which had been a recent addition to The Bastille. Here the Marquis often sat with his books, especially during summer, when through the wide open panes he could smell the strong salt air, and listen to the rhythmic hiss and boom of the waves below.

To the right lay the little port of Brightlingsea. Always gay with colour and movement, small fishing craft moved in and out of the harbour while the sea-gulls screamed and volplaned and dived for fish.

Fauna returned to the couch and lay still trying to collect her thoughts which were in considerable confusion. *What* was this splendid room? *Whence* came she here? She was warm, and the couch was luxurious. Across her legs lay a cashmere shawl of fine texture. She was clothed in a robe more beautiful than anything she had ever seen worn by the Lady Henrietta. It was of turquoise velvet lined with pure ermine. The wide sleeves had cuffs of the same rich fur. Around her neck hung ropes of creamy pearls which she guessed to be of fabulous value.

She stared at all these things, frowning perplexedly, and then suddenly noticed a tress of her hair which was spread over satin cushions of a bright turquoise to match her gown. *Black* hair. This fact confused her further. She sat up and glanced down at her hands. They seemed well cared for, with polished nails, and she wore several jewelled bracelets and one or two splendid rings.

Suddenly she gave a laugh. She must be mad or she had died and this was some curious paradise. But *why* should she have hair so black when hers had always been golden-red? She lay back on the cushions again, sighing, stretching her limbs voluptuously. She began to notice other things in the room. Rich tapestries, thick fine rugs on a floor polished until it looked like honey-coloured glass with sunlight streaming in upon it. An alabaster jar by the window filled with flowers. A French gilded clock on the mantelpiece. It chimed suddenly three times, so that she knew the hour. A buhl cabinet filled with choice ivories. A clavichord. A never-ending assortment of wonders each more beautiful than the last. Then she returned to fingering her velvet and furs and jewels again, struggling to co-ordinate her thoughts.

It was as though she had awakened from a long strange sleep punctuated by dreams; some sensual and beautiful; some sinister and horrible beyond words. Most of them had been nightmares, she told herself. Nothing could be real. So many faces had floated through her consciousness, so many voices both strange and familiar penetrated her hearing, she could ill remember them. Now, like frightened birds, her thoughts flew round and round her brain refusing to be captured for more than a minute. The terrible face of Mrs. Clack—yes, *that* she could recall. A memory of threats, of agonies, of wild tears and desperate heartbreak. Then the face of a man with green brilliant eyes. *That*, too, had floated through her mind in the more beautiful of her dreams. She had felt the strong touch of boyish hands; heard a low, beguiling voice calling her:

"Fauna! Fauna!"

Mingled with it came the sound of her own voice screaming; of a zither playing, and of hot vicious hands clawing at her ankles.

She sat up with a sudden cry, touching her throat. She felt an extremity of fear that had nothing to do with this beautiful tranquil sunlit room.

"*Harry!*" The name that meant so much to her burst from her lips.

Then came a man's voice from behind her.

"Hush, my child, do not distress yourself. You are in good hands. You have nothing to fear."

She looked through the slim fingers she had laced across her face. She saw the small but elegant figure of a man whose unpowdered hair was tied with a ribbon. He had a thin aesthetic face on which there were countless wrinkles. A gentleman of middle-age, she judged, handsomely attired in dark grey cloth with a flowered yellow satin waistcoat. There was fine lace at his throat and his wrists and he carried a lace-edged handkerchief. She let her hands fall and stared at him blankly but with the fear seeping from her. He obviously meant her no harm. In cavalier fashion he took her fingers, bowed and lightly kissed them.

"You are better," he said, "much better. That last physic given you by my good French physician, Monsieur Surenne, has done its work. This is the first time I have seen your eyes so bright: Now I want you to tell me who *Harry* is and why you call so repeatedly on that name."

He had drawn a gilded chair covered in gros-point to her side. He added:

"I have just finished my repast. Did you enjoy yours. You ate, I hear, quite well today."

Fauna's huge eyes gazed at him as though she could not believe what she saw or heard. She whispered:

"Did I—eat a meal? I do not remember."

He smiled.

"No. For the last two days and nights you have existed in a world of shadow and fantasy, like a marionette. I pull the strings and you move. You even eat and drink to please me. But I do not care overmuch for marionettes. I prefer that you should wake up and act of your own volition."

"Please, sir," said Fauna in a trembling voice, "explain more clearly. It is all so—so strange. I am without understanding."

Lucien took a small gilt snuff-box between his fingers, which were white and delicate, and applied the snuff to his nostrils. He sneezed thrice, then smiled in his cold fashion. But the eyes that watched her were not altogether cold. They were profoundly interested. He wondered if the child realized how perfect she was in that turquoise and ermine robe, the top part of which was moulded to her exquisite breasts. And she was not so pale this afternoon. There was a faint pink in her cheeks, a more healthy lustre in those wonderful eyes. He could never tire of looking at her. Many times since he had brought her to The Bastille, while she lay in her drugged sleep, he would come to look at her; with the cool criticism he levelled at all *objets d'art* in his possession. He never bought anything unless it was perfect. So he liked to look at this new treasure with the same cool admiration.

"Who is 'Harry'?" he repeated softly.

He saw a shudder go through her. A flame of scarlet dye her face and even the milk-white throat, which he found charming. Not since his youth had he seen a woman blush like that. The little slave girl was not, then, quite unawakened. For it was with a woman's deep passion and emotion that she answered him:

"He—*I—I loved him once.*"

"Once?"

Her head drooped. She was remembering things now with a vengeance. The turgid stream moved, the dam broke and there gushed out a veritable torrent of recollection of those days spent with Harry and her great love for him. Then her betrayal and the horrible foreigner who had driven her away from Pillars. The vile pink bedroom and Mrs. Clack . . . only after that did facts recede and go out of focus again.

The Marquis de Chartellet watched intently.

"You may speak with the utmost confidence to me," he said, "I must know everything from the start."

She sat up, pressing her hands against her agitated breast.

"But who are you, sir? Where am I? First tell me that."

He told her. He added:

"I bought you, my child, for the sum of one thousand seven hundred guineas. You are worth more, of course. You are, in your enchanting fashion, quite priceless. But I bought you, and you belong to me. Are you confounded by the idea?"

She looked at him with that doubt and confusion which he found so curiously disarming and pathetic. He was used to only two kinds of women—serving wenches (peasants of gross stupidity, dirty and ignorant) or high-born ladies, ignorant of all that truly mattered in life, but with the social graces—knowing how to make a Court curtsey, to coquette, to dally with their lovers or betray their husbands; to play at love—and at living. They bored Lucien de Chartellet exceedingly. But *this* kind of woman, this strange mixture of virgin and of innocent voluptuary, this born-slave with her imperial loveliness and the dignity that had clothed her even when she had stood naked and defenceless before that crowd of men on the night of her auction—was an entirely new phenomenon to him.

He leaned nearer her and spoke again.

"Is it displeasing to you to learn that you have become the chattel of the Marquis de Chartellet?"

Then she drew breath and glanced down at her jewels and her clothing. Her colour faded.

"It would seem you have been kind to me but——"

"Do you measure kindness by the value of the jewels and furs a man may give to you?" he broke in.

Now that life was coursing back through her veins, and her mind was clear again, she could argue. She became once more an individual.

"I care nothing for jewels, sir. They are beautiful. For their beauty, I like them—not their value. It is the kindness I crave, and that cannot be measured. It was good of you to let me lie here on this soft couch—to feed me and to bring me back to health. I cannot recall the fact that I was sold to you, but I do know that was the intent when . . . when that terrible Mrs. Clack and those men removed me from——" she broke off.

"From Harry?" the Marquis supplied the words softly.

"Yes," she said in a low voice.

"So it is kindness you ask for and jewellery you do not crave," went on the Marquis reflectively. "How refreshing and how rare in a female."

Fauna slid her legs over the side of the couch and stood up, immediately she felt giddy. With a gentle hand he pushed her back against the cushions.

"Lie there for a while longer. We will converse. These people who sold you were thieves. How did they get hold of you? What is your origin—and what is your name?"

She lay still a moment, then spoke in a low measured voice:

"I am called Fauna."

"Fauna!" he repeated, his eyes widening, " 'tis strange. Do you know what it means?"

"Yes, sir. Lord Pumphret, my former master, told me. It is from the Latin, and when he—when I was a child purchased from Bristol straight from a slave ship—my Lord Pumphret explained many things to me. He—was amused to call me 'Insect,' sir—but in jest, not unkindness. He was never unkind."

The Marquis brushed this aside. The name and its meaning was entirely unsuitable for her. He would find another. But Pumphret—George Pumphret, now dead—he had bought this girl when a child. That intrigued Lucien. He fancied he had met Pumphret once at the club and that he had also received an invitation to one of Lady Henrietta's drawing-rooms which he had not accepted.

He could see that the girl shied from answering questions about the man, Harry, whom she said she had loved. He was prepared to be patient. Now she began to tell him all that she could remember from the moment when, disguised as a boy, she had first been flung on to the slave ship with her grandfather.

"He was black," she added tragically. "I hate the very thought of that blood that runs in my veins, although my memories of *him* are of a noble and kingly person murdered by Englishmen more savage and cruel than any member of my unfortunate grandfather's tribe."

"Quite so," said Lucien, "there are degrees of savagery, and nobility can sit like a crown upon the brow of a black man as well as upon a white. The colour of your skin is not so important as you may believe, my child."

She beat one fist upon another, all the passion and hatred of her quadroon blood which had been fostered during the past few years, flaming into being.

"I hate it. *I hate it*. They would have married me to an African dwarf. I have been despised and beaten because of my black blood. Oh, I *hate it*!"

The Marquis's gaze narrowed. Coolly he said:

"You must learn, my child, to subdue your passions. He who smiles and retains a cold judgement when he most hates is most likely to vanquish his opponent. Keep your tears and intensities for moments of ecstasy—for a rapturous appreciation of great beauty. I smile while I run my sword through an enemy, but I could weep when I look upon true beauty—the perfection, for instance, of your delicate white body, the turn of your wrists and ankles, the rose-leaf curl of your lips, the luxuriance of your lashes and the satin mantle of your hair."

She only half understood a philosophy which in the years to come he was to teach her and which would become her own. But now, still pagan and untutored, she wept in her unhappiness and sobbed out her passion of her griefs, her resentment against those who had wronged her and the bitterness of her wounded love.

Soon de Chartellet knew all—piecing her story together like a jig-saw puzzle and finding that it made an immensely fascinating pattern. The quadroon slave, called Fauna, had the innocence of a child but was not virgin. She had for a few days been the mistress of a young man named Harry Roddney—nephew of the ex-Governor of Gibraltar—noted rake and habitué of London gaming rooms—friend of Beau Brummell. A foolish handsome headstrong young man of a type Lucien de Chartellet knew well and despised. The only thing he could not despise about Harry Roddney was the fact he held a reputation for being a fine swordsman, of that much Lucien was aware for he, in France in his youth, had held a similar position. He could not remember losing a duel.

So it was to Sir Harry Roddney this girl had belonged, and he had grown weary of her and returned her to her enemies.

She was sobbing openly now as though the flood-gates of her grief had opened up for the first time since she had been taken away from Roddney.

"I loved him," she kept moaning, "why did he not kill me instead of allowing me to live!"

The Marquis got up and with hands locked behind him began to walk up and down the room. A room filled with the sighing of the sea and the sobbing of the heart-broken girl.

He said:

"It is as well you were allowed to live. You will recover from this blow."

"Never," said Fauna in a hoarse voice.

"You will recover," he repeated coldly. "The mad passions experienced by human beings for one another are entirely transitory. The lusts in one's life are of no account. It is the affections that count. I have had but two—my love for my wife and my daughter, who are now both dead. With them died my love. Since which I have known only lusts—lusts of the eye, the ear, all the senses. These are appetites to be satisfied. If you will accept the fact that you have these appetites—satisfy and then forget them—you will be happy. You will cease to remember Harry Roddney as a young god to whom you gave your heart, and remember him only as the fool, to whom you gave your body, and who was ungrateful. I am glad that you live, for I shall see to it that one day in the future you will meet with Harry Roddney again."

"Never!" she cried in her bitterness, and added: "Oh God, my God, how could he have betrayed me?"

"That, my child," said the Marquis, "is a question that has been echoed by countless females throughout all the ages. It is easily answered. It is easy for human beings to betray one another but by no means one-sided. Women also betray men. For money, for vengeance, and sometimes out of sheer *ennui*. Another thing that I shall teach you is to put yourself always in the position of one who cannot be betrayed. That can be achieved only when you have built an armour for yourself, one without a vulnerable chink. Yes, *you shall meet Harry Roddney again.* But not until I have placed you in a position in which *you* will be able to look coldly upon him and make him pay the price of his betrayal; for it was ill done," Lucien added half to himself.

She shook her head. She was still not able to grasp how Harry could have done this thing to her. She could remember, even now, his last words to her: *"Till tonight. Then we shall exchange a thousand kisses to make up for those we must forswear while I am gone."*

But the kiss he had given her was the kiss of Judas Iscariot; a double betrayal.

"I would like to hate him, sir, but I cannot," she said in a pitiful voice to this new incomprehensible man who had thought fit to purchase her.

He came back to her side and took one of her hands, turning it over, examining the rosy palm.

"You will learn," he said, "when you have put such episodes into proper perspective. Meanwhile I would ask that you do not speak the name of Harry Roddney. I shall not forget it, I assure you. And from time to time I will give you news of him—if it pleases you."

"I do not want it. I wish to forget him," she said sulenly.

Lucien smiled.

"That is false. You must learn, too, to become emotionally honest; honest at all cost with yourself. Only then can you gain control and be master of your mind as well as your body. I will teach you these things. I am your master. You shall become my pupil. You shall be no slave in this house. I have more servants than I need. But I have a fancy for teaching—and being sick of idle amusement, and the feverish pleasures of our time—I shall find interest in training your mind. At the same time in seeing you grow daily more beautiful as you mature. I shall instruct you in my own method of living, and I can tell from this short discussion that you will be exquisitely receptive. This house shall become your school as well as your home. These next few years, the period of your education . . ." he paused and looked at her reflectively through half-closed eyes. The face of the satyr became the face of the aesthete; the artist. He went on: "You shall learn to speak and to write perfectly in English, and as perfectly in French, in Italian, and German. You shall be well tutored in all the arts. Music, painting and poetry. You shall become a connoisseur and a critic. You shall become, in fact, greater than the greatest lady in the land. And . . ." gallantly he bent and kissed the finger-tips that quivered in his own, "you will most certainly always be the loveliest!"

Fauna drew a deep breath.

"I hardly understand. Why should you do this for me, sir?" she said.

"It is my whim. But only if you will swear to give me your fullest attention and to work hard. Nothing can be achieved unless you cast aside the desire for frivolity and most industriously pursue your new studies."

She drew a hand across her hot tear-wet eyes.

"I think I would like it, sir."

He nodded, his mind darting this way and that, full of intrigue, with schemes for her. Then he said:

"Do not address me as 'sir,' but as *Lucien*. We shall not live together as master and slave—but as—friends."

Stupefied she looked up at him.

"Friends?"

His cool grey eyes smiled sardonically down at her.

"You expected, of course, that I would take you to my bed. But I shall not. I would not have you, warm and weeping, fresh from the embraces of Harry Roddney."

Now her cheeks were dyed with a hot blush of shame.

She turned her face to the cushions. But she felt the Marquis's thin hand lightly touch her hair.

"There is no need to feel thus. One of the things I would eradicate in you, my child, is a false sense of shame. You were not foolish to take Harry Roddney to your embrace—only to believe that he would be faithful to you. The one justification for shame is the knowledge that one has been a fool. You find that cynical? Yes, I am a cynic, and I am a devil and those who know me call me by the name of *Satyr*. But I will not have you afraid of me—ever."

Now she turned and looked at him with that languishing and haunting gaze which made such an impression on him.

"I do not think I will be afraid of you," she whispered, "and if you will endeavour to teach me all these wondrous things I swear I will be a most willing and devoted pupil."

"I wonder," he said reflectively, "what I shall make of you."

Then she said naïvely:

"I do not need the jewels."

He gave a low laugh.

"Then you shall have books, but wear the jewels to please me because I like to see them upon you."

"As you wish," she said.

"For the moment, it is as I wish," he nodded. "But I wonder how long it will be before it will be as *you* wish? I do not embark on this tuition without some danger. The pupil may in time outshine—even outwit the master. It has been known to happen. But I think if I make of you what I would—I shall go further. *I shall marry you.*"

Now Fauna gasped.

"Sir—milord—you are pleased to mock me!"

He got up, walked away from her and looked out of the open window down at the surging sea.

"No," he said, and his eyes for an instant held an expression of devilish glee. "If and when you achieve the intellectual heights I anticipate, coupled with your great beauty, you would not do badly as the second Madame la Marquise de Chartellet."

Her low astonished voice followed him.

"But my *black blood*."

"We will forget that, my dear, I forbid you ever to

mention it again, for I can see that it distresses you, and it plays altogether too exaggerated a part in your mind. I shall have the most immense satisfaction in introducing you to Society and in watching those who have hitherto ill-used you, tumble over each other in the effort to entertain or be entertained by Lucien de Chartellet's wife."

Fauna remained silent. The vista he opened up for her was too fantastic. The space between the now and the then still so wide she could not bridge it. It was not to be imagined. She could only lie still, her heart beating fast, and with the feeling gradually creeping through her that the tide in her fortunes had turned. This strange French Marquis was, perhaps, mad, but it was the type of madness she could welcome. She could think of nothing more wonderful than to be allowed to live here as his pupil; to learn all that he had to teach her; allow him to mould her into what shape his fancy bid. Whether he was good or evil she did not know, yet felt that she could trust in him. And for the first time since she had become a woman she could think obliquely about her own beauty and feel it an asset rather than a danger. Suddenly a new sense of well-being, of renewed hope coupled with the desire to go on living, pervaded her and calmed the turbulence of her spirit. As for the prospect of being raised from the degradation of her position as a slave into the exalted position he suggested—she almost laughed at it. It could never be. She touched the rope of pearls about her throat, and now, in anguish, remembered those pearls which Harry had given her, and which she had left behind in the house of broken dreams.

Lucien de Chartellet came and stood beside her. He had seen her expression. And he, who was beginning to know and understand her, tapped her hand suddenly, sharply with his:

"I forbid you to think of Harry Roddney. They tell me you sing. I will play the clavichord and you shall let me hear your voice."

"Yes, sir," she said gulping.

"Call me *Lucien*."

"Yes, Lucien!"

He pursed his lips. Slowly he beat his finger-tips together while he regarded her with his cool speculating gaze.

"No, *Fauna* does not suit you," he said. "From now onwards you shall be Helène. Have you ever heard of Helen of Troy, my child?"

She shook her head.

"Then you must learn. We shall touch on Greek history," smiled the Marquis.

"Who—was Helen of Troy?" she asked in a whisper.

"A goddess. Men went to war for her and died for her in their thousands. Paris gave to her the golden apple which signified her queenship of all beautiful women. The name *Helen* means in Greek—a torch. And Homer wrote of her 'She moves a Goddess and she looks a Queen.' The name comes from a Greek root whence springs the words *selené* meaning moon, and *helios* the sun. You have the body of a moon goddess. It is a pity that your hair is black because——"

"But it isn't," interrupted Fauna suddenly and unexpectedly. "They coloured it to disguise me lest I should be found by those who are searching for me in London. Oh, it isn't black, I do assure you. It *has* the colour of the sun."

The Marquis gave a cry of pleasure. His eyes glistened. He leaned forward, examined with a spy-glass the roots of her hair and saw suddenly close to the scalp a glint of red and gold. He gasped:

"*Parbleu!* It is true. Then indeed my Helène will be perfect. With hair the colour of the sun you are indeed the incarnation of the greatest of all Helens. I must send at once for the woman whom I have engaged as your maid. She is the first woman except yourself ever to live under this roof. I prefer to be waited on by men. Your hair must be washed at once. Do you feel strong enough?"

Fauna nodded and smiled shyly. It was the first time he had ever seen her smile. And her expression contained an element of coquetry which amused him vastly. So—the child was not so weary of life or so broken by love that all vanity had passed from her. She *wanted* him to see her redgold hair. By all the stars, it would be worth seeing, he thought, with such hair and those eyes, the newest and most absorbing treasure to enter his museum would be above price.

He pulled a tapestry bell. A middle-aged woman wearing stiff black silk muslin apron and cap and with soft Irish eyes entered and bobbed a curtsey. Aubrey Burkett had secured her services under his employer's orders, and brought her here from London. She had come with excellent references. Having no ties, she had agreed to the Marquis's terms, which were that she should be virtually incarcerated in this place whilst in his service, never leaving the grounds except to travel with his retinue to his London domicile. This for a number of years, having no contact with the outside world. She had confessed herself willing to live this nun-like existence, since she had lost all those near and dear to her and had no interest in the world's frivolities. She could save for her old age.

She turned now and curtseyed to Fauna who was relieved to read kindliness in the woman's eyes. She was all too accustomed to the reverse.

"This, my dear," said the Marquis, "is Hattie, your personal servant. Hattie . . ." he addressed the woman, "go with the Lady Helène to her bedroom. With the greatest care, aid her to wash and dry her hair."

"Yes, milord," said the woman Hattie, and advancing gave her arm to the young lady on the couch. She knew nothing about Fauna. Nobody within the confines of The Bastille ever knew anything of the Marquis's private affairs. None dared question his authority. Trembling a little, Fauna leaned upon the serving woman's arm and walked with her across the room. She turned and glanced over her shoulder, the Marquis put his heels together and bowed.

"I will await your return, *ma mie*," he said.

Like one in a dream, she walked out. Two flunkeys, magnificent, with powdered wigs and wearing the Chartellet coat-of-arms embroidered on their uniform—bowed as she passed, and closed the double doors behind her.

In the library, Lucien looked towards the closed doors and recalled the grace and slimness of the girl's exquisite figure. He was most impatient to see the false blackness of her hair turned to its natural gold. He thought:

"The Lady *Helène*. Yes—it suits her. I fancy that the next few years of my life will hold much interest. In you, *ma belle* Helène, at last, Lucien de Chartellet has found a fresh *élan* for existence!"

PART III

Chapter One

Four years later.

A cold bleak morning in mid-January. The Marquis de Chartellet entered the writing-room of his London house, spread chilled fingers to the blaze and rang for his secretary. When young Burkett entered the Marquis was seated at his rosewood desk sorting through documents. He knew the younger man's step. He had ultra acute hearing for a man of sixty years old and recognized every footfall in his house. Without turning his head, he said brusquely:

"Is all arranged, Aubrey?"

"Yes, milord," came the answer. But in a voice so changed from his ordinary measured accents—so full of what might be almost termed resentfulness that the Marquis swung round and stared at Aubrey. He put up his spy glass.

"What ails you, man?"

The boy—for he was still only in his twenties—flushed and turned away. His underlip hung sulkily. He muttered:

"Naught, milord."

Then Lucien gave a sharp malicious laugh and returned to the study of his documents.

"Ah, yes," he said. "You are distressed because I have placed upon you the unwelcome task of arranging my marriage to the Lady Helène tonight. Of course—it was thoughtless of me to cause you this pain. You are madly in love with her, yourself, are you not?"

"Milord!" The young man swung round, protesting hotly, his fair face burning, his eyes blazing with mortification . . . and some fear.

The Marquis laughed again. The laugh had a dry harsh timbre. If humorous, it was a humour of a wickedly sardonic kind. His nature was like that laughter, thought

Aubrey—dry, sapless, brittle. Yet not so brittle that *he* could ever be broken. He was as strong as steel. His character ruthless and determinate. He asked for no quarter and gave none. Yet strangely enough he commanded loyalty from those who served him and more—an affectionate regard, deep gratitude, from the most beautiful woman in all England. Helène—who had been the Nameless—soon to become Madame la Marquise de Chartellet. Perhaps, thought the secretary despairingly, the Marquis commanded fealty and respect because of his strong sense of justice. He had never been known to be anything but just —even in the measure of his punishment against those who offended him. But with him retribution came swiftly, and he never forgave a slight.

To Aubrey he had always been considerate—until this day. This day when he had placed upon him the detestable onus of preparing for the marriage which was to take place secretly with only two witnesses—in the crypt of a private chapel. It was to be performed by two priests. One of English denomination—and afterwards by a Roman Catholic, an exile from France who had at one time been Confessor to the de Chartellet family. It was not that Lucien had entered any church nor remembered his religion for at least twenty years past. But he wished this marriage to be correct in every aspect, to satisfy the most conventional taste.

The Marquis dipped a quill in violet ink, signed his name to a paper, and passed it over his shoulder to Aubrey.

"Take this to the French Consulate."

"Yes, milord."

"You have fixed the time?"

"At nine o'clock in the crypt, milord."

"You and the physician will be the sole witnesses. Or will it be too excruciating a sight for you to look upon?"

The cold voice penetrated the young man's reserve. He gave a quick, unhappy laugh.

"What matters even if it is so? I am your lordship's servant."

"You may resign if you so wish."

Silence, Lucien turned and gave the young man a quick searching look. Then a shade of kindliness gleamed in the eyes that had grown no warmer, and slightly paler in colour with the years—like the hair under the peruke, which was now almost white.

Lucien de Chartellet had aged these last two winters. He had developed a tendency to chest weakness. He coughed a great deal. The air at The Bastille suited him better than London. He intended to return to his stronghold by the sea until the spring. Once the season opened in Town he would bring Helène back here and have the exquisite pleasure of watching her make her début.

He said:

"Do not be foolish, Aubrey. You like your job with me, do you not?"

"Yes, milord," said the secretary hoarsely.

"Then why allow a woman's fatal allure to ruin you?"

"I—I—in truth there is no question of—of my being ruined, milord," stammered Aubrey. "I—my lady does not even dream——"

"Of your mad passion for her?"

The boy's head sank.

"If you call it that."

"What else is it?"

"Pray give me leave to retire, milord."

"Not until I have had my say. Look you, Aubrey—my lady knows well enough how you feel towards her. Maybe it does not concern her. I do not know. She conserves her thoughts and unlike most of her sex, preserves a rigid control over her emotions. Doubtless even if she returned your passion she would seek to curb it. You, too, should have learned self-control by now, my boy."

"I have endeavoured to curb my feelings, milord. And I am positive that you, alone, have guessed my unfortunate regard for my Lady Helène. It would be beneath *her* notice."

The Marquis gave a dry laugh. He looked the tall straight figure up and down.

"Is it ever beneath the notice of the fair sex when a handsome youth sighs when she enters the room or groans when she leaves it?"

"I crave your pardon, milord, if I have made any such exhibition of myself," the boy said with some spirit and pride.

Then the Marquis laughed again.

"Go—take hot spiced wine. 'Tis infernally cold out today. Forget your troubles and keep your counsel—and your job."

"Yes, milord," said the young man stonily and placed a paper in front of his master. Lucien glanced at it, raised his brows, nodded, then bent over his writing desk again.

The silence was broken by the sound of a rich imperious voice:

"Are you there, Lucien?"

The Marquis, cocking an eyebrow, glanced at his secretary and answered:

"Come in, *ma mie*."

Aubrey, unable to escape, stood by sulkily. He was a serious-minded young man and it was the first time that he had ever been in love, which he was—wildly and hopelessly—with his employer's protégée. He flinched from having his emotions dissected by the cold and analytical gentleman whom he served. But it was too late. The heavy carved mahogany door opened. Fauna—known as Helène—walked into the waiting-room.

She made a radiant picture; slim, trimly tailored in her bottle-green riding habit with touches of lace at throat and wrists. She wore a high-crowned beaver hat on her unpowdered curls, a butter-yellow veil floating from it. Her cheeks were pink and the frost twinkled on her. As she stood there pulling off yellow gauntlets, crop under one arm, de Chartellet looked at her proudly and possessively. It was the look of a man who admires his own work. He could, verily, be proud of this exquisitely poised young woman, so fashionable and regal, moving across the room so gracefully. Pearls hung from her small ears and a large diamond pin glittered on the laces at her throat. The small hand which she placed on Lucien's shoulder was also heavily jewelled.

"It is splendid out," she said, "but I could not ride for long. The ground is too hard and the Serpentine is frozen over. The people are skating."

De Chartellet nodded and smiled his cool enigmatic smile. He was amused by the way she used that word "people"—like an aristocrat viewing the childish antics of the common mob. He was amused, too, by the indifference with which she flung a nod of greeting at the secretary who immediately flushed violently and turned away. All that was left to *him* now, Lucien thought, was the ability to watch and dissect the passions of others for they could no longer destroy his own peace.

What a long way the child-slave had travelled, he continued to reflect as he gazed upon his *magnum opus*. There was no trace in this young woman today of the meek, heartbroken slave girl he had purchased. At twenty years of age, Helène was in the prime of her beauty. She was also highly educated. It gave the Marquis infinite satisfaction to consider the fact that she could speak French, Italian, and German like a native; her general knowledge was excellent; she could play the clavichord and harp and sing, divinely. Her dancing excelled that of any lady in the land. The pupil had—as he had prophesied—almost reached a stage where she could outwit her master. Nothing caused him greater enjoyment than their long debates and discussions; the way that quicksilver mind of hers—trained by him—could dart brilliantly and swiftly in so many directions. Her thirst for knowledge and her good use of it seemed tireless. If he had kept his word to educate her—she had kept hers to work hard. She had shown unflagging industry. What pleased him, too, was that she seemed to enjoy her arduous labours. So much for Helène the student. As for Helène the woman, the creature of flesh and blood, with warm primitive yearnings and hungry heart, she had been trained to self-mastery and was subdued. There were moments when even Lucien could not guess what lay beneath that unruffled surface, nor how long she would remain disinterested in physical pleasure. She never now referred to the past. She had not mentioned the name of Harry Roddney once since she came to live with him. Of one thing only Lucien was sure—that any man who hoped to re-awaken Helène to more than a fleeting sensual love, would get the worst of it. For *she* would never again be mastered. There was no weakness in her. She was all strength and if there was still fire, it was a fire held under supreme control. The slave could no longer be enslaved. Her personal obedience and loyalty to himself were not born of fear, she had no fear of him nor any living being. He had taught her to shoot, to fence, and to ride, like a boy. She had the courage of a lion. She was submissive and his to command only because she wished to be.

He found her a most engaging companion as well as an apt disciple and perhaps his greatest reward had come on the day when he had given her full permission, if she so wished it, to seek the company of younger men.

"My greatest joy is to look upon your beauty and to watch its further development," he had said, "but you are young and you have known passion. It is natural to desire it. Would you take a lover? I would be envious perhaps, but not jealous. Only fools are that. It is the most sterile of emotions. And, as William Shakespeare has said, cankerous. I shall not be jealous, but I hope you will find a man worthy of your attentions."

Then she had grown pale rather than red, and that proud disdain had flashed into her eyes which he, by his teaching, had infused into her. He knew then that she remembered Harry Roddney in that second but she did not betray the fact. She said:

"I am content with you. If you no longer need a mistress, then I will be mistress to no man."

"Yet there are many who look at you with desire," he had reminded her.

He alluded to the friends and acquaintances who had visited him at The Bastille during the last few years. None were from the society in which the Pumphrets had moved. They were for the most part gentlemen of learning from the Continent, from Denmark and Sweden where Lucien in his youth had many interesting contacts, from the Middle East, and America. Professors, scientists, art-collectors, musicians, and composers. Painters, and men of literature. Such were the types whom Lucien had received at The Bastille during the period of Helène's training. And whenever she joined them they were astonished not only by her beauty but her erudition; the brilliant fashion in which she joined in their arguments. The Marquis had been interested also in giving her instruction in occult matters and disclosed a deep strain of mysticism in her. She had spent long hours in his library. All his books were accessible to her. But with all this learning, he had never allowed her mind to become over-loaded or dull. He had taken her up to London, masked and veiled, to the Opera or the Play.

Aubrey had reported that London buzzed with conjecture as to the identity of the masked beautiful stranger glittering with jewels, always now to be seen at Lucien's side. It was rumoured that he had a new *maîtresse* to whom he was being extraordinarily faithful. But none knew her name, nor could guess from whence she came.

He had enjoyed all Helène's reactions to entertainment, and seen to it that her meditations should include every branch of philosophy; not forgetting to touch upon the erotic theme. And once she had learned to subjugate body as well as mind, he fostered in her a capacity for dragging every facet of her sensual side into the light, to be coldly and mercilessly dissected—then relegated to its proper place. At times now she amazed him by her own powers of self-control, and her frank scorn of hypocrisy, or the ordinary feminine lack of logic.

He had watched, with sardonic humour, the men who met and talked with her tremble at her touch and her own unconcern and indifference to their desire. Once a youngish man had come from Copenhagen to bring to The Bastille a rare painting which the Marquis had coveted. It had been quite an episode. The young connoisseur was to stay the night at The Bastille. The Marquis retired early, leaving the young people to talk together. At midnight he was awakened by the sound of horses stamping in the courtyard. Helène then entered his bedchamber and informed him that she had turned the young man out of the house.

"At such an hour," Lucien had murmured unmoved but curious. "Why? How did he offend you?"

"He tried to make love to me."

The Marquis sat up in his sumptuous bed yawning, chuckling.

"That cannot be enough reason to deserve ejection into the cold midnight air. And he *was* our guest."

Helène tilted her head. Her eyes blazed with sudden anger.

"I did not forget that. But I would not have him remain. He became like an animal. When he flung himself at my feet, I reprimanded him. Then he flung himself at *me*."

The Marquis chuckled further.

"He was not ill-looking—quite a fine young man in fact, and spoke excellent English."

"I do not care to be mauled by a Scandinavian boor who cannot hold his wine," she retorted.

He had thought then how beautiful she looked in her black velvet gown, gems sparkling at throat and wrists. She was a little taller than when she had first come to him. Her figure was the most voluptuous in curve that he had ever seen. Yes—she was a fascinating creature. He raised a brow and sighed:

"Poor devil! I could almost pity him. Would you not have found his ardour stimulating?"

"He disgusted me," she retorted, and added: "All men disgust me when they become carnal."

Then Lucien shook his head and with one eye closed, in his most satyr-like expression, chided her for an exaggeration. It was abnormal that she should feel disgust in all men, he said, and she must prepare herself for the day when she might meet one who would excite her erotic fancy, and learn to accept and deal with it.

" 'Twere best for you to admit that it might happen and be strong and not weak in submission. Then, and then only, will you enjoy the ultimate authority."

She had been pleased to debate upon this theme before she finally left him.

Now he was prepared to make the final gesture and give her his name—his fine time-honoured title—and along with it, a status of her own at last.

"Sit down, my dear," he said as she walked to the fire and spread her hands to the blaze. "I have several things to discuss."

"I will stand a moment," she said, removed her beaver hat and shook back the gleaming unpowdered curls. Her hair never failed to excite his admiration. He never forgot the living breathing wonder it had been to him when he had first seen her after Hattie had washed the dye from the slave's black tresses. How he had run his fingers through the brightness and rejoiced in such perfection.

He glanced towards Aubrey who stood there looking so glum.

"You may leave us."

The young man, not glancing in Helène's direction, bowed and made his exit.

She tapped her boot with her riding crop and frowned.

"Aubrey grows tedious. He sulks like a schoolboy whose sweetmeats are taken from him."

Lucien put his tongue in his cheek.

"Are you not sorry for him? He is in love with you."

"I know," said the girl calmly. "His fingers shake when he hands me a paper or a goblet of wine. But I liked him best when he was composed and indifferent to me."

"He was never that. I watched him from the hour you came."

She shrugged her shoulders.

"Well, then he concealed it. Now he openly adores me and is tiresome, for he cannot even talk amusingly. He must get over it."

"Is it not said that there are only two ways in which a man may recover from a great passion—to satisfy it, or to remove himself from the object of his devotion?"

"Then Aubrey must remove himself."

"Your pardon, *ma mie*, he is too useful a secretary for me to lose—he rarely makes a mistake. I would retain him. Truly, I should be annoyed with *you*, for you have ruined what was once a happy youth of balanced mind, with no feminine entanglements."

Now Helène smiled, and her large black eyes grew amused as they met the Marquis's shrewd gaze.

"La, la!" she said, "chide me then, dear Lucien, for being what I am—a woman whom men desire."

"You are a minx," he said calmly. "Now—your attention please. Aubrey has brought me a copy of the Bill that has been moved in Parliament this week by Grenville and Howick. It is carried, and Wilberforce has his way at last. Total abolition of slave traffic. It remains only for those pursuing the trade to emancipate the creatures whose limbs are still shackled."

Helène stood very still. Her colour was gone but not a muscle of her beautiful face twitched. She was remembering the agony and death of a man she had called *Grandfather*. That seemed so long ago now that it might have been in another life. She took the paper and folded it.

"I am glad," she said, "I will peruse the Bill when I am alone."

The Marquis sorted through some more papers on his desk and pulled out another.

"Mr. Rufus Panjaw," he said, "was, I believe, the name of the man who sold you to Pumphret."

She drew a deep breath.

"Yes," her voice was ice-cold. But her fingers holding the crop clenched.

"Aubrey has traced him. A year ago he moved from Bristol to Plymouth. He is still employed in the nefarious trade. But there is no doubt now that it has been made quite illegal even in the Colonies, he will be forced to retrench. He once beat you unmercifully, did he not?"

"Yes."

"He shall be beaten," said the Marquis softly, "and you shall watch it. I shall have him brought to The Bastille soon after our marriage. His house shall be burnt—as your grandfather's kraals were burnt. He shall be put in shackles, as you were put. I shall find it quite simple to arrange—privately, of course."

She inclined her head.

"The other name which interested you," went on the Marquis, "*O'Sullivan*—he who was kind to you. He is, unfortunately, dead, buried in Ireland over two years ago."

"I am sorry," said Helène and for the first time, her eyes were soft, "I would like to have rewarded him."

And she remembered the rough hands that had lifted her and the rough shoulder against which she had sobbed; and how the First Mate would have spared her, if he could.

"Captain Humbleby is also dead—of the plague," continued the Marquis. "You see, Aubrey has been busy with investigations. The woman, Mrs. Clack, has vanished. I fancy she was murdered by the Lopez brothers. For she has not been seen from that day to this. I refer to the day of your auction."

Helène maintained a cool silence. She knew that Lucien was watching her covertly whilst he pretended to read his documents. But she had learnt not to betray herself. Nobody could know the degree of disgust and even horror that she felt at the sounding of those names which had not been spoken for four long years. She said:

"Why do you tell me these things on our marriage day? Is it not a curious time to choose?"

"You must know by now," said Lucien, "that I often do what is least expected of me. But I felt this to be a suitable moment to deliver, shall we say, *the coup de grâce* at your past. For tonight that past will end and you will live again as *Madame la Marquise* de Chartellet."

Suddenly she came forward and laid a hand on his shoulder.

"You know, do you not, Lucien, that I am mindful of the honour you pay me."

He took that slim ringed hand and put his dry lips against it.

"The honour is mine, *ma belle Helène*."

"Nevertheless," she said steadily, "you marry Fauna, the quadroon."

He was pleased with her for he knew what it cost her to use those words. He admired an ability which she had not acquired easily, to be ruthless with herself as well as others.

"Fauna will be forgotten," he said, "long after Helène, Marquise de Chartellet will be remembered by all who come to know her."

"Nevertheless—the honour remains mine," she said smiling at him.

"We will not argue. Sufficient to say that everything is ready for tonight's ceremony. I cough a great deal, so I think it expedient, and so does the good Dr. Surenne, that we stay at Brightlingsea until April. Then I will hold the first big function in our London house when you will receive at my side."

She smiled.

This marriage would, she knew full well, be devoid of any sex excitement with this man who was old enough to be her father and finished with love. But there was some excitement in the prospect of her marriage all the same. She was on the brink of such a personal triumph that she would not have been human if she had not looked forward to it.

The four years of her training in Lucien's home by the sea had prepared her for this hour. Years that seemed to have passed slowly, yet been pregnant with learning, and with each day holding a fresh discovery for her eager mind. She had enjoyed every hour of it. And she cared in a deep if unemotional way for this man who had given her so much and asked nothing that she could not give in return.

But what now? She felt some strange sense of unease at

the idea of emerging from her retreat with Lucien into the society that had once spurned and humiliated her, and looked upon her as Henrietta Pumphret's plaything.

How could it possibly turn out? She knew that Lucien wished this revenge—this cynical gesture, introducing her as his wife. The amusement of it was to be his ultimate reward for the immense trouble he had taken to rehabilitate her. She was ready and yet . . . she caught her breath even now as she heard him mention the one name that she did not even allow herself to ***think.***

"Harry Roddney is in town," he said.

Quite steadily her huge heavily fringed eyes met the sardonic questioning of his.

"I am not interested," she said.

He drew a little breath as though relieved, but said:

"That is not strictly true. Let it pass. Roddney will be invited to our reception. I have a list here of the names to whom Aubrey will send invitations. It includes Lord and Lady Hamton."

"Hamton?" she repeated frowning.

"Henrietta Pumphret, George's widow, married a certain Edward Hamton. There are two children by him."

"Indeed," said Helène, and this time her gaze narrowed with some interest. "There were two by Pumphret—that makes four. Yes, I remember now—Edward Hamton, a gossiping idiot under her thumb."

"She will be made to regret very bitterly what she did to you in the past."

"I shall enjoy that," murmured Helène reflectively.

"The Rustingthorpes also will be invited."

The girl said:

"You seem to know everything. Aubrey is a good spy. What of Zobbo the dwarf?"

"He, it appears, *ma mie*, died recently in an unpleasant fashion. While buffooning with a scullery wench he hid himself in an oak chest, the lid of which fell upon him. His cries were stifled and when he was found he was dead. My Lady Clarissa organized a funeral in miniature, coffin, hearse, and black ponies to pull it. It was quite an entertainment and it appears that the Lady Henrietta was greatly envious."

A shudder went through Helène. Her rich red mouth curled with disgust.

"*Animals!* All of them," she whispered.

"You shall in the near future make them aware of their senseless depravity," said the Marquis.

"Think you, Lucien. Think you that they will recognize me?" she asked. And he could see that she had grown suddenly agitated.

Now he laughed.

"I hope so, or 'twould not be amusing. However, let us not worry about it today. The time is not yet ripe. We have a month or so in which to prepare for it."

Helène walked suddenly to the window and stared upon the cold grey London scene. She preferred life in The Bastille and the sight of the grey waves churning over the rocks. There were moments when she had time to reflect and became conscious of a weariness of the mind that had little to do with her vigorous health. It was as though she were sated with learning and with the cynicism, the remorseless logic of this strange man who was her constant companion; the only being with whom she had any real contact. As though in the persistent search for truth, and her conflict with herself, she needed relaxation; softness, comfort, *laughter*—things which she had experienced solely with the man whom she had once loved and to whom she had given herself. The man against whom she felt a bitterness even more acute than that which had festered in her against people like Henrietta Pumphret. *She hated Harry Roddney*. But she craved the joy he had once given her and which she felt she could never know again.

Was Lucien right? Were her occasional fits of restlessness due to a need for physical expression? Could she be comforted by a meaningless love affair—if love it could be called? Would she enjoy lying in the arms of some charming youth sharing in his transports of passion? But she felt a disquiet, rare for her, as Lucien mentioned Harry Roddney's name again.

"Aubrey tells me that both young Roddney's uncle and wife have died and he is now in possession of Porrington Abbey, and the Fayre fortune. Also he returned recently from India, where in company with a Mr. Wilberson, he has become a leading powerful spirit in the East India Company. It would seem that your dissolute young rake has mended his ways."

"Indeed?" said the girl stonily.

"Yes, Aubrey has it on the best authority that Roddney leads quite a useful and busy life, although once more to be seen on occasions at the clubs, playing at faro, or in Mayfair drawing-rooms."

Helène shrugged her shoulders. But she was asking herself with an icy bitterness if her first and only lover had ever given her a single thought through these years which had been so successful for him. She said:

"So he is not yet married?"

"No. Aubrey tells me he has little time for females."

"He has changed, then."

Lucien's wrinkled lids hooded the cynicism in his own eyes. He made no further comment but thought:

"So, somewhere in her deepest consciousness, she is still enamoured of the man. I wonder whether or not to go through with our marriage."

But he wondered it only for a moment. The exquisite pleasure of the revenge he had planned for her would be too sweet to forgo. And Harry Roddney's turn would come —with the rest.

Chapter Two

Helène walked with her light graceful step up the fine staircase, one hand on the carved rosewood bannister.

Reaching the top of these stairs she looked over and saw the sober figure of Lucien's secretary in the hall moving towards the writing-room door. He looked up. She had brief survey of his pale, unhappy young face. It was evident that he hoped to conceal his emotions but could not, for a crimson wave stained his cheeks and he dropped his gaze and hurried out of sight. But not before she had read the naked, hungry passion in his sulky eyes.

Truly, she reflected, as she went on to her own rooms, poor Aubrey was much enamoured, and very personable, and it was a long time—years long—since she had felt the warmth of a man's lips or the strength of his embrace. Tonight she was to become Lucien's wife. This was her wedding day. She would be a strange bride, she thought, with little right to a virgin's veil, and no expectation of a bridegroom's hot desire. Lucien had warned her of the impossibility of that; and in any case she had no feeling for him, save as her valued patron and friend, and the lack of feeling in this marriage had not seemed to matter when she had ridden through the frosty park this morning. She had been eager for it only as a culminating triumph. It was hearing Harry Roddney's name spoken again that must have unnerved her, she decided.

Frowning, she called to Hattie to bring hot water and towels and rub her down, then flung herself into a *chaise-longue* and picked up a book. It contained verses by Homer. She was reading in the original Greek. She was enjoying the pure intellectual beauty of the work. But today she could not apply her mind to it. Her thoughts were too confused. Her memory, out of control once more, dragged her back to another bridal night—illicit—stolen from time. The night she had lain in Harry Roddney's arms.

She was furious with herself that she could not eliminate that memory for all her savage attempts to blot it out. And it was with her that night when, finally, she stood in the dim, candle-lit crypt of the private chapel, with all doors locked, and was secretly united to Lucien Charloi St. Vincent de Chartellet. It haunted her even when the two officiating priests bent over her hand, gazed with due respect and reverence at her proud, beautiful face, and congratulated her.

"Felicitations, *Madame la Marquise*," they said.

Dr. Surenne also expressed his pleasure at the union. Then it was Aubrey's turn. The young secretary knew well that the cold, unwinking gaze of his employer was upon him. He had prayed wildly that he might receive the moral support of heaven during this most trying ordeal. But as Helène, the newly made Marquise de Chartellet, offered him her long fine hand, he began to tremble. He looked at her desperately. She wore a white dress of exquisite simplicity and over it a rich cloak of black velvet lined with ermine. At Lucien's request she had not come to this strange, secret wedding wearing the usual monstrous powdered head-dress now fashionable in London. Her wonderful red-gold hair fell naturally in curls on her naked shoulders. A gauzy veil was wound around head and throat. Her great dark eyes shone with a jewel-like lustre and there was a faint, enigmatic smile on her reddened lips. Aubrey—who had watched her gain in beauty over the last four years—had never before seen her look quite so alluring. It was enough, he thought, to make even the celibate priests turn their thoughts from beads and breviary. Her perfume was heady enough to drive away the very odour of sanctity.

"My—felicitations—*Madame la Marquise*," he stammered and touched her finger-tips with his lips.

Then to his utter astonishment she pressed his fingers with hers and whispered:

"Foolish boy—do not look so unhappy. I will see you later on."

He went pale as death. He was flung into a state of combined terror and delight. He did not know what to make of her words or the smile she gave him. *She would see him later on*, she said. What, in Heaven's name, could she mean?

Without daring to glance in the Marquis's direction, Aubrey hastened out of the chapel to call the chaise, which was to convey the newly married pair back to the house.

Later, in one of the smaller drawing-rooms of the great house, lit by hundreds of candles, warmed by two great fires and perfumed by roses, the married pair faced each other. Helène unwound her veil. Lucien gazed at her reflectively.

"I am not sure that I did the right thing in arranging so quiet and exclusive an affair. You look so enchanting, *ma mie*, I would wish all London could see you tonight."

She smiled.

"I prefer it thus. You did rightly."

"So," he nodded, "it is over. We have reached high water mark. The tide is in. You bear my name, and you are now chatelaine of this house and of The Bastille. One day, when the war is over I may take you to France to look upon the lost ancestral home of the de Chartellets. Would you like that?"

"Indeed, yes," she nodded.

"You are satisfied?"

She came and stood before him and held out both her hands with a rare gesture of affection, for demonstration between them was unusual. She said in a low voice:

"Very grateful, also, Lucien. Thank you. With my memories it means more to me than you can ever imagine."

"It shall mean more as time goes on. I, too, am grateful, for with the standard of perfection which you have attained I can be proud of my wife."

"I am assuredly proud of my husband," she returned the compliment.

"You will excuse me, *ma mie*, if I retire to my own rooms early," he went on, "I am somewhat fatigued, and my cough is worsening."

She looked at him with anxiety.

"Of course. But should you not retire straight away,

Lucien? I will not mind. I can dine alone. Truly I am glad," she added, "that tomorrow we return to Brightlingsea. Your health is better there."

"Your solicitude for me is charming," he murmured. "I, also, have striven to be solicitous for you. You are too young and ardent of temperament to be asked to spend a wedding night perusing your books or wandering through this great empty house alone. I have invited a guest. I met him for the first time today at the club and suggested that he should dine with us. He knows, of course, nothing of our bridal. I informed him merely that he would make the acquaintance of my new wife. Let him then inform London. It will whet the appetites of those who are going to meet you. He is an excellent chess player by the way. I thought that he might play a game with me, then later, when I am a-bed, with you. You can defeat me easily these days."

"Oh, Lucien, I do not know whether I wish to play chess with a stranger, this night of all nights. I should be at your side——" she began, frowning.

"God forbid," broke in Lucien with his dry laugh. "I desire no nursing—only sleep, my lady-wife, I do assure you. I am a weary old man."

"Whom have you invited?" she asked.

"Come, look and you shall see—I fancy I hear a carriage stop in the courtyard now," he said.

She was somewhat mystified by his manner but she walked with him to one of the tall windows. He opened it. She shivered as a gust of cold wind struck them.

"Pray go back—do not expose your chest to this raw air, Lucien," she begged.

He laughed again.

"I have a delightfully considerate wife. It is a new and charming experience," he said. "Well—can you see our guest?"

She did not answer. She had just caught sight of the tall slimly built figure of a man, handsomely dressed, stepping out of a smart private chaise. The moonlight, and the lights from the open doors and the torches carried by two postillions, illuminated his face clearly. A face so familiar and yet so strange that the girl on the balcony stared at it as though at a ghost. Her own cheeks turned ashy-pale. Her breathing almost stopped. She put a hand to the jewelled collar at her throat and stepped back into the room. She had to exert gigantic control as she addressed the man who had been her husband for less than an hour.

"It is Harry Roddney," she said.

The Marquis nodded.

"So! You recognize him. He has not then changed much?"

She licked her dry lips.

"Why have you asked him here?"

"To eat with us, *ma mie*. Was it not a good idea?"

"On—our wedding night?"

"As good a night as any for a sweet revenge."

"I see," she said, and added: "You have at least earned the name they give you, my dear husband. *Satyr*. Yes, you show a satyr-like satanic humour in this."

He eyed her closely, standing before the fire, hands folded under his coat, behind his back.

"And you, *ma belle Helène,* admirable self-possession. You are surprised, of course, to see him. But not much distressed?"

She hesitated. It was for such a fractional time that she imagined Lucien could not note her hesitation. Then she said, smoothly:

"Not at all. It will make excessively amusing entertainment—even if a little, shall we say, Rabelaisian, for a bridal night."

"You will, I am sure, play your part well and ensure that *he* finds the evening the very reverse of amusing."

She inclined her head, but her slender fingers curled into her palm and the points of her nails dug into the flesh.

He added:

"You will, of course, deny that you have any connexion whatsoever with the girl he remembers as Fauna the slave. You are Helène—daughter of an old friend of mine who died in exile, in England, like myself."

She nodded. Excitement was gathering in her, however greatly she tried to conquer it. The colour was stealing back into her pale face. Harry. *Harry*, after four long years. Oh, God, what an ironic jest on Lucien's part—and how typical of him to make it. But to protest, to show antipathy for the idea—that would be to disappoint him after his assiduous efforts to teach her the mastery of her emotional being. Besides, it might be an evening's sport worth experiencing—to watch Harry's surprise and discomfiture. She had all the weapons at her command. Her education, her new title and position, her bitter hatred of him. Her invulnerability, no matter what he might choose to say or do. Yes, it might be quite an entertainment, after all.

Lucien came up to her. He tried to read what lay in those great eyes, but they were strangely inscrutable even to him tonight. He touched her bare, cool shoulder.

"Can you go through with it, *ma mie*, or shall I send Aubrey with an excuse, and dismiss him?"

She drew in her breath sharply. Her eyes narrowed.

"No. Let him come. I can and will deal with him and you shall enjoy it."

The flunkeys threw open the twin-doors and announced: "*Sir Harry Roddney*."

He came quickly into the room. Standing erect, with head flung back and face expressionless, Helène gave him her hand. She was amazed to see no flicker of recognition in his eyes. Not even astonishment; only a faint look of undisguised admiration as he bowed over her outstretched fingers and touched them with his lips.

"Your servant, *Madame la Marquise*," he said.

Then he bowed in turn to Lucien who was watching with supreme interest—his fatigue and hacking cough forgotten in the cynical pleasure of this appointed hour. To himself, Lucien was saying:

"The boy has incredible self-control—or he does not yet know who she is? *I wonder . . . ?*"

Helène had shivered very faintly as she felt Harry's lips against her hand which she sharply withdrew. She did not honestly know whether she loathed and despised him for what he had done to her or felt a mad desire strike her like a lightning-flash, to fling herself into his arms.

Dear God, she thought, Harry, *Harry* after four long years! Such a yawning chasm stretched between them now as could surely never be bridged.

She found him little changed, older; faint lines about his lips which were sterner than before; crow's-feet at the corners of his eyes. But they were the same greenish-coloured brilliant eyes. He wore a periwig and was, as always, elegantly clad in dark brown velvet with creamy ruffles at his throat. When he smiled suddenly, as he exchanged comments with Lucien about the weather she felt a constriction of the throat. It was the remembered boyish smile. But, as well to remember, too, she told herself bitterly, the treachery that lay behind that seeming candour. Utterly, brutally untrustworthy; brutally callous; a man who could kill a woman spiritually, a moment after he had kissed her, and flung back to the tiger's claws what he had once been amused to rescue and possess, body and soul.

She sat still while a flunkey brought wine to the two men. Harry said:

"It is good of you, milord, to invite me thus and I do appreciate the honour of being able to make further acquaintance of you and your lady within your own domain."

"We are enchanted, sir," returned Lucien in his dry voice. "My wife and I are not over-gregarious. We entertain but little. Tomorrow we return to our seaport domicile but we intend to try and mend our ways and hold a reception for London in the spring."

Harry, with the facile flattery of the age, inclined his handsome head in Helène's direction:

"London will be the better, milord, for the presence of a new and most beautiful addition to female Society."

Helène remained silent but her fingers clenched over the gossamer lace handkerchief she held. So he was going to play *her* game and admit no previous association with her; show no surprise and offer no apology for the past even by so much as a single word or glance. He was monstrously cool. It was unbelievable that he should not acknowledge her. Was it, perhaps, that he feared the Marquis?

Baffled, she stared at Harry beneath those thick long lashes which he had once poetically described as the "silken curtain for twin-stars." Her breathing quickened. Lucien then made an apology to withdraw for a moment. He would return to supper, he said. To Harry Roddney he murmured:

"I am not over-well tonight, sir. You must excuse my indisposition."

"I must regret it, milord," said Harry.

Lucien glanced at his wife. She was sitting like a figure of stone. Then suddenly she rose and came to his side.

"Do not leave us, Lucien," she whispered.

"Do not let it spoil your evening," he whispered back with his faint sardonic smile.

"But it is our——"

"Yes—nevertheless it is the same as any other night in our lives, *ma belle*," he interrupted. "Let us not grow sentimental. I have given you the sword with which to do your enemies an injury. Use it——" and he bent over her left hand and significantly touched her wedding-ring with his lips.

As he vanished, she regained her control. She knew that he did not mean to return—he would send a message to say that he was ill.

And, indeed, it was not altogether untrue. She had never seen Lucien's thin aesthetic face more grey and drawn. She feared for him. But even though she knew him now so intimately, she could not grow entirely accustomed to that ice-cold, devilish humour that led him to do unexpected things like this and gnaw at them with the hunger of his inhibited impotent passions.

Truly, this was a strange bridal night for any woman. A night without a bridegroom, and with the spectre of a bitter passion for guest, and the knowledge at the back of her head that the crazily enamoured secretary slunk around the great mansion, waiting, hoping, spurred by the coquetry of the words she had whispered to him in the chapel. Had she meant to give Aubrey hope? Perhaps so—encouraged by the Rabelaisian Marquis who had so repeatedly advised her to take a lover.

But it was a confused Helène who ate supper alone with Harry Roddney that night in the small octagonal white and gold supper-room which she and Lucien used when they were alone. This room had been decorated by an artist of the period with painted ceiling and gay glossy Chinese paper on the walls. The gilded chairs were upholstered in scarlet and white stiff satin, the oval table was of gold and red and black lacquer. Lights gleamed from candles in gilt sconces against the walls and on the table. An enchanting, intimate little room which Helène preferred to the enormous dining-hall where they would, in due course, entertain large numbers.

An exquisite supper was served—turtle soup, sturgeon's roes; roast quail, venison from the Prince's preserves at Windsor. Pastries and confections of cream cake and fruit and nuts made into fantastic shapes by the Marquis's French chef who used to cook for him, also, in their native country.

At the end of this meal, Harry confessed he had seldom eaten finer food nor drunk more perfect wines. But it had not in his private opinion been an enjoyable meal. He had at first been somewhat surprised when the Marquis sent apologies that ill-health forced him to retire to his bedchamber. He experienced, of course, a man's natural pleasure in being left alone with so glorious and fascinating a woman. He had done his best to be gallant and amusing. Harry was aware that women liked him. He was used to easy conquests. And he had had a number of successes—a series of charming, pretty women for mistress—from the time he reached Delhi with James Wilberson, throughout their journeyings abroad, and later at home here in England. The company of pretty females stimulated him. Love given and received lightly is a necessity to most men at times. Harry was no exception. But it was not often now the extravagant passion of the Harry of the past according to those who remembered. He had more interest in the excellent, wealthy company of which he had with James Wilberson become a director.

He had surprised even that serious-minded gentleman by the arduous way he had carried out his apprenticeship and the intelligence he now brought to his present exalted position. He had not left the East India Company when he inherited his uncle's fortune. He felt able, from that time onward, to spend more money and live extravagantly if he wished. But he liked to work. He gambled only in moderation, and so far, had found no feminine allure strong enough to entangle him seriously.

Always the thought of the shadowed past fascinated but eluded Harry. He remembered nothing, save in occasional flashes, incidents of his childhood, rather than of his more recent past. He would enter a club that he used to frequent and feel it familiar, and be able to find his way about. He had thought he knew Mr. Brummell when the dandified Beau shook him by the hand and clapped his shoulder and said: "I'faith, Harry, you must recall *me*, my lad. Look well."

He had looked. He felt that he had, indeed, seen that extravagant foppish figure, famous throughout England, before. But his memory was not restored.

At first, after his strange accident down at Pillars he had tried hard to solve the mystery of the girl, Fauna, with whom he was supposed to have lived. The name perpetually haunted him. But his mind remained a blank and gradually even the unknown Fauna ceased to disturb him.

There was another puzzle which he would have liked unravelled. Who had taken the signet ring from his finger? His assailant, little doubt. But *who*? What enemy had so foully struck him down then bandaged his wound? That extraordinary fact remained unexplained through the years.

What small conceit Harry had in his own attractions for the fair sex, received a decided blow tonight. He did not make headway with the Marquise nor begin to understand her. She seemed as aloof and cold as the Himalayan snows. And incredibly erudite for a woman, he decided. There seemed no subject she could not discuss with force and knowledge. Yet she was more feminine and lovely than any woman he had ever set eyes upon, with those wonderful agate eyes deep and mysterious, betraying nothing of her feelings. That glorious shining golden-red hair, curling to her snowy shoulders, and which he found delicious after the preposterous wigs and headdresses worn by so many ladies of fashion. Her tall voluptuous figure in the fine white dress, with the wide sleeves ermine-cuffed; the gauze veil which now and then she looped about head and throat, were most intriguing. She wore fabulous diamonds. She was regal and most dignified; yet bore no resemblance to any lady he had come across in London society.

He found her disinterested in gossip—which was also rare—she seemed most entertained by discussion of music or philosophy. She was unfailingly courteous to him and yet . . . she chilled him. She did not, if he recalled rightly, smile at him once during the meal. He followed her back to the candle-lit drawing-room where the fire had been fed with fresh pine-scented logs and seated himself beside her on a gilded, satin-cushioned couch. She seemed quite disposed to play him at chess, and bade a flunkey bring the marquetry card table and some of the most beautiful carved ivory chessmen he had ever seen.

"Your husband is a great collector, I see, Madame," murmured Harry.

"He is one of the greatest connoisseurs of our time."

"So I have heard."

"Used you to attend the annual balls given here in this house by him in the past—ere we were wed and ere his health forced him to remain all the year in Brightlingsea?"

"No, Madame. But I have lived much abroad—I was in the Far East—until recently."

She nodded, watching him, brooding. She, for her part, had found no pleasure in the supper they shared. Nor could she summon any real desire to take him on at a game now. She was too restless and ill-at-ease even though she gave no outward sign of it. *They were as two strangers*, she thought. He played his part uncommonly well. How indifferent he must be to her! He meant to disclaim all knowledge of the past certainly, for to test him she had said:

"Is it of interest to you, sir, that the Prime Minister has achieved success with the Bill abolishing slavery?"

He had looked surprised by her question. So this fascinating creature interested herself even in politics, he thought. He replied:

"Glad, of course. There is no reaon why any poor creature, black or white, should be manacled and forced to submit to man's tyranny."

With a fast beating heart, Helène went on:

"Once I hear you—saved a young slave from abominable cruelties—is it not so, Sir Harry?"

She watched him intently but his face remained imperturbable. He answered:

"I think you have me confused with another. It was not I, Madame. I have never had aught to do with any slave that I know of."

She had sat back, her cheeks colouring angrily. So he did not choose to recall poor Fauna and that week at Pillars. How could he look at her so coolly?

Now as she was left alone with him and they seated themselves at the chess-board she had a sudden desire to probe him further. She leaned across the table fingering a magnificent star sapphire which she wore on a velvet ribbon about her throat. He followed her movement, and was fascinated by the slender perfection of that long swan neck.

"Sir Harry," she said, "have you and I met before this? Look more closely at me and *remember*."

He stared, astonished, and his finely cut face flushed a little with embarrassment.

"No, I do not remember having met you, *Madame la Marquise*—or is it——" he paused.

He had been about to add was it perchance that he had known her before his past had been blotted out by the wound in his head. But she interrupted:

"It is of no matter. Let us start our game."

He watched her long pointed fingers place the chess-men on the board. He fancied that they trembled. He was further baffled by her strange manner. But she did not look at him. Her teeth were clenched.

An almost uncontrollable rage consumed Helène. He must know her. He *must*. She had changed, of course, in manner and attire and taken on the personality and poise of a lady of high degree; but her face, her colouring, her figure *he must recognize*. By failing to admit recognition he had robbed her of much of the sweetness of her revenge. She had wanted him to cry out at the sight and the sound of her, then, in her turn to tell him that she did not remember *him*. How dared he reverse the situation? What a monstrous lack of real feeling he showed. And, indeed, she was filled with an intense disgust of herself, *because she knew that she still desired him* as she had never wanted any other man throughout the intervening years. He should pay for this humiliation, and for the callousness of his treatment of her, she decided. Yes, her hands shook but her voice was steady when she next spoke.

"I have moved—now it is your turn, sir," she said.

The game was long and complicated. The candles burned down and the ormolu clock over the fireplace chimed the hour of two in the morning before Helène made the final move.

"Check-mate, sir," she said.

He looked into her eyes. They were as unfathomable as dark pools but now for the first time her rich red lips curled into a smile. And for the first time tonight Harry Roddney was shaken to the depths. An extraordinary psychic recollection gripped him. He went pale and put a hand to his brow.

"What is it?" she asked, watching.

"I—I do not know," he stammered. "I . . . you have beaten me most magnificently. My congratulations, *Madame*."

She looked at him squarely.

"You are not easily defeated. You played once with the late Lord Pumphret who found you a formidable opponent, I believe."

"You knew—Pumphret," he was still stammering and confused but many others in London had told him of his friendship with George Pumphret in London and of their duels at chess. He had little use for the widow who had married that poor fool Edward Hamton. He and Henrietta Pumphret passed each other by disdainfully when they at last ran across each other at a Court function.

He said to Helène:

"Yes, that is so."

She turned away shaking. What a coward he was! Too much of a coward to come into the open and admit that not only did he know George Pumphret in the past but *her*, Fauna. Well—she would take her cue from him, but only for the moment. Soon she would trap him into an admission. For the moment she must be calm or ruin her own chances of victory. Suddenly she changed her mood. Harry was dazzled by the sudden full force of her charm she directed upon him.

"I should have allowed my guest to win—it was most inhospitable of me to be victor, was it not, Sir Harry?" she said with a musical laugh. "Come, let us drink to the next game we play—and play we must, quite soon."

He fell in with this delicious mood. He felt less confused and unhappy as he sat beside her now and feasted awhile on her smiles. Never had he met such an intriguing woman. She had so many facets to that diamond-like brilliant personality of hers. Eagerly he drank the wine which she, herself, poured for him. He was more at home with this new Helène. He could handle a fashionable flirtation. Yet he was in a queer way disappointed because the Marquise de Chartellet was not after all too exalted to disdain feminine coquetry. He had thought her above it.

He became a little drunk with wine and even more so by the voluptuousness of the woman who sat beside him. A thrilling perfume emanated from her. He set down his goblet, wiped his lips with a lace-edged handkerchief and gave a short self-conscious laugh.

"I'faith," he said, "that perfume that you use, *Madame*, is more intoxicating than the Marquis's wine."

"I am pleased you enjoy it," she said and closed her eyes an instant, shuddering with the recollection of something that he had said to her, long ago.

"I am weary of heavy artificial perfume, my Fauna. The odour of your hair and your skin is far more exquisite and not for any other man in the world save myself."

So he was becoming fascinated by her yet again, she thought with bitterness. Poor fool! He would pay dearly. But all in good time. Not tonight. Tonight she would send him away bewildered and uncertain of what she meant to do or *how far she meant to forgive or forget*, or perhaps tell himself that there was nothing that needed forgiveness.

"Do not be too long before you return to gladden the hearts of those who live in London," were his next words.

"There is nothing to prevent you, sir, from driving down to visit us at Brightlingsea."

"If I might dare hope that you wish to receive a visit from me, *Madame*, I shall assuredly come at once."

"The invitation is made," she said.

"And accepted," he said, playing the old game with ease and gallantry, and added: "I have heard, of course, of The Bastille. It is famous. So strangely named after that grim Paris gaol. It surprises me that *Monsieur le Marquis* cares to retain it."

"My husband"—she uttered the name drily—"is amused by sardonic humour."

"Have you been married long, *Madame*?"

"No," she said and laughed.

He probed feverishly in his mind for further explanation of this woman's mysterious manner. She had a perverse and unpredictable nature. Could she be in love with that dried-up little Frenchman? Lucien de Chartellet had the reputation of being learned but of an unpleasaing disposition. How came it that so exquisite and brilliant creature as this woman Helène could have agreed to share his bed and board—unless it was on account of his great wealth. Maybe in this respect Helène de Chartellet was no different from any other ambitious lady of modern society. Harry added:

"Are you French, *Madame*? You speak English with such perfection and yet——" He paused.

Now her anger kindled again. He went too far, to question her as to her origin. It was on the tip of her tongue to turn tiger-cat and snarl at him:

"Traitor! You who know well that I am Fauna, once a quadroon slave . . . !"

But once more she mastered herself. First, before she showed her claws, she would do even more exquisite damage with the velvet paw. The handsome young man at her side might be too ashamed or, more likely, too afraid to acknowledge her, but he still found her appealing to his senses. Her brow cleared. She became softly feminine and enchanting to him again.

"Would you like me better if I said I was French—or do you prefer me as an Englishwoman?"

He stammered:

"I wish you only to stay as you are, *Madame*, which is perfection."

She looked at him through her lashes, provocatively.

"And you? What shall I ask you, sir, in turn? You are unmistakably English. And you say you have travelled much lately. To what lands, and why?"

He told her of his work in India, of the journey he had taken also to Malaya, then to Holland, and of his connexion with the East India Company.

She nodded, a cynical little smile on her lips.

"Oh, yes, I have heard that Sir Harry has become a man of business. And what of the lighter side of life? What recreations do you pursue?"

"I play at cards when I am in Town. When I am in the country with Mr. Wilberson, my adopted uncle, I ride and shoot."

Something impelled her to say:

"You have—your own shooting?"

She wondered if now he would mention Pillars. There was no smile on her face as she watched him. But quite calmly he mentioned it though not by name, and informed her that he had inherited a place in Essex from his late uncle, General Sir Arthur Fayre, but never went there.

"Why?" she asked.

Now, she thought, with rising excitement, *now he will tell me. Now he will speak.* But he astonished her by dismissing the subject with a few brief words.

"I retain it for the sake of old association, but for me it is of sinister memory. I avoid going there."

Sinister, she thought. Ye gods, that is so. He must have some conscience, then, because he does not go there. But how has he the colossal insolence to maintain this farcical attitude, pretending that I am unknown to him?

Well, she would carry on as she had intended. She told herself that the challenge had been made, good and truly, and the glove thrown down. The duel between them had commenced.

Chapter Three

Harry had drunk a little too much. Not a great deal too much; but enough to make him feel light-headed, and tremendously happy. At three in the morning he was still sitting, beside the seemingly tireless Helène who made pretence of drinking with him but only sipped her wine occasionally, keeping a watchful gaze on him through the dark curtain of lashes.

He had grown daring and told himself that he had plunged headlong into love—a new, passionate, absorbing love—for the most beautiful woman in England—or France. He cared not that she was newly married, or that Lucien de Chartellet was a powerful man whom no man in Europe dared to treat lightly. He cared not whether or not *la belle Marquise* returned his sudden passion. He was used to lightning conquests and to yielding women. This evening had begun as a formal supper party and ended in an intitate tête-à-tête, the most entrancing he had ever spent.

He rose to leave at last, conscious suddenly of the lateness of the hour.

"I would not go, but should, most beautiful lady," he said unsteadily.

She smiled up into his eyes.

"Stay if you wish, sir."

"Will you not call me Harry?"

"Will you not use the name Helène—or do you prefer another?" she parried.

If he caught her meaning and remembered another, he did not say so. He was very cautious, she thought. He caught at a fold of lace against his throat. His handsome face was no longer calm and serious as it had been when he arrived, but hot with passion; eyes burning under their heavy lids. *Ah, God,* she thought, *never was a man like this one. May he burn in hell for the thing he did to a defenceless quadroon slave.* All the new importance and power given her by her new status, her rightful claim to position as wife to Lucien de Chartellet and mistress of this grand mansion, urged her to thrust the first point of the sword into Harry Roddney.

She swayed towards him suddenly, provocatively, so that a silken curl brushed his chin.

"What would you name me?" she whispered.

Then—emboldened—he caught hold of her. His arms gripped her fiercely and keeping her thus, her long slim body against his, he whispered back:

"Ah, Helène—so many names. Enchantress—siren—Helen of Troy returned to allure and destroy all men—and Harry Roddney in particular."

She let him keep her thus an instant longer, feeling his breath on her face. Hot, wine-sweet breath. The impassioned hands clasping her waist sent her mind reeling back to that night in Pillars—to that firelit, tranquil bedroom, with the snow falling outside, white and stainless, while he tore down the last flag of her maiden's resistance. Such a fierce anguish and resentment were hers, this moment; she who had become Lucien de Chartellet's wife, seared her very soul.

Fool—fool, she inwardly raged to think he could once more and so easily make a conquest of her, then glory in being able to abandon her a second time, when he grew weary. Did he imagine she was so ready to excuse what he had done that she would yield again thus—that she found him irresistible?

Now, mad with longing, he crushed her and laid his lips against the curve of her bosom, inhaling her perfume, leaving a little flower-like bruise upon the camellia perfection of her matchless skin.

She tore herself from him; white, shaking, she dismissed him.

"Go," she said. "How dare you touch me so. . . ."

He sobered up and stood panting, bewildered.

"Did I mistake your wishes? I beg to be forgiven. I thought——"

"Go," she repeated, in a strangled voice and put a handkerchief to her lips.

Harry, very sober indeed now, and most unhappy, for he supposed he had not read her aright, bowed low.

"Your pardon—I am your most humble servant, *Madame.*"

She could have willingly turned and killed him, watched him die at her feet. She could, she thought bitterly, willingly die herself, in this moment for very shame, because just now when he held her she had known a desire as fierce as his own; known that even after all the long years of tuition from Lucien, she still had not learned true mastery of herself.

"Oh, go, leave me," she said again wearily.

"Not until you tell me I am forgiven," he said. "Ah, Helène—you have driven me mad by your great beauty and the glory of conversing with you this night. You have no equal, I do assure you. Do not blame me if I lose my head. Permit me only to pay you my respects in the future. I would draw into my thirsty soul again and again the wine of poignant sweetness, the ineffable wit and wisdom that has source in you, and you alone."

This rhetoric on Harry's part brought her no comfort for she was shaken by the pangs of bitterness made worse by the knowledge that *he* chose to forget and was so monstrously eager to gloss over their past, and indulge in what could be nothing more noble than a mere revival of a carnal appetite.

She turned away lest he should see her disgust for him; self-loathing for herself. She had gained sufficient composure to remember that if her victory was to be complete she must not flee before delivering her final *coup de grâce*. She must lure him on—and on; play him at his own game—go on allowing him to believe she too wished to make no allusion to their former bond. She said:

"Very well. You may—wait on me again. Come to Brightlingsea—whene'er you wish."

He seized one of her hands and covered it with burning kisses.

"Then you do look upon me favourably?" he asked hoarsely.

She withdrew her hand.

"You grow presumptuous—and ask too many favours."

"Then permit me to retire—and accept my humblest apologies if I have offended you."

"Good night, sir," she said.

Once more she was as cold, as unapproachable as she had been when he first arrived. He was flung into a state of indecision, of strange, unbearable uncertainty of his position with her. Did she hate him—or was she merely teasing him? Was her frozen dignity a façade? And did a fire burn within her breast as violent as the one she had kindled within his? For assuredly she had not seemed unwilling for an amorous interlude. He could have sworn her beautiful body melted just now into his embrace. Yet . . . she had sprung away from his lips as from a serpent's kiss. It was most mystifying. Never in his life had Harry Roddney been more baffled.

He staggered out of the de Chartellet mansion into the frosty dawn, drunk not with wine, but with love and frustrated passion. Tormented with a desire which he was not sure would ever be returned. This new woman had flashed into his life like a meteor—brilliant, beguiling—yet as swiftly receding into the far distance. He muttered her name like a man possessed as he walked down the deserted purlieus of Piccadilly towards the small house in Knightsbridge Green where he now lived when he was not in Chiswick with his adopted uncle.

"Helène. Helène. *Helène!*" He kept repeating it.

Like a maniac, he felt impelled to stop, retrace his footsteps, and stand before the great silent house of the de Chartellets again, to watch the lights in the windows downstairs go out one by one, and visualize her mounting the stairs with the candlelight gleaming in her great wonderful eyes and upon that pale proud face. He had kissed the scented cleft between her breasts, but dear heaven, he longed to lose himself utterly upon her lips and in such consummation, be re-born, he told himself wildly. For the man who became Helène de Chartellet's lover, would be crowned emperor of the world.

Harry pressed his finger-tips to his burning eyelids. Assuredly some madness had entered him, he reflected—he, the serious-minded, practical man of business. Uncle James would not recognize him thus. He was worse than any callow, love-sick youth.

He turned again and strode home through the starlit night. A strolling watchman, calling the hour, stopped and greeted him, but he did not even see or hear the friendly fellow. He entered his quiet house and knew that the calm, even tenor of his formerly pleasant ordered life was at an end. From this night henceforth, Harry Roddney would know no peace of mind or body, no ambition save to love and be loved by Helène. And to achieve this ambition he was prepared to imperil his immortal soul. At whatever the cost, *he must possess her.*

The poison instilled into Helène by Lucien de Chartellet had passed through her—into Harry's veins. The poison of revenge. And it bore a most insidious dangerous sweetness—a force that carried Harry along on an irresistible tide. It was the second vital turning point in his career. Once having tasted that poison it began to work and must go on working to its secret fatal end. He would never now get her out of his blood—and he knew it.

She knew it, too. She had had the satisfaction of reading it in the last famished glance he had given her as he left her presence.

She felt tired to death when she walked up the broad staircase. Two yawning flunkeys, half asleep, followed in her wake holding candelabra aloft, then retired, murmuring:

"Good night, *Madame la Marquise.*"

Her new title. They mouthed it with awe, with respect. But the honour seemed to be suddenly empty and sterile . . . like her whole life. She paused outside Lucien's rooms. In there, her sick old bridegroom and teacher slept under the influences of the drugs the physician, old Surenne, prescribed for him. Yonder, at the far end of this fine corridor that was hung with priceless Gobelein tapestries, depicting exquisitely coloured sylvan scenes of French courtiers and their ladies in a woodland picnic—her own magnificent rooms waited. And Hattie, still her most trusted of the maids, ready to help disrobe her.

Endless luxury—a galaxy of beautiful objects to delight her eye—fabulous jewels—a London season of triumph soon to commence. Everything a woman could desire . . . everything *except love.*

Oh, God, *God* how she hated Harry Roddney—and herself for feeling utterly bereft now that he had departed. He would come back—yes—and she could go on playing with him—torturing him, before she sent him from her finally and for ever. But was the thought of revenge as sweet as she had expected—or as Lucien would wish it to be?

Suddenly a figure appeared from the shadows and waylaid her. Her eyes widened with astonishment, then she gave a low laugh. Aubrey Burkett; the poor love-sick secretary. Poor youth without his wig and with his golden hair tied back with a ribbon. His face looked thin and wan—no doubt because he languished through unrequited passion for her, she thought. He came and dropped on one knee before her, and catching a fold of her gown buried his face against it in speechless misery.

She put out a hand and touched his hair. His attitude made her feel vaguely compassionate. Yet, remembering Harry and her mistrust of all men and their passions, she grew cruel. She spoke with tempting sweetness.

"Have you waited so long to see me pass by, my poor Aubrey? 'Tis very late. You should be a-bed, with tomorrow's move from London to attend to."

He lifted his face but only to give her one look of hopeless love, then conceal it from her again.

"*Madame la Marquise*—I am in torment," he whispered.

"A pest on love if it is all torment and no delight," she muttered.

"To love you—to be permitted but to kiss your shadow would be delight for me," said the young secretary hoarsely. "Oh, Madame, *Madame*, and only yester-night I was witness to your bridal. I cannot endure it."

"Dear fool, you can and must. Besides, what bridal is it—*he*, my husband, sleeps and I am still awake and not even in my bed."

"I am not ordinarily emboldened enough to voice my love for you," went on the young man. "For years I have endeavoured to conceal it. But tonight——"

"This morning"—she corrected him—"like all men you want more than ever the thing that has become the unattainable."

"Ah, do not be cynical," he begged. "I do swear all loves are not born of perversity. I would love you to distraction even were it possible for Aubrey Burkett to approach so great a lady as *Madame la Marquise* de Chartellet."

She gave a brief ironic laugh.

"Pshaw—you know how I came to be so. You of all people know the full facts and should not be guilty of dissembling."

He bowed, seized one of her hands and held it, trembling, to his cheek.

"To me, you are still the greatest of great ladies. I forget the past."

"It would seem men prefer it that way and have a mind only for the lusts of the present."

Aubrey stared up at her bewildered by her strange words. She shrugged.

"You do not understand. What matter? You are a good child."

"Child? I am a man—older than you——" he began to protest.

"To *me*, you are a child. I am ages older."

He rose, pale, quivering with humiliation.

"Am I dismissed, *Madame*?"

"I am fatigued," she said, avoiding the question.

Now he eyed her covertly, resentment welling up in him.

"Sir Harry Roddney stayed long."

She grew suddenly angry. Aubrey knew about Harry. Aubrey, the confidential secretary, knew all things. Had Lucien not given him the task of delving into the affairs of all those who had been known to *Fauna?*

"If he did—what is it to you?" she demanded. "Good night."

He was dismissed and he stepped back, accustomed to a place of servitude, of inferiority. But his fair, long face crimsoned with mortification and his eyes filled with tears as he gazed after the beautiful, imperious figure as it vanished down the long corridor. He thought:

"She still loves him. I know it. I wish I may be permitted to kill him on her account."

Chapter Four

The next three months in the life of Helène, Marquise de Chartellet, were filled with movement, excitement, and a series of events which were to affect her considerably. The years of seclusion—of the almost nun-like existence she had led in The Bastille up till now—were, indeed, over.

Following upon that extraordinary evening spent with Harry Roddney, she grew a little harder, a little colder, and a little cruel which the Marquis noted with satisfaction. He preferred her thus. He found it amusing to watch her reactions. Every man she met became a fresh conquest. She played with each as a cat plays with mice. That also amused Lucien.

He had been in poor health since they returned to The Bastille. Unfortunately they encountered a spell of severe weather which tried him. The usually calm Colne estuary was an inferno of grey wind-whipped waves and that same salt icy wind tore round the miniature battlements of the grey domicile on the frowning cliff. Lucien lay much a-bed forced to take nauseous draughts, or soothing syrups, with Dr. Surenne in constant attendance. His beautiful gifted wife left his side only when he wished it. But he would not have her turn sick nurse, he said. He preferred her to find amusement and entertain their visitors in the usual way. It was she who dealt now with most of his letters and documents; the correspondence which he carried on with curators of museums or art galleries all over the world.

Lucien was aware of the state of mind suffered by his secretary during these early months of spring. Helène kept nothing from him. She knew him to be without jealousy and that his wicked sense of humour, which often had a vicious trend, could best be fed by stories that she could tell him. He liked to hear of her triumphs, and of the remarkable fashion in which those whom she scorned refused to be banished and came back for more torment at her hand. He knew every conversation she ever had with Aubrey and of the boy's despair.

He knew, too, what had happened in town between Helène and Harry Roddney. He congratulated her. She had definitely scored, he said. It was also his wish that Roddney should continue to come on her invitation to The Bastille. He approved of her plan of campaign. The affair had a tense atmosphere which intrigued Lucien. Every time Harry called here and spent a few hours with Helène, the invalid thirsted to have every detail afterwards recounted to him. He found it incredible, he said, that Roddney should be so long in coming forward and admitting that he knew Helène's true identity. But Lucien considered it right and proper that she should not make the first move. Under no circumstances was she to tell the facts to any of those who had known her in the past. Those who knew—and Harry Roddney surely must be one—might fear to raise the point lest they insulted so important a member of Society as the new Marquise. But doubt and the unsolved puzzle would fester within them, and there would be much whispering and rumouring. None would know the truth for certain—until Helène considered the time ripe for taking her final revenge.

The invitations to attend the de Chartellet reception in London, on 30th April, had gone out now to one and all—inscribed by Aubrey Burkett who found himself a much harassed and overworked man these days. A man who feared, too, to hear the Marquise's light footstep, yet longed for it with the madness of the passion which consumed him. Now and again she condescended to stretch out her hand to him, and receive the desperate kisses he pressed upon it.

"Foolish child," she would murmur and laugh and leave him.

He was eaten up with desire, driven mad by the cavalier treatment she meted out to him. Yet he worshipped her very shadow. He wrote poems to her; she read them sometimes to the Marquis as he sat up in bed looking shrunken and small, coughing and chuckling over the more extravagant lines.

Once, with a sly glance at Helène, he said:

"Do you not pity the poor imbecile?"

"I pity no man," she answered.

"Then pity *me,*" said Lucien with a dry rasping laugh, and momentarily laid his cold fragile hand upon her breast. He could feel the warm strong beating of her heart. Her face was expressionless yet her eyes softened a trifle as they looked up into his.

"*You* least of all, for 'satyr' though you are—you are even honest, Lucien."

"And only half a man," he grumbled. "There are moments, my dear delightful wife, when I badly wish myself the Lucien of the past, young and vigorous again. Then not one of these madmen who pursue you would have a single chance against me."

She gave a low laugh, took his hand and put it between hers, warming it. "They have no chance as it is, I assure you," she said.

"When does Harry Roddney come again?"

"Tomorrow. Important business keeps him today at East India House. But this was brought to me by a messenger."

She handed him a letter, bearing the violet seal and the crest of the Roddneys.

The Marquis unfolded and read the letter. It was couched in extravagant terms. Harry had grown lyrical. He compared Helène's beauty to all the goddesses who had ever charmed the gods of Olympus; or touched the heart of mortal man. He assured her that the writer was growing less and less concerned about affairs of the state or of money, and he lived only to be in her good graces. Each time he talked with her, he said, he became more completely enslaved.

Helène bent over his shoulder and marked a passage.

"Read that," she said, "it is significant, and brazen."

The Marquis quoted aloud:

> "The more I think upon you, O fair Helène, the more certain do I become that I was born to be your lover. That I loved you in the past, love you in the present, and will love you till death consigns me to my tomb. Have pity for I know no rest and no joy apart from you. . . ."

"So!" murmured the Marquis nodding, and with his most sardonic expression, tossed the letter back to her.

She walked up and down the room with quick angry steps, her face mutinous. It was an April day and the sunshine filtered through the windows and gilded her wonderful hair. She said:

"You see—he recalls the love he bore me in the past. He admits that it existed. *How dare he!*"

The Marquis coughed and leaned back on his pillows.

"Come, *ma mie*, you are not unduly harassed by this imprudent and insolent young jackanapes, are you?"

That restored her equilibrium. The old voice of her teacher expounding a philosophy devoid of any such emotional weakness as threatened her now.

"No. I am not unduly harassed," she said dully.

"What would you wish me to do for you?"

She narrowed her gaze. The last two visits from Harry had been as soul-searing as the first. He was now so completely in love with her that she held him in the hollow of her hand. It was not calf-love such as was tendered by the callow youth, Aubrey. It was the love of a serious-minded man, sure of himself, and confident of final victory. She played with him—yes, once even she had allowed him to touch her lips. That kiss had set the seal on his passion. He had told her that he would not rest until she accepted him for her lover. She had sent him away—the dismissal softened by the half hope she added for his success in the future. She knew that he would come back, and back again. His wild protestations of love were music to her ears. The sight of his face growing paler and thinner, and the knowledge that he was eating his very heart out for her, fed the hunger in her soul for vengeance. Yet with each fresh victory and each new proof he gave her that she had become his very life—she was also aware of her own sense of loss and fear. *She knew that she had never stopped loving him.* It was all she could do not to yield to his passion. She despised herself for this weakness and strove against it. The spiritual murder she was preparing for Harry could only end in her own emotional suicide—of that she was certain. Once she confided this in Lucien. He did not seem astonished.

"I thought this might happen," he said, "but do not be

over-troubled. Regard this as a period of trial. Make Harry Roddney your lover. Then banish him. It will make final separation from you harder to bear."

But she had shaken her head. She had thought:

I should die in his arms. I cannot and will not go so far.

But the torment she meted out to Harry became her own. In consequence she grew nervy and ate and slept badly. The natural sweetness of her disposition was frozen.

Lucien de Chartellet watched her and at times felt himself troubled rather than entertained.

What faithful creatures women are despite all that men do to them, he reflected. *She still loves this man who betrayed her. She will not falter in her endeavour to punish him. But in doing so she will cruelly punish herself. The sooner we go to Town the better. Let her be flung in all her beauty and grandeur into the heart of Society, presented to the Prince—given no time for introspection.*

He knew himself to be a very sick man and that his time on earth was not long. He would have to make a great effort to journey to London. He would have preferred to stay here a-bed in The Bastille, and listen to the surge of the sea; or with his couch by the window, watch the little boats come into the harbour. But in order to carry out all that he had planned for this, the last great jewel he would ever collect and place along with his treasures, he *must* make the move. Surenne bothered him with prescriptions and soothed him with prognosis of an optimistic kind. But Lucien de Chartellet, with the ever-increasing pain in his side and that rasping cough, knew that he would never again see the almond blossom break into pale pink bloom in the courtyard, nor would he live to watch the autumn leaves drift from the trees, or the winter rime glisten on his favourite statue of the rider with the captured girl upon the great French horse.

What was he doing for this young quadroon slave whom he had turned into a great lady? Often he asked himself. What would be her end? He did not want the sweets of triumph to turn sour in her soul. Ageing and ill, he fretted inwardly, which was strange for the Satyr. And although he would have died rather than voice it, he knew that in his heart of hearts, he, too, had grown to love this strange and lovely girl whom he had made his wife.

One sinister morning at The Bastille, towards the end of March, Rufus Panjaw was brought face to face with the woman whom he had so cruelly treated in her childhood.

Mr. Panjaw had been an extremely astonished man when, in the curricle which he was driving one afternoon towards dusk on a lonely road on the outskirts of Plymouth, he was waylaid suddenly by two masked men on horseback. Before he could draw and shoot at them they had captured him; one seizing the bridle of his horse and the other Mr. Panjaw himself.

Afterwards, bound and gagged, he had been driven by coach to Essex (and an exceedingly uncomfortable journey it was, over bumpy roads, and he gagged and gasping for drink and faint for lack of food). Why this had been done to him and by whom he could not imagine. It was certainly not the press gang. The two men who had assailed him remained masked and unrecognizable. He found himself eventually thrust into a cell in a house which he could see stood overlooking an estuary, although where he knew not. He could hear the sea lapping and the wind howling, and found his prison bitterly cold, and rat-infested. It had, in fact, been used as a dungeon for political prisoners during the reign of the last king.

Mr. Panjaw then had his gag removed, was given water and a crust and left to his own sorry reflections. He was an exceedingly frightened man. Like all bullies he had always been a coward. He shivered now not only with cold but terror. *Why* had this thing been done to him, by *whom*? The mystery gnawed at him. His handsome clothes were disarranged. The band at his neck had been torn in the scuffle which he had had long hours ago when first dragged from the curricle. He had lost his wig and felt foolish with his close-shorn head. He thought agonizedly of his luxurious house overlooking Plymouth Sound where he had moved when he tired of Bristol, his latest mistress, and all the comforts which he had been able to buy for years with the gold he had made. Made at the cost of the blood, the tears, the sweat, the groans, and the death-rattles of thousands upon thousands of tortured slaves.

He was left to a night's reflection, no sleep, and finally reduced to abject misery. In the morning the two masked men—who were, of course, servants of the Marquis—

entered his cell. He began to ask questions of them but they silenced him with blows, one of which made his lips bleed. Shaking like a jelly, he tottered between them up a circular staircase and was pushed into a small room hung with firearms, and in which there was only a wooden table and two chairs. A brazier warmed the air. Beside it at the table, sat an elderly man wearing a bob-wig, and heavily wrapped in furs. Mr. Panjaw did not know him. And for a moment he did not know the woman who stood beside this gentleman. Flustered and puzzled he stared at her. She, too, was protected from the cold by a fur mantle. She was vaguely familiar. That was all. Where, he asked himself, before had he seen that strangely beautiful face, those huge black eyes, and the gleaming curls as golden-red as the sunset. He stammered:

"Why am I brought here? Who has dared submit me to this indignity? I demand to know."

The old man spoke in a quiet and seemingly pleasant voice.

"You shall learn, sir. We will not long keep you guessing."

"I am Rufus Panjaw and well known in Plymouth——" began the prisoner.

Helène stayed immovable, expressionless, but her heart had turned over with a sick feeling as she looked at the remembered features of this man. He had played only a brief part in her life but it had affected her whole existence. The very sight of those crafty features and mean eyes, brought back vividly the memory of that day when he had come aboard *The Nauticas* and she had first seen him. He was little altered—except that he looked sadly dishevelled.

Lucien said:

"We are aware of your name, Mr. Panjaw. You were also very well known in Bristol at one time."

"I was."

"You owned a fleet of slave-traders among which was *The Nauticas* with a Captain Humbleby as master."

Panjaw, even more bewildered, stared from the old man to the girl.

"That is so, but——"

The inexorable voice broke in:

"On that ship in the year 1797 among the slaves was an

old Negro who died leaving his grand-daughter in the Master's charge. He brought her to Bristol where you met her and decided her fate. Do you recall that, sir?"

Mr. Panjaw began to tremble again and to sweat. He breathed hard. Then the beautiful young woman moved forward and spoke:

"Look on me, Rufus Panjaw," she said. *"Have you not seen me before?"*

His brain, in a flash, saw the connexion now. The past lived again. He gave a cry of amazement.

"The child, *Fauna!*"—he stuttered the words in a high-pitched voice—"you are *she*."

"I was that child," said Helène, "but I am now the *Marquise* de Chartellet."

"But how—how is it possible——?" began Panjaw, his eyes rolling and his face ashen. For he sensed now that he was to be the victim of revenge.

"Never mind, save your breath, for your curiosity will not be satisfied," broke in the Marquis coldly, "sufficient that you should remember how you tortured an innocent child. You thrashed her into a stupor, and shocked even a rough drink-sodden sailor by your brutality."

"I—I didn't know—I didn't mean——" began Panjaw.

"Silence," broke in the Marquis, "you have no excuse. None whatsoever; neither for what you did to that child nor for the long years of cruelty meted out to all the unfortunate human beings captured in order to enrich your coffers."

"I did not break the law. Slave trading has only this year been made illegal," screamed Panjaw.

"There was never any need," said the Marquis, "for slavery to be accompanied by the exteme sadistic cruelty for which you were noted, sir. The child, Fauna, was no ordinary slave, and you knew it. She still bears the scars of your thrashing on her back!"

Panjaw turned to the woman, fell on one knee and clawed at her gown.

"Mercy!" he stuttered. "Have mercy. I sold you to a kind gentleman."

"You knew not what her fate was to be," put in the Marquis, "and it so happened that the kind gentleman gave her to a woman who most cruelly misused her, and her fate might have been much worse had it not so happened that I discovered her."

"Mercy!" repeated Panjaw, his face bathed in perspiration.

Then Helène spoke again.

"You murdered my grandfather, Rufus Panjaw. At your command, he and his innocent people were dragged from their homes. Seventy-five per cent of them, on that hell-ship owned by you, expired. Mr. O'Sullivan himself told me (and I do not forget it) that Captain Humbleby asked over and over again, vainly, that you should scrap the ship and build better ones and export these hapless people under decent conditions. But that would have decreased your profits. Mr. Panjaw. It is always money that has mattered to you, is it not?"

Panjaw, panting wildly, looked from her to the Marquis. Then the Marquis touched a bell. The two masked men entered. One of them had a leather-thonged whip in his hand.

The Marquis said:

"Remove his coat, bind him to the bench face downwards, and give him fifty lashes."

Then Panjaw screamed.

"I shall not survive. I have a weak heart. Have mercy!"

"You had none upon me, and I was more helpless than you, for I was very small," said Helène in an ice-cold voice.

The Marquis said to his servants:

"Proceed."

After that the room was filled with the cut of a whip whistling through the air and the sound of a man howling like a beast. The girl stood there, motionless, stony-eyed and witnessed the thrashing, feeling that Fauna had been vindicated—in this quarter at least. But once more her triumph was as ashes in her mouth. She remained there until the punishment was over. Afterwards the half-fainting man, with his torn back, was given his clothes and told to make himself scarce, and to find his own way back to Plymouth, where he found his dwelling had been razed to the ground by an unexplained fire.

Weeping, and groaning and sorely subdued, Mr. Panjaw

staggered away from The Bastille never to show his face again—nor to be heard of again by the de Chartellets.

So ended one more episode in the life of the girl who had once been sold as a common slave.

Soon afterwards, the Marquis and Marquise de Chartellet moved to their town house and there came the night of the great reception. All London was buzzing and Society much intrigued and excited.

A reception and ball in the de Chartellet mansion was bound to be a fabulous entertainment. But this time spice was added to it by the fact that the invitation came not only from the mysterious French Marquis but also from his wife, Helène, Marquise de Chartellet. The Marquis was married. Nobody knew who or what she was, except that she had hair like a flame, was exceedingly beautiful and as cultured and highly intellectual as her husband. Also that young Harry Roddney had met her, was already *persona grata* in the house and reputed to be madly in love with her.

Of a certainty it promised to be a most intriguing evening.

Chapter Five

The night of the de Chartellet reception was fair and warm following a day of spring sunshine. In the Green Park that day the trees had never looked a more exquisite green, and the Dutch tulips, much loved by Queen Charlotte, made a riot of colour.

At night, under a sky studded with stars, the de Chartellet mansion was ablaze with lights from every window and the scene of great activity as carriage upon carriage rolled up delivering distinguished guests (and some less distinguished ones). For it had ever amused Lucien to watch people who hated each other, or who normally felt themselves to be superior—or inferior—forced to mingle amicably under his roof.

The Lady Hamton—formerly Lady Pumphret—came with her old friend, Clarissa, Marchioness of Rustingthorpe, who had during the last four years added two bows to her quiver and was now the mother of three sons. It was a bitter blow to Henrietta that her own marriage to Edward had produced only two more daughters. She detested the little girls of her second marriage and saw as little of them as possible. And she detested Edward who had grown fat and lazy and treated her with an abominable lack of manners. In addition he was extraordinarily mean to her and many was the day when she sighed for her good kind George who, when she had lived with him, she had never fully appreciated. Her second marriage had not been a success on either side.

Henrietta, grown fat and not nearly as handsome as before, hoped to impress tonight's gathering by her attire, if nothing else. She had chosen a most extravagant flowered satin gown made in the new Empire style—with one of the latest headdresses, in a confection of false hair arranged and hung with ropes of pearls, feathers, and flowers. Edward had sniggered but Clarrissa admired it; she, herself, still petite but a little dumpy, and smothered in the Rustingthorpe jewels. Both ladies chattered all the way to the de Chartellet mansion about Lucien's new mystery marriage.

"Who can she possibly be?" murmured Clarissa.

"Nobody knows," said Henrietta tapping a fan against her lips to conceal a yawn, for her liver was out of sorts. Her headdress was most uncomfortable, too. The feathers and ornaments wobbled and kept hitting the top of the carriage, and she had to crouch in an undignified position with her fat legs spread out. There was nothing left of her former beauty but her sparkling black eyes, and even they were habitually discontented.

She was fast losing her former position as queen of hostesses in London and she knew it. She attributed the fact to her marriage with Hamton whose wickedly gossiping tongue made him so unpopular and who perpetually humiliated her by his licentious habits with every maid who came into her service. Not only could she think of nothing new now with which to startle guests at her parties, but Edward screamed at her when she presented him with bills. The money left her by Pumphret had been tied up for his children which infuriated her. She could not touch the capital.

Everybody said that the new Marquise was bound to be the rage in London this season. So Henrietta was determined to make a good impression tonight. She had never before been a guest at the Marquis's house and longed to meet him. She had been surprised and flattered when she received the invitation. It was the first time, also, that the Rustingthorpes had been asked by the Marquis. Clarissa was likewise eager to meet and impress *Madame la Marquise*.

These feelings were shared by a great many other ladies of the Court and the name of Harry Roddney was whispered from one to another.

"How came Harry to know the de Chartellets, I wonder," Henrietta said to Clarissa as they drove down Piccadilly. "They say he is ready to die of love for *Madame la Marquise*. But surely he will not make much impression on so new a bride."

Clarissa was cynical.

"You never know, my dear soul. She is young and the Marquis is old."

"Well, Harry is sure to be there tonight," said Henrietta. "But we are not on speaking terms, are we, Edward?" She addressed her plump dissolute-looking husband.

Edward grunted. He was more interested in the thought of the food he would eat and the wine he would drink, than in the people he was about to meet. Henrietta had more to say on the subject of Harry Roddney. She could not excuse the fact that he had cut her dead when they last met. Everybody said how sadly he had changed since he returned from India and had come into his uncle's money. Some said that he had had an accident and lost his memory—but Henrietta did not believe that; rather that he had lost his manners, she said sarcastically. Now that he was wealthy and held a high position in The East India Company, he had grown too big for his boots.

"If I see him tonight I shall pass him by," she added, "and if I get a chance to gossip with the bride, I shall warn her not to pay over attention to his protestations of love. I shall drop a few hints as to his redoubtable past."

"How about me dropping a few hints as to yours, my love," put in Edward acidly, then guffawed.

She kicked him on the shin with the point of her slipper, whereupon he howled and threatened to tear her head-dress to bits. Rustingthorpe, a mild man, protested. Clarissa giggled. Henrietta was in a fine tantrum by the time they reached their destination.

Standing at the top of the famous staircase in that most beautiful of mansions which had faced the Green Park for the last fifty years, the Marquis and Marquise awaited their first guests.

Helène was in a strange state of mingled excitement and conscious also of strange apprehension. Tonight she was going to look upon Henrietta Pumphret again—Clarissa—the dead Zobbo's mistress—and many other people she had known in the past, but seen only from afar, keeping the respectful distance of a serving maid.

It was strange and bitter-sweet to find herself here tonight as the hostess about to receive these people, one of the richest women in England, bearing one of the finest French titles in history.

Her dress had been made by a leading couturier. It was of shimmering grey satin sewn with an exquisite pattern of gold thread, long and rather narrow in style showing the curve of her wonderful hips; and high waisted with short puffed sleeves and a low corsage revealing her perfect bosom. Over this she wore a mantle of gold lace. Around her neck glittered the most wonderful collar of diamonds in the Marquis's collection—the finest ever to be seen in London. There were huge diamonds in her ears and on her wrists, and long slim fingers. But once again, by the Marquis's express wish, she had not powdered her hair, but wore it simply in a profusion of long gleaming curls that fell on either side of her neck and in high puffs in front. Her lips were touched with red. Her face pale and her eyes looked almost unnaturally large and dark. She had never been more beautiful and by the very simplicity and elegance of her gown, must surely outshine any other woman who attended the ball tonight.

Upstairs, the great reception room glittered with lights from a thousand candles in swinging crystal chandeliers. The orchestra played, concealed behind banks of flowers. A great banquet was prepared and in waiting, for midnight. Uniformed flunkeys were ready with silver trays to serve sparkling wine, from the moment the guests entered.

Lucien knew full well how his young wife was feeling. He sought to divert her attention from herself by casual discussion of mundane things.

"Did Aubrey remember to tell you that according to a dispatch I received by a French ship Napoleon's admirers are already tiring of his system and France would like to resume trade with us here?" he asked her.

Helène attempted to answer calmly.

"Yes, I saw it. I feel sure that peace between France and England will be restored this summer."

"It will take years before our own disputes are settled," said the Marquis. "Napoleon is still too strong. However, you make your début in a great age, *ma mie*. If I can keep well, I wish to witness next month the launching of the first steam vessel ever to be constructed in this country. That should be intriguing. Also I am bidding Aubrey make inquiries about this use of the new-found gas as a means of lighting our houses. It will come. A Mr. Murdock has already used it for the illumination of a factory."

Helène tried to give him full attention.

"I am sure I shall always prefer candlelight," she said. Then drawing closer to him, hearing his incessant cough and seeing how drawn he looked—although most elegant in his black velvet coat with gold-flowered waistcoat—she added: "At times I fear that this kind of life will do you no good, Lucien. Do not stay in town on my account, I beg of you."

"I am well enough," he said abruptly, "taste your triumph tonight and relish the flavour, *ma mie*. I assure you it will cause me the greatest delight."

A flunkey announced:

"*Sir Harry Roddney.*"

Lucien's thin lips curled.

"First, and, no doubt, he will be last to go. Look to it, *ma mie*, that you give him the sort of evening he deserves."

Helène made no answer. The Marquis was still chuckling as Harry Roddney came up the staircase. She gazed down at the approaching figure. How tall he was and handsome; debonair in cream and gold brocade tonight, with powdered wig and flushed eager face. Despite all her efforts at control, her heart beat savagely fast. Hatred and desire like evil twins sprang to birth within her. The pangs became almost beyond enduring but she gave him her jewelled hand and her most enigmatic smile, murmuring:

"Welcome, sir, you are come pleasantly early."

"I could not wait to see you," he murmured and bent over her hand, then turned and bowed to the Marquis. He had seen little of Lucien de Chartellet either here in London or in Brightlingsea. And he had no conscience about him, for he was convinced that Helène did not love her elderly husband and was unhappy. Therefore she was to be consoled and he had sworn to be accepted as her prime consoler.

He murmured:

"The dove grey satin of your exquisite gown becomes you divinely, *madame*. I am magnetized."

She smiled, her velvet eyes caressing. At the same time there was a strange fire within them that made his whole being tingle with delicious thrills. He admired the smallest detail of her attire but in his mind, as for the last few weeks, he saw only the hidden secret beauties of that bewitching body which he ached to hold within his arms. He stood aside, watching her greet other guests who were now being announced, in pairs or alone.

"His Grace the Duke of Farthingaleshire."

"Lord and Lady Dunmorrow."

"The Hon. Mr. and Mrs. George Courtney."

"Lady Amelia Fitzgale and Miss Arabella Fitzgale. . . ."

The sonorous voice of the resplendent flunkey droned on. One after another the ladies and gentlemen answered the separate and exquisitely worded welcome from host and hostess. Lucien received a fleeting smile and word. But far more lingering glances were thrown at the young wife who stood at his side. As the guests passed on to the brilliant reception room, voices whispered and buzzed:

"What a beauty, my dear . . . did you see those eyes and lashes? Of Italian or Spanish extraction, undoubtedly."

"Remarkable—with those divine golden-red curls."

"What elegance and refinement of feature!"

"What *diamonds*! Good heavens—worth a king's ransom."

Proudly Helène accepted the bows, or curtseys from those of lower title; the undisguised flattery in the men's eyes; the surprised, over-awed expressions on female faces; the fawning words and murmured compliments that never ceased. Before half the people had passed by, Lucien whispered:

"Your success is assured, *ma mie*."

She made no answer. She was all too conscious of Harry, standing in the background alone, impatient to ask permission to partner her in the first quadrille. Lucien did not dance.

The flunkey called, nasally:

"Lord and Lady Hamton."

Now under the faint blush on her high cheek-bones Helène's face grew marble-pale. Her left hand picked at a fold of her flowing gown. The other closed over the ivory handle of her fan.

"*Henrietta*—at last," she said the words tensely to herself.

"Bon chance, ma mie," whispered Lucien and gave his staccato laugh.

Henrietta came up the wide glittering staircase. She was puffing, out of breath. She was so stout these days that stairs affected her. Her face was still red with rage after the scene in the carriage coming here. She paused in front of her hostess and curtseyed awkwardly.

"Madame la Marquise——" she began.

She got no further. Something had stopped her. Something—she knew not what—that robbed her of still more breath and heightened her ugly scarlet flush.

She stared speechlessly into a pair of huge dark eyes with fan-like lashes; at an exquisite face framed by shining hair. *Unforgettable eyes and hair* . . . carrying Henrietta back through the years . . . shaking her to the soul with wild amazement and still wilder conjecture. With gloved hand on her throbbing heart she repeated, in a faltering voice:

"Madame—la—Marquise——"

Helène smiled. An ice-cold smile.

"My Lady Hamton—welcome to our house."

Edward, roused from his usual lethargy and boredom by the stunning beauty of the new Marquise—bowed low. He had no remembrance whatsoever of the young slave whom he had tried to kiss in Henrietta's boudoir at Pumphret House. He was merely telling himself that Helène's elegance made his wife look like an overdressed turkey.

"Move on, can't you?" he whispered crossly in Henrietta's ear.

The feathers and flowers on her head shook. Her whole body shook. There was a fleck of saliva at the corner of her rouged lips; lips that Helène looked at now with disgusted recollection of their cruelty. Spinning through her brain were innumerable little episodes of those days spent in Henrietta's service; the long-drawn-out torture of being paraded by her ruthlessly through the long days, and the longer nights when her child's body had cried out for sleep. The bullying—punctuated by moods when Henrietta had pampered her carelessly. The jealousies and vicious cruelties of later years. The frequent banishments into hell with Mrs. Clack.

It boiled and bubbled in the cauldron of Helène's memory while the cold smile continued to curve her proud mouth and her huge eyes to burn into Henrietta's very soul.

Nature had already had a share in taking her revenge, she thought scornfully. Henrietta was so fat and overdressed; a travesty of her handsome self. Helène said coolly:

"You are not indiposed, I trust, my Lady Hamton? You tremble."

Henrietta gulped and lifting her handkerchief, wiped her wet lips. Her eyes goggled. She could not move on. She could not stop staring. Her lips framed the name, *Fauna . . .* but no sound came. Her mind was spinning. She felt quite sick, hot and then cold. To herself, she mumbled:

"It is the same. But no—it cannot be. I am mad or indeed ill. Yes mad. How can the Marquise de Chartellet be Fauna. She is dead. She must have died these many years ago. None has heard of her since."

Edward gave his wife a violent push. She staggered on.

Now it was Clarissa's turn. She inclined her *blonde-cendré* head in a coquettish little bow. She was a marchioness and on equal terms with her hostess. But not so rich. Everyone knew of the fabulous wealth and art collection owned by Lucien de Chartellet. Certainly the new wife was exquisitely pretty, reflected Clarissa, and her diamonds, *oh, la! la!* The features of the Marquise were vaguely familiar to Clarissa; those eyes and lashes; the colour of hair—yes. Familiar. But *why*?

Henrietta passed on, tottering. Clarissa joined her and whispered excitedly:

"Such *magnificence*. Such floral decoration and there must be a hundred servants in that dashing livery. It makes poor little Rustingthorpe seem insignificant."

Henrietta clutched her friend's arm, her bracelets jangled with the tremors that shook her ample proportions.

"Clarry—saw you the face of the Marquise? My pulses throb as though I am in a high fever. I sweat and shiver. *Saw you her face—her hair?"*

The hoarse voice disturbed the little Marchioness. Her big blue vacant eyes blinked. She shook her head.

"Saw you *not*?" persisted Henrietta. "Whom does she resemble so strangely? Great heavens, am I out of my mind, or is it true? *Think*, Clarissa."

Clarissa thought. Then her own mind received an earthquake shock. She paled.

"Great heavens!" she echoed Henrietta. "*Fauna, your slave.*"

"Ay. She is Fauna come back to earth. Fauna returned from the dead."

Clarissa's eyes widened.

"But you never knew that she died."

"I must sit down. I am about to swoon," gurgled Henrietta and sank into the nearest chair. The orchestra was playing softly. Brilliantly gowned women and handsome peruked men passed by, chatting and laughing. One name was upon all lips.

Helène. Marquise de Chartellet. Her beauty, her gown, her jewels, her charm of manner, her proud dignity. She was a sensation. Women envied the jewels and the looks. Men envied the French nobleman known as "Satyr"—such a bride. The satyr had found a heavenly spouse. It was Lucifer wedded to an angel, they said.

Henrietta fanned herself, as pale now as she had been red.

Fauna, the slave, must have perished that night she ran away from Pumphret House, she whispered to Clarissa, else she would have been discovered. She could not have vanished so completely. She must have been the victim of some ruffian or a pimp, or maybe was swallowed up in a bawdy house, later died and was flung into a cesspit or a pauper's grave.

"Of course, my dear soul, you are crazed to see any connexion between the quadroon and *Madame la Marquise*," declared Clarissa rather crossly.

"But saw you not the peculiar likeness?"

"I saw it—but——"

"It is uncanny. It haunts me. My evening is ruined," said Henrietta in a hollow tone.

Clarissa bit her lip.

"Of a certainty it is amazing. Let us ask *her*."

Henrietta smothered a scream.

"*Ask her?* If she be *Fauna*, black-blooded slave? 'Tis you who are crazed, my dear soul."

"No one knows her history," added Clarissa thoughtfully. "She has undoubtedly come from abroad. She has continental colouring. Though, mark you, *she* has no nigger-blood. It is impossible. And they say she is more instructed than the most learned professors."

"Look—she comes—and lord—look who is her partner," whispered Henrietta excitedly and rose.

Everybody in the room was on his or her feet now—watching—waiting.

The quadrille had commenced. The hostess was being led on to the floor not by Sir Harry Roddney, no—*but by the Prince* himself. This was Helène's final triumph. The dissolute young heir to the throne had consented to look in at the de Chartellet reception for an hour. Never in the days of her most supreme triumph as a hostess had a prince of England adorned one of Henrietta's drawing-rooms. Plump, smiling, good-tempered, the amiable royal gentleman conducted his beautiful hostess to the dance.

Harry Roddney stood in the background, watching. He refused to dance until Helène was free. He was thin, white, nervous, eaten up with his mad and, so far, unrequited passion for Lucien's young wife. Her dancing was perfection. Moodily he watched the grace and voluptuousness of her every movement. When the quadrille ended and the Prince moved away. Helène on his arm, Harry followed at a tactful distance, biding his opportunity to claim her.

For a moment as she passed by Lucien, he addressed his wife.

"Are you satisfied, *ma mie*?"

She whispered back, her eyes sparkling:

"Thank you, Lucien—as ever, I am in your debt."

It had been one of his surprises. She had not known that the royal prince had either been given or accepted an invitation. It meant *much*—to partner her future king. And he had not been slow to tell her that he found her most attractive.

"We must arrange for you to sup with us one night soon, *Madame*," he had said, beaming on her while she curtseyed to the ground.

Yes, it was a great night in her life. But once more Helène suffered a curious reaction to this dazzling success. Harry was here—she could not avoid the sight of his persistent following—waiting for her. And the meeting with Henrietta Hamton had unnerved her more than she had expected. It had dragged the past back so remorselessly. Yet in this encounter she had succeeded—Henrietta was not enjoying tonight and Helène knew it. She took care later to engage her in a conversation *à deux* which flung Henrietta into a pitiful condition of fresh doubts and even a sinister belief that the "dead" quadroon had returned to earth in a new guise to haunt her.

"Are you still indisposed, *Madame*?" Helène asked her with that ice-cold smile which froze Henrietta.

"N-no. I m-mean, yes," stammered Henrietta.

"Can I send for a cordial for you?"

"No, I thank you, *Madame la Marquise*."

"You stare at me—think you we have met before?" Helène persisted, watching the woman's scarlet troubled and all-too-familiar face.

Henrietta gulped.

"I—I . . . once knew somebody . . . who closely resembles you, *Madame*."

"Indeed? With my colouring, also?"

"Yes, albeit it is most rare, *Madame*."

"Who was this double of myself?" asked Helène smiling.

Henrietta clutched the pearls on her bosom. Why, she knew not, but that glittering smile and the penetrating gaze of the Marquise's huge black eyes terrified her. She could actually see the quadroon slave staring up at her, as Fauna had done on the last occasion they had met—outside the death-chamber of George Pumphret. The big black tear-filled eyes, terror-struck . . . anguished . . . and she could smell the incense and the sweet terrible odour of death drifting from George's bier. Henrietta felt horribly sick. She wished she had not drunk that hot spiced wine nor eaten so many cakes before coming out. She turned a greenish hue and looked frantically to the right and the left. Oh, heavens, she must not be sick here in this gorgeous ballroom, within sight of half London.

Helène watched. Vengeance was hers. She knew that Henrietta was sadly confused and upset and about to vomit. And she remembered the unfortunate miserable child who had defiled my lady's carpet and because of it been beaten almost to death by Mrs. Clack.

"You wish to retire?" she asked sweetly. "You look very sickly, *Madame*. Pray take my arm."

Henrietta clutched at the arm. She felt stricken with shame and horribly unwell. And the longer she stayed at the side of her hostess, the more certain she became that some diabolical fate had brought her in contact with a reincarnated Fauna. Her brow burned. The weight of her ludicrous head adornment became almost unbearable. She wished the ground would open and swallow her up. She tried to proffer an apology. Helène said smoothly:

"I know how you feel, my poor friend. As a child once I was sick over an exquisite carpet, newly arrived from Paris, too. I must get you to my powder-room. Let us hasten——"

But Henrietta could not hasten. Her fat legs would not carry her farther. Those last words spoken by the Marquise struck her like lightning flashes and shrivelled her up. Soundlessly she looked up *into the eyes of Fauna*. All her monstrous doubts culminated into a phantasmagoria of fear, the belief that she had suddenly gone out of her mind. Yes, she was mad, and the sins she had committed in the past were pursuing her. Guilt froze her speech. Her physical *malaise* increased. People were staring. She saw Edward's fat, worried face . . . Clarissa's anxious one. The handsome, disgusted countenance of Anthony Lennox, her one-time lover and now known to be one of her greatest enemies. What did the *Marquise* mean—telling her the story of a child's sickness on a Parisian carpet? *Her own carpet in the boudoir of Pumphret House. Fauna. Fauna, the first night she had arrived, carried in the arms of George, had been thus indisposed.*

Henrietta shrieked suddenly and fell to the ground. She heard "*ohs*" and "*ahs*" from those surrounding her. In her crumpled finery, her head feathers bedraggled, her skirts disarrayed, showing her garters so as to raise titters from the gentlemen—she lay struggling with her miasma. And she knew that she would never dare show her face in society again. Her day was finished. In complete, utter ignominy, finished and on this night, too, when she had intended to climb high again, as a bosom friend of the new Marquise. Henrietta's last memory before she swooned dead away, was of Helène bending over her, decorously pulling down her gown, of her voice saying:

"Poor creature. A sudden seizure I fear."

But from Clarissa—*Clarissa* her friend, the unkindest cut of all:

"*La! La!* Naughty Etta has had too many little drinkies, I fear."

After that—for Henrietta—kindly oblivion.

Chapter Six

Lady Hamton went home. It would be the stricter truth to say she was *taken* home by a husband who exploded with fury every time he addressed her. She arrived back—she had moved after her marriage to a new house in Fitzroy Square—in a semi-fainting condition, and wept and moaned hysterically about Fauna, her runaway slave, and the Marquise de Chartellet until Edward privately made up his mind his wife had lost her wits and must at once be attended by a physician.

So far as Edward was concerned—Henrietta was finished. He hated her. He had little love even for his fat, grizzling, guzzling daughters. He was finished with matrimony. Tomorrow he would go to Madrid to which capital a Spanish friend had invited him. He would never return to Henrietta. No—not after her disgraceful exhibition in front of the only people in London who mattered. Henceforth she could live alone; and little doubt most of her so-called friends would leave her to what Edward privately thought a well-deserved solitude.

After her departure, one of the so-called friends—the "best" in fact—made haste to sidle up to Helène and endeavoured to get into her good books. Helène—wandering among her guests, uttering a charming word here and there in the manner of a great lady and born hostess—listened with an enigmatic smile to all the tittering, stupid Clarissa had to say.

"You are, of course, a stranger among us, *Madame*, but I do assure you poor Henrietta has a tendency to take overmuch wine. Quite a shocking exhibition, was it not?" These were Clarissa's opening words.

"She seemed to have a confused idea that I resembled—someone she once knew," said Helène gravely.

Clarissa plucked at the buttons on her white kid gloves

and tittered again. Everybody was looking at her; envying her, of course, this tête-à-tête with the bewitching Marquise who had *quite* taken all London by storm. She felt so proud. Tomorrow she would be sure to tell Henrietta and watch that fat discontented face grow lachrymose and jealous.

"Oh, *Madame*, she was quite, quite off her head, and *I* know what she thought!" exclaimed Clarissa.

Helène fixed her with a long deep look and suddenly the foolish little woman felt uncomfortable. Helène was thinking:

False friend to one and all—weak and unscrupulous and you would have given an innocent sixteen-year-old child to a vicious dwarf.

Aloud she said:

"Pray whom do I so closely resemble, *Madame*?"

Clarissa bit her lip. The longer she stared at her hostess, the more uneasy she became. Truly, Henrietta was not to be blamed. Strip the Marquise of her fine clothes and jewels and she might be that very slave, she reflected.

"I—I would rather not say—it is unflattering—oh not from the facial angle, dear *Madame*—the—girl was exquisite—but of inferior birth to your noble self."

Now Helène's lips curled. Her lashes drooped. She said softly:

"You have three sons, I believe."

"Yes, was I not clever?" giggled Clarissa.

"Most clever, *Madame*. And once, I hear you had a black page—quite an amusing little monster."

Clarissa's eyes widened with surprise. But spurred on by this friendly talk, she said:

"La! That was three years back. Zobbo died—such a tiresome thing. Such a thwarted life, too. He had no mate. The one I had in mind vanished alas just before the wedding."

"The one you had in mind?" repeated Helène in a voice less honeyed, and with a dangerous glint in her magnificent eyes. Clarissa hurtled on—unaware of the cracking ice and the cold bath awaiting her.

"Yes, a pretty quadroon once owned by Henrietta Hamton (then married to Lord Pumphret)—the slave ran away, alack."

"Was she not happy in serving my Lady Hamton?"

"Who can tell, *Madame*, if a black slave be happy," the Marchioness giggled, fluttering her lashes.

Then Helène struck—her voice ice-cold—her beautiful eyes expressing such scorn, such anger that Clarissa was confounded, reduced to a state of petrification.

" 'Tis a pity, *Madame*," said Helène, "that you did not breed daughters instead of sons. For then you might have been amused to wed all three of them to Zobbo. As prince of a little harem, it would have made a vastly entertaining spectacle and been, do you not think, an excellent match for the girls?"

Clarissa went a greyish colour under her powder and paint. She quivered under this blow. Her breath quickened. She stood as though marooned in a flood, staring wildly up at her hostess. Those great dark accusing, contemptuous eyes filled her with fear. And oh, the *insult* . . . the ignominy—to have had such a thing said to her—for the Marquise to suggest that a daughter of *hers*—of *William's* . . . *a Rustingthorpe* . . . might have mated with an African dwarf. Oh, horror of horrors! Clarissa opened her cupid's bow mouth to speak, to protest. No words came. Helène smiled and bowed.

"Your pardon, *Madame*—I see my partner waiting for the next quadrille. I trust you will continue to enjoy your evening."

Clarissa stood staring after her blindly, transfixed, trembling from head to foot. A woman whom she knew, spoke to her. She did not hear. There was a singing in her ears; a terrible doubt in her mind—that same doubt that had recently felled Henrietta to the ground. *Fauna! 'Twas she!* It must be. How else could the Marquise have said such a thing? Why else had she spoken so bitterly, so cruelly? Oh, 'twas *monstrous* and the whole merry evening spoiled for Clarissa. No triumph would be little Clarissa's now. Never, never would she enter this house again nor indeed be asked to it.

Was it Fauna? *Could* it be? But, no! Impossible!

The Marquis de Chartellet, from a distance, saw Clarissa's face and chortled to himself. He knew that Helène had been speaking to her. His quick mind gathered that she must have shot a pretty bolt once more. The little

Marchioness was obviously in a state of considerable agitation.

He smiled and turned away. He felt tired and his side pained him. He coughed incessantly. But he was enjoying Helène's revenge with all the malice in his warped nature.

He stood watching her for a moment as she was led on to the dance floor by Harry Roddney. Harry's handsome winning face was radiant. He glanced down at his partner with all his soul in his eyes. Lucien chuckled. Soon it would be Harry's turn. *Soon*, now.

Clarissa recovered sufficiently to seek out her husband.

"Take me home, William—at once," she choked.

The Marquis, stout, uncomfortable in his hot wig and tight satin breeches was only too ready to oblige. He stared at his wife's altered countenance. He had never seen her look thus—ghastly under her paint—shaking.

"What in heaven's name ails you, my dear? Have you seen an apparition?"

She nodded.

"Yes, an apparition, William. Else I am losing my mind. 'His she. *'Tis she!*"

" 'Tis who, my love?" William asked, bewildered.

Clarissa pointed a shaking hand at Helène who, with matchless grace, danced the steps of the quadrille in perfect rhythm with Harry Roddney. William followed his wife's finger and then slapped his knee and guffawed.

"Zounds, my dear Clarry. Have you emulated Henrietta Hamton and had a drop too much?"

"Do not laugh," said Clarissa in a hollow tone. "Tell me about the Marquise de Chartellet—what is known of her background or whence she came? Speak!"

William tried to scratch his bald pate under the wig. He was sure there was vermin to attend to. Abominable little pests. He said:

"Tush, my dear, how can I know? Some say that de Chartellet met her on the Continent; that she is partly of Spanish blood—which accounts for her eyes. Deuced fine eyes, too; and a clever creature. We talked together of fauna and flora—my pet subjects—she has made a study of Nature and——"

He paused. Clarissa had swayed and caught his arm. In a terror-stricken whisper she murmured:

"*Fauna. Fauna*——"

He stared and guffawed.

"Know you your Latin, my love? I did not guess it. Come—let us pay our respects to our host if you have a mind to leave early."

She nodded. In all her spoiled empty life, Clarissa Rustingthorpe, had never been so upset—so frightened or confused. She could ascertain nothing—nothing concrete. On the face of it—her suspicions must be groundless. Yet that insulting barb shot from Helène's bow had entered her very heart. She left the de Chartellet mansion clinging fast to her husband's arm as though she had received a visitation from the Fiend himself. She shook and wept all the way home in the carriage. William could get no sense from her but heard her repeating wildly the names *Fauna* and *Zobbo* . . . until he, like Edward, made a mental note that what his wife needed first thing in the morning was the attention of a good leech.

The de Chartellet reception lasted until long past dawn. It was broad daylight before the yawning flunkeys saw the last semi-intoxicated happy guests into their carriages, and the sound of horses' hoofs clip-clopped gaily down Piccadilly.

It had been a tremendous occasion—not a guest departed but who—if sober enough—did not first smother the host and hostess with congratulations. Never had there been such splendour; such food; such wines, such fine dancing and amorous interlude when much liquor unleashed men's passions, and women's desires broke through the façade of court etiquette. At first it had been a grand affair, graced by the Prince himself. It ended as an orgy. It was talked of for months afterwards. And the main topic of conversation was the lovely witty young wife of the "Satyr." Helène de Chartellet overnight became the toast of London.

And what of *her*? . . . the recipient of this flattery—the new idol of Society?

She was well aware that she had, in a measure, avenged that other personality—Fauna, the slave. Henrietta and Clarissa had gone home two confused and frightened people. Henrietta Hamton was indeed ruined.

But what of Helène?

Pale, fatigued, almost overcome by her success, she was still bitterly conscious of her own deep failure to so much as touch the golden finger of her soul's content. But she continued to lure Harry Roddney on to his doom.

He had, as Lucien prophesied (Lucien had long since retired), stayed till the end. Now, alone with his *amorata*, he stood beside her in the deserted reception room, facing one of the tall balconied windows. The candles in the glittering chandeliers had been extinguished. The first gilt rays of the spring sunshine touched the trees in the park to a heavenly green. The Serpentine was a smooth silver mirror. The cool dawn air drifted into a room that reeked with perfume, smoke, and spilt wine. A great silent room full of rank disorder and emptiness.

Harry Roddney took Helène in his arms and pleaded as for his very life. With face drawn and anguished, he besought her to take him for her lover.

"This night has been agony to me. To watch other men so much as touch your hand and partner you in a dance—to see them receive your smile—to know that tomorrow not a man but will besiege you with flowers, with costly presents, with a thousand invitations. Oh, great God, Helène, how can I go on bearing this torment? Will you not put me out of my misery?"

She rested in the curve of his arm, her strange wonderful eyes looking up at him. How tired she felt—tired to the depths of her being. Conscious of the heavy weight she bore—the burden of the last four joyless years without love or at least the illusion of it. The triumphs which Harry enumerated were bitter to her taste. She shivered suddenly and he drew her away from the open window.

"My love—you are cold?"

She could have laughed. Cold? Yes. But not because of the fresh sweet air. The death-like coldness had settled in her very heart. She turned her melancholy gaze upon the man who had once disillusioned and abandoned her.

Was it not time he disclosed his knowledge of the past and gave one small sign of his penitence? How monstrously sure he was that he could lure her back into the silken web of her old passion and desire for him!

"Helène," he said huskily. "Look at me—let me but taste the nectar from your lovely mouth. Most beloved of women—if you would only fly with me, away from de Chartellet altogether—from all who know us—and be lost from sight and alone forevermore."

She gave a low laugh.

"Think you I wish to desert Lucien who has given me all?"

"I, also, will give you my all. He does not—cannot—make you truly happy. It is I whom you love, is it not?"

"Have I ever said so?"

"In my dreams, oh yes, yes!" he said fervently.

Her eyes glowed with sudden anger.

"And in the past?"

He mistook her meaning, and in any case saw no significance in what she said:

"It is as I wrote to you when you were at The Bastille. I believe that you and I have always loved each other, from all time. We were meant for one another, my dear delight."

She could have struck him across the face but she said nothing. Gloomily she noted his hollowed cheeks, the stains under his green, brilliant eyes. He suffered on account of her. Good! Never could his torments be as great as those he had caused her.

Suddenly she knew that she must kill him. First take him for her lover—afterwards destroy him, and ere he drew his last breath, make known to him the depth of her bitterness.

"Great God, I am mad with longing for his kisses whether they be his first or last," she told herself in horror.

She allowed him to caress her tumbled curls, to press his hot hungry mouth against hers. For a fierce moment she responded. Her mouth moved hungrily under his. Her arms wreathed about his neck.

"My delight, my soul's desire. I famish for you!" he almost sobbed the words. "Say that you love me, also, I do implore you. I have waited so long."

"And I—longer," she said bitterly.

Without understanding, he crushed her more savagely. She cried out:

"You hurt me."

"I am mad with love. I would hurt then make amends. *I would die* in your embrace," he added extravagantly.

"Die, then," she said, her lashes hiding the terrible despair in her eyes.

Once more he read another meaning into her words. Joyfully he caressed her.

"Helène . . . Helène . . . you mean it? You will give yourself to me? Oh, my wonder of the world, I shall not prove ungrateful even if I am unworthy!" he said passionately.

She shivered again and drew back. The time was not yet ripe. She said:

"Go, Harry—leave me."

His face grew anguished again. He began to speak.

"Go," she interrupted. "I will not see you for a week. In seven days' time I will send my messenger and tell you where we are to meet."

His brow cleared again.

"Sweet—*sweet*—wherever you wish! And I will send an envoy before me to carpet the ground with flowers ere you tread upon it. Dear heaven—is it true? Will you not come to me sooner?"

"No—in one week *you* will come to *me*. I shall get there first," she said, her gaze narrowed, her mind teeming with ideas.

"Where? Tell me now."

"No. I will send you word—one week from today," she said in a low voice.

Harry was still holding her in his arms; smoothing the silken hair back from her glorious brow. With his forefinger he traced the fine pencilled brows, worshipping her unblemished perfection. Yet, as usual, he was strangely baffled by this woman. He seemed always to be able to get so far with her and no farther—close—yet remained distant. It was as though he could never know or really understand her.

During these weeks and months which he had spent as her constant companion, he had grown to marvel not only at her beauty but at her erudition. At one time disinterested in serious matters, Harry Roddney had, himself, developed his intellectual powers since living with James Wilberson, who was not only a man of business but of letters. He had enjoyed every discussion with Helène—particularly at The Bastille—wandering with her in what she called her "kingdom by the sea." During the weeks of the Marquis's protracted illness, Harry had had the ineffable bliss of spending much time alone with Helène. They used to sit by the great wood fires on the cold evenings of early spring, reading or talking, or walk along the cliffs, or rode together. She excelled as a horsewoman. Harry spent unforgettable hours cantering beside her across the springy turf, watching the sea breeze toss her rich curls and whip the blood to her cheeks. He had discovered so many sides to her nature—so much sweetness. Yet that touch of hardness and, at moments, even cruelty when she dismissed him imperiously and the softness of her eyes could take on the sharpness of the rocks that lay beneath The Bastille. Rocks on which a man might dash himself to death. Once or twice he had accused her of being amused at his expense—of behaving as though she despised and resented him. Always when he asked her if she had any real regard for him her answer was noncommittal. He would leave her side torn with doubts and fears yet knowing that he must return to receive whatever treatment she might mete out. He who had scorned to become any woman's slave found himself slave indeed to *her*. When he dwelt on the thought of her he was a man bewitched and mentally confused. He knew her well, yet knew her not at all. Neither did she ever offer explanation as to why she had made this loveless marriage to the Marquis. Of one thing, Harry was positive—she had not made it because of her desire for material things. She was, like Lucien, more interested in the discovery of a fine picture or some other work of art than in any of the jewels that money could buy, craved by the average woman.

When Helène allowed him to take her in his arms, he was her master and she the eternally submissive female waiting to be conquered. But when they talked, she seemed so much older and wiser than he and he left her presence feeling foolish, like an ignorant boy.

He grew so restless and uncertain of himself that his work suffered. Only yesterday, Uncle James had called him to task and begged him, not for the first time, to marry and settle down.

"Your name is being linked now with that of the Marquise de Chartellet. And to what purpose?" Mr. Wilberson had inquired. And the kindly gentleman was much harassed. Harry was dearer to him now than his son had ever been. He yearned for the boy to take a wife, to have children and a more domestic life.

But Harry Roddney knew now that there was no woman he could wed unless it was Helène de Chartellet and that, seemingly, was impossible.

If there was one man in the world whom Harry hated it was Lucien. He hated him not only as the barrier which stood between Helène and himself, but because of the man's disposition. He loathed the perpetual sneer on the Marquis's thin lips and the strange hold which he seemed to have over the lovely creature he had married.

On this particular morning, Harry Roddney, overcome by the hopes Helène had held out, continued to wrestle with his thoughts and desires. He felt like a man drained of vitality yet burning with passion. He slid suddenly on to one knee and with his arms around Helène's waist, face against her. She could feel him shivering as though with fever.

"Dear heaven, I do love you so that I am suspended midway between heaven and hell," he whispered.

Her inscrutable eyes looked down at his bent head. She said:

"Is that all that you have to tell me, Harry? Have you not courage enough to speak openly to me even *now*?"

He raised his ravaged face. She so frequently made remarks like this which were incomprehensible to him. He said:

"What would you have me say?"

"Have you no shame?" she whispered.

Even then, groping blindly in the darkness of his bruised mind, he saw nothing significant in such a question but presumed that she alluded to her husband. He rose to his feet and laughed.

"The one thing that I shall never be ashamed of, is my love for you."

She drew in her breath sharply. Her lids narrowed.

"You are worse than a common traitor," she said between her teeth. "Shameless! Oh, *leave me*, leave me, I say."

Harry's face grew duskily red. She was ever like this—yielding at one moment and bitter the next. Maddening, inexplicable, *devastating* woman. And because he did not know what she *imagined* he knew, he answered her at cross-purposes.

"Hate me for it if you will, but let me stay shameless. I want you no matter what price I pay."

She wiped her lips—lips bruised from his savage kisses—and turned away.

"Very well," she said. "You shall have me, and you shall pay the price—*one week from now*."

After he had gone, she staggered upstairs as though drunk with weariness. That terrible mixture of hatred and desire which she felt for her lover consumed her like a white hot fire.

One light only burned now in the great silent house other than the candle in the silver stick which she carried; the light in Lucien's bedroom. The house was full of shadows. She looked with disgust at the litter which in a few moments the servants would be clearing away after the night's revelry.

Lucien's door was ajar. She heard him calling her and knew that his quick ear had detected her footsteps. She went to the foot of his bed. He had drawn the curtains and opened his windows. His face looked shrunken, much sharpened by illness, under his tasselled nightcap. He lay against a pile of pillows. She thought how much he had deteriorated even since their arrival in London. A quick pang seized her heart. Despite all the lack of sexual feeling, she knew that the day Lucien de Chartellet died, a part of herself would die also. That part which he had fostered and which had become his creature. The harsh wicked old man had been extraordinarily good to the quadroon slave, she thought, and suddenly came and clung to one of the carved bedposts and hid her face on the curve of her arm.

"My child, my child," said the Marquis, and put down the big volume he had been studying, for he slept little these nights. "What ails you? Why these tears when you should be crowing over your splendid triumph?"

Now she lifted her face. He saw her great eyes wild with pain and wet.

"Crowing," she echoed the word. "Yes, like a farmyard fowl on a dung heap. I hated them all—with their vanities and follies, their foolish snobberies—and the emptiness of their lives. Oh, yes, it was good to see Henrietta Hamton prostrate at my feet and carried like a sick sow from my house. And Clarissa Rustingthorpe hag-ridden with memories of the past that I evoked. Good to receive upon my hand the kisses of those who used to despise me when I was Lady Pumphret's puppet. Good to see Harry Roddney squirm like a fish with a hook in his gullet. But what is it all worth? Where does it lead? *What have I gained?*"

The Marquis closed one eye, and shut his book.

"Mercy on us, *ma mie*," he said drily, "I find your outpouring *triste*, but, at the same time, a little boring. You have grown too introspective of late. Or, like myself, too blasé. It is lamentable if you have out-lived your ambitions to look at your enemies' discomfiture. Or was I, perhaps, mistaken in imagining you would enjoy the sweets of revenge?"

She swallowed hard.

"The sweets grow bitter, Lucien."

"And you," he said sadly, "disappoint me. You admit failure. Failure is an expression of weakness, and I had thought you strong."

She came and knelt beside him, lifted one of his dry bony hands and put it against her hot forehead; it was a gesture of submission.

"Forgive me, Lucien. I do not care to disappoint *you*, of all men."

He sighed and frowned.

"You are my wife, do not kneel to me. The whole trouble is, of course, that you are still enamoured of that confounded young man."

This stung the blood to Helène's cheeks. She sprang to her feet, eyes flashing and teeth clenched.

"*I will not be*. I swear to you that I mean to *kill him*."

"Now you are my own Helène and far more entertaining," said the Marquis. "You will perhaps feel easier once you have removed him from your path."

"Yes," she said, teeth still clenched.

"What are your plans?"

She told him. He nodded and said:

"Good! Good! Let it be so. And let there be no more weakness or I shall feel," he added sardonically, "that I have married the wrong woman."

A ghost of a smile tilted her sad mouth.

"You always give me of your own strength. Trust me again and I shall not fail, Lucien."

"You are tired, *ma mie*. Go and rest."

"I do not wish to accept any social engagements during this week, just before my final meeting with Harry," she added in a low voice, "I wish to spend it beside you, sharing your studies."

"Very well, and incidentally," said Lucien, "once you have purged this poison from your system and are in complete command of yourself again, I have a treat in store for you."

"What is it?"

"I have been in correspondence with young Byron. He was interested in a book which he knew to be in my collection and is coming here to call upon us."

"I shall look forward to it," she said without conviction.

All London had begun to talk of George Gordon, Lord Byron. Despite his club foot he was deemed to be extraordinarily handsome and possessed of exceptional talent. Earlier this year, Lucien had given Helène a new book of Byron's poems which had been privately distributed. Lucien was one of the few men to possess a copy of that poem "To Mary" which had been proclaimed too indecent for general publication. She knew that Lucien had a high opinion of Byron.

Lucien added:

"The young poet has much success with women, *ma mie*, he may perhaps interest you."

"He may," nodded Helène.

The Marquis blinked. His head was aching badly. He wondered how much longer he was going to live. He felt suddenly so tired that he did not even wish to bother with his young and fascinating wife.

"Go seek your bed, *ma mie*, and draw my curtains again. There is too much sunshine," he said.

She drew the heavy velvet curtains and with a whispered: "*Good night* and *Good morning*," walked with her peculiarly gliding graceful step from the room.

Chapter Seven

The Marquis remained in bed most of that week. True to the variable English climate, the weather changed and became cooler. Torrents of rain, and a gusty wind swept the London streets and shook the budding trees.

Lucien never now seemed to feel warm. They kept great fires in his bedchamber and the room grew so hot that Helène could scarcely breathe in it, but she remained, as she wished, at his bedside most of the day. She read to him and shared his work upon a papyrus newly sent to him from one of the most recent excavations in upper Egypt. He was translating the Arabic into English.

She never once discussed her personal affairs; and if she looked pale and taut, her husband did not comment on it.

The result of the recent reception seemed to interest her little, although it was quite electrifying. The social papers were crammed with flattering reports. Letters of thanks poured in from all the guests, and gilt-edged invitations to many of the greatest houses in London reached *Madame la Marquise*. She bade Aubrey refuse all of them. Those who called—and there were a continual stream of admirers, anxious to renew acquaintance with her—were turned away. It was given out by the secretary that *Madame* was accepting no further social engagements until the beginning of May.

An effusive apology arrived with an enormous bouquet of flowers from Henrietta Hamton. This, alone, caused Helène's lips to curl. She tore the note in pieces and sent the flowers to the servants' hall. The great Henrietta apologizing to Fauna—this was as amusing as anything! But Helène did not reply to the letter. Aubrey formally acknowledged the flowers.

The Prince, himself, sent a basket of fine roses from the Palace, with a card signed by himself; enough honour to make the heart of any woman in Society beat fast with pride and joy. But when Aubrey set the great gilded basket of pink roses at Helène's feet and she saw the Royal signature, she remained unmoved. She began to wonder if ever again she would be moved except by the thought of Harry, and what she was going to do at the end of this week. She felt as though all roads in her life had led to this one sinister devastating episode. She felt as though she were being propelled towards her own doom as well as his. *Fauna, Helène,* whatever she was—had become a mere tool of destiny.

This week which she had set apart from the world was a strange period of waiting, of crisis. She was marooned within her own terrible emotions. They were in control, leashed, pent-up wild things waiting to burst their bonds.

She received a hundred or more gifts and missives from hopeful suitors with whom she had danced or talked, or smiled upon during the night of the ball. She was chronicled in leading journals of the day as *"La Belle Helène."* Her style of gown, the manner in which she dressed her hair, were to be copied. She was to become leader of fashion. She was to be queen of beauty, even high priestess of culture and wit. She read all these extravaganzas aloud to Lucien. They smiled over them together.

"If they but knew who I was!" Helène said.

"It will be amusing to let them know once you are firmly established," said the Marquis.

The slave, Fauna, was further avenged when the de Chartellets heard that Lady Hamton had been abandoned by her husband and, two days later, found dead in her bed of an overdose of veronal.

It was Lucien who first read of this suicide, then grinned and tossed the paper to his wife.

"So perish your enemies, one by one, *ma mie,*" he murmured.

She nodded. Henrietta's ugly end left her strangely unmoved. She walked to the window, looked out at the grey rain driving across Piccadilly and remained silent. The old man in the bed, watching her, knew that she was thinking of the arch-enemy—of the traitor, Harry—and of the approaching day of retribution. Lucien had an idea now that he need not worry much more about his wife, and that she would be strong enough to see the thing through to the bitter finality.

Towards the middle of that week, Lucien made a special effort to rise from his bed for he felt that if he did not, he would die in it. Racked by his cough, followed anxiously by Surenne, his physician, he wandered through the great draughty corridors and vast rooms of his mansion, examining each one of his treasures as though he were gazing upon them for the last time. He would sit for long stretches in front of his tank of exquisite tiny fish, watching, feeding them, until he slept and was carried back to his bed by his servants. It was perfectly obvious to Helène when she looked at his grey face and the skeleton-like frame under the fur bedgown that he was a dying man. But he would have none of her warnings and take few of Surenne's opiates. He was determined to drink the cup of life to the last bitter dregs and abide by his own philosophy—defy pain and weakness—defy death itself; that death that stalked him through the mansion—lean, hungry, horrible, amidst so much beauty and magnificence. Lucien felt the dread presence and cared not. Every time he awakened to a new day and found himself still breathing, and saw that lean figure still crouching, hungry and thwarted, he chuckled.

"Death must wait as we all wait for our triumphs," he told his wife one morning when she begged him to stay a-bed.

"You need me. I shall not carry out my plan for this weekend," she said, "I shall send word to Harry that our meeting is to be postponed."

"You will do nothing of the sort," croaked the Marquis, shaken by a spasm of coughing which left him breathless. "I forbid it. Proceed with the plans and then return to me and tell me all. I desire to hear it before I am laid in my tomb."

Now, suddenly near to weeping, she cried:

"Oh, do not leave me, Lucien!"

He, with rare tenderness, stroked the red-gold silk of her hair. He murmured:

"My most bright and beautiful of jewels, once I am gone I forbid you to grieve."

"What shall I do?" she whispered desolately. "My life without you will be utterly bereft."

"Tush—remember all that I have taught you of the transcience of human emotions. Besides, you will be the most sought-after widow in all England. And you will, I hope, find a husband, and reproduce your beauty. I do most devoutly wish it."

She thought of Harry's hands upon her waist and of his green hungry eyes, and of the terrible destructive love they shared.

"I shall never marry again, Lucien, neither shall I reproduce what might well be a full-blooded African with my tarnished blood," she said in great bitterness.

The Marquis scowled.

"You grow morbid. Send Aubrey to me. I would dictate a letter."

She sighed and rose. When the young secretary entered, the sight of his changed face brought her no consolation of vanity. One day soon, perhaps, she told herself with a cynicism worthy of her teacher, she would take the unhappy boy to her bed and cradle his golden head upon her breast lest he perish of his hopeless passion for her. When he handed her some letters he accidentally touched her hand, flinched and whitened. She knew how he felt, poor fool! The girl, Fauna, and the woman, Helène, both had flinched, suffocated by desire, at the touch of a hand.

Lucien was right. She would be better, maybe, when Harry Roddney was no longer in this world.

The day of reckoning came nearer. Death, like a wolf, sat on his haunches, waiting, tongue lolling, panting. His vile breath filled the Marquis's bedchamber with a stench which all the perfumed waters could not sweeten.

Then the Marquis with some of his former satirical humour—rousing body and brain to action—played his last sardonic prank—upon the unfortunate secretary.

Of late, Aubrey had wearied him exceedingly by his moods and depressions and the way he slunk around the place haunting Helène's very shadow; making one mistake after another in his work—which was a thing Lucien found hard to forgive. He knew that the boy was consumed with his passion, but time and time again had advised him, in crude terms, to seek consolation in other arms. This idea Aubrey always most stubbornly rejected. The wretched young man made it quite clear that since he could not enjoy the favours of *Madame la Marquise*, which he admitted to be impossible, he would never waste his manhood upon any other woman.

One night after Helène had retired, the dying Marquis sent for Aubrey. With all seriousness, he informed the astonished young man that *Madame la Marquise* had relented and admitted to her willingness to respond to Aubrey's affection.

"You have my full consent to seek her," ended Lucien, his sunken, marble-like eyes gloating over the expression that spread across the young man's smug young face. It was one of mingled anguish and delight.

"But, sir, *sir*! . . ." he stuttered wildly and clutching at the narrow Geneva band around his neck, fell on his knees beside his master's bed.

A low demoniac chuckle frm the heap of pillows. The Marquis, coughing terribly, gasped:

"Go—not to her own bedchamber, but to the Chinese room overlooking the courtyard."

"*Sir*——" repeated Aubrey, trembling violently, alternating between his desire and his horrified amazement at the old man's connivance. He had known him vicious in the past—but never as bad as this.

"Sir," said the Marquis in a dreadful voice. *"Would you keep Madame la Marquise waiting?"*

Aubrey Burkett recovered himself. Pale, trembling with wild excitement, he staggered from the odorous sick-room. He wiped the perspiration from his forehead as he walked through the cool corridors to the guest-chamber known as the Chinese room because of its glazed wallpaper of birds and flowers, its red lacquered furniture, and the hangings of peacock blue satin from Pekin. A room kept for the most distinguished visitors.

Aubrey reflected that Helène must have chosen to receive him there rather than admit him into her own sumptuous suite lest one of her maids should unwittingly surprise them. Why she should have climbed down from her pedestal and honoured him so suddenly and unexpectedly, he did not know. He dared not think. And if his joy was blunted by the uncomfortable knowledge that the Marquis had personally accorded him the privilege, he saw no reason to refuse what the gods offered. He was as a man under a spell as he turned the door handle of the Chinese room and it yielded to his touch.

The hour was midnight. The house was quiet and all the servants, save the Marquis's attendants, were a-bed. Aubrey had stayed up late and was still writing when his master's summons reached him. Then he had felt fatigued and unhappy. Now, flung into a state of exaltation—of supreme anticipation—he tiptoed into the bedroom. It was dimly lit by one single shaded light above the great lacquered bed, and a flickering fire. He saw nothing save the outline of a feminine form under silken sheets, and a cloud of red-gold hair rippling to the floor. The Marquise's face was hidden on her arm. The room smelled of attar of roses. All the choirs of paradise echoed in Aubrey's ears. He was like one possessed as he sank upon his knees, seized one of the white delicate hands just visible to him and pressed his lips to it. The fingers returned the pleasure of his. There came a muffled whisper:

"My love . . . you have come to me . . . extinguish the lamp I pray you."

He obeyed her, plunging the room into darkness. His heart was ready to burst with love and longing. His soul was faint with the depth of the gratitude he felt towards her. Now at last he could be truly glad that he had waited for *this*—that he had known no other love—no other embrace. Now, at last, the bitter sterile longing of the years since this divine woman had come under the de Chartellet roof was about to be assuaged.

"Helène—Helène—*Helène!*"

All the pride and glory of possessing his glorious exalted mistress turned Aubrey Burkett for this brief hour into a god; until at length he slept within her arms. He woke later to hear her soft, satisfied laughter.

"What a man you be!" she whispered. "Sweet Aubrey I am your most willing partner in this game of love."

Something in the timbre of that voice and the words used, roused the young secretary wholly from the stupor of his slumbers. *Something* . . . he knew not what . . . made his flesh suddenly creep and the hair on his scalp tingle.

He sat up and throwing back the bed covers, stared closely at the woman who lay beside him. It was the dark hour before the dawn; he could not quite see. She whispered drowsily:

"It is not yet the morning."

And then he knew that she was not Helène.

He sprang out of bed, drenched in sweat, assailed by furious doubts and a still greater terror. With shaking fingers he lit the lamp above the bed. The gay Chinese room took shape. So, also, did the girl lying on the pillows, arms laced behind tousled head, smiling at him wantonly. His unbelieving gaze noted the unfamiliar features. Pretty she was, yes, in a coarse way, with small blunt nose and small sly eyes. She had a big dissolute mouth, smeared with paint. But she bore no true resemblance to Helène de Chartellet other than that flame-bright, curling hair which had so deceived him when first he saw it tumbling over the edge of the bed.

She giggled at him.

"Sweet boy—were you not amused by the trick the noble Marquis played on you?"

He shuddered and said:

"*Who are you?*"

"My name is Caroline—more often called Carrie. I ply a good trade——" she laughed, her eyes shameless. "Was it not worth a golden guinea or so to you, sir, Aubrey? The Marquis paid me well. His minions found me in the Golden Cock Tavern in Shepherd's Market. They were seeking a red-head like me, they said. Once here, he, the Marquis, primed me in the part I was to play and *la! la!* what a to-do I had going through my paces, trying to remember to answer to the name of Helène, to hide my face from you and to whisper so as to deceive you. Faith, he is a merry old jester, the noble Marquis. What was in his mind when he did this thing? Were you enamoured of his wife? Mark you—I am a-feared of *him*, for I am cautioned not to tell one word about this outside or receive worse than a beating, he said."

Aubrey was listening to her in frozen silence. Body and soul were numbed by the knowledge of what he had done and how he had been tricked into doing it.

What was in the mind of the Marquis, this trollop had just asked? Aubrey knew, perhaps better than anybody else, what lay in the confines of that warped, sinful mind. Even at the gates of hell, Lucien de Chartellet chose to play an atrocious jest. He had sent him—a poor love-sick innocent fool—into the arms of a light-o'-love from a common tavern.

"Do not look at me so," the girl called Carrie tried to wheedle Aubrey. "The joke be over and the truth discovered. But I am still here."

He thrust away her hand and pushed her back from him as though she were malignant. He felt polluted. He was sick to the pit of his stomach. All that was decent in him revolted against this abominable trick that had been so successfully played upon him. His love for Helène had been ridiculed and defiled. He had been made to give all his first fine passion to a harlot—a wench who had nothing whatsoever in common with *her* except her sex and the colour of her hair.

"You be angry," Carrie pouted—and stared with perplexity at his ghastly face.

Then he turned from her with a smothered cry and rushed from the room. She shrugged her shoulders and lay down and went to sleep again, deeming all men peculiar and this one no exception.

Aubrey Burkett went straight to his own room. On his escritoire in an open leather case lay a gold-framed miniature of the Marquis which Lucien had presented to the young secretary one Christmas years ago. It was a fine work by a contemporary painter of merit, and valuable. Aubrey looked in horror at the sneering painted face, laid it upon the ground and set his heel on the glass. He crushed the miniature into powder. Then he took a poem which he had written last night to "*La belle Helène.*" This he placed in an envelope, and with it a note which said:

I loved you and you only until the end. Forgive me.
Aubrey.

Then he took a silken cord belonging to the window curtain, attached it to the high post of his bed and hanged himself.

In the morning the note to Helène was delivered to her by a white-faced Hattie who in trembling accents informed her ladyship that there had been a shocking tragedy in the house.

Helène sprang from her bed.

"Is it *Monsieur le Marquis?*"

"No, *Madame*—it is the poor young secretary," sobbed Hattie, who had known Aubrey for years—and informed her lady that the poor young man had been discovered by the valet hanging by the neck, and when cut down was found to be dead.

Helène paled. She bore Aubrey no particular love but he had been a clever, efficient secretary, and loyal and withal a handsome fair-faced youth.

She hastened to her husband's room. He knew already—for she saw the grim look on his face, a queer twisted grin on lips that bared his yellowish teeth.

"How came this about, Lucien?" she asked in shocked accents.

He looked at her, one eyebrow cocked, and with his most sardonic smile. His breath came with difficulty and his chest rattled.

"The fool," he snorted. "The weak fool. He had no red blood in his veins, only milk."

"Did he hang himself on my account?" asked Helène in a low troubled voice. "If so—I do most sorely regret it."

"He hanged himself because he could not take the excellent practical joke I played upon him," the Marquis informed her sullenly.

"What joke?"

He told her and shrugged his shoulders.

"God's death—why all the histrionics? I did not mean to drive him to do away with himself. It is an abominable nuisance—for he knew my ways and the whereabouts of all my documents. Now it is too late to engage a new secretary. He would arrive only in time to inscribe a certificate of my decease."

Helène kept silent. The familiar mocking voice had no power to amuse her this morning. She felt sick suddenly at the whole notion of what had been done. She could not bear to think of the young fair boy hanging from the bedpost. She said:

"It was a joke not in your usual good taste, Lucien. If you will pardon me, I will go and make arrangements for the burial."

"And for mine—damn you!" he flung after her. "You can weep for the pair of us. Helène, *Helène*—come back. How dare you leave me when I want you?"

But she did not go back. She was, for the first time, furiously angry with him, and ashamed; unwilling to do his bidding.

The wicked old man turned his face to the pillow. He chortled, then suddenly began to moan and gasp while the lean wolf, Death, crept nearer, and lay at the foot of the four-poster bed—so near that his foul breath mingled with the breath of the man called "Satyr" for whom he waited.

Chapter Eight

For the first time since he had joined James Wilberson in the East India Company, Harry openly clashed with him.

Harry had gone down to Chiswick after an urgent summons from his adoptive uncle. He had ridden there rather than be driven for it was a fine May morning. Bright sunshine touched Mr. Wilberson's formal garden, full of Dutch tulips, with a golden radiance. But there was no brightness to be seen on the countenance of either of the men who greeted each other, then walked up and down one of the flagged paths talking, while a groom rubbed down Harry's mare.

The older man, clad in sober black, and without wig, stopped a moment in his paces and, with hands locked behind his back, regarded his adopted nephew, his eyes sad but stern.

"Truly, Harry, you disappoint me. What valid reason can you possibly give me for not wishing to sail with me to the East Indies next month?"

Harry, who was also without wig, his dark chestnut hair tied back with a ribbon, muttered something about the heat of the sun, and discarded his coat. Standing there in his white shirt with the full billowing sleeves, and cravat, he looked still a mere boy, thought Mr. Wilberson, yet he was ageing fast. There were many new lines etched round the handsome eyes. What a strange character he was—such a mixture of strength and weakness. That accident over four years ago had at first reduced him to a gloomy morbid-minded, introspective man. He had abandoned all the sensual delights almost ready to shut himself away in the seclusion of a monastery. Yet—once having made up his mind to accompany Mr. Wilberson to India—his health had gradually improved and his mental balance been restored. It was as though that bullet had never lodged in his skull nor caused his lapse of memory. He worked hard and had done well and a few months ago Mr. Wilberson had fondly believed Harry to be a made-man. He had seemed normal and he had, like any other young ardent man, indulged in light love affairs. But now all was changed and for the worse. He was on the decline again; not this time an habitué of the gaming clubs, not wishful to enter tavern brawls nor seek the company of harlots. But worse, Mr. Wilberson pondered gloomily. For he was infatuated with a married woman. Mr. Wilberson had made his own inquiries and was fully aware of the danger of this mad passion. The Marquise de Chartellet was reputed to possess a fatal combination of beauty, of siren charm, and high intelligence. She was destroying the boy. With all his heart, James Wilberson wished *Madame la Marquise* farther. *The devil take her,* he thought this morning, and gave a sharp sigh. *And more fool Harry to allow himself to be thus ensnared.* Suddenly James broke out:

"There is only one reason why you will not come with me—it is this woman who has you in her toils."

Harry flushed.

"If so, then I am satisfied with my enslavement. I must crave your pardon, Uncle James, if it grieves you, but I love the Marquise de Chartellet and *I mean that I love her.* It is no passing fancy, I do assure you."

Wilberson stooped and examined one of his rose trees. In his spare moments, he loved to tend his garden. He loved this house which had been built in the reign of good Queen Anne; the house and all his possessions which would after his death pass to Harry.

"Why, *why* cannot you conquer your insane passion and turn to the love of a pure young girl whom you can make your wife?" he broke out earnestly. He laid a hand on Harry's shoulder, adding: "You know well the regard in which I hold you, lad. Do not let this terrible obsession wipe out the hard work and promise of four long years."

Harry was moved but obdurate—the older man could see that. He stirred restlessly under Mr. Wilberson's hand and averted his face.

"Forgive me, sir," he said in a low voiçe, "but I am pledged to *Madame la Marquise* now and for all time."

"But why, *why*?"

"To that, I myself do not altogether know the answer."

"I hear that she has a most disturbing beauty and great wit, but I beg you to recollect that she has also a husband."

"He is old and may die."

"Would you then wed his widow? Could she give you children? Is she not older than yourself?"

"No, she is younger. Young enough to be the daughter of the man whom she has married—even the grand-daughter. Any-how, there is no question of marriage at the moment, I assure you. But far from the lady ensnaring me, she is most difficult to approach and when you ask why I must love her, it is because there is a strange and inexplicable bond between us. Indeed, there are times when I do believe that I knew her before *this*——," and Harry touched the scar on his brow significantly.

Mr. Wilberson sighed.

"I fail to understand. I only know that you refuse to accompany me on an important business which would do you much good. You have money of your own, yes, but once you were ambitious and eager to take my place in The East India Company. I was even sure you would in time supersede me. Oh, Harry, the Governor-General in India, himself, is willing to grant you an audience. You could secure a position in Council of real power."

"Yes—but in India!" Harry reminded him.

"For a few years only."

"I cannot leave England even for a few years," said Harry in a low voice.

"So as to be with her?"

"Yes."

"Is this your final word?"

Harry hesitated. He saw that his adoptive uncle's face was worn and unhappy. He felt so ungrateful—loth to distress the kindly gentleman to whom he owed so much. Then he remembered *her*. He shut his eyes. In that instant, so strong was the power of memory that his whole sensual being felt the bewitching loveliness of that voluptuous body in his arms; he could inhale her perfume and feel the satin smoothness of her gleaming hair threaded through his feverish fingers. He could look into the inscrutable, velvety eyes—alluring, yet bidding him ever remember that she was not *his. Oh God!* he thought, *she has promised to send for me and if all the wealth of India were laid before me now, I would not take it, for it would mean abandoning the hope of making her mine!*

Ever since the night of the de Chartellet reception, he had waited for that message from Helène. None had come. He had not even been allowed to write to her, nor call at her house. She had forbidden it. At times he walked the streets like one possessed of the devil; or rode his mare out of town and across the common in a wild effort to fatigue himself so that he might sleep and, in sleep, forget his longing. For a long time he stood there, wrapped in gloomy passionate reflections.

"Uncle James——" he began, opening his eyes. But he found that the older man had slipped quietly away. He was alone. When he re-entered the house, one of the men-servants handed him a note. It said:

> There are many things that I can forgive a foolish wayward young man and you are as dear to me as though you are my own son but I cannot stand by and watch you ruin yourself for the sake of this woman. I shall not sail for India until the end of May. I give you until then to make up your mind. If you do not come with me I must ask you to move your things from my house and to consider our relationship at an end.

Harry lifted his eyes from this note and asked the man where Mr. Wilberson was to be found. He was told that the gentleman had left hastily for London.

Harry set his teeth. So it was to be war with Uncle James. That hurt. He was immensely fond of him and they had had great times together. He could never forget the tact or the patience shown him by Mr. Wilberson in those first months after his terrible accident.

The last thing he wanted was for the old ties with Mr. Wilberson and his home to be broken. True he had Porrington Abbey and his own means, but he had, in truth, always enjoyed his work in The East India Company. It suited his temperament to have an interesting job. *But he could not give up Helène.* Whatever the outcome of this terrible searing love that had swept like a tornado into his life—he could not relinquish it.

He bowed his head, wrote a swift note begging Mr. Wilberson to be patient and to bear with him, then left Chiswick. There was a lump in his throat as he rode away from the little house where the Dutch tulips flaunted their brave heads. He had spent many peaceful, happy moments there. But go to India and leave Helène—no—that was impossible!

If she does not send for me soon, my whole life will come to an end, he thought extravagantly.

As he rode through the outskirts of London, a flower-girl—pretty in a coarse way—flung him a carnation from her basket.

"God save you, handsome young gentleman," she laughed up at him.

He caught the flower, kissed it gallantly and tossed her a gold piece. Years ago he would have dismounted and claimed more than a kiss for that guinea for she had a ripe mouth and a challenging eye. But the Harry of today felt no desire for any woman in the world save one. He felt weary and depressed when he reached the small dwelling on Knightsbridge Green which he occupied during the winter. He had not yet moved to Porrington Abbey, his summer residence. All kinds of unhappy little details of his life and association with Uncle James kept nagging at his conscience. How dearly the older man liked to accompany him to the Opera, for he had an ear for music; or play a game of backgammon during the long winter evenings, or ask his help, as he had been doing before Christmas, in compiling his first book ever to be written on the history of The East India Company.

All would be finished, Harry brooded, if he would not give up Helène.

The servant who had replaced the faithful but forgotten Vincent, opened the door to Sir Harry and at once handed him a note.

"This came, urgently, for you just after you left London this morning, sir," he said.

Harry fingered the envelope. His name was written on it in violet ink and in a flourishing hand upon thick cream-coloured vellum. Turning the envelope over he saw a strange crest on the seal. Upon closer examination his heart gave a violent leap. Now he knew it to be the crest of the de Chartellets, for he recognized that heraldic design—a falcon with outstretched wings and claws gripping a gloved fist. He had first seen it carved in stonework over a fireplace in the hall at The Bastille. He had not recognized the handwriting, for it was the first time that Helène had ever written to him. *At last.* At last, he thought, and white with excitement tore open the envelope.

What he saw written staggered him, although at the same time it sent the excited blood mounting to his head. She *had* sent for him. But it was the place she had chosen for the tryst that astonished him. Nay, it was incredible, he told himself. Why, *why there*? He re-read Helène's imperious note as though he could not credit his eyesight.

> If you will go to Pillars at three o'clock on Sunday afternoon you will find me awaiting you. On no account are you to try to see me before, nor get to the house a moment earlier. If you do, you will never see me again. Till we meet, therefore,
>
> Helène.

Harry stared and pondered, his pulses racing madly, his mind much confused. Why *Pillars*, he kept asking himself; Pillars of all places? How came it that she knew of his solitary house by the lake? Of course she might have been told—or he in course of conversation must have informed her of the existence of the General's old shooting estate. But why in heaven's name pick upon *that* for their *rendezvous*? He could have chosen a hundred places more beautiful and idyllic for a lovers' tryst.

Harry remained both startled and dumbfounded but he had to console himself with the thought that she had kept her word. Obviously she meant to stay with him. *Tomorrow* was Sunday. Dear heaven how could he bear to wait these twenty-four hours. He would be driven insane. Best, he thought wryly, to go to the club and play faro all night for he would not sleep one wink. *Pillars!* It was indeed bewildering that Helène should have made that much neglected house her choice. Since his accident, Harry, himself, had avoided going there. Not only was it discoloured for him by the attempt upon his life and his subsequent illness, but by the fact he could remember nothing of the assassination, nor his existence before it. It somewhat unnerved him to think what a large slice of life had been cut right out of his memory. After his return from India he had grown self-conscious about it, and when old friends approached him, either pretended to remember them—or passed them by. But he never spoke of the past. If he strove at times to remember things now obscured from him, it produced a violent headache, and his physicians had forbidden him to make the effort. For that reason alone, he avoided Pillars. Yet he never tried to sell the estate. Without understanding the reason, something within the dark recess of his mind had rendered him reluctant to take any such action.

No one was there now who had known him or Sir Arthur. The Snellings had gone; the man dead and his widow, Martha, returned to her own people. Harry had installed an elderly caretaker, a widower, with a young son in his teens who attended to the garden.

Several times during the rest of that day, Harry was tempted to get in touch with the Marquise and beg her to reconsider her plan to meet him at Pillars. But each time he feared to do so lest he incurred her displeasure and she called the meeting off. Neither dared he follow his first inclination which was to go at once to the little house and prepare it for his lady's arrival. Whatever the strange reason, she seemed to wish to be there first. A woman's whim; well, let it be so! When Harry thought of her waiting there and of all it would mean, the house by the lake seemed to lose its sadness and take on the rosy hues of paradise.

Harry Roddney became a new man. Holding his lady's letter against his heart, he called for his servant and ordered wine and food. His eyes sparkled. His fine long limbs tingled with joyous anticipation. The rift between his adoptive uncle and himself was forgotten.

Chapter Nine

Helène was filled with the most inexplicable emotions when at last she drove through the wrought-iron gateway and up the drive that led to Pillars. She had come in a high travelling carriage, with two out-riders and two postillions wearing the de Chartellet livery. Once deposited at the portico of the house which was so familiar and the mere sight of which caused her intolerable pain—she dismissed the equipage.

"Return for me here this time tomorrow," she said.

The head coachman bowed low, replaced his cocked hat and whipped up the horses. It seemed a strange place to leave his lady but it was not for him to question what *Madame la Marquise* chose to do.

Helène stood motionless watching the handsome carriage roll down the drive. That avenue of limes, exquisitely green with the first leaves of the spring—how terribly familiar it looked—and those fine clipped yews shaped like birds, and the wisteria breaking into purple bloom across the portico. Turning, she caught a glimpse of the lake, shining silver in the sun. This Sunday morning was fair and warm with a blue sky. Spring was in the air. The place looked deserted, she thought, but well kept with clipped lawns and even flowers in the beds. The roses would soon be breaking into bloom. She saw a flight of heron moving gracefully across the sky and listened to their strange cries. The sound depressed her. No human being was in sight. All the windows were shuttered. The whole place had a forlorn, even tragic air.

She drew her fur-trimmed pelisse closer about her shoulders and with one gloved hand fingered, nervously, the ribbons with which her high calash bonnet was trimmed. At her feet, as instructed, one of the coachmen had placed her bag. She intended to stay here the night. Yes, that was what she had planned. Unless Harry was reduced to shame, and when he received her note and saw the name of the place she had fixed for their meeting, failed to come. There could be no dissembling for Harry this time. He must know now what she felt about the thing he had done to her here, four years ago. So far he had been so monstrously callous as to avoid the issue. He had hoped in his fine conceit and false pride to win her regard for the second time, without allusion to the past; wished to obliterate all memory of Fauna the slave.

But it was not Helène who stood here dreaming this May morning. The years rolled back and it was Fauna, tender-hearted, sensitive, innocent, most desperately in love. Fauna, abandoned to her fate. Here, she thought, shuddering, she had been forced into a hackney carriage by Miguel Lopez and found the loathsome toad-like Mrs. Clack waiting for her with her pinching fingers and vile tongue. *Here* she had learned to live and here had spiritually died; murdered by Harry Roddney. Yes, murdered by a sensual selfish heartless rake of a boy.

She began to tremble with anger, with the deep passions that the very sight of this place revived in her. It was almost too much, she thought; yet she must remain calm and strong; as strong as Lucien would have her be. She had come here to put an end to Harry Roddney's life—just as he had ended hers in a different way. But she felt infinitely bereft; never more alone in the whole of her life, even in those days when she had been Fauna.

What had she left to live for? Lucien was dying; Surenne gave him another two or three days—no more. It was a wonder, they said, that he had lived so long. Now at last he was fighting a losing battle.

She tried not to think of Lucien in connexion with the suicide of young Aubrey Burkett which had so shocked and disgusted her. She had not been able to hide her repugnance towards him for the infamous deceit practised upon the unfortunate boy.

The Marquis, however, showed no sign of conscience and he had looked, when she left him, like a malevolent old idol with his shaven head and wizened face, propped up in bed, grinning at her.

"The best of luck attend your lovers' meeting," he had croaked. "Would I were not a sick man and could be there to see you when all is over. Come straight back, *ma mie*, I have not long in which to enjoy your delightful society."

"I shall return at once," she had answered stónily.

"I beg you not to weaken," he added.

"I shall not weaken," she had replied in the same stony voice.

Within a tapestry bag she carried, there lay a hard cold weapon; her pistol. The same one with which Lucien, at The Bastille, had first taught her to shoot. She was a good shot. She was not likely to bungle it. No—and there could be no place for both herself and Harry Roddney in this world. Of that she was now certain.

But the coldness of despair settled upon her. A sickness as of a blight began to creep through her whole being as she knocked upon the front door of Pillars.

Almost she wished she had not dismissed her carriage. Almost she felt inclined to abandon this revenge, never see Harry again and return to Lucien's bedside. Lucien was about to die. Monstrously though he behaved, she supposed she must find excuses for him because he was, in his way, a genius and his mentality had become warped and abnormal. And he had been good to her. He had fought pain and his approaching end with a fortitude that commanded all her admiration. She had not really wanted to leave him this morning but he had insisted. He could not die happy, he said, until this thing concerning Harry Roddney was done.

She had expected to find the Snellings here and was disappointed when a strange man with a plump rosy face and iron-grey curls came round from the back of the house, a barking mongrel at his heels, to see who was knocking.

He touched his cap with respect as he saw the tall lady in her fine clothes. When she asked for Snelling, he informed her that Mr. Snelling had been buried this past year and that he, Caleb Finch, was the present caretaker for Sir Harry Roddney.

Helène considered this, then said:

"Sir Harry is meeting me here at three o'clock. I am early for the *rendezvous* and will wait."

Mr. Finch bowed and his rosy face grew redder. He looked pleased. It was a lonely life he led here with his young son. Nobody ever called, except Sir Harry's bailiff.

"It will be a pleasure to serve you, ma'am—milady——" he stuttered excitedly. "Nowt is prepared but soon will be, milady, I will send my boy, Tom, to the farm over yonder field to fetch victuals. Your ladyship will soon want a meal. It is nearing midday. What can I offer your ladyship? There are wines in the cellar, but I have not the key and——"

"Wine can wait until Sir Harry comes," interrupted Helène, "I require little—only a light repast. But I am cold and I know this house. It has been shut up; it will be damp. Light fires both upstairs and down. Prepare the big bed-chamber and the one adjoining it, overlooking the lake."

"Yes, milady—at once—at once!"

And the good Mr. Finch stared at the lady. In mercy's name, who was she, with her wonderful black eyes of a beauty such as Caleb Finch had never seen in his life before. She knew the house well, too, obviously. Wonders would never cease. He rushed away, calling for his son and vowing that he would immediately unlock the front door for her ladyship.

The mongrel lingered and sidled up to Helène wagging and seeking to lick her hand. She stroked the animal's dusty coat mechanically, then pushed it away. She did not want affection even from an animal. She did not want to be made to feel any kind of tenderness. For Fauna had felt great tenderness, yes—and all the generosity of first young love. For Helène de Chartellet there could be only a bitter passion, without mercy; and for Harry the kiss of death. It did not seem to matter what happened *afterwards*.

Within a few hours, Pillars had changed its aspect. The shuttered sinister house became once more a gracious dwelling, windows open to the sun and wood fires crackling in the grates. Caleb, who was something of a cook, busied himself in the kitchen, baking and roasting. The whole place was cleaned and garnished. Helène, without bonnet and pelisse, wearing a long close-fitting dress of rich brown velvet which had frilled ruffles at throat and wrists, and her unpowdered hair shining in the sun, walked in the gardens after her meal.

She looked like an ordinary, young, beautiful girl as she gathered flowers and put them in a basket. She arranged those flowers with unerring taste in the small library and upstairs in the big double room overlooking the lake.

She might have been the happiest of young women beautifying these rooms as for a bridal. A guileless maid waiting for her lover. With a touch of nervousness, she walked now and then into the library to look at the French ormolu clock. The last time she had noted that the hands were at a quarter-to-three. If Harry meant to obey her command, he should be here within fifteen minutes. *If he came. . . .*

Despite all her efforts to remain tranquil, there was no quiet in her heart, and no pleasurable anticipation. Neither did she feel as harsh or ruthless as she wished. Every now and then her nerve almost forsook her and she trembled as though with ague. She was pale under the delicate colour which she had applied to her cheeks. She wished she had never ascended the staircase and surveyed that room which the young Fauna had once shared with her lover. She hated every memory of that sweet shared passion, when the curtains were drawn around the great four-poster bed and the fragrant wood fire burned to ash in the grate and the snow was falling, falling, burying the grounds of Pillars under a white shroud. ***Oh, would God she, too, had died and been buried under that kindly snow***. It was ***Fauna*** who made that bitter cry. Fauna the quadroon slave who waited for Harry rather than the Helène whom Lucien de Chartellet had created.

She told herself that she must conquer these emotions or her schemes would come to nothing and all would be ruined. She knew, too, that if she weakened now because of Harry's charm or the old sentimental memories, she would ever afterwards despise herself.

She kept asking herself questions; how Harry would greet her, by what name he would call her, whether he would at once refer to the past and ask her pardon, or if he would continue to brazen the thing out and say nothing. She did not know; she could only make conjectures. But at a few minutes past three, she heard, suddenly, the clip-clop of a horse's hoofs. She ran to the front window and saw a yellow-wheeled curricle coming up the drive; and in it the lone figure of Harry, driving a high-stepping handsome chestnut.

The blood tore to Helène's cheeks and receded. Her pulses leapt—subsided. With a fatalistic look in her eyes she watched him come nearer—nearer, towards his doom. Then all pity, all softness left her. With her emotions culminating into a single desire to avenge that young Fauna whom he had so abominably betrayed—she went forward to meet him.

Chapter Ten

For Helène, that afternoon and evening, following the hour of Harry's arrival, were heavy with impending doom.

It was as though she could hear deep down within her the chant of a strange song, savage and sinister, commenced maybe in the kraals of her grandfather's village on the fringe of the African swamps. It had the slow repetitive beat of native drums. It had followed her all through childhood and adolescence just as surely as the blood beat in her temples. That portion of black blood in her could never be anything but primitive and compelling and hotly passionate and she knew it. The chant was swelling now to a crescendo. She could hear it drowning all other sounds, all the pleasant little melodies of civilization. The piercing sweetness of thrushes nesting in the high trees outside Pillars. The call of water-birds on the lake veiled in the lilac mist of twilight. The crackle of wood-logs in the grate —the tinkle of glass and silver and delicate china, as Caleb Finch laid the supper table and uncorked the wine that Harry had chosen. Helène had changed for supper from the brown dress which had made her look such a girl into a more sophisticated black velvet gown, unrelieved by jewellery. Her face was milk-white. Even her usually red lips were paler than usual. Her eyes looked immense under the languorous lashes, and were darkly sombre. She had brushed her hair into a red cloud—it floated to her waist in a profusion of rich curls.

When Harry first saw her enter the library thus, something about her appearance startled him. She seemed to bear no resemblance to the elegant, jewel-covered Marquise de Chartellet to whom he was accustomed. She was magnificent, yet the very severity of her attire gave her an air of new and extraordinary secretiveness. He did not want her so. He wanted a brilliant voluptuous Helène ready to melt into his embrace. He wanted the fire that simmered under the ice. This was a strange unsmiling stranger who made him feel uncomfortable.

And indeed, this was how Harry had felt ever since his arrival. At first he had been enchanted by the sight of the lovely girl waiting to welcome him into a warm sunny house full of flowers. He had feared to find the place full of ghosts with the chill of a tomb about it. He had laughed at such presentiments.

"I could not at first imagine why you wished to meet me here," he had told Helène, "but I quite like the place today. It seems as good as any, for here we shall most certainly be alone and undisturbed."

She smiled in that enigmatic way which never failed to intrigue him. He was in excellent spirits—greatly excited—like a boy, wishful to please her; warm, generous, full of the joy of life.

He brought her a great gilded basket of magnificent flowers; bonbons in extravagant be-ribboned boxes; a hamper of delicacies which he knew were not to be found in an Essex retreat. And other gifts which he laid at her feet, then covered her hands with kisses, behaving for all the world as though he had not a care on his mind.

This attitude, which would have enchanted any woman under normal circumstances, both astonished and irritated Helène. She found him monstrously insolent. She hardened her heart against the ardent handsome young man, despite his *largesse*. How could he act in such a manner, she asked herself, indignantly. Even *here* in this very place where he had abandoned her to an awful fate, he offered not one single word of contrition. He was shameless. This sin, alone, she could not forgive—this almost idiotic effort he made to gloss over the past; this game of pretence which he continued to play. While she watched and listened to him—he poured out to her in words his delight at being allowed to entertain her—and the unparalleled love he bore her—she imagined that she understood. It would spoil things for him to bring back Fauna and the past by so much as admitting their existence. Much better to live in the present as the acknowledged lover of the Marquise de Chartellet. He was a coward among other things. He did not wish to face up to unpleasant truths—more especially if they reflected upon his own character.

So the hours sped by for these two in complete misunderstanding, lacking all harmony except that neither could gainsay the terrible and potent magnet of desire which drew them to each other.

Ere darkness fell, Harry insisted on wrapping Helène in her fur mantle and walking with her down to the edge of the lake. The water looked almost purple now, with the dark sheen of metal, fringed by slender birches. A pair of crested grebes skimmed upon the surface, ruffling it for a moment, then vanished. The beechwoods and surrounding pastureland lay silent and beautiful.

"Spring lends this place a new enchantment," said Harry putting an arm around Helène's waist and drawing her to his side. "And you, my dear love, cast a spell upon Pillars more potent than spring. I grow more glad each hour that you suggested we should come here."

Her eyes narrowed. She said nothing. In one part of her being she suffered a deep desolation; the despairing wish that this thing had never happened; that she had been neither Fauna nor Helène but some humble peasant girl who could stand here with her simple lover. Harry went on talking, a kind of nervous excitement urging him on, not knowing how he blundered.

"When did the idea first come to you? Who told you of Pillars?" he persisted.

Now she moved away from his arm, angered.

"You know well, Harry," she said and looked at him bleakly.

He was without peruke, thick hair tied back naturally as she like it. He wore also the colour he knew to be her favourite—a coat of fine green cloth with high upstanding collar and huge pockets, knee-breeches and silken hose (Harry had a shapely leg and could be proud of it). Oh, he was handsome, yes—and more charming than any man she had ever known. She had met men wiser, richer and in more exalted positions. But never one like this, whose eyes, gay or serious, had power to touch her very heart-strings. It was as well, she told herself bitterly, that she had her emotions in check tonight, and well, too, that his pretended innocence, his silent refusal to admit past guilt, detracted from any pity she might have felt for him. In this fatal hour, she might still feel pity for herself, but not too much lest it turn her from her purpose.

"You are silent—I do all the chattering," said Harry suddenly. "I asked where you learnt first about Pillars?"

"And I answered," she said furiously, "that you *know*."

He pulled his ear in genuine perplexity then shrugged his shoulders and laughed.

"Oh, yes, I do remember now," he said and told himself that it must have been he, himself, who had spoken to her of the estate. But he saw no cause for her annoyance. Were she not his *belle Helène* who could do no wrong, he might have accused her of being ill-tempered this night. But if 'twere so, he thought, it merely made her more human, more attractive. He tried to put an arm about her again.

"Do you grow cold? Shall we walk back to the house?"

She went with him, silently.

So he had admitted that he *knew*. So much and no more; yet he still could be so callous. It passed her understanding and increased her furious longing to avenge that innocent young girl who had trusted him with her very life.

As they entered Pillars, mellow with the light from the candles which Caleb had lit throughout, Helène heard again the echo of that low sinister beat of approaching tragedy. She clenched her teeth and took a fresh grip on her emotions.

Harry placed her in a chair and poured her out a glass of wine. Then he raised his own glass to his lips.

"To my lovely lady," he said, drank the wine to the dregs, then let the goblet, which was exquisite, drop into the stone fireplace where it shattered.

"Will you do likewise with yours," he asked her, "so that no other lips save ours shall ever touch the two glasses with which we pledge our love?"

Now she went very pale.

"I cannot. You make it like a *sacrament*."

He knelt beside her, looking at her earnestly.

"Helène, is our love not sacred? Do you count it less?"

She avoided his gaze.

"You grow too serious," she muttered.

"Do you not wish me to be so?" he asked astonished.

"Have you come all this way to afford me so great an honour and delight, for *lighter* reasons?"

Suddenly she gave a wild laugh and rising, tossed down her own glass of wine and let it fall and smash in the fireplace, joining the fragments of his. Then she wreathed her arms about his neck.

"Very well. A toast to you, my lover. And what matter whether the passion between us be sacred or profane? I am in agreement with you, no other lips shall touch those goblets—and what happens tonight will never happen again; that, too, is a vow."

It was the first time she had made a physical gesture towards him since he arrived. He had been conscious of her coolness, but knowing her to be aloof and difficult, had taken it to be the usual sign of some remote shyness within her. But now she was warm and yielding. He whispered against her ear:

"I shall never altogether understand you, but I love you as Paris must have loved Helen of Troy and understand why a million men fought for her. Helène, *Helène*, say not that the love you bear me be profane."

"What matters?" she asked in the same wild mood and laughed in his arms, her long slender fingers caressing his hair. He felt himself drowning in those dark pools of her enormous eyes. He had never known her more crazy or provocative. He ceased to analyse or probe. For a moment they continued to embrace there in the candle-lit room. Caleb knocked on the door; the lovers did not hear and he went away again. Then Harry with some calm restored, said:

"Just now you suggested that this night might never be repeated. What happens will never happen again, you said. Is it then to be but one brief night of love? Ah, Helène, I would not have it so. I want you for more than my mistress for an hour or a day. I want you for my *wife*—till death claims us."

Tears of passion and of rage magnified her eyes but she laughed again.

"Why did you not speak such words to me years ago?"

He thought that she spoke now in symbols. He answered:

"Surely you realize that from the beginning of the world,

I have loved and wanted you for my own. My uncle has threatened to quarrel with me if I do not give you up. I do not care. If the Marquis knew that you were here tonight maybe he would wish to run me through with his sword. I care not for him, either."

"My husband is dying," she said, speaking harshly, and she thrust Harry away from her. "Tomorrow, when I return, he may be dead," she added half to herself.

Harry flung back his head.

"Then I can legitimately lay myself and my life at your feet."

She turned from him, shaking. He would have no life after tomorrow, she thought. *She could not bear him to live.* The strength of her own desire for him frightened her.

She said:

"Send for your manservant and let us eat. It grows late."

Supper was served on an oval table in front of the fire. An exquisite intimate little meal. Helène scarcely knew what she ate and she drank nothing. Harry was equally abstemious tonight. Across the silver candelabra, he looked at her pale bewitching face and floating hair. That hair was the only colour about her tonight. He thought her wild strange looks must be the outcome of her passion for him and adored her the more for such proof of her feelings. He quoted a verse for her:

"For over a hundred years, men have remembered Ben Jonson's poem and tonight it has a special meaning for me: *'Drink to me only with thine eyes and I will pledge with mine; or leave a kiss but in the cup, and I'll not look for wine.'* "

A little of Helène's wildness passed. She said reflectively:

" 'Twas a graceful verse, derived, you know, from Philostratus and dedicated to Celia, Jonson's mistress."

Harry's eyes kindled with admiration of her learning.

"I do not know which I love best—your glorious femininity or your scholarly love of learning which makes you second to none among the greatest ladies of today," he said.

Helène said nothing but twirled the stem of her empty glass and looked back to those days when she used to sit at

Lucien's feet in the huge library of The Bastille; listening to him, learning; through those long winters while the sea dashed upon the rocks and snow whitened the statue of the captive girl on the great stone horse. Lucien had likened her to that girl when first he saw her. Would God, she thought despairingly, she had never left The Bastille, but remained imprisoned there, like a nun, having no contact with the world. Would God she had taken no journey such as this, from which there could be no return. *Suddenly she knew now that when Harry died she must die with him.* She would never return to Lucien even if *he* still lived.

She got up, shivering from head to foot. Harry rose and anxiously approached her.

"My dear love, what ails you?"

"Oh, Harry," she said, and hers was the voice of a heart-broken girl. She put her arms around his neck and sobbed bitterly. He had never loved her more nor felt more completely enslaved by her, for this was Helène the true woman, and not a goddess whom he must fear to touch. He picked her up in his arms, covered her wet wild face with kisses, and carried her up the staircase to the room which had been prepared for them. A room full of firelight and gleaming candles and purple lilac which filled the air with intoxicating fragrance.

As he laid her down on the pillows an extraordinary feeling came over Harry. He clapped the back of his hand to his forehad. He felt as though someone had touched him with icy fingers and all the heat, the passion, went out of his body. Frowning he stared around him. *What did he remember about this room?* A pain started to throb in his temples; it troubled him exceedingly, because it was that same pain which used to attack him whenever he delved into the mists of his bruised mind. *He was trying to remember something now.* This was all terrifyingly familiar . . . the handsome firelit bedchamber, the four-poster bed and the girl lying upon it, half covered, with her cloud of red-gold hair.

Helène ceased to weep. She gazed up at him, once more mistress of herself, wary, resentful.

"Well?" she said in a sullen questioning voice.

"This room," he stammered, "you and I have been here before."

"*At last*, you admit it!"

But he was still confused. He answered at cross-purposes:

"Yes, yes, of course; this night was predestined."

She cried out:

"So you would betray me again!"

"God knows," he said astonished, "that I would not betray *you* nor could ever have done so even in another life, for I love you too well."

She pushed the hair from her face, panting, great eyes accusing.

"Harry, Harry Roddney, is that all you have to say to me?" she cried.

His confusion increased. He grew conscious of a sinister atmosphere creeping into the room, spoiling the moment which should have been the most wonderful of his life. Suddenly he bent down and kissed her lips so savagely that they were bruised against her teeth. He said:

"Let us have done with words. I can endure no more."

He walked from the room. She turned her face to the pillow, hands clenched, body convulsed. So he still intended to make her ignore what had happened between them before. Well—so far as she was concerned—it was the end; although a few moments ago, had he fallen at her feet and asked her forgiveness, she might have weakened sufficiently to grant it.

Now he should die. . . .

When Harry returned to her he found the room in darkness. She lay, as the girl, Fauna, had lain, white and defenceless in the great bed. But under the pillow one hand clutched the cold metal of her pistol. Her eyes were sunken in her face. But Harry did not see and did not care. It was for him the culmination of long months of hopeless longing. The world was blotted out. It was as it had been before—delight and ecstasy. But when he would have altered to a mood of tenderness, she thrust him aside and with trembling fingers lit the candle so that he could look upon her face.

"It is finished," she said, "I will have no more of you or you of me. *Now, Harry, you shall pay your debt.* Not to me, Helène, but to *Fauna the slave*."

He stared transfixed down at her beautiful terrible face. She sprang from the bed and tied her velvet robe around her. He, too, got up and stared at her. *Fauna. Why did she use that name?* He had heard it in the dim past during his illness here, four years ago, when he had lain in this very room. He had been told that he stayed with a girl named *Fauna* before he was found shot. He had thought then that the name was strange and intriguing; afterwards he had forgotten it.

Bewildered he continued to look at Helène. He found her complete and utter change of mood quite inexplicable.

"I do not understand——" he began.

But she had had enough and interrupted him. The savage beat of the mad music in her mind was swelling to such a high pitch that it drowned all other sounds, even that of Harry's voice. She drew the pistol and in a frenzy fired it. But her aim was far out, for her hand shook so that she could hardly hold the weapon. She heard the explosion and saw her lover stagger and fall. Immediately, like one demented, she flung away the smoking pistol and went down on her knees beside him. She forgot all that she had so long and coldly planned, and called upon his name.

"Harry, oh, God, *Harry*!"

She raised him in her arms. A trickle of blood poured down from his right eyebrow. She wiped it away, sobbing frenziedly. He opened his eyes and she saw now that the bullet had grazed his scalp but had not seriously wounded him. She sobbed again.

"Harry, *Harry*!"

To Harry Roddney it was as though he came out of a dark cavern of timelessness, of semi-oblivion. The bullet had narrowly missed a vital spot, and grazed the very scar made by that injury received four years ago. The sound of the explosion had seemed to crack through his head and temporarily extinguish the light. But now the light was returning, and with it a shock of remembrance. Time stood still. The years rolled back again. Suddenly Helène saw him smile, a wry boyish smile, and he put out a hand and touched her cheek.

"Fauna," he said, "my dear love, why did you wish to kill me? And how came you with one of my fire-arms and at this hour of night?"

She held her breath. She could neither move nor speak. The savage cadence throbbing within her deepest being was dying down. The drums grew fainter. The tempo of her heart resumed its normal count. She saw Harry rise to his feet and staggering a little, seat himself on the edge of the bed. She ran towards a powder-closet and fetched him a towel. She herself dabbed at the flesh wound over his brow. But still she could not find tongue. It was Harry who spoke again:

"You did not mean to to do it; of course you did not, my love. Do not fear, 'tis merely a scratch. If the sight of blood offends you, pray call Martha to attend me."

She put both her finger-tips against her mouth. She was dumbfounded. She whispered, in terror:

"Martha?"

A dazed look stole now into Harry's eyes. Holding the damask against his forehead, he frowned at Helène.

"I must say that I feel very unwell, little one. My head is decidedly odd. The shock, no doubt, has unnerved me. I will lie down a moment until the faintness passes. Open the window. 'Tis too hot in here. Tell me if the snow is still falling?"

Helène felt her spine creep. Her whole body began to tingle and quiver. *He was speaking as though they were here together as in the past.* Quite naturally, he used her name *Fauna.* He spoke of the Snellings—who were gone; of *the snow* as it had fallen when they were here on that winter's night. It was as though he did not realize that this was the month of May and that she had become *Helène de Chartellet.*

It was a shock for her and a singular one. She could be clear about only one thing—the enormity of her relief that he was not lying dead at her feet; that her attempt upon his life had failed. Once he was lying on the bed with eyes closed, she ran out into the corridor and called wildly for Caleb.

"Fetch a physician *at once.* There has been an accident," she breathed.

"Mercy on us, milady—I will saddle the horse and send Tom to the village this instant," the servant answered in a scared voice.

Thus it was that for the second time in his life, Angus Knox, Scots-born physician of the neighbourhood, was called out to Pillars to attend Sir Harry Roddney. But this time, not to dislodge a bullet from his brain, but to put a patch upon a graze of little importance once it ceased to bleed.

Helène, by this time fully dressed, did not reveal her identity. The old physician took it for granted that she was another of young Roddney's mistresses. Albeit, he decided, this one was an exceptionally handsome young woman who spoke with unusual authority and intelligence.

Harry had lapsed into a deep sleep which, the physician said, was good for him and from which he should awaken refreshed. Downstairs in the library, over a glass of wine, it fell to the lot of Dr. Knox to tell Helène the whole truth about Harry, that truth which had so far been hidden from her.

Knox described in detail the attempted assassination upon Harry four years ago and the arrival of the General and his young wife, and Harry's long illness that followed.

"Alack, the poor General and his lady perished before their time. 'Twas pitiful, and especially since Sir Arthur never lived to see the great change for good in his rake of a nephew," said Knox. "I was in correspondence once or twice with Mr. Wilberson who told me that my young patient had entered The East India Company and mended his ways remarkably."

Helène listened with bated breath. Her agitation and astonishment increased with every word the old doctor was saying. At last she exclaimed:

"So Sir Harry has suffered from loss of memory all these four years. He remembers *nothing* of what had happened before he was shot?"

"Nothing at all. And for a long time he was morbid—even suicidal; we feared the worst. But Mr. Wilberson renewed in him the will to live and make a new life for himself, and after that his natural intelligence and the resilience of youth came to his aid."

"He remembered nothing," repeated Helène in a whisper. "Nothing about *me*."

"You?" asked Knox and stared at her over the rim of his glasses.

She said in a low, choked voice:

"I, sir, was the red-haired girl who you say stayed here with Sir Harry before he was attacked."

The physician cleared his throat.

"Dear me, *tush, tush,*" he said, for he was a godly man of righteous habits and did not approve of such happenings.

Helène's heart beat madly fast. Through her exhausted body and mind there gradually stole a joy so great that she hardly knew how to bear it. For now she understood all. Now she knew how deeply she had wronged poor Harry. He had not been dissembling; he had not attempted to play a coward's game, nor to avoid the consequences of his sin. *He had never recognized her.* He had not in the past committed an act of betrayal. That was the most wonderful thing of all. She knew that it must have been Miguel Lopez who had struck him down. Had *that* not happened, Harry would never have deserted her.

And she might have killed him.

"Oh, God, God, have mercy on me," her lips framed the words.

Aloud she said:

"You think, sir, that he will remember everything when he wakes again?"

"Without doubt, for you say his mind reverted to the past when he first recovered from the shock of the bullet which you tell me—ahem—was fired tonight in accident," said Knox, coughing.

Helène nodded. The tears were rolling down her cheeks. It was her wish, she told Dr. Knox, that he should remain here until Harry awakened, in case he needed attention. But when, in the early hours of that morning, the young man unclosed his eyes, he seemed to be strangely well and refreshed and had not even a headache. Then he became aware of Helène sitting beside him in her brown velvet dress and with her hair tied back with a ribbon, and her face pale but inexpressibly tender. The old name immediately sprang to his lips.

"Fauna."

She had thought that word must for ever hold all the horror and bitterness on earth, yet now there was new magic in it. The very way he used it, and looked at her, freed him of guilt and put him back upon his old pedestal.

"Harry, oh, Harry, my love," she said and knelt beside him and laid her head on his bosom.

He put an arm about her. He grew confused again.

"Why did I call you that? I know you also as *Helène*. Great heavens, what does it mean? You are not *Fauna* but the *Marquise de Chartellet*."

"I am both," she said, "and both women love you dearly and beg your pardon for ever having doubted you. Oh, Harry, I shall never forgive myself. I so nearly took your life, which is dearer to me than my own."

He stroked her hair and lay silent a moment. Gradually more memories were returning and with them great wonder.

"I am vastly perplexed," he said. "I beg you to tell me everything."

She told him and as it was made clear, bewilderment cleared from Harry's mind. But still in a great wonder and daze, he looked at the lovely head cradled on his breast.

"Fauna," he said in an unbelieving voice, "*Fauna*, the slave, and she has become this remarkable woman, and the wife of Lucien de Chartellet! It hardly makes sense."

"Nevertheless it is true."

"Most extraordinary!"

"I should have realized all the way along that you did not recognize me," she choked. "I cannot excuse myself for the bitterness I directed towards you."

"You could not know. I never told you. Much of our conversation must have been at cross-purposes. You see—when I first returned from India—I said little to anybody about my accident or illness. My physicians forbade me to harass my mind and I thought it best that I should live only in the present and try to obliterate the past entirely."

She took one of his hands and kissed it.

"I love you," she said in a broken voice.

"There," he said, "speaks *Fauna*."

She raised her head and looked at him, her great eyes full of tears.

"No, here speaks Helène. I have no more pride. I know no other desire but to serve you, as once before."

"Hush," he said, "you have travelled a long way since then—you must never use the word 'serve' to me. It is I who shall be *your* servant, as well as your lover. All I would have you remember is that I would never in this life willingly have sent you back to such horror as you have recounted to me."

"I do know it now."

"And I," he said, "know such great love for you that I desire only to make you my adored wife."

"You would wed a quadroon?" she reminded him in a low voice.

He put a hand under his chin and tilted her head.

"The quadroon is my love. I desired her long before I was struck by the lightning glance of *La Belle Helène*."

"Bravely spoken," she whispered.

"And what now?" he asked. "For my Fauna remains Helène, wife to de Chartellet."

"Lucien is not long for this world," she reminded him with a sigh.

"Then you shall become my most honoured wife."

"No, Harry," she said in a choked voice, "with such blood in my veins, I could not bear you children."

"That is the one thing I wish to ignore and you must forget," he said. "It is of no importance whatsoever. I love you and you must never leave me. You have tried once already to kill me. Would you seek to destroy me again?"

She flung herself upon him, covering his face with kisses.

"Harry, do not remind me of it, for the memory congeals my blood."

For the first time a touch of humour lightened Harry's smile.

"My beautiful most erudite Helène, there is one thing that Harry Roddney will never teach you; how to shoot as well as you do other things."

Now it was her turn to smile, also.

"Believe me, Lucien looks upon me as a crack marksman," she said. "I *was*, Harry, I do assure you."

"Then I thank my stars that you did not exhibit your good marksmanship in my case."

She bowed her head, and he opened his arms to her.

"Come, sweet—kiss me, then bid the old doctor go home for I want no more of him; but only to be allowed to greet this enchanted dawn alone with you."

Suddenly she heard the sound of a horse galloping through the quiet countryside. It grew so plain that she rose from her knees, parted the curtains, and looked out. The sun was rising. A million cobwebs sparkled over the smooth lawns and there was a faint mist tangled in the trees. The birds were waking, piping. The lake was ruffled by a breeze. Then she saw a single rider coming at a full gallop down the drive. Leaning out farther, she saw and recognized him. She turned back to the bed.

" 'Tis a messenger for me, Harry. One of Lucien's men."

"Go, see what he wants, then return to me," Harry said drowsily and shut his eyes. He was feeling vastly content, and not yet used to the extraordinary change of his circumstances, nor to the never-ending wonder of realization that *Fauna* and *Helène* were one and the same.

When his love returned, he saw that she looked grave. She held a letter in her hand.

"It is from Dr. Surenne and written shortly before midnight," she said. "I had left this address with him in case of an emergency."

Harry said:

"The Marquis——?"

"Is dead."

A moment's silence, then from Harry in a low voice:

"I would be a hypocrite to say that I grieve for the Satyr, but I do say in all honesty: '*God rest his soul.*' "

Helène bit her lip. There was a strange brooding look in her wonderful eyes. She, too, could not turn hypocrite and weep for Lucien, but she knew that a great scholar had passed and with him, she had lost a great friend.

"He did not believe in God," she said in a low troubled tone, "and there have been times when I thought him in league with the devil. But he did much for me. I cannot be otherwise than grateful."

Harry nodded.

"For so much, I, too, respect him," he said.

Helène returned to her letter, reading it there by the open window, while the cool morning breeze stirred her curls.

"Surenne says that he died bravely, still jesting. He sent me a message. It is strange but I understand it as I always understood him."

"What does he say?"

Bid my wife farewell for me. Tell her I grieve that I shall never see her again, yet am I glad that I know not the outcome of her journey, for it would assuredly have proved a disappointment.

"What does that mean?" asked Harry.

She came to his side and looked down at him.

"Lucien was a strange, cynical and sometimes sadistic person," she said thoughtfully. "Yet to me, always kind, except that he could not bear me to grow sentimental. He was afraid, you see, that I might weaken when I came to you yesterday. That is what he meant in his farewell message—he was thankful he did not live to see me smile upon you again. He wanted me to be strong in my hate. A malicious man, yet one of his greatest worries while he was so ill was lest I forget to attend to his aquarium."

Harry frowned.

"A strange creature, indeed."

"Nevertheless," added Helène, "had he known the facts he would have accepted them. He might even have offered to release me in your favour. A queer, unpredictable man."

"God rest his soul," repeated Harry.

Helène stood up.

"There is but one thing I could have taught Lucien, my great teacher—that there IS such a thing as love—the kind of love that endures through all time, its roots untouched by cynicism or desire for vengeance. Had I done you any real harm, Harry, I would have put an end to my own life."

He stretched out his hand to her.

"For pity's sake do not refer to it."

She gave him a long look from her marvellous eyes.

"I do so love you, my own Harry. It is hard even now for me to realize that I am free and that the nightmare-past is ended and all made clear."

"I do not deserve your love but will seek a way of becoming worthy," he said.

She looked again at the dew pearled on the lawns, and all the fresh radiance of the new day. She thought of the wonder of this discovery that Harry had after all remained, first and last, her undoubted lover. She thought, too, of the cynical old man lying upon his bier in the great London house, infinitely alone in death, while the sad candles burned at his head and his feet. She said:

"Harry, my dear, I must leave you and return to my house. There is much for me to do and I think it best we do not meet again for a time."

Harry raised himself on his elbow, his face flushing.

"Let me come with you—oh, do not forbid me to see you for I fear you might be spirited away from me again."

She came close and put her hand in his.

"Nothing shall do that. I am for ever yours. But I must stay alone for a period of time and afford Lucien the honour and respect his wife should pay the dead Marquis de Chartellet."

"I understand. Then I had best go to my Uncle James in Chiswick and inform him of the Marquis's passing and of my intent to marry you. He will, perhaps, be pleased. More especially if I can tell him that you will accompany me on the business journey he wishes me to undertake for The East India Company. Would it be distasteful to you to sail with me to India, my Fauna?"

She fell on her knees beside him, hiding her face against his breast.

"Oh, that name, *that name*! . . ."

"It slipped out naturally, beloved."

"Call me what you will," she said, "I will go with you to India once we are man and wife."

They kissed now with more tenderness than passion. A moment later they heard the sound of carriage wheels and horses coming up the drive. Helène rose to her feet.

"That will be for me. Surenne says in his letter that he is sending my equipage to follow after the horseman. He knew that I would wish to return to London immediately."

"I will dress and see you away," Harry said. "Rest assured, sweet, I am quite recovered now. It will not be long before I, too, follow you."

They heard the shouting of the postillions and the neighing of horses in the courtyard. Helène drew on her pelisse and bonnet. She was ready to face, with dignity, the solemn part she must now play for the last time as *Madame la Marquise de Chartellet*. She felt strangely that there moved before her the procession of those Dead who had enacted the drama with her in the past and helped her shape her extraordinary destiny.

She could almost feel these shapes passing by as she walked down the staircase of Pillars to her waiting carriage. Shapes that would recede now into the mists of forgotten things, never to return.

O'Sullivan, the first man ever to befriend her; George Pumphret, weak, kindly creature, whose voice murmured as he passed: *"Poor Insect—they have crushed you cruelly. . . ."* But he was smiling at her, for he knew that she would never again be crushed or unhappy. She was secure in Harry Roddney's love. Farewell to Pumphret! To Henrietta who had paid the price for her fantastic follies; to the hideous Mrs. Clack; to poor Aubrey Burkett, unhappy suicide, victim of Lucien's most callous crime. And to Lucien, the Satyr—with his mixture of wit and cruelty—his exquisite taste—his generosity to *her*. He, too, was following the grey ghosts.

"*Farewell!*" Helène's lips murmured the word.

As she climbed into her elegant carriage she held out a small gloved hand. Harry bent over it and with the courteous formality necessary before her servants, touched it with his lips.

But his eyes looked deeply into hers. And it was the adoration in those handsome eyes that she remembered, and which out-soared all other memories for Helène as the carriage drove her swiftly away from Pillars through the bright spring morning.

BOOK TWO

Bride of Doom

PROLOGUE

Chapter One

The fierce sad baying of hounds echoed and re-echoed through the dark forests that frowned down upon the Vale of Aylesbury. Across the Chiltern Hills a mass of sombre cloud had been broken up by a wild wind and tossed across the sky. A sudden storm of rain blotted out the landscape. At three o'clock on this afternoon in October in the year 1836, the hunt organized by Denzil, Lord St. Cheviot, was at an end. Even now hounds had closed in on the limp exhausted body of the beaten stag. Its life-blood was welling from a hundred jagged wounds torn by the teeth of the savage dogs.

It had been a long disappointing day for the members of his lordship's hunt. The royal animal had given them a poor chase and only during the last hour or so had the pack found the scent and routed the wretched stag out of its hiding-place deep in the thicket.

St. Cheviot did not wait to watch the death-throes of his quarry. He was in one of his most sombre moods—in keeping with the stormy day. His friends who knew him well avoided him like the plague when he was in these evil tempers. Whispering together they looked after him as St. Cheviot wheeled round and pressing his spurs into the big black stallion whose sides were already foam-flecked and bloody, dashed like a madman along the thorny path that led out of the woods and into open country. Then he rode higher up the hill towards the summit on which stood the spectral outline of Cadlington House, the country seat of the St. Cheviots.

In all Buckinghamshire, there was no man with such a reputation as St. Cheviot's for lunatic riding—or indeed for such cruelty. He rode without mercy. It was whispered among the ladies that he had no mind whether he broke the heart of a horse or a maid so long as they satisfied him initially. His was not a pretty character. But his immense wealth and the grandeur of his ancient title made him *persona grata* in most of the Drawing Rooms in London—or Buckinghamshire.

Like a fiend, the rain lashing him, St. Cheviot with crop and spur urged his horse up the steep hill. He was in a hurry to get home to dry clothes, fires and strong wine.

Seen thus through the gathering gloom, man and mount seemed to be one hewn out of the stormy landscape.

There could be no denying the spectacular looks of the thirty-year-old nobleman. He was immensely tall and although slender of flank, had wide powerful shoulders. He had lost the green Austrian hat which he had been wearing earlier today. His raven-dark hair soaked with rain was curled, long and thick, plastered to cheek and brow. His deep-set falcon eyes had a penetrating stare. Just now they were bloodshot and angry. The anger was mainly the backwash of an incident which had taken place at Cadlington last night.

The place was full of guests whom St. Cheviot had invited to attend the chase today. There were one or two women among them—wives of the sportsmen who came to Cadlington not because of any love of the host but because they were satellites ready to fawn upon St. Cheviot and accept his lavish hospitality.

One of the ladies—Sybil Forminster—whose husband was welcomed to Cadlington mainly because he, Lord Forminster, was a crack shot and duellist, had recently attracted St. Cheviot's attention.

The Forminsters were not long married. Sybil was a beautiful girl—herself no mean horsewoman—with long golden hair and bright blue eyes. She was reputed to be as chaste as she was handsome and much in love with her bridegroom.

It was unusual for such a girl to visit Cadlington. St. Cheviot shunned matrimony and his mistresses, whom he frequently changed, were seldom either respectable or of his own class. Respectability bored St. Cheviot.

Last night, at the long rich banquet provided by the host, young Lady Forminster had been placed on the right of the host. Her husband, George, noted that St. Cheviot continually bent close to her and whispered in her ear, and that Sybil found it difficult to eat or drink. She appeared flushed and nervous. St. Cheviot had, in fact, drunk more than was usual and was in the throes of a sudden violent passion for the blonde beauty. George Forminster continued to watch gloomily—wishing, no doubt, that he had not brought his wife to Cadlington, no matter how splendid the chase or magnificent the hospitality. He had been in two minds about it. He did not like St. Cheviot but had been attracted by the thought of the stag-hunt—there were not many these days in the district.

Later, while the musicians played softly and the guests—most of them—gathered in the library to enjoy a game of cards—St. Cheviot had come upon Sybil, alone, in the gallery, where—a lover of painting—she had been examining some of the old portraits of the St. Cheviots. The "Black Barons" they had been called—for without exception they had the ebony hair and dark eyes which Denzil inherited.

Sybil greeted her host with innocent courtesy. He looked splendid in his dark red coat and flowered satin waistcoat, and shewing a well-shaped leg in silken hose. But he soon let her know the evil intentions in his inflamed mind. Then she tried to elude him—it was obvious to her that he was inebriated. But he seized her in his arms and embraced her hotly. When she struggled and protested, he breathed mad proposals to her, adding:

"I am crazed by your white and gold loveliness. I will give you the world if you will leave Forminster and elope with me." This he had said and looked so wild and passionate that the young girl uttered a frightened scream.

George Forminster heard the cry and came to his wife's aid. Both men were swordsmen and weapons were drawn. In a few moments the gay mood of the festive evening changed. Cards were scattered and forgotten. A circle of men gathered around the duellists and in the portrait gallery, in flickering candle-light, the outraged husband fought St. Cheviot.

In less than a few seconds the unfortunate George Forminster was down, bleeding from a serious wound which had only just missed his heart. St. Cheviot was the better swordsman of the two. Drunk or sober—he could use that flexible wrist of his with almost fiendish dexterity.

As for the fair-haired bride who now knelt weeping by her unconscious husband's form—she had lost any attraction she had held for St. Cheviot. He no longer glanced in her direction and was furious because he had been drawn into such a fracas. He had wanted amusement—not this. Livid, sweat pearling on his forehead, he smoothed the disordered lace and lawn at his throat and flung his sword on to the floor for scared-looking servants to pick up. Then he bowed to his open-mouthed, gaping guests.

"The party is over. Let us get to bed—we must be up early for the Meet," he said.

Nobody dissented. The people who gathered around him as a rule did what St. Cheviot bid and without argument.

An hour later the episode was over and must not be referred to. Forminster's carriage departed carrying the still insensible George and his wife away from Cadlington. St. Cheviot's own house-physician went with them.

But the memory of the episode remained with St. Cheviot and spoiled his day. He disliked weakness in himself—as well as in others. He was bitterly angry that he had drunk too much and thus insulted Sybil Forminster. The silly little fool's lips, so he reflected, had not been worth the kissing—or the consequence. It was a poor beginning to the week-end's sport. And now the party lacked one of the finest shots. Forminster would recover, but quite obviously he would never set foot in Cadlington again.

All through his life, St. Cheviot had made more enemies than friends. But though tongues wagged and women feared him—men found him interesting and the women vied with each other for his favours. It would be no mean triumph to pull off a marriage with St. Cheviot and become mistress of Cadlington, the most splendid mansion in Buckinghamshire.

The great park trees loomed out of the mist of rain and frowned upon St. Cheviot as he slackened pace and drew near the top of the hill. Lights flickered from the keeper's lodge beckoning him through the October gloom. He could no longer hear the huntsman's horn or the cacophony of the snarling blood-thirsty pack behind him in the forest. All was quiet. He paused a moment to take a swill at a silver flagon of brandy. He was wet and cold. He had a mind to leave his guests to their own devices. He would like to take a carriage and drive through the dismal evening to London. A game of cards at White's—a late supper with a pretty female more amenable than Sybil Forminster—they were decided attractions.

Down came the pitiless rain, ice-cold against St. Cheviot's face. He wiped his eyes with his sleeve. Suddenly his stallion reared, whinnied, and almost shot the unsuspecting nobleman from his saddle. Nevertheless Denzil kept his seat. Savagely he swore at the sweating frightened animal. Then, peering through the rain, he saw two figures: male and female. They had their arms around each other, huddled under sacks, like peasants trying to shelter from the storm. They must have been sheltering in the hedges, and St. Cheviot's mount had been startled by their sudden appearance out of the gathering mists.

"What the devil do you two think you are doing?" his lordship shouted furiously.

The sacks dropped from the heads of the pair who stood revealed to Denzil. One a stripling boy—no more than twenty or so at the most—supporting the figure of a hunchback girl whose head barely reached his shoulder. They were not ill-dressed; the boy in shabby suit and cloak; the hunchback also covered by a long cloak, and wearing a bonnet. But they were a wet bedraggled-looking pair, and St. Cheviot, looking down contemptuously, felt his temper cool. He gave a brief laugh.

"No wonder Apollo was startled out of his wits—never did I see such apparitions," he growled. "What the deuce do you two scarecrows do here in this weather, and on Cadlington Hill?"

The boy drawing nearer the horse and rider, spoke up: "Sir, whoever you are, you need not insult either my sister or myself," he said.

He spoke in an educated voice with a note of pride in it that surprised St. Cheviot, who dashed the raindrops from his eyes and looked closer. He noted now that the young speaker had a delicate but handsome face with large fine eyes; his mop of light brown curling hair was wet and tossed by the wind about his temples. No peasant this—but somebody of culture. St. Cheviot was suddenly curious.

"Who are you—why are you on my land?" he asked.

"My name is Peveril Marsh. This is my sister, Elspeth."

"What *do* you here in this storm?" Denzil repeated the question and now turned his attention to the hunchback. She suddenly gave a low moan and swayed. The boy supported her, then let her fall back on the side of the road and knelt beside her. He cried out:

"Ah! For God's sake, Elspeth, beloved sister! . . ."

Denzil scowled. He recognized the fact that this was no ordinary swoon. The unhappy girl was desperately ill. He hated illness in any shape or form but even he, who was not particularly charitable, could not ride on and leave such a youthful helpless pair to the mercies of the gathering night. The storm was growing worse. He shouted at the boy:

"What is wrong with her, in heaven's name? Why are you here?"

"My sister is dying," said the boy hoarsely and raised a white stricken face washed by the rain and his own tears. "Oh, God, I did wrong ever to allow her to leave London and journey this long way."

"To see whom did you come?"

"A Mrs. Ingleby, sir, of Whiteleaf."

"Whiteleaf? That is a mile away from here across the hill."

"Yes, sir. We got lost and we had no money for a conveyance, once having spent so much on our fares in the coach which brought us from London to Monks Risborough."

"Who is Mrs. Ingleby? I have not heard of her."

"An aunt of my mother's, sir," the boy began to explain. "But she has been dead this twelve months. We did not know. We hoped to find bed and board with her. When we found her gone we set out by foot, meaning to beg a lift. We were misdirected by a woodcutter and we are here, and have been walking until, as you see, we can go no further. My sister is on the verge of collapse."

And he added that Elspeth had been very sick for a long time and that it was in the hope that the country air might revive her that he had brought her this long way. He, Peveril explained, was an artist but had had little chance to indulge in his talent, for he was the sole support of the seventeen-year-old invalid. Their parents were dead. The boy earned a bare living working for a frame-maker in Cheapside.

This information bored St. Cheviot but he said:

"I will send two of my men down with horse and cart to pick you up. You can take shelter in the servants' quarters at Cadlington for tonight. But it seems to me as though the shelter of the tomb would be more in keeping with your sister's appearance," he added brutally.

The boy who called himself Peveril Marsh looked wildly up at the big dark figure of the man. His cheeks grew scarlet with anger, and with despair. Then he turned back to his sister's prostrate form. Tenderly he untied the bonnet. St. Cheviot, still peering, saw suddenly a face of astonishing beauty. It did not go well with the misshapen back, but of a certainty, he thought, she should have been a dream of loveliness. She had the same large eyes as the boy's and long golden curls. But her face was white as death itself and her lips bloodless. Feminine beauty never failed to interest Lord St. Cheviot. And being superstitious, hunchbacks invariably held for him a morbid attraction. To touch the hump meant good luck; this he had always heard. He slid from the saddle, leaned down and laid a hand on the girl's back. Immediately her large eyes opened and she looked straight up into his face. So peculiar and deep was her gaze that he felt a curious thrill run through him.

"Why do you stare at me so, poor soul?" he muttered.

"Destiny," she said in a thin quavery tone. "I know your destiny, sir—I am a seer."

"What does she mean?" Denzil asked the boy roughly.

Peveril, with a tender look at the hunchback, said:

"My sister has prophetic powers. She has always been able to look into the future."

Now St. Cheviot was vastly interested. Rain, wind, the icy darkness of this late October afternoon, all were forgotten. He had the supreme egotist's intense desire to know what lay ahead of him. He knelt down by the girl.

"Tell me what you see?" he demanded in the voice of one who is accustomed to being obeyed.

But now the boy artist spoke up bravely:

"Sir, I fear my sister is gravely ill. I must get her to warmth and cover."

"All in good time," said St. Cheviot and, fixing his black glittering eyes on the girl, urged her afresh.

"What do you know of my destiny?" he asked.

"Elspeth, are you all right?" put in the boy with feverish concern.

She gave him a wan smile but kept her extraordinary eyes upon the handsomely-dressed gentleman who was bending over her. Then in a sepulchral voice she spoke to him once more:

"Your name—what is it?"

"Denzil St. Cheviot, Baron of Cadlington, who lives at Cadlington House," he replied.

"St. Cheviot," she echoed that name in a hollow tone. "The black barons."

Surprised, he nodded.

"So they call us."

"Still unwed," she continued.

"By heaven, you are right," St. Cheviot gave a coarse laugh, "and likely to remain so."

"No," said the dying girl. She struggled to sit up and pointed a finger at him. "Within twelve months from now you will be wed. I, who can see into the future, do foretell this marriage. And with it comes disaster. Oh, horrible!" she added and shuddered.

St. Cheviot's lips curled.

"Marriage is for a man invariably a horrible disaster," he said and laughed at his own jest.

"A horrible disaster," repeated Elspeth Marsh. And now her breath came more quickly and with difficulty. "I see red-gold hair and violets. Yes. *Watch out for red-gold hair and violets*, sir . . . and for a black St. Cheviot."

"What, another?" Denzil gave another strident laugh. "And what is all this nonsense about red hair and violets?"

Then the boy interrupted:

"You will live to see that she has spoken the truth. Elspeth is never wrong and this is maybe the last prophecy she will ever make." His voice broke. He knelt down in the mud, his tears flowing as he tried to chafe some warmth into the hunchback's icy little hands.

Again a strange superstitious thrill passed through St. Cheviot's frame. Maybe it was true that the girl had vision. Sometimes, he knew, it was given to the dying to foretell what lay ahead. Again his hand touched the girl's hump. "For luck," he muttered.

But the boy did not hear. He had burst into bitter tears. "Elspeth, dearest sister," he cried.

Now St. Cheviot saw that the girl's head had fallen back. She was dead. His lordship recoiled and turned back to his horse.

"I will send my servants to assist you," he said curtly. "Wait here."

The boy did not answer but flung himself across the body of his sister and continued to sob her name.

Chapter Two

St. Cheviot dug his spurs into the stallion's flanks and urged the animal up the hill. He came to the great wrought-iron gates of his home. In the deepening dusk they took on a spectral aspect. Little could be seen at this hour, and in such weather, of the magnificent park surrounding the house. Two of the lodge-keepers, carrying lighted lanthorns, came running to open the gates for their master. He reined in his mount and flung a sharp order at one of the men.

"A few yards down yon hill you will find a lad—a stranger in these parts—and his sister, who has just expired. Have them brought to Cadlington and tell my footmen to see that they have attention."

"Yes, m'lord," said the man addressed.

St. Cheviot rode on between the sombre line of chestnuts that flanked the drive and were waving wildly in the gale. Soon he could see lights flickering from the windows of the House. Never had he been more glad to reach home. What a disappointing chase, he thought angrily—and what infernal weather. So far the whole week-end had been a disaster. Of a certainty he would return to London and leave his guests to their own devices.

Now he was outside the front door of Cadlington—shouting in his boisterous fashion for his groomsmen who came hurrying round from the courtyard. A footman flung open the door. Spears of light cut across the soaked lawns.

Cadlington House looked huge and forbidding in the purple stormy evening light yet it had a magnificence of its own—with the hill rising steeply behind, thickly wooded to the summit. In front of the house, the pleasure gardens were laid out in terraces. From here, tall windows commanded a magnificent view of the Buckinghamshire Weald.

Godfrey, first Baron of Cadlington, had built this house for his French-born wife, Marguerite. It bore the unmistakable Jacobean stamp—half stone, richly-timbered, containing some twenty-four or -five bedchambers, and a fine dining-hall surrounded by a musicians' gallery. At a later date, Roland St. Cheviot, Denzil's father, in atrocious taste, had added a wing. This stuck out from the rest of the building like a monstrous growth wrecking its beauty of design, for it was very lofty, rounded like a tower and turreted. It looked as grotesque as an illustration from a Teutonic fairy tale.

In the interior a winding staircase led to the highest turret which could be seen on a fine day for miles around. It had become a landmark.

Denzil, as a boy, had used it as a place of escape from parents or tutors. He had at one time kept up there wild animals that he had snared. One day a young maid-servant had been found on the staircase with her throat cut. How or why she came to such a sorry pass was never discovered. After that the tower had been shut up and the interior had fallen into a poor state of repair. It was now said to be haunted. Denzil was always intending to have the whole wing pulled down but some morbid fascination about the architectural excrescence held his hand.

Nobody ever went near the tower after dark. The local inhabitants regarded the tall frowning turrets with superstitious horror.

But the old house itself had all the graciousness and dignity of its age. And it was certain that no other in Aylesbury could boast of such fine linen-fold panelling or splendid fireplaces. The two staircases curving up to the musicians' gallery were built of rosewood, richly carved.

Throughout the last two hundred years, Cadlington had braved the elements on these wild wooded hills, buffeted by gales and storms—drenched by fierce rains. In severe winters the grounds lay buried in deep snow.

At such times the icy hills were almost impassable and then Denzil St. Cheviot would betake himself to London or go to a sumptuous villa which he rented in Monte Carlo.

But in the spring and summer, Cadlington would lose its forbidding and gloomy appearance and gain much beauty. It could, indeed, look mellow and welcoming against the green hills when the gardens were aglow with flowers and the orchards rich with fruit blossom. The time St. Cheviot loved best was the late autumn; the shooting and hunting season. Such a cold stormy October as they had experienced today was exceptional.

A few moments later, St. Cheviot was in the warmth and brilliance of the great hall standing, legs straddled, in front of a leaping log fire. He drew off his gauntlets and shouted for wine. A young footman came running with glasses and decanters. A huge wolfhound which was St. Cheviot's favourite pet, and so savage none but he dared touch her, had been lying in front of the fire. She rose and walked ponderously up to her master, wagging her tail. He looked down at her and patted the great head.

"Good bitch," he growled. "Where the deuce has everyone got to—the place is dead."

St. Cheviot had a loathing of being alone—even for a moment. Perhaps his conscience did not care for solitude—too much time for remembering—he had done evil in his life and had much to be ashamed of. At any rate, he liked company and grew ill-humoured when he was alone. If his female guests were resting at this hour before dinner, let them rest, he decided—later they might find him more entertaining.

Once inside Cadlington, the wind and the rain and the lonely countryside shut out, it was like being in another world; one of luxury and wealth—the enormous wealth of the St. Cheviots. The great house was stacked with treasures—a good deal inherited from the Lady Marguerite, Denzil's French ancestress who had been an heiress in her own right. The hall in which St. Cheviot was now standing was hung with fine Gobelin tapestries. The tall-backed pointed walnut chairs with their seats of multi-coloured gros-point were French. The fine thick curtains of vermilion silk brocade, sweeping across the windows, had been brought from Paris, hung in the time of the first Baroness and never changed. Some of these gay touches in the decorations amused Denzil St. Cheviot, who had a fancy for Paris and its fashions.

But beauty, colour, art, music, all things lovely crept into St. Cheviot's life only as a strange distorted foil to his inner spirit of darkness and depravity.

When he entertained here, he liked to do so with an ostentatious display of wealth and power. Tales of his astonishing banquets circulated through England. Those who had participated spoke afterwards of the lavish splendour. The long rich dinners eaten at a table laid with gold plate and rare china bearing the St. Cheviot crest—two eagles, with wings spread, their claws locked in conflict. The library in the west wing, filled with rare, handsomely bound volumes. Of a licentious nature, many were in Italian. But St. Cheviot was no great reader—the books had been appreciated by his father.

Within a few moments of the return of the master of Cadlington, the house blazed with lamp- and candle-light. He, washed and changed, sat before a fire in a small octagonal room, which he used as a private sanctum and kept particularly private documents under lock and key. When in here, it was more than any servant dared do than disturb him. Legs stretched before him, and with Alpha his wolfhound at his feet, Denzil sipped hot mulled wine. He began to feel more comfortable and agreeably-minded as the warmth crept back into his starved body. He had been soaked to the skin before he reached home.

He could not, however, forget the peculiar prophecy of the hunchbacked girl on the roadside. It haunted him.

Marriage . . . within twelve months from now . . . watch out for red-gold hair and violets, she had said, *and a black St. Cheviot.* Well, he had always been partial to blonde women and particularly to those with the white skin that accompanied reddish hair. As for the "black St. Cheviot," that was more than possible. No blond heir had been born to this family for centuries. But it was curious that a total stranger from London like Elspeth Marsh should know so much.

Before his meeting with the brother and sister, Denzil had fully intended to take himself off to London tonight. Now he had changed his mind and decided that he would stay here in the warmth and, later, join his guests for supper and a game of cards. But first he wanted to see the boy, Peveril Marsh. There were things on St. Cheviot's mind that he wished to ask the young man. Why, for instance, one who spoke so well and looked delicately bred should have come to such a sorry pass. Even as this question entered St. Cheviot's thoughts, a knock came on the door and the boy, himself, entered.

"Ah!" said St. Cheviot, "come in, my young sir. Stand here before me."

Peveril Marsh walked slowly towards him. St. Cheviot could not but be struck now by the boy's light graceful tread and extreme good looks. He was too thin—the face almost cadaverous—but the large grey eyes were brilliant and the forehead high and intelligent, crowned by that thick mop of brown curls which were now dry and glossy. He wore borrowed clothes, white shirt and a flowing tie. His eyes were red-rimmed and it was obvious that he had been weeping. St. Cheviot said:

"Have you had food?"

"Yes, sir, I thank you. Your servants have been very considerate. My sister . . ." his voice broke.

"Well?"

"Is no more," said the boy in a half whisper and choking. "They have laid her out in an empty room in the servants' quarters and put candles at her head and her feet. Tomorrow they say the parson will come and that a grave will be dug for her alongside Cadlington Church."

"Have you no kith and kin?" demanded St. Cheviot.

The boy seemed to struggle with his emotion. He could not answer for a moment. St. Cheviot added harshly:

"Come, you are no child—can you not conduct yourself in more manly a fashion?"

Now Peveril Marsh flung back his head and spoke with the pride that had first impressed St. Cheviot.

"I do not consider it unmanly to grieve for my sister, sir. She was all that I had."

"Pshaw," said his lordship, who was without sentimentality or, indeed, fine sentiment of any kind. He had only asked the boy to come and see him because he was bitten with curiosity to know how much power the hunchback really had possessed to foretell the future. He thrust jug and tankard across the table to Peveril and bade him drink.

"The wine is spiced. It will strengthen you. Take it."

Peveril drank a few sips and some colour came back into his cheeks.

"Your sister was misshapen—better that she should lie in her grave," said St. Cheviot suddenly. "She had singular beauty of the face but with her deformity no man would ever have taken her to wife."

But Peveril winced.

"She had me, her brother, always to love and protect her," he said in a choked voice.

"Tell me your story," said St. Cheviot.

"What can it matter to you, sir? Why not let me go whence I came?"

"You will do as you are told," snapped St. Cheviot.

Peveril Marsh looked at his benefactor in some surprise. He was soon to learn that here was a man quite merciless to those who offended him and who expected instant obedience. It could not be said that Peveril found Lord St. Cheviot kindly or a man of charm, but tonight the young artist was bemused with the pain of his loss, and with a despair that arose from the hopelessness of his position. He allowed the strong-minded wealthy nobleman to dominate him. At St. Cheviot's request, he related his personal history. He was about to celebrate his twentieth birthday. Five years ago, he had been in a very different position. He and his sister lived with their parents in a small but decent house in the neighbourhood of Holloway in London, where his father had owned a small haberdasher's shop. His mother was a cultured lady of more gentle birth than his father and she, herself, had taught the children from infancy. At an early age Peveril had shewn signs of genius with pencil and paint-brush. At twelve years he had painted a picture which had astonished even his parents. So at the request of his mother he had been given education at St. Paul's School and private lessons in painting from an old Italian artist, a friend to Mrs. Marsh. All had been set fair for Peveril's career. The one unhappiness in the family had been the sad deformity of the little girl, Elspeth. From an early age Peveril had learned to take care of her. Brother and sister were deeply devoted.

Then tragedy befell the family. Mrs. Marsh had suddenly been carried off by a fatal illness to which the doctors could give no name. But her demise, at the early age of forty-one, had not only caused intense grief to her young son and daughter, but altered the whole character of her bereaved husband. He had taken to drinking and neglecting his business. His son, trained only as an artist, and with little head for commerce, struggled to help keep the business afloat. But it had ended in misfortune. Poor William Marsh was taken to a debtor's prison where he languished for six months then died.

Peveril, at nineteen, found himself homeless and with a hunchbacked sister to support. Painting and selling pictures was too precarious a living, so he had taken a job in Cheapside with a firm of frame-makers. Brother and sister shared a home in miserable lodgings. From that time onwards it had become evident to Peveril that the delicate girl would never survive another winter. Thus he had taken the decision to leave London and take Elspeth to the country, to his aunt, Mrs. Ingleby, whom they had once or twice visited as children in happier days. Peveril had felt sure that she would care for Elspeth and allow her to stay in Whiteleaf where the good pure air might help to restore her failing strength.

"It was foolish of me," said the boy in a low voice, "not to have ascertained first that my aunt was still living, but as I had not heard of her death, I took it for granted that we would find her there."

After that, things had happened as formerly described to St. Cheviot. How the fare from London to Monks Risborough had taken all the money the brother and sister had saved; how Elspeth was taken ill during the journey and what had happened once they found that Mrs. Ingleby had died and her cottage was sold to another.

"I feel responsible for having hastened my beloved Elspeth to her grave," ended the unhappy young man.

"Nonsense," barked St. Cheviot, "the girl was already doomed, but I would have you tell me about her powers of prophecy. Am I to believe that she really possessed such supernatural knowledge or was she merely raving?"

"She was not raving," said Peveril. "She developed powers of fortune-telling even when she was a child. I've known her tell me even the exact number of marks I would get at school for certain subjects. Alas, she also foretold our mother's passing, only none of us believed her."

"Then you think she may be right and that I shall find myself wed to a female with red-gold hair, and within twelve months . . ." said St. Cheviot, rose to his feet and laughed harshly.

"Indeed, it will be so, sir."

St. Cheviot put his tongue in his cheek.

"We shall see."

"Have I your leave to go now, sir?"

"Go where?"

"I must no longer encroach on your hospitality."

"Would you not stay and see your sister entrusted to the tomb?"

Peveril shuddered.

"Yes—that I must certainly do, but after . . ."

"After, you will return to London and starve?"

"I will not starve if I can work with these, sir," said Peveril proudly and displayed his slender, well-shaped hands.

St. Cheviot locked his own fingers behind his back and frowned at the boy, who although tall was a head shorter than himself.

"How far are you skilled at painting, I wonder?" he drawled.

Peveril did not seem to hear. He stared into the flames with dull sad eyes. For so long now his sister Elspeth had been the one love and care of his life—he could not picture an existence without her. He dreaded the sad loneliness. Once, when they were talking together, she had prophesied that he would at a young age meet and experience a great love and passionate happiness. But that seemed almost impossible—so far Peveril's heart had never beaten fast at the sight of any woman. His affections had been claimed entirely by his family.

St. Cheviot's voice startled him out of his reverie.

"Supposing I keep you here at Cadlington and give you the wherewithal to paint my portrait? It is time my likeness hung on these walls amongst my ancestors . . ." and he gave his sardonic laugh; a laugh which Peveril found sinister rather than humorous. But regarding the nobleman's spectacular appearance, the artist in Peveril stirred. Indeed—what a portrait Lord St. Cheviot would make in rich and flowing oils, on a vast canvas worthy of his height.

"Well?" thundered St. Cheviot.

"I should like to paint your portrait, sir," said Peveril, and his grey eyes regarding the older man with an expression of cool confidence that St. Cheviot found intriguing.

One of those sudden whims of fancy which must always be satisfied in his lordship, seized him now. For no particular reason he decided that he would commission this unhappy youth who had so far suffered a disastrous beginning to a wished-for career as an artist.

"Then you shall stay here, and from time to time I will bore myself by reposing before you so that you can reproduce my likeness," he said. "Who knows but you are a genius in disguise? We shall see. Borrow paper and crayon and go into the hall now and draw for me a likeness of any one of my guests whom you see there, I do not care whom. Then bring it to me."

With some eagerness Peveril assented. For the past year while working as an assistant in a shop, he had had neither time nor heart to use his talents. He felt a sudden wish to prove to Lord St. Cheviot that he was, in truth, a real artist.

He was gone an hour, during which time St. Cheviot took a nap, overcome by the heat of the fire and the fumes of the wine he had drunk. Then his lordship opened his eyes to find the boy standing beside him. Respectfully Peveril handed him a sheet of white paper. On it was sketched in charcoal the head of a man; one St. Cheviot instantly recognized as that of Sir James Barnett—a bachelor of middle age who had come down from London for the shooting and was staying in the house. Unmistakable, the several characteristics of Sir James . . . the broad nostrils, the long face and the double chin, the pouches under the eyes, and the rather sheeplike expression. St. Cheviot burst out laughing.

"Gad! But this is quite remarkable. Yes—I can see that you have considerable talent, my young man. It is a dashed good likeness of that fool James, and if you get as good a one of the present Lord Cheviot—in oils on a full-length canvas—you need no longer starve. You shall become my portrait painter-in-chief. You shall also paint my house and gardens."

Peveril's cheeks flushed but the gleam of triumph in his eyes was short-lived. Too late, he thought sombrely, too late for Elspeth, whose tragic little body was even now lying on a bier. Peveril hung his head but St. Cheviot's hand clapped his shoulder.

"It is well done. I shall give orders that you be appointed a room in the tower, high up where you can have good light. You shall reside here. I will take you to London when next I go. There you shall purchase the necessary paints and canvasses, then return here to start your work."

"I thank you, sir," said Peveril in a low voice.

"First bury your sister," said St. Cheviot, in a voice of indifference, "and bury with her your melancholy. I do not like gloom around me. Now go get some supper and sleep. I've had enough of you for today."

Almost it was in Peveril's mind to reject the nobleman's offer of work even though of such a pleasant kind, for to become a great painter had always been his heart's desire. But he could not find it in him to like this man who had befriended him. There was something so brutal and callous about him. "Perhaps," Peveril thought bitterly, "I am over-sensitive and take my sorrows too much to heart."

So he decided to stay at Cadlington and accept the unexpected opportunity that heaven had sent him; even though that help came from what Peveril vaguely suspected a devilish quarter. He bowed and left St. Cheviot. But he went not to eat and drink, but to kneel beside the candle-lit lifeless frame of his sister; there to pray for her departed soul.

PART I

Chapter One

In the following year, 1837, on a fine cold morning in May, Hélène, Lady Roddney, sat in her boudoir reading a letter. The weekly mail arriving by post chaise had just reached Pillars. Sir Harry was out with one of his neighbours, shooting. The house was quiet except for an occasional peal of girlish laughter which made Lady Roddney lift her eyes from the closely written pages which she was scanning, and smile. It was as though she could see through the walls to the adjoining room where her young daughter, Fleur, was entertaining a friend. The merry laughter pleased her.

There was nothing she liked more than for Fleur to be happy. Ever since the child had been born on the twenty-fourth of this month, eighteen years ago, the Roddneys had lived with but a set purpose: to make beautiful the life of their daughter. The only child they would ever have, for Hélène had been told after that long and difficult birth that she would never bear another living infant. She had, in fact, never meant to have children—fearing the dark strain that might be inherited by the next generation and grievously embarrass them all. It was not that Hélène had any wish to forget the fine old African who had been her maternal grandfather. Indeed, he was unforgettable. Just as she could never totally eradicate all memory of her own terrible childhood and the sinister events that had followed. Those ghastly days of slavery, when, with her people, she had been sold into bondage.

But it was a period that above all things Harry wished her to forget. And now it all seemed barely possible that it had happened. Nearly twenty-eight years ago, it was in fact, since she had become Harry Roddney's cherished and adored wife. They had been so happy together that it had not seemed to matter that their union was fruitless for the first ten years. It was as Hélène wished. Then—Fleur had come.

Listening now to her laughter, silver-sweet and gay, knowing that Fleur was as beautiful as an angel and with a disposition as sweet and docile, yet with some of her father's fire—Hélène had no regrets.

She had been born on the very same day as a certain small girl at Kensington Palace; although just how great Victoria, daughter of the Duke and Duchess of Kent, and niece of William IV, was destined to be, nobody then could dream.

Hélène was only half way through perusing her letter—the pages of which were scrawled in violet ink. She was a little bored with the long epistle—and its writer. Dolly—Mrs. de Vere—was a cousin of Harry's. A silly, fussy little woman who cared greatly for money and position. She married Archibald de Vere, a wealthy business man much older than herself, but he deplored the manner in which she spent his money.

They had a house on Knightsbridge Green, a son younger than Fleur and a pair of fat daughters, twins, now nineteen, whom everybody except their mother found excessively stupid and plain. Cousin Dolly, nevertheless, from the very start of her cousin Harry's marriage to Hélène, then the widow of the famous Marquis de Chartellet—had proved herself a staunch friend. She had welcomed the advent of the beautiful and quite famous Marquise into the Roddney family and taken considerable pains to invite the married couple, on their return from Italy, to stay with her. This had pleased Hélène, who did not wish Harry to be totally cut off from the Roddneys. In addition, Archibald was a powerful member of the East India Company wherein Harry had started his life as a man of affairs—and from which he had only retired a year ago.

Harry got on well with Archibald who in character and demeanour very often reminded him of his uncle, James Wilberson. And Hélène tolerated Dolly, but she was a gossip and that sharp unkind tongue of hers often ran away with her. In Hélène's estimation one had to be careful of the things Dolly repeated.

Through half-shut lids, Hélène's dark velvet eyes

dreamed out of the windows at a white billow of cloud that drifted across the blue clear sky. It was so peaceful here, except for the light-hearted chatter and laughter of the girls next door.

And Hélène's heart was as a rule full of quiet. But today, for some strange reason, the past arose to haunt her. It was too terrible to lay for ever buried, and must at times disturb her peace. Sometimes she asked herself cynically how many of their present friends would accept her if they *knew*. Knew that she, the proud Lady Roddney, had been born in an African kraal of a white father and a half-caste mother. That as a fabulously beautiful quadroon girl of tender years she had been sold into slavery—become the chattel of a spoiled vicious society woman, by name Lady Pumphret, and that later when Lord Pumphret who had been her only friend, expired, been submitted to a terrible bondage from which she had fled to the protection of the noted young rake and charmer, Sir Harry Roddney. All these things that had happened she would not today allow herself to remember in detail. They were too terrible. And through a terrible misunderstanding Harry had gone out of her life again. So once more she had been sold—and this time to the erudite old Marquis de Chartellet. In his house, known as 'The Little Bastille,' on the Essex coast, she had found refuge and lived for some years. Her whole life had altered. Lucien had educated her and lifted her out of her misery. She had ceased to be the unhappy quadroon once known as *Fauna*. She had become *Hélène*—the name de Chartellet gave her, and in due course she had become his wife.

As *Madame la Marquise de Chartellet* she had been revenged upon the society that had once tortured her. But as far as she knew, not a living soul knew of that other hellish existence or of the dark strain in her blood.

After Lucien's death, when she had married her old love, Harry, she found all the happiness that had once eluded her. London accepted Lady Roddney just as they had once toasted her as *Madame la Marquise. Fauna, the quadroon slave, was to all intents and purposes, dead.*

But today as Hélène sat in her beautiful boudoir listening to her daughter's laughter, she was disturbed not only by the phantoms of the past but by the thought of Fleur's future.

The child was only seventeen but it was the day of early marriages and both Hélène and Harry realized it was time Fleur found a husband.

But whom? Who was there worthy of her, the mother asked herself this morning. Young Thomas Quinley—son of neighbouring Sir David Quinley, doctor and scientist—a nice boy, and Fleur liked him and rode sometimes with him and his sister. But he was to her no more than a brother—a companion. The Hon. Vyvyan Lockhart—a good-looking, amiable lad—would ride a good many miles from the Hertfordshire border to see Fleur for an hour. Fleur had convinced her mother that she would never accept a proposal from young Vyvyan.

This morning Hélène also fell to wondering who would care for Fleur should she be still unwed when her parents died. Death was not probable yet—but it was possible. There was, of course, Cousin Dolly. But Fleur had no great faith in the cousin, whose way of life Fleur herself despised. No—she would not want Fleur to make a home with the de Veres.

Other than that there was only Harry's lawyer (he had been legal adviser to Sir Arthur Fayre from whom Harry inherited Pillars). In case of an early demise, Harry had made Caleb Nonseale Fleur's legal guardian. Hélène found Mr. Nonseale polite, even servile, but deep down in her heart she did not trust him.

Chapter Two

Fleur Roddney bent low over a handful of exquisitely coloured silks with which she was embroidering a tea cosy for her mother's wedding anniversary. She chose a strand of deep violet and held it up to the light.

"Look, Cathy—is this not a pleasant hue?" she asked.

Catherine Foster—a pleasant, freckled girl with long brown curls—looked first at the violet silks, then into her friend's eyes. Catherine was—like many others—always fascinated by the shape and colour of Fleur Roddney's eyes.

"Truly, your eyes are more violet than blue—and like your silks," she sighed. "You *are* lucky! Your lashes are dark, yet you are fair—and they are the longest I have seen. Lucky, *lucky* Fleur!"

Fleur gave her musical laugh.

"Foolish Cathy—what have you to complain of? You have the dearest face," she murmured.

Catherine grumbled, glancing sideways at a mirror over the fireplace in her friend's boudoir. It was a charming room—white and madonna blue—Fleur's favourite colour—and full of spring flowers. Over the mantelpiece hung a painting of Hélène by a contemporary artist. To the young girl—who had received this on her seventeenth birthday—it was her dearest possession. Always she admired her lovely and fascinating mother.

Lady Roddney, superb in a grey velvet ball gown of that period, with low corsage; sapphires sparkling on her snowy throat and bosom; rich red-gold curls falling over the matchless shoulders.

Fleur's hair was a shade paler but she had the same contours; high cheekbones, small pointed chin and ripe curving mouth.

The girls chatted intimately as they worked. They were

vastly entertained by the prospect of the dance which Lady Roddney was giving at Pillars next week to celebrate Fleur's eighteenth birthday.

Suddenly Catherine remembered a certain gentleman who had figured at a dinner party which Fleur's Papa had given here, at Easter. He had not left Fleur's side all evening and had turned the pages for her while she played *Sheep May Safely Graze* on her spinet.

"Do you know whether Lord St. Cheviot is on your Mama's list of guests?" she asked, and looked slyly under her lids for Fleur's reaction. It was surprising. Fleur stiffened and her pink flush faded.

"I hope not," she said. Her voice was quite changed. She looked almost *scared*.

"But why, Fleur?" Catherine asked curiously. "He was so very handsome. You said so. You told me you were quite bowled over."

"Only at first—then almost at once I drew back," said Fleur and accidentally stuck her needle into her finger. She withdrew it, then, like a child, sucked the tiny pin-prick of blood.

"I do not think I want him to come to the Ball, nevertheless," she added.

"But why?" persisted Catherine.

"He—frightens me. And I do not find him sincere—he is too bold," said Fleur thoughtfully.

"But handsome."

"Oh, vastly so! I admire it."

"And entertaining."

"I do not know. We did not speak much together, but I believe he is greatly travelled," said Fleur. "He was originally of French extraction. He spends much time on the French Coast. Papa says he is a fine rider and a deadly shot. It was at a shooting party they met. The Baron is also famous at fencing, and I have heard it said that in Paris he once killed two opponents when he was attacked, on either side—ran them both through like this and this . . ."

And Fleur with a turn of delicate wrist, flicked her needle in the air from left to right. Catherine screamed.

"Ooh—how horrid!"

"I have a notion that Lord St. Cheviot, for all his gallant manner—is horrid," said Fleur frankly.

"But he sounds *fascinating*," breathed Catherine. "Wickedly, deliciously attractive, dear Fleur."

The other girl did not comment for the moment. She recalled her first meeting with St. Cheviot at a dinner party given by her Papa. Certainly, St. Cheviot had dominated the dinner. He was a witty conversationalist and *raconteur*.

When he had singled Fleur out for favour, she had at first been shyly flattered. Quite overawed, she had sat clasping her long slim fingers, listening while he bent over her chair and told her how her several beauties had enslaved him on sight.

"The white swan on your father's lake has not more grace than that which is yours," he had said. "The first time I gazed into the violet of your eyes, I was dazzled, and I am still blinded. I have never seen greater loveliness, Miss Roddney." Those were the sort of things he had murmured into her ear all through the evening. He had told her, too, about Cadlington—his vast residence. How lonely it was in all its magnificence—how wasted its army of servants—and the priceless jewels that lay in the family safe. All waiting for a bride; for the girl who would become the wife of Denzil, Lord St. Cheviot.

Heady, significant words—whispered throughout an entire evening—by the most dazzling man in the room. What wonder it had gone a little to Fleur Roddney's innocent head. Yet after he had departed, and she had discussed the evening with her mother, she had said:

"What is it about Lord St. Cheviot that repels me, Mama?"

Hélène had hesitated to answer. In her opinion, St. Cheviot was, despite his looks and title, too fierce, too coarse for her darling whom she and Harry had so long protected from the wickedness of the world.

"I do not personally care for him, my darling, and if you like, you need not see him again," the mother had told Fleur before they retired that night.

But Harry Roddney had other views. He was intrigued by St. Cheviot. Twice, since Christmas, Harry had stayed at Cadlington House as a member of a big shooting party. Hélène had of course been invited, but she declined. She preferred to remain at Pillars with her daughter.

When Hélène had suggested that strong rumour had it

St. Cheviot was not a good man, Harry had laughed and carelessly caressed the frown from the noble forehead of her whom he loved so well.

"Dear heart—he is a *man*—and unmarried. He cannot be expected to live the life of a saint. Was Harry Roddney's past life so speckless that he can afford to pick faults in others?"

"If Harry was not faultless in his youth—he was always kind—who should know better than I?" Hélène had answered. "But it is my opinion that St. Cheviot knows no charity."

"My dear love, do not worry your beautiful head about him."

"But he is enamoured of our daughter," sighed Hélène, "and makes every effort to see her."

Again Harry, with all the simplicity and gaiety of nature that Hélène had first loved in him, laughed.

"What man does not kneel at the feet of our Fleur? Let St. Cheviot fall. She will not have him."

"Would you wish her to?"

Harry pulled the lobe of his ear.

"N-no," he said at length, "I would not. He is, as you say—too worldly—and perhaps too old for her. Let her marry a simple youth—it is best."

With that, Hélène was content, and troubled herself no more about the master of Cadlington House. But since then she had discussed him with Cousin Dolly, and Dolly, the little gossip, shed further light on the magnificent baron —none too good a light.

"It is rumoured that a well-born girl recently drowned herself because he betrayed her," she had said. "Isn't it romantic? But I would adore to entertain him. He is so handsome and so *wicked*! They say, too, his house has a haunted tower where a crime was committed." She giggled. But her information did nothing to endear Lord St. Cheviot further to Hélène.

It was the last paragraph in the long gossipy letter from Dolly that finally made Hélène open her door and call to her daughter.

"Fleur—can you come to Mama a moment?"

Catherine, hearing Lady Roddney's voice, rose to her feet and said that she must depart. The carriage was waiting. Her Mama had sent the brougham for her, with Miss Spencer, her chaperone; and she must go.

"Come back tomorrow, dear Cathy, and we will finish our needlework," said Fleur, kissing her friend's cheek.

In her mother's boudoir, the young girl gazed fondly at the elder woman's grave, lovely face. To her it was a face that bore traces of deep suffering—but the mother never spoke of it, and Fleur never asked questions. She could only guess (dimly) that her mother had been through great pain in the past, and once her father had said to her:

"Be always angelic to Mama, my Fleur, for she has known tragedy that you are too young to understand—and come through her ordeal with flying colours. Now 'tis for you and for me to make sure she never sheds another tear on this earth."

Hélène put an arm about her daughter and began to read her what Cousin Dolly had written.

> "It might interest you, my dearest Hélène, to know that yesterday Archibald and I rode together in the Row and who should canter alongside us and greet us but the wicked St. Cheviot himself. He has grown handsomer than ever and wore a black riding coat and white breeches. He spoke of your little Fleur . . ."

Hélène paused and glanced enquiringly at her daughter. A carmine flush had crept up under the fair skin. Hélène continued:

> "Indeed he seems to find her so fetching that he is anxious to see her again and asked if I would not induce her to come and stay with my girls. Now if you would let me I could present her, providing his Majesty recovers and can hold a Court next Season. . . ."

Fleur listened attentively until her mother had finished reading the letter, then moved away from the encircling arm and thoughtfully touched the glossy leaves of a small palm which stood in a corner.

"Well, my love," said Hélène, "what about it?"

"It must be as you wish, Mama. If Papa wants the Baron at my dance, he must come."

At that moment there came the sound of horses' hooves in the drive. Mother and daughter exchanged glances of pleasure.

"Your father has come back," said Hélène.

Together they went down the handsome staircase and into the hall which had been greatly enlarged since the first day Hélène (then known as Fauna and a year younger than her own daughter was today) had set foot in it. Harry Roddney came through the door.

He kissed his lovely wife, and then his daughter.

"How is my Darling?" he asked, pulling one of the fair silky curls that fell upon her shoulder.

Fleur with the artlessness of youth plunged straight into the problem that was worrying her.

"Mama and I have something to ask you, Papa."

"Concerning what, my darling?"

"Mama will tell you."

"It is a question of the proposed guests for her birthday dance," said Hélène.

"Ah, yes," said Harry, "the great day when our Fleur becomes a woman of the world!" and playfully he swept a bow in cavalier fashion to his daughter.

Fleur laughed merrily.

"I don't think I shall ever be *that*, Papa, and do not want to be. Indeed, I do not want ever to leave you and Mama, and our home."

"Let us then talk of the guests for your Ball," said her father.

Hélène, who knew what the girl was struggling to say, said it for her.

"It is of Lord St. Cheviot she would speak, Harry. She is not sure in her mind that she wants him here again. She did not care for him."

Harry Roddney, who was inclined to be a little vague about people, put a finger against the side of his nose and reflected.

"St. Cheviot, ah yes, has he then been asked to Fleur's party?"

"Not yet. All the other invitations have already been

sent," said Hélène. "But we know, dearest, that you have been his guest at Cadlington and have said several times that you wished me to return some hospitality other than the once he dined with us."

Harry poured himself out a glass of sherry and sipped it, smiling amiably at his wife.

"It is for you to say, my angel. What do you want to do in this matter?"

But Hélène knew her husband. Harry was not always tactful and had no memory. She put a hand on his shoulder and looked at him whimsically.

"Are you quite sure that when you last went with St. Cheviot to the Anglo-French cock-fight you did not mention Fleur's birthday and suggest that he attend? It would be so like you, Harry."

His handsome face flushed. He looked apologetic and coughed.

"In truth, my love, now I come to think of it, I believe I *did* mention the fact. For St. Cheviot asked if he might be permitted to send Fleur a box of the orchids that they grow at Cadlington and for which the forcing houses in his garden have long been famous."

Hélène's expression changed. Fleur bit her lip.

"I hate orchids," said the girl under her breath.

"That's all right, my dear, you can receive them, then give them away," said her father grandly.

But Hélène shook her head.

"Harry, Harry, you were never a diplomat, although you are my heart's love."

"Have I done wrong?" he asked with so woebegone an expression that Hélène immediately took one of his strong fine hands and laid it against her cheek. The gesture of a young girl.

"My heart's love," she repeated under her breath. "If you have already made the invitation, do not trouble. We can entertain St. Cheviot once more and Fleur can receive the orchids, but it must be firmly understood that we are not interested in any serious advances from him now or ever. He is not for Fleur."

"Certainly not," Harry agreed promptly. "He is too old and a devil, but by gad, what a wizard with pistol or fowling piece or sword. I've never seen his like. Well, well—I will get changed. . . ."

He walked off. Hélène smiled at her daughter.

"Too late now to stop St. Cheviot coming—your naughty Papa has been so indiscreet. He is too lavish with his invitations."

"It is no matter, Mama," said Fleur. "I shall only give Lord St. Cheviot one dance and can send the orchids to Cathy's mother who likes them."

Hélène bent and touched her daughter's cheek with her lips.

"You need never be afraid of the Baron of Cadlington—or of any man. Your father and I will always be here to protect you, my angel," she said.

Not long afterwards, in the bitter agony of the storm that even now was clouding Fleur's horizon, the young girl remembered those loving words. They were words spoken from the heart, but in blissful ignorance. For soon neither her mother's devotion—nor her father's strength—could protect Fleur from the doom that awaited her.

Chapter Three

On May 24, when the Roddneys held a Ball to celebrate their daughter's eighteenth birthday, another birthday was being celebrated at Kensington Palace. Another young girl was entering her nineteenth year; Victoria with a royal destiny and a brilliant future before her.

All day it had seemed to Fleur that her own destiny was every bit as wonderful as that of any Royal Princess could be.

Hélène tried to make her rest but the excitement had conquered. Fleur wanted to have a hand in everything, and when all was done, had wandered arm in arm with her mother through the house. Never had the reception-room looked more magnificent. The Aubusson carpets had been rolled away. The floors were waxed and polished until they looked like golden glass. Banks of flowers, and tall palms, were placed in all corners and there was a raised dais for the orchestra that had been especially engaged for the night.

Three great chandeliers hanging from the carved ceiling glittered with light from hundreds of wax candles. All over the house, the candles burned in their gilt or silver sconces. Fires crackled in the grates, for the May night was cool. But it had been a lovely day and fortunately it was a lovely starlit night without the fog that Fleur had dreaded, and which might have kept some of the guests away.

The guest chambers at Pillars were full. Cousin Dolly had come to stay with the twins and her son Cyril, who was a little less gloomy and dumb than usual because he had just passed his entrance examination for Oxford. Nobody knew how he had managed it but it had given his mother something really to boast about at last with her dull-witted family. Now, she was telling everybody that "darling Cyril was the cleverest boy in the world and would *astonish* the dons, when term began."

The Roddneys had spared no expense to make this birthday party a perfect one for their idolized child. In the dining-room, the servants had already loaded side tables and buffet with every variety of food. Great dishes of stuffed veal in aspic, York hams, cold game, French and Russian salads; towering confections of jelly, fruit, and cakes with whipped cream and nuts; bowls of fruit salad; trifles in silver dishes and of course, in the centre, the birthday cake made by the Roddneys' chef who came from France and had surpassed himself. What a wonderful cake it was, thought Fleur. Three tiers of white icing like turrets, edged with pink, and studded with glazed cherries. And Fleur's name was written across it in pink icing, with "HAPPY BIRTHDAY" and the date.

The sight of the eighteen candles which she would light later this evening, made Fleur clasp her hands together like an enchanted child.

"So many! Oh, Mama, I am growing too old, and too fast. I wish now to go back and not forward."

But her mother had kissed her and laughed.

"We must never go back in life, my darling—always forward. For you, I pray, it will be ever upward, too—to the starry heights!"

Now Fleur was dressed waiting for the guests.

St. Cheviot arrived early. He was at the moment in residence in London. He was standing at the foot of the staircase when Fleur appeared to take her place beside her mother and father who were receiving.

She had a few moments ago run up to her room for a moment in order that her maid should put a stitch in the flounce of her ball gown which had a tiny tear in it.

Lord St. Cheviot's black eyes, which had been full of boredom and indifference, smouldered suddenly into an unholy glow of admiration. As his glance fastened greedily upon the girl who seemed to float rather than walk down the staircase, his pulses gave a wild throb—as they had throbbed and beaten upon the first night he had seen her at Lady Roddney's dinner party. Now, as *then*, he seemed to hear an echo of the prophecy made by the crippled girl who had died in her brother's arms that stormy October night outside the gates of Cadlington House.

"Within twelve months from now you will marry," she

had said before she expired. "I who can see into the future foretell this marriage. But with it comes disaster. Red-gold hair and violets—watch out for red-gold hair and violets. . . . It shall be . . ."

He remembered those words and tonight with more than ordinary excitement he continued to watch Fleur Roddney.

The dress chosen by her mother, and made by the French *couturier* who had come especially to Pillars to fashion it, was as snow-white as the girl's long neck and delicately rounded arms. Flounce upon flounce of the fine frilly lace—until it reached the tips of small white satin shoes. The corsage was cut low but modestly so, with rosettes of satin ribbons, drooping a little off the shoulders. A wide violet-blue sash was tied around the small waist. Her curls clustered silkily about her neck. Those large shining eyes, the hue of violets in her hair, made St. Cheviot catch his breath. In vain he looked to see if she carried the orchids he had sent, but she did not.

"Devil take it," he muttered to himself, "I do not think she fancies me."

As Fleur reached the last stair, and stood there a moment, he impeded her further progress. The thought flashed through his mind:

"*I must have her*. The hunchback's prophecy shall be carried out. Fleur, and Fleur alone shall be Lady St. Cheviot—Baroness of Cadlington."

He bowed low.

"Your servant, Miss Roddney . . ."

She looked up at him but she did not return his smile. She did not like it; it had the quality of ice—and behind the ice—the threat of fire. She did not like him. Yet he was the most handsome man in the room.

Black hair well oiled, curling across his brow, side whiskers, high collar, satin cravat; and like most of the gentlemen here, he wore knee breeches, silk hose and a cutaway coat. He was handsome and haughty and towered above the others because of his remarkable height. Fleur murmured a timid greeting; she felt at the same time as though his presence too greatly overshadowed her. She could no longer see the sparkling chatting laughing crowd—nor her parents who were near the front door. She had a wild sensation of terror, almost claustrophobic in its origin, and although St. Cheviot would have detained her, rushed past him and fled to her mother. She was pale and trembling as she reached Hélène's side, but said nothing of what she felt. Hélène was too busy welcoming late-comers to notice her daughter's distress.

Now the music was playing and young Tom Quinley thrust through the crowd to ask Fleur to open the Ball with him. She was about to write her initials on his programme when a tall figure slid smoothly between them. St. Cheviot, a hand on his heart, bowed.

"If you will grant me the pleasure, Miss Roddney . . ."

She wanted to say "*No*"; to cry to Tom to stay. But the boy was much too overawed by the age and magnificence of the well-known baron, and grimacing his disappointment moved off.

"Keep the next one—the schottische—for me, Fleur," he called as he went.

St. Cheviot crooked an arm. Fleur had no choice but to place a hand through it.

"I shall esteem this a very great honour," he murmured, "and might I say that tonight you look like the Spirit of all the flowers in the world?"

She made no answer. As before when she had listened to Denzil St. Cheviot, she was silent before his flattery. She was a little angry, too, because she felt this had been forced upon her. She had wanted to open the Ball with Tom, her friend. St. Cheviot was too masterful. Perhaps it was that he gave one such a feeling that he expected his wishes to be carried out instantly that she disliked. She, the least rebellious of people, wished suddenly to rebel.

The opening dance was a polka. St. Cheviot placed a kid-gloved hand at the back of the girl's slight waist. She placed her right hand on his. It might have been a snowflake, he thought, for all the impression it made. And when he considered what he had just said to her about being the Spirit of all flowers, he thought sardonically:

" 'Twould be a pity to cut her down and watch her die."

But immediately, as he moved with her on to the polished floor, a less merciful thought followed.

" 'Tis a pity, too, that I hold her here with formality and for all the world to see, and must contain myself, for I would like to crush her against me and bruise that meek young mouth with kisses; teach her that Denzil St. Cheviot is to be reckoned with."

Unmindful of any such hateful reflections, Fleur danced with the man whom her father had invited here. Those looking on were whispering what a handsome couple they made—the tall dark man and the slight fair girl. St. Cheviot was a graceful dancer and a good match for Fleur, who moved exquisitely. For a moment the other guests watched them and then Hélène, not wishing her daughter to be thus exhibited, followed with her husband. Soon the floor was crowded with couples.

The gay polka ended, St. Cheviot crooked his arm and escorted Fleur towards the conservatory. He manœuvred her through a doorway and she found herself seated on one of the red plush sofas.

"May I get you some refreshment, Miss Roddney?" he asked.

"Nothing, I thank you," she answered breathlessly.

His dark sombre gaze held hers. He saw how she shrank from him. It did not deter him. On the contrary it fired his longing to overcome her reluctance.

Fleur sat twisting the little painted fan which she held between her lace-mittened fingers. She attempted to discuss the crowd.

"Many people have come to my birthday," she murmured, "and I have had some wonderful presents. Look—my papa gave me this . . ."

Artlessly she held out a delicate wrist on which there glittered a little bangle of pearls, simply set in gold. St. Cheviot gave a smile that was more a sneer.

"A pretty bauble," he said, "but unworthy of that exquisite arm. At Cadlington there is a diamond bracelet that belonged to my French grandmother. It was Marie Antoinette's and is valued at thousands of pounds. I would like you to wear it."

Fleur swallowed. Her lashes fluttered. She looked to the right and left like a startled fawn.

"I—treasure my father's gift—but I—am not really interested in valuable jewels," she stammered.

But St. Cheviot was thinking:

"Her waist is so small I could almost take two of the old *Comtesse* Marguerite's bracelets and make them into a diamond belt for Fleur. One day I shall. *And I myself shall clasp it around her.*"

"Where are my orchids?" he asked suddenly with a bluntness that defeated Fleur. Once again she was distressed, not wishing to appear rude.

"The orchids were splendid, thank you. I—but I could not wear them, they—it was necessary for my attire tonight that I should wear violets," she said in the same stammering frightened little voice.

St. Cheviot folded his arms and looked down at her with his humourless smile.

"I will have more sent to you from Cadlington tomorrow. You can make a carpet with them and tread upon them with your little bare feet. I do not mind."

Such talk merely terrified her. She half-rose.

"No, sit down again," he said in a softer voice, and told himself that he must control his rising passion. He was used to putting out a hand and taking what he wanted. Such women liked force, but this one he could see must be wooed, *tamed*.

"Sit down, I beg of you, Miss Roddney," he repeated. "I apologize if I have said anything to offend your ears."

She put a hand on her fast-beating heart.

"I hear the strains of a schottische. I promised Mr. Quinley——"

"Will you not stay and talk with me?"

"No——" she began, and now saw to her utter relief the tall boyish figure of young Tom Quinley. He was not remarkable to look at and just now appeared rather red-faced and clumsy beside the magnificent baron, but to Fleur he was a sweet sight—a rock of refuge.

"Our dance, I think, Tom," she said.

He bowed and crooked his arm. She took it and walked away with him without so much as a backward glance at St. Cheviot.

He narrowed his lids until his eyes were like black slits. Up went his brows. A sardonic grin widened his lips. The first round to *her*. The first of many, perhaps, in the tussle that lay before them. Instead of returning to the ball-room, he called to a passing footman to fetch his hat and cloak. He was driving back to London at once. He left behind him a note for Harry Roddney.

> Your pardon but I have been taken ill and have called my carriage. I do not think your daughter likes me but I wish you to know that I would lay my life down for her gladly.
>
> St. Cheviot.

When Harry received this note he passed it, in some surprise, to his wife. Hélène shrugged her shoulders.

"I doubt if it was illness—I warrant it was pique. Fleur has just told me that she found him and his talk detestable, and shewed it."

"Dear, dear," said Harry and pulled the lobe of his ear, not pretending to understand his womenfolk in this matter. He saw only the loss of some very good shooting and entertainment if St. Cheviot should remain "piqued." But certainly if his darling did not care for the man, he must be allowed to go.

Chapter Four

A little less than a month later, on the 20th June, the star that had hung over the head of the Duchess of Kent's daughter flashed into sudden prominence. Her uncle, William IV, died on the 20th June, and the young Victoria became Queen of England.

When Fleur heard this news she was staying in London with Cousin Dolly in their tall narrow elegant house that faced Knightsbridge Green. They all heard it—the salute of guns—the newsboys dashing through the streets—the hurry and scurry of shopkeepers to put up the shutters and fix the crêpe to doors and hats. England was plunging into mourning for a King who had left no particular mark in the world. But that young fragile-looking girl with the lion's heart who had received the kiss of homage from her ministers in the early hours of this morning, was destined to rule over the greatest Empire history had ever known.

It was exciting news for England and for every family, including the de Veres. Archibald de Vere had gone out early and come back to tell them of the vast crowds surging round the Palace and the excitement that prevailed. Cousin Dolly immediately rushed the twins upstairs to find black dresses, and sent a message to Miss Golling, her dressmaker, to come at once. There were not many black gowns in Dolly's own wardrobe. Fleur, too, must get into mourning instantly, she declared.

Fleur meant to enjoy London but had not come here very willingly she had to admit to herself, although she behaved with the utmost sweetness and docility and tried not to let the twins—or Cyril—see how bored she was by their incessant vapid chatter.

Quite unexpectedly, Papa had been called to Paris, there to investigate the unfortunate death of a man who had worked for many years both for his old friend and benefactor James Wilberson; and for Harry while he had served in the Far East with the East India Company.

The man appeared to have died under particularly tragic circumstances and left a widow there, a helpless invalid. Harry Roddney, ever generous and conscientious, had deemed it his duty to go over and do what he could for the wretched woman; even bring her home. On a sudden impulse, Hélène had volunteered to accompany her husband. At this time of the year, the Channel crossing would not be rough and she might, she said, find it pleasant on a sunny day on one of the little paddle-steamers that took passengers from Dover to Calais.

"Papa shall drive me down the *Rue de la Paix* and I shall buy a new bonnet and choose one for you, my dearest," she had smiled at her daughter.

"Oh, yes, Mama, do," had been Fleur's eager reply, "for I hear the summer bonnets in Paris this year are very fetching."

They had had a happy dinner together the night before Harry and Hélène took their little voyage, although Fleur had found her Papa preoccupied with sad thoughts of the excellent head clerk who had come to such a sad pass on the Continent; it would appear through gambling.

But the next morning as Fleur had kissed them farewell and watched the carriage drive them away from the portico on their journey to Dover—a strange presentiment of trouble had shaken the psychic consciousness of the young girl. She had had an almost irresistible urge to fly down the path and scream after them:

"Come back—oh, my beloved parents, *come back*."

Cousin Dolly, who was with her, had been surprised when Fleur burst into hysterical weeping.

"Fie on you for being such a baby! Your parents will not be gone more than a week," she had said and led the girl back into the house, where the twins sympathetically offered their handkerchiefs!

Fleur had done her best to recover from this strange depression and to deem herself foolish and over-sensitive. Mama and Papa meant to stay in Paris only for a few days it was true—and then they would all be together again.

"I do believe you will weep at your own wedding!" Cousin Dolly scolded her.

Fleur had hastily assured Cousin Dolly that there was no wedding in sight, and that she meant to remain with her parents as long as she could.

With this, Cousin Dolly had little patience. Here she was, desperately trying to find suitors for the twins, and men from all sides milling around to get the beauitful Miss Roddney to smile at them. If *she* were Hélène, she would be positively annoyed with the obstinate young miss. As for the St. Cheviot business—that was more than annoying to Mrs. de Vere. For unknown to her Cousin Harry or his wife, she was in secret contact with St. Cheviot; in a manner which would have greatly angered both the Roddneys had they known.

St. Cheviot had not taken the slight he had received at Pillars very well. Dolly had heard reports that he returned to town in a towering rage and let everybody know it. He had even spoken of Fleur as a "spoiled pampered brat who needed a lesson." Nevertheless, he was so far challenged that he had, since the Ball, persisted in his advances. Lady Roddney gave him no encouragement, and when he saw Harry on occasions at the Club, the kindly jovial baronet spoke with him but seemed embarrassed about his daughter and avoided the subject.

Dolly knew that every morning now for four weeks, huge boxes of orchids had arrived at Pillars from Cadlington House. Valuable exotic blooms, purple and red and yellow-green—all shapes and sizes on long sprays. With each box, he sent a card always with the same words:

> Make a carpet of these if you so wish but do not ignore me.
>
> St. Cheviot.

Dolly would have given her silly empty little soul for this mark of favour from such a splendid and handsome person, devil though he was. Yet she had been told by the girl, herself, that as soon as the orchids came, she gave them away to anybody who wanted them.

"They are poisonous and they terrify me," she said. "I do not wish to receive tokens from *him*."

"But what have you against him?" Dolly asked, looking at the girl with round astonished eyes.

"I do not know," was the reply. "I just do not care for him."

But the orchids continued to come. Now, although Fleur did not know how he discovered it, St. Cheviot found out that she was staying in London with the de Veres. Every morning that same box was delivered at Knightsbridge from Buckinghamshire; brought thither by a rider on a sweating foaming horse. The very sight of the poor mount (Fleur had seen it arrive several times) disgusted her. He must be a cruel man, she thought, to allow an animal to be ridden almost to death in order that she should receive his flowers so early.

She refused to acknowledge her receipt of them, and once when Cousin Dolly suggested that St. Cheviot should be allowed to call, she turned so white that Mrs. de Vere had to capitulate with a shrug of the shoulders.

"As you wish, my love, but you are missing a great chance."

On this the morning of the King's death and the accession of the young Victoria, Fleur permitted Cousin Dolly's maid to measure her for a mourning gown and thought longingly of her parents.

At any moment now they would surely return from Paris and take her back to Pillars. She felt stifled in this fussy, ornate, noisy little house where it seemed to her that Cousin Dolly and the twins screamed all day.

Cousin Dolly, becomingly attired in black, with black bonnet and black fringed shawl, peered in to see what Fleur was doing. Fleur showed her a book that she was about to read. It made Cousin Dolly shudder. Gibbon's *Decline and Fall of the Roman Empire*. Heavens, she thought, what an uncomfortable girl! She enjoyed *history* instead of joining with Isabel and Imogen in the search for attractive mourning apparel.

"Oh, well," murmured Dolly, "we will gather together for the midday meal. I have an appointment with Miss Ply. *Au revoir*, dearest Fleur."

Little did Fleur know that Cousin Dolly was hastening to a rendezvous with Denzil St. Cheviot, himself. Veil over her face, and tiny parasol to shield her from the sun, the plump little woman sat puffing on a bench beside the Baron. He looked immensely bored.

"Is it not exciting that we have a Queen on the throne and when the time of mourning is passed, we can embark upon a brilliant social life in London," Dolly twittered.

"I did not come here to discuss the new Queen," said St. Cheviot in his most icy voice. "What of *her*?"

"Oh, it is tragic, but I cannot induce Fleur to see you or visit Cadlington," sighed Dolly.

St. Cheviot's lips drew into a thin line. He tapped his thumb-nail against the tall beaver hat to which was affixed a rosette of black crêpe. He looked taller and leaner than ever in his mourning clothes. He said:

"She receives my flowers daily?"

"Yes, my dear St. Cheviot, and throws them away."

"As she is trying to throw me," said St. Cheviot grimly.

Dolly floundered in her mind for a method of bringing Cousin Roddney's rebellious daughter to heel. St. Cheviot had struck a financial bargain with Dolly. He had discovered that she was heavily in debt.

At their last meeting, St. Cheviot had promised her a reward—handsome enough to make her senses swim—if she could aid and abet his courtship of her young cousin. The Roddneys need never know and it would be a solution to Mrs. de Vere's present embarrassment.

"Well," said Denzil curtly, and dug the end of an ebony stick which he carried, into the gravel, "have you no suggestions?"

"Oh, dear, it is so *difficult*," said Dolly. "Fleur is such a determined child."

"I, too, am determined," said the man coldly.

"Youth is temperamental," added Dolly. "She does not care for orchids."

"Bah!" said St. Cheviot, "then I will send—violets."

Dolly brightened.

"You might *try* them. I know she dotes on them. Meanwhile I will continue to sing your praises."

He bowed, escorted her to her carriage and left her.

He went down to Cadlington only at week-ends. His temper was frayed. The servants were in fear and trembling. Only Peveril Marsh dared speak to him. The young artist often received visits from the master.

Denzil would pace up and down the studio in the tower, gloomily watching the boy bring his splendid painting of Cadlington to life. He only half recognized the genius of the artist. It was in himself and his affairs that St. Cheviot was interested. Again and again he would question Peveril as to the validity of his dead sister's power of divining.

"Had she truly the gift of seeing into the future?" the Baron would demand repeatedly—tormented with desire for Fleur.

Peveril would look with his grave eyes at the bitter face of his strange patron and answer:

"I believe so, my lord. That is all I can tell you. Always when Elspeth told fortunes her prophecies came true."

Then Denzil would lose interest in the picture—and in his protégé—and return to his own quarters, to drink heavily until dawn.

Chapter Five

Fleur sat in the small writing-room at the back of Cousin Dolly's house, scanning the weekly newspaper which had just been delivered and which was widely bordered with black.

It was some forty-eight hours since King William IV had breathed his last.

This morning, Lord Melbourne had brought the first message from the Queen to the House of Lords, and Lord John Russell moved a similar address to the Commons.

Fleur, brought up by her father to be interested in her country's affairs, looked with interest at an article which described the present period as one of "perfect tranquillity." The young Queen had ascended the throne at a great moment in history. The country could look forward to a reduction in taxation, an improvement in the standard of living and a relaxation of the terrible severity of the present criminal laws.

It was expected, the paper said, that the young Queen would open Parliament in November; surrounded by wise elderly advisers there seemed little doubt that this new sovereign would inspire loyal devotion from her subjects.

Fleur continued to read the article, then lifted her eyes from it and thought deeply about this young Queen who was her own age. Henceforth Victoria Regina must live constantly in the fierce light that beats upon the throne. Nothing that she could do or say could be concealed. A husband would be chosen for her; she could not even fall in love and marry as Fleur Roddney hoped to do—a man of her own choosing.

"Who would be a queen?" Fleur asked herself and sighed in sympathy, wondering whether that very young girl, now immersed in state duties in her palace, ever felt lonely or afraid. *As I would feel in her place,* Fleur said the words aloud. *God bless and strengthen the poor little Queen!*

Then a feeling of happiness replaced the melancholy that Fleur had been enduring at her parents' absence. Last night a gentleman who knew Papa had brought a sealed message from Paris. A letter from Papa, telling his darling that they would be back in England tomorrow. Papa suggested that Fleur should drive with her maid to Pillars and there wait for the coach which would bring Mama and Papa from Dover. The little family would be reconciled in their own home.

"Oh, heavenly thought!" Fleur exclaimed and folded the newspaper which Cousin Dolly had said must be preserved for Archibald. Fleur had seen little of Cousin Archibald except during meal times. He seemed to her to be a docile silly gloomy man. He was always vainly grumbling at the cost of things and accusing the servants (if not his wife) of reckless extravagance in the house.

That evening, Fleur attended what she hoped would be the last family dinner with the de Veres. She was wild with excitement at the thought of returning to her own home. Cousin Dolly remarked on her colour and high spirits.

"It is not flattering to us," she pouted, "I hope you will not let your Papa think we have failed to amuse you."

"Oh, dear no, I have been much amused, Cousin Dolly," said Fleur with her exquisite *politesse.*

Dolly was growing more than a little afraid of the debts that were growing about her ears and terrified that Archibald would get to hear of them. She had warded off most of her creditors by assuring them that she expected to receive a fat legacy any day now and that "legacy" should have come from St. Cheviot—after his engagement to Fleur. Devil take the girl for being so obstinate in her dislike of him, and her stupid childish attachment to her family, thought Dolly.

This morning, the horseman from Cadlington had brought, instead of the usual orchids, a magnificent box of red roses lying upon a solid bank of violets. When Dolly had opened this box and shown the exquisite blooms to the girl (who declined the offering) she had screamed with rapture:

"How can you *resist*? *Really*, my love, you are rejecting a *great* passion from a *great* man."

Fleur had merely touched the violets with the tips of her fingers, a faint regretful smile curving her young lips.

"The flowers are beautiful, Cousin. One cannot help but love them, but I do not wish to accept favours from the gentleman who has sent them," she said.

Archibald de Vere rose from the dinner table and his family rose respectfully with him. As they trailed through the drawing-room, the master of the house glanced at Fleur out of the corners of his eyes. He said:

"So you leave us tomorrow, my pretty dear?"

"Yes, Cousin Archibald," said Fleur.

Dolly sniffed. Archibald never alluded to his own daughters as "pretty dears." Drat that girl! All men seemed to fall for her; even Archibald, who had little time for females.

"Let us hope," continued Mr. de Vere, settling himself in his favourite armchair in the drawing-room, "that the weather grows more clement for your parents' crossing. I fear they say the seas are running high."

Fleur walked to one of the windows and looked anxiously out at the rain. Yes, it was a wild drenching night. She could see the trees tossing on Knightsbridge Green, and the carriage horses slipping and straining in the muddy roads. Nobody would dream that this was June. She thought of poor Mama being tossed about on a rough Channel in one of those little paddle steamers. She bit her lips, Papa loved the sea but Mama would be *very* indisposed, indeed.

Fleur played a game of backgammon with the twins, then retired early to bed.

She wakened early and untying her little cambric cap, ran quickly to the window to look upon the weather. Alas, it was still blowing h rd and the park looked sad and sodden.

"Oh, poor Mama, how she will dislike the homeward journey," thought Fleur, and rang for her maid. Now to pack—delicious thought—to pack and prepare for the carriage which was to take them down to Essex at eleven o'clock. It was anticipated that her parents would arrive at Pillars before dark.

The farewells to her cousins were said. The twins blew

their noses and professed to shed a tear. Cousin Dolly said that she "regretted Fleur's short visit" and dared to murmur at the last, while a coachman tucked a plaid rug around Fleur's knees. "Do not be too harsh with poor Denzil St. Cheviot. He is eaten up with longing for you."

But all that naughty greedy Dolly got for her pains was a toss of Miss Roddney's lovely head and that mutinous twist of rosy lips that were usually so soft and smiling.

Dolly watched the carriage depart, feeling that she had failed on Denzil's behalf, and wondering miserably when the storm of debts would break over her foolish head and bring the wrath of her husband about her ears.

Meanwhile Fleur enjoyed every moment of the long drive from Knightsbridge Green to Essex; stopping only once or twice while her maid tossed pennies at the turnpikes as the young lady's carriage passed through. But she chatted merrily with her confidential maid. Molly had tended her since she was twelve years old. She was simple, direct and passionately devoted to Fleur's mother.

"There lives no finer lady in the land than my Lady Roddney, your dear mother," she would say to Fleur from time to time. "God's blessing be on her head."

Today Molly was a little more subdued and less talkative than usual. When Fleur asked what ailed her, the young woman blushed and drew a lugubrious sigh.

"I trust you are not sick, my good Molly!" exclaimed Fleur.

To which the maid then confessed that she was sick of heart, though not of body, and gradually there tumbled from her the confession that she had fallen in love for the first time, and with one of the serving-men in Mrs. de Vere's household. Noggins was his name. Vaguely Fleur called to mind the said Noggins who cleaned silver and worked mainly in the pantry. Decidedly a plain young man with a shock of red hair. But Molly seemed to think that he had all the graces. Well, well, Fleur thought, and smiled to herself; poor Molly was no beauty and Noggins appeared to be the first man who had ever paid serious court to her.

"Poor Molly, and you have been dragged away from your suitor. Alas, you must be very unhappy. What can I do for you?"

Molly fervently assured Miss Roddney that she could do nothing. Noggins had promised to remain sober and respectable and to save until such day as he could ask her to wed.

Once home, Fleur thought no more about love and Molly was too busy to remember to weep for Tom Noggins. There was much to be done. The lazy servants to marshal, special flowers to be arranged in Lady Roddney's room, a fine dinner to be prepared for the master and mistress who were returning home.

Later on Fleur attired herself in a dress of pale blue silk, which was a special favourite with her father. She fixed forget-me-nots in her bright hair. She sat in the withdrawing-room, an enchanting picture of maidenly loveliness, her ears strained for the first sound of horses' hooves in the drive. How late her dear ones were in coming. 'Twould be a pity, she thought, if the dinner were spoilt.

It was some time before Fleur began to be anxious. Then she rang the bell for Molly. She must talk to someone, for now the young girl was truly disturbed. Darkness had fallen long ago; still no sign of Sir Harry and Lady Roddney.

Fleur looked at her maid anxiously.

"Oh, Molly, there must have been an accident."

"No, no, miss," muttered the maid, although within herself she felt a rising apprehension.

Fleur clasped her long delicate fingers together.

"What else can have delayed them so? If only we were not so isolated and could communicate with Dover and find out what time the steam packet arrived. But, alas, we cannot."

"If it ever arrived," thought the maid grimly, although she dared not say so. But in the servants' hall they had been talking; Vyler, the butler, had recalled a terrible storm some years ago (Miss Roddney was still an infant) when one of the paddle steamers had sunk to the bottom of the sea.

It was nearing ten o'clock and at last there came the sound of carriage wheels. At once the colour returned to Fleur's face and she rushed into the hall.

"At last they are come, Molly. Oh, thank God!"

She did not wait for the servants. She herself flung open the heavy oaken front door.

A guest of wind whirled the flounces of her gay dress around her ankles. Then the chill, as of death itself, struck the girl as she saw the man who stepped out of the carriage and walked towards her. The greeting prepared for her parents died on her lips, never to be uttered. For it was her cousin-by-marriage, Archibald de Vere, himself, who walked into the hall. The man to whom she had said farewell early this morning.

He looked strained and grave, muffled in a thick grey cloak. He removed his high-crowned hat as he walked slowly towards the girl and shut out the rain-swept night behind him.

"Fleur, my dear child—" he began but stopped as though he could go no further.

Such terror seized Fleur's soul in that instant that she could make no movement, neither could she speak. Rooted to the spot she stared at Cousin Archibald. Before he spoke again she realized one thing—that he could be no harbinger of good news. She stared at him wildly, seeking mutely for the truth, no matter how terrible. Then de Vere, who was kindly despite his inherent meanness, and was desperately sorry for Fleur, cleared his throat and spoke again:

"Alas, my dear child, what I have to say to you can bring you nothing but great pain."

Molly, the maid, drew nearer, her hands clasped, her own face pale as she strained her ears to hear what was being said. But suddenly Fleur gave a piercing cry.

"*Mama! . . . Papa!* . . . What has happened to them?"

Archibald told her, faltering a little. The thing must be said. Dolly had sent him down here with two of their fastest horses to draw the carriage, in order that the news —which had already reached London—should be conveyed to the unfortunate girl.

The steam packet which had left Calais this morning had not reached Dover, nor ever would. One of the worst summer storms in history had broken over the small boat within sight of the English coast. The details were as yet unknown but coastguards reported that the steamer had sunk and that there were no survivors.

The unhappy Archibald, who had never been on a more distressing mission, fingered his hat, scowling at it. He dared not look at the young girl. He heard her low anguished cry:

"God have mercy . . . *have mercy* . . . do not let this terrible thing be true!"

De Vere spoke again.

"There is no hope. Of that we are certain, such is the violence of the storm—and it is still blowing—the seas were mountainous and even the strongest swimmer could not reach the shore."

Fleur only half heard these words. Her voice rose hysterically:

"They are drowned! My Mama and Papa are drowned . . . forever lost to me."

"Mary, Mother of God, have mercy," muttered Molly, who was a Catholic, crossed herself several times and went down on her knees in the hall.

Before Fleur's eyes she seemed to see those cold relentless waves . . . Mama, so beautiful, so delicate, sinking, sinking, choking for breath as the cruel water closed over her lovely head. Papa, so gay and handsome, trying to save Mama and failing. Death for them both. A cold watery grave—together still even to that agonizing end.

It was too much for the highly sensitive and imaginative girl—child of that great love which Harry and Hélène had borne each other. Darkness engulfed her. She fell senseless into Archibald de Vere's outstretched arms.

Chapter Six

Two months later, on a hot day at the beginning of August, Fleur sat in the writing-room opposite her Cousin Dolly in the little house in Knightsbridge which she had left so gaily that morning in June for the anticipated reunion with her parents.

For the last hour, Dolly de Vere had been saying the same thing over and over again.

"You have no choice, my dear. You must do as you are told, and you *must* remember that until you are of age, you come under Mr. Nonseale's jurisdiction, and my care."

Fleur made no answer. She had really hardly spoken during this conversation any more than she had spoken during the last eight weeks. It was as though the shock of the tragedy that had befallen her had robbed her of normal speech. She answered only in monosyllable. *"Yes, Cousin Dolly," "No, Cousin Dolly."* Mrs. de Vere found it most aggravating. She would almost rather have had an out and out quarrel with the girl.

"It's time you stopped this grieving," continued Dolly in a pettish voice, "and took a little more interest in life. A girl cannot weep for ever because her dear parents are accidentally drowned——" She broke off, for suddenly the silent black-robed figure of the girl jerked and moved as though she was a marionette, and this was the cue for her to come to life. She sprang up and turned on her father's cousin with such fury that Mrs. de Vere shrank back, flabbergasted. Fleur's face was colourless. Her eyes, dim with crying, flashed with a mixture of hatred and defiance that made even silly Dolly de Vere feel frightened. A hoarse voice said:

"Why do you not leave me alone? What have I ever

done that you should plague me so? Why can I not be left in peace to mourn for my darling Mama and Papa? Oh, I hate you, *I hate you*, Cousin Dolly, and I wish I had never been born!" And now the tears came in a flood, scorching down Fleur's cheeks. She rushed to the door. Mrs. de Vere, quick as an eel, wriggled herself there first and spread-eagled her arms to prevent the girl passing.

"Why, you ungrateful girl—to speak to me so," she panted, her own plump little face scarlet with mortification. "We took you in and gave you a home and this is your way of thanking us. I must say I feel very affronted."

"Let me pass," stammered Fleur, shaking. "Let me go to my own room."

"No, you will stay here and listen to me," said Mrs. de Vere. There were ugly thoughts twisting in and out of her foolish brain; thoughts very much connected with the future of this orphaned girl—*and* Denzil St. Cheviot. So far, despite all Dolly's efforts—her pleadings, arguments, or reproaches—she had not been able to induce Fleur to meet St. Cheviot. That gentleman, however, was now a regular visitor at the de Veres' house. And now Archibald was no longer in the way. His old business house in Calcutta had sent an urgent demand for his presence owing to a money crisis in the Company, and a couple of weeks ago, Mr. de Vere had sailed for India.

In consequence, Dolly had redoubled her efforts to pitch Fleur into St. Cheviot's arms. Her personal affairs were in such poor shape that she dare not delay any longer. She needed the golden sovereigns that St. Cheviot metaphorically rattled for her hearing, and she salved her conscience by telling herself that it was "for the twins," not for her own sake, that she wanted money so badly.

Dolly screamed at Fleur:

When St. Cheviot came to dine this evening, Fleur was pleased to be present. She was to take off that mourning gown and put on something more colourful and fetching. She was to sing and play for his lordship's amusement. Later, when she was alone with him, and when he proposed, *she was to accept him*.

This marriage had been arranged by Mr. Nonseale and Cousin Dolly herself. It had their full consent.

"But not Cousin Archibald's! He will protect me!" Fleur broke in at last, her lips quivering, her huge eyes tormented.

"Your Cousin Archibald is now upon the ocean voyaging to Calcutta and will not be back until Christmas announced Dolly triumphantly.

Fleur looked to the right and to the left, moving her graceful head with the frantic gesture of a hunted fawn. Mrs. de Vere added a few more sharp words.

"Understand, Fleur, that the time has passed when you can defy me."

"My parents would not have wished this. My Mama did not like Lord St. Cheviot any more than I do," said Fleur in a desperate voice.

"Regrettable though it is, I now stand in the place of your Mama," said Dolly arrogantly, and marched out of the room and shut the door behind her.

Fleur looked at the closed door. It might well have been barred and bolted like the gate of a prison. And Cousin Dolly was her jailer. The change in Dolly was incredible to Fleur. Never before had she experienced spiteful cruelty or ill-treatment. She had always lived in innocence and joy with her parents. Could it be only nine weeks ago, she asked herself, that they had so gaily celebrated her eighteenth birthday at Pillars? She was still only eighteen, but now no more young. Her girlhood had been murdered as though the dewy blossom were crushed by the heavy fist of the misfortune that had fallen on her.

Brought back to London by Mr. de Vere, Fleur had remained in bed, too ill to care what happened to her.

All England was shocked by the appalling disaster that had overtaken the little paddle steamer in that Channel storm.

Many friends visited her at first but Fleur had not been able to understand why her bosom friend, Cathy Foster, should have abandoned her in this hour of need. Later, the twins let out the fact that their mother had been very rude to Mrs. Foster. It was, of course, at the back of Dolly's mind to separate Fleur from all her closest friends. For this was, Dolly felt, a heaven-sent opportunity to get Fleur completely under her control and so bring about the engagement to St. Cheviot.

When, at length, Fleur rose from her bed, a pale ghost of herself, it was only to be hurled into a vortex of legal discussions and arrangements which were all being made over her innocent head. She was too bewildered to understand half of them. But she was at least forced to comprehend at last that life was not the simple happy affair that her parents had brought her up to believe. Now she began to suffer for the tender care that poor Hélène had taken of her beloved child. And she was the victim, too, of Harry Roddney's deepest failing. He had always been too happy-go-lucky and unwise in his choice of friends. Just as he had thought there was no real harm in the rakish St. Cheviot, so he had placed his trust in his Cousin Dolly. Fleur knew (for she had heard him say so) that he had always deemed her a butterfly, but had also believed her a fond kindly mother. He had never dreamed that she could be anything else to his unhappy daughter. Amongst the papers in the dead man's bureau, Archibald de Vere found his final Will and Testament. It declared that in case of the death of both parents, the young daughter was to be entrusted to the care of the de Veres and of Caleb Nonseale, Harry's lawyer. Hélène Roddney had never cared for Mr. Nonseale but Harry took no notice of the dislike. Nonseale had been adviser to his uncle, Sir Arthur—that was enough for *him*.

Fleur had so far had only one interview with Mr. Nonseale, and then every instinct had warned her that her good-natured father's trust in the lawyer had been misguided. So also must Harry's late uncle have been taken in by the wily, smooth-tongued legal gentleman.

When Caleb Nonseale spoke, he continually rubbed his hands together as though washing them. He never stopped smiling but it was not a smile that gave Fleur confidence. He discoursed at length and with much detail about affairs of her parents' estate which had no meaning for her. The only thing she could understand was that all her father's money, as well as the de Chartellet fortune (from her mother's side), would come to her when she was of age; and be entrusted to her husband should she marry.

At the end of the hour with Mr. Nonseale, he had said something to Fleur which had frightened her horribly.

"You are eighteen—already past the age when many young ladies are given in marriage," he observed, his beady eyes taking note of her several beauties (for beautiful Fleur must always be despite her sunken eyes and hollowed cheeks). "Mrs. de Vere and myself have discussed the matter, my dear, and decided that it will be a good thing for you to accept any—er—good offer that may now come along."

Nervously Fleur had made haste to assure Mr. Nonseale that she felt that it was far too soon after the demise of her dear Mama and Papa for her to consider a wedding.

"Besides, I have not yet met one whom I desire to wed," she finished.

Mr. Nonseale had frightened her still more.

"Now, come, come," he said, "your hand has, I understand, been asked for repeatedly by a fine nobleman. A great Baron—one who offers you title and riches beyond the expectations of most young ladies, I may say, my dear child."

Her blood froze as she judged his meaning.

"If it is of Lord St. Cheviot you speak, I will certainly never marry him," she said in a low voice.

The lawyer had continued to smile but he raised his bushy brows significantly.

"Ah well, we shall see!" he murmured.

From that time onwards, Fleur knew no peace. Dolly made merciless efforts to change her mind. Fleur thought she would go mad, listening to repeated praises of St. Cheviot.

When the poor harassed girl cried that she would sooner drown herself than become Lady St. Cheviot, Dolly called her conduct "disgraceful."

"What would your Mama and Papa have said to hear you make such an unchristian threat," she exclaimed.

To which Fleur, weeping, replied:

"Mama and Papa wished only for my happiness and said that I might choose my own husband."

Dolly answered that Miss Fleur Roddney was a spoiled brat.

Later on Fleur had gone quite humbly to Cousin Dolly and asked if she could draw enough money from the estate to live in retirement with her maid. If not at Pillars (dear, *dear* Pillars!) then in one of the cottages that had belonged to her father. This request was received by Cousin Dolly with a shrill laugh.

Fleur felt an increasing sense of despair and homesickness. She pined for Pillars but the place had been closed down. Donna, her mother's greyhound, picked up some poison in the grounds, sickened and died; so one by one the things that Fleur loved were being wrenched out of her life.

She did not feel well. The heat of London in August weighed her down.

Sometimes she considered running away. But to whom could she run? She was too proud to ask for succour from the Fosters since Cousin Dolly had affronted Mrs. Foster and Cathy was no longer her friend. And no gently nurtured girl born and brought up in the country could think of facing the sinister streets of London alone and penniless. One of the most outrageous of Dolly's acts had been to arrange with Caleb Nonseale that not one shilling of the fortune which was rightfully hers was to be paid to Fleur. Without money, she was powerless, and Dolly knew it.

Throughout the rest of this particular day Mrs. de Vere was more than ordinarily ill-tempered and spiteful. At last Fleur looked at her with beseeching eyes and said:

"Oh, Cousin Dolly, my unhappiness is too great to be borne. I do not feel I shall survive it!"

With a slight touch of anxiety, Mrs. de Vere regarded the young girl's sadly altered appearance. Drat it, she thought, she did not want Fleur to die. She controlled the wish to slap the girl. She tried once more to be affectionate, put an arm around Fleur and patted the poor bright head that drooped so piteously these days.

"My poor child, lean on my bosom," she said. "Oh, believe me I wish to comfort you and if I appear harsh it is only for your sake. I know what is best for you," she added with honeyed sweetness.

So starved was Fleur for a little love and understanding—so hungry for the warmth and devotion she used to receive from her parents—she flung herself into Cousin Dolly's arms in a touching manner.

"Oh, pray, Cousin Dolly, do not be harsh with me any longer, for my heart is breaking," she sobbed.

"Come then, do as I beg and consent to see his lordship at dinner this evening," cajoled the wily little woman. "You have built up in your imagination a false picture of him that has no truth in it. He is very splendid and would cherish you with his life."

A shudder went through Fleur's too-slender body. She kept her streaming eyes hidden against Mrs. de Vere's shoulder.

"Be sensible," Dolly wheedled, "and let him pay his respects to you, my love. Then you will be Cousin Dolly's own good little Fleur. And I am sure your Mama and Papa would rejoice if they knew that you were to make such a magnificent marriage."

Another shudder convulsed the girl. She whispered:

"And if I do not . . . will not . . . see him?"

Then Dolly played her trump card. Quite suddenly she went down on one knee before the girl, not caring what a ridiculous figure she cut, with her cap a little awry on her flaxen head; her big china blue eyes brimming with tears. She threw herself on Fleur's mercy. Now at last Fleur must be told how important it was that she should make an effort . . . if not for her own future's sake, for the sake of Cousin Dolly who had done everything for her since her Mama died. Dolly poured out to the astonished young girl the disgraceful story of her mad extravagance, and accumulation of debts; what disaster would befall her, and Isabel and Imogen, if those debts remained unpaid. Indeed so much did Dolly owe that she did not think Archibald would ever forgive her. He might punish her by leaving her to languish in a debtor's prison. Poor darling Cyril, he would have to give up Oxford. He would be ruined. *They would all be ruined . . . unless Fleur married St. Cheviot.*

Scarlet and confused, Fleur stared down at her father's cousin.

"But I surely have some means and could help you . . ." she stammered.

Whining and sniffing, Dolly explained that Fleur could not touch her money until she was of age—or had a husband, who would be able to control her fortune. Unfortunately, Harry Roddney had so worded the Will that Dolly could claim Fleur's money only with Mr. de Vere's consent; he being joint guardian. And him she dared not tell. Certainly she could not ask him to co-operate in drawing large sums of money from Fleur's estate.

Fleur was scarcely able to comprehend the legal facts that Dolly poured out. But she could and did understand that she might ruin Dolly and her children by refusing St. Cheviot.

"And is it only through my betrothal to Lord St. Cheviot that this money can be obtained?" Fleur asked in a low voice.

"Yes, my love," said Dolly, and she eyed the girl slyly, feeling that at last she might win the day.

A long sigh came from Fleur.

"You ask a terrible sacrifice of me, Cousin Dolly."

"Even so, I *do* ask it," said Cousin Dolly eagerly. "Oh, remember that I am your flesh and blood! Do not let me languish in a debtor's jail."

"If only Cousin Archibald were here," said Fleur in a despairing voice.

"But he is not," said Dolly. "My fate lies in your hands. Oh, my sweet Fleur, do not abandon me. I have been foolish, but it was for my children, and you know how well *your* Mama loved *you*!"

Fleur shut her eyes. She hardly dared think of her beautiful gentle mother and that love that was so cruelly lost.

To marry well seemed to be the first duty of a woman, she thought wearily. Not only Cousin Dolly, but many society matrons would think her crazy to hold out against Lord St. Cheviot.

Suddenly she felt that she could no longer go on fighting. She would at least consent to *see* and speak with Lord St. Cheviot again. In a voice of despair she said:

"I will dine with you tonight and—consider Lord St. Cheviot's proposal."

But when Dolly with an ecstatic cry sprang up to kiss her and called her "angel," Fleur shrank from her embrace. She did not even weep. She experienced an unutterable fatigue of body and mind; the loneliness of death, itself.

Chapter Seven

All through dinner St. Cheviot sat opposite Fleur and kept his dark desirous gaze upon her. He saw nobody else at that table. Even had Fleur not been there, he would not have bothered to look at Isabel and Imogen. Plump, giggling, they ate hugely, one course after another, and ogled the gentlemen beside whom they had been placed. Dolly had invited two young officers of the Dragoons, who were acquainted with the de Veres, to make up her numbers. She had also spent—in a wild gamble—a great deal of money on this important party. It was quite a banquet. The sombre, rather stuffy dining-room, was brilliantly illuminated with candle-light. The table shone with the best de Vere silver and glass. Dolly, herself was in pink taffeta with a little lace cap on hair done in coquettish ringlets that bobbed against her rouged and powdered face. She addressed St. Cheviot in the most servile fashion, complimenting him upon his looks, his taste in wines, etc.—or spoke in a voice of honeyed sweetness of her "beloved Fleur" as though she had never in her life nagged or bullied Harry's daughter.

To Fleur, the festive dinner was one long-drawn-out torment. Nothing that Cousin Dolly said could persuade her to change her mourning garb for a more colourful one. Her darling Mama and Papa had only been dead nine weeks. But she had never looked more alluring. The black evening gown made her skin look like the camellias that grew upon the south wall at Cadlington, he thought. Not once did she look straight into his eyes. She wore no jewellery, no ornament. Only two white roses. *His* roses, pinned to her corsage. He told himself cynically that no doubt Dolly had forced her to wear the flowers, but it was an encouraging sign.

When the dinner ended, Dolly marshalled her girls and

bade them take their escorts into the drawing-room for some music. To Fleur, she said:

"Lord St. Cheviot is most anxious to see that strange plant which your Cousin Archibald brought me from Covent Garden in the spring. Pray show it to him, my love."

Fleur's slight fingers twined convulsively around the little Dorothy-bag which she carried.

"Go along, my sweet child," said Dolly gushingly.

St. Cheviot crooked his arm. Fleur seemed to brace herself, as though for an ordeal, but she allowed the man to lead her into the conservatory. Useless to battle any more against this man's stubborn passion for her—or Cousin Dolly's determination. All day Fleur had thought about it—and of the reason why Dolly so much desired this match. All day she had asked herself if she could possibly bear her lot and make such a sacrifice; and if Papa would have wished it. To refuse and to send Cousin Dolly to a debtor's prison and disgrace the family—that would surely be too cruel.

Like a lamb to the slaughter she accompanied St. Cheviot and sank on to a small red plush sofa under a huge palm. St. Cheviot stood before her. Somehow the tremendous height of the man, and the breadth of his shoulders, frightened her. His ebon black hair was curled and pomaded. He held a lace-edged handkerchief in a white-gloved hand. Handsome, impeccable, and as Cousin Dolly kept reminding her, excessively rich, and always moving in that aura of wickedness which some women find mysteriously attractive. But not Fleur. After a moment she knew that he had seated himself beside her.

"It has been a long while, Miss Roddney, since we last spoke alone."

"Yes—oh—yes."

"Too long. A protracted misery for me. Why have you been so cruel?"

Her breath began to come quickly. The man's personality overawed her.

"I—did not mean to be cruel," she replied.

"You are very pale," he murmured. "Do you suffer so much? Is it an illness of the mind that weighs you down and has taken from you all the childish sparkle?"

Now she raised her eyes and gave him a long sad look. "That sparkle, as you call it, my lord, vanished for ever beneath the waves with my adored parents."

St. Cheviot scowled. He wished to let her think that he was a man of sympathy and understanding but emotions such as these displayed by this young girl were so foreign to him as to be incomprehensible. He had had no fondness for his own mother and father and regarded them in their lifetime only as barriers to his hunger for entertainment of a kind which they did not approve. And when they died he had mourned them only for the briefest possible time. He had been thankful for the freedom, the full control of money and possessions which their decease afforded him.

Now he cleared his throat and said:

"Alas, that sinking of the Channel steamer was a terrible tragedy. I know how you must feel."

"Do you?" she asked almost wistfully, as though seeking to touch one answering chord in him which might lead her to believe that this arrogant man had some real kindliness in him.

He bowed and answered:

"Most certainly. Who would not understand your grief? I respect it, also. But you are far too young to shut yourself away and, like Niobe, drown yourself in tears."

"Two months is not long," she said in a choked voice.

"For one who has so longed to look at you and hear your voice, it has seemed Eternity," he said glibly.

She sat silent. Her thoughts were with her parents. An Eternity, St. Cheviot said. Yes, so it seemed since she had looked upon Mama's beautiful face or heard Papa laugh, or walked beside them through the sunlit corridors of their country home. Long, so *long* . . . yet she did not want to emerge from her retreat in the shadows. The very sound of laughter or music hurt her now.

To her dismay she suddenly felt iron fingers grip one of her delicate hands. St. Cheviot had gone down upon his knee and was pressing his lips to her palm. It was a kiss so scorching that it terrified her. He seemed unable to control his terrible desire and continued to kiss the hand and to mutter wild protests of passion.

"I do so adore you . . . I beg . . . I implore you to thaw for me," he exlaimed. "You are all that is pure and perfect in my sight. I do most truly respect your grief and pain. I beseech you to turn to me for comfort. You are alone in the world now. Fleur, *Fleur,* take me for your husband. Give me the right to hold you evermore in these loving arms."

Well-chosen words. She listened to them dazedly. Deep within her she knew that had they come from the lips of a different man—one chosen by *her*—they might indeed have brought her the consolation she so badly needed. It would have been pleasant, indeed, to be able to lay her aching head against a heart that beat with tender love for her. But somehow every instinct in Fleur still recoiled from Denzil St. Cheviot. Now that she listened to him she knew that nothing could change her. She tried to drag her hand away from those greedy kisses.

"Lord St. Cheviot!" she protested faintly.

"Nay, do not shrink from me. Most lovely of flowers—all that I possess is yours for the asking. Marry me. Come to Cadlington House as its mistress, and my wife, and I swear that I will deny you nothing."

She sat there shivering. She knew that she wanted nothing that he could give her. A title, riches, all the furs and jewels in the world could not bring back her lost youth and happiness—or her parents. While she listened to St. Cheviot's frenzied appeals, two great tears rolled down her cheeks, sad twin diamonds glittering in the candle-light.

But the man did not note the tears nor had he it in his nature to show tenderness. He was consumed only with his longing to touch Fleur's young mouth. He spoiled the moment which might have been victorious for him, by suddenly sweeping her up into his arms.

"You shall not refuse me," he muttered. "I have your cousin's word for it that you will accept my proposal."

For the first time in her life, Fleur was kissed with a brutal passion that not only shocked her but decided her once and for all that she could never go through with this sacrifice, even for Cousin Dolly. Gasping, she pushed St. Cheviot away. She struck blindly at his hot face with one small clenched fist.

"I *loathe* you. How dare you insult me so!" she breathed and before he could speak again, picked up her flowing skirts and ran from him as though pursued by the devil himself. She rushed up the stairs to her room and locked herself in.

St. Cheviot stood still, panting, bitterly affronted. He was in a white-hot passion of rage. He sought and found his hostess.

For her he had only a few brief words.

"I have been refused and struck across the mouth by your charming cousin. Either you see to it that she retracts what she has done, and marries me immediately, or not one golden guinea will you get from me, Madam."

With this he left the house; Dolly wailing and shrieking after him in vain. Now it was her turn to be the bully. She darted upstairs and pounded upon Fleur's bedroom door, which was locked.

"Let me in at once, you wicked ungrateful girl!" she hissed.

No sound. Fleur was not weeping. She lay silent full length upon her four-poster bed, with the curtains half drawn. She had wiped her lips with a handkerchief again and again until they were almost raw, as though seeking to erase the vile imprint of St. Cheviot's kisses. She heard her cousin's voice reviling her, and threatening to turn her out into the streets, but she made no reply. She only knew that she would not be forced into St. Cheviot's arms, no matter what Cousin Dolly said or did to her. At length Dolly had to give up her efforts to gain entrance into Fleur's room. She was too afraid that the two young officers downstairs in the drawing-room with Cyril and the twins would hear and spread a scandal around town.

"Very well, my fine friend, we shall see who is to be ultimate winner of this battle," she flung at Fleur through the keyhole. "You have behaved like a lunatic. You shall be treated like one. I shall send you to a Madhouse. You shall finish your days among mad people like yourself."

Fleur did not reply but she heard, she trembled from head to foot. She did not know how to deal with the furious woman. As Dolly went away Fleur burst into tears and called helplessly on her dead parents. She sobbed: *"Mama, Papa! Why can I not die and come to you? Oh, look down and protect me now. Be with me in my helpless sorrow."*

Later, both Dolly and the twins tried to gain access to

her room, but Fleur refused to let them in. The last thing that Dolly screamed at her was a threat to take her by force to Cadlington House and leave her there. This froze the young girl's blood. She made no attempt to seek her bed but paced up and down the room alternately praying, and seeking in her mind for a way out of this horror.

Long after the de Veres were asleep, Fleur, a candle in her hand, quietly unlocked her door and tiptoed along the corridor down a small staircase to the servants' quarters. She roused Molly, her maid. The girl came out, hair in curl papers under a cap which was askew. Her red shiny face looked frightened and astonished as she saw the figure of her young mistress, wrapped in a cashmere shawl.

"Why, *miss*—what has happened——?" she began.

Fleur put a finger to her lips and beckoned the maid forward. Molly followed her. A moment later the two were whispering together in Fleur's bedroom.

"I rely on you, I must. I have nobody else in the world," Fleur ended pathetically.

Molly was five years older than her young mistress and certainly far more experienced after the many physical and moral buffetings she had received at the hands of both footmen and butlers in the servants' hall. She was quite a staunch young woman, and devoted to Fleur. With all her heart she detested Mrs. de Vere—and the de Vere household—with the exception of Noggins, who had made her romantic heart flutter.

But when Fleur told Molly that she wished to run away and that Molly must go with her the maid was at first hesitant.

"Oh, miss, but how would you do for money?" she gasped.

"Dear Molly, have you a little to lend me?" asked Fleur humbly, "and I could also sell the few jewels I have in my possession. I have a pearl necklace which belonged to my dear mother. Each pearl, I know, will be worth quite a few pounds."

Molly scratched an ear vigorously.

"I have my last month's wages not yet spent, miss. What would you have us do?"

"Leave this house before my cousin wakens, find a vehicle and drive to The Little Bastille," said Fleur.

Molly gasped again. She knew all about The Little Bastille. It had become a legend in the Roddney household. That fortress-like building on the edge of the cliff, facing the bleak wastes of the Colne estuary. It had been built by the Marquis de Chartellet soon after he had escaped from the French Revolution.

There, Hélène de Chartellet had spent much of her early married life. Because of its exceeding gloom, she had not used the place, after she became Lady Roddney, but kept it shut up and attended by caretakers because it was still full of Lucien de Chartellet's treasures.

Only once had Fleur been taken on a visit to The Little Bastille by her parents. She remembered, vaguely, narrow windows, thick stone walls and battlements that made the edifice look like a miniature prison fortress frowning down upon the sea.

It would be useless rushing down to Pillars; Cousin Dolly would obviously look for and find her there. But she might not trace Fleur once she locked herself within the walls of The Little Bastille. Fleur was certain that she could count on the loyal protection of Mama's caretakers. She doubted, too, whether it would enter even the head of her guardian Caleb Nonseale to seek her there.

"Once I am safely at The Bastille you can leave me, dear Molly, and return to your London life," Fleur told the maid, who looked as though she did not relish the thought of retirement to that peculiar house which had been built to satisfy a Frenchman's sardonic whim. But Fleur begged so hard that she should accompany her now, Molly could not refuse. Alas, the poor lamb looked like to die, as she told Noggins later on, and seemed properly scared of being forced into marriage with his lordship of Cadlington.

Fleur, feeling more hopeful now, returned to her own room, packed a small bag. She took all that she had of value and which she might need. She crept down the stairs and out of the house, accompanied by Molly who carried a small wicker hamper full of food that she had rifled from the kitchen, as well as her own possessions.

Before the de Veres were awake, and when the first vegetable carts were rumbling over the cobbles from Covent Garden, and yawning shopkeepers were taking down their shutters, the two fugitives were well away from Knightsbridge Green.

Now, Molly, half amused and half scared by the adventure, took the initiative and begged lifts towards St. Paul's. This, Fleur knew, was on the route to Essex. Noggins, being a Londoner, had informed Molly that there were livery stables not far from Paternoster Row. They could doubtless hire a private vehicle and coachman to drive them to the coast.

Sure enough, they found both stables and the coachman willing to convey them—at a price. That price took most of Molly's wages and a small brooch, offered by Fleur. The summer morning was warm and bright as they finally drove through the narrow streets on to the main Essex highway.

As they passed through the first turnpike, Fleur became almost hysterically gay. She clasped the rough mittened hand of her serving-woman.

"Dear Molly, I am for ever grateful and if my Mama were alive she would bless you," exclaimed the young girl, two hectic flushes on her cheeks. "I feel sure that once we reach The Little Bastille, I, for one, can remain lost to the world."

"But, miss, you cannot stay there alone for the rest of your life!"

"No, but at least I shall have time in which to consider what to do. I might eventually disguise myself and enter some gentlewoman's service," said the girl.

Molly glanced at her and sighed. Miss Fleur looked bad, she thought. What a terrible strain she had been under since her noble parents had been drowned! Molly was glad she had come with the poor soul. She began to open the hamper.

"You must eat, miss, and keep up your strength. See! . . . I have found a bottle of wine to bring a sparkle to your eyes."

Fleur shuddered. She seemed to hear St. Cheviot using that same word . . . "*sparkle.*" She said to the maid what she had said to *him*, "That sparkle has vanished for ever beneath the sea with my beloved parents."

But she tried to eat and managed a little of the loaf and

cheese, and a sip of the wine that Molly handed her. Then she sat back against the padded, musty-smelling cushions of the brougham and gave a long sigh.

"I am surely safe now," she murmured, "and oh, Molly, whatever happens, I beg you to be faithful and never to reveal to Mrs. de Vere the name of my hiding-place."

"Never, miss, or may I be struck dead!" exclaimed Molly. But she turned from her young lady and rather uneasily glanced out of the window at the first village through which they were passing, having left Whitechapel behind. She wished, suddenly, that she had not been so hasty as to whisper to Noggins, just before leaving, the very information that Miss Roddney wished kept a deadly secret.

"No matter, he won't tell. He promised," the maid salved her conscience. "And he begged of me to confide in him."

The coachman whipped up his horses. They broke into a gallop along the rough deserted road.

Chapter Eight

Three nights later, Fleur sat alone in a big bedroom in The Little Bastille, gazing out of an open window.

Twilight had fallen. The dark green sea moved steadily into shore and creamed over the rocks underneath the frowning cliffs. The sky faded from vermilion and purple into the dark mists of the night. The stars came out one by one. Fierce, sad and rugged though it was, this former stronghold of the Marquis de Chartellet had a beauty of its own. Fleur recognized and was comforted by it. She had small comfort else, for she was alone now—more alone than she had ever been in her life before.

But it seemed that her plan to escape from an enforced marriage with St. Cheviot had succeeded. Whatever the hue and cry in the de Vere household—no word of it had reached this solitary retreat. The helpful Molly had stayed here only forty-eight hours—long enough to get her mistress settled and to counsel Mrs. Leather, the caretaker's wife, to take good care of Miss Roddney. Then she had returned to London.

When, as she bade Fleur farewell, she had started to excuse herself for not remaining, Fleur in her gentle fashion begged her to say no more. She understood that Love (in the shape of Noggins) drew Molly like a magnet back to town. Possibly Mrs. de Vere would refuse to have her in her household, but Molly would soon find another job—and Noggins would go with her; he had said so.

Wistfully, the young girl had watched Molly drive away, feeling that with her vanished the last link with her old home.

Now the Leathers tried to serve her to the best of their ability. Jacob Leather was a goodly man; one-time butler in the service of the Marquis. Lottie, his wife, faithfully polished the furniture and silver, and kept dusted the beautiful pictures and tapestries and the thousands of books which the erudite Marquis used to read.

The Leathers had only been on the staff here since Lucien de Chartellet's marriage to Hélène, so they knew nothing of Lady Roddney's earlier life in The Bastille. But it was some comfort to poor Fleur to be with these amiable creatures who spoke of her mother as a great and beautiful lady.

"The spit of you she was, miss," Mrs. Leather told Fleur many times.

As soon as she was strong and well enough to tackle life, Fleur decided that she must earn a living. The first thing was to lose her identity as "Fleur Roddney" in order that Cousin Dolly should never find her again. She would take another name.

She finished the supper which Mrs. Leather had served, and sat now in her bedgown which was of broderie Anglaise threaded with blue ribbons. It made her look very young and fragile. Her glorious hair, unbound, flowed over her shoulders. Mrs. Leather had just brushed it.

"It would break my lady's heart to see you so forlorn," the good woman had murmured, " 'tis a cruel shame they should have treated you so, but do not fear; if anyone approaches, Leather and myself shall conceal you. There are many dungeons under The Little Bastille."

Fleur had wept in the woman's arms, hungry for love and understanding. What in heaven's name was she going to do with the rest of her youth? It was a question she could not solve tonight at any rate, she decided, as she leaned her aching head on her hand. She could hear the faint sound of music coming from a crowd of fishermen. They were singing a gay tune. It must be wonderful to be free—and gay—Fleur reflected. She envied the humble fisherfolk; she, who until a few brief months ago had envied nobody on earth.

"Indeed, Mama would never have left me to join Papa in Paris, could she have guessed the fate that has since befallen me," the poor girl mused.

Alas, alas, that one could not turn back the clock!

Fleur knelt beside her bed and prayed, as was her habit before retiring. A while later, she snuffed her candles and lay on her pillow, thinking. She had in mind that tomorrow she would have a conference with the Leathers and consider whether or not she could find a job in this district, as a governess. For she was well educated in many subjects, and especially good at the spinet, and with her needle.

It must have been close on midnight when she heard the barking of the dogs that were kept chained in the courtyard on the west side of The Bastille. This was followed by the tramping of horses' hooves and the shouting of men's voices. Fleur woke up and sat up in her bed, her heart beating violently. She lit a candle, slid into her wrapper and straightened the little muslin cap on her head. Then she stood near the door, listening attentively. It was useless opening one of the narrow windows which only looked down on to the sea. But dread had already entered Fleur's soul. *Had her hiding-place been discovered?* In God's name, had Molly betrayed her and told Cousin Dolly where she was?

While she mused upon this, she heard footsteps and suddenly her door was opened and Lottie Leather rushed in. She was a big-bosomed woman with a fat kindly face which was, in this moment, grotesque and ashen. She quivered like a jelly. Her night cap was awry, showing the curl papers over her grey head. In her hand she carried a tallow candle which was shaking so that the wax poured on to the floor.

"Oh, miss, *miss*!" she stuttered.

Every vestige of colour ebbed from the young girl's cheeks.

"Who has come? What is it, Lottie?" she demanded.

"It is Lord St. Cheviot," the woman gasped.

"Dear heaven!" whispered Fleur.

With a moan, Mrs. Leather continued: "His man, who rode here with him, has put a knife through my husband's back. Oh, miss, *miss*!" and she fell at Fleur's feet, sobbing wildly.

Fleur neither moved nor spoke. Rooted to the spot, abject fear consuming her, she stared down at the woman and listened to her babbling cries.

"St. Cheviot!" Fleur repeated the name again slowly, her eyes large and wild.

"Dear heaven, Molly must have told Noggins and he has played me false," she thought.

She was given no time to think further. She heard the heavy sound of footsteps. Then, and then only, she moved and tried to close and lock the door against the invader. But it was too late. A heavy fist crashed the door open and sent the girl reeling backward.

Denzil St. Cheviot stood before her. Fleur looked upon him with much the same terror as she would have gazed on a Fiend let loose from Hell. He was breathing quickly; garbed in riding attire. His usually well-pomaded hair was a little untidy; one black lock fell across a forehead that glistened with sweat. His cravat was awry. But he smiled. It was a smile so deadly that it made the young girl's spirit recoil.

Then he swept a bow; a mock flourish.

"Your servant, Miss Roddney!"

Mrs. Leather turned and began to claw frantically at his boots.

"Murderer, murderer of my innocent husband!" she shrieked. "You shall pay for it. I shall seek justice——"

But she got no further. He spurned her with the toe of his boot and called:

"Ivor!"

The man who had ridden with him appeared at once. Fleur, still frozen to the spot, unable to move or think, turned her attention upon him. Afterwards, she was to learn much more of this Welshman who had been Denzil St. Cheviot's confidential valet and close attendant for some years . . . and to fear him. A small sly little fellow with cunning eyes and a pair of hands that were freakishly big and powerful for his size. He was almost as good a shot as his master and utterly without scruple. He had but one loyalty and that was to the master he served, whether it be in the name of right or wrong.

St. Cheviot indicated the woman who was howling invectives at him.

"Bind this creature, take her down to one of her own cellars and leave her there. She will find it over-damp and cold, and rat-infested, but it will teach her to threaten me," he said.

Lottie turned and appealed to Fleur, her eyes bolting with fear.

"Do not let him murder me, too, miss!" she screamed shrilly.

Somehow Fleur found voice. This was the worst nightmare she had so far experienced since her former life ended. But she was no coward. Her spirit rebelled against the brutality of what was about to be done to the innocent and helpless wife of the caretaker.

"My lord," she said, addressing St. Cheviot, "this female served my mother when she was married to the Marquis. In their names, I demand that she should be spared. Already there is one murder on your soul this night; would you have another?"

St. Cheviot laughed. It was more like a growl in the thickness of his throat. Once again he swept her a courtly bow.

"As Miss Roddney wishes. . . . Ivor . . . let the female cool her blood in the dungeons for tonight only. Release her in the morning. But she is warned that if she mentions this night's work to any living soul she will die horribly. Do you hear?" He thrust his face nearer to that of the hysterical woman.

"*Silence*, or you pay with your life!"

Lottie nodded miserably, reduced to a state of abject fright. The Welshman, with a sly look at Fleur, saluted his noble master and retired, dragging Lottie after him.

St. Cheviot closed the door and smiled at Fleur.

"Will you not ask me to sit down?" he murmured. "I have ridden a long way—so fast, indeed, that my first mount burst its heart, which matter held me up at Chelmsford whilst Ivor found me a fresh horse."

Fleur did not speak. Her large eyes stared up at him.

Slowly St. Cheviot unbuttoned his cloak and threw it on the bed.

"It must surely impress you that I take so long a ride, and in such hot haste, to reach you," he continued.

Then with a hand at her throat, and every effort to still the violent trembling of her limbs, the girl spoke.

"My lord, I ask you in the name of decency to leave my bedchamber instantly."

He looked around. His tall figure in the light of the fluttering candles threw a gigantic shadow on the ceiling. Now that silence had fallen over The Little Bastille again, there could be heard the faint hiss of the waves on the rocks below. St. Cheviot glanced out of the window and then back at Fleur. He raised his brows.

"You have chosen a charming retreat although a trifle gloomy for one so young and fair. But up here it is warm and perfumed, and I am in no hurry to depart."

"Lord St. Cheviot, why are you come? On what authority have you forced an entry into my mother's house and done an innocent man to death?"

"He got in my way," said St. Cheviot coldly, "he sought to prevent me from entering. My man, Ivor, is quick on the draw—quicker than your protector—that is all."

"You are the devil himself," said Fleur in a dry whisper.

He drew nearer her.

"And you an angel. An interesting combination . . . we shall see what evolves when heaven and hell unite."

His words froze her blood. She backed away.

"Who told you that I was here?"

"Who else but your Cousin Dolly de Vere? But not until today could she bribe a fellow named Noggins into informing her of your whereabouts. You gave us all the slip in uncommonly neat fashion. When Mrs. de Vere first acquainted me with the news of your escape, I myself went to seek you at Pillars. But neither your servants there nor your friends knew anything. Then the good Noggins, who is anxious for the wherewithal to finance his marriage, informed your cousin of the facts. Until then, I must confess neither your cousin nor Mr. Nonseale, your guardian, had the slightest suspicion that you would fly to de Chartellet's Bastille."

Fleur put her finger tips against her quivering lips. She shook so violently that she could scarcely stand. So it *was* Molly who had betrayed her. Unwillingly, perhaps; but caught in the net of her own trust in the man she loved.

As St. Cheviot drew near to Fleur, she cried piteously:

"I beg and beseech you, Lord St. Cheviot, to have respect for me and leave my room. Tomorrow, I swear that I will be amenable and allow you to escort me back to London. I realize that I am defeated."

"Not quite," said his lordship with that deadly smile which made his handsome face assume for Fleur the features of incarnate evil.

"What do you mean?"

"That I intend to make quite positive, my sweet girl, you will never again refuse me as a husband," he said.

The black brilliant eyes which devoured her now were merciless, like the man himself.

When Dolly de Vere had informed Denzil of Fleur's escape he had consented to join with her in the search and to take measures to put an end to Miss Roddney's stubborn conduct. Measures that would never have been permitted were Archibald de Vere still in England. But Dolly, frantic for her own safety, showed herself willing to co-operate with St. Cheviot's vile plan. At first they feared Fleur had vanished for good. But once Noggins let the cat out of the bag, St. Cheviot immediately set out for the Essex coast.

"Leave all to me," Denzil had told Dolly, who had seemed a trifle nervous and ill at ease about the whole concern. "Tomorrow, when I return her to you, Fleur will do as she is told. Having regard to her reputation and her virtue, I do not think she will raise any further objections to our immediate marriage in her own interests."

Even Dolly had wavered before those sinister words. She had started to whine:

"I am a mother. I needs must consider my cousin's orphaned child. Oh, be gentle with her and remember she must not be too far driven or she may not live to become Lady St. Cheviot."

His answer had been:

"She will live. The maiden may languish in her grief and be sorely afflicted by her fate, but she is young and strong withal and will grow accustomed to her new status. Meanwhile I will not leave her side, madam. She shall be given no chance to do away with herself."

Now as St. Cheviot looked at the slight and exquisite girl, white as her muslin draperies, and with her soul's terror reflected in her large eyes, he knew nothing but a brutal desire; the determination to vanquish her utterly and thus force her to the altar-rails.

"My sweet child," he said, "do not waste your breath by

refusing me again. Tonight this solitary fortress chosen by yourself shall become a Cupid's paradise for us."

Fleur opened her lips to scream, but no sound came. It would have been useless even had she uttered it. She felt St. Cheviot's great arms crushing her, and the scorning passion of his kiss. Then he lifted her right up into his arms and laughed down at her.

"I think, my shrinking violet, that tomorrow you will be willing and eager to announce our betrothal, and to become my bride and the future mother of my sons," he said.

She was beyond answering, almost beyond caring in the extremity of her anguish. But the last sound that she heard before she temporarily lost her senses was the surge of the sea and a rising wind. The September night was passing into a stormy dawn. Seagulls wheeled uneasily over the battlements of The Little Bastille. Fleur wondered wildly if her mother's ghost would not arise from her watery grave to seek out and protect the daughter who had been so hideously betrayed.

PART II

Chapter One

On the fifteenth of September, 1838, Fleur, daughter of Sir Harry and Lady Roddney, late of Pillars, near Epping, was married at St. Paul's Church, Knightsbridge, to Denzil St. Cheviot, Baron of Cadlington.

It was a big wedding attended by innumerable relatives and friends, gathered from near and far by Mrs. de Vere, and almost every family of high degree from the county of Buckinghamshire. And London was gossiping about it.

Despite the fact that all England knew of the dissipations and vices of the Lord St. Cheviot, he happened to be one of the richest men in the country; hence those who were invited, and were disposed to whisper in shocked terms of St. Cheviot's excesses, forgot them today, hypocritically gushed over his magnificence and came willingly to see him married to his beautiful bride.

There had been a brief engagement. It surprised all who read the announcement. The affair was taking place a little soon, for conventional taste, after the tragic death of the Roddneys. But little Mrs. de Vere had explained to one and all that it was such a *love* match and the pair were so *anxious* to be together, and "poor darling Fleur needed a husband and home."

The church was packed. It was a pity, of course, that the late summer day was not mild and sunny. A wild wind tore through the streets bringing a shower of leaves down from the trees in Hyde Park. The gutters ran with muddy waters, and down came the rain just as the church bells started ringing. Handsomely clad gentlemen assisted their ladies to step from their carriages while coachmen held large umbrellas over them.

Mrs. de Vere played the "mother" beautifully, dabbing now and then at her eyes with a little lace handkerchief, twittering to her guests about her "broken heart" at losing her sweet little cousin. How "tragic" it was, too, that dear Archibald could not return from India because business kept him there. Mr. Caleb Nonseale, however, as the family friend and solicitor, gave the bride away. Even he—the sober-sides—had tried to clothe himself in a more distinguished way than usual for today's event. All Dolly de Vere's friends gossiped among themselves, *"Where is she getting all the money to give the Roddney girl such a show?"*

Which question might have been answered for them could they have heard the quick conversation which had taken place between Dolly and Mr. Nonseale just before setting out for the church.

"I must congratulate you, madam, on the way in which you have brought my young client to heel," said Caleb, and smiled significantly at Mrs. de Vere. She, resplendent in her blue velvet, with nodding ostrich plumes in her bonnet and a coquettish bow tied under her chin, looked a trifle uneasy, but managed to titter:

"Yes, indeed, but it's been a *great* responsibility."

"I have not asked how you achieved this change of front," he added.

"Pray do not," Dolly said, grimacing significantly, and fanned herself, growing first hot and then cold. Caleb then informed her that a large sum of money had this very day been placed by his lordship to her credit at the bank. An equal amount had been paid to Mr. Nonseale, himself. Mrs. de Vere could breathe again. Her debts would be paid on the morrow. She was safe. Archibald need never know how near she had been to ruin. And when the will was proven, the vast amount of money due to Fleur from the double estate of father and mother would be handed over to his lordship of Cadlington. He could deal with it as he thought best.

Kneeling in the church, after having uttered a hypocritical prayer for the welfare of the young girl whom she had ruined, Dolly tried to tell herself that she had really done the best possible thing for Harry's daughter. Nevertheless, Dolly de Vere could not quite erase from her mind the memory of the trust that Harry had placed in her and how she had abused it. Almost she could feel the cold horror and hatred with which he and Hélène would regard her if they but knew how the marriage had come about.

Of course, Dolly tried to argue with herself, Mr. Nonseale was equally culpable. It could not have taken place without his consent. He, too, had been in need of money. He, too, had broken faith with Harry Roddney.

"I must try not to think about it too much," Dolly de Vere muttered to herself. But when she looked at the altar before which the bride and bridegroom were standing, she licked her lips nervously. She was really quite haunted by the memory of all that had taken place during this last few weeks.

Unforgettable, the hour when St. Cheviot had brought Fleur back to her cousin's home. Even Dolly had felt a deep pang of shame at the sight of the girl's altered appearance. Deathly pale, with eyes that bore the stamp of despair, Fleur trembled incessantly and refused to answer any of the questions put to her. Dolly ordered the twins out of the way and sent the young girl straight to bed.

Molly, her former maid, and the treacherous Noggins, had been dismissed. A new woman, older and more reliable, had been engaged by Dolly to look after Fleur. She was told that the young girl was "sadly wanting" and must be closely guarded, and that no notice was to be taken of anything "odd" that she said.

From the moment of Fleur's return, the key was turned in the lock. She became Cousin Dolly's prisoner.

St. Cheviot, himself, seemed rather more angry than jubilant over the affair. The evil was done, but his lordship confessed himself dissatisfied. He was in a devilish mood. When Dolly in a quivering voice began to ask him what had happened, he shut her up.

"The girl has no fire in her," he said harshly. "She is made of ice. I think, too, unless she is carefully handled, last night's shock will unhinge her. Pray look after her with tact, madam. I wish her to be in better health and spirit when we come to marry. I will wait for her one month more and no longer."

With that he had departed. Dolly returned to the girl's side feeling more than apprehensive, wondering if they had not gone a little too far in their efforts to break Fleur's resistance.

The resistance, however, seemed to be broken. Fleur neither argued nor protested, nor complained of what had been done to her. It was as though all her spirit had fled forever and she wanted no more of this world. She turned her face to the wall and lay silent without so much as a tear or a sob. Mrs. de Vere had found it an exceedingly uncomfortable job ministering to her. Her patience was sorely taxed on many occasions during the weeks that followed, but she did at least extract from Fleur her promise to announce her betrothal to St. Cheviot.

"Yes," she kept saying every time Dolly asked the question. "Yes, I will marry him."

"You *must* now," was Cousin Dolly's assertion. "No decent young girl could do otherwise."

"No—no decent girl could do otherwise," Fleur agreed in a monotone. Her great eyes stared blindly ahead of her.

"It is all very unfortunate," stuttered Dolly. "I regret that it happened. Of course I had no *idea* St. Cheviot would dare to do—as he did."

Then and then only Fleur had turned and regarded Cousin Dolly with an expression of such scorn and bitterness that the older woman writhed.

"*You* knew, Cousin Dolly, *you* sent him. He murdered my father's servant. Then he murdered *me*," she added in a low voice. "If my father could return from the dead he would avenge me. You would not dare to look him or my mother in the face."

So Dolly had crept from the room, snivelling.

But for a long time Fleur was ill—with a sickness of the mind more than of the body. Archibald, ignorant of the black crime that had been committed against the unfortunate child who had been left in his wife's care, received only a much-delayed letter to say that "dear Fleur had consented to marry St. Cheviot." *Little doubt*, Dolly wrote, *you will rejoice.*

Physically, because Fleur was young and strong, she revived.

Once or twice when St. Cheviot came to see her, she received him and gave him her hand to kiss but refused to look at him. Dolly, watching, saw that she trembled and that the waxen pallor of her face was suffused by painful colour. However, she was extremely polite. The betrothal ring, which he had placed on her finger (three emeralds which Dolly imagined must have cost a fortune), was too big and heavy for her thin finger. But she thanked him for it and for a fabulous necklet of diamonds which he chose for her from the St. Cheviot collection. She had grown almost emaciated. This made St. Cheviot impatient.

"You must gain weight, my dear child," he told her. "I think you will benefit once you are living at Cadlington where the air is brisk and there is excellent fresh produce from my many farms."

"Oh, dear Fleur is a tremendously lucky girl," Dolly had chirped in.

And then Fleur's heavily languid eyes turned in the older woman's direction. Dolly found her cheeks growing hot. Really, it was awful, the scorn with which the young miss regarded her.

After St. Cheviot left, Dolly had been a little cross with Fleur.

"For the love of heaven can you not smile or simulate happiness—even if you do not feel it? Do you wish to be a bore? Take it from me, even St. Cheviot's patience with you will snap."

"I do not care," Fleur had replied, closing her eyes.

Exasperated, Dolly cried:

"Can we do nothing to please you? What do you *want*, you dreadful child?"

"To be alone," she had whispered, "alone with my shame and my sorrow. Were I a Catholic, I would wish to beg permission to enter a Convent and be removed for ever from this world."

"Upon my soul, you are a little fool!" was Dolly's rejoinder.

One day St. Cheviot sent Fleur a box of camellias in the centre of which sparkled a magnificent star sapphire. On a card were written the words:

> Let my care and my gifts make those sorrowful eyes of yours shine again with the blueness of this jewel. I will be good to you if you will let me.
>
> St. Cheviot.

She had—in obedience to Cousin Dolly's request—thanked him for the priceless sapphire—but a bitter smile had twisted her sad mouth when she saw how the sharp edge of the brooch had bruised the tender creamy petals of the flowers. Already they were brown and broken.

"Like my heart," she had whispered to herself. "Like my youth."

Today—on her wedding day—the bride was attired in an exquisite dress of palest violet satin, misted over with frills of exquisite lace. There were tiny lace-frills on the rim of the bonnet. A gauzy veil floated from the crown. A small violet velvet cape, lined with ermine, covered her thin shoulders.

In one lace-mittened hand, the bride carried a posy of violets and silver leaves. Diamonds sparkled around her throat. She looked so beautiful, so pure, so pathetically young and sad—the men felt curiously disturbed—as though suddenly they felt the grossness of man's appetite to be a shameful thing. But the women—knowing nothing of the truth—envied Fleur her marvellous jewels.

St. Cheviot was magnificent in dove-grey with floral satin waistcoat and a collar so high that his chin was almost in it. He towered above the young girl at his side. She *felt* that strong animal presence and loathed it.

She made the responses in the veriest whisper. Then it was all over. She walked down the aisle on St. Cheviot's arm. "His, *his* forever," she thought in anguish. From now onward, her life would be one long martyrdom. A *respectable* martyrdom, she thought with a cynicism that would have broken Hélène's Roddney's heart could she have known what lay in her daughter's mind this day.

Passively, the new Lady St. Cheviot accepted the kisses and congratulations of relatives and friends. There was but one person she would have liked here today—dear little Cathy, her childhood's friend, but this had been denied her, Cousin Dolly would allow her no communication with the former intimate friends of the Roddneys.

One of the things which Fleur had most bitterly resented was being escorted to her marriage by such a man as Mr. Nonseale. Loyal though she was to the memory of her beloved father, she had to admit that poor Papa had made a mistake in his solicitor. She was quite sure that Mr. Nonseale and Dolly were in league. She had had to talk with him and listen to a lot of dry legal matters which she did not understand. Wearily she had signed documents at his request. He had been suave, and servile, and made her shiver as he spoke of her "wonderful good fortune" in contracting so fine a marriage. Lord St. Cheviot, he said, would now decide what was to be done with the properties she had inherited. He hinted that his lordship had already made up his mind to sell Pillars and the de Chartellet estates. Henceforth all would be in St. Cheviot's hands to do with as he wished. All that she possessed. From this day onward he was her guardian, her trustee, her *owner*.

If her heart ached at the thought that she would never see dear Pillars again, she could at least be glad that never would she re-enter the freakish Bastille—that house of treasure which had once been Lucien de Chartellet's pride. It held for Fleur only the most appalling memories. When she ventured to ask what had become of poor Mrs. Leather, she had been told that the woman had been "pensioned off" by his lordship. The poor creature had been threatened to such an extent that she would never let it be known what had transpired at The Bastille that night. So she kept silent when it was announced that poor Jacob Leather had met his death "by accident."

Fleur tried not to think about these matters as she stood at St. Cheviot's side in the reception-room at Cousin Dolly's house. Footmen handed around Marsala and Madeira and the Bride-cake. The head chef at Cadlington had sent this towering confection of white frosted sugar—on it the initials "D" and "F," twined together with lovers' knots, and the Cadlington coat-of-arms in rose-pink ice picked out with sugared violets. Always violets, Fleur thought, weary of them. Yet once they had been her favourite flowers.

She was glad that the sun did not shine today. It would have been a mockery. She was glad, also, that St. Cheviot did not force her to travel at once. He had wanted to take her to Monte Carlo where the sun would be warm, but Cousin Dolly's physician had warned him that Miss Roddney's health was in such fragile state (he presumed due to the shock of her parents' death), he would not advise the long journey. Especially as she might have a natural horror of the Channel crossing. So Denzil had consented to take her straight to Cadlington. They were to leave Knightsbridge at midday in his lordship's famous "flying coach," pulled by four horses. This would mean a stop, midway, to Whiteleaf. It so chanced that St. Cheviot was friendly with a certain baronet, Sir Piers Kilmanning, who owned a fine shooting estate near the village of Fulmer. Kilmanning and his wife had offered the bride and bridegroom a suite in their house where they might rest the night. The next morning, they could proceed at their leisure to Cadlington.

The very name of "Kilmanning" had made Fleur feel worse instead of better. She had actually heard Mama speak of Lady Kilmanning; a woman she had known in the past when Mama was *Madame la Marquise*. One of the set that Hélène had despised; a middle-aged coquette who lived only for pleasure and whose husband was a famous buck during the period of the Regency.

As far as Fleur could see, any friends that she would have in future would be of the type that amused St. Cheviot, but against whom Mama and Papa would have shut their doors.

During the drive from the church, St. Cheviot with attempted gallantry raised her hand to his lips.

"May I not have one word, one smile from you, Lady St. Cheviot?" he asked.

She did not raise her lashes, nor answer. Then she felt his fingers grip her wrist like a vice.

"Answer me. I will not tolerate this contempt."

Now obediently she raised her magnificent eyes.

She said:

"What would you have me say, Lord St. Cheviot?"

"First, that you drop that odious method of addressing me. I am your husband and I have a name."

She bit her lip. *Her husband.* She found it hard to believe. On the rare occasions when she had talked to Cathy of a "possible husband," it had been in terms of exquisite romance.

St. Cheviot saw the working in her long slender throat. He was furious because whenever he spoke to her she looked ready to flinch as though before a threatened blow. For what he had done he had drowned his conscience fathoms deep. It had been the girl's fault for being so stubborn; anyhow, what had she to grumble at? Had he not given her his title and was she not in a position that his own mother before her had found flattering? He began to pity himself because of the difficulty of drawing one spark of response from this strange girl. Ignorant she could no longer be called but her innocence was still curiously unsullied. It was like an impenetrable wall between them.

"My name is Denzil," he said harshly.

"Denzil." She repeated the name as a child repeats what it is taught but without interest.

"Deuce take it," he said scowling. "This is not a good beginning to our married life. A bridal should surely be a happy affair."

"Happy?" That word was repeated most bitterly by the girl, and she laughed. It was not the first time that Denzil St. Cheviot had heard her laugh. Once at Pillars—months ago—he had stood watching her silently, listening to the light happy laughter of a radiant being. It was then that he had begun to desire her. Now she was his, but she had lost that radiance and her laughter was dreadful and humourless. The sound of it irritated him, when it should have filled him with remorse. He did not pause to consider that it was *he* who had murdered the soul in her, as surely as his man had plunged the knife in Jacob Leather's back.

"I will not have people think that I take an unwilling bride," he muttered.

Now Fleur spoke with a cold dignity that half annoyed and half amused St. Cheviot.

"I fear, Lord St.—I mean Denzil," she stumbled over the christian name, "I cannot be responsible for what others think. I have not supernatural powers."

He shrugged his shoulders.

"And you do not intend to be a willing partner?"

She looked at him with that loathing which he found so boring.

"I was *not* a willing partner," she said between her teeth.

St. Cheviot flung himself into his corner of the coach and folded his arms, scowling at her.

"Have it your own way. You are as obstinate as a mule."

She shut her eyes. As the couch rumbled along taking her towards her new home, she thought:

"Not only am I unwilling, but everything that is in me shrinks from carrying out my duties as Lady St. Cheviot. I wish I could die."

But she was denied the merciful oblivion of death—of joining those dear ones who were lost to her.

She carried with her a tiny sable and velvet muff. She locked her hands in it and leaned her head back against the cushions. Exhaustion claimed her. Utterly worn out in spirit and in body, she sank into a doze. Her bridegroom glowered at her from his corner but kept silent. There were times when to taunt Fleur afforded him sadistic pleasure, but for the moment he left her alone. He looked forward to what he knew would be an excellent meal with the Kilmannings. Sir Piers was a genial host and Arabella his wife had ever shown a willingness to receive St. Cheviot's attentions. She was a good-looking woman despite her age, with a pretty ankle.

St. Cheviot yawned, then he, too, slept.

Chapter Two

Cadlington House was bathed in sunshine. All morning there had been a scurry and a bustle among the servants both indoors and out. The master was bringing home his bride. They were expected home before midday.

Floors had been given an extra polish; stonework and plaster washed. In the immense kitchens, the head cook—he was a French chef—pompous and perspiring, chivvied his under-cooks, kitchen-maids, and scullions, and set to work on the superb menu which he knew, from practice, would please a difficult master.

Head of all the staff was Mrs. Dinglefoot, the housekeeper; a woman of character who ruled her big staff of females with a rod of iron. A steel purpose lay hidden behind a terrible smile. She was marshalling them all this morning like a general who knows that the enemy is about to attack. The enemy in this case was the new Lady St. Cheviot. Matilda Dinglefoot had held her position as housekeeper at Cadlington when Denzil's mother was alive. *She* had been a meek silly lady who suffered from wretched ill-health and was only too glad for Mrs. Dinglefoot to take entire control.

For years, Mrs. Dinglefoot (alluded to by all members of the staff in hushed and awed voice as Mrs. D.) had swept through Cadlington House imperiously, the keys of still-room, linen-cupboards and silver chests dangling from her waistbelt. Her strident voice issued commands which were instantly obeyed or immediate notice was given to the recalcitrant. Rarely did she come face to face with his lordship. His orders were, as a rule, passed to her through the medium of his confidential valet, Ivor. And Ivor, it could truly be said, was the only human being of whom Matilda Dinglefoot was afraid. She knew how high he was held in his master's esteem. His power was great and any woman servant to whom Ivor took a dislike would rapidly find herself outside the door. Mrs. D. hated and feared Ivor, and appeared outwardly as his friend. For him, in the servants' hall, were reserved the finest tidbits from the kitchens; the choicest wine. Linked in a curious and ferocious fidelity to the Baron, these two were, in truth, St. Cheviot's loyal servitors. But they would willingly have slit each other's throats.

This morning, Ivor had been busy giving orders at the stables and bidding the grooms make sure that St. Cheviot's hunters were in trim for a week's hunting. Then he had to attack the gardeners and see that the orchid house—the only part of the garden in which St. Cheviot took personal interest—was ready for inspection.

Ivor had just now come indoors to remind Mrs. D. that at any moment the bridal pair would arrive, and to warn her to make sure that the rooms for the new Baroness were ready.

"Don't fret yourself—all is prepared," Mrs. D. assured him and suggested that he might sip a glass of Madeira with her in her sitting-room. Over this drink, the crafty Welshman eyed the housekeeper with a touch of wicked humour.

"A little depressed are you not, Mrs. D.? It is many a day since there was a lady in the house to tell *you* what you may or may not do."

Mrs. D. smiled.

"I doubt if my new mistress will be greatly interfering—from what I hear of her. I tackled his lordship's mother—I do not doubt I can manage his wife."

Laughter gurgled in Ivor's throat.

To be sure, he thought, Mrs. D. could manage anybody except *him*. He knew too much about her and the way she feathered her nest in her master's absence. Never could she treat *him* as she treated the rest of them here. What a smile she had, to be sure! She had very big teeth like a horse. The smile was less an expression of mirth or pleasure than a drawing back of two lips which exhibited those fearful teeth. She was an immensely tall woman—a good head taller than the little Welshman. She had a poor complexion and used a kind of paste to cover her blemishes which gave her an ugly whiteness. Her hair, of a light shade of rusty brown, was dyed and done in a vast array of sausage curls always so neat that Ivor believed that she wore a wig.

To preserve an impression of youth, however, had become a passion with the grotesque old spinster, and when she had had a drop too much, she simpered and acted the coquette which was nauseating in the extreme. Ivor had suffered on occasions. To his master, he told tales of her gigglings and posturings. A coarse jest went down well when the Baron was in the mood for it.

"From what you say, her ladyship is not of too forceful a disposition," observed Mrs. D. as she finished her wine, and looked meditatively round her well-furnished parlour.

"You are right, ma'am, she is not forceful but she is of a stunning appearance."

Mrs. D., who had moved towards a mirror, patted one of her false curls and observed with dismay that more hairs than usual sprouted from her chin. The beauty of other females had power only to rouse the utmost hatred in the bosom of Matilda Dinglefoot.

"Well, well, Master Ivor," she said, "you have seen my lady—so you should know."

A mask fell across the saturnine face of the Welshman. *He* alone knew what wickedness had transpired in de Chartellet's Bastille, that turbulent night. In a curious way he had been disappointed in his master for he regarded it as a sign of weakness that a man should be driven to such lengths for love of any woman.

Mrs. D. took her leave of Ivor and went on her rounds. Underlings scurried away at her approach. There was none who wished to come under the lash of Mrs. D.'s tongue.

She marched up the stairs and into the rooms that had once belonged to her late mistress, Denzil's mother.

There were flowers everywhere. Big fires burned, in case the September evening should grow chill. All was spick and span.

But Mrs. D.'s face expressed a sour disapproval as she stood looking around her. Previously, these two communicating chambers were dark, gloomy and so filled with ornament that it took three servants at least a week to spring-clean the suite. The old Baroness had favoured rococo extravagance. Today the place was unrecognizable.

A miraculous change had been wrought—not by his lordship who had only paid the bills—but by Peveril Marsh, the young painter.

St. Cheviot had, in his moody fashion, grown to like the gentle young artist, and to admire his able work. Not only had Peveril executed a very creditable likeness of his lordship, but several large and wonderful paintings of his friends. It amused the Baron to boast that he had inaugurated a new member of the household as his "Painter Extraordinary."

The boy had taken a fancy to the old disused tower, from the top turrets of which one could command such magnificent views of the Weald; the Baron allowed him to occupy it. Here a studio had been furnished for him. The boy lived his solitary life there. When he was not painting, he was poring over his books. If he felt lonely, he did not complain. Once when St. Cheviot had told him that it was not good for so young a man to become a hermit and suggested that he should find a mistress to amuse him, the boy had blushed crimson and shrunk from the suggestion.

"I want no mistress, my lord. I crave only the opportunity to paint and to improve my mind," he had answered. Whereupon St. Cheviot, shrugging, left the boy alone.

Peveril had become a familiar figure at Cadlington—emerging from his turret studio only to take fresh air and exercise, and eat his meals in the servants' hall. The young girls of the staff tried to coquette with him. He had a kindly word for them but no mind to make love to any of them. They found him an enigma, but everybody liked him well. If there was any help needed among them, Peveril was the first to offer it.

He had extraordinary powers with animals. He could do anything with a wounded bird or injured dog. Even the ferocious Alpha, who never allowed any person but St. Cheviot to touch her, went willingly to Peveril. In fact, she often voluntarily climbed the steep circular staircase, and sat at the young artist's feet while he painted, through the long sunny hours.

But in Mrs. D., Peveril had a bitter antagonist. She was jealous of him and of Denzil's interest in him. As a rule if the Baron saw anything to admire in any one of the staff

Mrs. D. speedily found reason to send them packing. But this she could not do with Peveril Marsh. She was exceedingly indignant when his lordship instructed the young artist to rearrange the bridal suite.

"He is an artist—let him design for my lady the most beautiful bedchamber and boudoir that can be created and spare no money in the project," Denzil had commanded. So Mrs. D. was forced to stand aside.

Peveril had enjoyed the job. It appealed to the poet and the dreamer; this inauguration of beauty for a bride who was said to be the loveliest ever seen. He knew nothing of Miss Fleur Roddney's origin or sad story, just as he knew little of evil, itself. He knew little, really, about his master, the Baron. He could not altogether shut his ears to the wild stories that were whispered of St. Cheviot's misdeeds, neither could he altogether forget the callous indifference which his lordship had first exhibited towards poor Elspeth as she lay dying. But during his twelve months at the House, Peveril had had little cause to complain of personal cruelty from St. Cheviot. He was not a good man; he was not an amicable one; Peveril, the idealist, could never love such a master. But he was grateful for the protection and home St. Cheviot had given him after Elspeth died.

His one ambition now was to profit by his experience in painting, save what money St. Cheviot or friends in the district paid him for portraits commissioned, and finally leave Cadlington and start an independent life. He had no wish to accept permanent charity.

He had flung his whole heart and inspiration into the decorating and refurnishing of the bridal chamber. Mrs. D., who was as blind to beauty as a bat, stood now staring around her thinking only that it was all wasteful and foolish. It was a fairy-tale room and there was no part in Matilda Dinglefoot which could attune itself to gossamer fantasy.

All in white—glittering and delicate—the very reverse of the dark wine colours the old Baroness had favoured. The walls were panelled in ivory satin, frosted with silver thread. There were great white bearskin rugs stretched across the floor. Sweeping ivory-velvet curtains were looped back with silver cords on either side of the tall windows. From the windows one could look right across the green forest, or downwards to the blue mists of the valley.

The great four-poster bed had been stripped, repainted and hung with transparent, gossamer curtains. Overhead, painted cupids hung by silver chains, each one carrying in his chubby hands a silver lamp which would be lighted tonight for the bride. The bed was covered by a white satin spread smothered in an exquisite foam of lace. On the huge square pillows the bride and bridegroom's names had been embroidered. *Denzil and Fleur*. That name *"Fleur"* fell pleasantly on Peveril's music-loving ear. It was lovely; and he pictured her as a flower of beauty whom he would immediately wish to paint. Certainly his lordship would command it. A likeness of the new Baroness must eventually hang among her predecessors in the long gallery.

There was only one painting—it hung over the fireplace—a gilt-framed *Madonna and Child*, after Raphael; one of the many treasures in this fabulous house. Peveril had picked it out from the gallery and bade the servants hang it so that it could be seen from the bed.

Mrs. D. sneered, her arms akimbo.

"What does he think—that her ladyship will be inspired immediately to give birth to an heir, and so turn this mansion into a vast nursery for snivelling brats?"

She feared that his lordship had forsaken liberty and married in order to get an heir; there could be no other reason.

And she also presumed that there would be no more wild parties held here; no crowds of gentlemen for hunting and gaming. Mrs. D. would now be asked to run a milk sop, pious household, like most of them round here. Alas, it meant that the good old times at Cadlington were over!

The communicating chamber was her ladyship's boudoir (his lordship occupied the suite on the opposite side of the corridor). Here again, Peveril had allowed his artistic fancy full flight. The room was panelled in some light fruit wood. The predominant colour was olive green—carried out in the velvet curtains, and draperies on sofa and chairs. There was a little Queen Anne bureau by the window at which her ladyship could write if she had a mind; and a bookcase for which Peveril had chosen the books—the poets in particular. Portraits of the bride's parents brought from Pillars hung on either side of the carved wood mantelpiece. The ornaments were few—one or two delicate porcelain figurines and a pair of silver candlesticks. Much to Mrs. D.'s disgust Peveril had cleared away the many old framed photographs and pictures; the wax flowers under glass cases—the busts of previous St. Cheviots—all the sentimental trophies of the old Baroness who had taken a long time in dying and left an odour of decay in her rooms. But all that had gone now and the windows were open to the sunshine. In Mrs. D.'s memory so much fresh air had never before been let into this suite. A week ago Mrs. D. still hoped that his lordship would dislike it when he saw the new rooms. But St. Cheviot had approved—with certain reservations. A few days ago he drove down to make his final inspection and remarked to Peveril:

"Do you then think that a young lady will like such scarcity of ornament, and such simple design? By gad, it is too cold and chaste for *my* liking."

The boy had flushed and answered:

"It was my belief, sir, that the chasteness would please the bride."

That had brought a roar of laughter from St. Cheviot, but he had shrugged and said:

"This one—perhaps. We shall see. I must admit, at any rate, that you have achieved quite a stunning effect. Never before has Cadlington boasted such odd decoration."

This morning Peveril came up the stairs with an armful of lilies. He placed them in a silver gilt vase on a table beside the *chaise-longue*, over which he had thrown a white Spanish shawl. Masses of violets had been forced by St. Cheviot's gardeners, and were cut and ready for Peveril to bring in here as soon as the bridal pair were within sight. It was Peveril's idea to scatter them over the bed and the floor. His lordship had hinted that violets were the bride's favourite flowers.

"Stuff and nonsense," was Mrs. D.'s opinion, but she turned her back on the poetic bridal room and made her way down to the great hall. Thank goodness the interfering brat of a boy had not been allowed to touch *this* part of Cadlington and all was as before.

Chapter Three

Up in his studio Peveril Marsh thought much of the young bride who was being brought to her new home. All that was romantic in him favoured the day and the hour. He had been depressed lately, wondering when he would ever have enough money to go forth on his own and face the world. With all the benefits that Cadlington offered, he did not really like it here. But today his depression gave place to a pleasurable anticipation.

This turret was his only home. The circular room still had a slightly mouldy odour. The walls were shabby—half concealed by many paintings and sketches. A trestle bed, a table, two high-backed chairs and the artist's easel, served for furnishing. There were eight narrow windows in the circular turret. Peveril kept them uncurtained. He liked to look out on the landscape, in sunlight or shadow, in rain or snow. It was enthralling to him to watch the clouds race across the sky, to see at times the heavens open and let down a torrent of rain. He liked, at early morning, to glimpse the first bar of gold that cut across the darkness of the night and heralded the dawn. And in the summer he enjoyed gazing up at the stars, and marvelling at the infinity and splendour of the constellations. He was happy—yet unhappy—not knowing what lay behind his strange restlessness.

Gazing down on the sunlit vale this morning, he suddenly saw a dark shape winding up the hill towards Whiteleaf. The silence was broken by the unmistakable sound of horses' hooves, and the crack of whips. A look of excitement came into Peveril's eyes. *At last*—this must be the Baron's coach.

Peveril turned and ran down the stairs. Entering the great hall from the passage which led from the tower into the main house, he collided with Mrs. Dinglefoot. She tottered back.

"Careless young devil!"

"Your pardon, ma'am," he said, "but I have seen his lordship's coach coming up the hill."

Mrs. D. dived into a voluminous pocket for a handkerchief. She blew her nose loudly. Her small eyes—cunning, like an elephant's—blinked at the boy.

"Contain yourself, my good fellow. There is no need to knock over a defenceless lady in your transports."

A young footman, wearing the smart green livery of the household and who was drawing white gloves on to his sweating hands, sidled up to the young artist. He made an uncomplimentary gesture towards the back of the retreating housekeeper.

"Defenceless lady, indeed! It is the likes of us poor folks who need be defended from *her*!" he muttered.

Peveril spoke to the man with his usual kindness but with just that touch of dignity which proved his breeding.

"If I were you, Jukes, I would hurry to your post. I am going to fetch the violets for her ladyship."

And with his light quick tread, Peveril ran to the greenhouses where a gardener handed him a huge basket of the dewy flowers.

Upstairs in my lady's chamber, Peveril sprinkled the starry purple blossoms over the white rugs, and upon the foam of lace across the bed, until the whole room looked and smelled exquisite. Pleased with the effect, he ran downstairs again and presented himself with the rest of the staff who were lining up on either side of the hall. They were marshalled into position by Mrs. D. and the head footman, Mr. Wilkins; all present, down to the lowest scullery boy. Being a mild warm morning, the front doors had been flung wide open. In the sunshine, grouped around the portico stood the outdoor servants: the gardeners, the groomsmen, the stable-boys.

St. Cheviot's Welsh valet was well in evidence—smartly dressed in his best dark grey coat, pantaloons and Hessian boots. He occupied a foremost place of honour, and would be the first to receive the master and his bride. He beckoned genially enough to the young artist who had also attired himself in what was his finest apparel—a sober suiting of a dark cinnamon shade with which he wore a white frilled shirt; and, for once, a high collar and cravat. His frank handsome face was not as full as it should have been. He looked pale and haggard. There were shadows under his eyes. Peveril worked far too long and too late—sometimes in a fading light—and his whole expression was that of one who gave much time to philosophizing. He was for ever preoccupied with morbid reflections on the sorrowful loss of his beloved sister, his shattered family life. His, too, was the temperament of the artist whose work never satisfied him. He suffered (quite mistakenly) from the fear that he would never achieve a real work of art.

Now the coach with the four high-stepping greys appeared round the bend in the drive and was brought with a fine flourish to the front door of Cadlington House. A cheer went up from the staff.

A postillion climbed down and opened the door. From the coach emerged the tall haughty figure of St. Cheviot. His face bore no expression of pleasure or gratitude for the cheers that came from his retinue. He looked sour and rather yellow in the golden September light.

At Fulmer, he had sent his bride early to bed and stayed up, himself, until the small hours, dicing with his host and a few bloods who had been invited to gamble with him. He had drunk too much. His tongue was thick. He had no stomach for festive entertainment at home. But he had a new reputation as a husband to consider, and must make some hypocritical show of settling down to matrimony, or all doors in the district would be shut to him and his lady.

But last night when the amorous Arabella had whispered in his ear: "*'Tis but a child you have wed, my lord St. Cheviot. Truly, you will soon be bored,*" he had agreed with her. Now that he had got Fleur—he was already bored; more especially because of her lack of response. A prize obtained by St. Cheviot never possessed the same stinging attraction of things still out of reach. But he had a quick answer for Arabella. In the absence of her husband he had taken toll of her lips.

"I have married only for the purpose of getting me an heir, madam," he had whispered with meaning.

Which indeed he felt would soon become the sole *raison*

d'être for his excursion into domesticity. His passion for Fleur was likely to be washed away by her continuous weeping. However, with punctilious courtesy, he lifted her out of the coach and, holding her up in his arms, carried his bride across the threshold. He set her down on the tiny feet in their white kid, pearl-buttoned boots.

A roar of applause went up from the indoor staff. There were cries of:

"Welcome to his lordship and her ladyship."

"God bless the bride and bridegroom!"

"God bless you, my lord . . . and you, my lady."

Mrs. D., her eyes like gimlets, searching for what she could deduce from the bride's face, curtseyed to the ground, breathing heavily as she did so. The lesser servants peered over the shoulders of those in front.

And so Fleur, once Miss Roddney, beloved child of Sir Harry Roddney and of Hélène, one-time *Madame la Marquise de Chartellet*—came to Cadlington.

She came here as the Baroness, Lady St. Cheviot. She found herself in a great house of ornate magnificence. She looked at the rows of bowing, fawning servants; at the double staircases, and fine gallery, at the grand display of hothouse flowers. Even the banisters were entwined with exotic orchids. How she hated the orchids; she regarded them with horror. They reminded her of *him*.

Now at last Peveril Marsh set eyes on Lady St. Cheviot. His rapt gaze embraced her, marvelling at her pure extraordinary beauty. But what struck him most forcibly was the look of crushing sorrow stamped on that youthful face. How pale she was! How transparent! Was she very delicate? What was wrong? Never in his life had he seen hair of such a colour. It made him catch his breath; filled him with a mounting desire to reproduce immediately on canvas the rose-gilt hue of her curls. The slender perfection of her body was intensified by the fine cut of the lavender-coloured velvet skirt and short tight coat she was wearing. There was a drift of expensive lace at her throat. On her bonnet was a waving ostrich plume which made her look tall, but Peveril noted that she barely reached her husband's shoulder.

All that was true artist in Peveril rejoiced in this vision. He was not yet twenty. At his age many a young man had clasped many a woman in his arms, for lechery if not for love. But Peveril Marsh had had neither time nor money for the cultivation of female company. He had known, of course, that he could never become a true painter until he had fallen in love; for great talents and great passions are more often than not linked by a single creative force. The sight of St. Cheviot's bride struck at his being—like lightning—almost paralysing his senses.

St. Cheviot turned a jaundiced eye in his direction, and nodded.

"Good day to you, Peveril! How goes the latest masterpiece?"

"No masterpiece, I fear, my lord—but the new painting continues—I thank you," he answered. But he continued to look with awe and wonder at the young Lady St. Cheviot. Suddenly she raised lashes that seemed too heavy for the languorous lids. Her eyes met his. The deep violet of them astounded him. Once again that lightning flash struck at the trembling young man. Immediately he lowered his own eyes. Fleur did likewise.

During the journey from London, and last night at Fulmer, she had felt only half alive. The same deathly lassitude seemed to have settled on her limbs, and in her mind, this morning while they drove through the sunny Buckinghamshire countryside to Cadlington.

She could not raise one spark of enthusiasm when St. Cheviot had first pointed out the tower that rose above the forest of trees, and finally the park which surrounded the great mansion. He boasted of the many beauties of his ancestral home.

"Cadlington is all yours now, madam," he had said in a cold boastful voice, "and much more, if you would only appear a little less frozen in manner towards me."

She had answered:

"I care nothing for worldly possessions. I have already told you that, sir, and I cannot alter what I am."

"Sometimes I wonder *why* my choice ever rested on you," he snarled at her.

"Let it be remembered, then," she said with all her mother's dignity, "that the girl upon whom you first fastened your regard bears no resemblance to the one who was destroyed that night at The Bastille."

St. Cheviot had grown red, then pale. He said through his teeth:

"Do not mention that night—do not dare speak of it again."

Then Fleur, with her new unhappy laugh, said:

"If the memory shames you, my lord, that is one point in your favour."

He had sunk back in his corner of the coach muttering that the sooner my lady had a parcel of brats in the nursery to keep her busy, the better. Ensure that the race of St. Cheviot will be carried on; that was all now that he wanted. He took the trouble to tell her so. She said nothing but looked at him with a fresh disgust. Everything that she said or did proved to him that she had gone through with this marriage only in bitter revulsion.

Now she was being asked to admire the magnificence of her new home—the luxury of the life that she would lead here. But it did nothing to comfort her. She wished bitterly that she could be like Cousin Dolly or the twins, who would gladly have accepted the pollution of this husband for the sake of worldly possessions.

Who, she wondered, was the grey-eyed boy who had looked at her just now with such deep respect and admiration? She seemed to notice none of the other faces; only Peveril's alone. Then she passed on. She came to the foot of the staircase. Here, a gigantic woman wearing a frilled bonnet came and bobbed and spoke to her, mittened hands meekly folded over her breast.

"Your servant, my lady. I am Mrs. Dinglefoot, the housekeeper; here when the sainted Baroness, his lordship's mother, was still alive."

"I give you good morning, Mrs. Dinglefoot," said Fleur with the exquisite politeness which she never failed to show to the lower classes.

Mrs. D.'s malevolent gaze travelled critically up and down the girlish figure. The beauty that had struck Peveril Marsh's soul and ravished it, filled her with new sensations of malice and spite. Truly, my lady was a great beauty. But she looked tired—almost *crushed*—the housekeeper thought with some pleasure. Maybe already she had been brought to heel by the Baron. He was not one to suffer any nonsense, nor bow to a woman's whim. Perhaps Mrs. D.

need not anticipate that she would receive opposition from this quarter. Fawning, her lips drawn back to show the horse's teeth, Mrs. D. murmured something to the effect that she hoped her ladyship would be pleased with her rooms; and would she like to inspect the kitchens and the rest of the house now or later?

"Later, please," said Fleur.

She was tired—always so tired. She craved to be alone; to be left to sleep. Only in such oblivion could she find relief from the misery and degradation of what was now to be her life. Through the laces at her throat was thrust an arrow of large white diamonds. Diamonds sparkled around her wrists and on her fingers. Not one of these maid-servants but envied her, she knew—and she would rather have been the very least of them than Lady St. Cheviot.

Denzil came forward and put a careless hand on her shoulder. Immediately she flinched away from it. That gesture did not escape Mrs. Dinglefoot.

"Ah ha!" she thought, "there is not much love lost between *them*. I fancy my lady has not come here as a willing bride. So much the better. She will not want to rule me or my domain, for she will not be particularly concerned."

And hugging this observation to herself, Mrs. Dinglefoot bobbed, withdrew and whispered fiercely to the rest of the female staff to get on with their business. Lunch was not to be served in the big dining-room but on a small oval table *à deux* in a morning-room; a more intimate meal for the "bridal pair." Tonight there would be a banquet to which many guests from the district had been invited. Fleur knew about this and her fainting spirit shrank from having to be presented to St. Cheviot's friends and acquaintances so soon; and from playing the part of the blushing bride. She hated hypocrisy; but she knew that she must go through with it. She thought, *This is only the beginning.*

When St. Cheviot had carried her into the hall just now she had felt as though his strong brutal arms were pitch-forking her into a prison. Henceforth there was to be no escape for her, no privacy, nothing left of *Fleur Roddney*. Within these walls, as Lady St. Cheviot, she must "love, honour and obey" this terrible man—until she died.

Suddenly there came the deep-throated bark of a big

dog. Fleur saw a white wolfhound bound through the open doorway. She liked animals, but she thought this one had a ferocious aspect. It sidled up to St. Cheviot and licked his hand. He caressed the dog's head and said:

"So! Always a welcome from my favourite! This is Alpha —Alpha, go to your new mistress and show that you are pleased to greet her, too."

Fleur held out a hand. Alpha moved forward, gingerly, sniffed at the extended fingers and then backed, snarling. She preferred men. She had never made friends with any female at Cadlington. But she saw Peveril Marsh and went up to him for a caress. St. Cheviot laughed.

"A true woman," he said. "You must have a care, Fleur. Cross her and she will show her fangs."

"She has already shown them, my lord, and I shall not seek to cross her," said my lady coldly.

The bitter and sometimes misplaced humour that lay in St. Cheviot moved him now to exhibit his power over the animal—and over Fleur, herself.

"Alpha will guard you at my bidding. And if I say so, she will allow no one else to approach you. Watch!"

He spoke and gestured to the wolfhound, who immediately turned and caught a fold of Fleur's skirt between her yellow fangs. Fleur stood stock still, a frozen expression on her face. There was no fear in her eyes. Of this ferocious dog she was less afraid than of her amorous master.

"Now," said St. Cheviot, and beckoned to Ivor, "try to take her ladyship by the arm," he commanded.

The Welshman obeyed sourly. He knew the bitch's temper, but he was no coward. When he was almost within a few inches of taking Fleur's arm, however, the wolfdog sprang at him, snarling horribly. Ivor retired, muttering that one day he would cut the beast's throat. St. Cheviot rocked with laughter. The rest of the staff joined in. Everybody seemed to think it a fine joke. Fleur had not moved but her face had grown a shade whiter. Then Peveril Marsh dared to speak to her.

"Do not fear, my lady. Alpha's bark is worse than her bite."

"I am not afraid," said my lady in that same cold little voice, but her eyes held kindness for the young man who tried to put her at her ease.

St. Cheviot whistled off his hound. He was tired of the sport.

"Now, my sweet child, I have a surprise for you," he addressed Fleur in a dulcet voice intended for his staff to hear, although his dark eyes were still full of the resentment which he felt towards his young wife. "Let me present to you, Peveril Marsh—the young man of whom I have already spoken. A genius in our midst. My Painter Extraordinary. You shall sit to him for your portrait—all in good time."

He beckoned to Peveril, who came forward a trifle shyly and bowed low to my lady. At once she felt drawn to him. He looked so youthful and gentle beside the dark massive figure of St. Cheviot. Art in any form appealed to Fleur. Both her parents had cared greatly for beautiful paintings and she, herself, in her early teens had been commended for her brushwork. (Ah, heavens, she thought, with a sudden anguished pang, how far away those dear dead days at Pillars. Oh, gone for ever, those happy blissful days!)

"I am honoured to meet you, my lady," said the young artist. His voice was low-pitched and as gentle as his expression. Instinctively Fleur held out a small gloved hand. He looked at it as though not knowing what to do. St. Cheviot gave a sarcastic laugh.

"You may kiss her hand. She will not bite you," he said with a return to humour.

The boy's thin face burned. He took the little kid-gloved hand. It looked very small and white lying against his brown palm. He noted with some dismay that his own long fingers bore smears of paint that no amount of scrubbing with soap and water had been able to remove. He barely touched his lady's little hand with his lips—then dropped it as though it was a hot coal. St. Cheviot roared.

"Our young artist has not the cavalier touch. But you will mark, my lady, that he can use a brush with great perfection. Damme, if his portrait in oils of myself is not the finest in the collection of St. Cheviots. Come, show it to her, boy."

Fleur said:

"If you will excuse me, my lo——" she stumbled and added, "Denzil. I would go to my room. I am a little faint."

"Women are always faint at the wrong moment," grumbled St. Cheviot, and turned and shouted: "Which one of you is the temporary maid to her ladyship?"

In a day or two there would come from Paris a French woman whom St. Cheviot had engaged as his wife's personal maid, but for the moment Mrs. Dinglefoot had found a nicely-spoken girl from the village who understood the care of clothes and would not be too clumsy.

This maid—younger than Fleur—stepped forward and bobbed.

"I am Phoebe Withers, my lady—daughter of Reuben Withers who is head gardener at Cadlington, so please you."

"Good day to you, Phoebe," said Fleur kindly. "I shall be glad of your services."

St. Cheviot glanced at the little maid and told himself coarsely that he, too, might one evening be glad of them. She was a pretty wench who had not so far come within his notice. Reuben Withers had charge of the orchid house and was second to none at his job. Little Phoebe had a trim figure and a pair of sparkling eyes. Behind Fleur's back, Denzil chucked the girl under the chin. She blushed and giggled. These actions did not pass unnoticed by Peveril, who frowned and felt some astonishment if not disgust. It seemed an extraordinary way for the Baron to behave. Did a gentleman, then, bring home a bride and within twenty-four hours of his wedding, pay attention to a female servant?

Peveril looked a trifle anxiously at Fleur. She turned and said, "I would be glad if Phoebe would come and show me to my rooms."

"Not so. I shall show you the rooms myself," said St. Cheviot, "and with us shall come the one who has so cleverly designed them. To this young artist, I entrusted my decorations. All has been newly done in the attempt to please you, Fleur." He added the last words in a low voice meant only for her ears. She did not answer. She walked up one of the fine thickly carpeted staircases, a small hand on the rosewood banisters; her head held high.

Peveril followed, his heart beating fast. Now that he had looked upon Fleur St. Cheviot's face, he hoped passionately that his decorations would please her. And he was glad that he had spent so much time and effort in making the rooms beautiful for her. For now he knew that he had chosen well. The virginal, sugar-white loveliness of the bridal chamber was the right background for Lady St. Cheviot's cool flawless beauty.

He had the satisfaction of hearing a cry of approval fall from her lips. Indeed, Fleur wakened suddenly now from the nightmare of her thoughts, and came to life if only for a few moments as she looked upon the enchantment conceived and carried out by the young painter. Despite her misery, her profound despair, all that was feminine in her was gratified by what she saw. The glittering lace-covered bed, the cupids overhead with their gleaming silver lamps, the painted ceiling, and most of all the sweet-smelling scattered violets—violets for her to tread upon. What a charming idea!

"It is indeed bewitching," she murmured and some colour crept up under her skin.

Peveril bowed low. He was ready to kiss her feet for joy.

"I am rewarded—and more—by the mere knowledge that it pleases you, my lady," he said.

Now she looked him straight in the eyes. She even smiled.

"Thank you," she said. And she was glad that *he* had done this thing and not St. Cheviot.

But almost at once the towering form of St. Cheviot came between them, blotting out of sight the boy's happy face. Denzil encircled her tiny waist with the long fingers of his two hands.

"So you are really pleased? You are blushing. At last, perhaps, you begin to realize what I feel for you and all that I would do for you if you would be a little kinder," he said under his breath.

At once her pink colour faded. She shrank away. The glorious shining bedroom was veiled from her as though by a mist of loathing and despair. If this had been prepared for her by a bridegroom whom she had loved, if in this heavenly room she could have been bride to any other man than St. Cheviot—how different it might have been! Little did Peveril Marsh dream that this pretty chamber could be only another setting for her abasement—her martyrdom—

and that when St. Cheviot's hands touched her, it was as though they grasped those lilies yonder, staining the matchless whiteness to a bitter brown.

Indeed, Peveril Marsh, knowing nothing of such reflections, walked happily with the bride into the communicating room. This, too, satisfied her. Once again in her gentle way she smiled and thanked him.

"I have never seen lovelier rooms," she said. "This one in which we now stand reminds me a little of my parents' home; of the boudoir that belonged to my dear mother. She, too, favoured pale wood panelling, and this same shade of green."

Peveril looked at Fleur, speechless with gratitude. His searching gaze noted that the girl's full underlip trembled and that a tear glittered on the longest lashes he had ever seen. Once again he was sorely troubled. Why, why did Lady St. Cheviot look so sorrowful; so *defenceless*? What was her history? What had led her to marry the Baron? Did a woman not give herself for love? What in heaven's name lay behind this curious atmosphere of disaster which the sensitive young artist was quick to sense?

He felt that it was time he absented himself. Bowing first to Denzil, then to the bride, he murmured a few words and departed.

Phoebe tripped into the room.

"Mrs. Dinglefoot wishes to know if my lady would like a cup of camomile tea or a cordial before her luncheon——" she began.

But St. Cheviot interrupted.

"Leave us."

"Yes, my lord," said Phoebe and hurriedly shut the door again.

Fleur began to untie the ribbons of her bonnet. She walked back into the exquisite bedroom, moved to one of the windows and stared down at the wonderful gardens; at clipped yew hedges; the flower borders, pink and scarlet with late summer roses, or magnificent chrysanthemums; the upper terrace with its Italian marble balustrade; an artificial lake embroidered with water-lilies. Then she stared into the distance across the blue-green mist of the forest down into the valley.

She was an exile, utterly alone, as though in a foreign

land—far removed from everybody, everything she had ever known. Her spirits were so low that she even felt she would like to be back in Cousin Dolly's house; at least with her own kith and kin. Yet no! Cousin Dolly was her enemy, and poor Cousin Archibald knew nothing of her betrayal. There was no one to protect her from any further infamy to which she might be subjected. She had been made a respectable wife—yes—now she bore a fine old title—and she was mistress of this palatial home. And she wanted none of it.

The slow tears began to trickle down her cheeks. With a heart-broken sigh she brushed them away. She knew that it angered her husband to see her cry.

Now he was at her side. His eager fingers began to unbutton her little jacket. His face was flushed with the passion she had grown to dread.

"You are a lovely thing," he muttered. "It is a pity you are also an icicle."

She stood dumb. She had little spirit with which to fight. What was the use, anyway? She was his wife, she had her duty. Always Fleur had been conscious of her duties in this life. Thus, she had been brought up by her mother.

"Can you not say one word of thanks for everything I have done for you?" St. Cheviot demanded savagely, his black eyes glowering at her.

"I thank you," she said in a low voice.

Enraged, he pushed her away—so roughly that she stumbled and fell. She lay still on one of the white bearskin rugs—crushing the violets—her face hidden on one curved arm. But she did not cry.

Chapter Four

Two months later, one cool wet morning in November, Fleur climbed the circular staircase that led up to Peveril's studio. She climbed slowly for one so young. She could not overcome that lassitude that had fallen on limbs and spirit since her marriage to St. Cheviot.

At the moment she was feeling better than usual, because St. Cheviot was away. He had had a fiery row with his head gamekeeper over some shooting incident. Cadlington had been full of gentlemen enjoying the shooting last week-end. All day, the forest had resounded with the crack of guns. But following this row, St. Cheviot, in one of his black moods, had taken himself off to London. There, Fleur knew he would spend his time at the clubs, playing cards or supping with his mistresses. She knew that he had mistresses. He had told her so, to add to her shame and horror.

"Man cannot live with a block of ice," he had told her one night, "and I can easily find attractive females who think me a fascinating lover."

To this Fleur had made no response. Always when he insulted her, she remained dumb. It was this very patience and resignation in the face of her misery that angered him most.

Once, and once only, he had muttered an apology when, after a peculiarly unhappy scene between them, she had faced him, driven beyond endurance, and cried:

"Oh, God! The day will come when the ghosts of my beloved parents will rise from their watery grave to haunt you. Your monstrous behaviour cannot go unpunished—you will see."

She had noted the way he backed from her. She knew that he was superstitious.

After a week or two of trying to accustom herself to her new life at Cadlington, Fleur consented to sit for her portrait to the young artist, Peveril. She saw him quite often—either in the house or wandering in the grounds. She never failed to stop and speak to him. His great gentleness—coupled with a certain boyish dignity—appealed to her. He seemed the one member of the household she could like and respect. On the whole she disliked the Baron's staff. It had not taken her long to discover that the housekeeper was her enemy, and a most unpleasant one.

Phoebe had long since been replaced by a French woman of over thirty years, by name Odette; sharp-featured, sharp-tongued and not at all the pleasant or motherly type that Fleur's mother used to employ at Pillars. But Odette was a clever needlewoman and took excellent care of my lady's wardrobe. This satisfied St. Cheviot—so Odette remained. One of the many burdens of Fleur's existence was the number of times the Baron liked her to change her clothes. She was dressed up like a doll to amuse him, she thought bitterly.

She disliked not only her husband, but his friends. Many people had called—one or two matrons with young daughters who might have been pleasant company and were highly respectable. But the mothers seemed to fear the Baron (rightfully, Fleur told herself with irony). In such a way did he look at their virginal daughters! So the nicest of the neighbours came rarely to Cadlington, some not at all. It was left to the unfortunate young bride to find but one modest friend; Peveril, the painter.

She grew to look forward to her hour of sitting while he painted. They talked fluently together nowadays. They found much in common—these two young things who were much of an age. She learned of his early life, his struggles, his misfortunes. His knowledge amazed her. He was a scholar and a poet as well as a painter.

There were moments during these last two months as autumn drifted into the beginning of the winter and the weather kept her much indoors, when Fleur had wondered how she could have borne her life without Peveril's company.

This morning she was a little more breathless than usual when she reached the top of the tower.

She, like Peveril, found in this turret studio a refuge, a retreat from the rest of the world. In her own rooms she was suffocated by the very magnificence with which he surrounded her.

Peveril heard her light slow step. He went quickly to the door and opened it. As he watched Fleur climbing up the last few stairs, his eyes bore the expression of one who looks at a sacred image.

In all his nineteen years, the young artist had never experienced a rapture more intense than that which he felt at the sight of the beautiful young Baroness; nor a respect more profound. But whereas hers was burdened with an intolerable sorrow, his was disturbed only by the anguish of love.

As she reached him, he bowed low, touching with his lips the slender hand she extended. *This* was how he liked her best; in the simple gown in which he was painting her. It was of madonna-blue velvet, the violet-blue hue of her eyes; she wore no jewellery. She seemed to him to look no more than fifteen or sixteen years old. The pearly quality of her skin like the rose of her lips was nature's masterpiece. A thrill of pure joy would frequently shoot through the young man while he painted her.

The Baron, one morning, had said to Peveril:

"Mind you execute the portrait of my lady in gay mood. I want no hint of tears. Women cry too much and too often!"

Peveril had repeated this to Fleur and been horrified by the bitter little laugh which had escaped her. She said:

"Paint me as you see me, Peveril—a true artist can only reproduce what he sees with his own unfailing vision."

But he feared that St. Cheviot might not be satisfied. He begged him not to look at the painting until it was finished.

Peveril led Fleur into the studio. She seated herself in the high-backed chair in which she always posed for her picture.

"Will you feel a draught, my lady?" he asked anxiously.

"No," she said, "I like it here."

And she laid her hands on the arms of the chair, crossed her small ankles, and shut her eyes, while Peveril knelt before her and arranged the folds of her blue velvet gown. He looked up. That perfect head was drooping like a lily overweighted on its slender stem. As ever, he marvelled at the length of her silken lashes. This morning the shadows beneath those huge eyes were deep. Seen thus with sealed eyelids she made his heart ache. Oh, that tragic curve of lips! Now, and every day of his life, he brooded over the mystery of her. Knife-points of doubt and anxiety entering his tender heart until he felt that he was bleeding from a thousand wounds. What was wrong with her? *Oh, what?* He loved her so deeply that he would gladly have died to bring one smile of true happiness to her dolorous mouth. But he hardly ever saw her smile.

Her lashes lifted. Peveril trembled. He could not look too closely into the purple depths of Fleur St. Cheviot's eyes. Sometimes he felt that he did not *want* to learn what lay in them.

"The morning is grey," he said hastily, "I will start to paint while the light is good," and he turned to the canvas. It was nearly five foot high. He felt it would be his masterpiece if ever he was to paint one. Today he was concentrating on that sweet mouth with the divine cleft in the lower lip. He dipped his finest brush into rose-madder and began to paint.

She watched him and talked a little.

"It is dreary at Cadlington when the rains come."

"Yes, my lady. Last winter it was worse after Christmas. Fearful gales come sweeping across the valley. The whole house seems to rock with the thunder of the storm."

"I shall not mind the storms. But the vapours—the autumnal mists add to my gloom," she said.

"There should be no gloom for you, my lady, only the joy of spring," said Peveril.

One of her brows lifted. She said:

"It is a long time since I have tasted the joy of spring."

This was the sort of reply which he hated to hear.

"The Baron is away for long?" he asked.

"Until the end of this week, I believe."

Now it was Peveril's turn to raise a brow. How could any man leave such a bride for a whole week? he asked himself.

Said Fleur:

"Tell me, Peveril, have you any supernatural powers such as your poor sister possessed?"

"None, my lady. Elspeth, alone, was born with that psychic spirit."

"I laid a flower upon the poor child's grave when I was in the churchyard, yesterday, with my maid."

"I thank you, for my sister's sake. She suffered much and I often reproach myself that I brought her all this way from London and hastened her death."

"You did it for the best," said Fleur who had heard his story so often that she knew it well, "and at least the strange fate that led you here did you also a kindly turn. For it gave you work and a domicile at Cadlington."

To herself, she said:

"And it gave me my one, my only friend in the world."

The young artist murmured:

"I owe much to his lordship."

Fleur shut her eyes for a second. It was well, she told herself bitterly, that anyone had anything to thank *him* for. Oh, she knew that St. Cheviot could be free with his money—even tolerant when the mood took him; but as a rule his whims and fancies turned in the wrong direction. He was more prodigal to those people who amused him, than to the ones who deserved his generosity. Least of all was he generous to *her* in the only way she wanted. He did not wish to give her peace, or let her lead the kind of life that she wanted.

"How long do you think you will stay at Cadlington, Peveril?" she asked him.

"I do not know, my lady," he answered. "There are moments when I feel I must get away. I do not wish to be beholden for ever even to such a good master. But when I have spoken to his lordship he has refused to allow me to leave."

Fleur nodded. She knew from what Denzil had said to her that he like to keep Peveril here because others envied him his young "Painter Extraordinary." For St. Cheviot, he was just another treasure in the great house, but if and when Denzil tired of the boy—he would ruthlessly abandon him. That was St. Cheviot's way.

Peveril continued to paint. He was not working well and he knew it. He was strangely restless. Fleur had become the inspiration of his life yet, today, he felt uninspired. He would like to stop work, throw himself at her feet and ask her a hundred questions about herself.

He was not altogether ignorant of what was going on. There was much gossip in the servants' hall, to which he could not entirely stop his ears.

There was always intimate gossip, too, from Odette, the French maid. Odette was a Parisienne, not averse to some coquetry and, although twice Peveril's age, had an eye for the handsome boy with his singular talents. Once or twice she had waylaid him in the gardens and whispered that she could teach him much if he was interested. He rejected her advances. Subsequently she grew spiteful and never missed a chance to tease him. And although she dared not speak her mind, she was quite sure that the young artist was genuinely enamoured of my Lady St. Cheviot. So she took special pleasure in letting Peveril hear the kind of talk that would make his spirit recoil.

She carried tales of his lordship's overwhelming passion for my lady. Of his terrible rages. She, Odette had seen him rush out of my lady's room, cursing her. And later found my lady in tears which she tried to hide but could not. Once, Odette whispered to Peveril, she saw livid bruises on my lady's slender arms; imprints of his lordship's fingers. There must be dark terrible scenes in that enchanted bedchamber that Peveril had design for the "happy bride." Scenes of unbridled passion on the Baron's part—of reluctance from my lady.

Such tales drove Peveril into a state of deep distress. Each fresh story only confirmed his dread suspicion that my lady had come here as an unwilling bride. More than that, it began to destroy what had been his boyish respect and homage for the man who had befriended him.

This morning, Peveril talked to Fleur of the Queen.

On the 20th November, he told her, the young Victoria would be going in state to open the Houses of Parliament.

"I wonder," said Fleur, "whom she will marry."

"No doubt it will be whosoever her statesmen choose for her," said the artist, leaning forward to smear with his thumb a tiny coil of thick oil paint.

"Alas, that most women must marry the men chosen for them rather than make their own choice," sighed Fleur. "I shall pray every night that our young Queen's fate will be happier than——" She broke off, crimsoning from brow to chin. How nearly she had let that disloyalty fall from her lips. *Happier than mine*, she had been about to say.

Peveril dropped his brush. He grew suddenly pale. His brows contracted. He walked to the fire and kicked a log into position, making the sparks shoot up the chimney. He knew exactly what the unspoken word should have been. And today he knew beyond all doubt that Lady St. Cheviot did not love her husband.

"If my lady will forgive me, I am not in the mood to paint well today. I would sooner leave it till tomorrow," he muttered.

Fleur stood up and stretched her cramped young body, moving towards the warmth of the fire. Now the wind had changed. Spear-points of rain tapped against the several windows of the turret. In here it was warm, but outside it was cold and bleak. As bleak as the future that stretched before her, Fleur reflected. She could hardly tolerate the thought of the Baron's return.

"Would it disturb your work, Peveril, if I stayed here with you a little longer?" she asked with the meekness of a very young girl, not conscious of her dignified status in this vast establishment.

Peveril sprang to his feet. Nervously he fingered the Byronic tie which he favoured.

"But, my lady—it is for *you* to give *me* orders," he stammered. "If my humble studio pleases you, it is an honour and delight for me to entertain you here."

She looked at him with sweetness, and a faintest uplifting of her sad lips.

"I like to be here," she said gravely and spread her chilled fingers to the flame.

"My lady," he said, "to paint you is my privilege. To converse with you also is like a strange unfettering of all my thoughts."

"And mine," she whispered.

It was the first time the two young things had ever dared openly to express such pleasure in one another's company.

Peveril continued:

"I would like to do more—so much more! My dear lady, tell me, how best I can contribute to your happiness?"

She turned the small head with a movement both graceful and proud. But there was all the sadness in the world in her voice as she answered him.

"I have not known what happiness is since my Mama and Papa were taken from me by a monstrous cruelty of fate."

Then suddenly they heard above the sighing of the wind and the rain the sound of heavy footsteps. Someone was coming up the circular staircase. Fleur was first to recognize that step. All the colour that both the fire, and the sweetness of Peveril's words, had raised in her face, drained from it now.

"It is my husband. The Baron has come back earlier than intended," she said.

The full frightfulness of his suspicions broke over the young painter's head, for he could not help but read the stark misery and dread that had so suddenly aged and blanched that young fair face before his very eyes.

"Oh, God," he thought, *"she hates him."*

And immediately there followed another thought: *"Then I must hate him, too."*

Chapter Five

The studio door burst open unceremoniously. In sober but fashionable clothes, St. Cheviot stood there. He wore a cape and carried gauntlets in his hand. He looked as always after he had been away in London for a few days; dissolute, moody, his face ravaged by the excesses in which he had indulged. His great height made it seem as though he filled the doorway. There was a sinking sensation in Fleur's heart at the sight of those broad shoulders and that florid handsome face. He looked her up and down and then a lightning glance round the studio—a glance that barely included Peveril. Then he turned to his young wife again.

"Well, well, *well*, so this is where my loving wife has hidden herself. I looked for her in vain in her own apartments."

She moved forward.

"I did not expect you home so soon."

"Obviously," he said with a sneer, loosed his cape and flung it on a chair. He ran his fingers through his thick ebon-black curls, still smiling in that cold cruel way.

"I came early because Mrs. Dinglefoot sent for me," he said.

Fleur started.

"*Sent* for you? On what grounds?"

St. Cheviot did not answer at once but moved across the studio to the easel. He examined Fleur's portrait. Legs straddled, hands in his pockets, he rocked to and fro, on toe and heel. His eyes narrowed. He said:

"Mrs. Dinglefoot, the excellent creature, always has my good at heart. I asked her to communicate with me should she see anything amiss down here."

"And pray what does she see amiss?" asked Fleur, putting her hand to her breast. Her heart was beating violently.

Peveril stood rigid and silent.

Said St. Cheviot:

"The good Mrs. D. sent me a carefully worded letter to the effect that she did not think you look well and that you spend too much time in weeping."

Fleur, with a nervous glance at Peveril, said:

"I do not consider that my health—or my tears—should concern Mrs. Dinglefoot."

St. Cheviot took no notice of this. Staring harder at the painting, he said:

"She deemed it her duty as an old and confidential servant of this household, to express the opinion that you expend far too much time and energy upon climbing these steep stairs, and remaining in this studio. You might be better employed out of doors in the new phaeton, driving through the countryside or calling upon the neighbours. That conduct would, of course, also be more fitting to your ladyship's dignity. More in observance with the conventions, shall we say."

The inference behind St. Cheviot's words brought the hot blood to the young painter's sensitive face. But Fleur remained deathly white. Then she said:

"I consider it none of Mrs. Dinglefoot's affair if I come up here. I resent such interference."

St. Cheviot turned to her. His dark eyes glowered.

"My dear Lady St. Cheviot, Mrs. D. acts under my orders."

"As a spy——?" began Fleur with passionate resentment, but cut the sentence short. "Nay—we must not embarrass Peveril by discussing our private affairs before him."

Suddenly a new suspicion smote St. Cheviot. *Could it be . . . was it possible* . . . he threw a slantwise look at the girlish figure in the madonna-blue gown. It was early days . . . of course . . . but that *might* just be the good reason for her ladyship's sickness in the mornings.

He rose, yawned, and turned a sour gaze on young Peveril.

"You have been making too many demands upon her ladyship's time. There have been sittings enough," he said. "Finish the portrait without her ladyship."

"As your lordship pleases," said Peveril, but his breathing quickened.

To cut short these moments of joy . . . to see Lady St. Cheviot only at a distance . . . to talk with her no more . . . what cruel deprivation! He looked at Fleur anxiously. She stared at the ground, as though not wishful to meet his gaze. Heavens, how pale she was, how she trembled, he thought.

"Incidentally I have some criticism to make of the portrait now that I have at last seen it," added Denzil. "The flesh tints and the hue of the hair have that remarkable quality which even old Clarissa Rustingthorpe (and she is a connoisseur) declares is reminiscent of the Venetian masters. But why no adornment? I will have the St. Cheviot jewels sent up to you. Paint them into her ladyship's picture, if it is ever to hang in the gallery beside the other ladies of quality."

The harshness of the command did not disturb Peveril. Indeed, both he and Fleur had suspected that this was what his lordship would say. But he could not bear to see the look, as of a drowning woman, that came into Fleur's eyes as his lordship put an arm around her.

St. Cheviot said:

"You do not appear well, madam. Come—let us go. Mrs. D. is right. It is high time I came home and personally organized your life. Come!"

She opened her lips as though to protest but closed them again. Her whole body seemed to shiver from the contact with him. She was stricken dumb by the thought that he had returned. That after today these little moments of innocent happiness spent in this studio must end.

Peveril said:

"If your lordship would permit *one* more sitting . . ."

"No," said St. Cheviot in a rough voice, "and remember to paint in the jewels. I give you good morning." He added: "The Marchioness of Rustingthorpe is sending her carriage for you the day after tomorrow. She has a granddaughter in residence at the moment. I have given my word you will accept a commission to paint her. She is an ugly brat, but you can do your best."

Now Peveril spoke up:

"It is my earnest wish, my lord, that I start to make my

own way. If I can add this fee for painting the Marquis's granddaughter to my small savings, I shall have enough to enable me to set up a small studio in London."

St. Cheviot, who had been walking to the door with Fleur in the circle of his arm, looked at Peveril over his shoulder and frowned.

"It is for me to say when it is time for you to leave Cadlington," he snapped.

Fleur thought:

"St. Cheviot is only happy when he is curtailing liberty—imprisoning a human being for some vile or egotistical reason of his own. Alas—poor Peveril! He has outgrown the pleasure of accepting charity *here*."

The boy saw that this was no time for argument with his lordship. But anger was bubbling in him—a proud resentment against tyranny.

Suddenly Fleur felt faint and put a hand to her temples and murmured:

"Oh, pray support me, sir—I fear I am about to swoon."

St. Cheviot's arms lifted her from the ground.

"The devil take it, she is, indeed, indisposed," he muttered.

Peveril, sick with pity and anxiety, looked to the right and to the left.

"Alas, I have no vinegar—no feathers to burn . . ."

"No matter. I will carry her downstairs."

And without even saying farewell, he turned and began to walk slowly down the stairs bearing the unconscious form of his wife.

Slowly Peveril shut the studio door. The rain was coming down in torrents now, lashing against the windows, blotting out the Vale of Aylesbury. He walked to the easel and looked at the portrait in despair. Then he turned to the chair in which Fleur had but recently sat. He clasped it as though he were clasping the shade of her living presence.

In Fleur's exquisite bedroom, Fleur was laid upon her bed. Imperiously, St. Cheviot called for servants, cordial, burnt feathers, and vinegar. He also sent a footman hurrying down the hill to fetch the parish doctor. This pyhsician, an old man by name Dr. Boss, was adequate at his job, if not up to date.

Fleur struggled back to consciousness reluctantly. She

found her room full of people. She was at once conscious of the presence of her husband on one side of the bed, of Odette bathing her temples and applying burnt feathers to her nostrils and of the menacing figure of Mrs. Dinglefoot in starched apron and bonnet, giving orders to the lesser maids to bring in hot water, warming pans for my lady's cold feet, and to remove the lilies which were filling the bedchamber with their overpowering scent.

St. Cheviot bent over his young wife.

"So, my love, you are reviving," he said in the smooth voice which he sometimes used to her when in the presence of his staff. Let it be said in the neighbourhood at least that he was a devoted husband.

Fleur felt faint and sick. There was a frightened sensation in her heart and the moment she was conscious, she *remembered*. Never again was she to be allowed to go up to the studio in the tower and sit with Peveril Marsh. Her last and only happiness had been taken from her. A tear rolled down her cheek.

"Courage, my love," said St. Cheviot in his most dulcet voice. "Dr. Boss is on his way."

"Lawks, ma'am, my lady, but you gave us a fright," began Mrs. Dinglefoot who was in some triumph because she had managed to get her master back to Cadlington and upset what she called "the apple cart." The wily woman had become well aware of her young mistress's desire to spend a great deal of her time conversing with the young painter.

She had sent for the Baron not from a spirit of loyalty nor any genuine anxiety for her ladyship's health, but out of the spiteful wish to rob my lady of any joy that she had found in life. Gentle, long-suffering though she was, Fleur inspired nothing but hatred and malice in the heart of the ugly old woman. Only last night, Mrs. D. had remarked scornfully to the French maid, who was her friend and ally, that her ladyship was a poor sickly thing who would no doubt die bearing her first child.

Mrs. Dinglefoot had served the late Baroness when she was first *enceinte* with the present Baron. She knew the signs of pregnancy in a female. She was sure that accounted for my lady's nausea in the early mornings.

Fleur's eyes looked with distaste at Mrs. D.'s hairy chin. The sight disgusted her. She whispered:

"Denzil, please to clear my room. I wish to be alone."

"With me, of course, my darling," said St. Cheviot in a breezy voice, clapped his hands and dismissed the maids who were running to and fro like a lot of silly useless hens.

Outside the door, Mrs. D. eyed Odette.

"You will see. Dr. Boss will confirm my suspicions."

Odette tittered. She was thin with a foxy face, a woman of inordinate vanity. She wore a frilled cap with long streamers, perched on the top of her mountain of coarse black curls.

"*Oo la! la!* It will tie down *Madame la Baronesse.* She will not be able to carry on with her intrigue with ze young *Monsieur* the artist."

"I would dearly like to find out if it *is* an intrigue," muttered Mrs. D. "Come, my girl, I hear Dr. Boss's carriage."

The physician from Monks Risborough examined Fleur carefully.

She did not dislike him. He had white hair and beard and a noble forehead. Anything of nobility—that quality which used to surround her in her childhood but seemed now so rare a thing—appealed to Fleur. She lay against her huge lace-edged pillows looking wan and pathetically young, her beautiful hair tumbled about her throat. The old doctor was much moved by the sight. When he told her the reason for her swoon and for her *malaise* of the last week, he was perturbed to see how badly she took the news. She went scarlet then pale . . . then turned her face away. The physician held one thin little wrist between his fingers, feeling the flutter of a weak pulse. He heard a low sob from her. Bending over her, he said:

"Nay—my dear child (your pardon, my lady Baroness, you seem such a child to me, for I am a very old man), but you must not grieve over what is an entirely natural state of affairs. The Baron will be delighted and surely you——"

"I am not delighted," she broke in. "But I do realize that it is my duty to bear my husband an heir."

"When it is born you will love the infant," Boss encouraged her.

She shuddered. She could not imagine herself loving any child of St. Cheviot's. What a monstrous thing nature was, arranging to unite her shrinking flesh with that of a loathed husband and thus conceive a new life. Monstrous that from her reluctant body there would emerge flesh of his flesh. . . . A son or daughter? Who could tell? But it would be a St. Cheviot *through her.*

Dr. Boss continued to offer comfort and counsel in his kindly way. She must rest a great deal, take a little exercise —not much—and plenty of fresh air. She must conserve her strength for the approaching birth which Dr. Boss reckoned would be early in June.

Of course the good doctor knew a great deal about St. Cheviot. He had, in fact, brought the Baron into the world. And he had attended the old Baron and Baroness and closed their eyes after they had died. He could not say that he cared overmuch for the family; and, like others in the neighborhood, he had heard ugly rumours of the excesses to which the present young Baron was prone. But like everyone else, Dr. Boss waited upon St. Cheviot with deference and civility because of his wealth and title. It was expected of a physician who had his living to earn. St. Cheviot paid well—better than the villagers who called Dr. Boss to their stinking hovels—only for death—seldom to attend a birth. Many a medical service he had to render around here for no payment at all. The farmers and most of the local inhabitants were ground down by heavy taxation. The cost of living was high and wages disgracefully low. The country, in Dr. Boss's opinion, was in a sorry state. Pauperism was spreading through England like an ulcer. In recent months, cholera had almost wiped out several of the adjoining hamlets. Maybe now with Queen Victoria on the throne and Lord Melbourne in power things would grow better. Meanwhile such autocratic and wealthy landowners as the St. Cheviots or the Rustingthorpes continued to wield a despotic tyranny over the lower classes. Dr. Boss deplored such facts but could not escape from them.

Suddenly Fleur turned to him, her eyes unnaturally bright and wild.

"Some births are difficult and even dangerous. Maybe I will die when my child is born."

He looked up from the bag in which he was packing his instruments and clicked his teeth in a shocked way.

"I beg you, my Lady St. Cheviot, not to consider any such calamity. You are not well. You need a tonic which I shall prescribe for you, but you are excellently fashioned by the Almighty, and should bear a fine child. With care, my lady, *with* care."

He made his exit. He would come again in a few days' time, he said, to ensure that her ladyship was making good progress.

A moment later, St. Cheviot burst into the room. There were many times when Fleur asked herself why the crystal loveliness of the bedchamber that Peveril had designed for her did not shatter to fragments whenever that dark powerful figure thundered into it.

She felt Denzil pick up one of her hands and cover it with kisses—an act of homage rare from the Baron.

"My love . . . my dearest! So it is true! Mrs. D. has not brought me home for nothing, You have conceived. That is the reason for your present delicacy and lack of appetite. Ah, my love, this is a happy day for your devoted husband. What could be finer than to know that in seven months' time an heir will be born to Cadlington!"

She lay motionless. St. Cheviot's kisses left her unmoved. But she permitted herself to give a humourless smile.

"Do not be too sure of a son, Denzil; it may be a daughter," she said.

"No, it must be a son," he said, rubbed his hands together and stuck his thumbs in his waistcoat. "It would be a new and amusing thing, my dear, if we should have a redhead like your own in the family. It would be the first red St. Cheviot. Well, well, I would not mind."

"Maybe," she said in a barely audible voice, "the babe will not live."

St. Cheviot frowned and seating himself on the edge of the big white bed, imprisoned both her hands in his strong hard fingers.

"I forbid you to speak in such vein," he said loudly. "You know my burning ambition to have an heir. It was for this that I married you. Besides," he added with a slight laugh, "the rest of the hunchback's prophecy has still to be fulfilled. And now I recall that she promised that it will be another black St. Cheviot. Yes . . . it cannot be red-haired but black like myself."

"Pray leave me to myself for a while," said Fleur.

"Not, madam, until you have reassured me that you will do all in your power to conserve your health and strength and give me a fine son. It shall not die, do you hear, Fleur? *It must not!*"

"That will be as God wills," she whispered.

"Bah!" said his lordship, and taking a tiny gilt box from his waistcoat applied snuff to each nostril. He sneezed violently several times.

Fleur thought:

"If only he would go away and leave me alone."

But St. Cheviot raved and ranted about the fine race—the former Barons—and what he would do with his son. How he would teach him to shoot, and to ride, and to be a man.

"None of your namby-pamby artists," he ended, "and thinking of artists—if that young genius Peveril likes to flaunt his independence in my face now that he makes money through my benevolence—I may well bid him go before the child is born. I fancy, too, that I shall pull down the tower, and wipe out its sinister ugliness once and for all."

Fleur made no answer. She only knew that the tower had never seemed sinister to her. As for sending Peveril away, the very idea chilled her and made her frighteningly conscious of how dear he had grown to her. She was human enough to allow herself, for a moment, to remember Peveril and the unspoken sympathy that ran like a golden electric current between them. If the studio and the little winding staircase were demolished her dearest joy would be buried under a heap of stones.

St. Cheviot took her hand again.

"Come, Fleur, I am pleased that you are *enceinte*. Ask for whatever you want. Some new pearls? Another emerald for your finger? Speak! I will send to Paris for whatever you desire."

"I desire nothing," she whispered.

"Do not be so foolish," he said impatiently. "There are

many women who would envy you the magnificence of this house, my gifts, and even of my embraces," he ended with a significant look.

She looked up at him. He was uneasy before the expression in those huge sorrowful eyes. Dammit, he thought, must she always make him conscious of his villainy towards her? He shouted:

"I give you everything. What more do you want?"

"Nothing, I tell you, save to be left alone."

He glowered around the virginal bedchamber.

"You have become as frozen as this sickly white room. After your child is born these decorations shall be altered. A new setting shall be created—more fitting for my wife. There shall be scarlet satin, a gilded bed, erotic pictures. No more of such religious stuffs as *that*. . . ." He pointed at the Raphael Madonna over the fireplace. "You need to be encouraged if you are to participate in passion's pleasures, my dear; that is obvious."

She set her teeth. To destroy this beautiful room would be only one more act of violence and unkindness on Denzil's part.

"Do you think, my lord, that a changed environment could alter my feelings towards you?" she suddenly asked him. Through their long lashes her eyes glittered, rejecting him. "Oh, go away, go away," she added, and flung herself face downwards on her pillows.

"You are a fool!" he shouted at her, "and unwise to show so much contempt. You belong to me. Take care that I do not exert my rights and keep you chained to one room as I would chain a slave, and allow you no further contact with the world."

No answer from Fleur. St. Cheviot's blood cooled. He reminded himself that if she were to give him a healthy babe he must curb his passionate temper and leave her alone. Yes—he would take himself off to London again where flesh-and-blood women were waiting to receive him with open arms. He could be bothered with her ladyship no longer. As he walked to the door, he said:

"Perhaps you wish that I should send for your Cousin Dolly since you have no mother of your own to advise you."

Now Fleur sat up, her feverish face bathed in tears.

"No—no—on no account do I want to see her. I could not endure her presence. *You* know why, my Lord St. Cheviot."

His sombre gaze fell. He shrugged his shoulders, striving as best he could to be tolerant because of her condition.

"Then is there anyone you would like to see during these coming months? I daresay I shall be much in London," he growled.

She hesitated. Into her mind had flashed the awe-inspiring thought that she wished only for the sweet comfort and friendship given her by Peveril Marsh. Her cheeks flushed a deep crimson at the very idea. She hung her head.

"I know of no one," she whispered.

"Then good day to you and I bid you take care of yourself, my lady," he said gruffly and walked from the room.

Chapter Six

Christmas came.

Cadlington was cut off from the rest of the countryside, once the long winding hills were covered with snow and the puddles were blue with ice. It was a severe winter. Nobody in the district called on the poor young Baroness although all the ladies knew from gossip that she was bearing a child. One or two of the more kindly ones might have bothered to take a glass of cordial with her, but the weather conditions made a good excuse for not doing so.

Fleur, therefore, was left very much alone. This she did not mind. And in particular she was relieved because St. Cheviot spent much of his time with his cronies in London. Also, when he came down she was not so much as before subjected to his violence, his possessive passions. For now she was advancing in her pregnancy he was so anxious that she should bear a living child, he controlled himself and acceded to a few of her wishes.

He even went so far as to put the brake on Mrs. Dinglefoot. The very sight of the woman's ugly countenance upset Fleur. She told her husband so. He laughed and tried to make a jest of it and called her fanciful, but she insisted that she would not have anything to do with the housekeeper. Fleur did not like Odette overmuch but she preferred the French woman who sewed so well and had begun, with Fleur, to stitch exquisite tiny garments for the coming infant.

When Mrs. Dinglefoot received orders from her master not to force herself on her ladyship's presence but to send word on matters concerning the household through others—her hatred became overwhelming. If she could do anything to spite Fleur for daring to snub her in this fashion (for it became a matter of jest and snigger in the servants' hall) Mrs. D. intended to do so.

Fleur received Christmas greetings from Cousin Dolly and the twins. She knew that Dolly wanted to come to Cadlington. But such was Fleur's loathing of the woman who had betrayed her to St. Cheviot that she tore Dolly's Christmas letter in two and left it unanswered. She wanted no more to do with her. Dolly was a widow these days. Cousin Archibald was dead. He had succumbed to the cholera in India a few months ago. One of the twins—Imogen—wrote to Fleur and said that Mama might possibly give them a step-Papa in the spring—a gentleman of some means and wasn't it "a pity that Cousin Fleur would be *hors de combat* and unable to attend the wedding."

Fleur did not send congratulations to Cousin Dolly. Even were she able to go—nothing would have induced her to attend such a wedding. Cousin Dolly was a wicked woman. Perhaps it was as well that poor Archibald de Vere had died before he could return and discover why, in truth, Harry Roddney's hapless daughter had been forced into marriage with St. Cheviot.

One letter only at Christmas time brought some warmth to Fleur's starved heart. An unexpected communication from her girlhood's close friend, Catherine Foster. Catherine informed Fleur that a month ago she had married their mutual friend in Essex, Tom Quinley.

Catherine wrote:

I have often thought of you, Dearest Fleur, and the happy days we knew together at Pillars when your dear Parents were alive. Mama and I were exceedingly Distressed to hear of your Misfortunes and I would have communicated with you before now but you did not answer the letter which I wrote to you just before your Marriage. I thought perhaps that you had no more time for our Friendship. But now I am Mrs. Thomas Quinley and dear Tom makes me an excellent Husband. We reside in a very elegant house not far from Bishop's Stortford.

I feel an overwhelming desire to look upon you again and to know your news. To think that you became the Baroness of Cadlington after all. Do you not remember how uncertain you were about your Affections when first St. Cheviot came to pay his attentions to you? One hears things but I trust they are not all True. I would prefer to believe that you are happy and not too fine a lady now to remember Mr. and Mrs. Thomas Quinley . . . .

When Fleur read this letter—the day after Christmas—she was sitting by the fire in her boudoir. She had been reading, trying to pass the time. It grew dark early on these winter afternoons; the nights seemed long and dreary. Already one of the footmen had lighted the candles and set a lamp upon her table.

Fleur seated herself at the bureau in order to answer Catherine's letter. Alas, she thought, if Catherine but knew the truth! It was because of that ugly truth that she had not written to her before now. She did not wish the Fosters to know her dreadful fate and subsequent unhappiness. And she was afraid that if she saw Cathy she could not conceal from one who had known her as a child, the dreadful havoc that had been wrought in her.

She was writing to Cathy when she heard a knock upon her door. Without turning her head she said, "Come in" thinking it one of the servants; Odette perhaps, to help her change into a loose velvet gown which she wore before the evening meal. She was always cold in spite of the fires. Cadlington was so huge and draughty that during this severe weather it struck chill at her very bones. She felt perpetually ill. Dr. Boss promised that she would begin to have better health once the child had quickened but as yet she had not felt the stirring in her womb.

"My lady . . . do I disturb you?" said a boy's low voice.

She dropped her quill and swung round. Her heart leaped for pleasure as she saw the unaccustomed sight of Peveril Marsh. He stood before her, smiling—a parcel under one arm. He was dressed plainly in a velveteen suit with wide cravat. He looked changed, she thought, fatigued and curiously older; a new maturity sat upon him though she knew not the reason. She had not seen him face to face for six weeks now.

Peveril advanced and bowed respectfully.

"It is to give my lady my Christmas greetings and to give

her this humble offering," he said fingering the parcel. He added: "I did not come yesterday. When Mrs. Dinglefoot saw me approaching your apartments she informed me that it was no use making any attempt to see you because you were too ill to receive me."

Fleur stood up. Her cheeks coloured angrily.

"Mrs. Dinglefoot was not acting on my instructions," she exclaimed.

"Today I dare to steal, unnoticed through the house and up to this door," Peveril confessed. "I have been so concerned, my lady to hear many tales of your indisposition."

"My illness is—natural. I am in no danger, I thank you, nevertheless," she said in a low voice.

"I am much relieved," he said.

They stood silent now, surveying one another. The blood was flowing fast through the veins of both these young creatures who had been denied the consolation of each other's presence for so long. The boy with his keen artist's perception noted little indication of her approaching maternity. Somehow he was fiercely glad. It had brought him the most strange repugnance to hear that she was to give the Baron an heir.

He had missed her friendship sorely and hungered for a glimpse of her. He lapped up every item of news of her that he could gain from the servants' hall, even though it was news he did not wish to hear. With the greatest reluctance he had altered her portrait and painted in the jewels the Baron had sent him, upon Fleur's throat and wrists. But for the artist, the whole significance of the painting had lost its meaning. It was just another to take its place in the gallery amongst the former ladies of Cadlington. The sad Madonna had become a bejewelled, tragic figure. Peveril could no longer bear to look upon it.

Reading his thoughts, Fleur said:

"My portrait is now being framed, I hear."

"Yes," he said and lowered his lashes.

"I did not care for your picture once I had painted in the jewels," he confessed.

"One day, perhaps, I shall sit for you again, Peveril," she said.

"I wish I could think so, my lady," he exclaimed before

he could restrain the impassioned impulse. To cover his embarrassment he handed her the parcel he had brought. "A humble offering for Christmastide," he said.

It was wrapped in white paper and sealed with wax. Opening it, she found a small painting in a carved wood frame which, afterwards, he told her he, himself, had fashioned. The painting was of such perfection that it drew a cry of pleasure from her lips. A pair of delicate, slender hands clasped as though in prayer, resting upon a tiny cushion of ruby velvet with tassels on each corner. Against the rich red material the hands looked very white and fragile. The long fingers, with nails almond-shaped, were entwined, upraised, suggesting intense supplication. *They were her hands.* Fleur's face grew rosy with a sudden radiance that Peveril had never seen before. It made him catch his breath. She looked so young and so startlingly happy.

"Oh!" she exclaimed, "what matchless work!"

"You know whose hands they are?" he said in a low voice.

She laid down the gift and spread her two hands to the fire by which she was sitting. They looked transparent in the light. She answered:

"Yes."

"I remembered every line, and wished to reproduce their beauty. I trust that you are not annoyed."

"Annoyed," she repeated, "but how could I be? It is a charming compliment and the little painting is a gem—like a Dutch masterpiece. With all my heart I thank you for it."

Now Peveril said awkwardly:

"I trust his lordship, also, will like it."

Fleur knew that those formal words were forced but that he had painted her hands for her alone.

"It shall hang in this room," she said.

"Thank you," he said.

Now they held each other's gaze with a look of almost frightening concentration. Each was stirred by the sudden glorious warmth of feeling which ran so positively between them. Neither spoke.

At this juncture Odette knocked on the door and walked in. She tossed her head, her long muslin streamers fluttering as she saw Peveril. She eyed him wickedly out of the corners of her slanting eyes. He did not return the look but hastily took his departure knowing how vile Odette's tongue could be. Knowing too, that Mrs. Dinglefoot from some secret spying place must have seen him steal up here and sent Odette further to spy.

Fleur said nothing. But long after she was alone again with her thoughts and dreams, she studied the exquisite little painting of her folded hands. Then she folded her own flesh and blood fingers in the same anguished entrancing manner that he had reproduced, laid her forehead upon them and wept bitterly for all the joy of life and love that was forbidden her.

She did not see Peveril again for a long time.

A bitter February came—cold, savage weather, holding the Buckinghamshire countryside in its icy grip.

Wrapped from head to foot in rich furs, the lady of Cadlington was taken for a short drive in the sledge which St. Cheviot had imported from Russia and given to her as a present. It was a gay affair, painted in red and white, and drawn by two sturdy ponies with bells on their tossing heads. It amused Cheviot to present his wife to the world as some fabulously rich Russian Princess who might have appeared thus driving from her palace in St. Petersburg. When he had first shewn this equipage, with two groomsmen from his stables, in the new livery, he had said to Fleur:

"This will enable you to go out more often. Horses slip much on these roads. It is a unique gift. I trust you are grateful."

She thanked him in the cold proud but courteous way in which she always acknowledged his extravagant presents.

"It is an amusing idea," she said.

St. Cheviot looked at her gloomily.

"One would not think to look at you that you are amused."

She turned her face away. She could never look upon him as a friend, a kindly husband, but only as the man who had slain her youth.

In this, the fifth month of her pregnancy, much of the original nausea had passed. She would have felt quite well but for her deep depression, the perpetual hunger of her heart. The worst thing of all was her dread of the future, when she knew she must share St. Cheviot's bed and board again.

However, he did not nag at her nowadays, but tried in his selfish fashion to be conciliatory. On this February morning he himself took her for a drive in the gay sledge and was pleased when the villagers turned out to wave and cheer as they passed by. They called: *"God bless you, my lord." "God bless you, my lady."*

Fleur looked sadly at some of these people who were her husband's tenants. Their threadbare garments and cadaverous faces—their sickly infants—saddened her. How gladly she would have thrown them all the jewels that weighed down her throat and her hands. She wanted to visit their dwellings, to act the lady-bountiful. But St. Cheviot had forbidden her to go near any of the cottages on his vast estate in case she caught a fever. He had a dread of contagion.

During that drive in the sledge they met Peveril walking alone with Alpha, the wolfhound, padding behind. St. Cheviot bade the sledge driver (whom he had fitted up in character, in bearskins) to pull up the sledge for a moment. He called to the boy:

"Is it not time you put the final stroke to the portrait of that Rustingthorpe child—you have been far too long over it. Do you grow lazy, my young friend?"

The young painter doffed his cap. He allowed his gaze to linger for a single pulsating moment on the beautiful girl who sat with lashes downcast—silent, motionless in her sable wraps. He said:

"The portrait was finished this morning, my lord. I am on my way now across the fields to Rustingthorpe. The Marchioness has sent for me."

St. Cheviot puffed at a cigar which he had just lighted. He pulled the fur rug closer over his knees. A few snow flakes were drifting down from the grey sky and it was very cold and raw. He said:

"The old woman seems satisfied with what you have done. She is a lewd old harridan and likes a handsome lad. . . ." He laughed coarsely. "She wishes you to make other studies of her family to which I have given my consent."

Avoiding Fleur's gaze, Peveril said:

"If your lordship would grant me the time, I wish greatly

to converse with him about taking a final leave from Cadlington."

Fleur felt a knife go through her heart. She opened her great sad eyes. But her face remained expressionless. Yet she could not restrain the relief that seized her when St. Cheviot, himself, thwarted Peveril's desire for independence.

"Rubbish," he snapped, "why show such longing to leave Cadlington, ungrateful fool? Stay where you are until my friends, who are also your patrons, want no more of you."

Then without waiting for the young artist to answer, he ordered the driver to whip up the ponies and go ahead. Peveril stood still, watching the sledge slip over the narrow glassy road till it was out of sight. The bells on the ponies jingled faintly through the frosty air. The bleak wind cut the boy's sensitive face. He put his cap back on his head, shivered under his cape, and went his way uneasily. The desire to be near *her* was growing too strong. He had seen her sometimes from afar—watched the slenderness of her waist thicken. He knew, indeed, that she was heavy with St. Cheviot's child. But he adored her. Night and day he craved to lift some of the burden of sorrow from her young shoulders. Night and day, his hatred of the tyrannical Baron intensified. But he decided that he would accept St. Cheviot's despotic orders to remain at Cadlington until he knew that the birth of the heir was safely over. Far too often he had heard whispered gossip among the staff that her ladyship was delicate and might not survive. The idea appalled him.

February passed. The snows melted and ran in muddy streams down Cadlington hill, and Fleur was still to be seen moving about her garden, or out driving in the phaeton. Her spectacular Russian sledge could no longer now be used.

Peveril lingered at Rustingthorpe—working on a new portrait. But sometimes in the evening, after the Marchioness's carriage (graciously lent for the occasion) brought him back to Cadlington House—he saw Fleur. They would wave to each other. If they passed in the gardens, then they would pause to converse—but only for a moment. My lady was sensitive to her increasing size and too much the victim of conscience. For she knew now, that she loved Peveril with all the tenderness of her woman's heart and her sad despoiled youth. Just now passion could have no part in her life, and because she was a deeply moral being nothing would have induced her to forsake the dignity of her present position as St. Cheviot's wife.

Then later when the savage winds of March shook the great house and kept the young mother-to-be huddled before her fires, her mental and physical sufferings increased. Sometimes St. Cheviot stayed with her, but he seemed always ill-at-ease now in her company. He was, however, exceedingly careful of her health, continually giving orders and countermanding them. She must not do this, she should do that. He had heard that a prospective mother should drink special milk, and eat rare food. He sent for new cows from Jersey. He ordered delicacies from the London stores—even from Paris. Fleur was surrounded with his gifts—suffocated by them—wearied by his incessant hectoring. He even badgered her to smile.

"You must be gay or the babe will be born as melancholy and as sickly a being as yourself," he flung at her one evening when he was spending a few days at Cadlington. He quite enjoyed the spring weather now. A fair April had drifted into a warm sweet May. The forest was green and the sun shone often over hills and valleys. "Do you not find some humour in these new books I brought you?" he added irritably. "I am told they are amusing."

She looked at him with her grave eyes and fingered the novels he had chosen.

But she was obedience itself. She said:

"I will try to smile, Denzil. It is not easy if you do not feel in good humour. But I beg you to cease troubling yourself over my health. It is very good at the moment and Dr. Boss tells me that we have nothing to fear."

"He will get a bullet through his throat if he isn't right," muttered Denzil.

She looked at him with scorn in her clear eyes. How violent he was in his loves and his hates!

It was on this particular evening that he mentioned Peveril's painting of her hands.

"Our young genius grows impudent. He did not ask my permission to present you with this. How came he to portray your hands so faithfully? Have you been posing for him—have you dared——"

"He remembered them from the big portrait. He thought that in giving me the little painting it would be a gesture of gratitude—towards us both," she added.

"I do not care for it," said St. Cheviot, "a pair of hands—what a dull subject!"

"Perhaps they suggest the act of prayer in which you are disinterested," she said with unusual sarcasm.

He frowned at her. She lay on a couch by the fire in one of the smaller drawing-rooms which they used when they were alone. A Cashmere shawl was thrown over her. She looked, he thought, less sickly than usual. She was damned handsome. It was a never-ending irritation to him that he could not entirely break this young girl's spirit.

"Ah, well, if you like religion proceed with it, Lady St. Cheviot. You are too saintly for me. But no doubt your saintliness will make you a fond mother."

She did not answer. "Fond mother," alas she thought bitterly. Far advanced in pregnancy though she was, she could not yet feel one grain of longing for St. Cheviot's child. Poor little unwanted thing! Of a certainty she would be good to it, and no doubt grow in time to love it. She had but one more month to wait, then it would be all over. She had ceased to yearn for death because she believed it to be wicked, for if the infant lived and she died, who then would mother it?

St. Cheviot began to walk restlessly up and down the room.

"This is the 28th May," he said. "Boss said that the child should be born ere another month is over. It is as well, for I hope to be in London for the Queen's Coronation."

Fleur showed a modicum of interest in what he said. She was always entertained by stories of the young Queen Victoria. She listened while St. Cheviot began to discuss the Coronation. It would, he said, be one of the most colourful and brilliant affairs in the history of the nation. Already the Duke of Dalmatia, Ambassador Extraordinary from France, was at the Embassy. All the crowned heads in Europe would follow. There were to be fêtes and banquets more splendid than the metropolis had ever known.

"They say," added St. Cheviot, "that the expense of this affair will be in the nature of £70,000. I myself am having a new fine suit made for the occasion."

And he described at length the French brocade chosen for his waistcoat; as he smoked, and sipped his after-dinner brandy. Just for a moment it was as though they were a happily married couple, Fleur thought sadly. St. Cheviot was quite genial. But only for a moment. Then he tired of her and took his leave. He had invited Sir Edmund Follyatt, one of his few friends in the district, to sup with him and play cards.

He picked up one of Fleur's hands and pressed his lips against it. Immediately he felt the shrinking of her flesh, so he flung the hand down again and laughed.

"Very well, my dear, if you prefer it—twine your fingers in prayer. I do not care. Good night. Do not forget your hot milk. I will send Odette to you."

She nodded.

St. Cheviot added:

"By the way, I have had a talk with Mrs. D. She greatly resents the fact that you will not receive her, and it is my wish that once our child is born, you alter your behaviour towards my good Mrs. D."

"Oh, Denzil," said Fleur suddenly, "could you not find me another housekeeper? I cannot tell you what disgust Mrs. Dinglefoot inspires in me."

"We have already had this argument," he said coldly.

She looked up at him with her soft lovely eyes.

"You give me so much that I do not want, would you not do this little thing for me?"

He hesitated. It was the first time his young wife had ever made so direct or intimate an appeal to him. The old violent passion stirred in him. Turning he flung himself by the couch, put his hot face against her neck and feverishly kissed one of her long silken curls.

"I will do anything—*anything* once you are well again. I will even turn poor Mrs. Dinglefoot from Cadlington—only swear to love me," he breathed.

But she shuddered away from that embrace. The very infant seemed to move in protest. She felt sick with her old fear and disgust. Always she must see him as he had been that night at The Little Bastille, satanic in his merciless passion.

"Leave me alone," she panted, "go away. Go back to your mistresses."

He stood up, brushed his sleeve and gave an ugly laugh.

"As is customary, your virtue freezes me. But I apologize, my dear. This is not the time for advances. If our young genius in the tower were a sculptor, I would suggest he fashioned you out of marble."

"So that you could take a hammer and smash the statue?" she asked him, and flung back her long throat and looked up at him. He avoided the scorn in those huge eyes and marched to the door.

"Good night," he said.

After he had gone the proud head drooped. Fleur could be brave in his brutal presence but not once she was alone. Her thoughts moved irresistibly towards the magnet of that high tower—so near yet so far from her. It was long now since she had spoken a bare word of greeting to the "young genius" whom St. Cheviot mocked, yet in whom he took such a possessive pride.

"Ah, Peveril, dear, dear Peveril," she whispered.

The child leaped again. Fleur sighed, placed her incomparable hands upon her stomach and began to weep bitterly.

Chapter Seven

In the last two weeks before St. Cheviot's child was born, such a summer settled over Cadlington as no one living in the district could remember. The keen winds that blew so incessantly across the Chiltern Hills died down. There was a lushness in the meadows; a stillness over the dreaming woods; a warmth in the high-walled gardens around Cadlington House almost tropical in its languor. So long and hot were the days that even the birds seemed to grow dumb and to cease their singing as they dozed on the leafy branches. The herbaceous flowers in the great borders shot up too rapidly in the sun. The rose petals were scattered by the heat before twilight, despite the efforts of a small army of gardeners to keep the place watered. Many plants perished. Only the orchids that Fleur hated, flourished and grew more fat and wicked-looking. The great lawns changed their velvet green for the hue of burnt-gold. The servants grumbled at the heat. The windows of the big house were opened wide; doors, too, so that a draught could blow through the corridors.

St. Cheviot no longer drove to London because Dr. Boss had warned him that any day now the child might be born. So, for the time being, he abandoned his haunts in Piccadilly and his new mistress. Bored, yawning, he stayed at Cadlington and slept or drank away most of the golden summer hours. He saw little of his wife but had installed two midwives recommended by the doctor. Fleur was never left alone for a single moment now. Always she was under the watchful eye of the trained women. The Baron did not intend that anything should go wrong with his lady's confinement.

A few months ago when Fleur had asked if her old friend, Catherine Quinley, could stay here, Denzil had acceded to her request, thinking that the visit might be good for her spirits. But fate did not allow her even that small pleasure for Catherine was laid low with the smallpox a few days before she was due to take the journey.

Now with the birth of her infant imminent Fleur was very much alone in spirit. The constant presence of midwives and servants tormented her. She was irked by the mere knowledge that St. Cheviot, too, was hanging around the house . . . waiting . . . ready to spring upon her like a tiger in case she should do something to annoy him . . . something that he did not deem good for the child. It was always of the child he thought. Never of her.

She no longer went downstairs but stayed up in her bedchamber or boudoir. Just a little longer she could enjoy her romantic fairy-tale bedchamber—knowing that once the birth was over, St. Cheviot meant to destroy Peveril's creation.

"Queer in the head, I'd call her," Mrs. Dinglefoot snorted one evening while the servants were eating supper —they were all gasping in the heat which drifted from the kitchen. "Maybe the infant will be half-witted. My late mistress would turn in her grave."

As usual Peveril was forced to listen to this kind of talk, though he finished his meal as quickly as possible and went back to his solitary tower to continue painting until the light faded.

Upon this occasion, he made one of his rare protests. Fixing the malicious housekeeper with his clear candid gaze, he said:

"No one who has spoken with her ladyship would call her 'queer.' She is reserved but has many talents."

Mrs. D. fanned herself, and with the back of one red hand, wiped the sweat from her forehead. She looked particularly repulsive in this heat. She said:

"Ah ha! Listen to our young artist. Always a champion for my lady."

Odette, who still cherished a secret passion for the handsome painter, leaned near him and nudged his arm.

"You are wasting your time, Mr. Peveril. *La la!* If *Monsieur le Baron* thought that you held my lady in such high regard he would shoot you through the throat like this——" She pointed a fork at Peveril and clicked her teeth.

Mrs. Dinglefoot snorted. Ivor had loosened his cravat and was fanning himself but his sharp eyes cast a side glance at Peveril. He was bitterly jealous of Peveril and had been since the first day that Peveril had come here to live. He was equally jealous of he beautiful young bride who took up so much of his lordship's time and attention. Like Mrs. Dinglefoot, he greatly preferred the old days at Cadlington and the excitement of the wild parties that the young bachelor used to hold. He said in his sing-song Welsh voice:

"And it is swollen-headed our Master Painter is getting—painting all the Quality in this district."

"I am not swollen-headed," said Peveril quietly.

"But you have ideas above your station, Master Peveril," put in Mrs. Dinglefoot folding her arms over her enormous bosom and eyeing him sourly. "Creeping up to her ladyship's bedchamber when his lordship was away. Don't forget that we know about it."

Peveril sprang to his feet.

"You are vile and unspeakable," he said.

Odette caught at the boy's fingers and tried to pull him back beside her.

"*Tiens, tiens,* sit down and eat your pudding, *chéri.* They only tease you," she said.

He wrenched the hand away. He was quivering with an indignation which was for Fleur—not for himself. The valet cocked an eyebrow.

"Better take care. Let it be known to his lordship that you have such a fancy for my lady and he will not take kindly to it."

"Do not interfere in matters about which you are totally ignorant," said Peveril passionately.

The Welshman's eyes slitted.

"Beware also of my ill-humour. I am not a good enemy but I can shoot as straight as his lordship. In fencing, also, I am an expert. Might one ask, *Sir Peveril,* if *you* could fight a duel?"

"I am no swordsman and I have no wish for fighting. I am a painter," said the boy.

"Or a coward?" suggested the Welshman softly.

Silence. The other servants ceased their noisy chatter and set down tankards, knives and forks with a clatter. A meagre-sized pantry boy wiped his greasy hands on his apron and came forward to listen. Everybody was agog to see what line the young painter would take after Mr. Ivor's open insult.

There was only one line that Peveril wished to take. Delicately made, totally unfit for physical violence, nevertheless Peveril Marsh was not going to be called coward by any man. He sprang at the Welshman. The next moment Peveril found himself down on the floor and Ivor's thin steely fingers were at his throat, his thumbs pressing cruelly into the flesh. None of the other men dared interfere. The Welshman was too much in his lordship's favour. If ever a chef, or footman had dared to cross the Welshman, he regretted it. But Odette screamed and pulled at Ivor's arm.

"Leave him alone—*mon Dieu!*—you will kill him. He is no match for you."

"Let them fight," said Mrs. Dinglefoot, her eyes blinking with pleasure as she saw the young painter's frantic efforts to extricate himself from those merciless thumbs.

Then suddenly the doors of the servants' hall were flung open. One of the midwives, a stout rosy-cheeked little body, her cap awry, ran in waving bare dimpled arms at the housekeeper.

"Mrs. D.! Mrs. D.! Hot water and plenty of it, pray. *Her ladyship is in labour.*"

At once an excited clangour of voices broke the silence. All the servants, including the housekeeper, stood up. So the Great Moment for which the whole household had been waiting had come. It saved Peveril. The unfortunate boy had almost lost consciousness. Ivor released his grip. This was no time for delivering punishment to the young painter. He prodded Peveril gently with the toe of his shoe.

"See, my fine gentleman—I am your victor. Next time I shall squeeze the life out of you."

Peveril stood up, swaying on his feet, one hand at his bruised throat. He was scarlet with mortification. This night, the gentle painter had become a man who wished to God he had learned to fight and could give Ivor as good a punishment as he meted out.

The infatuated Odette put an arm around the boy, steadied him, and held a glass of wine to his lips.

"Foolish one to have roused the Welshman's temper," she whispered. "*Zut alors!* You show too openly that you are her ladyship's admirer."

Peveril drank the wine. Ivor had disappeared. The staff were scampering in all directions.

"What has happened?" Peveril muttered.

Odette informed him.

"Her ladyship is in labour. I, too, must go, I shall be wanted. Come—Peveril, do not waste your time on a fine lady who will soon be closeted with her nurses and physicians and later with a new-born babe. A fine boy like you needs a fine girl for kissing. . . ." She giggled and sidled close to him. "I'll steal over to the tower and visit you tonight. Folks will be too busy to see which way I go."

"Thanks, but I do not want you in my tower," said Peveril shortly, and he walked through the hall conscious of nothing but a tearing blinding anxiety.

She was in labour. Oh, God, what an atrocious thought! From that sweet body which he worshipped with the same homage that he adored her mind and her soul, tonight or tomorrow there must come forth St. Cheviot's child. She would suffer. The young man was ignorant about these matters, but imaginative. He could not bear to dwell on the details. Burning as one in a fever, he escaped from Odette and ran up the circular staircase to his studio. Kneeling down by the open turret windows, he began to send wild prayers up towards the stars that glittered over Cadlington.

"God in heaven, do not let her die this night."

From every window of the great house lights were glowing. Since the midwives had informed him that her ladyship was about to be confined, St. Cheviot had been in the throes of mingled delight and apprehension. Delight because he could thank God (or the devil) that the long waiting was over. But his apprehensions were sinister. Fleur might die in labour and the child with her. Or it might be deformed.

He marched up and down, through the long galleries, the corridors and the big drawing-rooms, pausing only to shout for more wine and drink it. He told himself that if Fleur did not bear him a fine son he would make her suffer for it. He would drown the two midwives in the pond at the bottom of the garden. He was filled with crazy murderous thoughts, his brain inflamed by much wine. Then he would start thinking of the handsome boy who might be born tonight; how he, Denzil, would repent his evil ways and become a good father and better husband. He would even give money to the Church and attend to religion. He would turn into a leader of respectable society—have done with his Hungarian mistress, his dicing, his secret sins. He would make Peveril paint the new-born child.

Dr. Boss told him that the thing was taking its normal course but that her ladyship was very narrow and it would be a difficult birth; to which both the midwives agreed.

The doctor then looked a trifle awkwardly at his lordship and added:

"It is customary, Lord St. Cheviot, to ask the husband if things go badly and a choice must be made between the life of the mother or the child, which am I to save?"

Without hesitation, St. Cheviot answered:

"The child. I can always find another wife."

The old doctor recoiled, deeming this a savage reply. But he bowed and went back to his patient. Coatless, sleeves rolled up, he waited in the boudoir for the midwives to inform him that the birth was advancing and that his help was needed.

When he had last seen Lady St. Cheviot, the old man was filled with unspeakable pity. She was as white as the cambric nightgown in which the old women had dressed her. The shining hair was bundled up into a white cap. Already she was enduring those sharp rhythmic pains which succeeded one upon another with remorseless regularity. One midwife exhorted her to pull at a rope which she had tied on the bed post; the other bathed her temples with perfume and vinegar. Fleur made no sound. That was what distressed old Boss who had delivered many a shrieking lady in the district. Fleur, her face contorted, bit on her lips and stayed silent save for that low moaning in her throat.

"Why do you not call out, my dear?" Dr. Boss had

asked her gently. "It would greatly relieve your feelings."

She opened her large eyes, purple, wild now with pain. The sweat poured down her cheeks. She answered:

"I do not care for his lordship to hear me cry. The pain is severe but less terrible than all the agony I have lately suffered in my mind."

Those low words, for him alone, made the old doctor draw back in shocked silence. St. Cheviot was a devil, he knew. The old man could do nothing to comfort Lady St. Cheviot.

"His lordship will be delighted once you give him his son," he said hopefully.

Fleur made no answer. She battled dumbly with her travail.

That was the beginning. But the night merged into the dawn and the labour continued.

Every now and again St. Cheviot stalked up and knocked upon my lady's door and asked for news. When Fleur heard his voice, she shuddered and bade the women in attendance upon her keep him out at all costs.

By three o'clock Cadlington was hushed, though few slept. Still the babe had not been born. Dr. Boss was anxious. Her ladyship was more exhausted than any of them and her pulse was feeble. It seemed that the child would never come, for all her brave efforts to bring it forth.

Now such hideous suffering engulfed the young mother-to-be that she prayed to die.

She implored the old doctor to give her chloroform.

"I cannot endure much more," she gasped.

He shook his head, muttered to himself and kept a finger on her fluttering pulse. He was sorely tempted to give my lady a drug to ease her pain but dared not in case it harmed the infant. The Baron was in such a state of nerves and ill-temper that the old doctor was afraid of his own life. He would not put it past his lordship to do some violence this night, if things went badly.

Downstairs in the great hall, Denzil marched up and down, his clothes disordered, his shirt stained with wine and his eyes wild and inflamed.

Alpha, the wolfhound, padded after him. Once in a fury,

he lashed out at her with his foot and she cowered away, bitch-like, submissive.

Into St. Cheviot's drink-inflamed mind came one of his crazy notions. He sent a footman to the tower.

"Bring Master Marsh to me. Bid him come immediately."

Chapter Eight

Peveril presented himself to his lordship, feeling taut and nervous. St. Cheviot tried to force wine on him.

"Drink with me, you white-livered young fool," St. Cheviot snapped, fixing the boy with his falcon eyes. "Painter or not, you are still a man, are you not?"

"Must one then drink in order to be a man?" the boy asked quietly.

"Yes, and get drunk, too," said Denzil, and added coarsely: "and tumble a pretty female in your bed."

Peveril said nothing. He stood silent, feeling a profound repugnance agianst this animal-like person. How could he act thus with that sweet saint upstairs struggling for her life? The boy's grey eyes lifted to the musicians' gallery, beyond which lay her ladyship's apartments. Denzil followed the boy's gaze and gave another harsh laugh.

"You, too, wait for news, eh? Well, none is forthcoming, so you can settle down to drinking and I will teach you to play a game of cards. According to Boss, it may be hours yet before the child is born."

"I grieve to hear that the waiting is so prolonged," said Peveril in a low and scarcely steady voice. How much more could Fleur St. Cheviot endure, he wondered.

"Sit down, sit down and do not annoy me," muttered St. Cheviot, and flung a pack of cards on to the table beside which they were standing. "Here, cut—let us see if I have any luck?"

Peveril sweated. With all his heart he wished to escape from this *tête-à-tête* with the Baron.

St. Cheviot goaded the boy into drawing a card. He would not be satisfied, either, until Peveril had drunk a measure of wine. For the first few moments the boy was the winner. When finally he drew the Ace of hearts against

St. Cheviot's King, the Baron tossed the whole pack on to the floor and laughed scornfully.

"So! Beginner's luck! You should take to gambling, my young friend. You seem fortunate."

"I would not consider it good fortune to win money in this fashion," said Peveril quietly.

"Bah! You painters—with your namby-pamby fancies—what then would you consider good fortune?"

"To paint a great masterpiece."

"So you have said before. But you have painted many masterpieces, have you not, my little genius?"

"There can be but one in an artist's lifetime."

"Then it shall be the portrait that you paint of my son. Yes, I have decided that as soon as he draws breath, you shall paint a great portrait of the new St. Cheviot," said his lordship. He spilled more wine on the frilled front of his fine lawn shirt. He had divested himself of his jacket. The heat did not seem to mitigate with the dawn.

Peveril kept silence. He felt sick and bewildered. He only knew that the last thing he wanted in the world was to look upon the newly-born baby even though it was partially *hers*; neither did he wish to add a single portrait more to the gallery of St. Cheviots. He knew now that they were a bad race and that this one was the worst of them all.

St. Cheviot walked unsteadily to the windows and flung back the curtains.

"Ah!" he muttered. "As I thought—this appalling sultriness heralds a storm—look yonder!"

Peveril went to his side. Together these two men who made such an incongruous pair—the great broad-shouldered Baron and the slender boy—gazed upon an awe-inspiring sight. It was five o'clock. The stars had faded. The paling moon was obscured by clouds. Dark monstrous clouds rolling up from the valley. A great storm was approaching Whiteleaf. Even while they watched, there came a low growl of thunder and the first streak of lightning tore a livid jagged fork across the sky.

Peveril stood in silent appreciation of the magnificence, but when the first rain drops spattered down, St. Cheviot gave a drunken laugh and wheeled around.

"So—my son and heir comes in on a clarion note; born in a storm like his father! Yes—old Dinglefoot remembers if none else—that I made my entry into Cadlington while a thunder storm was in progress. She told me that my mother screeched because she feared lightning—and as her lungs gave out that note—I, her son, joined with her, uttering my first cry."

Peveril shuddered. A nausea seized him. Perhaps it was the wine, or perhaps the abominable thought of St. Cheviot's birth. Once more Peveril was filled with wild and feverish imaginings of what went on upstairs. No cry would come from *her*; he knew that . . . not though she died.

"God be merciful to her ladyship," the words were torn from Peveril's lips.

St. Cheviot laughed, staggered to the foot of the staircase, and called out:

"Are you there, Boss, my good old fellow? Have you no news?"

Thunder crackled over Cadlington. The hall was illuminated by sudden blinding lightning. Down came the rain; in torrents now. At least it would cool the air, thought Peveril. Already the temperature was dropping. With the back of his hand, he wiped his damp forehead and sighed.

Suddenly there appeared at the head of the staircase the figure of the white-bearded doctor. He looked ghastly pale. But St. Cheviot leapt up the stairs, two at a time, and seized him by the shoulders.

"The birth is over? I have a son?"

Dr. Boss trembled. The old man was not a coward and he had been through many terrible moments in his career. He had seen birth and death in its ugliest aspects, but this night would be one that would live in his memory, for ever.

He stuttered:

"Your lordship . . . St. Cheviot . . . the news is bad. . . ."

Peveril caught those words and his muscles tautened. The colour forsook his tired face. He heard the Baron shouting.

"You mean the child is dead?"

"Alas, *yes*, my lord."

"Dead!" repeated St. Cheviot furiously. "Ten thousand devils! I knew that my lady would never bear a living child. The poor imbecile!"

Peveril Marsh hearing those brutal words was roused to

such shocked resentment that he gave tongue to his feelings.

"Great God, my lord, but what of *her*?" he exclaimed.

St. Cheviot did not answer. The old doctor intervened.

"Lady St. Cheviot lives, but only just. She is very weak, your lordship. The child was ill placed and has almost cost her her life."

"What was the sex?" demanded St. Cheviot.

"It was a son," said the doctor in a low voice.

"That makes it worse. You old fool, could you not have saved it?" St. Cheviot said savagely, and raised a fist as though to strike the physician in the face.

Boss looked fearfully into the enraged face of the Baron.

"The infant never breathed," he stuttered. "There was naught I could do, *and it is as well*," he added to himself.

St. Cheviot did not hear the last words. He said:

"So I am the father of a dead son. This is fine news. A fine end to my hopes."

"Have you no thought for your lady?" asked the old man timidly.

"It was a mistake that I ever married such a weakling," said Denzil.

Peveril put his hands to his ears as though to blot out the sounds of the Baron's voice.

"My lord!" Boss uttered the protest.

"Well—how is she? How is she?" asked St. Cheviot impatiently. "I suggest Dr. Boss, sir, that you apply all your medical skill to ensure that my lady will bear other, healthier children to me."

"She will never bear another child," said Boss sombrely.

"Never another? What do you mean?"

"What must be said, though I deplore it. This is the first and last child that Lady St. Cheviot will bring into the world."

"She is dying, then?"

"No. You mistake me. She will live, but motherhood is not for her in the future. All hopes of that are over." And once more the old man muttered the words, *"It is as well."*

St. Cheviot let out a roar of rage.

"Then she is utterly useless to me, and the hunchback was wrong, for she promised there would be another black Baron of Cadlington."

Peveril heard this allusion to his sister's prophecy. His

whole body had flamed with a secret and forbidden joy when he heard the doctor announce that Fleur would never bear another child. Thanks be unto God, thought Peveril, that there would never be born of her flesh, another vile St. Cheviot.

St. Cheviot was beginning to sober up. His first violent rage was cooling. But he was sick with disappointment. He tried to pass by the doctor.

"I wish to look on the dead body of my son."

Then the older man, visibly shaking, stayed him.

"Do not do so, Lord St. Cheviot, I pray you."

"Why not?"

"It would—only distress you," muttered the doctor.

St. Cheviot hesitated, then shrugged his shoulders.

"Very well. Tell Lady St. Cheviot that I am thankful that she is spared to me and that I will see her after I have rested," and he lurched past the doctor, down the corridor and into his own apartment.

The old doctor walked slowly, descended the stairs pulling down his cuffs. He looked with red-rimmed eyes at the young man in the hall.

"This is a sorry night," he said wearily.

"Indeed, yes," agreed Peveril with a deep sigh. "How is she, sir?"

"Weak but not critically ill. She bore her travail with amazing fortitude. Truly, in these moments the most frail woman seems to possess the courage of a lion."

"She, in particular, is courageous," said the young painter in a moved voice.

The doctor peered at him.

"You are the artist who has executed some exceedingly fine portraits in recent months."

"I am Peveril Marsh—yes, sir."

"Then if you live here you must see and hear much of what goes on at Cadlington?"

"Too much," said Peveril in a low voice.

"God grant that worse is not to come," muttered the doctor.

"What do you mean?" asked Peveril, startled.

"I must hold my tongue," said the old man, "and I can but pray that those two good women who assisted me will hold theirs."

"You speak mysteriously," said Peveril.

"What I know, I wish that I did not know," said Dr. Boss.

Before Peveril could speak again, Cadlington House resounded with a crash that was not of thunder but of a slamming door. There came the sound of St. Cheviot's voice echoing through the lofty corridors. The doctor turned pale. He avoided Peveril's startled gaze and muttered:

"Great heavens, I believe he knows—*one of those women has talked.*"

"What is it——?" began Peveril.

Now the figure of the Baron appeared. He wore a striped silken bed-robe, and a night cap on his head. His eyes were black slits. Uncomprehending, the young painter watched this malignant figure come slowly down the stairs. When the Baron reached the bottom of the staircase, he fixed the old doctor with a menacing gaze.

"So," he said softly, "*do not go and see the child because it would distress you!* Yes, yes, my good Boss, now I can well understand your concern for my feelings."

The old man licked his lips.

"I tried only to spare you, my lord St. Cheviot."

"You tried to deceive me, you old liar," snarled St. Cheviot. "You would have let me think that my lady had given birth to a normal still-born son."

"Who has said that he was not normal?" asked the old doctor, playing for time.

"My good friend and counsellor—my one and only loyal servant—Mrs. Dinglefoot. One of the midwives whom you tried to bribe, told her the truth, and my good Mrs. D. deemed it in my interest to enlighten me."

"The child was no monster. It was beautifully formed, and with the violet eyes of her ladyship."

"And it was *black*!" Now St. Cheviot's voice rose and her thundered the words "*black as ebony from top to toe.* Mrs. Dinglefoot saw it. *Black as the child of a full-blooded negro, even though he had the features of my lady*. I know all now, so do not try to dissemble. *Beware of a black St. Cheviot*, eh?" He swung round to Peveril, drawing his lips back from his teeth. "Now I see that your sister's prophecy held a deeper significance than I understood. We are known as the Black Barons, but this misbegotten infant to which my lady gave birth has *coloured blood in it.* I have been inveigled into marriage with a female who has black blood in her veins. Ten thousand devils!" he added, his face contorted and fearful to see, "if that child had lived, I would have stained my soul with a double crime for I would have murdered both the child *and* its mother."

Peveril and the doctor recoiled. St. Cheviot continued:

"Is it not true that this is a throw-back? That if the history of the Roddneys were unfolded, I should find that somewhere a Roddney has sprung from Africa?"

"It could be so, your lordship," said Boss, trembling.

"Very well. Do you dare suggest that the *faux pas* can be laid at the door of a St. Cheviot?" thundered Denzil. "No—*you* know that that cannot be so, for my line is pure and unbroken. It is the breeding of her ladyship which is at question, and it shall be examined." He added more to himself than the other: "Mrs. de Vere shall pay for this. I shall see her tomorrow. I shall leave no stone unturned in order to discover the full facts."

The doctor dared to lay a hand on the arm of the enraged Baron.

"Pray, Lord St. Cheviot, listen to an old man who has known you and your parents from birth. I deplore this terrible thing. It is not your fault, nor that of the hapless young mother. She lies in her room, semi-conscious and unknowing of the tragedy. Treat her gently, and with mercy, I implore you."

"If I find that her family was aware of the strain that she brought to her marriage, she shall receive no mercy from me," said St. Cheviot in a blood-curdling voice.

Then Peveril Marsh, who had been an unwilling yet fascinated listener, was stung to speech:

"Good God, it cannot be my lady's fault. She is as innocent and pure as the driven snow."

St. Cheviot did not so much as look at the boy.

Peveril turned and walked across the hall and out of the house. The horror of the whole night had laid a mark on him from which he would never recover. At last, the poet, the dreamer, and the painter had come face to face with knowledge of the terrible things that could happen in the life which he had deemed so beautiful.

He knew nothing of heredity, or of the possibility of a "throw-back." But at least he was positive that if such a thing had happened, it could not be any fault of *hers*. She must once more be an innocent victim; and this time victimized in so terrible a fashion, thought Peveril, that the very angels must be weeping for her.

Chapter Nine

After that night of the storm the weather changed. It grew cold for the time of year. Rain swept across the vale and washed hills and forests. The trees dripped around the great house. The sodden flowers were beaten into the muddy earth. The lawns were bogged. Carriage wheels stuck in the ruts on flooded roads; there was little of summer left; the whole place was sunk in incipient gloom.

For Fleur St. Cheviot, too, everything changed. Following that night of fearful pain when she had so nearly died in childbirth, she was flung into a new nightmare of fear—without any understanding of what was going on around her.

She recovered consciousness, asked to see her child, and was told that it had died. St. Cheviot did not come near her. She found that bewildering. She had expected him at least to pay her a courtesy visit. One of the midwives bent over the bed and told her that the Baron had left the house early, before breakfast, taking with him his travelling coach and four servants, including the Welshman.

For a while Fleur was relieved. As for the infant, she thought of it, the tears trickling down her cheeks. She had never wanted it because of its monstrous father. So she gazed up at the midwife—an Irishwoman—and whispered, *"It is better so."* Even then she was conscious of a peculiar look cross the woman's face, when she repeated those words.

"Yes, my lady, it is better—indeed to goodness it is!"

But they would not let her see the tiny corpse.

For a few days she lay dozing, gaining strength, nursed by the Irish midwife. The other one had gone. Nobody came near Fleur, not even Odette, which surprised her. But on the fifth morning, when she asked for her maid to come and dress her hair, the midwife told her that Odette had returned to France.

This was the first of many astonishing episodes which Fleur could not fathom. Sometimes she heard carriage wheels; lay listening and imagining that there were callers, come to leave flowers and express their sympathies. Long afterwards she found out that this was so.

She supposed that St. Cheviot must be in a towering rage, because the heir he wanted had not lived. But it seemed abominable that he should be so unkind to her. It was not her fault that the child had died.

Dr. Boss came to assure himself that my lady was being properly looked after. Fleur tried to talk to him, but the old man seemed ill-at-ease and would not meet her eye. Neither did he make more than a vague reply when she asked him for details about the poor little babe.

Timidly she asked about St. Cheviot.

"Perhaps he went to London expressly to attend the Coronation."

But she knew, and Dr. Boss knew, that the Coronation of Queen Victoria had taken place a fortnight ago—on the 28th June. Now it was mid-July.

While her ladyship was recovering from her confinement, the village of Whiteleaf had taken part in the Coronation celebrations. All over the Buckinghamshire countryside there had been dancing and singing. But the gates of Cadlington remained closed.

Boss had had his orders from the Baron. He was to ensure that her ladyship regained her health, then not to enter Cadlington again.

After the last visit, as he rode home, Dr. Boss met the young painter, Peveril Marsh. He reined in, and spoke to the boy, who looked strained and unhappy, but asked about my lady. The doctor told him that she was recovering.

"I thank God!" said Peveril in a voice of relief. "I have been unable to get news of her from any of the staff."

The old doctor leaned down from his mount and added in a low tone:

"Have you seen his lordship?"

"No—not since he went away. But I fear for Lady St. Cheviot. When he left Cadlington, he looked like the Fiend himself."

The doctor sighed.

"Alas we can do nothing but trust in Almighty God that her ladyship will be spared further misery," he said.

"I have tried to visit her," said Peveril. "They will not allow it. One by one the old servants are leaving. A new and rougher lot have come, and Mrs. Dinglefoot grows more and more difficult—and more powerful," he added sombrely.

"Take my advice, young man, and get out of the place. It has a curse on it," muttered the doctor.

"I shall not leave Cadlington whilst I may be of service to her ladyship," was the reply.

"Take care!" warned the old man.

He did not visit his patient again.

All these things remained unknown to Fleur. Revelation came for her only on the first day that she was allowed to leave her bed.

It was a cool misty morning in July. She had walked into the boudoir which she had not seen since her confinement. She had grown so thin that the velvet negligée which she put on hung on her loosely.

The first thing that struck her startled gaze was the sight of her bureau. It looked as though it had been ransacked. Personal papers and letters scattered on the carpet. Quills broken, ink spilled, seals broken, sealing wax smashed to powder. And what horrified her even more was the sight of the gilt-framed portraits of her mother and father which she had brought from Pillars. These had been ripped across with a knife. The faces were unrecognizable. It looked for all the world as though a lunatic had entered the room and wantonly destroyed everything in it. In particular Fleur was agonized by the desecration of that superb painting of Hélène Roddney in her grey velvet gown.

Fleur felt shocked and bewildered. She managed to pull the bell and summon the midwife who was still in attendance on her. She pointed to the chaos.

"What do you know about this?"

The Irishwoman looked uncomfortable. She knew all—but dared not tell her ladyship. There were in fact many things that the old woman knew and about which she dared not speak. For like Mrs. D., who shared with her the terrible secret of Fleur's child, she had had her lips sealed by dire threats from the Baron. She was, in fact, looking forward to the day when she could get away from this house of horrid tragedy.

She did not answer Fleur.

Fleur put her clasped hands to her fast-beating heart.

"Was it his lordship?" she persisted.

"Do not ask me," said the woman.

"I do not understand. I must go downstairs," said Fleur. "Help me dress."

Then the midwife, nervous, curtseying, stammered:

"Impossible, my lady. Oh, pray, my lady, do not blame me but your doors are locked from the outside."

Fleur stared. Her face had grown very white.

"You mean I am a prisoner in my room, and by his lordship's orders?"

The midwife gulped again.

"Yes, my lady."

"Who holds the key?"

"Mrs. Dinglefoot, my lady."

Fleur drew a breath. She sank wearily on to the edge of her bed. Her knees were shaking. Now she imagined she understood exactly what was going on. Denzil was mad with fury because she had not borne him a living son. This was his revenge. But why ransack her bureau? *What had he been trying to find?* And why by slashing those poor portraits desecrate the memory of her beloved parents?

"This is too much," Fleur said aloud. "I shall not stay at Cadlington and submit myself to such abomination. Under no circumstances will I remain the prisoner of Mrs. Dinglefoot."

She put out a hand and gripped the midwife by her plump arm.

"Will you take a message for me?" she asked breathlessly. "If I write a note will you keep your counsel and see that Mr. Peveril Marsh receives it?"

"The young painter in the tower, my lady?"

"Yes," said Fleur, and two hectic spots burned on her hollow cheeks. "He, I know, will help me. I must secure a carriage. I have been degraded and ill-treated long enough. I must leave this terrible place and seek the protection of my friend, Mrs. Catherine Quinley."

The midwife fell on her knees before Fleur and burst into tears.

"My lady, do not ask me to take a letter to the painter or to anybody outside this house. It is more than my life is worth."

"I implore you," Fleur wrung the woman's hand. "Look—I am young and helpless and you can see how I have been treated. Only confined three weeks ago, and my husband has not yet come to utter one word of regret for the loss of our child, nor to enquire after my health! Will you not assist me to escape from such a man?"

After a few moments, the midwife consented. She was not unkind and she was touched by the helplessness of the poor young lady. She, herself, did not understand why his lordship should treat his wife in such a manner, although, of course, there was that dark-skinned infant which must be explained away. (God help the little Baroness, for no one else would, the Irishwoman thought, and crossed herself, being a good Catholic.)

Fleur found a piece of broken quill, and enough ink with which to scratch a note to Peveril.

> Something is going on which I do not understand and which fills me with fear. You are my only friend here. After dark, I pray you come beneath my window and I will speak with you.

She signed this *F. St. C.*

But that note was not destined to reach Peveril. The midwife, terrified that she was being watched, carried out her promise to the hapless girl she had nursed. She took the letter up to the studio. Finding no one there, she pinned it to Peveril's pillow and went down again, intending to tell my lady she had done this. But she never saw Fleur again. On her return to the house Mrs. Dinglefoot paid her off and bade her leave. Dr. Boss had said that my lady required no more nursing.

Nobody went near the tower, so for the moment, nobody found the note. Peveril, himself, was in fact at Rustingthorpe. The Marchioness had received an unexpected visit from one of her married daughters, and insisted upon Peveril staying to paint her likeness before she left again. She offered double fees if Peveril would remain. The young painter had grown weary of hanging around Cadlington, knowing that the implacable Mrs. Dinglefoot would not allow him to pay my lady a visit, so he saw no reason why he should not spend a couple of days at the home of his patroness. Each painting upon which he worked meant more pay. And a new desire had come over Peveril. Idealism and artistic fancy had given way to the human need for storing up money. It was almost as though he sensed that he might one day need every golden guinea that he could earn—for *her*.

The tragedy of Fleur's marriage to Lord St. Cheviot was drawing to a swift and terrifying end—of that he was positive.

Meanwhile Mrs. Dinglefoot, supremely triumphant, entered Fleur's apartments and took control of her.

"Pray, ma'am, do not continue ringing your bell for the other servants for they will not come," the housekeeper told Fleur. Her small eyes blinked at the girl malevolently. "I have his lordship's orders to serve you myself."

"I do not wish to be served by you," began Fleur. "Kindly leave my bedchamber, Mrs. Dinglefoot."

But Mrs. D. stood her ground.

"It is foolish of you to order me out, and it would be worse for you if I obeyed, my lady. You would starve—and quickly. For I, alone, shall be bringing you your food in future."

Fleur looked at the woman with a proud attempt at defiance.

"I am Lady St. Cheviot. Do you forget that?"

"No, but first and foremost I remember that I am the humble servant of his dear lordship."

"And do you tell me that it is his wish that I remain locked in these rooms, and that no one comes to clean them and that I am to have my food thrust in here as though in a common jail?"

Mrs. Dinglefoot shrugged her shoulders.

"It is not for me to give you any information, my lady, nor to find reasons for the Baron's orders."

Gathering her strength Fleur spoke again.

"What have I done to deserve this? What crime have I committed that I should be submitted to this outrageous indignity?"

Then Mrs. Dinglefoot gave her an ugly scornful look.

"Better ask his lordship when he returns," she said. "You'll hear—*you'll hear!*"

Cackling with that horrid laughter, she walked out of the room. Fleur heard the key turn in the lock again.

She ran to the window and looked down. The gardens were deserted. The countryside presented a melancholy aspect. So high up was she, that she could not jump from these windows except to dash her brains out on the marble balustrade underneath. A frightful despair engulfed her. Her life seemed to go from bad to worse. At least before her baby was born she had been allowed some dignity here as the Baroness. She had given her orders. She had been free to walk the grounds, to drive into Whiteleaf, to talk to Peveril.

Oh, God, now that she remembered *him*, her one and only friend, her heart was torn with misgivings. Had the midwife delivered that note? Would he come? *Was he still here?* She dared not ask that question of Mrs. Dinglefoot.

For the rest of that day Fleur stayed alone in a state of suspense and puzzled misery. She even began to wish that Denzil would return. She could not endure being left at the housekeeper's mercy.

The food brought up to her now became unappetizing and obviously not cooked as usual by the chef. The wine was watered. A tray was put on her table by Mrs. D. who flung her an ugly look and departed, without a word. No hot water was brought nor any attempt made to clean or tidy my lady's apartments.

Fleur began to wish that she had died with her child. She walked around the room, clutching in her hands the torn faces of her father and mother which she had tried in vain to piece together, like a jigsaw. She wept over them, as a child over a smashed treasure. There was nothing left for her to look at with pleasure but the Raphael, and Peveril's painting of her hands. She feasted her hungry gaze upon these, and waited for darkness to fall. Then she walked to her windows and watched for Peveril. She felt if she did not see him and know that she still had one friend left in the world, she would go mad.

But Peveril did not come. And she did not know the reason why he stayed away. So she thought that even he had deserted her. She no longer wept. She was too bitterly unhappy. Nobody came to light her candles. She sat in the darkness until her body ached for weariness, her mind grew numb with misery and she fell upon her bed. Then at last she slept, wretched and uncomforted.

She awoke at midnight to hear the sound of horses galloping through the grounds, then closer, the scrunch of wheels on the drive. She sat up, listening, her heart pounding. A few moments later her door was unlocked, and St. Cheviot, in sombre travelling attire, carrying a lamp in one hand, walked into her room.

Fleur's heart beat fast. She sat up, reached for a little shawl and folded it modestly over her breast. She looked like a sleepy lovely child but as the man approached her bed and set the oil lamp down upon the table, not one spark of tenderness lit the satanic darkness of his mind and purpose.

"Ah! I find you awake, my love," he said in a pleasant tone. "I bid you good evening."

For a few seconds she was deceived by this tone and the smile which made him look devilishly handsome. She had been so lonely, so unhappy, her starved heart went out even to *him*, the cause of her downfall and oppression.

"Oh, I am glad that you are back, Denzil," she began. But she got no further, for although the smile lingered on his lips, now that she had become accustomed to the dim lamp-light, she could see the expression in his eyes. It froze her very marrow. He turned from her, walked to the wall facing her bed, and unhooked Peveril's painting of her hands. He came back to her, and held up the picture.

"Your hands, madam, your beautiful little hands which, when I saw them first, seemed to be those of a high-born lady sprung from excellent stock. I kissed the rosy tips and, on the correct finger, I placed my marriage ring. In the hollow of those hands I placed my hopes. The hopes that my charming wife would bear me a fine new St. Cheviot——" He paused and drew in his breath with a sucking sound.

Clutching her shawl to her bosom, the young girl looked up into the face of this sinister man whom she called husband, and knew that she need expect neither kindness nor tolerance from him. She was thrust back into the bottomless pit of her despair. But she spoke quietly:

"From my heart I beg your forgiveness, Denzil, that our child died——"

He interrupted her, using a low but venomous voice.

"If it had not died naturally, my lady, I would have provided the means for its demise."

She shrank back further against her pillows.

"How can you say such a terrible thing?"

"Firstly," he said softly and his smile broadened, "I intend to destroy this painting of the charming lily-white hands that Master Marsh would have handed down to posterity. Already his portrait of you lies in ribbons. Mrs. Dinglefoot took much pleasure in burning the pieces. No likeness of the present Lady St. Cheviot shall ever hang in the picture gallery at Cadlington among ladies who were more worthy of their titles. Your portrait must be forgotten—wiped out of memory, *like yourself*."

These words froze Fleur's blood, but she neither moved nor screamed. She was too paralysed with fear. Her dilated eyes watched while he smashed the little, exquisite painting of her hands; first the frame, then the canvas which he tore from end to end. The rasping sound of the ripped material grated on her every nerve. She shuddered and whitened. Despite herself, a low cry broke from her.

"You are mad—you have destroyed a masterpiece."

"To the devil with that," he said through his teeth. "Now for your bridal chamber, my fine wife. Peveril spent his genius and my money on preparing this nest for you. He made a grave error."

"But what have I done?" Fleur cried. "Is it so desperate a crime to bear a dead child?"

St. Cheviot seized her by both wrists and jerked her out of the bed. He stood her up before him. From his towering height he glared down into her eyes.

"*It is as well it died*," he said savagely.

"You—its father, say so!" she panted.

"Its father, yes—and one who sought to raise fine sons through you. You, the virginal Miss Roddney—the innocent maid, so modest and so fine that she could scarce endure a lover's caresses. It makes me laugh. Do you hear? It makes me *laugh*."

She thought, truly, that he had gone out of his mind. She would have fallen, only his steely fingers held her up, shaking her now and then like a doll until her teeth chattered.

"The infant's skin was black," he said in that low and sinister voice, "*Black*, my dear, do you hear? *It was a negro. My* child—yes, no doubt I fathered your vile spawn. I cannot accuse you of adultery. The child was conceived at The Bastille. It was yours—and mine."

Fleur gasped: "What are you saying? Oh? Monstrous, abominable thing. It is not true?"

He shook her again.

"You married me knowing what blood ran in your veins. Knowing that the taint was there and might well be passed on to your offspring."

She stared up at him with eyes so terrified, that St. Cheviot, crazy with rage though he was, could not pursue this line further. He realized that she did not understand one word of what he said. But her ignorance made him no less violent in his anger against her. He released her, throwing her on to the bed. He added:

"Then if you did not know—I curse the memory of your mother. *Your quadroon mother*, my dear. Do you hear that? Proud beauteous Marquise de Chartellet—later Lady Roddney—was a *quadroon*. Through her, you committed this enormity, and I was nicely fooled into giving you my name."

Fleur could not begin to take in the significance of what he was saying to her. She still thought that he was out of his mind. He began to prowl around her room like a malicious animal seeking what he might kill. He ripped the delicate laces from her bed and her dressing-table; the satins and the bows, all the feminine fripperies that had made it such a charming nest. He trampled on the gleaming, snowy draperies, defiling them with his heavy riding boots.

"Tomorrow they shall burn," he said.

He smashed the ivory brushes and perquisites of her toilette. Unlocking her jewel-cases, he took out the gleaming jewels and thrust them into his pocket. "These," he said, "my family heirlooms, shall never be worn by you again."

Then he took the Raphael painting down from the wall, and studied it a moment, sneering.

"This shall be spared for it is valuable. But it shall no longer hang in here. There is no link between you and any Madonna; nor, they tell me, will you ever bear another child. It is as well, lest it be another throw-back from Africa—abominable evidence of your maternal history. *Now* I understand the hunchback's warning, '*Beware of a black St. Cheviot.*' Great God—how inspired she was—infernally so. We are the Black Barons—but your son's blackness came from hell itself and scorched my soul!"

The unfortunate girl lay where he had thrown her, her eyes glittering up at him through the tangle of her hair. Her face, her form were damp with sweat. She shuddered convulsively. She kept moaning:

"I do not understand, *I do not understand.*"

When he had completed the thorough destruction of her room, it presented a spectacle of terrifying disorder, and bore no resemblance to that gracious lovely chamber which she had first entered as a bride. Even her clothes were pulled from the cedar-wood closets, and flung into a heap. Henceforward, he added, she would need no fashionable garments. She would need very little, in fact, *for she would never leave this room again.*

For the moment that dire threat passed over Fleur's head. Neither did it trouble her to see her valuables wrecked before her eyes for she had never wanted them. But suddenly the implication of what he was saying about her dead child became too terrible to bear. She sat up and with sudden spirit blazed at him.

"You say that my child was *black*. You call my mother a *quadroon*. These can only be the ravings of a maniac."

Denzil came to the foot of the bed. He flung at her several sheets of paper closely written upon in a small hand.

"Read this. Now, every word of it," he said.

"Denzil, I am ill——" she began.

He thundered, "*Read*, I say, and *then* tell me that I am mad!"

Fleur, who felt her reason tottering, took the papers. Her fingers shook so that she could hardly hold them. She dragged herself nearer the lamp. St. Cheviot stood motionless, a dark vengeful figure, watching her out of his cruel eyes.

She began to read. . . .

Chapter Ten

The document which Fleur devoured that midnight, set the final seal of sorrow on her unhappy young life. A revelation of her dark inheritance—contained in a letter written to the Baron by a firm of London solicitors. They had been approached by his lordship, on the day after the Coronation, when their offices had re-opened. His lordship had demanded that they should trace the history of the Roddneys, late of Pillars in Essex, near Epping Forest.

Dolly de Vere, cousin to Sir Harry, had sworn on her oath that she knew nothing of Hélène's past and neither threats nor bribes could make her revoke that statement. Denzil had to seek elsewhere for his information. It was known that Sir Harry Roddney had married the widow of the French aristocrat, Lucien, Marquis de Chartellet. But the firm of lawyers had their sleuths. By various means, old newspapers and diaries were unearthed. Once, much had been written in fashionable journals about the fabulous Marquise whose wit and beauty had taken London by storm.

Note had been taken of the fact that two of the well-known ladies who attended the first reception given by the de Chartellets were the Lady Henrietta Hamton and the Marchioness of Rustingthorpe. Discreet enquiries were made—first of the Hamtons. It chanced that Lady Hamton's daughter (by her first marriage a Miss Pumphret) had married a young gentleman who was also a client of the very firm dealing with St. Cheviot's affairs.

Mr. Groves, the junior partner, noted for the remarkable fashion in which he unearthed secrets of the past—betook himself to visit this Miss Pumphret who was now a Mrs. Cuthbertson, residing at Kew. She was the elder of two daughters and could remember that her father Lord Pumphret had brought home from Bristol a female quadroon slave whom they called *Fauna*, and who remained for some years in the service of Lady Henrietta Pumphret.

Mrs. Cuthbertson could, indeed, remember quite a lot that went on in her mother's lifetime—the Balls, the Drawing Rooms, and the quarrels between her parents. In particular, a certain incident which had been described to her gleefully by a maid-servant (recounted in turn by a footman who witnessed it). The cutting of a monster cake by Sir Harry Roddney. Out of this cake had stepped a small girl of incredible beauty with long red-gold hair. She was called Fauna, and was a quadroon slave. She became the talk of society. For although she had black blood in her on her mother's side, her own skin was as white as driven snow. Mrs. Cuthbertson could recall even though it must be over thirty years ago, seeing this little slave girl and hearing people chatter about the splendid blackness of her eyes and the gold-red glory of her hair.

When Fleur reached this part of the document she paused a moment to wonder what this had to do with Hélène Roddney. True, her beautiful mother had been noted for that strange combination of red-gold hair and dark eyes, *but what could be the link between a quadroon slave and Lady Roddney?*

Fleur read on. As she did so, her blood turned to ice in her veins.

Mr. Groves discovered many more things from the one-time Miss Pumphret. He could tell his lordship how Fauna, the slave, had run away from the Pumphrets' house in London never to be seen again *until* the night of the great reception given by the Marquis de Chartellet in order to introduce his new young wife to society.

Miss Pumphret related a further story of how her mother, after being received by *Madame la Marquise*, was brought home in a dying condition. She had had a stroke. But before she closed her eyes she swore to all in her household that *Madame la Marquise and Fauna were one and the same.*

Mr. Groves—a little sceptical about this matter—passed on from Mrs. Cuthbertson to the Marchioness of Rustingthorpe who resided in the same district as his lordship.

From the fat, pock-marked little Marchioness he heard a similar story. *She* had whispered to him that she was *posi-*

tive that *Madame la Marquise* was once the slave. She imagined that Fauna must have found some Gentleman to raise her from her lowly state and later had the singular good fortune to marry de Chartellet. She, Clarissa Rustingthorpe, old though she was, could recall her own vast astonishment at the sight of Hélène de Chartellet. There could be no two such women alive, she said—with those eyes, that hair and those features.

She had not dared to impart this information to St. Cheviot, however, since she had no proof. But Mr. Groves was not long in finding that proof. He turned supposition into certainty.

He paid a visit to The Little Bastille, which in these days had become derelict. But in one of the dungeons there remained a strong-box bearing the Marquis de Chartellet's name. This Mr. Groves had forced open. Therein he had found papers which he sent on to St. Cheviot. An account written by a man who signed himself Aubrey Birkett—one-time secretary to the Marquis. This separate document (read with such horror by Fleur thirty-four years later) struck the final nail in her coffin. After all, St. Cheviot was no maniac—his accusations had hideous foundation. For Mr. Birkett described in detail a purchase made by his master, the Marquis, at a secret auction in the East End of London—the sale of a young quadroon slave named *Fauna*. Then how she had been taken back to the Marquis's residence, and her name changed to Hélène, and her original identity changed. How during the next few years she was secretly educated by the erudite Marquis who finally married her and helped her to revenge herself upon society. Particularly to revenge herself upon a certain nobleman named Sir Harry Roddney whom she thought to have betrayed her, although this was not a fact. Later, of course, Harry had married her.

All this was set down by the secretary, including a faithful account of the loveliness, the sparkling mentality of the one-time slave who had been so cruelly ill-treated by her purchasers. Now at last, Fleur learned of her ancestry. Of how her mother—then the child, Fauna—had been taken on to a slave ship from the African coast to Bristol. And how her grandfather, a gentle negro of Christian upbringing, had died before reaching his destination.

"He was *my great-grandfather*," Fleur looked up from the papers and whispered the words inaudibly. "So I have an eighth of black blood in me. The dark stain escaped my mother and myself but was handed down to my unfortunate babe."

She knew little about matters of heredity but she knew her Bible; that terrible warning. "*The sins of the father*" it began, and something about "behind handed down to the third and fourth generation." Her poor darling mother! Even now Fleur could think of her only with tenderness. She was not to blame for her ancestry. But if only she had warned *her* that she should not marry, and why—what a lot of misery she might have been spared! Fleur could only presume that her parents had hoped that as they had been lucky, she, too, might escape the curse.

Oh, shameful, shameful doom! Fleur reflected. God be praised that the old doctor had promised that she would never bear another babe.

Utterly exhausted by the enormity of the truth which had been unfolded to her this night, Fleur dropped the paper and fell back on her pillows unconscious.

When she opened her eyes again, St. Cheviot had gone. She stared at a scene of utter devastation. July sun poured into the outraged bedchamber and struck cruelly against the eyes of the young girl who must have lain unconscious through the small still hours of the morning. Then beside her bed she saw the overpowering figure of Mrs. Dinglefoot. Her face bore a formidable expression. She set down a tray on which there was bread and milk.

"Come on, my girl, sit up and eat," she said tartly. "No playing the fine lady with me. I'll not bring burnt feathers or vinegar for any of your swoons."

Fleur could hardly struggle into a sitting position. Her whole body ached and she fancied she had some fever.

"Where is his lordship?" she whispered.

"Gone back to London—the poor gentleman—he could not bear to remain here and breathe the same air with you, who should not call herself by the proud name of St. Cheviot."

"I will not argue with you as to that," said Fleur, "but I wish to know when his lordship intends to return."

"Never," said the housekeeper, and gave her high-pitched laugh as she looked around the ruined room. "A nice nest—and suitable for the daughter of a slave," she added, and the hairs on her monstrous chins quivered with secret and malicious mirth. "I wish our fine young painter could see his work now. I was aware at the time it was wasting my Lord St. Cheviot's money and that his marriage to you was a calamity."

For a moment Fleur was silent. From the woman's words it was obvious that she knew everything. What respect could she demand now, the poor girl asked herself hopelessly.

"*Oh, my mother, my poor mother, what have you done to me!*" she inwardly cried.

Out of her apron pocket, Mrs. Dinglefoot produced a letter written in his lordship's flourishing handwriting.

"I was told to give this to you. When you've read it, please to make some order out of this bedlam in here. You will be cleaning it yourself in future. There will be no more maids to wait on you." She walked toward the door.

Fleur called after the housekeeper: "Am I to be kept a prisoner then?"

"Yes, and it's what you deserve."

"Shall I be allowed to see nobody?" asked Fleur faintly.

"Nobody," was the answer.

Fleur struggled with the anguished desire to ask what had happened to Peveril. *She dared not mention his name* in case he should be implicated—and the terrible man who was her husband would also visit his wrath upon the innocent youth who had been her friend.

She had not seen or heard of Peveril for so long now that she could only suppose he had left Cadlington. So, she thought, she was deserted by all, at the mercy of Mrs. Dinglefoot.

Once the key turned in the lock she read what St. Cheviot had written. It was a cruel letter and did not add to her comfort.

Madame,

Any kindly feeling that I ever had for you died when I discovered what you are and of the wrong you and your family have done me. At a later date I may seek annulment for I consider that your relatives deceived me by marrying me to one of black blood without warning me of the menace to my issue. At the moment I am unwilling for this horrible scandal to become public. I have, therefore, told all and sundry that the birth of your child has unhinged you and that you must in future be kept away from the world, and nursed like a mad-woman. Nobody will be allowed to visit you. My faithful Mrs. D. will be your sole attendant. Had you extended a greater generosity to me in the past I might now feel more tolerant towards you. However, the thought of your beauty fills me with disgust, aware as I am of your tainted blood. I shall spend most of my time henceforth in London or upon the Continent. As your husband I remain in control of your fortune and have acquainted Mr. Caleb Nonseale of the sad fact of your insanity.

This monstrous letter was signed *"St. Cheviot."*

The young girl looked up, stared around her with dull apathetic gaze.

She could expect no better treatment from the Baron of Cadlington, she thought bitterly. After nearly a year's intimacy with him she could believe him capable of any abomination.

> Had you extended a greater generosity to me in the past I might now feel more tolerant towards you.

Those words stood out in St. Cheviot's letter. Yes, he might have still desired her had she fawned upon him. But now—no longer desiring her, he could sadistically gloat over the thought of her unhappiness. She had no weapons left with which to fight.

There stretched before her an endless vista of loneliness. If Cousin Dolly or her family or Mr. Nonseale, her trustee, asked for her, they would be told that she was out of her mind. In truth, if she stayed here long enough, she might lose her senses.

Dropping Denzil's note, Fleur flung herself upon her disordered bed, and with tearless eyes pressed against the rumpled pillows, lay without moving for a long time. Later that day Mrs. Dinglefoot came into the room. The woman looked at the girl on the bed and snapped at her:

"Still too lazy, my fine lady, to start tidying your bed-chamber, eh? Well—you will learn. Here, take this and get into the next room and begin to clean up there. . . ." She flung Fleur a mop and duster. "I have two good souls here who are to measure your windows for bars."

Fleur slipped into her muslin wrapper, threaded with blue ribbons, one of the few garments which St. Cheviot had not destroyed.

"Meanwhile," continued Mrs. Dinglefoot, "you shall have somebody to watch you and ensure that you do not attempt suicide."

And suddenly she opened the door. Alpha, the wolf-hound, bounded in. Fleur stood still, her gaze riveted on the animal's ferocious mask. Lover of animals though she was she had never been able to make friends with Denzil's pet. That was not the poor dog's fault, she knew, but that of Alpha's master who had maliciously trained her to snap and snarl at his bidding.

Mrs. Dinglefoot had red raw meat in her hand. With this she tempted the hungry dog. He went to her, greedy, slavering. But now the woman pointed at Fleur.

"Hi! Alpha, let me see what you can do," she said.

Alpha sprang at Lady St. Cheviot. The animal's teeth closed into a fold of the muslin negligée. She growled in her throat, pulling at the frills, keeping her eyes on Fleur. The girl trembled but refused to cry out. Mrs. Dinglefoot laughed.

"Come, Alpha, sit down and wait for it," she said. "Later you shall be on guard, my good creature."

Fleur put a hand to her throat.

"Am I to be left to the mercy of this animal?" she asked faintly.

"Alpha will not touch you unless you make an attempt to reach those windows," said Mrs. Dinglefoot.

Fleur shut her eyes and shuddered.

Came the sound of men's voices. Mrs. D. bundled her into the boudoir. After a moment, huddled against the communicating door, Fleur heard the voices of two of the workmen from the estate. In their strong Buckinghamshire dialect, they chatted about the size of the windows and the type of bars that must be cut at Whiteleaf Forge.

Fleur closed her eyes. She tried to pray. Oh, fearful fate—locked behind closed doors and barred windows and treated like a poor deranged creature! *Peveril!* her lips formed his name. *Peveril, if you but knew you would not let them do this to me.* What had happened to *him?*

Peveril had, in fact, been told little by anyone at Cadlington. For since the fearful night when Fleur's baby had been born, the boy had spent much of his time at Rustingthorpe. It was from the old Marchioness herself that he finally heard the whole sordid story.

Clarissa Rustingthorpe, approaching her sixtieth year—bore little traces of the beauty which had once won for her a wealthy husband with a great title. Her hair was always dressed nowadays in dyed auburn curls, and she wore bright coloured dresses and too many bows. She was very fat and waddled on high heels. But she was quite amiable and had taken an enormous fancy to young Peveril Marsh.

The Marquis was an invalid and remained in his own rooms attended by his gentlemen. Clarissa coquetted with the handsome young artist. He found her repulsive but pathetic. She was always trying to induce him to leave St. Cheviot and establish himself here in one of the rooms of her vast mansion. She chatted to him endlessly while he painted, feeding him with bon-bons that he did not want, or trying to force wine on him. This, Peveril found very trying, but she paid well for his work and without saving money he could never hope for the independence he craved.

Clarissa also plied him with endless questions about Lady St. Cheviot. She was never tired of hearing Peveril describe the Baron's wife. He spoke with eloquence of Lady St. Cheviot's beauty but more guardedly of her personal life. Clarissa stubbornly persisted in trying to find out the true state of affairs at Cadlington. She even tried to whisper malign stories about Hélène Roddney and her mysterious life before she became *Madame la Marquise de Chartellet*. But Peveril politely but firmly shut his ears to them.

After the birth of the child, however, a certain Mr. Groves visited Rustingthorpe. He had a long session alone with the Marchioness. Afterwards she waddled back into the room in which Peveril was putting the finishing touches to the portrait of the little Victoria Rustingthorpe.

"My goodness, now the fat is in the fire," the Marchioness giggled.

"With whom, my lady?" Peveril asked only vaguely interested.

"The St. Cheviots."

Then Peveril's expression changed.

"What has happened, my lady?"

Clarissa seated herself beside him. She allowed herself an ecstasy of gossip. She made no effort now to guard any secret she might hold but poured out the whole story into the boy's ears. That same story that she had told Mr. Groves.

So Peveril heard in detail the scandal of the Marquise de Chartellet. And now at last he understood the nature of the tragedy that had taken place at Cadlington a few weeks ago.

"They say Lady St. Cheviot has been deranged ever since her confinement," chattered Clarissa.

"*Deranged!*" repeated Peveril.

"So they tell me," nodded the Marchioness fanning herself. "Poor creature! From what you say, so like her mother, and she was uncommonly handsome."

Peveril stood up. His eyes held a stricken look.

"God be merciful to my sweet Lady St. Cheviot," he said in a low voice that held much of horror.

Clarissa waved a lace-edged handkerchief at him. From it floated a cloud of scent.

"Oh fie!" she said, "do not tell me that you have a naughty fancy for Lady St. Cheviot. It would do you no good. The poor soul is out of her mind and they tell me St. Cheviot has left Cadlington and gone upon the Continent. Everyone knows he keeps a mistress in Monte Carlo."

Peveril remained speechless. He could think of nothing but Fleur. He was shaken to the depths of his sensitive being by the thought of her terrible sufferings. *Out of her mind?* Maybe so. But maybe it was only one of the Marchioness's fancies. Her imagination often ran away with her.

He could scarcely bear the flirtatious perfumed old woman. But for once in his life he felt the need to dissemble. He must go to Fleur St. Cheviot's aid, and without money he was lost. He had some savings but he would need more. He threw down his paint brushes and bowed low to the Marchioness.

"Your servant, my lady," he said hoarsely. "I beg you to excuse me. I have urgent business to which I must attend. What you have told me leads me to suppose that it were better for me to leave Cadlington. I will go and pack my things."

"And come back here to Rustingthorpe?" asked the silly old woman, peering at him from short-sighted eyes.

"I will consider it, my lady."

"You want money? I will give it to you."

He flushed.

"I want only payment for my work."

"Yes, yes, little Victoria's portrait. You shall have twenty guineas for that. Wait—I will give it to you now—but only if you promise to return here."

Peveril bit his lip. Twenty guineas was a small fortune and could do much for him. He must be in a position to place himself and his services into Lady St. Cheviot's hands *should she need them.*

He permitted himself the lie and hinted to the infatuated old Marchioness that he would return. Later with the money in his pocket he set out to walk to Cadlington. He refused the phaeton offered by Clarissa. He felt that it might be better for him to make an unobtrusive return after his two days' absence from the tower.

Chapter Eleven

The day was warm and the hedgerows sweet with wild flowers. Fleecy clouds hung like cotton wool in the blue sky. The countryside was green and pleasant after the recent rain. While he walked the long road toward Cadlington hill, Peveril was bathed in sunshine but his heart was filled with misgivings.

What would he find at Cadlington?

He unbuttoned his coat and loosened his cravat as he began to climb the steep hill to Whiteleaf.

For the rest of his life, he was to thank God that he refused the Marchioness's offer of her phaeton. For halfway up the hill, he was waylaid by a young girl who darted out from the woods and caught at his arm.

"Oh, Mr. Peveril, zur!" she exclaimed. She was well-spoken and had only a slight Buckinghamshire accent.

"Why, Rabbina, good morning to you!" he returned her greeting.

She was a young servant—one of the between-maids on St. Cheviot's staff. She had only come here a month ago, just before my lady was confined. She was a timid little thing, small for her age and easily bullied; the daughter of a low-born cowman on St. Cheviot's farm. Mrs. Dinglefoot, recognizing that Rabbina was poor and ignorant and also very nervous, had immediately picked upon her. Peveril had witnessed some of the bullying and tried to help her. From that time onward, the humble Rabbina became Peveril's slave. In her adoring way she performed many small services for him. She answered his greeting today, her small freckled face puckered with anxiety.

"I thank God that I have seen you in time and can speak to you, Mr. Peveril, zur!" she panted.

He looked with surprise at her hot perspiring face.

"What is it, Rabbina?" he asked in his kind way.

She clasped her hands together and plucked at the strings of her sunbonnet.

Last night, she said, she had been given orders to serve cooled cider in the housekeeper's private sitting-room. The child knew that Mrs. D. was entertaining Mr. Ivor. Ivor had gone to London with his lordship, but returned yesterday to fetch some important documents which his lordship had forgotten and which he would not trust with any but his personal servant. Rabbina had spilled some of the cider just outside the housekeeper's door. While stopping to mop it up, fearing that the irascible housekeeper would see the puddle and cuff her, she had overheard a conversation that was going on between Mrs. D. and the Welshman.

"Well?" asked Peveril tensely. "What has this to do with me?"

"It is of you they spoke, zur," she peered up at Peveril with adoring gaze. "You wuz always good to me, sir, and this is my chance to give you a warning."

Aware suddenly of danger, Peveril took Rabbina by the elbow and drew her into the shade of the glade. There hidden from the road, he listened intently while Rab repeated what she had heard.

Mrs. D. had been describing how the bars were now being made, down at the blacksmith's, for her ladyship's windows.

"How fearful . . ." muttered Peveril. "It is worse than I anticipated."

Rabbina continued:

The pair in the housekeeper's room mentioned Peveril Marsh by name so Rabbina remained outside to eavesdrop. *Fleur had written to him.* Ivor had informed Mrs. D. that his lordship had discovered a note which Lady St. Cheviot had sent, appealing for Peveril's help—for Denzil had ransacked the studio before leaving Cadlington.

At first St. Cheviot instructed Ivor to seek Peveril out at Rustingthorpes and horsewhip him. Then his temper cooled. Peveril was for the moment under the patronage of the Rustingthorpes. Even St. Cheviot did not fancy creating a scandal under the Marquis's roof. The wealthy Marquis was too close and too powerful a neighbour. And as Denzil had destroyed Fleur's indiscreet letter, Peveril would never now receive it. When Peveril returned to Cadlington, Ivor had his lordship's permission to thrash the painter within an inch of his life, then despatch him from Cadlington. Lady St. Cheviot would never look upon her poetic painter again.

"So you will see, zur," ended Rabbina, "you must not return to the House. Mr. Ivor may kill you."

Peveril stood silent a moment, racking his brains. He was a man of peace but no coward. He had learned neither to wrestle, to spar, to shoot nor to defend himself from physical attack. It would be madness to pit his strength against the trained Welshman. *That* was not the way to help Fleur. No—he must be more wily. With cunning, he might rescue Fleur St. Cheviot from terrible doom that had hung over her since she came here as a bride.

Rabbina remembered something else to tell Peveril.

"Zur, there is a great fierce dog guarding her ladyship day and night until the bars have been made for the windows."

"Ah?" exclaimed Peveril. "A white wolfhound?"

"Yes, zur, Alpha, and I heard Mrs. D. say that it sits by the window and if my lady moves towards it and so much as tries to open it, the bitch will fasten her teeth in my lady."

Peveril shuddered. He knew well how fierce the wolfhound could be. Even the Welshman was afraid of her. His poor sweet lady! Oh, what a monstrous man was Denzil St. Cheviot! To think that there had ever been a time when Peveril Marsh had thought him fine and noble. Then a sudden thought struck the boy. The colour returned to his cheeks. With *him*, Alpha had always been astonishingly docile and submissive. Many of the old servants had remarked that they had never seen the bitch more friendly towards any one. *That might prove vastly useful.*

Rabbina was speaking again, her roughened fingers plucking firmly at a bunch of nettles that grew close to them.

Peveril followed the action and muttered to himself:

"Grasp firmly at the nettles and they will not sting. Yes, I must emulate this little maid's example. I have spent too much time painting fine portraits—gathering the lilies, dreaming my foolish dreams. Now I must take action even if it is violent. For violence is being done to *her* who is the idol of my soul. God give me strength and wisdom for I am in sore need of both!"

He had not heard what Rabbina said to him but he gripped her arm.

"Have you ever seen the Baroness? Would you do her a kindness even though it endangered you?" he said hoarsely.

Rabbina nodded.

"Aye, I saw her once and thought her most beautiful and pitiful. I would willingly do her a kindness and you, too, Mr. Peveril, who have been so kind to me."

"Then you shall," said Peveril.

Chapter Twelve

In her great bed lying under the tattered linen and lace Fleur lay motionless. She had not dared to stir since darkness fell. Earlier she had drunk some soup that Mrs. D. brought her, only because the woman forced her to do so.

"We'll not have you starve to death and let folks say his lordship has done you a cruelty," the woman had snarled at her. "Drink every drop of it!"

Afterwards, when Mrs. D. had left, locking the door behind her, Fleur became horribly conscious of the white wolfhound lying by one of the windows. Mrs. D. had opened that window in order to give the animal air, for the night was particularly warm. Until now Fleur had scarcely been able to support the atmosphere.

Another storm was gathering; heralded by those black clouds that could be seen rolling up from the valley. Mrs. D. had brought her no light. Fleur could only dimly discern the shape of the wolfhound but could hear her panting.

Fleur felt the sweat pour down her limbs. She did not particularly wish to have the animal spring at her again and, perhaps, sink her fangs into her flesh and draw blood. She lay in a stupor. She was singularly uncomfortable. She had been allowed neither to wash herself nor comb her hair. She felt begrimed. Her lips were dry and sore. She had not yet fully recovered from the effects of her confinement. Brought up like a delicate lady she had never before experienced such rough usage or deprivation of things like warm water and soap, a brush and comb for her hair, or clean linen. She wondered indeed, if any gentlewoman alive had ever experienced such a fate as this in the hands of her husband.

She wondered if it was St. Cheviot's intention that she

should be driven insane so that he could ease his conscience and feel justified in locking her away from the world. Yet even during the worst of her torments she kept telling herself that she preferred to lie here like this, forsaken and neglected sooner than submit—as she had done in the past—perfumed and bejewelled, and in loathing, to his demands.

The night was silent save for the hooting of the owls down in the forest.

The night seemed uncommonly long. She could not sleep. She could not bear this tension—this feeling that she dared not move because of the animal guarding her.

Then suddenly she heard a low growl rumble in Alpha's throat. Fleur sat up, her heart beating faster. What did the animal hear? *Something—somebody*—but what—who—at this hour, for it must be well into midnight.

Rubbing her eyes, Fleur saw the shaggy creature pad to the window, still growling. But all of a sudden she saw an astonishing sight. Alpha, having ceased to growl, began to wag her tail furiously. Dully, Fleur told herself that it must be that the animal heard familiar footsteps.

Now there rose above the window-sill the dim outline of a man's head. She heard a whisper:

"Alpha . . . good soul . . . good girl . . . lie down, Alpha . . . take this. . . ."

Fleur put the tips of her fingers to her lips. Huddled on her bed she stared, not daring to believe that she had recognized the voice.

Alpha padded into a corner and began scrunching some tidbit that obviously pleased her. The next moment a slimly built man vaulted into the room and moved soundlessly towards Fleur. Once beside the bed he paused. He looked down at Fleur. She stared up at him. Then a low sound issued from her throat. She uttered his name.

"Peveril!"

"My lady," he breathed.

"Oh, God!" she whispered, and held out both hands to him, frantic with excitement and joy. "You have come to take me away."

He knelt by the bed, took those outstretched hands and raised them each in turn to his lips, covering them with kisses.

"My sweet lady, what have they done to you?"

Her head sank. Her forehead touched his shoulder. Both his arms supported and held her. She wore still the crumpled muslin negligée which she had not been allowed to change. He could barely see her but he could feel how hot, how feverish she was, and the dampness of her silken tangled hair. He held her not in passion but in love—a love that was profound; full of pity. For the moment he knew that it was what she needed and what he must give. He pressed his cheek to hers. With his own heart beating wildly, he dared to kiss her hair.

"My dearest—my beloved lady—oh, *Fleur,*" he whispered.

"Peveril," she spoke his name again, and by the frenzy with which she clung to him, he measured the extent of her pleasure at this reunion. She trembled in his arms. Her tears drenched his face. He heard her hoarse whispering.

"How did you come? How did you know where to find me? Is it safe? Have you not endangered your very life by coming here, like this, to me?"

He answered only the last question.

"If I have, it is worth while—I am privileged to risk such an unworthy life for you."

She said:

"You cannot be aware of the truth about me?"

"I know everything," he said. "I loved you before I knew. I love you still more now. Your husband has forfeited the right to protect you. I beg to be allowed to do so."

"You are the only true friend I have in the world." She wept and Peveril felt her lips against his cheek. He said:

"We must be quick. At any moment Ivor or Mrs. D. may wake and hear us."

"How did you get here? Where have you been?"

He told her everything that had led up to his meeting on the hill with Rabbina, the between-maid. Fleur learned how the little maid had also risked terrible punishment and met Peveril underneath Lady St. Cheviot's window. Rab kept watch below there now while Peveril climbed the strong creeper that grew as high as her ladyship's bedchamber.

"Praise God," said Peveril, "I am agile and have a good head for climbing."

During the afternoon he had bought stout rope. This he would tie to the bed post. He would let Fleur down first, then follow. None of this could have been achieved had he not made friends with Alpha.

"How thankful I am that the hound was my constant companion before you came here," whispered Peveril. "I have only to tell her to lie still and she will not move."

Wild excitement gathered in Fleur's heart.

"What clothes have you?" Peveril asked her.

"Alas, only a shawl for my shoulders. The Baron . . . in his rage . . . destroyed everything that I have."

"He is indeed a madman," muttered Peveril.

"Worse than that."

Peveril struck a match. The tiny light illuminated Fleur's face and figure. Almost he uttered an exclamation of horror. She was so emaciated. Her hair was tangled and matted, her lips cracked. It broke Peveril's heart to see her. But she pulled the shawl over her breast and smiled at him. A smile of unearthly sweetness. He extinguished the match, took her hands in his, and covered them with kisses.

"If heaven has given me the right to call myself your protector, I am the happiest of mortals. Henceforth my life is dedicated to you," he said.

Then quickly he tied the rope to the post of her bed, gave an order to Alpha who wagged her tail and continued to gnaw the delectable bone he had brought to her. He moved to the window, looked down and whispered:

"Hist!"

Rabbina's voice floated up to him.

"Yes, zur, all is quiet."

Then Fleur St. Cheviot became once more the vivacious spirited fleet-footed girl who had once graced her parents' household and for whom nothing ever held terrors. He tied the rope round her waist. He lowered her safely to the ground. She felt a pair of strong young arms receive her.

"Oh, my lady, my lady," whispered Rabbina, the little maid, and then let her ladyship go and curtseyed and bobbed, much embarrassed. It appalled her to see a lady of quality in such a state. Why, the poor young thing, thought the raw country girl, she is not much older than myself—all eyes and a bag of bones.

Fleur caught the little servant's hand in hers.

"With all my heart I thank you for the risk you have taken for me tonight," she breathed.

Peveril had swung himself down beside them.

"Ssh, still a moment," he whispered.

All three of them stood tense, listening. Fleur felt that the beating of her own heart must make a noise in the quietness which had fallen upon Cadlington. Even the owls had stopped hooting. Now they heard the church clock from Monks Risborough strike the hour of one. But the great House remained wrapped in an almost uncanny silence as though it would aid and abet Peveril's rescue of the Baron's ill-fated wife.

Peveril breathed again.

"Come—all is well—let us go," he said.

Fleur took the arm he held out to her.

"What are your plans?" she asked.

He told her. His paints and a few clothes were in a carpet bag which had been collected from the tower by Rabbina and left in the bushes.

They must not pass through the main gates, for the lodge-keeper might waken and see them. They would turn off the main drive and make their way through the hedgerows leading out on to the road towards Great Missenden. If Lady St. Cheviot could walk so far as half a mile, Peveril had organized a horse and gig to wait for them at the cross-roads.

"Once we are in the thicket we shall be safe," added Peveril. "Our only danger is lest somebody should awake and see us running across the lawn into the trees."

"Oh, let us hurry!" exclaimed Fleur frantic with longing to be gone.

Peveril took one of her arms, Rabbina the other. The next moment the three shadowy figures flitted across the lawn. They they were gone, and safe behind the shelter of the tall trees.

An immense thankfulness filled Fleur's heart and warmed yet more of life and vitality back into her. She moved as swiftly as the little servant girl in her home-spun cloak and stout boots. Once the fleecy shawl fell from her thin shoulders. Peveril picked it up and wrapped it tenderly about her. She felt his gentle touch and smiled up at him. He had never seen her thus before. It was as though the sorrowful statue of his madonna had come to life, with the blood surging through those alabaster limbs. Her new feverish beauty enthralled the painter.

But they were not yet out of danger. Once on the high road bearing the wooden sign-post "To Great Missenden" Peveril picked up the carpet bag which Rabbina had packed for him and hidden beside her own modest bundle. Rab, too, was leaving Whiteleaf for ever. It did not particularly grieve her to know that she must remain away from her family from now onward.

Her apprenticeship at the great House under Mrs. Dinglefoot had offered little so far but ill-usage and hard work. She had begged Peveril to allow her to go with him when he left Whiteleaf and become maid to her ladyship.

Now it was Rabbina to whom Peveril and Fleur must turn for immediate help. She had an aunt in Great Missenden; by name Mrs. Tabitha Gomme, who was sister to Rabbina's dead mother. She had always been a favourite with Rabbina, but the child had the chance to visit her only rarely. Mrs. Gomme, a widow, was a respectable body, a lace-maker, who occupied a tiny tumbledown cottage on the outskirts of Great Missenden. She would, Rabbina knew, give a haven tonight to the runaways.

Peveril then bribed a man named Amos from Monks Risborough, who owned horse and gig, to convey them all to Missenden. He would not recognize the Lady of Cadlington. Nor did he know the young artist by sight. He was a dull-witted fellow who minded his own business and would not ask questions or give information even if it were demanded. What he wanted was gold. Peveril had offered plenty for the journey and received his promise of complete discretion. He fancied that Amos would not bother to tittle-tattle about his nocturnal passengers, and in any case, even if Amos was suspected, Peveril and Fleur would be well away before he could be accused.

Peveril outlined his further plans for Fleur as they walked swiftly along the long dark road to the cross-roads at the top of the hill.

Rabbina was to introduce them to Aunt Tabitha as an

"eloping couple." Peveril apologized to Fleur with humility, for this impertinence. At once she replied:

"As if I could take offence since you plan all for my wellbeing," she said with her loveliest smile.

"Thank you," he said in a low voice and pressed her arm against his.

It was when they reached the cross-roads and the end of that half-mile that they first encountered a setback.

As arranged, Amos, from Monks Risborough, sat with his gig and piebald mare, chewing a piece of straw, waiting for them. He eyed the two females with small interest.

He was anxious to get on and earn the full purse the young gentleman had promised him.

" 'Tis sta-army, zur," he said with his broad accent. "I'll be fair aggled if does ra-ain afore we git to Missenden."

Rabbina giggled suddenly and whispered to Peveril.

"He means he'll be angered, zur. *Aggled* is what we calls it in Buckinghamshire."

"I shall be 'aggled' too, if the rain starts and my lady is soaked," muttered Peveril drily. "We will get poor shelter in this tumbledown gig."

"I am very happy—do not bother about me," Fleur begged him.

But when she was settled inside the gig and seated snugly between her two rescuers, a man suddenly sprang out of the hedge at them. He shouted that he wished a lift if it was to Whiteleaf they were going.

Fleur smothered a scream. She clutched Peveril's hand. He covered it with both of his, reassuringly.

"Ssh—do not move or speak," he whispered.

The sudden apparition was a thin, sandy-haired man wearing gaiters, and with half a dozen rabbits slung over his shoulder and a fowling-piece under one arm. He started a controversy with Amos. Amos having explained that they were bound for the opposite direction, the stranger began to argue that Amos should first turn back and take him home. He was obviously inflamed from a plethora of raw gin, for now he offered a swig from a large flask to Amos, who rejected it.

Peveril cut in sharply:

"Come, my good fellow—we are in a hurry—do not delay us, if you please."

The man began to mumble that he had caught his foot in a hole, wrenched an ankle and wanted a lift.

He was causing Peveril some real concern, revealing himself now as Jack Hommock, nephew of old Hommock one of the lodge-keepers from Cadlington. Jack began to climb into the gig and peer at the three occupants. He recognized at least two of them. (Fleur had hidden her face against Peveril's shoulder. He could feel her trembling violently.) Hommock said:

"Well, if it isn't little Rab—the cowman's girl—and with the young gentleman-painter. Where are you two a-going might I a-ask?" He drawled the question.

"Get down and mind your own business," said Peveril sharply.

Hommock swayed, and peered closer to him.

"Taking a night trip wi' the cowman's daughter, eh, my master painter?" he sneered.

Peveril felt in the darkness, the feverish clasp of Fleur's fingers.

"Do not start trouble, for dear God's sake," she whispered.

But it was too late. The poacher lurched towards her and rudely snatched her scarf. The silken tangle of curls fell across her bosom. Hommock instantly recognized her and gave a shout which was half in fear.

"Lawks-a-mussy! It is the Lady of Cadlington, herself. I be scrummerous to have laid a finger on you, my lady."

Fleur gave a cry of despair.

"We are lost, Peveril."

But not so, for Peveril Marsh—who all his clean pacific life had been a gentle lad and averse to acts of violence—sprang at the poacher, who with a hoarse cry, fell back on to the road. He lay there groaning. His fowling-piece had clattered to the ground. The rabbits followed. Peveril sprang after him. He dragged the poacher to the side of the road. The man looked up at him with inflamed, malevolent little eyes.

"Helping the Baron's mad lady to get away—is that it, my master?" he gasped. "I'll raise a hue and a cry once I'm back at Cadlington and you won't get far, I warrant."

"As I expected," said Peveril darkly. "Well, my man, you are unlucky this night for if it is a case of you or my lady—her life—or yours—you must be the one to suffer."

The clouds parted—for a moment the moon shed a ray of light and Peveril saw a flash of steel in Hommock's upraised hand.

The next moment the two men were rolling in the dust. Peveril's fear for Fleur lent him an unnatural power; a frenzied purpose to shut the fellow's mouth.

Amos sat watching sullenly. He had no part in this quarrel neither did he comprehend it.

Fleur and Rabbina clasped each other. Fleur said in an anguished voice:

"Oh, God . . . if he is injured now . . ."

"Take heart, my lady," the little maid tried to comfort her. "Jack Hommock is in drink and will not be as slippery with his knife as usual."

Such was the case. Hommock pitted his brawn against the painter only for a few moments. Peveril, his fingers about the poacher's wrist, forced him back. They wrestled and panted in the darkness. Fleur could only see dim shapes and hear the heavy breathing.

Then suddenly came a sharp cry from the poacher. The knife clattered on to the roadway. Peveril reached for the fowling-piece and brought the butt down on the other man's skull. It was the first savage blow he had ever struck in his life. Hommock rolled over and lay still, Peveril pulled him into the hedge and left him there.

"Oh, thank heaven—you are safe," Fleur exclaimed as Peveril sprang back into the gig. "Alas, you have had to commit a crime for my sake."

"I do not think the fellow is dead. I heard him groan. But it will be some time before he is found and can betray us," he said.

His face was pale. He caught Amos by the arm.

"Remember—once you return to Monks Risborough you will say nothing of this to a soul or I shall seek you out and make sure you never open your lips again," he said fiercely.

Amos hunched a shoulder and whipped up his mare.

"I wao-on't talk, master. I'd be a-feared. All I want is the gowld," he said.

"You shall have it," said Peveril.

The gig rattled on down the other side of the hill in the

direction of Great Missenden. Now a few drops spattered from the sky.

"The storm's a-coming," said little Rabbina.

But Fleur and Peveril did not hear her. They were clasping hands again. Once more Peveril felt her breath against his cheek. She whispered:

"My dear, dear Peveril—if indeed you have stained your soul this night for my sake, it will be forgiven you. The fellow would have set all the inmates of Cadlington upon us."

"And still will—if he lives?" said Peveril in a low voice. "We must seek a refuge where the Baron can never discover you."

She sighed. Her head leaned against his shoulder as they jogged along through the ever-increasing rain. She felt weary beyond caring, yet at peace.

"Oh, how happy I am to be with you . . ." she breathed.

Then he forgot the violence he had committed. All his manhood was vibrant for Fleur. He kept her fingers locked in his as they journeyed on to their destination and she did not seek to withdraw them.

Chapter Thirteen

The storm which growled over the Chiltern Hills all night broke with some ferocity at four o'clock in the morning. By that time the runaways had reached the cottage belonging to Rabbina's aunt.

Now Fleur sat in Tabitha Gomme's rocking chair, her small feet on a stool, drinking herb-tea from a blue and white china mug. Mrs. Gomme had found a more manly drink of ale for the young gentleman. While he drank, and ate the bread and cheese Mrs. Gomme had served, he kept his enraptured gaze upon Fleur.

Mrs. Gomme and her niece had taken Fleur upstairs as soon as she arrived, removed the crumpled negligée and helped to dress her in a grey homespun gown which belonged to Mrs. Gomme. Once more her fair fell in gleaming ringlets about her neck and bosom. Difficult, thought Peveril, to believe she had ever been wife to St. Cheviot, or borne a child—she looked so young like this.

He seated himself on a stool at her feet and began to talk to her.

"My lady——" but she interrupted, gently pressing his fingers.

"I wish never to hear that odious title again. The very sound freezes my blood. To you, henceforward, I am just —Fleur. And for me, you are my friend, Peveril."

"*Fleur,*" he repeated the name as though it were something sacred. His reward was great when he saw the faint uplifting of her sad mouth.

He discussed the future.

They must press onward to London. It would be wiser, because of the poacher and what might follow the discovery of his body. As soon as Fleur had rested, they would breakfast and catch the first mail coach of the day from Great Missenden, to London. Only there—among millions—could they lose themselves and stay hidden from their pursuers.

Peveril now spoke of a great friend who lived close to the river, near the Royal Vauxhall Gardens. By name Luke Taylor, he was, like Peveril, an artist in his spare time. He was a year or two older than Peveril whom he had met first at the Grammar School. He worked in a firm of merchant bankers in the City. The last that Peveril had heard of him was that he was doing quite well.

"Luke and I have always been much attached. He has my way of thinking and Alice, his wife, is one in whom you could put your trust," Peveril told Fleur. "She is in fact some ten years older than my friend. She has the most amiable nature. With the help of a little servant of Rabbina's age, Alice keeps the house uncommonly well for my friend. I propose to take you there. I shall tell them everything—that is if you permit it—for I know that they will offer us shelter and that Luke will help me to find work. Does the idea please you?"

"I am sure I should like your friends," said Fleur, "but I do not know why they should be bothered with me."

"They have but to see you, to love you," said Peveril, with a look that brought the warm pink to Fleur's hollowed cheeks.

"Alas," she said, "I cannot—dare not—approach my own dear friend, Catherine Quinley, or any who has known me in the past."

"Agreed," said Peveril, "and although it is best for us to be frank with Luke and Alice, it is essential that you at least change your name immediately, for it is certain the Baron will make a desperate bid to find you and take his revenge."

A shiver went through the girl.

"Yes, I can imagine his rage." She nodded.

"Let us then take asylum with the Taylors. When the excitement has died down, no doubt his lordship will seek to have the marriage annulled."

Fleur looked blindly at the boy.

"Once," she said, "I believed in the sanctity of the marriage vow. But now I no longer feel pledged to him. *Let* our marriage be put asunder. I do most heartily desire complete severance from a monster such as St. Cheviot."

"Amen to that," said Peveril.

Then he stood up and drew her on to her feet.

"You must have some rest," he said and smiled down at her.

All her heart went out in gratitude to him.

"Oh, what can I ever do for you who have done so much for me!" she exclaimed.

He was silent a moment, then said in a low voice:

"It is too soon to speak of such things for I feel you must shrink from any man's protest of affection. But I stand here and protest unashamed, my love for you, most beloved Fleur. If you would do something in return for me, I ask that you permit me to stay for ever by your side."

Now her tears fell thickly but with touching gesture she laid her cheek against his hand.

"I do not wish you to leave me," she whispered. "Through all my anguish I have remembered you. When I first went as a bride to Cadlington, the only happiness I knew was in your presence, listening to your voice."

He covered her hair with kisses. For a moment they stayed close. Then he drew away, walked with her to the casement window, and pulled aside the curtains. The little kitchen was at once filled with pearly light. Peveril snuffed the tallow candle. They looked out at the dawn. Meadow and road were white in the mist. From the distance came the crowing of a cock, and the sound of a dog barking.

The young artist turned to Fleur. She looked pallid and frail in her grey gown. He gazed at the sheen of her wonderful hair, and received from her the smile that he, and he alone, seemed able to bring to her lips. Then he dropped down on one knee and leaned his forehead against her folded hands.

"You are my saint and I worship you," he said.

She could not answer. Her heart was too full but she read in Peveril's eyes an end to her despair; a promise of a happiness greater than she had ever known.

That hope still kept her spirits high when—a few hours later—she sat between Peveril and Rabbina in the mail coach which was being drawn by four fast horses *en route* for London.

In borrowed cape and bonnet, heavily veiled, she had

little fear of recognition. With every mile that they covered, she began to feel less strained. There seemed no likelihood now that they would be overtaken.

Peveril, too, was in high spirits, but the financial angle troubled Fleur.

"I am totally dependent upon you. It seems all wrong," she told Peveril. He laughed at her. He had saved for this very purpose, he kept reassuring her, and he brought a few more smiles from her by describing for her his painting of Victoria Rustingthorpe and the coquettish antics of the elderly Marchioness.

"I fear," ended Peveril, "her ladyship will be sadly disappointed when I do not return to her, but I gave her good measure of work for the money she paid me, so I need not feel guilty."

Fleur looked at Peveril with a new and personal pride in him.

"You are a great artist, and should easily be able to make both name and fortune in London," she murmured.

"I dare not offer a painting under the name of Peveril Marsh," he reminded her, "for my work is individual and might get into the hands of a dealer where it would in turn be noticed by the Baron. Thus he would trace me—and you. No, I must begin life again. I shall find other means whereby to earn our livelihood."

Fleur reflected upon this and sighed.

"I have spoiled your career——" she began.

"Hush," he interrupted tenderly. "You have spoiled nothing. You have given me the sun, the moon and the stars, by placing yourself under my protection."

She was too moved to answer.

The coach rolled grandly along the highway. It was a sunny day and there were many passengers. Some well-attired gentlemen and their ladies, chattering about the state of the country under the new Queen, and recently assembled Parliament. There was a brisk genial atmosphere in the coach which did much to hearten Fleur who had never before travelled in a public conveyance. It seemed to remove her far from the old life she had led as Lady St. Cheviot. This new freedom and the happiness of being loved and cared for by Peveril brought her a deep pure joy.

Only once, Fleur allowed herself to dwell on the grim

horror of that night when St. Cheviot had destroyed her room.

"Your painting of my hands—that little gem—oh, how it grieved me to see it smashed!"

He looked down at the perfect hands in the lace mittens which the kindly Mrs. Gomme had given her.

"Do not grieve," he said. "I shall paint you again."

They paused outside the first toll house, while the guard paid his dues to the turnpike.

Afterwards on the high-road again they sat with their fingers tightly locked, while the coach wheels rumbled through Uxbridge. Fleur stared out at the outskirts of London—the crowded dwellings, the dirty streets, the milling crowds of people. This scene flung Rabbina into transports. It was the most thrilling day of the little country girl's life.

"Lawks-a-mussy—I am in London!" she kept saying.

So at length they came to St. Martin's le Grand where everybody got out of the coach. They took the final journey in a hansom cab which was the latest thing in private conveyance. It carried them to the Royal Vauxhall Gardens. Fleur was unutterably relieved when at last Peveril conducted her into the presence of his good friends, the Taylors.

This couple occupied a small shabby house in a genteel but modest terrace constructed in the reign of George III. Sydney Terrace led off a broader and more elegant row of houses, about two minutes' walk from the river.

When Peveril rang the front-door bell, the Taylors were up in the room which Luke had made into a studio and where he painted in his spare time. This being Saturday, he was home earlier than usual.

Luke's pleasure was genuine and unbounded when he saw who stood upon the doorstep. He loved Peveril Marsh and had held his family and hunchback sister, Elspeth, in respect and affection. Luke had deeply deplored it when Peveril took the decision to abandon London and seek a home in the country for his invalid sister's sake.

Alice joined her husband. They looked with some surprise at the young woman in grey, and her servant who accompanied them. Peveril clapped an arm over his friend's shoulder and said:

"I have much to tell you. I would be uncommonly indebted to you if I might beg your hospitality, not only for myself, but for this lady and her servant."

"Most certainly," the Taylors chorused, being both of warm and hospitable nature.

Luke was not an inspired artist like his old school friend but sufficient of one to recognize the extraordinary talent shewn by young Peveril Marsh.

Delighted to see him again, Luke led the way through a narrow hall into parlour. Mrs. Taylor followed, keeping an inquisitive eye on the young lady. She wondered if she could possibly be wife to Peveril.

Rabbina was sent down into the basement, there to give a hand with the evening meal which was being prepared by Emma, the Taylors' own maid-of-all-work.

Now in Alice's little drawing-room, which Fleur could see at once was furnished as tastefully as a poor pocket would allow, Peveril spoke, running nervous fingers through his bright brown curls.

"It is a long story, my friends," he said. "But first I ask you for your complete discretion. It is imperative that no one should know that I am here, nor must you divulge the name of the lady."

"Pray untie your bonnet and be at home, my dear," said Alice Taylor, turning to Fleur. Fleur did so and at the sight of the singular beauty of the delicate face in the frame of rose-gilt curls, both the Taylors forgot their manners and stared. Peveril smiled. He read their minds. He nodded at Luke, who was a short, stoutly built, merry-eyed fellow, with long hair brushed into a curl over his forehead—and the side whiskers much affected by gentlemen in London these days.

"Yes," said Peveril, "she *is* beautiful, is she not?"

"Quite out of the ordinary!" exclaimed Luke, the appreciative artist in him stirring as he looked into Fleur's violet-blue eyes.

"Have the goodness, you two, not to raise the poor girl's blushes in such a manner!" Alice chided them. Fleur looked gratefully at the older woman who had a pair of sparkling eyes under a fringe of dark brown hair, and seemed both motherly and kind.

"Go ahead—tell us all, boy," said Luke. "I do assure

you we can find room for you both, can we not, Alice, my love? You can sleep in my studio and our one guest chamber is at the service of this lady whom you wish to protect. But we are tremendously inquisitive to know what this means, and what you have been doing since you left London."

Peveril took one of Fleur's hands in his. . . .

"All in good time," he said. "To start with I must make this lady's true identity known to you."

"Whatever secret you have to tell will be safe with us," said Luke.

"Listen then," said Peveril. "This is Fleur, Lady St. Cheviot—wife of the Baron of Cadlington in Buckinghamshire, whence we have just come."

The Taylors preserved a respectful silence whilst Peveril outlined for them the story of his first meeting with the notorious Lord St. Cheviot and later with his bride.

When it was finished, Luke Taylor rose, and putting his hands behind his back, scowled quite ferociously out of the window.

"By heavens, Peveril, your story has made my gorge rise!" he exclaimed. "The Baron of Cadlington must surely be insane."

"Sometimes I thought as much," whispered Fleur.

Alice—a warm-hearted, friendly young woman—forgot Fleur's title and high estate and flung both her arms around her.

"Poor blessèd lamb!" she said and tears sparkled in eyes that rarely found occasion for them. "What you have endured moves me to grief for you and loathing for him whom you call husband."

"I knew you would both feel this way," said Peveril, his handsome face flushed and grateful. "But you see the mess we are in. For all I know, I may have committed a murder last night. In any case all the devils in hell will be let loose if Hommock lives and St. Cheviot hears that his wife has gone away with me."

"I rejoice that you rescued her!" cried Alice. "And the poor lamb shall stay here in my care for just as long as she likes. You, too, Peveril, who are Luke's dearest friend."

Luke, also, turned and put a hand on the younger man's shoulder.

"Yes—stay with us and share our humble home," he said. "Great discretion is needed. You must lie low for some time to come. You, Peveril, can grow a beard and set to work a-painting under an assumed name."

Peveril fingered his chin and laughed ruefully.

"Yes—a beard would be a useful disguise. As for painting—I must make that a sideline, as you do, Luke, and earn my bread in the world of commerce."

"You have a good education and a quick mind—I am confident I can find you something," said Luke.

"But what of Lady St. Cheviot?" began Alice. Fleur put a finger against her lips.

"Not *that*—I beg of you—ever again. To you I am Fleur."

"Bless you," said the emotional Alice embracing her. "And I must set to work to fatten you up—you are most abominably thin, poor dear. Some weeks of rest in my little home and my strengthening jellies and home-made cordials and you will soon recover health and strength."

"But how shall she be called?" asked Peveril. "She dare not even return to the name of her youth—which was Roddney."

"Alas, no," said Fleur.

Peveril gave her a long yearning look.

"Would that I could give her *my* name," he said in a low voice.

Her cheeks coloured. Her gaze met his then she turned away for she was afraid of her own heart's throbbing. He added:

"One day—*one day it shall be*, please God."

"I have an idea," said Alice brightly. "She can for the moment pass as a young widow and call herself by my maiden name, which was Trelawny—I am Cornish by birth. There—Fleur Trelawny—does it not sound nice?"

"Very nice," said Fleur. "And I cannot tell you how much more I like it than *Lady St. Cheviot*," and she shuddered violently.

"It is an excellent plan, Alice. Mrs. Trelawny she shall be," seconded Luke.

"As for her own kinswoman—Mrs. de Vere, who betrayed her into that dreadful man's hands—*she* deserves to be roasted," added Alice, tossing her handsome head.

At the memory of her weak and wicked Cousin Dolly, Fleur shuddered again. She would not dare to be seen in the vicinity of Knightsbridge Green where her cousin and the family still lived.

"I, too, must find work of a kind. I cannot be entirely beholden to you, Alice, or to *you*," she added, looking at Peveril.

But he caught her hand in his and kissed it.

"Fleur, dearest, do not take from me my greatest privilege—or my hope for the future," he said in a low ardent tone.

She sighed but her eyes filled with tears—of happiness this time. To be here with these good cheerful people who were ready to cherish her was sweetest balm to her deeply injured heart.

That night, supping with the Taylors and with Peveril, she felt a contentment that she had not known since her parents' death.

Chapter Fourteen

All through this same day—the day which marked a new and better existence for Fleur—chaos reigned at Cadlington House. It smashed the peace of the golden summer's morning from the moment that Mrs. Dinglefoot's piercing scream brought most of the staff scurrying up from the kitchens and pantries to her ladyship's bedchamber. They all thought at first that the housekeeper had entered the poor "mad lady's" room to find her lying dead on her bed.

Nothing would have pleased Mrs. D. more. But instead when she unlocked the door, she found the apartment deserted, the bird flown, and the wolfhound whining and scratching to be let out.

Ivor had been just about to saddle his horse and ride to London to deliver the papers to his master who was awaiting them. They were intending to cross the Channel on the next packet to Boulogne.

He stood watching Mrs. D. ransack the room—screaming and spluttering like an outraged hen. The woman could not get over the fact that Alpha had allowed my lady to go.

"Out of the window—and someone down below to aid her. But the bitch was trained to savage her if she went near that window. I cannot comprehend it!" wailed the woman, her hairy face red and perspiring.

"Alpha was friendly with the young artist," Ivor reminded her and added: "His lordship will cut your throat for this."

Mrs. Dinglefoot put a hand to her flabby throat and groaned.

"I did all I could—what more could I have done, except sleep in the same chamber as that wretch. Oh, if I ever lay hands on her again, I shall make her suffer for this."

"You never will," prophesied the valet darkly. "I warrant my lady has friends whom you know naught about."

"Who?—tell me," spluttered Mrs. D.

"The painter is certainly one," muttered Ivor. "Who else could it be? He has eluded *me*—the cunning young reptile."

"*Your* throat will be slit, as well as mine, you cockerel," screamed Mrs. D. in a passion of rage, as she flung the bedclothes from Fleur's abandoned bed on to the floor.

"You were in charge of her ladyship—not I!" Ivor snarled back. And the two stood there, bickering, snapping at each other—shrinking with fear of the master to whom they were responsible.

Then one of the younger servants came running into the room and bobbed to the housekeeper.

"Please ma'am—Rabbina, the new between-maid, is missing and has not slept in her bed last night."

"What can that have to do with her ladyship——?" began the housekeeper. Ivor interrupted harshly:

"Imbecile—*there* you have the help from within—the painter and this girl, Rabbina, have spirited Lady St. Cheviot away."

"Then go after them!" screamed Mrs. D. "Do not stand there wasting time, you fool."

The rest of the staff who overheard, fled along the great corridors of the house, whispering together excitedly. It was plain that there was going to be trouble. But more than one of them spoke with compassion of the Baron's martyred bride.

"I for one am glad the poor thing has escaped," said a young footman who had received kindness in his time from the Lady of Cadlington.

"I, for another," whispered a scullery wench. "I saw her in the gardens before the baby was born and she looked like an angel."

Throughout the rest of the July morning the staff, headed by Mrs. D., searched the house, the tower, the gardens and the surrounding park, in case they should discover the body of her ladyship. She might have taken her life.

Later they learned the truth. At noon Seth Hommock's nephew was discovered lying in a ditch half a mile from the great gates. He had a nasty wound on his skull and was semi-conscious when picked up and brought home by a carrier.

Not until sundown did he open his eyes and speak—then it was to tell his uncle what he knew. The older Hommock conveyed the information to Ivor and Mrs. D. Lady St. Cheviot had been driven away in a gig, drawn by a piebald mare, and in the company of Peveril Marsh and Rabbina.

Mrs. D. ground her teeth and called down hell's vengeance on Peveril—and on young Rab. The next thing was to discover who had driven the gig. Jack Hommock could not remember. He was addled in his mind and said he had never before set eyes on the fellow. It was no one from Whiteleaf—that was all he knew.

The cowman had no notion where his truant daughter could have gone, so he was no help. It seemed that the truth could no longer be kept from his lordship. Someone must tell him of his wife's escape.

That "someone" had to be Ivor.

When the moment came, Ivor, the bully, became a craven coward. He stammered excuses as he stood before his master in the coffee-room of the inn in Folkestone where St. Cheviot impatiently awaited him.

"Idiot—fool of fools!" St. Cheviot shouted. "You and that old imbecile Dinglefoot—letting my wife escape while you lay in bed snoring like the sloths you are. I could slit your gullets—the pair of you."

His face was livid with rage. His mind crawled with bitter, venomous thoughts that writhed around the memory of his young wife.

It was not that he wanted her back in his embrace. He harboured too strong a hatred of her appalling heritage. His former lechery had turned to a sadistic desire to break her proud spirit and humble her to the dust.

In Denzil's evil mind—incapable of a pure or high motive—he was positive now that the young painter had been Fleur's paramour. As such, he must be routed out and the insolent flame of his life extinguished. As for Fleur, she should end the rest of her days disgraced and destitute. And St. Cheviot would find a more suitable wife to bear him an heir.

Meanwhile, Denzil's fury was further inflamed by the

mental pictures he drew of those two together. All Fleur's pale slender beauty was for Peveril Marsh now—a humble youth hardly yet grown to full manhood. All given to him willingly, with the heat, the rapture, the desire she had denied St. Cheviot himself.

"I shall kill them both," St. Cheviot said through his clenched teeth.

He swung round to the valet and blazed at him.

"Get out. I shall cancel my passage to France. We return immediately to Cadlington."

PART III

Chapter One

Two years later. In London, on the 8th February, a cold gusty day, a tall prematurely white-haired gentleman wearing side whiskers and sombrely dressed in a dark overcoat and cape, with flat oval-shaped hat, stepped out of the coach which had just brought him from Plymouth to London.

When he took off his hat one could see many scars—of jagged and livid hue—spoiling what had once been a fine and noble countenance. A face darkly bronzed as though the owner had been exposed for a long time to tropical suns.

For a few moments, he stood shivering in the biting wind which blew down Newgate Street. One or two feathery flakes of snow settled upon his cape and hat for an instant then vanished. But sombre though the weather, the streets were full of people and much decorated. In some places workmen sat astride the lamps, busily polishing the glass. It seemed to the new arrival that there were preparations in progress for some big event. He, having just arrived from Australia, and out of touch with his own country, knew nothing. He felt that he must make some enquiries. He walked into a nearby tavern and joined some of the gentlemen who sat drinking and smoking in the Commercial Room.

What he heard surprised and interested the returned traveller.

The day after tomorrow the young Queen Victoria was to be married to Prince Albert, son of the Duke of Saxe-Coburg-Gotha.

The returned traveller raised his tankard of foaming ale. "Long live the Queen," he said respectfully.

Later, as he emerged into the bitter streets again, he

found it odd to remember that he had not set foot on his native soil since the young Victoria succeeded to the throne.

"All is changed in England. And heavens knows what further changes I shall find," he thought.

Buttoning up his collar, he then made his way to a firm of solicitors whose offices were situated not far from St. Paul's Churchyard. The name was engraved upon door and dusty windows. *Nonseale, Nonseale & Duckett.*

Once inside he asked a clerk if Mr. Caleb Nonseale were in. He received the disappointing reply that Mr. Caleb was out of town attending the funeral of a country client. He would not be back until tomorrow.

"So be it, I will return tomorrow," said the traveller.

"What name shall I say, sir?" asked the clerk.

"You do not recognize me?"

The clerk, a gangling lad, peered shortsightedly at the tall gentleman's scarred face and shook his head.

"No, sir."

"Then I have changed a great deal more than *you*, young Benjamin Drew, who are much grown in height since last we met."

"Lawks, sir—then you know me?"

"Yes. You have received me here many times—my uncle before me. But no matter—I will not divulge my identity for the moment. It shall be kept as a surprise for Mr. Nonseale."

And smiling, the gentleman turned and walked from the office leaving the clerk to gape after him.

The traveller did not stand long in the cold greyness of the winter's morning. He stopped a passing cab, stepped into it and gave the address of a house on Knightsbridge Green.

"I fear this will be a shock for Dolly, too," he thought, "and for Archibald and the others."

It was snowing fast by the time the scarred gentleman pounded the brass knocker on the door of the narrow house facing the Green.

He was astounded when he was told by the butler who answered his enquiry that Mrs. de Vere no longer resided there.

The butler went on to inform the visitor that Mrs. de

Vere had married again, some eighteen months ago, and was now called Lady Sidpath.

"Lady Sidpath!" The returned traveller repeated the name with astonishment. "Then Mr. de Vere died?"

"Oh yes, sir, in India—it would be two years ago."

"Alas, poor Archibald! This is the first loss of which I am to hear," thought the stranger.

Once or twice at White's, the traveller in the past had played a game of cards with Sidpath and lost to him.

The traveller now heard that Dolly—Lady Sidpath—lived in Berkeley Square. The butler added that the two young ladies, Miss Imogen and Miss Isabel, were still unwed, and lived under their step-papa's roof.

The scarred gentleman wasted no further time but made his way to Berkeley Square.

He was lucky enough to find Lady Sidpath at home. The powdered footman who received him, ushered him into a handsome, if ornate drawing-room. The caller said:

"Be so good as to inform her ladyship that I am a relative—from abroad."

The next moment, he heard Dolly's familiar high-pitched voice out in the hall. The door opened and she walked in.

She was dressed as though about to go out. He could see at once that she had put on much weight and was no longer at all attractive, despite the richness of her velvet dress and jacket, her handsome sable muff and tippet, and smart plumed bonnet.

On high-heeled boots she tapped across the parquet floor towards him. She began:

"You must pardon me, sir, but I cannot understand what Jenkins means when he says you are a relative from abroad. I have no relatives——"

Then she stopped. For she had come close to the tall gentleman and was peering up into his face. All her colour had vanished, leaving only the redness of the rouge upon it. She put a hand to her lips and gave a scream.

"Mercy on us! It cannot be—it *cannot*."

"Yes, Dolly, it is. Harry Roddney back from his watery grave," said the man in a sombre voice. "Back, alas, without my beloved wife who lies for evermore beneath those cruel waves. My poor beautiful Hélène!"

But he was speaking to himself now for the fat little woman with her furs and jewels and feathers had screamed again and crumpled up in a dead faint at his feet.

He picked her up, placed her on the sofa and rang for a servant. The footman fetched her ladyship's maid who came rushing down with burnt feathers to apply to her ladyship's nostrils. Dolly moaned, spluttered and opened her eyes. Those greedy furtive eyes from under their blackened lashes stared wildly at the man who had just revealed himself as Harry Roddney. She shivered like one with ague, and stuttered his name.

"Harry! Merciful Heavens, *Harry!*"

"I must ask your pardon for subjecting you to such a shock, Cousin," he said.

Now she sat bolt upright, her face suffused with colour and her eyes bolting. She looked like one in the throes of a ghastly fright. She waved the maid aside and bade her leave the room. Then she looked up with that same wild gaze.

"Yes, it is he—scarred and grey, but all the same it is he. The closer I look, the more certain I become."

"You can indeed be certain," said Harry Roddney with a brief laugh. "I assure you, I am no ghost."

With trembling fingers, Dolly pressed a handkerchief to her lips.

"But you were drowned!" she wailed. "You perished in the storm that swamped the Packet on that Channel crossing, three years ago!"

He seated himself by the sofa and crossed his arms over his chest. "No, Dolly, I did not perish. The others did—all—including my adored wife. I was the sole survivor."

"Then why did we not know? Where have you been? Explain to me or I shall go out of my mind and still believe that you are some dreadful apparition."

Dear Heaven, she thought, if he but knew the ugly terrors that swamped her guilt-stained soul. For now another apparition stood beside Harry Roddney—although this one was indeed in her fancy—the slender form of the young girl whom Dolly had so abominably betrayed. Fleur, whom she had sold into the hands of the vilest of men, in order to get her miserable debts paid by the bridegroom. Ever since Fleur's wedding-day when Dolly had knelt with hypocritical piety in the church her conscience had pricked her. She had never heard a word of Fleur, until after the birth of the child. What had happened *then*—the scene with St. Cheviot, who had in fury and indignation snarled at her—Dolly hardly dared think about in this moment. Neither dared she dwell on the horrible possibility that since then, for all she knew, Fleur might have been hounded to her death.

She sat trembling and sweating, listening to her cousin's story.

It appeared that once in the water, after the Packet sank, he had tried to hold up his drowning wife, but in vain. Hélène's lovely head sank beneath the waves and for all his endeavors, was finally sucked under, lost to him. After, he clung to a floating spar, and although tossed and drenched by the terrible waves in the teeth of a cruel storm, managed to keep alive for several hours. He shuddered as he recalled the awful scene; the capsized Packet sinking, settling to her doom. The screams of the injured and dying; the last gurgling moans of those who fought the waves but went under, when all strength was gone.

Harry drifted awhile and when he was at the pitch of exhaustion, found himself within short distance of a sailing vessel which—although reeling—seemed able to ride the storm. Afterwards, he learned that it was a Greek merchant ship bound from the Port of London to Athens. Of his actual rescue he remembered nothing. For it was then that he had received the terrible injury to face and head which had so altered his appearance, and impaired his memory.

One of the ship's officers who spoke a little English described the rescue to him. How the officer of the watch had seen his head bobbing there on the water and they had thrown a rope to him. Harry had managed to tie it round his waist successfully, but as they hauled him up the ship's side a sudden gust of wind, which was blowing at gale force, hurled him against the ship's side. He had known a searing pain. The blood gushed down his face and blinded him. Then for him—total darkness while the Greek sailors pulled him up on to the deck. He did not recover consciousness for nearly a week. By that time the ship had sailed away from the English coast, well on its way to

Greece. Because of his fine health his body recovered rapidly, but his face remained badly scarred and his mind confused and wandering. He could remember nothing whatsoever of his past—neither his name nor his history.

Strange bitter blow to descend twice upon a man who once had a fine intelligent brain. Once before in his youth, set upon by assailants, he had been reduced to the same sorry state. As before, he wandered in a mist. Since he had neither money nor papers upon him—for he had removed his coat in the effort to save his wife—no one could discover who or what he was or whence he came. Only when he began to speak, they judged he was of English extraction.

He was invited to remain on board and give a hand if he so chose, because there had been an outbreak of smallpox and they were short of crew. So for a month or two Harry Roddney turned sailor and worked with a Greek crew on a dingy ship, and under conditions that should have killed him but did not. Fate willed that he should survive.

He suffered severely, much given to fevers and fantasies. However, he recovered and even grew attached to the sea and the life on board. So he continued to serve under the Greek captain. Because he was a gentleman of breeding and intelligence, they found him useful as an interpreter at the English-speaking ports which they visited.

A year went by. Those at home had presumed him dead and at the bottom of the Channel. But Harry remained on board the Greek ship. They called at Botany Bay, Port Jackson and finally sailed into Sydney Harbour. Ashore here, Harry encountered an Australian doctor who took an enormous interest in the bronzed scarred Englishman with the lost memory. He prevailed upon him to remain in Sydney. The doctor felt that he could help him recover his memory. And so Harry stayed behind and became much attached to the Australian physician and his wife.

It was just before Christmas that another and lesser accident changed his whole life again. He was driving in the doctor's gig through the streets of Sydney. The horse took fright and bolted. The gig overturned. The unfortunate doctor was killed instantly but his passenger escaped with a broken collar bone and slight concussion. Upon regaining consciousness, Harry found that he had also recovered the memories of his past. It was a tremendous and awe-inspiring moment for him. Once again he knew himself to be Sir Harry Roddney.

He soon recovered from the shock of his return to normal. But he was at first anguished when he remembered how he had lost Hélène, his idolized wife. However, he soon experienced deep happiness recalling that he had somebody to live for now—his own dear daughter, Fleur. He pined to get back to her, and to Pillars—their home. He could only imagine what grief it must have been for her to presume that she had lost both parents. Poor beloved orphan! And it would be months before he could complete the voyage around the world and reach England again.

The doctor's widow provided him with the means, and he boarded a new clipper ship belonging to some American builders and which was on its first voyage round the world. This vessel was modern and fast and if uncomfortable, had at least the virtue of speed, which was what Harry Roddney needed.

The clipper had put him ashore at Plymouth twenty-four hours ago, and here he was.

Walking up and down the drawing-room, Harry addressed himself as much to the air as to his Cousin Dolly who had listened to this astounding story in profoundest astonishment.

"It seemed that I would never reach you in whose care I left Fleur," said Harry, "and with whom I hoped to find her again. Just now I called upon Mr. Nonseale in order to get my own money. But Nonseale was away so I came straight here."

He paused and stood looking down at Dolly, hands locked behind his back.

"Fleur is with you still?" he asked. "My own darling! Barely eighteen when I left her, she must now be nearly twenty-one years. Ah, Cousin, speak to me and tell me how my little dear has fared all this time without her loving parents."

Dolly did not answer. She seemed struck dumb. Indeed, the wicked heartless little woman looked as though she were about to swoon again. Then for the first time Harry felt a thrill of fear.

"What is it? Why do you look at me like that? *What has*

happened to Fleur? Speak!" And now it was as though an icy hand clutched his heart. "In God's name, *is Fleur no longer living?*"

Dolly groaned. She could see there was nothing for it but to tell the truth, or half the truth, and whitewash herself as best she could.

"So far as I know, Fleur lives," she stuttered.

Harry's eyes, still the blue handsome eyes of the man whom Hélène had loved so madly, regained their sparkle.

"Thank God," he said. "Then is she here?"

"No. She . . . she was married soon after your . . . your . . . you were drowned, I mean, thought to be drowned."

"*Married*—to whom?"

Dolly gulped.

"To . . . to the Baron of Cadlington, Lord St. Cheviot."

Harry Roddney uttered an exclamation.

"Good heavens, my little Fleur become Lady St. Cheviot? Impossible!"

Dolly shut her eyes tightly as though to shut out the sight of Harry's altered face. She could only sit there gibbering, wishing that she had never arranged that shameful marriage.

She stuttered:

"Indeed, Harry . . . yes . . . Fleur was married a few months after you left her—an orphan as she believed."

"Where is she living?"

"At Cadlington. Her husband's country house."

"Then I shall not see her today. She is in Buckinghamshire," exclaimed Harry in a disappointed voice.

Dolly nodded. She must be the unluckiest woman in London, she groaned to herself. How could she possibly have guessed that Harry would return to this life? And everything else was going wrong. The twins were "on the shelf." The one or two gentlemen who had proposed to them, they had rejected, either because they were too old or too ugly. No young and good-looking suitors had approached them. Cyril, her son, had done badly since he left Oxford and eloped with a common actress—which had greatly upset Dolly and discouraged her, for she had so longed to shine in society with her new title. And her second husband, Bertie, since his fit, had become a horrid slavering old man, who was so jealous that he kept her chained to his side and allowed her little chance to enjoy herself as the rich Lady Sidpath.

"I must know more!" exclaimed Harry. "Is my darling happy? Does St. Cheviot make her a good husband?"

Dolly panted and waved a burnt feather in front of her nose again. She stuttered and stammered: She didn't really know how Fleur was, she had been anxious because she had not heard from the child for so long. St. Cheviot was a strange, inhospitable man. Neither he nor Fleur had answered her letters. Nobody in town had seen St. Cheviot lately. And so on.

Harry grew anxious. He wondered why Fleur had retracted all she had said when last he had seen her. To him and to her mother she had repeatedly stressed her reluctance to receive St. Cheviot's intentions.

"I must go at once to Cadlington," began Harry in a low voice.

But Dolly had fainted again. Now, feeling it a certainty that all was not well with Fleur, Harry handed Dolly over to her maid and left the house.

When Dolly recovered, she had screaming hysterics which brought her invalid husband out of his bed, demanding to know what it was all about. While Dolly concocted a dozen feeble answers and set to wheedling the old nobleman to take her to a watering-place on the Continent immediately, Harry betook himself to the house of an old friend. He could get no more out of the hysterical Dolly but he *must* endeavour to secure the latest news of Fleur. He could not wait until Caleb Nonseale returned to London. Tomorrow of course the family lawyer, who was Fleur's guardian, would be able to enlighten him.

Harry was singularly unlucky, for the friend he called upon with eager hope, a man with whom he used to play cards and who also knew the Baron—had died a few months ago. His widow had sold up the place.

Deeply depressed, Harry turned into Piccadilly, shivering a little in the cold air. It was no longer snowing but the wind blew gustily and he was used to the heat of the Australian sun. What should he do now? It was too late to get a coach to Cadlington. He must wait for tomorrow, by which time he would also be able to see Nonseale which was essential, for Harry needed his papers—and money.

God alone knew what had happened to Pillars and the affairs of his estate, he thought gloomily. Alas, could it be that Fleur—the innocent darling—had mourned her dead parents to bitterly that in her desolation she had turned to St. Cheviot?

"God grant that he has been good to her. If he has not—*God help him!*" Harry Roddney muttered the words grimly as he walked down Piccadilly.

Now luck favoured him—at the same time bringing him face to face with the truth. He was just about to pass a young couple who were standing by a hansom cab (the gentleman was paying the driver) when the young lady turned her face towards him. At once Harry recognized her. He gave an exclamation as he saw that homely but pleasant countenance, faintly pitted after her attack of smallpox.

"Why, Catherine Foster!" he cried, and doffed his hat.

The young lady, who wore a fur-trimmed bonnet and pelisse and was holding her dark brown velvet skirts above the snow-wet pavement stared at him, then gave a gasping cry:

"*Sir Harry Roddney!* But no, it cannot be. It is his double. It is is a ghost! Sir Harry is dead!"

The hansom moved off with a jingle of bells. Now the young gentleman turned to Harry and was recognized by him.

"Tom Quinley!" Harry greeted him.

Tom put an arm around his wife and in his turn exclaimed:

"*Sir Harry Roddney!* It is scarcely possible. . . ."

"Oh, Tom, have I seen an apparition?" stuttered poor bewildered Cathy who was beginning to doubt her own eyesight.

"You are right, Cathy dear, it is indeed I," said Harry. "I fear that this is a shock to you and will be to all who knew me. I must explain to you what has happened. Where are you bound? Where can we talk?"

The young couple exchanged glances. Tom Quinley said:

"Cathy is now my wife, sir. We were about to call upon my aunt, Lady Quinley, who occupies this house. We are on a visit to London. My uncle, Lord Quinley, has a seat inside the Abbey in order to be a witness of the Queen's marriage, the day after tomorrow."

He paused, for Harry Roddney, clapping a hand on the boy's shoulder, interrupted:

"Yes, yes. And I most heartily congratulate you on your marriage, Tom. But I am mad with anxiety about my daughter. After three years' absence—with no news of my dear one—you can picture my mental anguish. I have just now been told by my cousin, Dolly, that Fleur is married. But for some peculiar reason she could give me no news of Fleur. Cathy—you were my child's dearest friend. *You* must be able to tell me something of her?"

Once again the Quinleys exchanged glances. Harry's quick eye noted that Cathy looked distressed. He was prey to the deepest anxiety. But young Tom intervened.

"We cannot stay out here in this bitter wind. Dear Sir Harry, all of us who knew you will rejoice at your return from the grave. But I fear that any news we can give you of Fleur is far from good."

"Reassure me that she is alive!" Harry turned to Catherine. Her eyes filled with tears.

"Alive, yes, but——"

"When did you last see her?" the father cut in again, profoundly agitated.

"Six months ago," said Catherine, "when Tom and I were in London. We reside most of the year in our country home."

"Then Fleur is in London? Can I see her tonight? Is she not at Cadlington?" Harry asked one question after another.

"Come inside, sir," said Tom Quinley, "we will go into my aunt's house and talk." A footman opened the front door. The three of them walked into the well-lighted hall.

Lady Quinley was informed of what had happened. She at once offered hospitality to Sir Harry, whom she had not actually met but about whom she had heard much from Tom's mother.

A few moments later, Harry was seated in the drawing-room, sipping a glass of wine, spreading his hands to the blaze of a fire and hearing the awful truth—as far as Catherine Quinley and her husband knew it.

Chapter Two

On this same day that Harry Roddney sat listening to what the young Quinleys had to tell him, Fleur, one-time Lady St. Cheviot, picked her way daintily through the snow which lay thickly on Sydney Terrace and knocked on the front door of the home which she and Peveril shared with the Taylors.

Rabbina let her in. The little maid from Whiteleaf looked much the same except for her new uniform striped cotton dress, starched apron and little frilled cap.

Fleur was flushed and breathless. A hat box dangled from a ribbon on one wrist, and she carried a parcel under the other arm. She greeted Rabbina with:

"Mercy on us, what a day! It has started to snow again and the wind is bitter cold! Are the master and mistress in?"

"No, ma'am, they're both out," said Rabbina and took the boxes from the young lady who walked into the little house, appreciating its warmth. So dark had the February day become, that Rabbina hastened to light candles and place them on the table in the dining-room where Fleur untied her bonnet.

"I have everything I need now. Where is Mr. Marsh?"

"He was painting an hour ago but just after you went a-shopping he called to me and said that there was not enough light and he could not finish the portrait."

"And then?" enquired Fleur smoothing the folds of her grey cashmere dress.

"Then, ma'am, Mr. Warren—that gentleman who so often comes here—called to see Mr. Marsh. They went off together in a hurry. If you please, ma'am, I thought Mr. Marsh seemed put out."

"*Put out*, Rab? What do you mean?"

"I heard him say: 'Good heavens, Warren, you have me much puzzled and not a little disturbed.' And then Mr. Warren said something about some gentleman of title whose agents had refused to accept Mr. Warren's word that this picture was not for sale. But I heard no more, ma'am, and I hope I did not do wrong to listen."

"That is right, Rabbina. Now you may go," said Fleur.

She stood a moment, puzzling out what she had just heard. She leaned a hand on the mantelpiece and looked thoughtfully into the fire. It was cosy in here. The gloom of the February day was dispelled by the firelight and the gentle gleam from the three-branch candelabra on the dining-table. Fleur's reflection in the mirror over the mantelpiece showed little alteration in the great beauty that Peveril had adored and painted in the tower at Cadlington. Now, at nearly twenty-one years of age, Fleur retained the exquisite transparency of skin—the lustre of fair hair with the curls pinned to one side. But she was no longer the terror-stricken girl whom Peveril had first seen and adored. She had found peace here in this modest happy-go-lucky home with Peveril and his artist friends.

She began once more to try and understand what Rabbina had just told her. Why should Peveril have gone off in a state that Rab described as "put out"? What had Warren come to tell him?

Arthur Warren was the owner of a small but prosperous art gallery in Ludgate Hill, and Luke Taylor's godfather. After seeing Peveril's work it had not taken Mr. Warren long to recognize the touch of genius in the young man's work. In particular he had praised the portraits Peveril had painted over the period of the last two years, both of Fleur and Luke's wife, Alice. Whenever Warren came here he tried to induce Peveril to let him exhibit his work, and could never understand why the young man refused. His painting was only his hobby, Peveril maintained. He would neither display nor sell. But the more he painted, the more Arthur Warren argued with him and endeavoured to make him change his mind. Added to which Peveril refused the job which Mr. Warren offered him in his business. But gratefully he accepted as much work as Mr. Warren cared to commission, which could be done at home.

Later on, Luke had explained to his godfather that

through no fault of his own, Peveril Marsh was forced to lie low for a time. Also that it was imperative that his name should not be mentioned in any art circles lest he might be traced to this address. Mr. Warren, who was very fond of his godson, accepted this explanation and gave his assurance that he would never divulge Peveril's identity. But he sent all the masterpieces which were in need of restoration to the young painter to work upon. Also orders received from clients for great paintings and portraits to be copied. Peveril faithfully carried out these commissions. It was work he did not care for, but he was glad of the money.

Looking back over the last two years, Fleur thought with deep tenderness of the young man whom she had grown to love more than life itself. It was for her sake that he had to remain *incognito* and abandon all hopes of becoming a great portrait painter. For her sake that he rarely went out in public, save to walk with her and their friends; or take a coffee or tankard of ale with Luke in one of the city taverns.

How wonderful he was! thought Fleur. Uncomplaining about his existence as an *inconnu*, seemingly contented so long as he could be with *her*. She owed him not only her freedom from a living death at Cadlington, but now her livelihood, for it was he who by his efforts for Mr. Warren, paid for her keep as well as his own in this household.

After her arrival here, Fleur had collapsed. It had taken all Peveril's devotion and Alice's tender care to bring her back to normal. After some months of recuperation, Fleur then insisted upon doing her share of work. She, once the spoiled daughter of the Roddneys, brought up as a great lady who would never need soil her hands, became "Mrs. Trelawny," a teacher of pianoforte. For this was where Fleur's own talents were of vast use. Her dear mother's insistence that she should be taught to play and to practise, bore rich fruit in these days of necessity. She advertised for pupils, and found them. After her initial success in preparing one small candidate for examination, she was much sought after in the neighbourhood. While Alice went about her duties in the house and the men plied their particular trade, Fleur sat daily at her piano, coaxing and teaching her small pupils. Within a short space of time she grew to be much loved for her patience and charm. But few ever saw her out of doors during that first year, save in black and heavily veiled.

That Fleur and Peveril had dangerous enemies, they were well aware. St. Cheviot, Caleb Nonseale, Cousin Dolly, who, they feared, might not hesitate to betray Fleur a second time. These were the dark spectres of the past which Fleur wished to eliminate.

Eighteen months ago, quite by accident, Fleur ran into her old and much loved friend, Catherine Quinley. It had been on a sunny day—a Sunday morning, when strolling in Kensington Gardens. Fleur, Peveril and the Taylors were approaching the Round Pond when they came face to face with the Quinleys. Catherine had at once rushed to Fleur and greeted her, delightedly. Fleur was equally pleased to see her friend, but immediately warned Cathy how essential it was that St. Cheviot should never discover her or Peveril's whereabouts.

When Cathy had heard the long sorry tale of all that had taken place since Fleur's marriage she had been shocked to the bone. At once she gave her solemn promise—seconded by Tom—that she would keep "Mrs. Trelawny's" secret. But the Quinleys were horror-stricken by Fleur's story.

"You had every right to escape and seek a new life," Cathy assured her friend. "I always feared that you were not happy, my dearest, but could never dream that St. Cheviot was such a sink of iniquity."

And then to have given birth to a baby of dark skin—*what an appalling disaster*. Stupefying, indeed, the knowledge that there had been this black strain in the family through Fleur's mother whom Cathy remembered as the proud, dazzling Lady Roddney. Cathy wept with Fleur, convulsively pressing her fingers.

"My poor sweet friend, how you have suffered! It rends my heart. What can I do to help?"

Fleur had answered:

"Nothing—only keep my secret for I could not bear Denzil to find me. Still less could I support it if Denzil found Peveril and did an injury to him."

Cathy had questioned her about the young painter and gleaned from Fleur's rosy blush that it was in this young man now that all Fleur's hopes were centred, all her joy in life renewed. Because she was another man's wife, he had so far stemmed the tide of his passion. He was her friend and counsellor, but never once had he tried to take his reward from her lips.

"How you must admire and love him!" Cathy had exclaimed.

And Fleur had replied:

"Yes. Till I die, I shall love him and only death, itself, could separate us now. But alas, even though I am chained to a monster, I am still his wife and cannot break my marriage vows."

"That," Cathy had said with a sigh, "must be hard for young lovers passionately in love with each other."

However, a year after the meeting with the Quinleys who came often to see Fleur, Cathy herself had been able to convey the best of news to her old friend. For young Tom had heard news of St. Cheviot from Lord Quinley who frequented the same Clubs. St. Cheviot now openly stated that his wife had dark blood in her and had tricked him into marriage. He had approached the Ecclesiastical Courts in order to secure an annulment of his marriage.

This news had flung both Fleur and Peveril into a transport of joy. Safe in their hiding-place with the Quinleys to watch and listen and inform them, they waited to hear that the Court had granted the Baron of Cadlington his release.

Her whole body trembled with emotion in this moment as she remembered how, that evening for the first time, in this very room where she told him the news, Peveril had taken her in his arms as a lover and kissed her.

"Will you marry me when the day arrives that you can become my wife?" he had asked her. "I have waited so long, and I love you so well."

Whereupon she had looked up into those grey, deeply intelligent eyes, wound her arms about his neck, and answered:

"Yes, yes *and yes*. Oh, my dearest, this promises a joy almost too great!"

So for the first time their lips had met with a fervour—a hunger, that could at last find appeasement. She had thought never to know the thrill of passionate love—never to be capable of it; she, who had learned to shrink from the base and ruthless sensuality imposed upon her by Denzil St. Cheviot. She, whose wifehood had from the very start been degraded and outraged. But this was a new heroic love—the reward of Peveril's loyalty and patience. This was passing from a long nightmare into a golden dream. Peveril held her close. His firm lips insatiable for hers, restored her womanhood. There awakened in her that glorious desire to give, to *him*, her heart's love, her dearest friend.

Luke and Alice were quick to utter congratulations. They opened a bottle of wine and toasted the young couple's future.

Peveril and Fleur planned also to find a home of their own; perhaps a cottage at Richmond. Peveril was in a position to earn enough money to support his own wife. There would be no further need for her to continue with her teaching.

"I cannot give you the sort of home you deserve, alas——" Peveril began sadly. But Fleur, radiant and glowing in his arms, laid a finger across his lips forbidding him to sigh again.

"To share the smallest cottage with you, my dearest, will be more to me than a splendid mansion with any other man," she had assured him.

So for the past six months they had lived in blissful anticipation of their future. Gradually, through Tom, more rumours had reached them—fresh news of St. Cheviot. The annulment was signed and sealed. St. Cheviot was taking to himself a new wife. No doubt he meant to get his heir, Fleur observed to Peveril, and shuddered and blanched at the memory of things which Peveril preferred she should forget.

So she had tried to put them out of her mind and thinking of St. Cheviot's second wife—although not knowing who she was—could pity her.

After that, Fleur and Peveril began to move about more freely—once they even attended a Mozart concert in company with the Taylors—for they were all musical.

The day came when Arthur Warren at last persuaded Peveril to lend him a small painting which Peveril had done of Dorothy Dickins—a small pupil of Fleur's. A girl of eight years old, with long golden hair and a peculiarly sweet intelligent face. Peveril had made a lovely portrait of the little girl in her blue merino frock and white frilled pinafore, her hair tied with a blue ribbon, and Mr. Warren praised it highly. He begged to be allowed to exhibit it in his gallery. So it hung there, but unsigned. Mr. Warren, this very week, had received a dozen or more handsome offers for it from Collectors, and Connoisseurs.

Fleur pondered over the possibility that Peveril had gone off in a pother about the portrait because he feared the gentleman of title had persuaded Mr. Warren into selling it. Peveril was meticulous about keeping his word. No matter how handsome the price offered he would not wish to disappoint Dorothy's mother to whom it was promised.

Then suddenly a new fear smote Fleur—like a blast. *A gentleman of title* had made the offer. . . . Good heavens, it was surely not . . . *not* . . . but Fleur's thoughts carried her no further. She began to tremble. She could not endure the possibility that Peveril's painting might have been seen—and the masterly style recognized—by St. Cheviot, himself. But surely Mr. Warren would know the name of his client and would have told Peveril, she thought.

She and Peveril had been so happy. They had decided to solemnize their marriage a long way out of London. They had been singularly fortunate because Arthur Warren, himself, owned a small house on the outskirts of Bath. He had suggested that Fleur and Peveril go down there and be married in Bath, then borrow his home for the honeymoon. Like this, they could avoid publicity in London. So Peveril had arranged to take the coach down to the West Country tomorrow—see the parson, and make the necessary arrangements.

This morning Fleur had gone out to buy a new bonnet and fashionable shawl for her wedding. It was all deliciously exciting—so different from that nightmare time at Cousin Dolly's three years ago when she had lived in the grandeur of Archibald de Vere's house and been fitted by fashionable dressmakers and hated it all. For then it had been for *him*, the object of her loathing and contempt.

But now a feeling of oppression replaced her gaiety of spirit.

Luke and Alice—returning for dinner—found Fleur pacing up and down the studio. She at once rushed to her good friends and told them all that she knew.

Luke offered to go to Ludgate Hill and see Mr. Warren. He might find Peveril still there.

"You must eat first——" began Fleur.

"No—let him go—the food will wait but you cannot—I know your loving heart," broke in Alice. "Do not unduly distress yourself, my dear. I am sure your fears are groundless. No doubt Peveril, in view of his coming marriage, has decided to see the would-be purchaser who so greatly admires his work and is arranging to paint a portrait for him."

Fleur bit her lip. Alice added:

"Naturally your first fear is that some danger threatens him whom you love so dearly, but I do not for one moment think the titled gentleman is aught but a stray client of Arthur's. Do you, Luke?" she turned to her husband.

"I do not," he said.

But to comfort Fleur he departed forthwith. The two young ladies toyed with the light meal prepared by Alice's cook, and served by Rabbina, after which there was to be another period of anxious waiting for Fleur.

The afternoon seemed in itself to be forbidding. For soon after two o'clock the sky grew black with storm clouds. Spires and rooftops were blotted out. Indoors, the Taylors' little house was gay enough with the fire, and the lamp-light, but Fleur could not settle down to her sewing. She kept looking at the clock—or out of the window, peering down the length of Sydney Terrace which was shrouded in the winter gloom. Oh, where was Peveril? How come he had not even returned for his meal? What had *Luke* discovered when he reached the Warren Art Gallery?

"It is to be hoped," said Alice, "that there will be brighter weather for the marriage of our beloved Queen."

Suddenly Luke came home. A Luke less cheerful than he who had left home. As soon as the two young women saw him they felt a premonition of disaster. Fleur uttered a cry:

"Merciful heavens—*you come alone.* Where is my Peveril?"

"Courage, dearest," said Alice, although her own heart sank when she saw the change on her husband's countenance.

Luke quickly told them all he knew.

When he had reached the Warren Gallery he found his godfather alone, ill as though with shock.

Yesterday, he told Luke, two gentlemen arrived by private carriage and examined the pictures which Mr. Warren had for sale. One announced that he was the agent of a famous collector. The other, of less noble mien, gave no account of himself but was of Welsh extraction. They seemed particularly intrigued with the painting of Dorothy. The agent—he, too, gave no name but remained *incognito* —had heard about this portrait from a friend. Mr. Warren at once explained that it was not for sale. The gentleman then asked the name of the artist. That information was refused by Mr. Warren.

At this juncture of Luke's story, Fleur went as white as the snow outside and clung to Alice's strong arm.

"Dear God!" she gasped. "*A Welshman.* It may be *Ivor* . . . Denzil's valet. And the would-be buyer must be an agent from Denzil himself. He has remained our implacable enemy and even though our marriage is annulled and he is to remarry, his malice has not been assuaged. I believe that he has ferreted us out at last. I see it all! Until now, no work of Peveril's has appeared in public. But the gentleman who was with Ivor, and who has been paid to use his skill of detection, may have recognized the painting of Dorothy as Peveril's work. It bears the singular stamp of his genius. The lustre of the hair—the rich blue of the dress—the classic background, after the Italian school which Peveril favoured. They are outstanding qualities. I mentioned to you, Luke, and to you, Alice, that the whole thing was executed with just that same brilliance Peveril showed when he painted *my* portrait at Cadlington."

She finished this speech breathlessly, her very ears assailed by the horrid sound of the name *Cadlington.* It conjured up a hundred sinister memories.

Luke went on to tell her that the agent had grown angry —even offensive when Mr. Warren persisted in his refusal to sell, or even give the address of the painter. Finally the Welshman drew a pistol and threatened Mr. Warren, warning him not to attempt to seek police protection. Luke said, with a heavy sigh, his godfather was not a brave man but easily intimidated and this threat of violence to his person had terrified him. On his own admission he had been a coward. He agreed to fetch Peveril to the Gallery.

Here Fleur interrupted—clutching at the gold cross and chain which she wore about her throat.

"Did he then not realize that the Welshman might be Ivor—and that the Baron was surely behind all this?"

"Yes," said Luke. "And my godfather is now greatly remorseful for having dragged Peveril into danger. But his own life was in peril and when Peveril heard it he was determined that Mr. Warren who had been his friend and patron for two long years, should not suffer in his place. So Peveril went to the Gallery to face the music."

"Oh, Peveril, my love!" muttered Fleur, and her great eyes held a look of anguish.

Arthur Warren had been obstinate only on one point—that no ill should befall "Mrs. Trelawny" or the Taylors. He insisted that he went to find Peveril alone. The would-be purchasers must not follow, but wait in the Gallery until he and Peveril returned. The Welshman had said:

"We agree. But you are warned—any attempt to betray us or spirit the painter to a new hiding-place, and you, yourself, shall forfeit your life."

So the trembling art-dealer gave this promise and rushed to fetch Peveril. The moment he entered the Galleries Peveril saw Ivor, turned to Mr. Warren and said:

"You have brought me to my enemy. But whatever befalls me now, I pray you never while you live and breathe divulge to these men *her* whereabouts."

"Meaning me," breathed Fleur. She was ashen and Alice had to support her, she trembled so violently.

"Yes," said Luke. "And Mr. Warren said: 'As God is my judge I never will betray her address. My poor boy, I shall not forgive myself, but I feared to die.' "

Luke continued his story.

"The Welshman looked long and hard at Peveril then gave an ugly laugh.

" 'So—we were right. At last, Master Painter! Vile seducer of Lady St. Cheviot. At last we have found you.'

"Peveril answered:

" 'I am no seducer. It is your master who has earned that name. Do not dare to lay the crime at my door.'

"Ivor took little notice of this denial but added:

" 'For two years this good gentleman who has knowledge of the arts, and I, myself have searched the country seeking for a trace of you—we have searched all galleries and shops that might have held work that could be attributed to you. Lucky my lord kept the portrait you painted of *him* so that the expert was able to acquaint himself with your style.' "

Fleur, hearing this, uttered a cry:

"So I was right. Oh, God in heaven, St. Cheviot's hatred and fury have pursued us to the bitter end. Why did we ever think ourselves safe!"

Luke nodded miserably. He repeated all that Arthur Warren had told him. The good dealer would have come to see her, Luke said, but was prostrate from the shock of the outrage.

Ivor, it appeared, had said to Peveril:

"His lordship has ordered that you be taken to him at Cadlington, there to fight a duel, for he intends to wipe out the wrong you did him. You will accompany us, Master Painter, by coach to Whiteleaf."

"*A duel!*" Fleur repeated those words, her blood curdling. "Good heavens—St. Cheviot is the finest swordsman in England, and my poor Peveril a man of peace who has never learned to use either foils or pistols."

Luke, his honest face pale and agitated, nodded.

"I know. But Arthur said he put up no resistance against these gentlemen."

" 'I am willing to accept St. Cheviot's challenge. I will fight for my lady's honour,' said Peveril, and then turned to Luke, and added: 'Give my dear love to *her*. Tell her I could not, as a gentleman of honour, avoid this fight—deeply though I deplore it.' "

"When is it to be?" Fleur asked faintly.

"I do not know," said Luke. "As you know, my poor godfather swooned and when he recovered, his assistant told him that Peveril had been taken away by the two strangers. We presume—to Cadlington."

Luke added that Ivor had also told Peveril that the Baron intended to marry again in a month's time but he wished to vindicate his honour before installing a new wife at Cadlington.

"Who is the unfortunate lady?" It was Alice who asked this, her feminine curiosity coming to the fore. Fleur was too tongue-tied with horror to speak.

Luke answered that it was a young girl of noble blood, by name, Lady Georgina Pollendyne.

Then Fleur lifted her head. For the first time in her life she spoke with bitterness:

"I know her by repute. She is but sixteen. Once again, St. Cheviot covets the innocent. God forgive the parents who are handing poor little Lady Georgina over to such a villain."

Turning to Luke, she added:

"If Peveril dies at St. Cheviot's hands—for my sake, I shall hope also to die. I had thought we escaped—but the world is not wide enough in which to hide from St. Cheviot's monstrous cruelty. From the beginning I have been doomed. *I* do not matter, but he—my darling—my love—oh *God*, hear me!" She clasped her hands. "Be merciful and spare *him* who has done no wrong."

And she staggered out of Alice's arms to a sofa and lay upon it with her head on her outstretched arms, weeping as though her heart were broken.

Luke and Alice exchanged unhappy glances. This evil had struck—at last. The black shadow of Cadlington hung over the once tranquil little house. A house that had been gay with preparations for the joyous wedding of Fleur and Peveril. They knew not what to say—what to do—how to comfort or counsel the weeping girl.

Suddenly there came a knock on the door.

"Tell Rabbina I will go," said Luke who was a very worried man. "This may bring us news of Peveril."

Fleur's head shot up. Through the tears, her eyes glittered with a wild hope.

"Yes, yes—perhaps he has come home after all."

But Luke met with disappointment. It was not Peveril but a tall, well-built gentleman with a scarred face browned by tropic suns who stood on the threshold. As he courteously removed his hat and bowed, Luke could see that his hair was white, but not on account of age for he was obviously still in his prime.

He asked if a Mrs. Trelawny lived here.

"Yes, sir . . . but she cannot see you. She is indisposed

. . ." began Luke. Then he stopped. For Fleur had heard the voice and, deeply puzzled by its familiar cadence, moved into the little hall. The February day was drawing to a close. But by the shadowy light of a flickering lamp, Fleur could discern the visitor's face and form. The tears dried on her lashes. She stared wildly as though at an apparition; drew nearer and stared again, peering more closely up at the stranger. Her heart pounded in her breast. Her body shook. She whispered:

"No—I am out of my mind with my grief and anxiety. *It cannot be.*"

Then the tall man moved forward and held out his arms.

"Fleur, my little darling, it is I, Papa," he said huskily. He, like the young girl, trembled with extreme emotion.

For an instant Fleur stayed motionless, as one might hover between the gates of paradise and the jaws of hell. She continued to search that scarred countenance—examining one familiar feature after another.

Harry Roddney, on his part, looked through his tears at his daughter and found her no longer the laughing child he had left but a mature young woman with the mark of tragedy on her brow. Her still slender beauty, those rich curls, that divine grace, recalled for him, with painful vividness, the comeliness of her mother. It gave him a deep pang. Then while the Taylors looked on confused, they saw Fleur fling herself into the stranger's arms. They heard her voice, almost hysterical with delight.

"It *is* you! You did not die. You have come back to me. Papa, *papa*, my dearest, my most beloved father!"

The Taylors, not waiting for further explanations, linked hands and stole away. Alone, Harry Roddney and his daughter clung to each other, the tears raining down their cheeks.

Chapter Three

While Fleur, seated at her father's knee, recounted all that had happened since he last saw her—Harry Roddney sat motionless. He listened with an ever increasing sense of horror coupled with an intense indignation as she blurted out the dreadful story. Her voice faltered, her cheeks burned, when she reached the point of her betrayal at The Little Bastille.

Coming home from Australia, Harry had built up a memory of Fleur as the fair, joyous child whose laughter used to echo through their quiet country home. His dearest Fleur, the treasure of his and Hélène's lives; with the dew of her budding womanhood fresh upon her.

How could either of them have guessed that a terrible doom sat upon that pure unclouded brow? Harry smote his forehead with a clenched fist, remembering that it was *he* who had insisted upon returning St. Cheviot's hospitality. He who, in an idle moment, had invited St. Cheviot to Fleur's birthday party. He could picture the man, haughty, handsome, suave. But now that picture was blotted out by the other that Fleur had conjured up for him while she told her harrowing tale. He saw the Baron as a cruel ravisher of his young and innocent darling. Having made her Lady St. Cheviot, Denzil had subjected her to appalling sufferings—in particular during her imprisonment after the birth of her child.

It was almost more than Harry could stand. His whole body was shuddering. For now he had to realize that the stigma which had escaped Fleur had spread to Hélène's grandson. The poor infant heir to Cadlington had not survived his birth. But the strain, the shame, must remain. Oh, monstrous brutality of an inexorable fate that it should have been a young and innocent girl who suffered because her mother was born a *quadroon*.

At length he interrupted Fleur.

"Stop, do not go on—I have heard enough!" And he buried his face in his hands and sobbed without restraint.

Now Fleur forgot her own sorrows and made haste to comfort her father. She kissed the tears from his cheek, smoothed his hair with loving hands and begged him not to grieve.

"It is all over now, Papa. We are together again. Even though we have lost dearest Mama, God has restored *us* to each other."

Harry raised his head.

"My child, if your mother knew but a portion of this terrible thing, her heart would break."

"If she had lived, dearest Papa, it would never have happened."

"That is true," Harry nodded. "One cannot foresee the future, and when your mother begged to be allowed to accompany me to France, I could not guess that in agreeing, I signed her death warrant—and your worse fate!"

"It was not your fault, you must not blame yourself."

Harry Roddney wiped his eyes.

"Yes, dearest child, but of one thing we were guilty—we should have told you the family history as soon as you came of marriageable age."

"But, Papa, who was to know the strain would go down to the third and fourth generation," said Fleur in a low voice. "Mama's skin was white as the dazzling snow and her hair more red than mine. But why, *why* should the native strain have passed through *me* to my unfortunate babe?"

"Only doctors or men of science could explain, my darling. But it was an appalling heritage and I know now that your dear mother was right when she said, before we ever married, that we ought not to have children. Yet we so longed for a child of our great love—and when you were born, all seemed well. The possibility of this happening to *you* did not enter our heads."

Fleur seized her father's hand and put it against her cheek.

"I beg you not to blame yourself. Never through all my miseries did I reproach you or my beloved mother."

"You are an angel," said her father and once more

found it hard to check the difficult and unmanly tears.

"Did many people know that my great-grandfather was an African?" asked Fleur in a low voice.

"None for certain. One or two who were acquainted with your Mama when she was the Marquise de Chartellet, may have guessed: because of the singular likeness between her and the young quadroon Fauna, who was Lady Pumphret's slave."

Fleur stared blindly at her father.

"Mama—a slave—oh, how difficult for me to believe!"

"Yet it was true. And you must always revere her memory. Even as a young girl—and held in shameful bondage—she remained pure and unsullied. She gave her love to me alone. Her marriage to Lucien de Chartellet was marriage in name only. Till her death she was mine, my dear and most faithful wife."

He bowed his head. Fleur's tears fell thickly but she wiped them away and began to talk of Peveril. Harry listened, nodding once or twice.

"There can be no doubt that this young gentleman is of the finest mettle, and worthy of your love. He shall receive nothing but affection and assistance from me."

"Then you do not object to my remarrying?"

"I want nothing but your happiness, my poor little darling," he said.

He rose and began to walk up and down the room, hands clenched at his sides. His scarred face bore a look of repressed anger. He broke out harshly:

"Dolly—my own kith and kin, sold you to St. Cheviot! Well—she shall pay; before God I swear it! She, who is herself a mother, must surely be the lowest creature on earth to have committed such a base crime against a motherless girl."

Fleur did not answer. Harry added:

"And Nonseale—my own uncle's friend and my lawyer in whom I also put my trust. He, too, is guilty. My home sold—my money and estates handed into St. Cheviot's keeping—oh, the infamy! Caleb Nonseale shall be called to account."

But Fleur's mind turned to Peveril and his immediate danger.

"Papa, I beg of you to help me save Peveril," she said. "He must not be allowed to fight this senseless duel with Denzil. *You* know how expert Denzil is with the foils. Peveril is gentle and peace-loving. He has offered to fight St. Cheviot for my honour and his own, but I tell you he has no earthly chance against Denzil. And if Peveril is killed you will lose your daughter, for I could not survive his death."

Harry Roddney strode across the room and took his daughter's hand in his.

"You shall not lose him. Thank God I am come in time. It is I, your father, who have the right to avenge your wrongs. *And it is I who shall meet St. Cheviot in the dawn tomorrow.*"

Fleur put a hand to her throat. Her eyes gleamed with mingled hope and terror.

"You!"

"Yes. What I have to say to Dolly and to Mr. Nonseale can wait. But this matter is vital. I know St. Cheviot's worth as an opponent! The very last time I was at Cadlington I struck the foil from his hand twice in succession. I can remember how discomfited he was. He said, then, that Harry Roddney alone could do such a thing to him. Oh, merciful God!" Harry raised a clenched fist above his head, "Be Thou on my side and let it come to pass as it is written in the Scriptures: *'an eye for an eye—a tooth for a tooth.'* For every moment of horror that you, my child, have endured at St. Cheviot's hands, let mine draw the blood from him, even though he fall bleeding from a thousand wounds!"

Fleur breathed quickly.

"You were once called the finest swordsman in England. Do you think, Papa, that your wrist will have lost its magic?"

"No," he said grimly. "*I shall kill St. Cheviot*—and before he has time to take a new bride to Cadlington."

Fleur glanced wildly at the clock on the mantelpiece. She rushed to the window and peered out. She saw to her relief that it was no longer snowing. The sky had cleared during the last hour. It was cold but crystalline stars winked high above London. She turned back to her father.

"The weather is grown clement. Can we get to Whiteleaf in time? Oh, Papa, Denzil's creatures have already gone and taken Peveril with them."

"The duel will not be fought until daybreak," her father reminded her. "Whatever St. Cheviot does, he will respect the formalities. For his reputation's sake he will not attempt to kill the young painter in cold blood tonight."

Fleur shivered.

"Let us go quickly!" she said.

Harry Roddney passed a hand over his brow.

"Wait, my dearest. I am financially embarrassed. I have landed with little money and——"

"You need not lack money. I have my savings and Luke will assist us," broke in Fleur.

"He shall be rewarded. In time the law will restore to us all our lands and my fortune," said Harry Roddney.

"Do not let that trouble you now, dearest Papa. Oh, I implore you, let us go."

"Are you sure you wish to come with me?" he asked, looking doubtfully at the girl who appeared so fragile, so deeply in need of care.

"Yes. I must be there."

"Then you shall be, my darling."

At that moment, Luke knocked on the door and entered, offering wine and refreshment to Fleur's father. Harry Roddney said:

"I thank you, my boy. A little wine and food will not come amiss while we wait for a conveyance."

He then told Luke Taylor what he proposed to do. Peveril's friend was, as usual, most helpful. He, himself, would go at once to the nearest livery stables and secure the fast coach that Sir Harry needed.

"No expense is to be spared," said Harry, in the old voice of authority that Fleur remembered in her father. "Hire four of the fastest horses available. In five to six hours, with a change of horses half way, we shall be at Cadlington soon after the Baron's men get there."

Luke ran to carry out this order, while Alice helped Rabbina serve a quick supper to Sir Harry and his daughter. Alice looked with some anxiety at Fleur.

"It is a bitter night. You must wrap up well. Would you like me to go with you?" she asked.

"No, I shall be all right. I have my father now to look after me," said Fleur, and flung a tender grateful look at the white-haired man, who lovingly returned it.

Harry then spoke to Alice:

"Some other time, ma'am, I will thank you in more detail for the inestimable service you have rendered my poor child."

"Peveril was our friend," said Alice, "and Fleur holds an equal place in our hearts."

"Oh, and you, too, will love Peveril, Papa," put in Fleur.

"If he is your choice I know he will also be mine," said Harry Roddney.

Fleur kissed him then hurried upstairs with Alice to change into a thicker dress, and put on her travelling cloak and bonnet.

Left alone, Harry Roddney picked up the stick he had carried when he arrived. His eyes narrowed. With a turn of his wrist he swished the cane through the air—pointing it this way and that as though at an invisible opponent. Finally he lunged forward, lower lip caught between his teeth, breath coming more quickly.

"Die," he muttered, "die, dog, *die*!"

Then he drew back, flung the cane into a corner and laughed a little, grimly, in his throat.

Chapter Four

It was three o'clock in the morning. The coach bearing Peveril and his captors neared Whiteleaf.

Peveril was stiff and half-frozen with the cold. The drive had been a long, arduous one over bad roads. The snow had held off and the heavens glittered with frosty stars. But the cold was intense and the pace slow; the horses continually slipped on the icy surface. One animal broke its forelegs. Another was brought to replace it but the delay was considerable. Ivor cursed and swore—he, himself, found this wintry journey unattractive. But they stopped at the *Saracen's Head* at Beaconsfield, where drivers and passengers were heartened by strong hot rum before they continued towards Wycombe.

Ivor and the art-connoisseur who was in St. Cheviot's pay, kept up a running flow of conversation when they were not attempting to doze under their rugs. Peveril sat apart from them in a dignified silence. Neither spoke to him and he did not wish for conversation. With folded arms he leaned back in a corner of the coach, brooding over what had transpired. It must be confessed that when he faced the thought of what was likely to happen, he could not be anything but apprehensive. Cowardice was not in Peveril Marsh, but he had always been something of a fatalist as well as a philosopher in his quiet artist's way. It seemed probable to him that he had signed his own death warrant when he agreed to accompany these men to Cadlington. But how, he asked himself, could he have faced his conscience—or a future with Fleur—if he had tried to evade the duel? He even felt a queer exultation at the thought of facing Fleur's one-time husband. It would be an honour to fight—and, if necessary, to die—for her sake. But he could not altogether overcome his grief at the thought that he might never see her again.

Tomorrow he should have been on his way to Bath to arrange for their marriage. Now all was over and *she* might be alone in the world save for their kind friends.

A thousand poignant memories assailed him as the coach climbed the hill and he saw the dark tower of Cadlington House pointing towards the luminous sky. Whiteleaf again; the familiar little village asleep at this bitter hour of early morning. Ah! . . . *his* tower! He had never thought to set eyes upon it again. Up there in that studio, his love for Fleur had been born. There, the boy had become a man—capable of deep and passionate love.

Peveril felt his heart sink as the coach rolled through the wrought-iron gates and the lanthorns, raised aloft by the lodge-keeper, shed a rosy glow across the snow. It lay a foot deep. The carriage wheels stuck to the surface and the horses strained and pulled but did not slip. As Peveril stepped out of the coach, he thought of former days when he had roamed through those magnificent gardens—and painted in freedom and tranquillity, days before St. Cheviot had brought Fleur here as a bride.

Was she never to know peace?

The front doors were flung open. A sleepy footman, buttoning his coat and yawning, admitted the visitors. Peveril glanced at him. He did not know the fellow. No doubt most of the staff here had been changed. The Baron's wrath had descended upon those who had allowed my lady to get away.

But now suddenly Peveril saw an all-too-well remembered figure approaching him. Mrs. Dinglefoot moved into the hall. She carried a lamp. It threw her vast shadow behind her. She was wrapped in shawls and wore a nightcap on her head. When she saw Peveril, her eyes blinked first with astonishment and then with an evil delight.

"Lawks-a-mussy! Peveril Marsh! So you've got him at last," she exclaimed to Ivor.

"Yes, and we're all frozen and need refreshment, Mrs. D.," said Ivor, rubbing his fingers.

Mrs. Dinglefoot, keeping her gaze on Peveril, said:

"Well, well, my fine little painter—and how does it feel to be back in the house that once gave you shelter, in return for which you did his lordship such abominable wrong?"

Peveril, weary and cold, tried to unfasten his cloak with numbed fingers. He answered the woman briefly:

"I have nothing to say to you or to anybody in this place."

She came closer to him, peering into his face.

"And what of my lady? The pasty-faced little hypocrite with her native blood—did she find your bed more to her taste than her lawful husband's?"

But here she stopped for Peveril raised a clenched fist.

"Say one more word like that, you female monster, and whether you are woman or not I will strike you!" he said.

The housekeeper shrank back. So, she reflected, the gentle artist had become a man. The glare in his eyes frightened her. She gave a teetering laugh and turned to Ivor.

"He will change his tune once his lordship sets upon him. Better take him to the tower. Let him sleep in his old bed. It is running with damp and the rats are up there. Maybe that will cool my young gentleman's hot blood."

Ivor spoke in the housekeeper's ear.

"I presume his lordship has not heard us arrive."

"No, he was dicing and drinking until late last night with his friends and I imagine he is snoring," Mrs. Dinglefoot whispered back. "He wouldn't be down here at all, but that Lady Georgina's mother and father wished to come and see the place yesterday. We had them here preening around like peacocks. They drove back to Aylesbury just before dark." She added confidentially: "I do not fancy the new Baroness will interfere with me for she's a silly simpering creature who giggles a great deal and is madly in love with his lordship. She will do anything to please him. She calls me 'her dear good creature' and will leave the running of the house to me, little doubt. None of my former lady's airs and graces or icy innocence."

She flung a wicked sidelong glance at Peveril.

"But the icicle thawed towards *him*, hey?"

Peveril glared at Mrs. D. so fiercely that she moved away, muttering.

The Welshman eyed Peveril and yawned.

"Come—better lock you in the tower," he said.

"There is no need to lock me in. I am here of my own free will and willing to meet your master on his own terms," said Peveril coldly.

"All the same I'm not risking losing you after the long search and trouble you put us to," said Ivor, drawing his upper lip back from his teeth.

At that moment there was the crash of a door and the sound of footsteps. Those in the hall looked upwards to the musicians' gallery. There appeared the flickering light of candles. Then came the tall figure of the Baron, himself. Wrapped in a thick velvet gown and holding a three-branch candelabra aloft, from which the grease dropped as the draught played with the spears of flame—Denzil St. Cheviot came slowly down the staircase.

Peveril's heart started to beat more quickly. Some colour flowed into his pale serious young face. For the first time for two years he looked at the man who had been Fleur's husband. St. Cheviot, he noted in some surprise, had aged during the last twenty months. There was a touch of grey in the raven locks tossed untidily about his brow. Roused suddenly from his sleep and with the stubble on his chin, he looked blear-eyed and vicious.

Slowly he set the candelabra on the long oaken table in front of the fireplace. Then, tightening the girdle about his dressing-gown, he turned and surveyed Peveril from head to foot in a slow critical manner that could not be other than offensive.

"Well, well, *well*," he drawled, "so it is indeed you. My good Ivor was justified when he sent me word that he fancied he had traced the work of the master painter. Welcome back to Cadlington, my young cockerel. You have been left in peace long enough to crow on your dung heap."

Peveril made no reply. Steadily his grey eyes looked up into the glittering black ones of St. Cheviot. He caught a whiff of sour alcoholic breath. With all his soul, he loathed this man.

St. Cheviot continued:

"So, after all, the stroke of genius in your brush gave you away—or shall I say your vanity? For at last you were compelled to display your work to the public gaze. Or was it that you were in need of funds?"

"I needed nothing, thank you," Peveril rapped out the words.

"Are you not ashamed of yourself?" continued the

Baron. "Just now as you came up that hill on which your sister breathed her last, did you not remember how willingly I gave you succour, and afforded you, my young painter, the opportunity to practise your talents and save your gold? Does your conscience not smite you knowing how you turned upon the one who showed you this generosity and came like a thief in the night to steal his wife?"

Peveril clenched his hands. His forehead was a trifle damp under the crisp brown curls of hair but his voice was steady and clear as he answered.

"If we must talk of conscience, my Lord St. Cheviot, would it not be more fitting for you to examine yours and ask yourself why I grew to despise you. If I aided the escape of her—the lady who was once your wife—you even more than I—must know the true reason why it was done, and that I acted with full justification."

St. Cheviot gave a short laugh.

"Young fool. Do you think to hold yourself up as a crusader, imagining that you had the Almighty on your side when you assisted the lawful Lady St. Cheviot to climb down from the room into your lecherous embrace?"

The scarlet blood rushed to Peveril's cheeks.

"There was no lechery between us, nor has ever been and well you know it!" he said.

"I know nothing of the kind."

"Then you are informed of it now. It is the absolute truth and may the Almighty, whose Name you have so little right to use, my Lord St. Cheviot, strike me dead if I have spoken a falsehood."

"Bah!" said his lordship, but his malicious gaze fell before the young man's clear shining eyes.

"What is more," continued Peveril, "you are aware that you subjected Fleur to insupportable anguish, and that she had neither kith nor kin to champion her. I was her only friend. As such, I befriended her."

St. Cheviot raised his voice a trifle higher, working himself up into a passion against Peveril which he knew to be unjust.

"Sir—you abducted my wife and for that I am going to take your life."

"Sir," said Peveril, "you have locked up that defenceless wife, treating her as a lunatic and leaving her to the mercies of a fiendish woman who does not know the meaning of the word 'mercy.' It was from that fate that I saved my lady. I am glad of it and ever shall be—come what may."

"Come what may!" repeated St. Cheviot with a loud laugh. "Well, it is your last hour which is coming fast towards you, my little painter! I shall fight you as a gentleman—pistols or swords, I do not care—you shall have the choice. But I shall feel the better when I have rid the world of you."

"His lordship gives words to sentiments I would like to express towards himself," said Peveril.

St. Cheviot laughed again and turned to his servant.

"You hear that, my good Ivor? Does our young genius hope to match me in a duel? Shall he plant a bullet in my head, or the point of a sword in my bosom?"

Ivor echoed the laugh.

"Your adversary is as good as dead already, my lord."

If Peveril's blood froze a little in that moment, it could not be held against him, but he showed no sign of fear. His only terror was for Fleur; lest the long arm of St. Cheviot's spite should reach out and destroy *her*.

St. Cheviot's next words considerably alarmed him.

"And I warn you, I shall not rest until I find that flower of purity for whose sake you are about to die. And to trace her, now that we have found you, should not be impossible."

Peveril's heart sank.

"But why—why, my Lord St. Cheviot, do you wish to extend your vengeance to *her*?" he broke out in a low poignant voice. "The religious Courts have severed you from your matrimonial ties. You are about to take a new bride. Can you not leave poor Fleur alone? Have you not done her harm enough already?"

"What I do or do not do about the former Lady St. Cheviot, is my affair," said St. Cheviot harshly. "You will not be alive to attempt interference."

For one wild moment, Peveril sought in his mind for a means to escape—to reach the side of her whom he adored and protect her as had always been his dearest wish. Just for a moment he regretted that he had ever allowed himself to be drawn into this trap. He could not, must not die and leave Fleur alone. Then he pulled himself together. If it was the last thing he did, he would prevent St. Cheviot from thinking that Fleur had given herself into the keeping of a man less courageous than himself.

He said:

"Let us proceed with the duel."

"It is not yet the dawn," said St. Cheviot shortly. "I shall return to my bed. You, too, can sleep if you have a mind to do so. Ivor will call you. We shall meet in the meadow—beyond the south wall. It shall be a fair fight, correct in every detail. Dr. Boss is dead, the old fool. The new one, Dr. Barnstaple, shall attend us and since you have no seconds, I will provide you with them. This gentleman for one . . ." he turned to the art-collector who had assisted in the discovery of Peveril . . . "shall act for you."

"I thank you," said Peveril stonily.

St. Cheviot put a hand up to his mouth to conceal a yawn. He was feeling cold. His liver was out of order and he was aware that it was going to bring him little satisfaction to put an end to this young man's life. He had even admired the nerve and skill with which Peveril had spirited Fleur away from this house. The full measure of his vengeful feelings were directed not so much against the young painter as against Fleur, herself. Through these long months before he had secured the annulment he had thought of her with a mixture of loathing and desire. Loathing for the black strain that had tarnished even for a few seconds of life, the pure blood of his son and heir. Resentment against the barrier of pride and coldness that she had erected between them from the very moment he had first snatched her into his embrace. Yet his desire for her remained. For a while it had died but it had re-awakened; in his dreams, even in his waking hours, he remembered that incomparable beauty; the ice that he had never been able to thaw. It had driven him mad at times to remember his frustration and her spiritual triumph even in the hours of her deepest degradation at his hands.

Now, as he was so soon to take another bride, there seemed little reason left for his malice. He had cast Fleur off absolutely. He had a new fancy. Georgina Pollendyne was a pretty child with a handsome dowry behind her. But her somewhat infantile adoration for himself had brought him little satisfaction. She would be a pliable wife—no doubt she would bear him healthy children. But she did not appeal to him as that *other* had done. There was nothing in him for Georgina of the wild, hot passion that had stirred his blood when first he looked upon Fleur; Fleur with the violets twined in her rose-gilt hair, and in the dazzling loveliness of her maidenhood. Even now on this cold grey February morn he felt the old gnawing anger because she had never really been his. He could and would kill Peveril.

He snarled at the young man.

"Well—which is it to be? Swords or pistols?"

The painter, who had no knowledge of either weapon, made a valiant effort to answer with nonchalance:

"It would give me much pleasure to run the point of a sword through your throat, my Lord St. Cheviot."

"Idiot!" exclaimed St. Cheviot, shaking now with a fury roused by the black demons of his own vile memories. "You have only a few more hours in which to live. You . . ." he swung round to the valet, "lock him in the tower and let him stay there until six o'clock."

Peveril started to argue but St. Cheviot, seizing the candelabra, turned his back and walked up the stairs.

"Come along," said Ivor roughly, addressing Peveril.

The young painter turned and followed.

Once again he climbed that well-remembered circular staircase while the Welshman followed with a lighted lanthorn. Nobody had entered the haunted tower since Fleur and Peveril left Cadlington. The place lay hidden under a thick coating of dust. The studio, itself, presented a grim and forlorn aspect when the young painter entered. Cobwebs, opaque with filth, hung across the dirty panes of the turret windows. Peveril's own easel still stood in the centre of the room. One or two old canvases lay on the ground full of holes—gnawed by the rats. Even as Ivor opened the door—squeaking on its rusty hinges—a dark object scuttled across the floor-boards. Peveril followed its progress with a thrill of horror. He had no liking for rats. Ivor said:

"Not nice, eh—but good enough for you, my little painter. You have a few hours left in which to think about the life which you are so soon to leave. Good night—or shall I say good morning!" And with a mock bow, he departed, closed the door and turned the key in the lock.

He took the lanthorn with him.

Peveril stood a moment in darkness until his eyes got used to the lack of light. It was not pleasant in this bitterly cold room with the sound of rats squeaking and scuttling in the corners. Such surroundings would have struck gloom into the stoutest heart. Peveril's spirits dropped now to zero point. Dear God, he thought, what a way in which to spend the last hours of life—if they were to be his last. He knew every inch of this room. He groped his way to the windows and threw one open. The air was piercing but fresh and he drew it gratefully into his lungs. The studio had been long shut up and stank. Peveril could not bring himself to lie down on the rat-gnawed couch. So he stood at the window staring out at a view which once he used to find so glorious but which filled him now with the utmost gloom. Slowly but surely the night was passing; dawn had already laid a glimmering finger across the eastern sky. It would not be long before he must go down there to the meadow to meet his opponent in what would be the first, and surely, the last duel of his life.

How white and still it was over the countryside with the mists curling through the forest, half obscuring the Vale of Aylesbury from sight. Accustomed to the sombre light, he turned now to look for the high-backed chair in which Fleur used to sit. Yes, it was still here. He could almost see her there in all her delicate loveliness; feel the rich velvet of her blue gown; catch the fragrance of her hair as he arranged a silky curl before starting to paint her. He remembered her grief, recalled the terrible punishment that her vindictive husband had inflicted upon her when she most needed love and care.

Peveril had hoped once he was Fleur's husband to give her the devotion and happiness which she had never known. Now probably it would never be. Down there in that white meadow beyond the south wall he would do his best, but, as St. Cheviot well knew—it would not be a fair fight.

Peveril sank down on his knees and laid his feverish forehead against a curved arm.

"Oh, Fleur, my best beloved, how hard it is to leave you now," he whispered.

The cold was intense. He reached up a shaking hand to

shut the window. Crouching thus he stayed for a while until his eyes closed and an urgent need of sleep overpowered him. Being young and strong—even with that degree of discomfort and so much on his mind—he could still fall into a brief uneasy slumber.

He was wakened from it by the grating sound of a key being turned in the lock.

Ivor and the art-collector, who had been detailed by St. Cheviot to act for Peveril, had come for him.

Dawn was breaking over Cadlington.

Chapter Five

Out of the curling mists of the morning, Cadlington rose like a dark spectral shape, the grisly tower pointing as though in vengeance to the sky.

A little wind suddenly sprang to life and chased the clouds across the heavens. The sickle moon was paling fast before the rising sun. The forest still lay sleeping, but down in the valley, smoke wreathed upwards from the chimneys of the cottagers. They wakened early. The cattle from their byres began to low mournfully; the sound was like a protest against the cruelty of man—of birth and of death.

In the meadow which was approached through the orchard, a small group of men were gathered.

The Baron of Cadlington stood with his seconds behind him, and the new young medical man, Dr. Barnstaple, who carried his little black bag and looked nervous. He was gloomy about the whole proceedings for he was a peaceful country physician, but newly qualified, and unused to violence. This was his first attendance upon a duel.

St. Cheviot appeared to be in excellent spirits. He continually showed his fine white teeth in a smile while he divested himself of his upper garments and stood at length dressed only in his small clothes and silken hose. He began to roll back the full white sleeves of his fine lawn shirt carefully over each elbow. As he saw the slenderly-built figure of the young painter walk towards him, he continued to smile but his eyes narrowed. Peveril came nearer and bowed. The younger man looked pale and heavy-eyed but showed no sign of fear or embarrassment. Denzil St. Cheviot returned the bow punctiliously. A slight feeling of admiration once more entered his heart for this young man who was so nobly offering up his life on the altar of honour and human love. No such sacrifice, to St. Cheviot's meaner mind, could be worth while. It might be that he would fight for his so-called honour, but always with the confidence of victory.

Now, swords were brought forward by Ivor. The art-dealer and a young gentleman who had been staying at Cadlington and had been roused from his bed for the occasion, presented themselves to Peveril as his seconds. He, too, divested himself of his outer garments and rolled up his sleeves. He shivered as the wind stirred his hair. Raising his face to the sky he saw a rift of blue. A sudden shaft of sunlight pierced the green glade fringing the meadow. Almost it might have been the dawning of spring. The first promise of an end to the long bitter winter. How strange, mused Peveril, that this was the eve of Her Majesty's wedding. London today would be chaotically engrossed in preparations for the ceremonials. It was entirely irrelevant to his own tragic situation that he should pause to utter a silent prayer that her dear young Majesty would be happy with her chosen prince. Then he forgot everything but Fleur. He drew a long sigh and, with fatalistic courage, made pretence of testing the quality of the sword which he had been handed.

One of the seconds whispered to Dr. Barnstaple:

"Do you know what this is about? I have no notion."

"Nor I," the doctor whispered back, "save that there is some question of the Baron's honour being involved, in respect of the former Lady St. Cheviot. Their marriage was recently annulled." And he added: "But I have heard that this young gentleman, Mr. Marsh, is an artist by profession and has little knowledge of duelling. Lord St. Cheviot will kill him."

"May the Almighty have mercy on him," muttered the other.

This young gentleman who was St. Cheviot's guest of honour at the moment was a Frenchman by the name of the Marquis de la Poeur. He now took control of the situation. He was experienced in duelling. He warned the two antagonists of the rules and placed them face to face with their swords pointing to the ground. In every respect now, Peveril struggled to follow the motions and actions of the Baron. But he wondered grimly if he would be allowed to strike a single blow, or even once hear his sword echo against the other's blade before he was disarmed. But when the Marquis asked if the antagonists were ready, Peveril was the first to utter the word "Yes." The Marquis said sharply:

"En garde, messieurs."

The two lunged towards each other. With a swift blow the Baron struck the sword from Peveril's hand. He laughed and said through his teeth:

"Pick it up."

Peveril, face and ears dyed scarlet with impotent shame, picked up the weapon. Once more he lunged desperately in the direction of his adversary.

"For *her,*" he said, desperately.

"Imbecile," said St. Cheviot, and made a swift parry. Once again the weapon spun from Peveril's hand. The blood began to drip from his sword arm.

The Baron arched his body.

"What now?" he snarled.

Peveril's heart hammered almost to bursting but he took no notice of the blood that was fast dyeing his shirt and again stooped to retrieve the weapon.

His next movement was lightning quick—not so much a thing of skill as of despairing desire to make at least one creditable stand against Fleur's husband. The two blades clashed. Even Denzil St. Cheviot was surprised by this sudden slight display of swordsmanship. But it could not last. It could only be a question of St. Cheviot playing cat and mouse with the unhappy young painter. Dr. Barnstaple watching anxiously, uttered a low cry of protest.

"My lord—it is not a fair fight—it will be murder!" he said with spirit.

"I shall kill him all the same," said St. Cheviot.

The sweat ran down Peveril's face. There was a second wound in his shoulder now but he shouted at the Baron:

"Continue! On guard, my lord!"

Now with grudging respect (for he could not but admire great courage when he saw it) Denzil lunged again. The fine point of his sword pierced Peveril's right hand. For the third and last time the sword fell from his bloody fingers. He staggered and would have fallen had his seconds not sprung forward and supported him. The young man's face was ghastly. His eyes bore a look of chagrin and despair.

"Let me go," he muttered, "I will fight with my left hand if need be."

"Fight then and die——" began St. Cheviot who was growing sick of such poor sport.

But at that moment the silence of the countryside was broken by the cry of a man:

"Stop!"

The duellists and the rest of the little party gathered there in the meadow, turned and saw three people coming through the arched doorway that led from the gardens of Cadlington. Two were men—one tall and wrapped in a cloak, one shorter and sturdier, and the third a female whose face was heavily veiled.

St. Cheviot stared in amazement at the intruders. It was highly improper that a duel should be thus interrupted. Besides—who were these strangers who dared enter his grounds? St. Cheviot handed his sword to one of his seconds and walked forward as the two men advanced towards him, leaving the female standing alone by the gate. Dr. Barnstaple was busy trying to staunch the two or three wounds which Peveril had received. They were superficial but he was bleeding profusely. He, with startled gaze, stared at the short curly-headed younger man of the two. It was Luke Taylor. What could Luke have come here for, Peveril wondered dizzily. Then suddenly he turned and saw the girl who stood by the gate. The young woman had raised her veil. Peveril was some way away from her but he would have recognized her from any distance. His whole heart seemed to turn over. He cried:

"Fleur!"

Now the taller of the men was face to face with Denzil St. Cheviot, and he removed his hat and stood a moment with his sombre gaze fixed on the Baron.

With every moment that passed it was growing lighter. The pale February sunlight was fulfilling its promise of an hour ago, drinking the snow from the long wet grass. St. Cheviot, nonplussed by the unexpected digression, stared at the scarred face and white hair of this gentleman whom he did not recognize.

"May I ask the meaning of this, sir . . . who are you?" he began.

"Look closer at me, St. Cheviot," interrupted the other, "look close *and remember.*"

St. Cheviot stared. Anger was replaced by a vast astonishment. At first he told himself that it *could not be.* Then his very tongue seemed to dry against his teeth. He said in a gasp:

"*Harry Roddney!* No, not he but his ghost, come to haunt me."

"I am no ghost," said Harry, and unfastened the clasp of his cloak which he let fall to the ground. "I have been away for three long years—at the other side of the world where for reasons which I have no time to explain to you now, I was unable to communicate with my daughter. I have come to avenge her, sir. We have had trouble with the horses or I would have been here before. Thank God I am in time," he added with a swift look at Peveril.

Peveril, pale and shaken, leaned on Dr. Barnstaple's arm and stared at the tall gentleman.

"*Fleur's father!*" he exclaimed incredulously.

"Yes, my boy," Harry said in a more gentle tone. "I know all that has happened. You can rest assured that I am your friend as well as *her* father."

Denzil St. Cheviot continued to stare at Sir Harry Roddney in dumb amazement. Harry again addressed him.

"I know all, Denzil St. Cheviot. For what you did to my defenceless daughter in the absence of her parents you shall answer to *me.* Not to this lad who would have avenged her if he could, but is without knowledge of duelling."

St. Cheviot put a hand to his throat. He was momentarily robbed of his usual arrogance.

He began to bluster:

"I protest. The Ecclesiastical Courts granted me my Annulment admitting I had grievance, being tricked into marriage with the daughter of a common quadroon slave."

Harry changed colour. He took his glove and slashed St. Cheviot across the face and mouth with it.

"You shall not say such things and *live,*" he said in a voice of rage.

St. Cheviot stepped back, eyes glittering.

"Not so fast. It may well be *you* who shall die. That young lecher abducted your daughter from her lawful husband's side. Where is her innocence? As soon as my back was turned she took the low-class painter for her paramour. What of that?"

Speechless with fury, Harry snatched the sword that one of Peveril's seconds was holding.

"You were not tricked!" he said through his teeth. "For a sum of money you purchased my daughter's innocence when she had none to defend her."

"And what of her black blood? Have I no cause for indignation? Was I told of this abomination?" demanded St. Cheviot.

"There was none to warn you of Lady Roddney's ancestry. But once you knew—had you acted as a gentleman of honour—you would not have punished a wife who bore her child in helpless ignorance."

St. Cheviot opened his lips to say more, but now suddenly, the veiled female by the gate came running towards them. The raised voices of the men had reached Fleur across the quiet meadow. She approached St. Cheviot. After two long years she looked once more upon his hated face. Her eyes flashed.

"You know well, Lord St. Cheviot, that I was faithful to you, even though you would, if you could, have broken my spirit," she said.

For a moment the Baron was unnerved. Least of all had he expected to look upon *her* again. He tried to brazen it out and gave a mock bow.

"My compliments, madam. You look well, even at this early morning hour. Welcome home to Cadlington," he sneered.

Harry Roddney put a hand on his daughter's shoulder.

"Go to the coach with Peveril, my darling—he needs your care. He is hurt."

Fleur uttered a cry and ran to her lover who put his uninjured arm about her.

"It is nothing," Peveril said, "but I protest against the interruption of this fight that was solely between Lord St. Cheviot and myself."

Sir Harry took him up on those words.

"A one-sided fight is not good sport, my boy. I am better

equipped to deal with St. Cheviot. You have but lately entered my daughter's life—I am her father, and it is I who have first right to challenge the Baron to combat. Stand back. . . ."

The seconds whispered among themselves. The doctor shrugged his shoulders helplessly. He understood nothing and wondered if he were in a bad dream. Ivor, St. Cheviot's servant, who had been watching from afar, had heard enough; more than he wished, for his own good. The miraculous and mysterious reappearance of my lady's father upon the scene boded ill for *him*, should Sir Harry win this fight. For Mrs. Dinglefoot, too.

Harry Roddney, now prepared, stood still—with his sword pointing to the ground. He had tested the quality of the steel, his face a mask of hatred and resentment, as he bethought himself of the evil that St. Cheviot had practised upon his young daughter. As for those words "*common quadroon slave*" that had fallen so scathingly from the other man's lips . . . they, apart from anything else, thought Harry, had sealed St. Cheviot's doom.

The Marquis, who enjoyed a duel between well-matched opponents, and had known Harry Roddney in the past—and his prowess as a swordsman—looked eagerly from one man to the other. This would be something to talk about in the London clubs—and in Paris. He would not have missed it for worlds.

"En garde, messieurs," he said gaily.

Fleur led Peveril away.

"You have lost a lot of blood—you must come back to the coach and rest," she said.

He bent his head and kissed her hand. His face was flushed and his eyes bright with fever. "I have failed you," he said, "I shall never recover from the shame of it. I was beaten before I started. But I meant to kill him for your sake."

Fleur seized the hand that St. Cheviot had injured and pressed it to her lips.

"My dearest, you must not regret Papa's decision to take your place. He deems you chivalrous and gallant for ever having entered upon this contest."

"But I wanted to kill the Baron," groaned Peveril.

"With God's help my father shall kill him for you. And think what it would have meant to me, my dearest love, if *you* had paid the price this morning with *your* life!" exclaimed Fleur.

For a moment Peveril stood looking down into her tender eyes, his mind whirling.

"Last night I believed it to be the end, and that I would never see you again," he whispered.

"Now we shall never have to leave each other," she whispered back. "We have my father to champion our cause."

"Dearest, do not ask me to return to the coach just yet," Peveril begged her, "I must stay and witness what takes place."

She nodded.

So they stood there with their arms around each other, watching. The pallid sunlight flashed upon the swords of the two men as they lunged towards each other. There was a sudden sharp clashing of blade upon blade.

All of them who witnessed that fight, and the Marquis de la Poeur in particular, were to remember it as a remarkable affair, both men being superb swordsmen.

Every time Harry Roddney lunged with parry or *riposte* the name *Fleur* was upon his lips.

For ten full moments, they fought and thrust—neither man drawing blood. On and on—magnificently matched—lunging and parrying, breathing heavily until both panted and the Baron's face grew livid and his upper lip drew back in an animal-like snarl. He, better than anybody, anticipated what he might expect. He had fought with Sir Harry for the love of the sport in the days that were past. But this was no idle sport. This was a fight to the death and he knew it.

It was St. Cheviot who drew first blood—and pierced Harry Roddney's arm. Harry's sword clattered on to the ground but with remarkable celerity he picked it up again and fixed St. Cheviot with a murderous gaze.

"For *Fleur*," he said again in a gasping breath.

The spectators looked on, holding their breaths. The Marquis muttered:

"*Dieu*, but this is a most excellent sight."

Fleur and Peveril, their fingers convulsively entwined, regarded the duel with less pleasure and with anguished intensity.

"Oh God—do not let Papa be beaten!" Fleur sent up a voiceless prayer.

Now the two men fenced again with deadly and ferocious intent.

"This," said Harry Roddney, "for what happened at The Little Bastille. . . ."

And with a lightning turn of the wrist he drove the point of his sword into his opponent's right shoulder.

This time it was the Baron's sword that fell to earth. He muttered an oath. Harry stood panting while his adversary picked the weapon up again.

Once again the two gentlemen engaged. Now only their heavy breathing and the clash of steel upon steel could be heard in that quiet meadow. Both men poured with sweat. Into the dark eyes of St. Cheviot there had crept a new look—an expression of failing confidence in himself. *And the first fear he had ever known.*

"This for the black brat your fine daughter spawned," he snarled as he attempted to gain mastery. But they were the last words Denzil St. Cheviot was ever to utter. For with a fearful cry, Harry Roddney lunged and with all his strength drove forward; the point of the sword passing straight through the Baron's heart. And Harry cried out those words that he had uttered in the Taylors' house last night: *"Die, dog, die!"*

Without a cry, with only a pink froth bubbling from his lips, Denzil St. Cheviot dropped his sword and sank on to the grass. The red blood slowly dyed his fine shirt. The melting snow on the grass turned a deep crimson.

Dr. Barnstaple rushed forward and knelt beside the Baron. He examined the fallen man for a brief instant, then looked up at the others, his face scared.

"His lordship is dead," he said in a sepulchral tone.

"Deo gratias," said Harry Roddney, and wiped his bloodied sword on a handkerchief, and the sweat from his brow.

Ivor turned and slunk through the archway. He began to run towards the house.

Fleur and Peveril came forward. The girl disengaged

herself from her lover's embrace and ran to her father. He folded her to his heart.

"God has been merciful. I have avenged you and the dear mother who bore you," he whispered.

There was a brief silence while Harry dressed himself and Dr. Barnstaple covered the dead Baron with his cloak.

A while later, one of the gentlemen who had been witnesses, after staring in silence at St. Cheviot's corpse, looked up towards the house.

"Great God—there is a fire—*look!*" he cried.

All eyes turned to Cadlington House. Sure enough, a flame like an orange tongue flicked up into the morning sky, followed by a billow of black smoke. Peveril exclaimed:

"*It is the tower*. The tower is ablaze!"

Fleur, very pale and avoiding the sight of that body that lay so still on the grass, trembled from head to foot.

"Something must have happened there, we ought to go back and see," she said.

Dr. Barnstaple said:

"I will give orders for his lordship's servants to carry his body to my house. Let us all go to the House, for every hand will be needed."

What accident had occurred remained a mystery to them. The Welshman was at this very moment running like a rat down Cadlington hill seeking to escape from the vengeance which he knew would fall upon him.

As soon as he had realized that all was over and that he could no longer hide behind St. Cheviot for protection, he had hurried to tell Mrs. Dinglefoot what had happened.

Hearing of her master's death, that terrible woman had uttered a cry of grief. She and she alone had truly loved the vicious young nobleman upon whom she had waited on since his infancy. But sorrow speedily gave place to a desire for self-preservation. She, too, was horrified and startled to hear that Sir Harry—father of the one-time Lady St. Cheviot—was alive—and here. She had just been regaling herself with a tankard of stout during her breakfast, brooding upon the thought of young Peveril Marsh's impending death which would afford her great satisfaction. Ivor's news came as a horrid surprise. St. Cheviot *dead*.

Peveril alive. And with a rich and powerful man like Harry Roddney behind him! What a calamity!

"Say nothing to the rest of the servants, but let us two get away," she said to Ivor. The very moles on her face quivered; her small eyes almost disappeared in the wobbling fat of her cheeks.

"Such is my intention," Ivor replied grimly.

But although Ivor made his escape, Martha Dinglefoot was not so lucky. Out of her own avarice and greed, she managed to destroy herself.

For many years, Mrs. D. had been stealing in a quiet and unobtrusive fashion from the hand that fed her. She had always controlled the domestic purse-strings for Lord St. Cheviot's household, and she had managed to fill a deed box with gold. She did not keep the box in her own room. She did not trust the servant girls who cleaned or entered the apartment in her absence. So she had conceived what she thought to be the brilliant idea of hiding the money in the one place where it was least likely to be found; the studio in the haunted tower. For none of the staff dare venture there except when Peveril was in residence.

Up there, under one of the loose boards, was a hole in which she had placed her box which every week grew heavier with the golden guineas she pilfered.

Now that she knew St. Cheviot was dead and that she, herself, might be called to account by Sir Harry Roddney for her cruelty to her young mistress, she made haste to find her savings. She must escape.

She took with her a small oil lamp, for there was little light in the long neglected passage which ran between the main portion of the house and the tower.

Panting and puffing, Mrs. D. climbed the circular staircase, reached the studio and went down on hands and knees. She found the loose board and drew out her treasure. Her eyes glittered with triumph. All was well. She could live comfortably on the money she had so carefully put away. She might, she thought, even have time to pocket one or two of the jewels which St. Cheviot, in his careless fashion, used to toss into a drawer. Jewels he had intended to give to his second bride. But the foolish giggling Georgina would never now become Lady St. Cheviot. The Master of Cadlington lay dead and there was no heir.

It was the end, thought Mrs. D. and managed to squeeze a tear, blinking her sandy lashes as she hurried downstairs again.

Holding the lighted lamp in one hand and the heavy box in the other, she could not cling to the banisters for support. In her haste, she caught the heel of her boot in a hole that the rats had bored. That for Mrs. Dinglefoot was dire calamity. She stumbled, clutched at air, and pitched down the stairs, uttering a fearful cry. The box clattered before her. The lamp broke, the oil spilled and caught alight. In a moment, the dry rotting wood of the narrow banisters ignited.

When Mrs. Dinglefoot recovered consciousness a few minutes later it was to a satanic world of hot darkness, of black suffocating smoke; and with the crackle of burning timber in her ears.

A wail of despair was drawn from her throat, ending in a gurgling moan. *The tower was on fire.* She was pinned here with her legs broken under her. She could not move. Soon she would not be able to breathe. Her voice was inaudible above the terrible sound of that ever-increasing furnace. Her cries could not be heard. As the flames drew nearer to lick at her face and singe her hair, the housekeeper uttered a last frightful cry. It seemed that every crime and abomination of cruelty that she had practised, rose to confront her now. It seemed, too, that she caught a glimpse of a young pale face with violet eyes full of pain and grief. It was as though Fleur St. Cheviot, the young bride, who had been brought to Cadlington three years ago, stood beside her now with clasped hands, watching; crying aloud for vengeance.

"Mercy . . . *mercy!*" yelled Mrs. Dinglefoot, writhing in her torment and feeling that hell, itself, was already her portion. Then a piece of timber from the ceiling fell from a great height and crushed her skull. She knew no more. The purifying flames melted her fat and frightful body.

Later, when the tower had burnt itself out and scavengers came, they found the twisted box of gold; but of the woman who had hoarded it, and who had caused so much suffering to others, nothing remained save a few charred bones.

The rest of the servants escaped from the big house with

ease. One or two attempted to show loyalty to a dead master by throwing a few treasures out on to the lawn. Gardeners and farm hands attempted to pour water on the flames that advanced all too rapidly from the direction of the blazing tower. But it was futile. A brisk wind this cold February morning fanned those flames into a merry conflagration.

The heat from some buildings nearby which had also caught fire shattered the panes of glass in the famous orchid houses. The lovely poisonous blooms writhed and danced in the hot blast like horrid marionettes jerking to their death. They shrivelled and blackened until nothing was left.

As the smoke belched into the heavens and the fire rose higher, licking greedily through the dry old wood of the great hall, hundreds of people in the valley saw it and watched in awe and horror. It was an epic fire; that great fire of Cadlington which burned and smouldered late into the night. It was to be chronicled in history and remembered by old and young in the district as long as they lived.

Little remained of the famous mansion in which generations of St. Cheviots had been born and had died; it became a charred ruin with yawning apertures for windows. One by one the painted smirking faces of the barons and their ladies that had hung in the galleries, had melted, crumpled and become thin black fragments to be tossed by the mischievous wind into complete disintegration.

Chapter Six

In the humble parlour of the small house in Monks Risborough occupied by Dr. Barnstaple, the dead Baron of Cadlington lay on a bier like a figure of wax, his nose already thinning with the sharpness of death. And even in death, the expression on that face remained arrogant and brutal. The upper lip was drawn slightly back from the teeth in a sneering smile.

Candles burned at the Baron's head and feet. White linen covered his body—drawn up to his chin. But those on his estate who came to pay their respect to Denzil St. Cheviot did not find him a pleasant corpse. Few truly mourned him save one creature, and that, a dog.

Alpha the wolfhound had escaped from the burning mansion and nosed her way to the doctor's house. She laid herself down beside the bier of her master and refused to leave it, showing her fangs, until at length one of the men on the estate, in obedience to the doctor's orders, put a bullet through her head.

Meanwhile, Harry Roddney and his daughter, with the young man who was her chosen love, and Luke Taylor, travelled in their coach back to London.

Harry, despite his age and the exhaustion that had followed his fight with St. Cheviot, was in good spirits. Peveril bandaged and pale from loss of blood, was also capable of smiling, for his fingers were locked in Fleur's, and her warm sweet presence remained close to him while they rolled through the deserted countryside.

None spoke of St. Cheviot. Death had wiped him out. In Harry Roddney's mind there remained only two more things to be done—to settle an account first with Caleb Nonseale, then with Cousin Dolly, Lady Sidpath. Neither should go free, he decided. For they were the two who were most culpable. Had they not sold Fleur into the hands of the monster Baron?

Pillars, The Little Bastille, all his and Hélène's possessions, would in due course be restored to Harry. Once again he could live in comfort and elegance as a gentleman of means. And already Fleur had expressed the hope and wish that she and her young husband might share the beauty of her old home with him, the father, to whom she owed everything.

This new day for Fleur had dawned like a miracle of joy and renewed hope. Nature itself was rejoicing. The snows were melting. All the way through Buckinghamshire and into London, pale sunlight persisted, and with it the golden promise of the approaching spring.

Behind them they had left Cadlington in ashes. Her dear Peveril had been spared to her. She felt that her cup of good fortune was overflowing, and that the doom had been lifted at last from her head.

It was afternoon when they entered the busy city and drew near to St. Martin's le Grand. They saw the final touches being put to the array of flags, banners and bunting. A spirit of excitement rippled through the entire populace this afternoon. Then the little party in the coach turned to each other, remembering the circumstances and the date.

The marriage of the Queen! This was her wedding eve. Tomorrow, the young Victoria would stand beside Prince Albert. The young sovereign would have a Consort to cherish and support her in the tremendous duties that lay ahead of so great a queen.

Fleur's heart beat quickly. Her shining eyes turned to Peveril.

"Let us pretend that the bells are ringing for us, too, my dear love," she whispered.

"It is no pretence. They shall also ring for us very soon now, my love," he said.

"Oh, Peveril," she said, "what happiness to know that I have a father to turn to before I take you for my husband. For now I need not walk alone to the altar. *He* will walk with me."

"If his lordship is willing," put in Luke, "we will now

proceed direct to my house where Alice will give us refreshment."

"I shall be happy to receive it, my boy," said Harry kindly, "and afterwards to rest awhile before I call upon Mr. Nonseale."

Fleur shivered.

"I always hated that man."

"I owe you an apology, my darling," said Harry ruefully. "Your dear mother abhorred him, too. It seems that my judgment (and my uncle's) were at fault."

Peveril had felt the tremor that went through the slim form at his side. He pressed Fleur's arm close to him.

"Turn your thoughts from all things sad and let us remember our love and contemplate our future together," he said.

She lifted his bandaged hand and put her lips to it.

"Alas that your wonderful fingers were mutilated for my sake," she said, "I cannot get over *that*."

"But, my dearest, Dr. Barnstaple said that in a few weeks both shoulder and hand will be healed and I shall soon be able to paint again," he comforted her.

Harry Roddney opened sleepy blue eyes and smiled at the young man who was to become his son-in-law. The more he saw of Peveril Marsh, the more he liked him. There was nothing dashing or spectacular about Peveril. But the lad was charming and an idealist. He adored Fleur. He had helped her to escape from what might have been a terrible martyrdom at Cadlington. Added to which, Harry had been moved, as only a much stronger man could be, by the thought that the young artist had embarked upon that fearful duel with St. Cheviot, knowing that he had not the slightest hope of winning it.

"You shall paint me when your hand is recovered, Peveril," he said with the old gay smile that used to enchant Hélène. "Scars and all, eh?"

"Scars can be truly honourable, sir," said Peveril.

"Quite so," said Fleur softly and once more raised her lover's bandaged hand to her lips.

As the little party stepped down from the coach a merry fellow, arm linked with that of another, passed by them. One well in drink paused and clapped Peveril on the back.

"Long live the Queen and her Consort!" he ejaculated.

Peveril winced a little from the pain of his wound, but smiled and echoed the good-natured young gentleman's words:

"Long live the Queen and her Consort."

And then it seemed that all the church bells in London were ringing. Fleur linked hands with her father and her lover. She thought of the young Victoria in her Palace preparing for tomorrow's great event.

"Oh, my dear young Majesty," she whispered the words to herself. "God bless you and may your happiness be as great as mine!"

And she could no longer see the faces of the two whom she loved so dearly; for at long last Fleur wept, not for sorrow, but for the joy of being alive.

BOOK THREE

The Flame and the Frost

BOOK THREE

The Flame and the Frost

PART I

Chapter One

On that bitterly cold afternoon of January, in the year 1870, London was enveloped in a thick yellow fog.

Sounds were muffled. Boys holding flares ran ahead of slow moving vehicles. The drivers tried to lead their bewildered horses.

Figures emerged suddenly out of the blanketing vapours, bumped into each other and moved back muttering apologies. By four o'clock, darkness had fallen. Few were out. Sensible folk stayed by their firesides. It was raw and uncomfortable out of doors.

A girl, aged about twelve, moved slowly and uncertainly along the Thames Embankment not far from Battersea Bridge. She was lost. She had gone out an hour ago while there was still light, to buy a reel of cotton for her aunt who took in dressmaking. They occupied the ground floor of a shabby house in the Pimlico Road.

Charlotte had not yet bought the cotton. Having a penny in the pocket of her pinafore which she still wore under a hastily donned coat—she had gone further afield, lured by the anticipation of filling a somewhat empty little stomach with a few sweets. Mr. Ingleby's confectionery shop was only two blocks away. But Charlotte, surprised and somewhat frightened by the swirling fog, missed the turning and now found herself actually alongside the river. The dim lamplights made no impression in such thick darkness. Charlotte tried several times to recross the main road, but each time she stepped off the kerb, she was forced back by the sound of clip-clopping horses' hooves, as some vehicle loomed out of the shadows.

She had a little hood over her head but no gloves. She was rapidly growing colder. The poisonous gases of the "peasouper" made her eyes smart. She coughed and gasped and the tears were not far away. She wondered what Aunt Jem would say. Poor Aunt Jem—she would be waiting for the red cotton and unable to proceed with the new merino dress for Miss Potter. It had been promised for tomorrow morning because Miss Potter was off to Brighton to visit her newly-married sister. She would be so disappointed if Aunt Jem failed her. But Aunt Jem would sit up all night, sewing and pressing and finishing the dress with those fine, tiny stitches which Charlotte thought so wonderful.

The child knew that the effort would be bad for her aunt whose eyesight was rapidly deteriorating. Miss Darnley suffered from dreadful headaches. Sometimes she could hardly go on with all that endless sewing. Poor Aunt! She was the sole support of the little household which consisted of herself, and Charlotte who was her orphaned niece. Then there was Aunt Jem's only brother, Albert, who had lately come to live with them. He was a widower. At one time he had been comfortably off with a little business in Shepherd's Bush. But the business failed after Uncle Albert's wife died. In her lifetime she had stood between him and his weakness for drink. After her death, he went downhill, got into debt and had to sell up in order to appease his creditors. He had only enough money left to pay his sister, Jemima, ten shillings a week for board and lodging, which barely kept him. But he was a kindly, harmless man when sober. As far back as Charlotte could remember, Uncle Albert had been especially kind to her; reading story books or taking her out for walks while Miss Darnley plied her trade as a dressmaker. Charlotte, in fact, loved Uncle Albert except when he had a drop too much and his breath smelt of beer when he kissed her, or tickled her cheek with his long drooping moustaches.

Charlotte wished heartily that she had waited till Uncle Albert got home and let him go and buy the red cotton. How could she be so foolish as to miss her way like this within a few hundred yards of home? Neither she nor Aunt had dreamed the fog was so thick.

If only she could meet a policeman who would help her to find her way back. She was afraid of strange men. Aunt Jem had so often cautioned her never to speak to one. She sometimes hinted at the Fearful Things that might happen to a young, unattended girl. When Charlotte asked for an explanation it was never given. Aunt Jem just pursed her pale sad lips and said tartly:

"Never mind, miss. One day you will understand."

Charlotte was always being told that "one day she would understand." She lived in a constant state of being mystified. Grown-ups were forever hinting at Fearful Things in front of her. Beginning to say something and stopping, glancing slyly in her direction. Once Uncle Albert had come home rather merry, and started to tell his sister about a "young lady who had been taking a glass of port and lemon with him at The Three Bells." What a fine bustle she had, and violet kid boots and gloves. Aunt had interrupted, her cheeks red, and said:

"Be quiet, Albert. In front of the *child*. You ought to be ashamed."

But what he ought to be ashamed of was never made clear to Charlotte. By nature she was intelligent and inquisitive. But when she appealed for explanation as to why she could not hear more about the young lady in The Three Bells, Aunt clicked her teeth and muttered: "Young *lady*, indeed! I know better!" Uncle Albert laughed and winked at Charlotte who was promptly sent to bed because she innocently winked back.

Charlotte, however, was deeply attached to her aunt. And Aunt Jem loved her in her way, quite fondly, considering her cynical mistrust of human affection.

Life had not been kind to Jemima Darnley. First of all, the only man she had ever cared for jilted her cruelly, after which she had lost both her parents and had to take in dressmaking for a living. Then Lottie, her only sister (Charlotte's mother), a beautiful girl, happily married to Oliver Goff, a valet in the service of a duke, died tragically when Charlotte was three. Oliver had been taken ill in Paris where he was with his master at the time. Mrs. Goff rushed across the Channel to see her beloved husband but he died without recognizing her. He had typhoid fever. Charlotte's young mother contracted it and within a couple of weeks, she, too, was dead, and lay beside her husband in the cemetery in Paris.

Jemima, who had adored her sister, never recovered from this blow. Poor Lottie had been so gay and sparkling. A trifle too sparkling, at times, to suit Jemima. Charlotte closely resembled her mother. Her good-looking father, Oliver Goff, had been decently educated, and Charlotte inherited his quick grasp of things, his thirst for knowledge. From her mother, those long slender limbs and charming contrast of colouring. Eyes, the colour of dark honey, and tawny curling hair. At the moment she was overthin and pale. Her high cheekbones jutted out. Her long fine fingers were always red—half frozen with cold from which she suffered intensely. There was no margin for rich food or piled-up fires in Aunt Jem's household; every shilling had to be watched, every penny saved.

Charlotte received no education beyond that which her aunt and uncle gave her, but, once able to read, she read hungrily. She continued to do so and to improve her mind when her aunt was not calling upon her to help with the housework. The cooking was done by an elderly respectable woman living in this same house, who volunteered to come for a few hours daily in order that Miss Darnley should be free to ply her trade. For this assistance, Miss Darnley parted with the ten shillings a week given to her by her brother. It was a hard struggle. And, alas, Charlotte had no aptitude for sewing. Aunt Jem had hoped to train her as a dressmaker, but Charlotte could not sit still for long, and if and when she sewed, her stitches were big and her little fingers would grow hot and greasy. Aunt Jem could not risk her wrecking the delicate fabrics which belonged to her customers.

Charlotte's footsteps quickened. She began to run through the fog. She *must* get home. She panted and the tears chased down her cheeks. Turning left, she stumbled off the kerb. Her terror drove her on, despite the fact that she heard the warning clatter of horses' hooves on the roadway and caught the glow from the flare held by a lad who was leading a smart landau, pulled by two handsome greys. But suddenly she stopped, hesitated and was lost. For the horses seemed to bear down upon her with terrifying suddenness. Like spectral shapes they materialized, tossing their heads, whinnying as the coachman pulled hard on the reins. Charlotte heard the shouting of men and her own thin scream. Then she was knocked down and she lost consciousness.

Chapter Two

Charlotte recovered to find herself in the comparative warmth and shelter of a well-padded carriage. She was lying on the seat, her head pillowed in the lap of a woman richly dressed in black velvet, with sable-lined cloak. A sable-trimmed bonnet framed a noble and beautiful face which Charlotte was never throughout her life to forget. It was that of Eleanor, Lady Chase, the subject of several of Sir John Millais' most famous portraits. In the same year that Millais was elected a Royal Academician, Eleanor Chase's portrait with her small son, Vivian, standing by her side, became the rage of London. It now hung over the fireplace in the dining-room of Clunes,—the Chase family seat in Hertfordshire.

But for the last six years Lady Chase had been living in retirement from which she emerged only occasionally, mainly from a sense of duty to her son, Vivian. Vivian's father, Lord Chase, had been attached to the 13th Light Dragoons and mortally wounded in the Crimea. Since then, Lady Chase had devoted herself entirely to the boy. Vivian was now seated beside her. The landau had just brought them from a luncheon party. They were returning to their house in Eaton Square, trying to fight the regrettable fog. When the coachman pulled in the horses and the landau stopped, it pitched Lady Chase into her son's arms. Startled, she leaned out of the window, and saw to her consternation that one of the horses had knocked down a little girl. She at once ordered that the child be lifted into the carriage, although Vivian protested.

"Really, Mama, she may be verminous! No gently-nurtured child would be walking alone on the Embankment."

His mother chided him.

"Pray remember, Vivian, my darling boy, the quality of mercy."

Young Lord Chase shrugged his shoulders, crossed his arms and sat watching gloomily while his mother's orders were carried out. Charlotte's insensible form was lifted on to the cushioned seat.

"Home, Perkins," commanded Lady Chase.

Vivian pulled a handkerchief from the pocket of the dove-grey coat which he was wearing, and interested himself in smoothing the curled brim of his fine top hat.

Then Charlotte opened her eyes. She stared up at the face of the woman who bent so solicitously over her.

"Aunt Jem," she whispered.

The landau moved on. Lady Chase, with her own lace-edged handkerchief dabbed gently at a cut on the child's left cheek. It was bleeding. A nasty bruise was already swelling on the white forehead. The shabby cloak was streaked with mud but Lady Chase spoke to Charlotte as tenderly as she would have done to any child of her own.

"There, poor little creature, do not be alarmed. You are safe now, and in my care."

Charlotte sat up. Her head was swimming but she had the youthful faculty of being able with rapidity to throw off the effects of such an accident as this. In the gloom of the landau she could barely see the occupants, but she noted the saint-like loveliness of the face which bent down to hers. Charlotte blinked and gasped. Such a fine lady!—and this splendid carriage—how came she to be in it?

Lady Chase explained to her.

"Do you feel better, my little one?" she murmured.

"Much better," whispered Charlotte and stared through her lashes at the youth on the opposite seat. With a child's natural curiosity she admired his finery, and thought how handsome he was. But Vivian glanced out of the window as the coach moved slowly through the thickening fog, towards Eaton Square.

Lady Chase pulled a little gold-stoppered bottle from her pocket, uncorked it, and shook a few drops of scent on to Charlotte's forehead. This she smoothed with her long delicate fingers.

"Lie still, child, you must be in a daze. Why are you out in such bitter weather and unattended?"

Charlotte suddenly gasped:

"Oh, lawks-a-mercy, Aunt Jem will be waiting for her red cotton. She has to finish Miss Potter's dress tonight. Oh, I must go home immediately."

Lady Chase, only vaguely comprehending, shook her head.

"You are not fit to walk yet awhile. I shall see that you have dry clothes and a cordial before you are taken home. But how is it possible that your Mama ever let you venture forth in such a fog?"

"I have no mother," said Charlotte. "No father either," she added sorrowfully.

Eleanor Chase touched her son on the shoulders.

"Do you hear that, Vivian? This poor little girl is an orphan. How very sad!"

It did not seem sad to Lord Chase who had gone into a reverie and was considering the beauties of a certain young woman of quality who had excited his fancy during the luncheon.

Soon after Vivian's sixteenth birthday, less than a year ago, he had been initiated into the mysteries of sex by a pretty servant girl at Eton College where his lordship was receiving his education. Today he had been greatly smitten by the charms of the young lady seated next to him. It annoyed him that he was forced to live under the roof of so saintly and righteous a being as his widowed mother. All the world adored Eleanor Chase. But her only child was a supreme egotist; he was fast growing out of control. He had a callous and deceitful streak which made him unpopular once people became familiar with him. But his mother was blind to his true disposition. It was his boast to the "young bloods" who were his friends that he could "twist dear Mama round his little finger."

He enjoyed these jaunts to London when for his sake alone, Mama emerged from her retirement. He enjoyed life at Clunes only when the great house was filled with friends. Much to his mother's regret, he inherited none of his father's fondness for country pursuits. He rode well but was neither a good shot nor a keen fisherman.

As he followed his mother into the well-lighted hall where two powdered footmen waited upon them, Vivian wondered how he could persuade Mama to take up permanent residence in Eaton Square. The red-haired young miss who had excited his fancy at the luncheon was, he knew, resident in town.

Vivian handed hat, cloak and gloves to one of the footmen and simulated an interest in the little girl who was now able to walk beside her ladyship into the library.

"I trust you are none the worse," he said in his haughty voice.

Charlotte bobbed a curtsy. She looked up at the tall young gentleman, her lashes fluttering. Vivian's imperiousness overwhelmed her. She thought that he looked as splendid as a prince in one of the fairy books read to her by Uncle Albert. Yes, he was princely with his well-pomaded golden waves of hair, his heavy-lidded eyes, blue as turquoises—and the flashing ring on the hand which rested on his waist. A hand as slender and white and womanish as his mother's.

Lady Chase unclasped her sable-trimmed cloak and handed it to her maid.

"We must find something to fit this child, or wrap her in one of my shawls, and then send her home in the carriage. Her dress is soaked through. She fell in the gutter," Lady Chase told the maid.

"My lady, she shouldn't be standing in her muddy boots on your carpet—" began the grey-haired Hannah who was privileged, having been long in the service of the Chase family. Hannah was fond of his young lordship but had never been quite taken in by his facile charm. But my lady admonished her servant.

"Tush, Hannah, the child is God's creature, as are you or myself. She shall not be denied the comfort of our fireside. See—the rent in her stockings—the blood. She is so small and so brave. She neither cries nor complains."

"I could take her down to the servants' hall—" began Hannah with a severe look at the bedraggled Charlotte.

"She shall stay here. I, myself, will bandage her," said Lady Chase coldly. "Be so good as to fetch hot water, towels, and my medicine-chest."

Hannah curtsied and departed, muttering.

"Pray pull the bell, Vivian, and order the fire to be made up. It is chilly in here," added Lady Chase.

Charlotte did not think it cold. She found herself in a

warm and wonderful world. A world of magnificence hitherto unknown to her. Despite bruises and cuts and the shock of the accident, she had hardly suffered. She was entranced by the marvels that she now gazed upon. The heavy satin curtains shutting out the fog. The hothouse flowers. The thick rugs on the polished floor. The splendid pictures against dark crimson-papered walls. Over the mantelpiece hung a great French gilt mirror with candelabra in which six tall candles were burning like golden spears of light. There were handsomely shaded lamps elsewhere. The perfume of smouldering pine logs was pleasant to her nostrils, as was the lingering scent of violets from Lady Chase's hair. Fascinated, the child regarded the wondrous rings sparkling on my lady's hands. Her smart bustle, the silky-brown curls only just threaded with silver, falling on either side of her face. Such a wonderful face, like a sad cameo. Charlotte was intrigued by it. Indeed, she was dazed by all that she saw and most of all by the thousands of books. Handsome leather-bound volumes reaching as high as the ceiling. This was the library. Charlotte could not resist uttering an excited exclamation.

"Oh, my lady, what splendiferous books and so many of them!"

Lady Chase smiled down at her.

"Do you like books, then, my little one?"

Charlotte bobbed and blushed and nodded. Lady Chase felt it was strange that a small creature of this class should be so interested in reading-matter. She remarked upon it to her son. He, spreading his hands to the blaze from the logs, yawned a little.

"I suppose some of these paupers have brains," he drawled.

"Vivian!" admonished his mother and shook her head as though at a naughty child.

Vivian strolled out of the library and into the dining-room to pour himself out a glass of wine, because he dared not order it to be brought to him at this hour in front of his mother. He fell to thinking about his red-haired young lady and the exciting curve of her bosom under her sky-blue taffeta dress. He flung himself into a chair, stretched his long legs and wondered how he could get out of this house without being discovered, once Mama was abed, and go on a spree with another young gentleman who was equally thirsty for adventure.

When he returned to the library, however, he received quite a shock. For he saw a new Charlotte. She had had her cuts dressed and Hannah had found an old cashmere shawl of an Indian red which suited the child's lovely skin. They had wrapped it around the slender figure and pinned it over one small shoulder as though it were a sari. My lady intended to put another woollen shawl over her, and thus send her home. They had taken off her wet buttoned boots and torn stockings. Her feet were bare and, so Vivian noted, like alabaster, with high arches.

She was scrupulously clean despite her poverty. And now with her face and hands washed and her long bronzed curls brushed and shining, she presented a very different picture from the mud-stained waif upon whom Vivian had first gazed.

"By gad," he thought, "she is quite pretty."

He drew nearer her. Amused, he let his naturally lascivious gaze wander over the girl whom he judged to be older than she was. She held promise, he could tell, of exceptional looks. She was exceedingly graceful. And never before had he seen such a pair of eyes.

"By gad," he said again aloud, and chuckled at his hot boy's thoughts.

Lady Chase, innocent and gentle, smiled at her son.

"Is she not sweetly pretty, dear Vivian?"

"She certainly looks better than she did," he admitted.

Charlotte tried to thank them both and curtsy. Her bare toes caught in the fringe of the shawl which was much too long for her. She stumbled. The young man reached out and caught her. For a moment he held her up in his arms, grinning down into her rosy charming little face. She had a wonderful curve to her lips, he thought; a pity that *she* was not being trained as a servant girl at Clunes.

"Shall I myself take you home, little one?" he said lazily.

Charlotte, frozen with nerves, over-awed by the young gentleman who was holding her aloft, now gave a little cry.

"Pray set me down, sir."

"Yes, put her down, Vivian. She is terrified of you,"

smiled his mother, and added: "Perkins will drive her home. There is no need for you to venture out again."

His young lordship shrugged his shoulders, set Charlotte on her feet and moved away from her. Already he had ceased to be intrigued by her childish beauty. He gloomed at the prospect of an evening playing piquet with Mama. Tomorrow term would begin. He would be quite amused to return to school and indulge in a few daring escapades in the village with his companions.

Snugly wrapped in thick wool, Charlotte was at length carried by a coachman out to the carriage. She was wildly excited. What a lot she would have to tell Aunt Jem. In her hand she clutched a box of bonbons given to her by Lady Chase. A beautiful big round box tied with rose-pink ribbon. It had a glorious rose painted upon the lid. It was the sort of box that Charlotte had seen in the windows of fine shops but never dreamed she would ever possess. As for the beautiful kind lady, she had actually kissed Charlotte on the brow and pressed a sovereign into her hand as well as the bonbons. She said that she would call upon Miss Darnley tomorrow to discuss what might be done for her niece.

"If you so love books, it would seem a pity not to help you to receive some education," my lady said.

So, tomorrow, before her ladyship returned to the country she was going to talk to Aunt Jem. Oh, thought Charlotte, if she could but be *educated*. If she could but read some of those splendid books in that library; what utter bliss!

Charlotte was still in a transport, far removed from earthly things, and having almost forgotten the red cotton which poor Miss Darnley so sorely needed. The reluctant coachman set forth again in the fog which was just beginning to lift a little. As they moved towards Pimlico, the child dreamed again of all that she had just seen and of these exalted personages who had befriended her. It was well worth a few painful cuts and bruises.

The young gentleman—she thought more of Vivian than of Lady Chase, being true female—how handsome he was! The figure of the young lordship had impressed itself upon her mind. In her romantic childish way she had quite fallen in love with Vivian Chase. She was the beggar maid of the story books. He was the prince who lifted her up in his arms, laughed down at her with his light blue eyes, and turned her into a princess. Oh, if she could but return, and become not a princess but his slave. Oh, would she *ever* see him again?

Chapter Three

All too soon, Charlotte found herself back in the depressing ill-lit draughty rooms which constituted her home. She was received by Aunt Jem with floods of tears and loud lamentations in which a semi-inebriated Uncle Albert joined, loudly blowing his nose.

"Dear heavens, I thought you were lost to us, stolen by some Terrible Man. I never should have let you go forth in that fog," sobbed Miss Darnley.

The good soul was genuinely relieved to see her little niece again. She plied the child with questions, all of which Charlotte answered to her satisfaction. It was obvious that except for that cut on her forehead, a scratched cheek, and the grazed leg, she was little the worse for being knocked down. And Aunt Jem grew almost as excited as Charlotte as she drank in every detail of the child's description of the fine carriage and the house in Eaton Square.

"Imagine!" exclaimed Miss Darnley turning to her brother, "*Lady Chase* and her son. They are wealthy and famous. And her ladyship means to call here to see me tomorrow. Albert, I am all of a-flutter."

"We must polish the linoleum and the furniture," said Mr. Darnley mournfully.

Mr. Darnley had just come from The Three Bells. His breath exuded the bitter tang of the ale he had just consumed. But nobody noticed. Miss Darnley was far too excited in what her niece was telling her.

"Oh, fancy! Albert, listen to the child's description of the house in Eaton Square. Look—she owns a sovereign. Our Charl is rich!"

"And what about the handsome young gentleman who tossed her in the air, eh?" chuckled Mr. Darnley winking at Charlotte.

She winked back with youthful devilment, risking a reprimand from her aunt. She and her uncle had an understanding and if he was in liquor she did not realize it. Yes, she had plenty to say about young Lord Chase. She grimaced at the threadbare carpet. Her toes sunk into the deep soft pile of the rugs in Lady Chase's library, she said. Holding up the trailing shawl, she pirouetted, giving a performance as a fine lady.

"Hannah," she mimicked Lady Chase's aristocratic voice, "pray fetch the little creature a cordial—"

And she put a hand on her waist, looked through her lashes and gave a fair imitation of Vivian Chase, whereupon both aunt and uncle laughed until they wept. After which they all tasted a chocolate from the big round box, although Charlotte hated to untie the bow. She cherished the pink rose in her hands and kissed it.

"Oh, my lovely rose! Aunt Jem—it was all like one of uncle's fairy tales. I wish—I *wish* I had not to come home!"

At that, silence fell. Miss Darnley looked down her long thin nose and bridled, but with sadness in her eyes. Uncle Albert sighed and turned away. Charlotte, with her natural love of beauty had been dazzled by the luxury of the great house belonging to the Chases and now saw clearly the poverty of this place. Oh, how untidy and ugly it was with the poor furniture—the bits of material, threads and pins all over the floor. The darned, coarse lace curtains looped on either side of the dusty window which looked upon the roof tops of the poor street in which they lived.

But this was the home in which Charlotte had been brought up. Here, she had received all that she had known of love and care, for she remembered neither of her parents. Charlotte was too sweet-natured to allow the feelings of Aunt Jem to be hurt. She rushed at her and flung her arms round the angular form.

"Dear, dear Aunt Jem, forgive me. I did not mean what I said, I like it here best. I would not exchange our little home for the glories of Eaton Square."

At this, the good woman burst into tears. Uncle Albert became maudlin. They all had a good cry together. Finally Charlotte was given a bowl of bread and milk and sent to her bed. First of all Aunt Jem rubbed her chest with camphorated oil in case she had caught a cold out there in the fog. Before the candle was blown out in the icy cold bedroom, Charlotte knelt beside her aunt to thank God for her merciful escape from death under the horses' hooves.

Charlotte lay wakeful for some time. Her injured leg and cheek felt sore. Her little mind teemed with excited memories which kept her from her usual healthy sleep. She kept seeing the beautiful grave face of Eleanor Chase; then the bold blue eyes of Vivian, Lord Chase, as he had picked her up in his arms. Would she ever, *ever* see him again? Blissfully she hugged the dream of enchantment to herself. Terrified lest it should for ever escape her, she lay wondering whether her ladyship would keep her word to call upon Aunt Jem tomorrow. At last Charlotte fell asleep. But her uncle and aunt talked well into the night.

Miss Jemima, whose fingers were never idle, continued to ply her needle. At last her eyes were so sore, she had to stop and lower the lamp. Fearing to wake the little girl next door, the two whispered together about Charlotte's accident. Sadly Aunt Jem reviewed the potentialities in her sister's child.

"Alas, Bertie, our little Charl is a great beauty and has a talent to amuse. She could be a fine lady, herself. Did you not see how she looked when she acted for us this evening? It was indelicate, perhaps, with that shawl draped over her naked shoulder as though she were a heathen princess. But quite charming. And she is so tall, she will all too soon be a little woman. If only we had the means to educate her properly. To give her the chance of life she ought to have!"

"Agreed, agreed," mumbled Albert. He sat rocking in his chair, toying with his watch chain, hankering after the warmth and pleasure of The Three Bells. But he dared not go back there. Jemima kept the purse and doled money out to him only in small quantities. Miss Darnley returned to the subject of Lady Chase's visit.

When Mrs. Skipper came up in the morning, she said, to cook the midday meal, there would be no time for cleaning. She, Jemima, and Albert must try to get a little law and order into their apartment tonight. Much against Uncle Albert's will, he rose and lent his sister a hand. Miss Darnley, half dropping with weariness, nobly exerted herself. By midnight the sitting-room had been transformed. Tomorrow morning, Miss Darnley announced, she would move the sewing machine into the bedroom, and there continue with her work so that this room would remain garnished for her ladyship's visit.

Mr. Darnley then bade his sister good night and betook himself to the attic in which he slept. Miss Darnley crept to her own bed feeling every bone in her body aching, and a strange pain in her breast. Yes, she had felt very ill for some long time. She wondered how to carry on and what would happen to Charlotte if anything happened to *her*.

She stood a moment beside the truckle bed in which her niece was lying. Shading the candle with one hand, she peered down at Charlotte's recumbent form. The tawny curls were tossed upon the pillow, the pale young face was flushed in sleep and the lips parted to show a dazzle of pearly teeth. It was a remarkable face and Miss Darnley knew it. In a vague way she felt bitterly afraid for Charlotte. As she had once been afraid for her lovely Lottie, her sister. Lottie had been just such a one for luxury and gaiety, and just as generous in spirit. She had loved Oliver Goff passionately, given her whole heart to Charlotte's father. What would happen to little Charlotte who, like her mother, had so few leanings toward quiet domesticity. What work could she do and still keep her refined ways? What chance had she in such quarters as these to meet or marry a gentleman?

"I must speak to her ladyship, if indeed she comes tomorrow," Miss Darnley thought feverishly. "Perhaps she will patronize our Charlotte. And now I must try to get some sleep and be at my best to receive our distinguished visitor."

But Jemima Darnley was never to look upon the beautiful face of Eleanor Chase; nor to know the excitement of welcoming a lady of the nobility to this modest home. The long drawn-out torture of sewing and pressing all through the tedious hours of day, and half the night, was ended for Miss Darnley. Ended, the bitter struggle for existence, with no one beside her save a useless inebriate of a brother. Long years of semi-starvation, trying to save a little money for the child, added to a congenital weakness of the heart, cut short Miss Darnley's life. Tonight's particular effort to clean and tidy the room had been too much for her. She had time only to blow out the candle and stretch herself upon her bed—and it was the end. A gasp for breath—a convulsion—and her courageous spirit fled.

It was Charlotte who discovered the awful tragedy—the first real tragedy in her life—when she awakened next morning. She yawned and stretched, then by the light that filtered through the yellow blind, saw Aunt Jem lying in a peculiar way, staring at the ceiling as though her gaze was transfixed. She was so ghastly a hue that even the child's heart plunged with horror. She screamed for her uncle. Mr. Darnley, wearing his night-shirt, and with a cap askew on his head, accompanied by another lady in the building, came running in answer to that piercing cry. But it was too late. It was only a cold corpse that they found. The frozen smile of the dead lay upon Miss Darnley's lips.

A neighbour took the horrified, sobbing child into her own quarters. Later, Mr. Darnley answered the questions put to him by a hastily summoned doctor, and while he wept into a handkerchief, wondered slyly how soon he could extract a shilling or two from his dead sister's purse, and take himself off to The Three Bells.

And this was the scene that Lady Chase found when, true to her word, and accompanied by Hannah, her maid, she arrived at the Darnleys' dwelling.

Chapter Four

Four years later.

Clunes, at any time of the year, was a magnificent place. It had been built three hundred years ago by the first Lord Chase who had married a French Countess. To please his bride, this nobleman had designed what might be taken as a small French chateau, with a marble terrace overlooking superb grounds. The dove-grey of fretted stonework was glorious against the sombre green of the trees. The last Lord Chase had spent a great deal of money upon the grounds. A small army of gardeners toiled daily, cutting the velvet lawns, clipping the hedges into the strange shapes of birds beloved by the French. And then there was the famous fountain, a miniature lake, the rose arbours, the herb walks, and the orchards.

Clunes lay like a jewel on the borders of Hertfordshire and Essex, and one mile from the sleepy little village of Harling, with its fine Norman church. The late Lord Chase had been revered by all its inhabitants as was his beautiful and saintly widow who regularly visited the sick and suffering. There were rumours that the young Lord Vivian was not quite so noble as his sire. Gossip from the servants' hall at Clunes suggested that the handsome and charming young man could, when he chose, be a young devil. But on the whole the Chase family was popular and the villagers looked with awe towards the great lodge gates.

In winter, when the grounds were deep in snow and the turrets of Clunes gleamed as though with crusted diamonds, the place looked like an illustration from a story book. And it was in winter that Charlotte Goff had first come to live in the Lodge—a little grey stone house with diamond-paned windows, standing sentinel by the gates. It was spring when she had first grown to love Clunes with passion and think of it henceforth as the most gorgeous house in the world.

On this particular day in April, Charlotte walked down the famous elm drive, and enjoyed the warmth of the spring sunlight on her upturned face. After the years spent in the grime and soot of London, cooped in Aunt Jem's room, country life never failed to appeal to Charlotte.

This carriage drive was nearly a quarter of a mile in length, flanked by tall trees and great rhododendron bushes soon to burst into crimson bloom. Up on the tall trees the rooks cawed and circled around their nests.

Under her arm, Charlotte carried two books—one on French history, and one of Keats' poems. It was half past two. This was the hour that she usually spent with her benefactor, Lady Chase. For the last four years her school had been the library which was twice as large and filled with twice as many rare books as the one in Eaton Square.

Thanks to Lady Chase, the little girl of twelve had developed into an erudite young lady who would soon celebrate her seventeenth birthday, who was proficient in French and English subjects, able to play the piano, to dance and to paint. But still the same Charlotte who could not sew. Lady Chase had given up trying to interest her protégée in the embroideries and tapestry work which she herself executed so well.

As Charlotte neared the broad marble terrace of the house, she paused a moment to look upon a sight of which she had never grown tired. At this time of year the lawns were like emerald velvet. Every tree was in bud. The beeches a tender green which would eventually mature into tawny gold. On either side of the terrace stood two magnificent tulip trees which were Lady Chase's delight.

For four long years now, Charlotte had lived with Mr. and Mrs. Forbes, the lodgekeepers. She never mixed with any visitors who came to Clunes. Only vaguely now she remembered her old life—and Uncle Albert. He had soon followed his sister to the grave. A drop too much liquor one night, and, outside The Three Bells, the old reprobate had swayed across the road and been knocked down by a passing cab. Charlotte then had no one of her own flesh and blood left in the world.

Since Aunt Jem had passed away, life had been transformed for Charlotte. Lady Chase, having discovered the state of affairs in the Pimlico dwelling house, had at once approached Uncle Albert and offered to take his niece down to Clunes.

"I would like to see that she is properly educated. She is a charming, beautiful child, and interests me," her ladyship had said. And Mr. Darnley, not knowing what to do with a small girl on his hands, gratefully handed Charlotte over to the great lady's care.

Nan and Joseph Forbes, the lodgekeeper and his wife, were uneducated but respectable folk with no family of their own and only too pleased to adopt her ladyship's protégée. They found Charlotte easy to manage and very affectionate, and she soon won their hearts with her beauty and charm.

During the years that followed, she grew tall and strong. She adored the country and quickly learned the names of all the birds and flowers and trees. Her greatest delight was to learn her lessons at the knee of her benefactor. Her ladyship often said to her: "It is a pleasure to teach you, my little one, for you assimilate knowledge as the sun drinks the dew."

But it was not her ladyship's intention to allow Charlotte to move too freely in a *milieu* which could never be hers. Charlotte shared her foster parents' simple pleasures. Visitors to Clunes rarely saw the beautiful young girl. Vivian was nearly always away. He had left Eton and gone up to Oxford.

When Charlotte saw him—which was rarely—she still looked upon Vivian as the prince of her dreams. Now that he had grown to manhood, he had much to occupy his time. During the holidays he filled Clunes with the young friends in his own set. But there were occasions when he condescended to wander down to the lodge and speak to the pretty girl whom his mother had befriended. At such times Charlotte listened, enthralled, while he boasted of his conquests and confided some of his escapades, just in order to see the rich blood whip her cheeks and hear her gasp: "Oh, my *lord*!"

He teased her, shocked, and delighted her in turn. Occasionally he would tell her that she was growing "deuced attractive." Then she grew a little scared. But she did not understand why the Forbes, when listening to her rhapsodies about the golden-haired young gentleman, glanced at each other, then looked down their noses. She could see they did not like his lordship. And once Mrs. Forbes said: "Do not believe all that young man tells you, my little dear. Her ladyship is an angel but there is a devil in his lordship."

Charlotte only laughed merrily. She thought the world and everyone in it wonderful. She could see no real harm in Vivian. Innocence shone out of her golden eyes. But she did realize quite soon, that once *he* returned to Oxford, Clunes seemed empty and a little sad.

When his lordship was home, she sometimes watched him ride through the lodge gates with his companions and she would envy the beautifully-dressed young ladies who had the right to ride beside him, and call him *"Vivian."* And she wished passionately that she could go to some of the splendid balls and dinner parties up at the house and share *his* life, *his* pleasures. But such thoughts she kept deep in her heart.

This afternoon as Charlotte came up the marble steps to the terrace, gay with vivid colour from the flowers in the big stone vases, she came upon Vivian. He was dressed casually, wearing a light velvet jacket and flowing tie. He looked, she thought, her heart beating as it always did at the sight of him, like a young god. Her inexperienced eyes did not note the dark smudges under his eyes—the looseness of his mouth—the twitching of his slender fingers, betraying the fact that his lordship's nerves were bad.

He had been leading a secret life of debauchery, undreamed of by his saintly mother. He could still manage to deceive her—if not his tutor at Oxford. Last term he had been in danger of being sent down and only escaped by virtue of the fact that the senior proctor had known and loved his father, and had pity on Vivian's widowed mother. But a grave warning had been issued to him.

For a while Vivian, subdued, had resolved to turn over a new leaf. But he was too great a rogue at heart to stay penitent for long. He had not got it in him to study assiduously, or moderate his habits. Drink and women had already taken a hold of him.

However, today, he felt as he put it "deuced fatigued." After his mother had gone to sleep last night, he had strolled through the woods to a certain house presided over by a lady on whom his mother would never call. A divorcée, named Roma Gresham. At one time Mrs. Gresham had been a respected member of London society. After her divorce she had turned to a way of life which to a pure woman like Eleanor Chase would seem appalling. The man for whom Mrs. Gresham had abandoned virtue had died before she could marry him. She was still handsome and vivacious in her early thirties. Her lover had bequeathed to her enough money with which to lead the sort of life that amused her; for she was both sensual and avaricious. She passed from one admirer to another. Her latest lover, a dissolute baronet, had rented this house for her—and himself. The countryside was a good "cover-up" for his excesses. Mrs. Gresham held wild parties, with gambling, drinking and dancing to amuse him and his friends. They also amused Vivian who was more often to be found in Mrs. Gresham's house than in his own.

He threw away his cigarette as he caught sight of Charlotte. Each time he returned from Oxford, he was struck by her fast-maturing beauty. Spoiled as he was by the world of women in which he moved, and growing a little tired of the painted faces in Mrs. Gresham's set, he was equally bored by the empty-headed, well-brought up young females in his own circle. But Charlotte Goff intrigued him. She had, as he so often told himself, a *"Je ne sais quoi"* that fascinated him. She was a mixture of the artless child and the intelligent student whom his mother was teaching. The sun touched her bright bronzed hair to a deep gold. She moved with unconscious grace. Her pale blue dress was plain homespun and without distinction, but, Vivian, the young sybarite and philanderer, saw in her one of the nymphs of the Greek classics which he had to study—much to his *ennui*. However, he felt little *ennui* as he looked at Charlotte. He stood up and bowed as low as he would do to any fine lady.

He quoted:

Had I the heart to slide an arm beneath her,
Press her parting lips as her waist I gather slow,

Waking in amazement she could not but embrace me:
Then would she hold me and never let me go?

Charlotte with crimson cheeks and a pounding heart tried to laugh.

"Your lordship should not say such things to me."

Vivian laughed lazily.

"My dear child, it was not I who conceived those romantic lines but the poet, George Meredith."

She nodded.

"Her ladyship has given me many of Mr. Meredith's beautiful poems to read."

Vivian let his gaze, critical and voluptuous, wander over the pearly texture of Charlotte's skin; her rounded arms, her delicate wrists, and ankles, her long tapering fingers. Often he wondered from what stock this lovely girl had sprung. She seemed to him more of an aristocrat than many of the girls in his own set. His mother, too, had remarked on the fact.

But they knew little of Charlotte's ancestry beyond what the old reprobate, Albert Darnley, had told them about her lovely mother and her good-looking father, who had both died so tragically young in France.

Vivian put out a finger and touched one of the silky ringlets that lay upon Charlotte's shoulders.

"Sweet thing," he said. "Mr. Meredith must certainly have been thinking of you when he wrote those words. Tell me—would you *'come with me to a beech tree'* and lie like the lady in the poet's verse—*'couch'd with her arms behind her golden head'*—He wrote that, too. I care little for poetry but this was brought to my mind as I watched you walk toward me this afternoon."

Charlotte meditated. Except for her visits to the great house, she led a strictly secluded life. She had no knowledge of the world and could not begin to deal with the flattery of a man like Vivian. But she could not ignore the compliment. It went a little to her head.

Vivian watched how her curving lashes flickered. He was no longer inclined to sulk out here on the terrace. A remorseless wish to teach this pure and unsullied girl the meaning of man's passion gripped him. He was positive that she would respond if he could but woo her into his arms. He could see how deeply even his words affected her.

"What time do you finish your lessons?" he asked suddenly in a low abrupt voice.

She fingered her books nervously.

"At half past three, I think, my lord."

"How many times have I told you not to address me so."

"I cannot call you 'Vivian.' "

"You can and shall."

She was rendered speechless, for his look was burning. Suddenly she was afraid.

"Your mother will be waiting for me—*Vivian*," she whispered the name which was so often on her mind, and in her prayers. Yes, she prayed nightly for this golden-haired prince of her dreams and if anybody had spoken ill of him she would not have listened.

"I will be here when you come out," said Vivian, and touched her curls again with a caressing finger.

She hurried away through the long open French windows into the library where Lady Chase was waiting for her. The young man seated himself astride the balustrade again. He took a cigarette from a gold box which he carried, and lit it. His eyes narrowed. His thoughts were lascivious. This was not the first time that he had felt a dangerous desire for Charlotte Goff. So far in his young spoiled life he had denied himself little that he wanted. Looks and money and his title secured what he craved. The cloak of virtue which he wore for his mother's benefit and also for the benefit of Sir Harry Cawder, his guardian, was soon dropped once Vivian was out of their sight. Fortunately for Vivian, Sir Harry had long been ailing and only once in recent years had the young man come under the General's jurisdiction. Then, he had received a strong caution.

Charlotte was not the first innocent girl whom Vivian had desired and seduced. Already one unfortunate of sixteen summers had borne a child to him. The babe had died and the miserable ruined young female was spirited away by her parents, Vivian having paid them a sum of money. The boy was devoid not only of morals but of respect for purity. Nothing barred him from indulgence save his fear of losing the money that came to him through the generosity of his mother.

He knew exactly what his mother had planned for Charlotte. Once she was seventeen, she was to go to France. Eleanor Chase's greatest friend, the Princesse de Larolles, who had a family of small children, wished them to be taught English. It was arranged between the two ladies that the young Charlotte should live for a year or two in the big chateau at Fontainebleau and teach the little Larolles all that she knew.

When Vivian had first heard of these plans he had deplored them. He had grown so accustomed to seeing the bewitching young girl down at the Lodge, and talking to her when he was bored. Besides, he thought of what might happen to her in France. Doubtless some hot-blooded young Frenchman would pay court to her beauty. Vivian wanted to be the first to touch those rose-red lips which were curved so splendidly for kissing. He had a sensual knowledge of women which led him to believe that for all Charlotte's childlike, lily-white innocence, she was by nature passionate. She would have much to give a man. Vivian Chase did not intend to let this prize drift out of his reach to France.

He flung himself into a long basket chair. Quite heartlessly, he planned the seduction of Charlotte.

Chapter Five

In the cool library amid the books that she loved so well, Charlotte sat with Eleanor Chase. She read first an English essay on Keats; then a short résumé of the French Revolution. Later she would receive a lesson at that magnificent grand piano in the drawing-room. Charlotte loved her piano-forte lessons, given to her by an elderly lady named Miss de Wynter who resided in Harling.

As a rule, Charlotte gave her whole heart to her lessons. Today, Lady Chase found her young pupil unusually *distraite*. She kept stumbling over her words and looking out of the windows; then, flushed and apologetic, would return to her books.

"Your thoughts are not on your studies, little one," her ladyship remarked gently.

"I beg your pardon, my lady," stammered Charlotte.

"Never mind," said Lady Chase and smiled in her sweet sympathetic way, "I cannot expect an old head on young shoulders. You are progressing well, but the sunshine must be tempting to you today. Perhaps you wish to be out in the wood gathering primroses? I forget that you are still only a child."

Charlotte bit her lip. *Only a child!* That made her feel guilty. For they were not childish thoughts that distracted her from this afternoon's lessons. They were the exciting, troubling, terrifying reflections of a girl in her seventeenth year; *a girl in love*. And it was the handsome face of Vivian Chase which she kept seeing. The memory of the pretty things he had said to her—especially his announcement that he would be waiting for her when she went out again—haunted her imagination.

How horrified her ladyship would be if she could but guess! *Oh, dear*, thought Charlotte, *I am wicked and un-*

grateful. It is not fitting that I who am nobody at all, should think so much of him.

But the thoughts were not to be banished. And at last when she spoke a wrong line as she recited *"The Eve of St. Agnes,"* Lady Chase stopped her.

"There, my dear, enough for now; go back into the sunshine. It is better for you than learning the verses even of so divine a poet. I will ask Miss de Wynter to excuse you, also, your music lesson. You can take it tomorrow."

Charlotte collected her books; her expression was downcast.

"Alas—I have disappointed you, my lady."

"Not at all. Do not make so much of it. You are far ahead of most pupils of your age."

"I thank you, my lady," said Charlotte gratefully, and curtsied low.

Eleanor leaned back in the winged armchair which was her favourite. She smiled benevolently at Charlotte. The girl was turning into a real beauty she thought. But what Eleanor liked still more was the fashion in which Charlotte's character had developed. All who knew her spoke well of her. The good couple at the Lodge were never done praising her qualities of piety and obedience, coupled with that charming natural warmth and gaiety which made her such a general favourite.

"I did not make a mistake when I took her out of that sad house in Pimlico," Lady Chase mused. "She has amply repaid me."

Almost Lady Chase loved her young protégée as a daughter—the daughter she had wanted and never had.

As the girl returned her ladyship's glances, she felt, not for the first time, a tinge of anxiety. The years had not sat kindly upon Eleanor Chase. The celebrated beauty of the sad "Madonna" was still there, but the brown curls had turned to silver grey, the eyes were sunken. She had aged; grown excessively thin. Several times during lessons, Charlotte fancied she saw a look of pain cross that serene and noble countenance. Once, one of the wonderful diamond rings which her ladyship liked to wear, slipped from a finger become too slender.

Charlotte had, on one occasion, questioned the son of the house about his mother's health, but he seemed unconcerned.

"Mama has always been delicate. She does not complain to me," he had said with a shrug.

But even the inexperienced girl could not fail to note today the sinister marks of some secret malady on my lady's face, revealed by a sudden shaft of sunlight that fell on her.

"What is it, my child?" said Lady Chase as she saw Charlotte's expression.

The girl was too shy to say, but suddenly picked up one of the lovely hands of her benefactor and pressed her lips upon it.

"My lady, I thank you from the bottom of my heart for all that you have done for me," she breathed. "I fear I have been inattentive today. Do, pray, forgive me."

"There—think no more about it," smiled her ladyship. "We all have our moments of day-dreaming. As a rule you are a very diligent pupil. Go out and take the air, my little one."

Charlotte curtsied and bade her farewell. Lady Chase did not move but followed the graceful figure with her brooding gaze. Dear little Charlotte! Not once had she ever shown ingratitude or grown too bold. Indeed Eleanor Chase could have wished that her son possessed many of the girl's excellent qualities. She loved Vivian but could not at times fail to see that he was very egotistical; that there was a certain wildness in his blood. She had always hoped that, with the years, he would gain stability and become more like his splendid Papa. She used to shut her eyes to his shortcomings. But she did at times fear for Vivian's future. The best thing that could happen would be for him to make an early marriage. But not to a silly frivolous child like Harriet Dawnay who occasionally stayed down at Clunes, and hunted with him. Indeed, so far none of the young ladies who partnered Vivian seemed to Lady Chase at all suitable. She wanted him to marry a young woman of sterling qualities, as well as of noble birth.

Ah, well! that day would come, she mused, and it was her dearest wish that it would come soon.

In her innocence, Lady Chase even allowed herself sometimes to think what a pity it was that her protégée was not of good birth and breeding. She would make some man an excellent wife. But Lady Chase never connected Charlotte and Vivian. So far as she knew they rarely saw each other. If Vivian ever spoke of the girl it was in a patronizing way. He counted her as his social inferior. His mother had never been able to persuade him, even when he was a small boy, to be kind or considerate to those beneath him in station.

So it never entered her ladyship's head that Vivian would be likely to take a serious interest in Charlotte. In any case, Charlotte in her ladyship's opinion was still in the "schoolroom."

Eleanor sat quiet for a moment and let her mind dwell with pride and affection on the thought of her son's good looks and his charm, rather than his faults. Then, suddenly, pain struck at her. It struck so cruelly that for a moment she thought she was going to faint. Gasping, with closed eyes, she sat clutching at her breast. And now, suddenly, she knew that it was the coldness of death itself that chilled her on that sunny afternoon.

Lady Chase had known for a long time that she was going to die soon but she did not know when. So far it had been mere instinct, coupled with long wakeful nights, and days when her courage had faltered because of the pain in her heart. Her mother had died of *angina pectoris*. Maybe this same fate awaited her. Eleanor did not know but accepted the possibility with the same calm stoicism that she had accepted all her sorrows. But she did not want her end to come *too* soon; not until Vivian was more stabilized.

Somehow she managed to get up and stagger to the long tapestry attached to the bell and pull at it. A footman entered. She sent him for Hannah, her maid. When old Hannah came in and saw her beloved mistress's ghastly face, she fell on her knees and burst into tears.

"My lady, my lady, you cannot go on like this. You must let me call your physician."

"I suppose so," whispered Lady Chase.

"Indeed, my lady, I will send one of the men for Dr. Castleby at once. Now you must let me help you up to bed."

The terrible pain had passed. Lady Chase was breathing normally again and even able to smile. She drew a long deep sigh.

"Alas, Hannah, I think my end is approaching."

Hannah, with streaming eyes, said:

"Do not say it, my lady. I could not bear that aught should happen to you."

"My faithful Hannah, death must come to all of us. And I shall see my beloved husband again. Is that not a joyful prospect for me?"

Hannah nodded, wiped her eyes and straightened the little muslin cap on her grey sedate head. But as she helped her mistress up to her bedroom, the old servant could see for herself that her ladyship was mortally ill. Alas that they were not in London, for old Dr. Castleby from Harling, although a godly and righteous man, was not a specialist in diseases of the heart.

Hannah helped her mistress into bed and tried to be comforting.

"This is maybe only one of your attacks, and it will pass, my lady."

"Yes—and it will return," said Lady Chase in a hollow voice. She looked mournfully around her beautiful bedroom.

On the wall before her, hung a huge painting of her husband in uniform, one hand on his hip. So like Vivian in face and form, she thought, as she gazed at the fine figure with her world-weary eyes. Difficult to realize that two men could in character be so different. Alas, that the boy was not more like his father. Alas, too, that his godfather who might have counselled him well, was also stricken down. Soon there would be nobody left to guide the young man's footsteps.

At the doorway, Hannah turned and said:

"I will go and make you a cordial, my lady. Shall I send his lordship to you?"

The colour rose to Lady Chase's pale cheeks.

"Under no circumstances is my son to be told that I am so ill. Inform him, if you must, that I have a migraine and that because of that I have asked Dr. Castleby to come and prescribe for me."

Something urged the old retainer to frown at this.

"Would it not be better that he should know the truth, my lady?" she muttered.

"No, Hannah. The worry might interfere with his lordship's final studies at Oxford. And God in his mercy may spare me a little longer, so why bring needless worry and grief to those who care for me?"

Hannah sighed. She bobbed a curtsy and departed. On her way downstairs she paused on the landing in front of one of the big windows, in order to pull a fold of curtain into place. She had peculiarly good long sight for one of her years. And as she stood there—peering out of that window—she clicked her tongue against her teeth. For she saw something that was not to her liking. It was the figure of his lordship vanishing through the rosary which led past an ornamental lake into the woods. Nothing unusual about this, except that Hannah had also seen that other figure which preceded Lord Chase. Her ladyship's protégée, Charlotte Goff.

Hannah stood still. Her mind was full of unease. She was an old woman, but not ignorant of life and she knew the young master only too well. Had she not seen him grow up, and witnessed many of the youthful follies which had been kept hidden from her ladyship. The whole staff was for ever covering up for the handsome boy. But Hannah knew perfectly well that he would have little respect for a pretty girl in Charlotte's station.

Hannah did not particularly care for Charlotte; she had always thought it over-charitable of her ladyship to bring the orphan to Clunes. The old servant was jealous, too, of the many hours which the girl spent in the company of her ladyship. But she was a good woman, and would not want any harm to come to Charlotte; especially not through Vivian.

Hannah was quite sure those two young things were up to no good; but, of course, she could not so much as mention the fact to her sick lady. Nor could even she, as a privileged maid, speak to Lord Chase. If she did, she knew that she would receive nothing but a laugh and a denial. Vivian either teased her or was rude to her. There was no love lost between them. The old servant uttered a prayer.

"God grant that her ladyship will never know what I and many others know about her son. Better that she should have a peaceful death now, than live to suffer a terrible awakening."

Chapter Six

Through the beechwoods, dappled with the bright sunshine that filtered through the young leaves, Charlotte walked beside Lord Chase.

The young girl was unspeakably happy. She felt, too, unspeakably wicked. It was really the first time she had ever done such a thing as this. And she seldom left the Lodge without letting Nan know where she had gone.

"I dare not—" she had said to Vivian when he had begged her to take this stroll.

"Nonsense," he had broken in. "*I* shall be responsible for you."

Vivian felt no sense of responsibility in this hour; only an ever increasing desire to be the first man to take this radiant young creature into an embrace.

He knew that she was, in her innocent way, already his slave. He also knew that he must go warily at first. So as they walked, he spoke not of love, but of life. Into her enchanted ears he poured stories of things he had seen and done. Of ceremonial visits to London and Paris. Of a holiday spent with an Oxford friend in Monte Carlo; of others in Rome and Venice.

"Oh, Lord Ch—I mean Vivian—it all sounds so glorious!" she exclaimed, when he drew breath. "How well you describe it all. Indeed, I think *you* should write my essays for me. You have such imagination."

With a careless smile he accepted her flattery.

"Do not dwell always on the thought of studies, Charlotte," he said. "You are young and beautiful. You should be dreaming of more romantic things. Is it not time that you saw life as other young girls see it? That you went to dances and parties? I think it is all wrong that my mother keeps you so firmly shut away from pleasures indulged in by other young girls."

Charlotte looked quite shocked.

"But I am a *nobody*. Her ladyship has shown me great honour by giving me an education. It would not be fitting for me to go to the fine balls like the young ladies in your set."

They had reached a little clearing in the glade where the mossy ground was tawny with last year's leaves. Vivian caught hold of one of Charlotte's hands. Before she could decline, he pulled her down beside him.

"Come—let us sit together and rest awhile," he said.

"Oh, Vivian, I ought not—" she began.

He interrupted:

"I shall be the one to say what Miss Goff ought or ought not to do today."

She continued to protest, her cheeks hot and pink, her eyes dancing. He broke in again:

"Tush! You are only too ready to take instruction from others. Will you not take it from me?"

"You are very masterful," she said in a low voice.

"A maid likes a man to be masterful, does she not, Charlotte?"

"I know nothing of men," she said, her heart beating madly fast.

"How old are you?" he asked abruptly.

"Seventeen in August."

"Still sixteen and so sweet," he said.

Now he fingered a fold of her light dress confined at the narrow waist by a belt with an old buckle. It had been made by Mrs. Forbes. The young man said dreamily:

"I would like to see you wear a bustle."

Charlotte giggled.

"I cannot imagine myself in one. It would be far too fashionable for me."

"And I would also like to see you in a corsage slipping off those creamy shoulders," he said boldly, and touched her warm white neck. Immediately alarm seized her. She moved away; yet not too far, for his touch thrilled her immeasurably.

"Let us walk on," she whispered.

But with a single movement he pulled her down to him and held her against his breast.

"Let us stay here. Charl—little love—you are so sweet. It is delicious to be here alone with you—at last!"

"Vivian, please let me go," she said, and turned quite pale. She was, he thought, like a bird that found itself in a snare.

"Lie quiet. Let us speak together of love," he said. His face was flushed, his voice husky with the passion that consumed him. "Tell me your dreams, your thoughts, your hopes. Surely they cannot always be connected with dry, dull learning."

She was too scared to answer. But she trembled with delight, lying close to him, while his hands caressed her hair.

Unconsciously she had always wanted him with the natural warmth of her budding womanhood. When suddenly he drew her down to his lips and touched them, his kiss—her first—destroyed the innocence of her childhood.

She struggled, first white then red, torn between tears and laughter, between fear and surrender.

"This is wicked—wrong—you must let me go—dear Vivian, *please*."

"Do you not love me, my little darling?"

"It is not permitted that I should love you," she breathed in terror.

"That is for me to say. Forget those others who would control your existence."

Vivian felt her whole body quivering. Anyone but he might have had compassion for her. With rougher passion he began to kiss her mouth and her throat. He tangled his fingers through the thick masses of her chestnut hair. This lovely child was completely in his hands, and if to satisfy his own desire he must break her heart, what matter to Vivian Chase? It amused him to remember more of those verses read by him at Oxford only a few weeks ago. With lips wandering across her face, he came to one small ear. He murmured in it.

> You, my wild one, you tell of honied field-rose,
> Violet, blushing eglantine of life. . . .

A desperate bid for sanity, coupled with her natural modesty, led Charlotte to fight him again. She tried to beat off his kisses. He seized her hands, kissed and imprisoned, and laughing, silenced her lips. He quoted again:

Oh, the golden sheaf, the rustling treasure-armful
Oh, the nut-brown tresses . . . oh, the girdle slack about
the waist.

Then he spoke no more but gathered her closer, his hands exploring her slim waist. He was intoxicated by her unblemished perfection. For him it was another conquest. But for her, farewell forever to the purity of her body, to the tranquillity of her mind. Now—an ecstatic surging of her senses. Afterwards would come the anguish of remorse —the darkness of despair. But not yet, not while she lay in Vivian's arms, possessed and enchanted.

As he grew more daring, alarm shuddered through her. She pressed his hot desirous face back from her, the palms of her hands against his cheeks.

"No, Vivian, no, this is wicked."

"There is no wickedness in love," he said blithely and touched the silk of her lashes with his lips.

"Let me go," she whispered.

"To escape me forever?—no." But she was frightened now and cried out as he none too gently untied the ribbons at her throat and moved his lips across the matchless purity of her shoulders. She trembled, caught between her rapture and her fear. Suddenly the cry that broke from her was of pain as well as ecstasy.

"Ah, no, for God's sake, Vivian. I implore you."

But it was too late. The handsome boy was crazy to possess her; careless of her age—her pitiful innocence.

"You shall belong to me," he said against her bruised lips, "you *shall*, you heavenly child!"

It seemed to Charlotte that all the pathways of her life had led to this one moment—led her to her fate, be it for good or evil. Vivian Chase took her in passion, but she gave in compassionate love, true to her sex. Later, when he lay at her side, content and sleepy-eyed, the tears tumbled through her long lashes but he kissed them away with a careless affection. He laughed at the shame in her eyes. He found her state of mind stupid rather than deserving of compassion. He had long since forgotten what it was to be ashamed in such matters as these.

He lay humming under his breath, his hands laced behind his head. He was satisfied and triumphant. Charlotte re-tied the bows at her throat and looked down at him like a stricken doe. Suddenly she threw herself upon him.

"I never meant that to happen. It was truly wrong. Vivian, Vivian, what shall I do?"

"Stupid—there is nothing you should do," he said. His smile was half scornful, wholly victorious. "You are mine now, and shall be again many times I hope—that is when it is expedient for us to meet."

"No," she said under her breath, and shook her head violently.

"Yes," he mocked her and pulled her lazily down upon him.

As his lips met hers, the salt of her tears trickled upon them. He sat up and brushed the leaves from his bright gold hair. He was impatient of her. He had had enough of this love-play. For her it was the beginning and end of a life. To him an interlude.

"Why must women always cry and spoil things," he grumbled.

"Say that you truly love me, say it, *please*!" she begged.

"Of course I do. I love all pretty girls."

Wounded to the core, Charlotte's great eyes reproached him. She said under her breath:

"Am I one of so many? Merciful heavens, do not let me hear you say that again."

He yawned and stood up, smoothing his crumpled suit.

"What would you have me tell you, foolish girl? That you are the *only* woman in my life? It would be a damnable lie."

She stood before him hurt and dumb. She looked as though she had been shot straight through the heart.

"I do not understand you," she whispered, "there is no sense in what you say. I only ask to be allowed to love you and never any other man. Can you not promise to love only me?"

"Oh, stop trying to pin me down. Be satisfied with what you have had," he said in a hard, mocking voice.

Now her eyes were so piteous that even Vivian softened. He pulled her into his arms. With a fresh spurt of passion, he kissed her long and hard. He whispered between the kisses. "Never mind, sweet Charlotte. You are very lovely and I do, indeed, love you. I will see you soon again. Now I must take you home or Nan will wonder where you are. Come!"

He held out his hand. Charlotte put hers into it, trying to check the turbulence of the grief which had replaced the ecstasy of an hour ago.

The Spring day had lengthened into the violet dusk of evening when at last the young lovers emerged from the wood.

Outside the oak doorway which led into the orchard through which Vivian could reach the big house, the young man stopped and smiled down at the girl.

His face was flushed. His eyes were full of satisfaction, tempered only faintly with guilt. He knew he had committed a monstrous sin which, if his mother were to find out, might bring disaster upon him as well as Charlotte. The only thing that worried him was his own danger. Over this beautiful child, not yet seventeen, whom he had so heartlessly seduced, he had few qualms. All girls were the same, he thought cynically; fools, ready to comply with a man's requests. Charlotte was a little *special* perhaps, and he had enjoyed her beauty. He had been pleasantly surprised, too, by the ardour of her response. He had, of course, always imagined that hers was an ardent nature. Now he knew it.

"We must meet soon again and repeat today's splendid idyll," he said carelessly, and touched her cheek with a careless finger.

She was silent. There was no vestige of colour in her face. Her eyes looked huge and scared. She was looking neat and demure again; she had smoothed her dress and brushed away the leaves and twigs. But she could not brush away the consciousness of her fall from grace. Now that the overwhelming excitement was over, she was horrified at what she had done.

"No—no, never to be repeated," she breathed, and bit hard on lips that were bruised from his mad kissing.

"Stupid child, why not? Did you not return my kisses and love me as I loved you?"

"Love," she stumbled over the word, "yes, but not *that*."

"Nonsense," he laughed, but frowned at her out of the corners of his eyes. *Afterwards* a girl never seemed to him so desirable as before; not even this one.

"I should never have permitted such a thing," she whispered, and tears hung like diamond drops on her lashes.

The sight of those new tears irritated Vivian.

"Come—you are not going to make a scene, I trust," he said.

Her poor heart, her dazed mind were shocked by this display of indifference.

"What would her ladyship say?" she breathed the words, then suddenly put her face in her hands and wept.

"Oh, good heavens," said Vivian angrily, "how perverse you women are. You laugh with desire as you come into a man's arms and then when you leave him, you weep with regret. Why not strive to be more like us male creatures who accept these things as part of Nature's great scheme."

Her tears dried. An arrow seemed to transfix her heart. In that moment—scarcely able to credit the fact that the wooing and tender love could so quickly become harsh and dictatorial—Charlotte's first sweet illusions were shattered.

Very pale and in a quiet voice, she said:

"I do not mean to anger you. But in my own mind I have done something terrible."

"Good heavens, you wanted it just as much as I did—is that not so?" he demanded brutally.

She flung back her head and looked at him unsmiling but proud.

"Yes."

His gaze turned from her. For an instant he felt some contrition. He patted her shoulder.

"There, there, foolish little Charl—let me see you smile again. As I say—I found you deuced attractive and I have every intention of strolling with you through those woods again. I must go back to Oxford tomorrow but I will return home for the summer. A pity," he added, "that I cannot ask you to one of the Commemoration Balls, but your position makes that impossible."

Her position! For the first time, humble though she was, Charlotte was nauseated by his use of that word, particularly in this moment. She realized in that terrifying instant, how utterly mad, as well as bad, she had been to give herself to Vivian Chase.

Uttering a cry, she turned suddenly and ran from him. She ran as fast as she could across the meadow. She would not pass through the grounds. She would find her way back to the lodge by a circuitous route. Vivian called after her a trifle angrily.

"Charl, you little fool, come back!"

But she had vanished—like a wild scared creature into a thicket.

Vivian shrugged his shoulders and walked into the orchard banging the door behind him.

"I hope she is not going to do something senseless, such as throw herself into the village pond," he muttered. "Perhaps I have been foolish to trust her. If she speaks of this, it will be singularly unpleasant for me."

In the great hall he met Hannah. She gave him a queer look.

"Hullo, Hansie," he said, using a childhood's name for her.

The old woman knew that he only used it when he wanted to curry favour. She sniffed at him. She longed to tell him that his mother, these days, walked hand in hand with death. But her lips were sealed.

"My lady is not well," she snapped. "She has a bad migraine and Dr. Castleby has just been to visit her."

"I will go to her," said Vivian.

"Pray speak gently and try not to disturb her too much," said the privileged old woman.

Vivian first slunk into the dining-room to pour himself out a glass of wine. He needed a stimulant. He felt thoroughly nettled about Charlotte. What business had she to run off like that, crying and carrying on like a servant girl; she was, of course, little more than a servant despite her education. She ought to consider it an honour that her first love should be Lord Chase of Clunes.

And now Mama was ill. How tiresome! He must go and sit with her—hold her hand and dab eau-de-Cologne on her forehead and trust that she would be well enough to pay him that money he needed before returning to Oxford. He had incurred quite a few debts last term.

Complying with Hannah's wishes, he tip-toed into Lady

Chase's bedroom where he conducted himself like a model and affectionate son.

Down at the Lodge, in Nan Forbes' spotless little sitting-room where the casements were gay with frilled muslin and there were pots of geraniums on every sill, Charlotte faced her foster-mother.

"You are terribly late, Charlotte. Whatever time did you finish your lessons? Why did her ladyship keep you so long today? Where have you been?"

These and many other questions were put to Charlotte by the anxious woman who had been awaiting her at the door.

Charlotte answered at random. She found it difficult to prevaricate and could not explain that she had left Clunes several hours ago, and had since been in the woods with Lord Chase.

Mrs. Forbes eyed the girl anxiously. How pale she was. She had been crying.

"You have not given her ladyship cause to reprimand you. I hope," the good woman exclaimed, "I have never seen you so tearful."

"Please leave me alone—it is just that my head aches—I have been for a—a long walk," stammered Charlotte. "Her ladyship sent me out to enjoy the sunshine. I—I did not realize it was grown so late."

"Uncle Joseph will be in for his supper in a moment," said Nan. "Better wash, my dear, then come down to eat."

"I want no supper," said Charlotte abruptly.

Nan stared the harder. She had certainly never seen Charlotte in such a state. Why, the girl was trembling, as though she had a fever. Was she ill? There had been two cases of scarlet fever in the village.

"Perhaps you had best go to bed and let me bring you some hot gruel," said Nan.

Charlotte tried to gain control of herself. She was really very fond of this little woman with whom she had lived for the last four years. Nan was a dear lovable person; round, plump, red-cheeked as an apple. She was a woman without education but spoke well, and at forty-five years old was a respectable and pious matron. Joseph, her husband, was equally religious and a kindly diligent man, devoted to his job, and to the Chase family. Not only he, but his father and grandfather before him had served them. The great regret of the Forbes had been that God had not sent them children. But during the last four years they had been happy in their affection for the beautiful little girl whom Lady Chase had entrusted to their care.

"Truly, I feel that it might be best for me to call Dr. Castleby to see you and send word to her ladyship that you are taken ill," began Nan.

Quickly Charlotte protested, her cheeks a burning red.

"No, Nan dear, do not dream of it, it is just that I do not feel myself. But it is nothing to be agitated about. Tomorrow I will feel quite well again. Now I should like to go to my bed, if you do not mind."

Nan did not mind. She fussed and brooded over her like an anxious hen until Charlotte felt ready to scream.

At last she was tucked up in bed in her small room. Charlotte, feverish, troubled, lay rigid and tormented by her memories. She was no longer a child but a woman. Lord Chase was her lover. She could not bear the heavy sense of shame and guilt. It weighed her down; all the more so because she truly loved her patroness, Lady Chase. She *knew* that Lady Chase would look at her in horror if ever she discovered what had happened. And dear, good honest Nan, and Joseph—"Uncle Joe"—they, too, would be amazed and scandalized. With all her heart and soul she regretted her weakness.

Turning her face to the pillow, with a little moan, the young girl fought against her inclination to sob bitterly, lest Nan should hear her and come up and ply her with questions, and once more threaten to send for Dr. Castleby.

Chapter Seven

A hot July morning at Clunes, with the sun beating down. The flower beds looked parched, despite the efforts of the gardeners; for the last week there had been a drought. The blinds were continually drawn in the big house to keep out the heat.

Lady Chase had never known a warmer summer. Normally she would have enjoyed it. But this year she felt too ill; she could only lie languidly on the *chaise-longue* in her boudoir most of the day.

Hannah fussed and worried over her. Friends who called exclaimed at her pallor and increasing loss of weight.

Dr. Castleby came often and had lately prescribed stronger drops. He also begged her to see a specialist in London, but Lady Chase declined. No doctor, however good, could cure her now, she said; she knew it. It was just a question of time—of how many more of those terrible bouts of agony her poor heart could endure.

Meanwhile, Vivian knew nothing of his mother's condition; she would not have him told. Nor did he bother overmuch about her. He had only returned from Oxford this summer for a brief twenty-four hours, then rushed away to join a friend, the Earl of Marchmond whose parents had a yacht. Vivian had been invited to sail with them to Brindisi.

Greatly though Lady Chase longed for the company of her son, she was almost thankful to let him go. She could no longer bring herself to act a part for Vivian; to pretend to be well and enthusiastic about his pursuits, or bear the noise of the young gay friends he brought to Clunes.

She was dying. She knew it.

The one person whom she continued to see daily and whose presence never irked her, was Charlotte. To a woman as erudite as Eleanor Chase, the high intelligence shown by the young girl, her progress as a pupil, remained a deep satisfaction. But in these days, the lessons more often than not took place up in the boudoir—with my lady resting on her *chaise-longue*.

This afternoon, as Lady Chase waited for Charlotte, her mind was heavy with the burden of trouble. First of all, she was being forced, inch by inch, to tear aside the veil of illusion; to see that her son's character was deteriorating with the passage of time. His laziness, his refusal to accept responsibility or curb his mad extravagance and love of wine, all were growing more apparent. A letter from his tutor, received at the end of the summer, stated in strong terms that Lord Chase needed the firmest discipline; that it was to be hoped that he would mend his ways, especially as he would so soon be coming of age.

Vivian's mother mournfully echoed the tutor's "hopes." Secretly she dreaded Vivian's next birthday with all its implications. She had only one lever left that she could use if necessary. Unbeknown to the boy, the late Lord Chase had been wise enough to word his Will so that his son could not assume control of the capital until he was twenty-five. Until then, his allowance would increase but his mother and the General remained his trustees. Thank God, Vivian's father had had this foresight, she thought.

Not only was Lady Chase conscious of disappointment in her son, but also of a strange apprehension about Charlotte. The girl had changed during these last two months. She was growing tall and thin which, perhaps, accounted for her intense pallor. But her pinched face alarmed Lady Chase. The girl looked as though she spent much of her time in weeping. She would come to her lessons with heavy, red-rimmed eyes. When her ladyship asked what was wrong the reply was always the same: "Nothing, my lady—it is only the heat that tries me."

That might be so, but it did not seem right to Lady Chase that Charlotte, at sixteen, should not be able to stand a little extra heat. Besides her whole demeanour had altered. She used to laugh, to dimple, to delight in life, talk gaily to her instructor. Now she was over-serious, even nervous; she would never stay and talk once her lessons were over.

Hannah, reluctant as usual to allow the young girl to enter my lady's sacrosanct boudoir, opened the door and admitted Charlotte.

Lady Chase extended a white hand, which as a rule, the girl kissed before she sat down and opened her books.

But today she did not take the hand. She stood still, trembling in every limb. So ghastly did she look that Lady Chase half rose from her cushions and gave a cry:

"Charlotte, my child, what is it? Are you ill? What has happened to upset you?"

Charlotte did not answer. Her lips moved but no words came. Lady Chase noted that there were marks not only of physical malaise but of a mental disturbance upon the young face. The lashes were sodden with tears that made them seem too heavy, fringing eyes from which all brightness had fled. She did not even look as neat as usual. Her long cotton skirt was crumpled as though she had been lying on it. As Lady Chase stared, Charlotte tried to gather her courage in both hands and speak.

She had been lying on her bed for the last hour or two, sobbing bitterly after the doctor's examination, while the grim facts were disclosed to her.

Every day for the last couple of months, Charlotte had suffered from nausea; from a physical condition which, in her ignorance, she barely understood. The kindly Nan and Uncle Joe had taken it for granted that she was the victim of a bilious attack. At last they had called in Dr. Castleby.

He, of course, soon discovered what was wrong. After he left, the girl passed through a hideous hour of interrogation. Nan, overcome, told her what the doctor had meant when he said that *"Miss Charlotte was in the family way."* It was beyond all doubting.

"Better find who this cur is, responsible for our poor young maiden's misfortune," he had muttered as he snapped his bag together and went forth to re-mount his horse.

Again and again Nan had hurled questions at the girl, followed by bitter denunciations.

How could she have done such a dreadful thing?—she must be sly and deceitful—and ungrateful—oh, how badly had she repaid her foster-parents' tender care! And, again and again, Nan flung at the unfortunate girl this question: *"Who is the man?"*

With whom had she been consorting? A farm labourer? A gardener? One of the young game-keepers? Nan mentioned all the possible names. Never, so it happened, that of Lord Chase.

Finally Chrlotte threw herself at Nan's feet and begged for tolerance.

"Do not condemn me so utterly—I know I have done wrong but I did not understand what might happen," she sobbed piteously.

At that, and seeing the young girl's face so woeful and streaming with tears, Nan herself broke down. The woman and the young girl wept together.

"It was only once," Charlotte kept moaning, "I had but a few brief hours with my—my lover. Merciful heavens, what have I ever done to deserve such a cruel fate? Oh, dear good Nan—I am covered with shame. Let me die. Help me to find some means to do away with myself."

At that, Nan had gathered the girl close and forbidden her to repeat such a threat.

"You are not to die. You shall marry the man responsible for your condition. Your uncle and I will see to it," she exclaimed. "Only tell us who it was. We will not blame you. I believe you when you tell me that you did not understand. Some evil man has taken advantage of my poor Charlotte's innocence. *Who is he?*"

But the girl would not utter the name of her seducer. She thought of him, God knew, with bitterness. Love no longer played much part in her memories of Vivian. He had not written one word to her since his return to the University. Nor had he called to see her once he had come home again. So much for *love*, the poor child had thought in anguish.

Now that the facts had been made clear to her, she despised Vivian. *He* must have known the dangers—the possible consequences of that ruthless passion with which he had taken her.

When Charlotte persisted in her refusal, Nan grew antagonistic. Once more she accused Charlotte of being uncooperative as well as wicked.

"Since you refuse to tell us, then we shall go to her ladyship," she threatened.

"Never, never *that*!" cried Charlotte in a wild voice.

It was then that the truth suddenly struck the good woman. She put a finger on her lips.

"Dear God—*the young master*—it is him. Oh, yes, yes, I know it," she went on as Charlotte shook her head, and turned red then white again. "Now I understand. Fool that I am not to have thought of it before. That day that you were so late in coming home, *you were out with his lordship*. Oh, that monstrous young gentleman! It is *he* who got round you with his winning ways and handsome face. He, who has brought about your downfall."

After that it was useless for Charlotte to try and hide the truth. The time for weeping was over. With the coldness of despair, she admitted, at long last, that it was young Lord Chase who had seduced her on that April day.

Another consultation between Nan and her husband, and the pair agreed that her ladyship must be told. Neither of them realized, of course, how ill Lady Chase was nor knew about her heart trouble, or what effect such news might have on her. They were good, pious people. They had never liked the young master and they were of the opinion that her ladyship should be informed.

"If you do not go, I myself shall do it," announced Nan.

But to this Charlotte would not agree.

"I will not be a coward," she said dully. "It is my sin, so I shall confess to it. Even though her ladyship will recoil from me in horror. Never again will she admit me to the house, or allow me to benefit by her teaching. Doubtless she will have me sent away from Clunes altogether; and from you, too, dear Nan, dear Uncle Joe. From this home in which I have been so happy. But that must be my punishment. I shall accept it."

These words reduced Nan to further tears, but she wiped them away.

"Indeed! And where does his lordship come in?" she snorted. "Shall *he* not be made to account for his crime?"

Charlotte from whom all childishness had fled, suddenly learned to be cynical. She gave a wretched laugh.

"Ah, no! Remember—in his eyes I am just another village girl who has been seduced; a privilege I no doubt share with many other unfortunates."

"Well, we must make certain the babe—and you—are provided for," put in Nan, being a practical woman.

Charlotte kept a bitter silence. She did not want to hurt her benefactor. She would rather have run away and told no one. But the Forbes insisted.

So now here she was in Eleanor Chase's lovely cool boudoir, scented with lilies—facing the most terrible ordeal of her life. This was the last time she would ever look upon Lady Chase's lovely gracious face and form. She dreaded having to say that which would make her ladyship's smile change to a look of horror and scorn.

Lady Chase spoke with great kindness.

"Come, Charlotte, my dear, speak! What is so sorely troubling you? I have noted of late you have seemed poorly, unlike yourself. Perhaps it is that you study too hard. You must take a longer holiday from work than the one I gave you in June, I—"

But she got no further. For with a groan, Charlotte stumbled to the couch and fell beside it. She crouched there, sobbing, her face hidden in her hands.

Lady Chase's tender heart was deeply distressed by this sight. She let the girl cry for a space while she delicately stroked the thick satiny hair. She said:

"Hush, Charlotte. Control yourself, my child. Share with me the grief that troubles you. I am, I assure you, both your mentor and your friend."

At this Charlotte raised a face disfigured by tears, scarlet with shame.

"Do not touch me, my lady. I am not fit to be touched—least of all by you."

"Charlotte—what words are these?" exclaimed my lady, growing uneasy.

"Oh, what shall I do, what shall I do?" moaned the young girl.

"Speak, for heaven's sake and explain these wild words."

"I cannot bring myself to say it, my lady. Oh, believe, before ever you hear my wretched story, that I have loved and revered you most deeply," said poor Charlotte, "and that I never meant to dishonour your house."

A bright flush now stained Eleanor Chase's cheeks.

"Dishonour my house?" she repeated. "Come, Charlotte, this is too much; it cannot be as bad as that."

"It is—my lady, it is! Forgive me. I beg you to pardon me!" said Charlotte. Her big golden eyes burned so crazily, her expression was so wild that Lady Chase was frightened. She put her hand to her heart. It was beating too unevenly.

"Charlotte, my dear, you have ever been a passionate little thing, given to exaggeration. Pray, now restrain your emotions and speak quietly to me. Whatever it is that has befallen you, I cannot but swear to befriend you, as I did when first we met. As I shall always do, my gentle, clever child."

Such kindly words did little to comfort the girl. They heaped coals of fire on her head. Now, face hidden in her hands again, she blurted out the dread words.

"My lady—oh, my lady—I have sinned. *I—am going to bear a child.*"

At this, Eleanor Chase felt such astonishment, such a dire sensation of calamity, that she sat bolt upright. Her cheeks turned crimson. For a few moments she could hardly gather together her thoughts or consider the full significance of Charlotte's revelation. It was so utterly unexpected. Charlotte—self-confessed—*enceinte.* Oh, no, it was too dreadful!

Little Charlotte, who was only in her seventeenth year, going to be a mother! *That,* then, accounted for her change of countenance, her strange bouts of sickness this summer, her vanished mirth. And it was her sense of guilt, of shame, that had prevented her from lingering for the old happy, heart-to-heart talks which they used to have, once the reading, the learning, was over. Now Lady Chase recalled how Miss de Wynter, the music mistress, had come in one day and announced that poor little Charlotte had had to go home because she had been taken ill.

Another thing—a mysterious veiled warning given her by old Hannah, only yesterday. At the time Lady Chase had taken little notice—she was used to Hannah's jealousies. The old woman had said:

"I'd like to know what ails Charlotte Goff. Very queer she looks and behaves. Very queer. You mark my words, my lady, our young Charlotte is a dark horse. One day you'll be astonished. You will find out something, sure as eggs is eggs, my lady."

Eleanor had laughed.

"Fie on you for an old misery, Hannah, always speaking in riddles. Why should Charlotte be a dark horse? What next?"

But now the blindness had fallen from Lady Chase's eyes. She could see Charlotte more clearly—understand what Hannah had hinted. But what did *Hannah* know?—

Lady Chase began to tremble. She caught between her long fingers a bunch of the mauve ribbons trimming the muslin tea-gown which she was wearing.

"Charlotte, stop crying! Get up, and tell me at once the name of your seducer!" she said in a high, authoritative voice.

The girl rose. She dabbed her eyes with a handkerchief and stood there, meekly, trying to control herself.

"Tell me everything. I insist," went on her ladyship in the sternest voice Charlotte had ever heard from her.

Then in a halting voice, Charlotte described the April afternoon when she had accompanied her lover into the woods; and still more falteringly she described her seduction. Sick with shame, she stumbled over the story.

"He was so masterful, so strong, he insisted—and I was in ecstasy. Oh, I know that it was shocking of me, but I loved him. I had loved him for long. It seemed so magical that he who was so far above me should wish to love me. So I surrendered, my lady; but once I understood the full meaning of such passion, I came to my senses. I wished it undone. It no longer seemed like perfect love—but something brutal and destructive. It has destroyed *me*, my lady!"

Charlotte's head sank. The tears started to flow again. She could speak no more.

Lady Chase had kept her glittering gaze upon Charlotte, listened to the whole story with a painful intensity. She herself, so tender, so loving, could not fail to be moved. It was pitiful—that one so young, so gentle, should have been so cruelly used by a wicked man. For he must be wicked, he who had not hesitated to despoil a young maiden's innocence. According to Charlotte's woeful tale, he had deserted her. Where had he gone? Where was he? *Who?*

Charlotte seemed reluctant to betray him. More loyal than her betrayer, thought Lady Chase.

Then going over in her mind, everything that the unhappy girl had said, and considering those words "so far above me," Lady Chase almost swooned. What could such humility mean but that it was a gentleman of birth and breeding who had seduced her? Pray *what* gentleman? Where had she met any such person?

Lady Chase found herself shivering. She addressed Charlotte.

"Pull the bell immediately," she commanded.

Charlotte did so, one hand shading her hot and aching eyes. Hannah appeared almost at once.

"Do you want me, my lady?"

When the old servant saw the wild and terrified expression in her mistress's eye she hurried to the *chaise-longue* and bent over her.

"Oh, my lady, I must fetch your smelling salts. You have been taken ill again?"

"Stay, I wish to question you," said Lady Chase. Her fingers gripped Hannah's arm. She looked up into the troubled face of her faithful maid. "Hannah, you are in my confidence and have been ever since his dear lordship died. In you I place my confidence. A dire catastrophe has overtaken little Charlotte. You are not ignorant of this. You *know*. Yes, do not deny it, for only yesterday you muttered a warning that I did not comprehend."

Hannah put a hand to her lips; she felt scared and showed it. She began to whimper.

"I know nothing really, my lady."

"Hannah, you are to speak, or I shall send you from my service this very day," said her ladyship in a stern voice such as the old servant had never before heard.

"Oh, my *lady*!" exclaimed Hannah and sank beside the couch on one knee. Turning her head, she glanced at the young girl. Yes, she knew what had befallen Charlotte Goff. It was written there for Hannah and all the world to see. Hannah whined a fresh denial but Lady Chase had no mercy on her. She was determined to get to the bottom of this thing.

"Charlotte has been betrayed. Which gentleman has she been meeting? Who has dared to lay a hand upon a young girl who has been beneath my roof for so many years?"

"Oh, for dear heaven's sake," broke in Charlotte, "do not ask any more, my lady."

"No, do not ask, and pray, my dear lady, compose yourself or you will have another heart-attack," said old Hannah, her voice breaking.

Lady Chase looked from one face to the other. Then, indeed, it did seem that that heart of hers ceased to beat, so terrible was the pain that gripped it. *For suddenly she knew the truth.* Before she fainted dead away, she guessed it. And she wondered with bitter grief why she had not known before. She gasped:

"*My son!* It was—Vivian, *my own son!*"

She fell back on her cushions, so still, so waxen pale, that the others feared that she was dead. All thoughts were now directed to her. Charlotte was forgotten. Hannah flung orders at the girl.

"Send one of the grooms immediately for Dr. Castleby. Call Millie and tell her to bring burnt feathers. Hand me the drops, there, on her ladyship's bed-table."

Charlotte obeyed. As she ran to the door, the old woman maliciously called after her:

"God forgive you. You have killed a great lady."

Those terrible words followed the unfortunate girl as she hastened to do Hannah's bidding. After that, Clunes seemed to be in an uproar. Servants were running from one end to the other in the vast mansion doing this, that and the other. Dr. Castleby was traced to the home of a patient two miles away. He at once spurred his elderly nag to a gallop, in order to reach Lady Chase's bedside. It was rumoured throughout the district that her ladyship was dying, if not already dead.

Hannah was not to be torn from her lady's side until Dr. Castleby, fingering the delicate wrist, assured her that there was still a feeble flicker. Lady Chase had had another of her attacks but not yet, he said, a fatal one.

Meanwhile Charlotte, suicidal with grief, made to feel wholly responsible for all this trouble, crept into the woods and hid herself from the rest of the world. But it was not long before Nan and Joseph, her foster-parents, who knew her habits, came to find her. She lay face downwards on the mossy ground, eyes blind with weeping, body ice-cold.

She had passed beyond tears and passion. She was like a dying person—finished with this life.

"Poor crazed creature," muttered Nan as she helped the girl on to her feet. "Dear God, what his lordship has to answer for! Come home, my dearie, come with us. It will not make matters better for you to catch your death of cold, and starve to death.

"Is her ladyship dead?" asked Charlotte in a dull voice.

"No, she lives and has asked to see you."

With glazed eyes, Charlotte regarded Nan's plump and worried face.

"She *cannot* wish to see me. She knows—"

"Yes, she knows," said Nan with a meaning glance at her husband who hardly returned it. The good man was unnerved by these happenings.

"She *cannot* wish to see me," repeated Charlotte.

"But she does," said Nan. "Hannah sent us to search for you."

"If it is to reproach me, I cannot bear any more," said Charlotte. She was shuddering from head to foot.

Now Nan put an arm around her and comforted her.

"She will not reproach you. Hannah says she herself wishes to tell you what decision she has reached."

They had walked out of the woods now into the clearing. The sun was still shining at the end of this long day—the longest it seemed to Charlotte, that she had ever known. Joseph muttered a few words to his wife and walked off in the direction of the Lodge. Nan guided the girl into the orchard and through the gardens to Clunes. All around Charlotte lay the superb beauty of that familiar garden—she could hear the soft cooing of doves in the dovecote—the evening song of the thrushes. But for her there was no warmth, no beauty, no song, only a deathly sickness and distaste for life; a feeling that she would rather that Nan had left her there to die in those woods. For what could Lady Chase wish to say to her that could bring her anything but fresh guilt and pain?

Chapter Eight

The Lady of Clunes lay in bed in a room darkened from the sun and smelling of aromatics and the sharp sweetness of the eau-de-Cologne with which Hannah had been bathing her fevered wrists and temples. Dr. Castleby had gone, satisfied that the poor harassed heart was beating once again with more vigour, if not normally. He would have preferred her to have seen nobody, but she insisted that Charlotte be sent for.

While she had waited, Eleanor Chase had reviewed her whole life and wondered what she had ever done to deserve this anguish, this terrible discovery of Vivian's guilt. It was a guilt that she must, she told herself, forever share with her son. She was a most unusual woman; one who entertained the highest ideals and acted only from the highest motives. The very last trait in her character was snobbery. Although so well born, she was without class-consciousness. Unique in her day, she possessed a strong sense of social equality. She did not believe in one law for the rich, and one for the poor. She did not think that a peer should be forgiven a crime for which a labourer would be condemned. She did not, therefore, see why Vivian should be allowed to get off scot free, whilst Charlotte suffered. When she had first recovered her senses, Lady Chase had forced Hannah to admit that Vivian was Charlotte's seducer. The old woman would have denied it, but Lady Chase made her swear upon the Bible. Then Eleanor Chase had said:

"I must not die. I must live to see this wrong righted."

She sent for Nan and talked with her. The lodgekeeper's wife, weeping bitterly, said:

"Pardon poor Charlotte, she did not know. I had never warned her, so maybe it's me you should blame, my lady, not the girl."

"Nobody is to blame save my cruel and heartless son," had been Lady Chase's response. For she knew that had Vivian loved Charlotte, he would never have deserted her. Love, his mother could have forgiven, but lust was ugly and unforgivable in her sight.

Nan could not understand her ladyship's attitude. Any other great lady would have driven the girl from the house, or paid her off. She said so. And it was then that Eleanor Chase felt indignation kindle within her. In a loud clear voice she denounced her own son.

"He is a grown man. He knew better. Charlotte was still a child and in love with him. She is romantic and tender. She was ripe to fall for a handsome boy's flattery. And she, herself, told me that the love she had thought so sweet, destroyed her. My son has brought about that destruction. He shall not be allowed to sneak out like a cur and leave Charlotte to pay the price."

That was the way that Eleanor felt and those were the words she repeated to Charlotte herself, when at length the trembling girl stood beside the big canopied bed and heard the astonishing verdict passed by this humane, extraordinary judge.

"I have sent for Lord Chase. He shall return from the Mediterranean and marry you immediately," announced Lady Chase.

"It is not possible—it would not be right!" exclaimed Charlotte in great agitation.

Lady Chase took one of the girl's slender hands.

"Charlotte," she said, "I admit that you have sinned, my poor child. But your sin was less of a crime than the outrage committed by him who understood what evil he perpetrated. You were frail; too loving, too giving. I, who have known you so long, realize that you were always over-generous and hasty. Have I not often chided you for that tempestuous streak? That lack of reserve?"

"Yes, my lady," whispered Charlotte.

"Nevertheless you knew not what you did," murmured Eleanor Chase, "and you must have suffered unbearably all these weeks. I can well believe the extent of your torture, my poor child."

"Yes, oh yes," said Charlotte and buried her face against the counterpane, "but why do you not cast me out?"

"Because I wish to see justice done, and because you will bear my grandchild," said Lady Chase. "I refuse to lose sight of that fact. That child shall be given its proper name. When it comes—if it seems premature in the eyes of the world—a seven-month child, what matter? Those who gossip must hold their tongues. You shall be Lady Chase and you shall bring up your child here in this house, where it belongs."

Charlotte could hardly believe her ears.

"But my lady, it is not fitting that I should become Lord Chase's wife," she said trembling.

"Other ladies of title and good family might agree with you. I do not. You are fundamentally good. You were pure until Vivian's passion sullied that purity. But he, my son, has defiled not only you but his noble name," her ladyship added.

And now she put her delicate hands over her face and her tears began to flow, breaking through the façade of her dignity, her resignation. It had been fearful to her to learn that Vivian, son of that dear and noble husband she had loved, was a common seducer.

"It is a terrible thing to despise the son I have loved," said Lady Chase suddenly, "but he must pay the price of his crime against innocence."

Charlotte, trembling, had a swift vision of Vivian as she had last seen him; bored and haughty and anxious to get away from her.

"For mercy's sake, permit me to leave Clunes," she broke out. "Vivian will hate me now, more especially if you force him into marriage."

"He shall marry you," said Lady Chase inexorably.

"But his proud name—this great house—I could not take my place here in your shoes," said Charlotte wildly.

"You can and shall," said her ladyship. The extent of her disappointment in Vivian impelled her to enforce this justice. In their circle Charlotte would be considered a "nobody." Let him raise her up by giving her and his child the name of Chase. If he hated to do it, it was only what he deserved. The knife-edge of her anger was turned towards *him*. Suddenly, with deep bitterness, Lady Chase said:

"You have more intelligence, and more courage than the

one who has wronged you. In my opinion it is Lord Chase himself who is not worthy to have *you* as wife, instead of the other way round."

The young girl knelt beside the bed speechless and bemused. She was beyond fighting or arguing. Lady Chase took her hand and pressed it.

"Go back to Nan and Joseph, my dear. Stay with them and do not leave their care again until I send for you, which will be when his lordship returns."

"Yes, my lady," said Charlotte in a very faint voice.

"You will swear," added her ladyship, "to do no harm to yourself. You must remember that the child you bear is of my blood as well as of yours."

"Yes," said the flabbergasted Charlotte, "yes, my lady."

As she moved across the room, Lady Chase's voice followed her.

"Stay a moment. I have something more to ask you."

"Yes, my lady."

"Do you still love my son?"

Silence. Charlotte knew not what to reply. But she felt a sickness come over her and hid her face in her hands.

Lady Chase saw and understood. She gave a deep sigh. "He has killed your love. It is little wonder. Alas, that this marriage must have its roots in hatred. Charlotte, my child, do not let it be so. It is love that conquers all. Love that casts out all fear. Are we not told so in the Bible?"

"Oh yes, my lady," said Charlotte weeping again. But she added with some of her old spirit: "Nevertheless it is hard to love when one no longer has respect."

Lady Chase nodded. "Yet we must both love and help him for he is in need of love and strength. You must master your own desires and become so strong, spiritually, that you will be able to strengthen *him*."

Charlotte ran back to the bed, took one of Lady Chase's hands and pressed her quivering lips to it.

"Oh, my lady, it is I who need strength. How shall I be able to give it to Vivian?"

"Because I believe you have the courage. You are not a poor witless girl. Develop your fine character. Earn not only his thanks but the regard of all his friends. Then I shall feel that the horror and shame of this thing may pass.

You will be a better wife for my son than many others he might have chosen from a higher social circle."

"Oh, my lady, you are an angel," breathed Charlotte, "an angel whom I shall worship all my life."

"Nay, Charlotte, you should worship none but God."

Abashed, Charlotte dropped her ladyship's hand.

"I will try to do, to be, as you wish, my lady, and pray forgive me for the part I have played in your unhappiness," begged Charlotte.

"I do most freely forgive you. Now go and wait quietly, in meditation and prayer, until I send for you again."

Charlotte hesitated. In a pained voice, she whispered:

"If he—if he is very against it, which he will be, do not consider me, only yourself and him. Oh, anything, my lady, rather than that I should be a trouble to *you.*"

She saw Lady Chase's pale face flush. The dark wonderful eyes glowed with fire and pride. In a quiet firm voice, Lady Chase said:

"I have made my decision and I shall not alter one word of it. If you would please me, keep a quiet mind and prepare yourself for what is to come."

Charlotte choked back a sob and walked slowly out of the room. In the corridor she stood a moment leaning with her back against the closed door, trying to regain composure. This decision taken by Lady Chase was so fantastic, so unexpected, she could not even now believe it. In one way she felt a wild relief. She need no longer fear that her babe would be born illegitimate. But she did not want to marry a man who did not love *her. And to become Lady Chase*—Perhaps at this very moment beneath her heart she carried the future Lord Chase.

It frightened Charlotte. It set up a kind of paralysis in her mind.

She tried to think of Vivian as she used to do, as the Prince Charming who had first ravished her childish dreams, as the handsome and fascinating young hero who had taught the maiden, Charlotte, all the ecstasy of love. Alas—her mind and her heart had changed, gone beyond that love; grown critical of him. The feet of her idol were turned to clay.

She heard footsteps. She shrank from the doorway as

Hannah approached, carrying a copper can of hot water and soft lavender-scented towels for her ladyship's evening ablutions. The old servant and the young girl came face to face. Charlotte's cheeks turned to crimson. Hannah's withered ones were colourless, but from underneath the white brows the sharp eyes peered at Charlotte with fierce hostility.

"How is her ladyship? Have you done more harm?" she asked under her breath.

"Nay, Hannah, I pray not," Charlotte whispered back.

Hannah looked her up and down with such a glance that made Charlotte feel more than ever the burden of her guilt.

"So! In trouble, and with the master of the house. It was only what might be expected of you, Charlotte Goff."

But they were the last words of the kind that Hannah was ever to speak thus insolently to Charlotte. Suddenly all that was dignified and imperious in Charlotte asserted itself under the lash of the old servant's tongue. The look she fixed on Hannah now was full of mingled grief and pride.

"You shall not speak to me so, Hannah. I know that I have sinned but it is to my Maker alone I shall pray for forgiveness. I am forever beholden to her ladyship for all that has been done for me since I came to Clunes. But if you do not already know it, I will enlighten you. I am to be married to his lordship as soon as he returns."

"Merciful heavens!" exclaimed Hannah, and nearly dropped the can and the towels.

With a choking sob Charlotte rushed away and down the wide staircase and out of the house. Hannah hurried in to her mistress. When she asked for confirmation of what Charlotte had said, Lady Chase quietly gave it. She added:

"Do not argue or protest, for it is my wish. Charlotte Goff was my protégée, I am responsible for her. Let everybody think that I am out of my mind, but I am doing what I consider best not only for Charlotte but for *him*."

"For *him!*" repeated Hannah in a quavering voice, "Oh, my lady, but what of her lowly station compared with his?"

Lady Chase gave a curt laugh.

"She is God's creature and far from lowly. Wait and see how she develops. Her brain will go beyond his lordship's.

Her character is such that I wish to God that he had one similar. Oh, believe me, Hannah, what I do is for the best."

Hannah made a gesture of despair, and moved to the windows to pull up the blinds and let a little light into the dim room before she washed my lady's face.

Alas, her ladyship looked shockingly ill, Hannah thought, as she returned to the bed and saw more clearly the pinched and grey countenance of her beloved mistress. Surely she would not live long.

Lady Chase read her thoughts.

"My end is coming, but not yet. I shall live to see this wrong righted," she said, "and you, Hannah, who have ever been my loyal servant, must carry out my wishes to the end."

The old servant sniffed. Gently she began to brush the brown tresses which were now so plentifully streaked with silver. Oh, what a heavy burden of shame and disgrace had fallen on this once proud happy household! How could Hannah do aught but hate the young girl who was responsible? Never could she bring herself to do as her ladyship, and place the blame at the door of his young lordship.

Once again Lady Chase seemed to read Hannah's mind.

"The child did not understand the full significance of loving. *You* know the extent of his lordship's great charm and power over women. All too often I have watched him exert it. Poor Charlotte had no chance. It was as though he laid a snare for the tender bird, then brutally wounded it."

Hannah muttered:

"You are too kind, my dear lady."

"See to it that you are kind to her, also, once I am gone," said Lady Chase in a warning tone. "Treat her with the respect due to the one who carries his lordship's child."

The old woman fiercely blinked away tears that she found hard to shed.

"Oh, my lady, what will his lordship say when he comes home?"

"I have sent a message by telegraph, to await him at Monte Carlo which he reaches next Thursday," said Lady Chase looking out of the window with her sunken eyes. "He is ordered to return to Clunes at once. He should reach London three days later, by train and packet. Meanwhile, Hannah, not a word of this to the staff, or to anyone outside this house. You shall swear on my Bible never to betray how this marriage, when it takes place, came about. I count on your integrity."

"You can, my lady, oh, you can!"

Lady Chase leaned back on her pillows. She felt desperately tired. While Hannah continued to smooth and braid her heavy hair, she fell asleep.

Chapter Nine

During the next three days, Charlotte stayed in bed and was devotedly nursed by Nan who, with her husband, could not get over the shock of realizing that their charge was to become the future Lady Chase. Nan, however, in her way, was as high-principled and reliable as Hannah, and she kept her mouth shut. She said not one word to anybody else of what had happened. Joseph went to his work in the grounds. Nan stayed indoors. And Charlotte, exhausted and quite overcome, spent most of the time sleeping. Those early days of pregnancy brought her a nausea that she found hard to control. With all the will in the world, too, she could not acclimatize herself to the fact that she must soon face Vivian. She dreaded meeting the young man. She dared not think what *he* would have to say.

When, at length, she was sent for by Lady Chase, Charlotte was so terrified that Nan had to coax and then scold, in order to get her to go up to the big house.

More dead than alive, she stood, at last, facing her former lover. They stood side by side before Lady Chase who lay on the sofa in her boudoir. Charlotte gave Vivian one swift scared look, then her heart seemed almost to stop beating. Faintness seized her. She sank on to a chair, and laced her nervous fingers together.

"Pray pardon me, your ladyship—" she began.

"That is all right—do not distress yourself," came Eleanor Chase's gentle voice. "All has been made clear to my son and I have announced my intentions. Your engagement will be public news tomorrow. I shall give it out that an immediate marriage between you two will take place because of my grave state of health. It shall be thought that I wish to see my son happily married before I die, the doctors having stated that death for me is not far off."

At this, Charlotte's head shot up. She looked with deep concern at her beloved patroness. Words failed her.

Lord Chase stood silent, scowling. Under the tan which he had acquired during the cruise, his face was a yellowish grey. There was nothing handsome about him at the moment. He looked sick with fury and chagrin. And it was with this sickness and fury that he returned Charlotte's gaze.

"Traitress!" that glance seemed to say.

But he was given no chance to say it. Instead, a pallid kind of smile wreathed his lips and he muttered:

"I hope I find you tolerably well, Charlotte."

She made no answer. She could not. Came a voice from the couch, clear and cool and controlled. Nothing in it to show the agony of Eleanor Chase's true feelings.

"Charlotte is very poorly, Vivian," she said. "It is nothing to be alarmed about. She will soon recover herself. But she commands your pity and concern."

Vivian crossed his arms. He was a very crestfallen young man without his usual *hauteur* or insolence. When in Monte Carlo he had received the telegram from his mother, he had presumed that it was because of her sudden illness that he was recalled to Clunes. To reach home and be told that Charlotte was *enciente* by him, also that his mother knew it, had been a hideous shock to Vivian. Still more so her ultimatum. Never had it entered his head that his mother would uphold Charlotte rather than *himself*. Of course, he thought, it was just another of her crazy acts of idealism. He had ranted and raved, argued and protested, for a couple of hours. He would not marry the slut, he said. He would not mess up his social life right from the start. Who would receive Charlotte as his wife? What had he done after all, that a dozen other lusty young men of good families had not done before him?

But always, Lady Chase made an obstinate reply.

"Charlotte was as a daughter to me. You shall make an honest woman of her. If you find things difficult at Clunes, for a time, that will be less punishment than you deserve. But Charlotte will make you a wife of whom you will one day be proud. You have only to give her the opportunity. And I would remind you that *you* were a seven-months' child although born two years after my marriage. Why should Charlotte not emulate my example? People will not find it amiss."

Vivian lost his temper and grew ugly. He said things that made his mother put her hands to her ears and shut her eyes. Now indeed, the velvet gloves were off. This was the Vivian she had suspected but never so far known.

But no bullying or shouting from the enraged young man altered her purpose. It was inflexible. She considered that what she was doing was the right thing. She had to help her, she informed Sir Harry Cawder—Vivian's godfather and co-guardian.

"It's a bit hard on the lad," the General had written in reply to her letter telling him what she meant to do.

She had written back to him:

> What of the young girl who is to bear my grandchild? It would be much harder on her if the father did not see her through.

The General was old and ill and disinclined to make an issue of it. He had adored Eleanor Chase since she was a young girl and he, her husband's Commanding Officer. He was not certain that she was doing the right thing, but he bowed to her wishes.

So Vivian faced the fact that if he did not go through with this marriage and acknowledge his child, his allowance would be cut. The sum of money which he would inherit when he came of age would barely pay his wine-bill these days. Clunes would be his but it was entailed; he could not sell the place. This meant virtual poverty for him. Until Lady Chase died, she must remain in authority. She could and would, she assured him, make things difficult for him if he refused to right the wrong. But if he married Charlotte, she would sign what cheques he demanded. Later she would leave Clune, go to a small secluded house with Hannah and her staff (if she lived!) and Vivian would be master of his own home.

The young man gnashed his teeth. He was cornered and he knew it, and like a cornered rat he bared his teeth. He even tried to bluster words to the effect that he could not be sure that Charlotte's child was *his*.

"You know you lie! Heaven will strike you dead if you repeat that lie. Can you, my son, repeat that foul implication with your hand upon the Bible?"

Vivian mumbled that he could not swear to anything.

"Because you know that you are responsible for Charlotte's condition," Lady Chase had said quietly.

Now and again Hannah had crept in, terrified that her mistress's heart would not stand up to the strain of this terrible scene. Each time Lady Chase sent her away.

"God will give me the strength to see justice done," she said.

Once during the argument, Vivian stormed at his mother:

"Is the future of this wretched girl more important to you than mine?"

"No more and no less," had come the answer. "I used to love you as a mother loves her son, more deeply and proudly than anybody in the world; but your recent conduct has broken my heart. I die, a sadly disillusioned mother. I can only leave you to the unfortunate girl you make your wife and to your Maker."

Never before had Vivian Chase heard such terrible words from his once gracious and loving mother. He was reduced to silence. Then to a muttered apology.

"Forgive me, dear Mama, I lost my head," he grunted.

"That is no excuse, my son. I would rather you had been a thief than a despoiler of innocence."

Now Charlotte and Vivian stood, side by side, listening to Lady Chase's arrangements for their future. She had everything planned. Dr. Castleby already knew the staggering facts. His assistance and his silence could be relied upon. There would be no attempt at a high society wedding. Distant relatives and friends would be at once informed that a wedding between Vivian and Charlotte was taking place in strict seclusion, in the little chapel at Clunes, which had long been shut up. It could be opened for the ceremony. Afterwards, said Lady Chase, Vivian could take his bride for a brief honeymoon to a quiet watering place in France. Then, she told her son, he must return here to take up his duties as the master of this house. She would hold a reception for the pair on their return. It was a pity, she added, that Vivian could not return to Oxford. He must forgo obtaining his degree. But she doubted, she said with a sarcasm he had never before heard from her, if he would have obtained one anyhow.

Vivian gnawed at his finger-nails. If looks could have killed, both the women in this room would have been dead. He hated Charlotte with all his soul because she was the instrument of what seemed to him a ghastly punishment. He hated his mother for enforcing the penalty. When she mentioned that her health was such that she was not likely to survive the marriage, he secretly wished for one frightful second she would die before it need ever take place.

Lady Chase lay back on her cushions. She closed her eyes. She felt so very tired, but she was still fighting Death, the last enemy. She could not, would not go in peace, until she had restored Charlotte's honour to her.

"Now, Vivian, take Charlotte back to the Lodge," she commanded. "Later this afternoon Mr. Meadows, our Vicar, is calling on me and will arrange with me the necessary formalities."

Charlotte moved towards the couch, her handkerchief to her lips.

"What can I say to you, my lady?" she whispered.

"Nothing, Charlotte. You have suffered enough. Now be at peace, and for the infant's sake keep calm. You have a trying time ahead of you."

Downstairs in the library, as the shadows of afternoon lengthened, Vivian and Charlotte faced each other alone. The moment the door closed on them Vivian turned upon the wretched girl.

"I suppose you realize," he said, "that it is the money that impels me to go through with this marriage. I am not prepared to be reduced to poverty and to have to earn my own living because I have made one mistake too many."

"I do not wish to marry you," she said in an ice-cold voice, and the look in her eyes as they turned towards him now was one of scorn and even loathing. "It is for the sake of my child that I intend to go through with this dreadful marriage."

He sneered again:

"Surely you are glad to have hooked so fine a title and home." He swept his arm arrogantly around the handsome library.

"I will not listen to your insults," she said.

"My dear," he said, "as soon as we are married you will listen to whatever I say and put up with it. As my wife you will have saved your honour in the eyes of the world but to me you will be the lowest of my chattels."

She knew that he had an evil temper but she could scarcely believe that any man could say things so base to a woman who bore his child. Charlotte Goff was no helpless maiden in distress in this moment. She, herself, was reduced to fury. She came at him suddenly, her eyes blazing, her teeth clenched, her long trembling fingers clawing at him.

"You vile wretch. Oh, how I despise you!"

Now Vivian was amused. Weeping and cringing, a woman had no attraction to him. But he decided that Charlotte looked deuced handsome in her fury. He caught at the fingers that would have torn his cheeks, and imprisoned her against him. When she once more gasped out her hatred, he laughed and closed her lips with a kiss that seared and nauseated her.

"No, my beauty, I shall not let you have it all your own way once you are legally mine," he said. "You shall be taught who is the master. You gave yourself willingly enough that day in the woods. Are you too pure now for my kisses?"

But Charlotte Goff had bade a long farewell to meekness, and the shy tenderness of virginity. She kicked at him, and kicked again until she caught him a blow against his shin which made him release her.

"I do not think I shall marry you even for the sake of my child," said Charlotte in a strangled voice. "I cannot bear you to touch me."

"That would suit me," said Vivian, "but unfortunately my lady mother has other plans for us. She is a great believer and always has been, I seem to remember, in marriage in such a case as ours."

Charlotte tried to smooth back her dishevelled hair. She felt horribly ill. The library was swimming around her. But the young man no longer tried to force his attentions upon her. The brief renewal of his physical interest in her had faded. He walked, hands behind his back, to the window and stared gloomily out at the approaching twilight.

Charlotte, trembling, looked with hot resentful eyes at Vivian's unyielding back. Hatred was festering within her very soul; in her, who had never before in this life disliked any human being. The hatred was so strong that it surpassed her dislike of herself, of the frailty that had led her to this pass. For a few brief seconds in his hateful embrace, she had genuinely considered the idea of running away from Vivian, and from Clunes. Then a new sensation seized her. It was almost as though she felt the urge within her to avenge the babe he had begotten. Let *him* take his punishment. Let him be burdened with her as a wife, since he so disliked the idea. Let him give a name to this poor infant whom, in the fullness of time, she must bring into this unhappy world. She spoke aloud:

"I thank my God that I can look upon you without love, Vivian Chase. If it is hatred that you feel for me, then your feelings are reciprocated."

He did not answer but she heard the snarl of his laughter as she walked out of the library, and out of the house.

At the Lodge Nan met her and began to ply her with anxious questions. What had happened? What had his lordship said? What had been arranged?

Charlotte looked at her stonily. Nan gasped a little as she saw the changed expression in that once tender and innocent face. It was the face of a woman grown hard and bitter.

Then said Charlotte:

"I shall become Lady Chase as soon as arrangements have been made with the Vicar."

The little lodgekeeper clapped her hands. She looked like one crazy with joy and triumph.

"Oh, my dear life, what an honour! You, my little Charlotte, to become a great lady and live at the big house."

"To me it is no honour, but a sign of my degradation," Charlotte said.

"Are you mad?"

"No, I was so, but I have grown sane. I shall marry Vivian Chase only for the sake of my unborn child. He hates me as much as I hate him. It is a fearful humiliation for him. I have tasted the very dregs of suffering these last few weeks. Now it is his turn to suffer."

Nan stared.

"Come, come, dearie, you are the luckiest girl alive. Think what her ladyship has done for you."

"I shall love *her* always, and spend the rest of my life trying to expiate my sin, and any grief that I may have caused her," said Charlotte in a low voice, "but I shall never be happy again."

Nan, following the girl up the narrow staircase into her bedroom, tried to treat this as a joke.

"You are but sixteen, my dear. You will mature and learn to regard your position differently."

"We shall see," said Charlotte. "Now, please dear Nan, leave me alone."

The little woman found the door shut in her face. She shrugged her shoulders and went back to her kitchen, but she paused now and then in her work to remember the look in Charlotte's eyes and the sound of her voice when she had said those words: *"I shall never be happy again."*

Chapter Ten

The sudden and private marriage of Vivian, Lord Chase, to Charlotte Goff, foster-daughter of the lodgekeepers at Clunes, was a nine days' wonder in the district.

People had of course been warned, after the announcement of the betrothal. From that time onwards, gossip seeped through house after house, both down here in Hertfordshire where the Chase family resided, and up in London.

Not one amongst the many distant relatives or friends seemed to know just how or why this engagement had come about, and been sponsored by Lady Chase. No invitations were issued for the wedding. The wildest rumours circulated. The only information that threaded its way through the gossip was what had been given out by Lady Chase, herself. Her secretary sent formal notes to meet the many inquiries, and Vivian confirmed them; to the effect that this was a long-considered love-match. Because of Lady Chase's failing health, it was decided to expedite the ceremony. Also that the London specialist sent for by Dr. Castleby confirmed his opinion that Vivian's mother might die suddenly and without warning. It was her dearest wish to see Vivian and Charlotte joined in marriage. The only people outside the family who knew the whole truth were Vivian's guardian, Sir Harry Cawder, the Forbes, old Hannah, and of course, the doctor.

Over the teacups and dinner-tables tongues wagged and conversation buzzed.

Everybody knew Charlotte by name, and in what high regard Lady Chase held her. Many in the district had caught a glimpse of her, from time to time, and spoken of her beauty—those fabulous golden eyes and curling chestnut locks, that dazzling complexion which many a high-born lady could envy.

A few ladies lowered their lids and whispered suggestively that there could be *other* reasons for the hurried wedding. In the London clubs, young Lord Chase was discussed by the men who had known his father. They also knew his reputation at Oxford. They confessed themselves puzzled.

There were one or two snobs in the district around Clunes who were affronted by the fact that the future Lady Chase had "sprung from nothing." But such folk were in the minority. The Chase family were so distinguished and so enormously rich it would not be in the interests of friends or acquaintances to refuse when the time came to call on the bride.

There was perhaps one other person who guessed at the truth even though she did not know for certain. That was Roma Gresham who knew Vivian and his vices so well.

Vivian had scarcely dared to leave the house in that interim between his return from the cruise and his wedding. It had not taken him long to guess that Hannah had been the spy who had betrayed him, rather than Charlotte. The old servant continued to spy for her mistress, and Vivian was kept at the latter's bedside. Eleanor Chase submitted him to long lectures on morals, and appeals to him to alter his ways and make Charlotte a good husband.

Vivian had plenty of private troubles. He had run up debts of honour in the gaming-rooms in Roma Gresham's house. He was forced because of this urgent need for money to knuckle under to his saintly mother's rule. That he had hurt *her* and made her last few days on earth a tragedy, he hardly cared. He was too filled with self-pity, too resentful of her power over him.

On one or two nights, he walked across the fields to Mrs. Gresham's house and held what might be considered a farewell party to his bachelorhood. When Mrs. Gresham politely congratulated him on his forthcoming marriage, he could see that she was surprised that he should marry this country girl. But he did not, for his own sake, tell her the truth. He would have to reside at Clunes. Decorum and etiquette would insist upon his leading a respectable life and ensuring that Charlotte should be given her due as his wife. No, he was not going to give anyone like Mrs. Gresham the sordid facts.

But Roma Gresham was too experienced a woman of the world to believe that Vivian meant to settle down.

"Shall we see you no more, then? And will you spend your evenings sitting virtuously with your little wife rather than come here where you are ever welcome?" Mrs. Gresham asked him, fluttering her lashes.

Those words fired Vivian as they were meant to do. He looked down into her wicked, painted face and laughed arrogantly.

"Do I seem a man to make the kind of husband never to leave his wife's side? No, rest assured, Madam, I shall often come to your enjoyable parties. And I shall *not* encourage my wife to ask questions."

Roma looked relieved. Even more so, when my Lord Chase pulled out a handful of sovereigns to pay bills that had been long outstanding. She had no scruples about ruining young men, nor for that matter, young women.

"I have a new attraction for you tonight, my Lord Chase," Mrs. Gresham murmured. "She is from Paris, a dancer who is to give a performance at the Crystal Palace this Autumn. She is immensely popular in Paris, and in Cairo, from which she originally comes. I have persuaded her to spend a few weeks down here to enjoy the pure country air." And with a tinkle of laughter Mrs. Gresham moved away, fashionably attired in an expensive evening gown with red carnations in her hair and long lace gloves. To look at from a distance Mrs. Gresham might have been a lady of high degree but Vivian knew well that all respectable doors were closed to her. Moodily he considered her divorce and how far she had sunk since she went through the Courts. But he enjoyed her hospitality. As for the young dancer from Paris:—It was not to enjoy pure country air she was here, but to amuse Mrs. Gresham's clients. This house, hidden away in the woods was little more than a high-class brothel.

Divorce in this period was fearful disgrace. It struck Vivian here and now that he was tying himself up in the matrimonial prison for good and all. And in his twenty-first year.

Gone, for ever, all his hopes of enjoying marriage with

a rich dazzling young woman chosen from his own set.

But at least Roma Gresham's house remained near Clunes. If and when life became too boring here, he could still pursue his secret sports. Mrs. Gresham was nothing if not discreet.

Chapter Eleven

On the 20th July, five weeks before Charlotte's seventeenth birthday, she was married to Vivian Chase in the chapel at Clunes.

No bride is likely to forget her wedding. For Charlotte it was an affair so fantastic that she was certainly not likely to forget it.

After the events of the preceding week, she had been as one in a daze, acting like an automaton, speaking only when addressed, living in a kind of nightmare world from which she hoped in vain to awaken.

At Lady Chase's command a dressmaker had been sent to measure and make her a few dresses fitting for her station. Charlotte took no interest in clothes as in happier circumstances she might have done. It was Nan who was excited and pleased. Nan, who kept trying to coax the girl to be thrilled with the many lovely things Lady Chase sent her. But she stood like a marble statue while the dressmaker and her assistant fitted her and barely admired the glossy satin of the bridal dress, or the exquisite Limerick lace veil which had belonged to Vivian's own mother. She only knew that she felt ill and tired. But Nan kept telling her that she must rest and try to look beautiful for the marriage ceremony.

"Beautiful for what, for whom?" Charlotte asked herself bitterly. Her whole being cried out against this wedding. She had felt a hypocrite when at length they had attired her in the gleaming dress and veiled her face with the foaming lace. Apathetically she pulled the long white kid gloves over her hands, and took the bridal posy of white roses and stephanotis, grown in one of the Clunes's greenhouses.

She had no right to wear this gown or to go like a virgin

to her marriage and she knew it. Eleanor Chase knew it, too, but she had insisted.

"There are other moments in life when a lie must be acted for the sake of others. It is for your child's sake that I wish it to appear in the eyes of the witnesses as though there is no babe on the way. I will not have it known that my first grandchild was conceived in sin."

Charlotte had wept bitterly at those words but it was not often now that she cried. Her grief was too deep. She was thankful that she saw little of Vivian. Once or twice only before the ceremony, they met in his mother's boudoir. When he escorted her home they had nothing to say to each other. In silent hatred they separated.

To one of such warm and affectionate nature as Charlotte's, it was a ghastly state of affairs.

Then the wedding itself.

The gardeners had filled the little disused chapel with flowers. There was an overpowering scent of roses that made Charlotte feel sick. But Dr. Castleby had been attending her and made sure that she would stand up to the ordeal of the day. He had scolded her, too, just before she left the Lodge with Nan and Joseph (the good pair both attired in their Sunday best and hugely elated).

"You are a strong young girl," the doctor said, "in perfect health. This *malaise* from which you suffer is a nervous tension. You must be strong-minded for the sake of all."

So it was a white but controlled Charlotte who finally stood beside the young lord of Clunes that sultry summer morning. There was no sunshine. Dark clouds were gathering. A big storm was on the way. It seemed to Charlotte ironic and correct that such a marriage as hers should be solemnized to the accompaniment of thunder and lightning instead of hymns.

Lady Chase, leaning heavily on the arms of the doctor and Hannah, came up the aisle. She sat in the front pew, alone; that was how she wished it. She could scarcely see the proceedings because of the tears that continually blinded her eyes. She thought of Vivian as a curly-headed, small boy, so full of charm and promise; yet even then with the temper and moods that had made him difficult to control. She thought of the gallant soldier-husband who had died in the Crimea, and she thought of the splendid wedding which should have taken place in a far bigger church with all the glitter and pomp befitting the wedding of a Chase.

But there was just this sad ceremony in the little chapel which struck cold even on a summer's morning and was filled with the shadows of the approaching storm. Mr. Meadows, the aged, white-bearded vicar of Harling, officiated alone. He looked ill at ease. He felt that something was wrong even though he was not in her ladyship's confidence. But he presumed with the rest of the district that this curiously hasty marriage was taking place solely on account of Lady Chase's failing health. Indeed, he wondered if she would even survive the day; she looked so ill. Every now and again she raised the veil she wore and lifted a gold-stoppered bottle of smelling salts to her nostrils.

Sir Harry Cawder had not been well enough to leave his home and attend this wedding. The only occupants of the other pews were members of the staff. All were thunderstruck to see his young lordship being joined in holy matrimony to Charlotte Goff.

Whatever they thought, none dared say it. But there were few smiles; and no air of gaiety. Charlotte trembled violently as she repeated the words dictated to her by the old clergyman. Her voice could scarcely be heard. Vivian's was audible but exceedingly surly and now and again he tossed his golden head, looking to the left and right as though he wished to escape but could not.

Not once did he glance at his bride. But as he slipped the ring on her finger he felt a shudder go through her. Then they turned to one another. Vivian was quite thunderstruck by the beauty of Charlotte in her bridal gown, despite her ill-health. But the huge eyes were cold and hard, they even made him feel uneasy.

Now Lady Chase's head sank into her hands.

"It is done," she thought. "Charlotte has been vindicated. My son has paid the price. As for me, his most wretched mother, *I think he has cost me my life.*"

Mr. Meadows gave the final blessing. The bridal couple, Charlotte's gloved hand through Vivian's curved arm, turned and began to walk slowly down the aisle.

Charlotte was thinking:

"So I have been made an honest woman and I am Lady Chase. I am also the most loveless unhappy being in the world, hated by a husband whom I despise."

And Vivian reflected gloomily:

"So now I have a wife! Ye gods, what a wedding for Vivian Chase! *She shall pay for it*—that I swear!"

A quiet family lunch had been arranged at Clunes after which Vivian and Charlotte were to take the brougham to Harling station. There, a train would carry them to London, and they would stay the night in her ladyship's London residence. Tomorrow it was arranged that they go by steamer and train to Monte Carlo where a villa had been lent to Vivian by one of his mother's friends.

As they moved down the corridor, still in a sullen silence, the first flash of lightning illuminated the darkness. The bride gave a faint cry and raised a hand up to her eyes. There followed a low rumble of thunder.

"So the storm is come. A happy augury," said Vivian with a derisive laugh.

Charlotte made no reply. She felt, as she had felt for long, that her heart had turned to stone.

She was silent and unsmiling while the unhappy wedding breakfast took place in the morning room which the staff had dutifully decorated with flowers.

The Dowager Lady Chase maintained her stoic calm and determination throughout the "celebration." The Vicar remained with them. Wine was drunk and sandwiches eaten. There was no wedding cake. No friends or relatives to toast the bride and bridegroom, save Vivian's mother supported by Hannah and the somewhat baffled and embarrassed clergyman, who raised a glass and murmured:

"To the bride and bridegroom."

Charlotte merely touched the ice-cool wine with her lips. She nibbled a sandwich when Nan whispered to her that she must do so. The bridegroom drank a great deal and laughed and talked a little too loudly. He mentioned the inclement weather and discussed the most trifling things with Mr. Meadows. He reminded the Vicar that there was to be an amateur race for bicyclists on the new machine.

"I'm told that it has a driving wheel of sixteen inch diameter," Vivian drawled, looking immeasurably bored but feeling his mother's dark and gloomy gaze upon him.

"Ah, yes," murmured the Vicar, "the Honourable Keith Falconer from Trinity College, Cambridge, has been much talked of as a possible winner of the contest."

"I must say bicycling does not interest me. I prefer riding," went on Vivian and walked across and looked out at the teeming rain. "Our drive to the station will be a stormy one," he added.

The bride followed his figure with her gaze. She wished that she could rouse herself from the terrible lethargy into which she had fallen. This ring upon her finger could not be a wedding ring. That tall, handsome, cruel young man *could not* be her husband. She dreaded the thought of going away from Clunes with him. She would rather have stayed with her newly-made mother-in-law. Now she turned her large despairing eyes to the Dowager who gave her an encouraging smile and beckoned to her.

"Come here, my child."

Mr. Meadows moved to the window. He stood there talking to Vivian. Eleanor Chase took one of the bride's ice-cold hands.

"Courage, poor dear little Charlotte," she said in a low tone, "you must pray to Him who resolves all things in order that He may strengthen you. Do not look so tragic. You are now a wife, and will, in the fullness of time, I am sure, become a happy mother."

Charlotte shuddered, but made no response.

"Try," continued the older woman, "to grow well and strong in the sunshine of Monte Carlo. The sea should do you good. You will see much of life beyond Clunes and Harling hitherto unknown to you. Remember your learning, all that I have tried to teach you. Do not forget, if only for *my* sake, to be a good wife and a helpful comrade to *him*," she indicated Vivian.

Now the bride went down on one knee in all her shimmering draperies and with that look of despair still stamped on her young face, picked up one of Eleanor Chase's hands and laid it against her cheek.

"My lady," she began.

"I must now be 'mother' to you."

"Oh, Mother," said Charlotte in a wild voice, "I do most deeply revere you. I am not worthy to call you by that sweet familiar name but I beg for your forgiveness. Whatever I can do to please you in the future, I will do it. Alas, my love for *him* seems to have vanished beyond recall. It is that knowledge which freezes my mind and torments my heart."

The two women were speaking in lowered voices and could not be heard by the others at the far end of the room. Eleanor Chase's features worked. Tears were not far from her eyes but she stroked the bride's chestnut head and rearranged a fold of the lace veil.

"You are my own dear daughter now," she whispered. "I do most freely forgive you for I know that you remain innocent at heart. But try, oh, try, to love my son—no matter how hard or painful it must seem to you in these terrible circumstances. Now Nan must help you to change. Your train is at four-thirty, and I am very tired. I shall not be able to endure much more fatigue."

"Beloved Mother," said Charlotte with fresh agony in her voice, "pray take care and rest, and be here to welcome us when we return. Oh, do not leave Clunes yet awhile. I could not do without you now."

"One day you *must* do without me," said Lady Chase with a wan smile. "Come, rise from your knees, my dear little Charlotte. Be at peace, and send Vivian to me."

When Vivian stood beside his mother, she looked up at him with a long penetrating stare which seemed to search his very soul. He moved uncomfortably.

"In the name of your dead father and for the sake of your mother who may not much longer be with you—be kind to your young wife," she said. "Cast hatred out of your heart. Turn from thoughts of self. Only by love and kindliness can you ever obtain the true peace of mind which we all seek in this world."

Vivian grunted rather than replied.

"Oh, Vivian," added his mother with anguish, "you are my only son. Can you not let me die in peace, believing that you mean to act like a gentleman, and a Chase."

He shrugged but muttered:

"I will do all I can. But remember, Mama, that you have done my reputation no good by enforcing this absurd marriage."

She dropped his hand.

"I regret that the legal union seems to you absurd,

whereas you were willing enough to enter upon an illicit one," she said abruptly.

"Well, I am married to Charlotte now," he said sullenly.

"Respect that marriage bond or you will for ever lose my affection," said Eleanor Chase, coldly.

Thus ended the wedding of Vivian and Charlotte. Her ladyship retired to her bedroom. An hour later the newly-married couple left Clunes in the carriage which took them to Harling Station.

Charlotte sat rigid in her corner, staring out at the rain. It continued to fall heavily although the storm was abating. Only an occasional flash of lightning lit up the grey sky and made the bride shut her eyes tightly. As a small child she had always been frightened of storms and she particularly hated this one. It was, she felt sure, a presentiment of future evil.

Nan had kissed her good-bye tearfully, trying to comfort her by reminding her of the dazzling future awaiting her when she returned from her honeymoon. Charlotte had made no comment. *She* wanted nothing except the peace of mind that she had lost—the essential peace of an innocence which Vivian had destroyed.

Her husband sat at her side as silent as herself. He barely glanced at her. Yet she was beautiful in her fine blue suit with its coquettish bolero jacket, fashionable just now; fine *guipure* lace at the throat. A charming blue straw bonnet, with silk flowers and a little French veil hanging down from the back, was tied with a little bow under her chin. She carried a small folding fan which she used continuously. A pleated taffeta coat lay across her knee. The afternoon was steamy and close after the storm.

On her way to France! Hard for Charlotte to believe it. In the carriage, following, were their servants. Browning, Vivian's valet and Hester, one of Eleanor Chase's servants who had worked under Hannah for some years. She was excellent with her needle, and was now to be Charlotte's personal maid.

Charlotte gazed out of the window as they passed the Lodge. She thought sadly of the happiness she knew there in her childhood. One or two of the estate workers waved and threw flowers to her. They were standing in the rain to see the bridal couple go away.

Charlotte waved back at them, trying to smile and be grateful, but she felt that the whole affair was one long continued farce. What kind of a bride *was* she? What happiness could she hope for? And with Vivian as her lawful husband and master, was she not facing a veritable martyrdom rather than the brilliant future that Nan prophesied? Eleanor Chase had done what she believed to be the right thing. Ethically it might be so, but from every other standpoint Charlotte felt it must be wrong. It was an enforced wedding between two human beings who had passed from mad passion to mutual hatred and contempt.

She thought with melancholy of the bliss she might have experienced today had she felt about him what she used to feel; had *he* loved *her*, had this been a true wedding in every sense; with no disgraceful memories to pursue her, no apprehension of the future.

She felt even worse when at length they entered the great house in Eaton Square where they were to spend the night, for she was pursued by a sharp recollection of the little Charlotte who had been brought here by Lady Chase and her young son on that night of fog. She thought with pain of poor old Aunt Jem and Uncle Albert, of the old life in Pimlico which had been uncomfortable, poverty-stricken, yet in its way happy, with the happiness of ignorance.

Today she entered the big house on the arm of her husband, remembering how Vivian had charmed her in this same house when he was a mere boy. How fantastic and impossible it would have seemed to her then, had anybody said that one day she would become his wife.

The footmen bowed; the staff had ranged themselves in rows to curtsy and welcome the bride and groom, and stared inquisitively at the beautiful newly-made Lady Chase.

Charlotte bowed and smiled as graciously as she could. Vivian acknowledged the greetings of his servants with the haughty bored smile he assumed for menials.

The valet, Browning, and young Hester attended to the boxes. Charlotte and Vivian passed up the staircase into the rooms that had been prepared for them.

Charlotte looked around the enormous bedroom. It had a floral wallpaper and deep blue satin curtains. It seemed to her unfriendly, chilling. Vivian made things no better by indicating the huge four-postered bed with its brocaded curtains and saying:

"I was born in that bed, so they tell me, my dear. The confinement should have been at Clunes, but I believe my sainted mother came up to London to be with my father for a State occasion and I arrived with deuced lack of consideration, so my Mama had to remain here."

"Indeed," said Charlotte coldly as she unfastened the strings of her bonnet and drew off her gloves.

She had no wish to consider the birth of Vivian or the sufferings of that poor mother whom he might well call "*sainted*." It made her feel queasy. She longed, too, to be alone so that her new maid could come and unfasten her tight stays. She could not breathe. She was unused to tight-lacing. She deplored the necessity of it for fashion's sake. Her bustle felt strange and a little absurd.

It was terribly hot in London. There must have been a storm here, too, she thought. The pavements were wet. The trees in the square looked sodden.

She had not seen London for more than four years. With her memories crowding down upon her, she moved to one of the windows, pushed aside the lace curtains and stared out. She had never felt more lonely. Already she was homesick for Nan and the Lodge, for the great avenue of trees leading to Clunes. For the daisy-starred meadows, the grazing gentle cows, the peace of the Hertfordshire countryside. For her books, her dear books, and last but not least, her most *dear* teacher who now lay dying, bitterly disillusioned.

Oh, thought poor Charlotte, if one could but turn back the clock! If only she had never met Vivian Chase, never felt the sheer animal magnetism of the handsome young man and listened to his honey-sweet flattery.

She let the curtain fall and turned round, her bonnet still in her hands, her eyes blinded by tears.

She saw her husband lounging against one of the bedposts, his hands in his pockets. He eyed her almost malevolently, she reflected.

Suddenly she came towards him. It was as though her loneliness, her abject misery on what should have been the happiest day of her life, broke through the surface and overflowed.

"Oh, Vivian," she said, "can we not start afresh? Do not look at me with such hatred. I am, after all, the mother of your child."

"You cannot expect me to be glad of that, especially when your betrayal of me has meant my ruin."

"Oh, Vivian," persisted the poor young bride, "I did not willingly betray you. But consider my years, only sixteen, and I knew nothing of what passion meant until you taught it to me. Surely you do not blame me entirely for what took place?"

"If you had loved me you would have died before you blabbed to my mother," he said with superb egotism.

"And what would have become of me?"

"No doubt I would have paid to see you through your trouble," he drawled.

Charlotte's mind, still so young, so fresh and idealistic, could not fathom the depths of such utter selfishness. It appalled her.

"Then does this new young life for which we are both responsible mean nothing to you?" she asked.

His eyelids drooped. He kicked the point of a boot against the bed-post.

"Pff! You women sicken me with your sentimentality."

Young though she was, Charlotte had character. For a little while her horror and astonishment at the discovery of her own condition, and of Vivian's callous attitude, had subdued her spirit. Now, her courage and determination were returning. She was the old Charlotte again. She felt a rightful indignation against this young man who seemed to have no respect for virtue.

"What kind of man are you?" she demanded with scarlet cheeks and brilliant eyes, "*what kind*—that you can remain so indifferent to human suffering?"

"Are you suffering?" he sneered.

"More than you will ever know. Being made your lawful wedded wife this morning has saved my reputation but it has not eased my conscience. Neither can it wipe out my sorrow that in a moment of madness I helped to wound that mother whom you have rightly called a saint."

"Oh, come, come," he said, "you were not always such a pious little miss. You returned my kisses very prettily in the woods at Clunes that day!"

She flung back her head.

"I do not deny that I loved you. But I was in your hands—your cruel hands—so experienced and remorseless. Yet you have not one spark of conscience. It is that which amazes me."

"Good God," said Vivian in a violent voice, "you are not the first female to be put in the family way by a gentleman."

This coarse and brutal remark sent an even deeper crimson into the girl's pale, tired face. She stepped back a pace.

"How disgusting you are!" she said in a low voice.

He laughed loudly.

"Really, my dear, your refinement of spirit is most touching. A moment ago you asked me if we could not start afresh. Well, *well*, I fear I am in no way paternal, and I have no interest in this babe that we have begotten. Of course I rely upon your giving me a son. I trust, too, that it favours my side rather than yours."

"What is wrong with mine? The Goffs were good decent people," she flashed. "My father would have scorned to treat my mother as you treated me."

"All the same you did not scorn my embrace when you were in my arms that day at Clunes," he reminded her, and with a lecherous expression he advanced and caught her to him. He let his hand slide down her back to her waist that was still so small, so alluring. The exploring fingers went on to crush the rustling taffeta of her bustle, and up again to her warm, white neck. Playfully he began to pull the lobe of her ear and nibble at it.

"Pretty Thing, I am not unwilling to break the ice," he whispered. "For I can see that it will be dashed uncomfortable if we start off this honeymoon like two antagonists. Besides, London is too hot for quarrelling. Sweet, I'd forgotten how long your lashes were, how silky your skin. Ye-es, I fancy I could be kind to you, providing of course, that you rest as willingly in my embrace as any ordinary bride would do on her wedding night."

For a moment Charlotte stayed stiff and unbending in his embrace. She did not like the things he said, nor the way he said them. She felt that there was no real love in his heart—nothing of the tender romance for which she yearned. The Prince Charming whom she had once so blindly loved, seemed more like a satyr, eager to hurt—to ravish. He did not quote poetry to her today. He covered her face with kisses that wounded, instead of comforted. She broke down and wept.

"Oh, Vivian, Vivian!" she sobbed his name.

"No tears," he said, "if you wish us to make something of our marriage, I want neither tears nor recriminations. If I have sinned, you and my mother between you have made me pay for it. Now it is *your* turn to give, rather than take. Cease this nonsense about my cruelty. You are no innocent maid, you know. You are a *wanton.*"

"That is a vile lie!" she stammered wildly, and tried to push him from her.

"Oh, do not make any mistake, I like wanton women," he said with a grin.

Tired to death, Charlotte made no further protests but despairingly surrendered. His fingers tore at the little buttons on the back of her dress—at the rich silk and the lace on her petticoats. He seized a handful of her curls, pulled her head up against his and kissed her with violent passion. After a time he picked her right up in his arms and carried her towards the big bed.

"I am behaving like a model bridegroom," he said and laughed. "Is this not as you would wish things to be, my dear?"

She went limp in his arms and hid her face against his shoulder.

All the heartbreak and pain within her were centred in the one sobbing cry that came from her lips.

"It is love that I need from you, Vivian. *Oh, my husband, it is love that I need.*"

But if he heard that cry he did not answer it. He laid her on the pillows, walked to the door, and turned the key.

Any hope that had flickered feebly in her heart that he would give her such love, died during the hour that followed.

Chapter Twelve

The honeymoon was over.

Lord Chase's carriage, drawn by two beautiful greys, rolled down the broad drive that led to the house. The bride and bridegroom were home again. They had left that home in a thunderstorm. They returned on a mild evening, after a golden day of sunshine late in August. Not yet had the beech leaves turned to gold, but the Michaelmas daisies were already colouring the herbaceous borders with royal purple. The Virginia creeper over the west wall of the old house was beginning to turn red.

Once again for Charlotte, the old formula of welcome from the retinue of servants. The curtsies, the deep bows. This time, no stopping at the Lodge. It was Vivian's wish that his wife should not see too much of Nan and Joseph nor remind anyone that she had once lived with them. She was to take her rightful place at Clunes and must develop, he had told her more than once, some degree of snobbery. For he knew that this was missing from her true nature.

With mixed feelings, Charlotte walked into the familiar hall at Clunes, and, followed by Vivian, went straight into the library where they were told that the Dowager awaited them.

Charlotte had felt thankful while she was at Monte Carlo to receive a note from her mother-in-law stating that, after rest and care, she was better. Equally was Charlotte relieved to approach the house this afternoon and find Vivian's mother still alive. She had almost held her breath for fear that she might find the blinds down. Now as she looked upon the beloved figure on her accustomed sofa by the fire, Charlotte hurried across and knelt beside Lady Chase.

"Dearest Mother, we are here at last," she murmured.

"At last," echoed Eleanor Chase and gave a deep sigh of relief as she looked into her daughter-in-law's golden eyes, then up at her son.

Whatever had happened, it seemed on the surface, any how, that they had reached some kind of compromise. Indeed, they looked quite well, the mother thought, gratified. Vivian was bronzed and good humoured and Charlotte did not look nearly so white or strained as she had done when she left here. She had gained in poise and dignity. It was also evident that Vivian had been generous to her in Paris for she was fashionably attired in a new travelling dress, wine-coloured, with a three-quarter-length coat bordered with silk fringe. A little tilted hat of palest green, with a long veil floating down the back, sat on the chestnut head. She looked mature, and of course, Eleanor Chase reflected, her figure was fuller. She looked much less of a child.

Lady Chase whispered to Charlotte:

"Is all well?"

"Yes, dearest Mother, all is well," Charlotte whispered back.

Then Lady Chase held her arms out to her son.

"Embrace me, my dear boy, it is very good to see you," she said in a voice of deep emotion.

Vivian graciously bent and kissed first his mother's hand then both her cheeks.

"Splendid to see you looking so much better, Mama," he said and coughed.

"Oh, I am not feeling too badly," said her ladyship. "Hannah has taken good care of me and Dr. Castleby comes every day. Hannah," she turned to the old maid who hovered as usual in the background, "do our young couple not look wonderful? Monte Carlo has benefited them."

"Yes, my lady," grunted Hannah.

But there was no pleasure in the look which Hannah directed at the young Lord and Lady Chase. She still felt that Charlotte ought not to be here in this exalted position. She told Vivian bluntly, out in the hall when they were alone, his mother's looks belied her. Dr. Castleby was most concerned about the state of her heart. But she had insisted upon rising from her bed and coming down to welcome them home.

Vivian pretended an anxiety he did not really feel. It was not in his nature to worry over things before they happened.

He felt depressed, mainly because he was back in England. Clunes held no joy for him, and it irked him to have to act the penitent and anxious son. Just as it had irked him to simulate the adoring husband while he honeymooned in the South of France.

He was no more in love with Charlotte than he had ever been. He could be excited by her beauty when in the right mood—but he found her no companion. She had too fine a mind, too deep a nature. He liked women to be lighthearted and frivolous. And he had seen to it while he was in Monte Carlo that he had obtained as much such female society as he wished. There were plenty of gay *demimondaines* to be found hanging round the Casino. He also spent much time and money at the Tables. He had come home "broke" but knew that if he played his cards properly with Mama, he would soon be able to replenish the coffers. In fact he had grown to look upon Charlotte as something of an investment. His mother seemed so attached to her and the idea of the coming child, she would deny *him* nothing so long as he conducted himself well towards his wife.

Meanwhile Charlotte sat beside her mother-in-law and the two women exchanged news, while they sipped the China tea that had been brought to them. Lady Chase looked at Charlotte with the old tenderness in her dark sunken eyes.

"Is it possible that the Almighty led me to do the right thing and that you and Vivian have found some common interest, a new contentment?" she asked the girl in a yearning voice.

"Yes, yes, we—we get on very well now," said Charlotte lightly. "The villa was enchanting and I was stunned by the beauty of the French Riviera. You see my new clothes—" she laughed and indicated her costume. "Vivian was generous. Little Charlotte Goff has quite vanished."

"I do not want the little Charlotte *I* knew ever to vanish," said the older woman, "I liked her too well."

"Toward you, Mother, she will never change," said the girl with feeling.

"I do not think an exalted position will do much to spoil you," agreed Lady Chase. "And I feel in my bones that you have a good influence over my son. You do not know, Charlotte, how thankful I am for this day."

Charlotte murmured a reply and went on drinking her tea. So great was her desire to spare Eleanor Chase further pain, that she drew a veil over so many bitter memories of that honeymoon just spent in Monte Carlo. Please God, if his mother had only a short time to live, Vivian would be man enough to play *his* part and so make her happy until the end.

But for Charlotte the future stretched bleakly and without hope. After a few weeks of intimacy with Vivian Chase she knew that she could never find happiness with him. She knew just how base he was, how utterly ignoble.

The honeymoon had been a period of bitterness and disgust for man, man as revealed to her by marriage to Vivian Chase. At times, when she came up against his stubborn determination to master her, she had wondered in despair if he had inherited a single one of his parents' qualities. It seemed incredible that two such noble people should have conceived this monster of egotism.

Most evenings she had spent alone, either wandering through the beautiful orange-scented grounds of the villa or sitting in sad solitude on the terrace looking down at a sea that shimmered like blue silk. Hour after hour, she lay lonely and forsaken in the splendid Italian bed in a room of Rococo magnificence. Day after day, accompanied only by her maid, she wandered through the Casino gardens to see the flowers, or sometimes she visited the glittering, expensive shops. More often than not she stayed at home where it was cool and restful and she could read.

Vivian spent the whole of his honeymoon enjoying himself in the way he desired, which was mainly apart from his wife. He lingered at the Casino with his men-friends and played roulette or baccarat. He amused himself with the *demi-monde*. He drank too much champagne. He would return to his villa at dawn to sleep heavily until mid-day. When he was with Charlotte his mood was usually surly. He taunted her and reminded her that he had married her by force and not by inclination.

Her delicate condition awoke no pity in him. Gradually

she stopped hoping for love or tenderness from Vivian. When he demanded what he called his "marital rights" she accepted his attentions coldly and silently, believing it to be her duty. On her seventeenth birthday, two days before they returned to England, he threw her a jewelled bangle which he had bought in one of the Monte Carlo shops, but he did not dine with her, or show her any special consideration.

"You are not well. You should go to bed," he said.

"Today I am seventeen," she thought, "and already an unhappy, disillusioned woman."

The gay and warm-hearted Charlotte who had once found life an intoxicating mystery, seemed to have died. This Charlotte, Lady Chase, knew only a dreadful loneliness.

While together in public, they had met one or two people who knew the Chase family. Vivian, who could be so utterly charming when he wished, put a hand through his wife's arm and introduced her with a loving expression as, *"My beautiful bride."*

The honeymoon couple returned from Calais on the newest Channel steamship, the *Castalia*. The journey to Dover took one hour and fifty minutes—a tremendous speed, which caused a sensation. But the sea was choppy and Charlotte retired to her cabin with her maid, deathly sick.

Once mistress of herself again, and during the train journey to Harling, she summoned up her courage to discuss their future with Vivian.

"Whatever you feel about me, I beg you to make her ladyship happy whenever we are in her presence," Charlotte said. Vivian scowled.

"How many times must I remind you to call her *Mother* —or Mama. If our friends hear you say 'her ladyship,' they will think I have married a servant girl."

In this vein they returned to Clunes.

But Vivian was making an effort today and it was not an unhappy meal, of which later the three of them partook. The Dowager was quite delighted because her tall son insisted upon carrying her, himself, into the dining-room, and placing her in her usual chair at the head of the table.

"You are still mistress of Clunes. Charlotte and I will sit on either side of you, as your devoted children," he said gaily.

Eleanor Chase was sublimely happy, confident that a miracle had caused this change of heart in Vivian. But Charlotte knew what a hypocrite he was. Earlier, while they were dressing, he had come into her room and grumbled because his poor mother was still at Clunes.

Now her gaze rested for a moment, fascinated, on the big portrait over the fireplace—the Millais masterpiece. Eleanor Chase, youthful, gloriously beautiful, wearing a ruby red crinoline dress; Vivian leaning against her in a velvet suit with lace collar and cuffs; looking angelic with his large blue eyes and golden curls.

Too early in life Charlotte was becoming a cynic, aware of the painful gulf between good and evil. Almost she found it impossible to believe that any child who looked like that one in the portrait could grow up into such a demon.

Tonight she had the right to live here at Clunes—mistress of this splendid house. When the Dowager was gone, it would be *she*, Charlotte, who would sit in that tall-backed armchair, facing Vivian at one end of the long table.

A perfect meal was served ceremoniously by Williams, the butler, and Lucy, the head parlour maid. Charlotte did not look at them but could feel their inquisitive glances frequently upon her. They, who had known her in the past, must find it strange, she reflected, to wait upon little Charlotte Goff from the Lodge.

At Vivian's request, Charlotte had put on one of her new Paris gowns: dark rose silk with a yoke of black lace, and black lace frills frothing round the bottom of the skirt. She looked much older in such a frock but it seemed to please Eleanor Chase who complimented her daughter-in-law upon her dignified appearance.

Over coffee the Dowager discussed the plans she had made for her son and daughter-in-law. Tomorrow, Sunday, she was holding a small tea party and reception for them in the garden. Invitations had gone out to their closest friends. Alas, she said, Sir Harry was still not well enough to come down to meet the bride, but Eleanor's cousins, the

Miss Ida and Miss Mary Foulkes, were presenting themselves. These old spinsters were said to have made their wills in favour of Vivian.

The most important of local guests would be Sir Claude Glover whose house, Hamfield Court, was two miles distant from Clunes. He was still only in the late forties, but had been forced to retire from the diplomatic service owing to ill-health. Alicia, his first wife, had been Eleanor's dearest friend. Two years after her death Sir Claude married again. This time to a woman considerably younger, without interest for Lady Chase. A pretty prattling little thing but Lady Chase, ever gracious and understanding, had invited the new Lady Glover, more for Charlotte's sake than for anyone else's. Gwendolen Glover was not much older than Charlotte and might make of her a friend.

Vivian, listening to the list of guests in a bored way, perked up at the mention of Gwendolen Glover.

"I know that you find Sir Claude a bore but he is a fine man and the type to do you good," his mother reminded him.

It was Vivian's private opinion that the new Lady Glover would do him much more good. He had taken her on at a game of archery last summer and remembered her trim figure, her flaxen curls, and narrow, laughing eyes. He was quite sure she had only married old Glover for the title. She had given him, Vivian, many an inviting smile.

Charlotte also listened and felt her heart sink a little. It was not that she did not want to meet the Chases' friends. She was sociable by nature. But she felt such a hypocrite at the moment with her Deadly Secret which must be hidden from all the ladies. Soon she could no longer wear these elegant gowns and then, *what?* She would have to pretend illness and lie up for a while, and come down in loose tea gowns; négligées which would hide her condition.

After dinner, Vivian carried his mother up to her bedroom. Charlotte sat with her a moment while Hannah fetched hot water and towels. Charlotte thought that Lady Chase looked mortally tired and ill.

"Oh, pray do not do too much, dearest Mother!" she begged. "Do not hold this tea tomorrow just for Vivian and me, if it is beyond your strength."

Gently, Lady Chase chided her daughter-in-law.

"It is not for nothing that I take this course, my love. It is for Vivian's *reputation*. Your marriage was solemnized in secrecy because I feared that I was about to die. But now, while I still live, it is expedient that you should play your part for the visitors with a natural air. Whatever they think now, after tomorrow they will be forced to accept you as Vivian's honoured wife."

"Would that I did not feel such a hypocrite," said Charlotte and put her face in her hands.

"That must be your cross, my poor child. You must bear it with courage. Do not give way to your innermost feelings. Hide then and continue to make my son happy as he now appears to be. That is all I ask."

"Dearest Mother," said Charlotte and kissed the white hand extended to her, hardly able to restrain her tears.

"In my bureau," went on the Dowager, "you will find a bundle of letters which are the answers to my invitations. Nobody has refused. Everyone is anxious to meet you. Take these letters, read them and familiarize yourself with the names and addresses of the writers."

"I shall do so."

"And you will not fail me tomorrow? You will be my old, sparkling Charlotte, without a care in the world?"

"If possible, yes," whispered the girl drying her eyes.

"Lady Glover has asked if she might bring two house guests who are spending the weekend at Hamfield Court which is the Glover residence. They are a Mr. and Mrs. Peveril Marsh. He is a portrait painter of considerable reputation. They live in Essex. She was the daughter of Sir Harry and Lady Roddney, now dead, and was once wife to the Baron of Cadlington who lived in Buckinghamshire. There have been considerable rumours about the romantic nature of the Marshes' meeting and marriage, but I never listen to gossip so cannot repeat it. I have, therefore, informed Gwendolen Glover that she has my permission to bring her friends to our tea party."

Charlotte kissed Lady Chase good night and went to her own room. It was the most elegant of the guest chambers —furnished in palest grey. It had been prepared with magnificent flowers for the bridal couple. Vivian's suite adjoined. Charlotte wondered if he would hold any conversation with her tonight; or if the pleasant mood put on for his mother's benefit would be reversed once he was alone with her.

But he did not come to her room nor did she see him again until morning. After the rest of the inmates of Clunes were abed Vivian had slipped out of a back entrance and made his way to his old haunt—the house of Roma Gresham.

Chapter Thirteen

Sunday was a disappointment as far as weather was concerned. All hopes of a garden party had to be abandoned. At dawn the weather changed, and a rain storm swept across the countryside accompanied by a high wind. By breakfast time the grounds were in a sorry state. The new Michaelmas daisies were flattened and bedraggled. The branches of the tall elms tossed and creaked. The tempest sent a shower of leaves scurrying across the puddled lawns.

Eleanor Chase announced that Vivian and Charlotte must receive in the drawing-room. The whole staff was kept busy helping to prepare for the event. The Crown Derby tea service was laid out. For hours, cook and kitchenmaid cut delicate, fine rolls of brown and white bread-and-butter, and made *pâté* sandwiches. There was a fine array of iced cakes which had been made yesterday, one of which was in the nature of a bridal cake—three tiered—and with the initials "V" and "C" entwined in a circle of lovers-knots.

Charlotte would ordinarily have enjoyed it all, even felt the tiniest spurt of pride in her new dignity of position as the young mistress of the house. But Vivian took care to spoil whatever pleasure she might have extracted from the party. They had a bitter dispute before descending from their rooms—on the subject of Nan.

The affectionate and grateful Charlotte had wanted to run and see her foster-parents at the Lodge. Vivian forbade it.

"Now that you are my wife, you will kindly forget that you ever lived in the lodge," he said in his haughtiest voice.

"But Nan and Joseph cared for me for many years. I cannot treat them now as though they are dust just because

I have become Lady Chase," said Charlotte indignantly.

Vivian, whose face was puffy after a night of debauchery, flung her an unpleasant look.

"You will do as you are told."

Charlotte's heart began to beat fast.

"But it is my *duty* to pay my respects to the Forbes."

"Your duty is to *me*, alone—" thundered Vivian.

Charlotte, for once, defied him.

"I refuse to hurt my good and kind friends. I shall call upon them and prove that I am still their loving Charlotte."

A moment's silence, then Vivian said with a freezing smile:

"You have forgotten that *I* am the master of Clunes. Whoever my mother sides with over this, you shall do what I wish. If you dare go near the Forbes I shall turn them out and engage new keepers for the Lodge."

"Oh," gasped Charlotte. "I would not have that happen to them for the world. They love their home and they have always done their job conscientiously. Why, *why* should you forbid me to visit them?"

"Because it must be forgotten that you were ever a nobody from Pimlico and brought up here by common employees; that is, if you wish to be held in respect by our friends."

"Would I be respected for turning my back upon those whose lowly station I once shared?" she persisted.

"Go to the devil," said Vivian, "and do as I command, or the Forbes receive their notice to leave—tonight."

Knowing him so well, she realized that he would carry out his threat. It was a sickening start to her day. She could not even explain matters to Nan without being disloyal to her husband. All the morning she thought of Nan, waiting for her visit; hating the thought that the little woman would be deeply hurt and disappointed when she failed to put in an appearance.

Then came the party.

Charlotte stood at the drawing-room door beside her husband and received the guests who shook hands and filed past her to the couch on which the Dowager sat, covered with a light cashmere shawl.

The inclement weather had brought the temperature down so low that it was decidedly cool in the house today.

Log fires had been lit. Autumn seemed already to be here.

As the Dowager had anticipated, the entire neighbourhood buzzed with excitement and curiosity to see the young girl whom Vivian Chase had married. There had, of course, been a veritable flood of rumours.

The more kindly and well-disposed accepted her ladyship's explanation that the wedding had been a sudden and secret one because the doctors feared for her life. The less charitable whispered to each other that there might be *another reason* for so hasty a wedding.

All knew about Lady Chase's protégée, but few had met Charlotte Goff. *Extraordinary,* they thought, that the wealthy and highly eligible Lord Chase should wish to marry a girl of lower station than his own. However, it was agreed that Eleanor Chase was devoted to Charlotte and found her intelligence of a high order. Certainly Charlotte *appeared* to be well-bred, even if she was not. She looked every inch a lady, and behaved with the utmost decorum. Her manners were exquisite. It was generally thought that she looked older than her seventeen years, being a little full in the bust. The ladies cast many envious glances at her dress. For this reception (her mother-in-law had made the choice) the bride wore one of her most beautiful yet simple gowns, in the latest mode from Paris. White sprigged muslin, cut rather low in the *corsage,* with bunches of the crisp material flounced back into a bustle. Pale blue bows on the wide bell-shaped sleeves; ruffles of blue on the hem. Little blue satin slippers. White flowers were pinned to her hair which was dressed in a *chignon,* with long glossy curls cascading down the back of her neck. She was pale but her large eyes looked brilliant under their narrow arched brows. She gave an impression of fresh, innocent youth, a semblance of the purity which nothing that Vivian had done could pollute.

"She is uncommonly handsome, is the little bride," the men whispered to each other.

"Not so guileless as she looks," suggested the more shrewd among the women as they gossiped over their teacups in the corners of the drawing-room.

One or two matrons, disappointed that they could not now snatch Vivian as a husband for their daughters who were just about to come out, were less charitable.

So much nonsense, they murmured, about *intelligence*. Intelligent females were always under suspicion. A woman's true place was in the house attending to her servants or (discreet cough) in her nursery.

One discerning lady, who deeply respected the Dowager Lady Chase but had never trusted Vivian, came nearer the mark by suggesting to a friend that young Vivian was a "real rake" and that perhaps his mother had thought this marriage to a pure young girl would steady him.

However, most of those who had come to pick holes in the bride were forced to admit that Charlotte was charming and interesting. She seemed able to talk on most subjects as well as to look beautiful. Congratulations were poured upon the couple.

But the guests were unanimous in their fears for the Dowager. She looked like a wraith, they said. Not long for this world; they could well believe it! This fact did much to foster the one impression Eleanor Chase meant to convey that the quiet, hasty wedding of her son with Charlotte Goff had been on *her* account.

The Misses Ida and Mary Foulkes, both in the early seventies, garbed from head to foot in the black which they had worn after the death of Prince Albert and never abandoned, asked too many awkward questions to please Vivian. He had to wriggle out of one or two decidedly difficult moments. One on either side of him, the old ladies sat upright, as stiff as pokers, on the edge of their chairs. They barked at the handsome boy whom they did, in fact, adore.

Why this sudden marriage to a nobody?

Why hadn't *they* been informed?

What had induced Cousin Eleanor to give her approval, while Vivian was still at Oxford?

Vivian, however, answered the questions lightly and made all his explantions sound feasible. The Misses Foulkes clicked their teeth and tut-tutted, but finally coated the pill of suspicion with the sugar of a grudging admission that they admired his young wife. But they still thought he should have made a better match.

Charlotte was frightened to death of the old ladies. She felt that they saw through her; must *know* of her condition. She went pale when they approached her. But the Dowager saved the day by calling her cousins to her couch.

In her serene, tactful fashion, she brushed aside the dagger point of their critical attack upon Vivian.

"My son fell in love," she said calmly. "That is the long and the short of it, dear cousins. I am soon to be called to the Judgment Throne. I wished to see my son wed to the girl of his choice before my departure. Charlotte is a dear girl and will make him very happy."

Half-way through the afternoon, Charlotte began to feel exceedingly fatigued; at times a little giddy. Oh, heavens, she thought, she must not swoon. She must not in any way draw attention to her state of health. Vivian would be furious. Once she drew him aside and whispered:

"Do you think I could find an excuse to withdraw for a short time? It has become so hot in here with the fire on. I am feeling dizzy."

Vivian hissed into her ear:

"Kindly take a hold of yourself. You must remain. Do you want everyone to *guess*, you little idiot?"

She stood where he left her, as near the window as she could get, nervously fingering her Dorothy bag which was made of artificial forget-me-nots. She felt stifled. Soon she *must* put an end to this tight lacing, she thought. She ground her teeth trying to control the faintness that threatened to overcome her.

It was then that she felt a gentle hand upon her arm, and, turning, looked into one of the most beautiful faces she had ever seen. The face of an elderly woman in a dove-grey lace dress and coat, and wearing a small plumed hat.

"I note that you feel a little indisposed," said a soft kindly voice, "these receptions are so trying for a bride. I wonder if I might ask you to show me the portraits in your gallery. There, you will doubtless find it a little fresher."

"It is uncommonly kind of you," said Charlotte.

Gratefully, she walked with this discerning lady out of the hot, crowded drawing-room.

In the gallery, there was a gilt and brocade sofa of the *Louis Quinze* period. Charlotte's new friend insisted upon Charlotte sitting down upon it, and offered her a bottle of smelling salts.

"You are too kind," whispered Charlotte, sniffing the salts and closing her eyes. "I do feel poorly, I must admit. Pray tell me your name, I fear I have forgotten."

"I am Mrs. Marsh—Fleur Marsh, I came with our good friends, Sir Claude and Lady Glover. We are staying at Hamfield Court."

"But of course," said Charlotte who was beginning to revive. "Your husband is the great painter."

Mrs. Marsh smiled.

"I do not know about a *great painter*—but he is a very great man—in my estimation at least," she smiled.

How Charlotte envied her the cause of that smile. Easy to see that Mrs. Marsh adored her husband. Love glowed in her eyes; and what magnificent eyes, thought Charlotte. Of the most unusual shade of violet-blue. She must be fifty, at least, for her red-gold hair was lavishly streaked with silver and the delicate face was lined. But she still possessed an almost unearthly beauty and there was something about her sympathetic manner which instantly drew Charlotte to her.

"I know little about paintings save what I have learned from my mother-in-law," said Charlotte shyly, "but I have often heard mention of, and read about, Mr. Marsh and his portraiture."

"My husband, as soon as he saw you, said that he would like to paint *you*," observed Mrs. Marsh. "Could you sit for him? I am sure Lord Chase would be pleased—" Mrs. Marsh indicated the long gallery—"he will want your likeness to hang here with his predecessors."

Charlotte stayed silent. She could not imagine Vivian wishing to have a portrait of her. The older woman stayed silent, too. When she had first set eyes on the young bride she had thought that those big golden eyes held far too melancholy an expression for one so young—and a newly-made wife at that. She had formed an impression—and had passed it on to Peveril—that the new Lady Chase was unhappy. Now she felt sure of it. Fleur Marsh, remembering the anguish of her own first marriage, the terrors that awaited her at Cadlington House when, as the Baron's bride, she had been forced to entertain his friends, felt a deep sympathy for this girl. All marriages were not made in heaven, like *hers* with Peveril. All men were not as fine or gallant. She had been married to Peveril these thirty-five years, and they were still deeply in love.

What was the secret behind young Lady Chase's look of

despair? Of all the guests, only Mrs. Marsh, who had herself tasted the pangs of hell, sensed tragedy.

"You must come to Pillars, our home, and see us," she told Charlotte. "We live just across the border, not far from Epping. We would be happy if you and Lord Chase would spend a few days with us. The partridge season has begun. We have some fine shooting."

"I fear my husband is not fond of sport," said Charlotte sadly.

"Nor, in fact, is Peveril, my husband. He is an artist," said Mrs. Marsh with a smile. "It was my father, Sir Harry Roddney, who liked shooting so well. Pillars was my girlhood's home. It has many lovely memories for me."

Charlotte nodded dumbly. She, too, had her lovely memories. The four years at Clunes as Eleanor Chase's pupil, before her mad passion for Vivian had stormed into her life.

"One day," continued Fleur Marsh, "I would like to tell you the romantic story of my parents, and my old home."

"Perhaps one day I will tell you mine," said Charlotte in a low voice.

"At any rate, pray count me your friend, my dear," said Mrs. Marsh, laying a hand on hers.

The kindness of this charming grey-haired little woman thawed some of the ice around Charlotte's heart. She returned the hand clasp warmly and said:

"You are exceedingly kind, Mrs. Marsh."

Vivian suddenly appeared. Fleur noticed at once how Charlotte sprang to her feet; how the young girl's whole face and figure seemed to stiffen as Lord Chase sauntered up towards her. There was something in the young man's turquoise blue eyes from which Fleur shrank. Despite his looks, she found him repellent. She saw, too, how resentful Charlotte looked when Vivian slid an arm round her waist.

"He is doing it only to impress me," thought Fleur. "I do not like him, and the poor child looks as *I* must have looked when that monster to whom I was first married, touched *me*."

Vivian drawled:

"If you will pardon me, Mrs. Marsh, I must take my sweet Charlotte away. She has to say good-bye to some of our guests who are departing."

Fleur answered politely and turned to Charlotte.

"Do not forget, my husband and I will be most happy for you to visit Pillars," she said.

Fleur stayed alone for a while in the cool picture gallery. She felt no particular desire to join the crowd in the drawing-room. She wanted to think. She had received such a vivid impression that the new Lady Chase was stalked by tragedy.

After a few minutes she was joined by her husband who had been searching for her.

The artist was a slightly built man with grey curls. He had still a boyish look, although his face was much lined when one inspected it at close quarters. He had been for some years now racked with rheumatic pains which caused him great suffering. He stooped a little. But he never complained. He still worked hard at his painting which was his dearest occupation, and the dearest of all people in this world to him was this wife of his. As he reached Fleur's side he picked up one of her hands and kissed it.

"You have been away from my side for nearly an hour. That is exactly one hour too long," he smiled.

"Dear Peveril," she leaned her head on his shoulder.

He looked tenderly down at that beloved head. Once it had been a glorious auburn; he could not count the number of times he had painted it. But he loved her none the less today because she had grown old.

She began to talk to him about young Lady Chase. She spoke of her involuntary dislike of Vivian and the queer psychic intuition that led her to believe that Charlotte Chase was an unhappy bride.

"Like myself when first you saw me, Peveril," ended Fleur, and her slender fingers closed convulsively around her husband's.

"Hush," he said, "do not let the sadness of the past depress you now, my beloved."

She bit her lip. Peveril Marsh gazed at her anxiously. He knew that there were many moments when his wife did, indeed, brood upon the terrible things that had happened to her, more than thirty years ago. The horror of them had set an indelible stamp upon her. He grieved that this should be. As they stayed there a moment, arm in arm, he could follow her train of thought. It would not be untrue to say that he, too, remembered every detail of the past. It had a way of creeping in to ruffle the surface of their now tranquil and happy life.

Unforgettable for both of them that day, thirty-six years ago, when Fleur, the hapless daughter of Sir Harry and Lady Roddney, had entered Cadlington House as a bride on the arm of Denzil St. Cheviot, one of the most wicked and notorious noblemen of his day. He, Peveril, then a mere stripling, and protégé of the Baron, had painted the first and most beautiful portrait of his life of the Baroness. This one and many others, were destroyed in maniacal rage by the Baron after the birth and death of his son. The subject of that ghastly tragedy was *taboo* in Peveril's household. For even after this long time Fleur could not bear to speak of it. The poor little infant which she had never seen (for it had died at birth, so she had been told) was unmistakably of black blood. That blood could be traced back to her African great-grandfather, and had been transmitted through the veins of Fleur's mother, Lady Roddney; she, who had once been called *Fauna*, born a quadroon slave, and had later become the Marquise de Chartellet, wife of the French Marquis of that name. After the Marquis's death she had married Sir Harry and Fleur, their only child, had been born to them.

Of Fleur St. Cheviot's martyrdom during the brief period she had lived with the cruel Baron, of the latter's death by the sword at the hand of her father, Sir Harry, of the destruction by fire of Cadlington House, and of her elopement with him, Peveril, there was both good and bad to remember.

Good had triumphed. For thirty-four years these true lovers had lived in happiness at Pillars. And then, ten years ago Harry Roddney died, an old man, adoring his daughter, respecting the son-in-law who had risen to great heights as a painter, and much loved by them. With his dying breath Sir Harry had murmured the name of Fleur's mother.

"I am going to her," he whispered, "my beloved Fauna."

De Chartellet had re-named her, *"La Belle Hélène."* But Harry had called her "Fauna" with his final gasp of breath. *Fauna*—the unforgotten name, Fauna, even now remembered by the daughter who had learned about that African strain—too late.

The Marshes were without children. Much as Fleur had longed for a family, she had known after the tragic events of the past that it must never be. Fleur maintained that she wanted none but Peveril. But sometimes the sensitive and affectionate man who loved her so well wondered if their lack of children had not left a hunger and void in her life. For somewhere, he believed, in the deep recess of her memory, there lingered a yearning sorrow because her ill-fated babe had died.

Now Fleur spoke to him imperiously, as though a sudden and psychic knowledge had been imparted to her. Clinging to Peveril's arm, she said:

"*There is to be a child*—yes, Peveril, the stamp of motherhood already sits on the brow of that girl who has just been speaking to me, and all will not be well."

"Oh, come, my angel," said Peveril with a laugh, "you let imagination run away with you. Besides, such an idea casts a slight upon the newly-wedded pair."

"Nevertheless," said Fleur, "it is so. You will see. Meanwhile it is my earnest wish, dear heart, that you ask Lord Chase to stay with us. Yes, I know you do not like him. Neither do I, but I *must* give what I can of friendship to Lady Chase. You will discover how much she needs it."

"Your wish is my command," said Peveril, and touched his wife's cool cheek with his lips.

But just how much Charlotte was to need the Marshes' friendship, and just what true cause Fleur had for her instinctive fears, neither Peveril nor anybody else this afternoon at Clunes could dream.

Chapter Fourteen

August was an emotional month for Charlotte.

Then came September.

Fortunately for all concerned the changes wrought by her pregnancy were few. She no longer laced quite so tightly and a clever dressmaker helped to make her new smart dresses looser without losing their essential *chic.* During the fortnight after the tea party at Clunes, any fears that Charlotte might have entertained that she would be cold shouldered by the neighbourhood were laid to rest. Invitations to the newly-married pair poured in from all quarters. A succession of luncheons and dinners were held for them. Charlotte dreaded them but was forced to accompany her husband. They were, of course, rather too conventional to please Vivian's fancy, but they were consoling to his pride. He need no longer feel that his marriage to Charlotte Goff had wrecked his social life. The beautiful and intelligent girl seemed to have made a hit with everybody.

If Vivian craved amusement after his own fashion there was still Mrs. Gresham's house, so discreetly hidden among the trees. But just now it was the gambling there that interested him rather more than the women. And he had money to burn. By behaving outwardly, anyhow, as his mother desired, he found her generous with her purse.

Charlotte did not feel well and went perpetually in fear that one or other of the ladies would recognize the signs of her condition.

But as that terror lessened, she became absorbed wholly by the darkest dread of all; those wrapped around her mother-in-law. Lady Chase took to her bed and did not leave it again, as though she felt that she had done what had to be done and was now ready to give up the ghost.

Dr. Castleby's visits increased to both night and morning. Two distinguished specialists drove down from London, only to tell Vivian that nothing more could be done for poor Lady Chase. She was growing weaker and it could only be a matter of weeks before the end.

Charlotte hoped secretly that the impending loss of his mother would rouse the best instincts in her young husband. So distressed was Charlotte, herself, by the prospect of losing the great lady she had loved so well, the tears were never far from the surface. But Vivian took it all casually. On several occasions he lectured Charlotte for weeping. "Death must come to all of us and my mother is no longer young," he said loftily. "Her time has come. It cannot improve matters for you to creep around the place snivelling. I find you most unbecoming with your shiny nose and puffy eyelids."

Charlotte had grown used to the callousness of this extraordinary young man.

"But do you not *love* your mother?" she asked, staring at him incredulously. "Do you not *feel* grief?"

"My dear Charlotte, Mama is not dead yet," he drawled. "I shall save my tears for the event."

"You are monstrous," she said in a whisper.

He laughed.

The Dowager had two trained nurses, one of whom was a good-looking woman with some fame attached to her, for she had nursed in the Crimea with Florence Nightingale. When Miss Parkinson was present, Vivian sat by his mother's side and made himself excessively charming. He would hold one of the invalid's long white hands, sighing deeply, murmuring endearments which would impress anybody, and certainly a female. Miss Parkinson often glanced quite tenderly at the fair debonair young man. She mentioned to her colleague that she had never known a more devoted son than Lord Chase.

"And he is handsome as an angel," Miss Parkinson sighed romantically.

But the dying woman, herself, was not impressed by any of these exhibitions from her son. Alas for her, Eleanor Chase's perceptions seemed to sharpen with her fast-approaching end. The love that she had once borne her only child changed to suspicion and contempt. She listened to him in silence when he spoke to her. Day after day when Charlotte visited her, the older woman saw how pinched and pale the young girl's face had grown. How sad she was, despite all efforts to be bright. Eleanor Chase knew the worst. Vivian's marriage had not changed him, nor ever would. Her deepest grief now was the knowledge that she must leave Charlotte to bear her cross alone. And she even asked herself in the small hours one morning, when she lay sleepless, if she had done right in making Vivian marry Charlotte. She had saved the girl's name. The child would be born in wedlock. *But had it been for the best?*

If only she could die feeling that he would be good to poor little Charlotte. *If only*—

Suddenly Lady Chase heard a cry.

She struggled into a sitting position, her thin sick body breaking into a sweat.

"What was that?" she panted and pulled the little night shawl over her head, and sat taut, shivering, straining her ears. The night nurse had slipped downstairs to fetch herself a plate of biscuits to eat with her morning cup of tea. Hannah was not yet up. It was still only half-past five.

Again that sharp cry. And suddenly Lady Chase recognized it. *It came from Charlotte*—from the direction of the rooms occupied by the newly-married couple.

Lady Chase pressed both hands to her rapidly beating heart.

What was wrong? Had Charlotte been taken ill? The girl had looked so ill lately; could it mean that this was the beginning of a miscarriage? If so, one of the nurses must go to her immediately and a footman be roused and sent for Dr. Castleby.

Again that cry and then a laugh, *a horrible maniacal laugh*, that seemed to freeze the Dowager's blood.

"Nurse! *Nurse!*" she called frantically, in a high thin voice.

No answer came. Eleanor Chase was bathed in perspiration, confident now that something terrible was happening at the end of the corridor. Suddenly she flung off her bedclothes and slid her legs over the edge of her bed. Hers was the false final strength of a desperate dying creature, the last terrible effort Eleanor Chase was ever to make.

Without slippers, with only a shawl wrapped over her voluminous white nightgown, she tottered out of the bedroom. She swayed as she went. Once in the corridor, she had to put her hands against the wall in order to keep her balance. She uttered little sobs and moans under her breath as she went. Her heart beat so fast and caused her such agony that she could hardly bear the pain. Yet she prevailed. She propelled herself on and on, whilst oblivious of this crisis, the night-nurse lingered downstairs, searching in the pantry for delicacies that she fancied.

Meanwhile, in Charlotte's bedroom, chaos reigned.

A few moments ago, Vivian had returned to Clunes from Roma Gresham's house. He was drunk and in a venomous, belligerent mood.

Charlotte, who had been fast asleep, had wakened to find him standing beside her bed, holding a candelabra at a tilted angle so that the hot wax dripped on to the carpet. The gleaming light showed up the sweat on his pallid face. He no longer looked angelic or handsome, but hideous in her sight, with loose lips, damp dishevelled locks, all the marks of his debauchery. His fine clothes were disarrayed, his shirt stained with wine, his cravat untied. As she sat upright, clutching the bedclothes to her, he laughed down at her.

"Do I disturb your innocent slumbers, my puritanical wife?"

Quickly she slid out of the bed and into a blue velvet gown. She looked young and intensely sad. She was still half-drugged with sleep but she managed to speak calmly.

"Vivian, for mercy's sake, where have you been?"

"That is my affair. I want no questioning."

Wide awake now, she stared up at him with wide-eyed disdain.

"You have been keeping poor company, sir, that is obvious."

"Do not dare to criticize me if I have had some amusement; that is only natural. Do you think I can live and breathe in such a rarefied atmosphere as this," he waved an arm drunkenly around the cool, fragrant bedroom. The curtains billowed in the strong wind. Charlotte felt cold and began to tremble. He added:

"It is a freezing in here as well might be, since it is *your* bedchamber. I was brought up by a damned saint, and now I find myself married to a bedamned icicle."

Pale and horrified, Charlotte tried again to soothe her husband. Her one concern was lest the invalid at the other end of the passage should hear Vivian's loud hectoring voice.

"I beg of you to control yourself," she said, "and if you do not like my bedroom, you have your own. Pray go to it."

He ignored this dignified appeal and set the candelabra down on her bed table with a clatter. Unsteadily, he walked across the room and pulled at the cord of the open window, making a crash that was enough, thought Charlotte, to waken anybody.

"I like warmth," he said, "warmth and gaiety, and an impassioned invitation from a flesh-and-blood woman."

Charlotte made no answer. Her pulse rate increased. She was nervous of Vivian in this state. She had seen him drunk before, but never quite as bad as this. She knew, of course, that on occasions he left the house and did not return until the early hours. But never before had he come into her room to disturb her rest. She could see that he was half crazy with the strong liquor he had consumed.

"For the life of me I do not know where he goes to get in such a state," she thought miserably.

She had deemed it fortunate during the time that she had lived at Clunes, that she did not have to endure much of Vivian's company. But she had suffered from an increasing loneliness which had not been lessened by his spiteful refusal to allow her to visit her foster-parents. Twice in secret she had met Nan in the gardens, then only for a few moments, and had tried to give Nan a tactful explanation. But she had seen that the kindly woman was deeply hurt because she went to the Lodge no more. Nothing Charlotte could say could convince Nan that it was not because she had become too high and mighty for them.

She played her new part as well as she could, as a lady of quality. But she remained at heart the simple child who had given all for love's sake, and to whom all love was now denied.

Vivian staggered back to his wife and stood leering at her a moment, swaying from toe to heel.

"Damned hypocrite. You weren't always an icicle, were you?" he said with a laugh that chilled her.

She wondered in despair if he would ever allow her to forget that tragic passion which had brought her to this pass. She felt now that the very idea of kisses or caresses from him was abhorrent. He had killed romance, desire, and all natural warmth with his fiendish malice.

Glancing at the travelling clock by her bedside she said:

"In half an hour from now the servants will be waking. Will you not go to your bed and sleep, Vivian?"

"So you want to get rid of me, do you?"

She backed away from him.

"I implore you, go to your room!"

"Damn you!" he shouted, "my wife shall be my wife if I so desire it."

"But I do *not!*" she said under her breath.

"Your wishes are not to be considered. You live in my house and I am your lord and master."

"Vivian, your mother will hear," Charlotte began.

"Your mother, *your* mother," he mimicked, "forever throwing my mother at me. While she forever reminds me that I have a dear little wife. I am sick of the pair of you."

He lurched at her and caught her by the arm, wrenching it in the strength of his drunkenness. His mind was inflamed. He wanted only to prove his mastery over this young lovely girl who looked at him with scorn and loathing. How dared she look at him like that?

"We will see who is master! We will thaw the ice!" he said thickly and wrenched her arm again, this time forcing that first cry heard by the Dowager.

Now there followed a shameful struggle which lingered in Charlotte's memory for many a long dark day. Vivian, with ruthless fingers, tore at her dressing gown. As they struggled, he leaned his full weight against her. The side of her face caught the bed-post as she fell, wrenching another scream from her lips. He kissed her brutally. She sobbed and cried:

"For God's sake, Vivian, oh, for God's sake—!"

"I am master of my home and my wife and shall prove it to you!" he said and burst into wild laughter as he flung her across the bed. The laces at her throat were in tatters.

She lay panting. One cheek had been lacerated by a sharp edge of carving on the bed-post. She tried to regain her feet but he bore her down. Her fingers clawed at the satin quilt and pulled the frill from one of the linen pillows. It was as though the fiend himself had entered that quiet room, she thought. It was a devil who grinned down at her with Vivian's features, and clawed at her with Vivian's hands.

"You are really mad!" she sobbed.

"Mad or not, this shall teach you not to argue with your husband," he said, and struck her across the face.

She cried out again in hot protest:

"For God's sake, can you not remember that I am with child—?"

"*Vivian!*" Now it was another voice that protested. The anguished voice of Eleanor Chase from the doorway, ending in a gurgling moan.

The young man sprang to his feet and stood swaying. He tried to pierce the swirling mists of his inebriation, and saw the spectral shape of his mother wrapped in her white shawl, horror in her accusing eyes. Clinging to the lintel of the door, she stared dreadfully from him to the prone figure of the girl who had turned her face to the pillow and was weeping bitterly.

"So it has come to this," said Lady Chase in a hollow voice, "to *this*. May Almighty God forgive you, my son, for I never shall."

Then the Dowager collapsed in a heap on the floor. She had spoken her last words on earth. Vivian rushed across and knelt beside her. He was sober now. As he turned her over, he saw his mother's blind, staring eyes and he knew that she was dead.

For the first time in his life he knew, too, both fear and remorse. He went cold. His teeth began to chatter. Those had been terrible words to hear from a mother's lips.

"May Almighty God forgive you, for I never shall."

"Mama," Vivian cried hoarsely, "Mama, speak to me again. Mama, I did not know what I was doing. I went to a party. I had too much to drink. I will do everything from now onward to show my contrition, oh, I swear it. Dearest Mama—!" He stopped and in anguish kissed her cold, limp hands.

But no answer came from Eleanor Chase. The light in

her eyes was for ever extinguished. She neither saw nor heard her son as he knelt there, sobbing.

Charlotte became aware of what had happened. Aghast, she knelt beside her husband and added her pleas.

"Mother, dearest mother, it is I—your Charlotte—speak to us," she implored.

By this time the whole house was roused. The night nurse came running in, terrified when she had found her patient's bed empty. Hannah, a shawl over her night clothes, ran in too, and waved Charlotte and Vivian aside. She crouched there on the floor, cradling the Dowager's lifeless form in her arms. Already that ivory face had settled into an expression of tragic serenity, her limbs assumed the frozen immobility that belongs to the dead. The faithful old servant, tears streaming down her cheeks, muttered: "My lady, oh, merciful heavens, my lady!"

"Oh, alas, oh mercy me!" whimpered the night-nurse, her fingers uselessly exploring the dead woman's wrist, "What happened? What made her come along here, my lord? I fear it is the exertion which killed her."

"Yes, what happened, my lord?" echoed Hannah, and looked accusingly from Lord Chase to his young wife, the tears streaming down her wrinkled cheeks.

The young pair looked, not at her, but at each other. On Charlotte's left cheek an ugly bruise was swelling. There were drops of blood trickling from the cut. She did not seem to notice it. Vivian, completely sober now, was spokesman. In his cowardly way he cast aspersions on the unfortunate nurse.

"My mother should not have been left. She must have had a fright and come along here to rouse us. You have failed in your duty, ma'am."

"I left her only for a moment, your lordship," said the nurse, her eyes terrified.

Charlotte said:

"Hannah, send at once for Dr. Castleby."

"It is too late," said Hannah with a deep sob.

"Yes, it is too late, but he must come all the same."

"I will take her back to her bed," said Vivian. And even he, callous though he was, felt shocked as he lifted his dead mother up in his arms. She weighed little more than a child.

Charlotte was left alone. Shuddering in the cold room, she sat down and put her face in her hands. She was so shocked that she was beyond tears. But she whispered:

"Oh dearest Mother, my dearest Lady Chase, would to God that I had died with you in this hour."

But death was not for one so young and strong. Even in that moment—ironic fact—for the first time, Charlotte felt the child quicken and leap within her. Trembling from head to foot, she lay down and covered herself with her quilt, nursing her injured cheek. Her whole body ached. Her mind, even more than her body, was bruised and shamed by what had occurred.

When a few moments later, she felt Vivian touch her on the shoulder and utter her name, she shrank away.

"Go—leave me alone," she whispered.

He spoke quite humbly.

"Charlotte, dearest wife, I am not going to hurt you. I have come to beg your pardon."

She lay still, too unhappy even to feel astonishment at this *volte-face*. Then the tears came, scalding, rushing through her fingers, soaking the pillow case.

His apology came too late, she thought; too late by weeks and months. In a broken voice she said:

"You are the cause of her death. I do not want to see you. Oh, go away and leave me alone."

But he stayed. He sat on the edge of the bed. He was grey in the face and there was a sick look in his eyes. For once in his life, Vivian Chase knew what it was to feel frightened.

"Hush, Charlotte," he said, "a man does not wish to be told that he has killed his own mother."

She turned her head and looked up at him, her eyes flashing through the tears.

"Nevertheless it is true."

"It was accidental," he muttered, "I was mad with drink. I did not realize what I was doing, or that she would hear. I did endeavour to explain, but poor Mama had gone beyond recall."

"Pray do not speak of her," broke in Charlotte. "Or argue with me, Vivian. Tonight at least, while *she* lies dead, let there be peace under this roof, or do you wish your hatred and selfishness to extend into the very tomb?"

He bit his finger-nails.

"I tell you I am sorry," he muttered, "is that not enough?"

"Nothing that you can do will ever be enough. That heart which ceased to beat was the most noble we shall ever know."

"I will make up for it. I will try to be a better husband to you, Charlotte," Vivian said, and, completely unnerved, he suddenly began to whimper like a child.

Charlotte drew a long shuddering sigh. She was so stunned that she could feel no pity, and because he had stooped to ask her pardon, he seemed no more acceptable in her sight. Eleanor Chase had departed, and with her all that Charlotte had ever known of the heart's true affection and happiness.

Vivian, however, was as egotistical in his desire to show a contrite heart as in his cruelties. He could not leave well alone. He pulled Charlotte up from her pillows and held her in his arms.

"Tell me that I did not hurt you or our poor child. Tell me that you will forgive me and let us start again," he implored, weeping in a maudlin fashion.

She stayed, reluctantly in his embrace, her eyes shut, her body unyielding.

"You had best tidy yourself and wait downstairs for Dr. Castleby," she said.

He tried to control himself and taking her hands, kissed them.

"Alas, I hurt your cheek. It is bleeding."

"It is nothing, I assure you."

"Say that you will forgive me and do not accuse me of being my mother's murderer. Her heart was weak, it was the effort of getting out of bed, coming down the corridor that killed her, not anything that she saw or heard in this room."

Charlotte had no spirit left to argue. Vivian added:

"Promise that you will never make that accusation against me again. You shall—you *must*."

Too weary, too sick to hold out against him any longer, she promised.

The colour returned to Vivian's cheeks. He began to feel better.

"And we shall try to be better friends, shall we, my own Charlotte?" he said quite tenderly.

Still she found it difficult to surrender. It was too sudden a metamorphosis. But as Vivian stroked her hair and continued to use endearments and show the first affection she had received from him since the hour when their child had been conceived, she gave way. She was still so young, so pitifully in need of tenderness. She flung her arms around his neck.

"Oh, yes, yes, if you really mean it, I do indeed want to be reconciled with you, Vivian," she wept.

"Then it shall be so," he said, kissed her on the forehead, and then laid her gently back on the pillow. "Rest, dear Charlotte, while I go to meet Dr. Castleby. My mother will see from Heaven that I am reformed. She will forgive me, will she not, Charlotte?"

The girl was silent a moment. She was no fool. She could not help but see that Vivian's present surprising mood of kindliness sprang more from a superstitious horror of the last words his mother had spoken, than from genuine concern for her, his wife. He was afraid of the Unknown. With his mother's corpse lying here in the house, he did not wish to feel that her spirit would haunt and condemn him. Like all braggarts and bullies, he was, at heart, a coward. He appealed for his wife's sympathy, her moral support, and hoped for absolution from his sins. He would not leave Charlotte until she actually declared that she was positive Lady Chase would hear and forgive him.

Then Charlotte heard him sigh with relief.

"I must go and bath and change my clothes," he muttered.

Charlotte looked at him with tired eyes.

"Will you really try to love me and the child—*your* child—for I have, for the first time, felt the life stir within me?" she whispered.

He stood up, rubbing his tousled head, yawning. Gentleness and sympathy did not come easily to Vivian Chase and once more he was beginning to feel tired and cross; the effects of last night's orgy in Mrs. Gresham's house. At the same time he also began to realize that he would have complete control here now that his mother was gone. That old fool, Sir Harry, was on his last legs. Physicians did not expect *him* to last the winter. After that, there would be nothing between Vivian and his fortune but the family solicitor, Mr. Trueby, whom he felt sure he could manage easily. William Trueby was not a strong character.

As he walked to the door, Vivian gave another loud yawn and said:

"Pray remember, my dear, if the doctor questions you, that it is that night-nurse who was at fault for letting Mother get out of bed in delirium."

"But Vivian, that would not be fair—" began Charlotte.

He swung round. The turquoise eyes were cold as stones again; his manner regained its arrogance.

"Little fool, do you wish the whole world to be told that it was *I* who killed my mother?" he snarled at her, "or shall I lay the blame at *your* door?"

Her heart sank. A cold hand seemed to clutch that heart again. It had beaten for a few moments with the real hope that she might, after all, find peace and solace with her husband. But she now realized such could never be the case. The leopard could not change his spots. She spoke no more, but turned her face to the pillow again, blinded by her tears.

Vivian marched out of the room, his nostrils distended, his lips curved in a cruel, self-satisfied smile.

Chapter Fifteen

On a cold wet night in January—it was the year 1875—Charlotte's child was born.

Had the child been a son, perhaps Vivian would have been a little proud and pleased, more ready to show his charming side to his poor wife. But alas for Charlotte, it was a daughter.

It was four months since Eleanor Chase had been laid to rest in the family vault at Harling, Vivian soon broke his pledge to renew the old love and tenderness for Charlotte. He seemed to have little respect for her condition and no interest in her as a woman. He was still vain enough, however, to wish to make a good impression on their immediate circle of friends. In their presence he was gay, chivalrous and affectionate toward Charlotte, who had speedily become a favourite.

Less than a month after the Dowager's death, Vivian brutally ejected the Forbes from the Lodge. Nan had been seen too often in the new Lady Chase's company for the liking of his arrogant lordship. He refused to be moved by Charlotte's tears or entreaties.

"I wish it to be forgotten that you ever resided in the Lodge in the care of those simpletons," he said. "They shall go. My bailiff has found me a new lodgekeeper."

It was a bitter day for Charlotte when the Forbes departed. Heavy with child, sad of countenance, she defied Vivian and went down to the cottage to bid farewell to the poor couple. Nan was in tears. Joseph was grey-faced and bitter. He had done his job honestly and efficiently and he, like his father, had been in the service of the Chase family for over forty years. Nan clung to Charlotte.

"Alas, we have no choice but to go away; his lordship

refused to give us our money unless we agreed to go far afield."

They had been forced to seek new work in Suffolk, where Joseph's only brother lived and worked.

"I ask your pardon for this indignity—but it is not my fault," Charlotte wept in Nan's arms.

"We understand. Our chief sorrow is that we shall not see your babe nor be there to comfort you in times of stress," Nan replied.

Long afterwards, Charlotte had thought:

"There will *be* no comfort for me in the future—now my mother-in-law and my foster-mother have been taken from me."

She stood alone; lonelier than the meanest servant in the great house wherein she now lived so exalted a life.

Then came the day of her confinement.

She returned to consciousness from a mist of physical agony that she had for a short space found unendurable. It had been a hard, long labour. The first pains, which had sent one of the footmen scurrying to Harling for the physician, had started at three o'clock in the morning. At first, Charlotte had wrestled courageously with the pangs, relieved to know that at last the long waiting was over. It had been a dreadful nine months for her.

The monthly nurse, Miss Dickson, was a plump cheerful Lancashire woman in her forties, from St. Thomas's Hospital. Fortunately, Charlotte had taken a fancy to her. She was a kindly woman and good at her job. It was kindliness that young Lady Chase most needed in that hour of her trial. She had received none from Vivian who, once awakened by his valet to be told that her ladyship was in labour, turned on his side and sent the message that he was to be called only when the child was born, and that he was not otherwise to be disturbed, unless anything went amiss.

When these words were conveyed to Lady Chase by her personal maid, Charlotte had given a cynical little smile, not unnoticed by Nurse Dickson. The latter had drawn her own conclusions about this wealthy titled pair. Lady Chase was charming, a mere child, not yet eighteen. His lordship was handsome and agreeable when he chose, but a devil at heart; Nurse Dickson had taken note of the young man's villainous temper and his lack of concern for his beautiful young wife. She had, too, heard it rumoured among the gossips in the servants' hall that Lord Chase had married "beneath him" and that his bride had been only the foster-child of lodgekeepers who had since departed. But Nurse Dickson cared nothing for gossip. She knew goodness when she saw it, and it was her firm conviction that Lady Chase was, or had been, the victim of tragic circumstances. As for the infant—well, it was obvious to the experienced midwife that it was a fine, fully-grown child. It weighed six and a half pounds. But Dr. Castleby had tipped her the wink that she was to answer all inquiries with the information that the infant was a *seven months'* child.

Charlotte leaned heavily on Nurse Dickson during the terrible protracted confinement which lasted a full day and another night. The infant was not born until near midnight on the 16th of January.

By that time Charlotte was in a delirium of pain and totally exhausted. She was narrow in the pelvis and the old doctor was unskilled at the job. He gave the poor young mother no sedative, no help, until it seemed that she could bear it no longer. It was a wonder that he contrived to deliver the babe alive, and the mother had a severe haemorrhage which nearly cost her her life.

Vivian was sent for once or twice and then, resorting to the bottle, retired blind drunk. He excused himself on the grounds that he could not stand the anxiety and did not visit his wife or give her a word of encouragement because he hated the sight of suffering.

Miss Dickson sniffed as she repeated the message. The nurse had come by chance upon the master of the house late last night in the library where she found him, semi-intoxicated, in the embraces of a girl, whom the scandalized nurse recognized as the lady's maid.

It was the last straw for Vivian when he heard that the ill-begotten child was a girl. But he reached his wife's side soon after the infant arrived, looked down at her with a smile put on for Nurse Dickson's benefit, and raised her hand to his lips.

"I am heartily glad it is all over for your sake, my dearest Charlotte. It has been a nightmare," he drawled. "You look very poorly, my love."

"Poorly" would hardly describe Charlotte's state. She

was milk-white, devitalized, still harrowed by the memory of her appalling labour. Her great golden eyes, dark with pain, looked at the handsome flushed face of the young husband who should, in this hour, have been her great consoler.

"Forgive me, I apologize that the poor baby is not the heir you hoped for, Vivian," she whispered.

He dropped her languid hand and whispered back:

"What can be expected of our unhappy marriage, madam? I admit to my bitter disappointment."

She bit her lip. The tears rolled down her cheeks. What of *her* feelings. She was disappointed not only for him, but worn out. She had never needed tenderness more, nor so greatly missed the noble lady who had died. *She*, at least, would have taken her granddaughter in her arms and blessed it, and Nan, dear Nan, would have rejoiced.

The late-night hour was bitterly cold outside. In the big, handsome bedroom a huge fire blazed and it was warm. The curtains were cosily drawn. The infant slept in a wicker bassinet which was trimmed with fine lace and satin ribbons, blue for a boy. Everything was blue. There lay the poor little girl, a pink and crumpled object, with her father's narrow shaped forehead and a thatch of darkish hair. Not much like him, but like his mother, Charlotte had noted when first she took the infant to her breast.

The tiny creature was hers, her own, and she would love it, she told herself, if nobody else did.

Vivian threw only a cursory glance at his child. He was annoyed to see that in colouring of complexion and hair she resembled his mother and not himself. Miss Dickson said, also, that she would have dark eyes.

"Your mother's eyes," Charlotte told him and expressed the hope that he would allow her to call the infant *Eleanora.*

"Call it what you like. I am not interested," was Vivian's cold reply as he left the room.

Charlotte began to cry wretchedly. Miss Dickson came to her side and exhorted her to keep calm for the baby's sake.

Charlotte nodded. Lifting a weary hand she pushed the heavy waves of hair back from her damp aching forehead. She could foresee nothing ahead save unhappiness with

Vivian. This must be accepted as stoically as possible as her punishment for the weakness of her first illicit surrender to him. But at times like this the thought of the future appalled her.

One of her few pleasures lay in her friendship with Mrs. Fleur Marsh. In October, and again in December, Vivian had consented to drive with Charlotte over the border into Essex to pay a visit to Pillars, the loveliest house Charlotte had ever seen; full of charm and happiness. Sitting in front of a big log fire in Peveril's studio, Charlotte felt peace and a true appreciation of all things beautiful.

Nobody was more astonished than Charlotte that Vivian had allowed her the pleasure of this friendship. The Marshes were too simple and artistic, too quiet, to suit Vivian's taste. Fleur's beauty was fading. The two men had nothing in common. But it was Vivian's immense vanity which had actually won the day for Charlotte. He wanted to have his portrait painted. Since the Millais, executed when he was a small boy, no portrait had been done of the master of Clunes. Peveril Marsh was now hailed by the critics among the finest painters in the land, so Vivian condescended to give him the commission.

When Peveril announced that he must do the painting in his own studio, Charlotte guessed that dear Mrs. Marsh had had a hand in this, too, and she was thankful. It meant that she could accompany her husband and spend quite a number of happy and peaceful days with her delightful friends.

The portrait went well. Vivian was painted in Court dress. It was a full-length canvas. This, too, Charlotte learned, had been cunningly contrived by Fleur in order to protract the sittings. It promised to be one of Peveril's finest works. Vivian was certainly an absorbing subject for a painter. As the likeness unfolded—the splendour of his waving golden hair, the proud nostrils, the strange turquoise blue of the cold eyes, in contrast to the sensuality of the full lips impressed themselves upon all who looked at it.

One morning, while the two women had been sitting together, talking, Fleur Marsh for the first time mentioned her past. For, she told Charlotte, Vivian's portrait brought out certain qualities all too reminiscent of Fleur's first husband, the Baron of Cadlington.

By now Fleur knew the exact position between the Chases. Poor Charlotte, agonizingly lonely and longing for someone in whom she could confide had poured out the whole sad story. Whereupon Fleur had at once taken the girl in her arms and when Charlotte begged her not to feel outraged, she had said:

"My poor child, you have little reason to feel so deeply ashamed. You were more sinned against than sinning. In your innocence you were grossly betrayed. Your love has turned to loathing, and little wonder, for Lord Chase behaved in a most heartless manner. I can only say that I revere the late Lady Chase for taking the attitude she did, towards you. It was most unusual and indicative of a fine, just nature."

"Then you will still be my friend?" Charlotte had asked, with streaming eyes.

"Ever at your side should you need me, dearest Charlotte," was Mrs. Marsh's reply.

Not then, but later on, discussing the portrait, Fleur spoke of her own life with her first husband.

"Lord St. Cheviot's true character was exposed by Peveril's brush. It showed all his worst instincts. I never, *never* mention the Baron now, nor speak of my dreadful experiences at his hands. But since you have confided in me, I will return the compliment."

So Charlotte learned about the ill-fated young girl who had once lived happily in this very house with her beautiful mother, Hélène, and Sir Harry Roddney, the father who had later fought a duel on Fleur's behalf and wiped off the earth one of the most notorious and wicked men in England—Denzil St. Cheviot.

Charlotte learned how the joy had been crushed from Fleur's life, when she was little older than Charlotte. How—still worse—she had never known the joys of her motherhood, only the horrors of the birth, and her punishment, after the infant died, at the hands of the disappointed Baron.

"At least Vivian is human at times, but St. Cheviot never was," Fleur declared, shuddering. "We must hope that your babe will live to be a great comfort to you, dear

Charlotte. My happiness with Peveril has been marred only by the fact that I could never bear him a son. I love children."

Charlotte tried to take cheer from that conversation, but it seemed to her shocking that so sweet a lady as Mrs. Marsh should have suffered so cruelly. She had to admit that Vivian Chase was not always brutal. He could, when he chose, be the delightful boy she had first loved with blind passion. The trouble was that his good moments were few and far between. But as she had advanced in her pregnancy Charlotte began to feel a subtle and mysterious bond between her and her unborn babe.

She felt sure that she would, as Mrs. Marsh prophesied, find her child a real comfort.

Mrs. Marsh encouraged her to think this and it helped Charlotte through many of her difficult moments with Vivian.

Now, as she lay a-bed with her new-born infant, peace gradually stole through the unhappy wife and drew a kindly veil over the memory of her tortures, both mental and physical.

Let Vivian despise his daughter. Let her, Charlotte, for ever have to forswear passionate love. She now had this tiny creature, sweet-smelling and swathed in flannel, lying in the curve of her arm. Suddenly a smile of pure joy overspread Charlotte's face.

"Eleanora," she whispered that sacred name to the slumbering babe, "you are mine and nothing shall ever take you from me."

In the stormy years that followed she was to remember those very words and the critical hour in which she whispered them.

Miss Dickson, tidying up the room, and arranging some flowers which had been sent up by the housekeeper, saw the expression on Charlotte's face and was spellbound by it. Down in the servants' hall that evening she remarked to the staff that young Lady Chase looked extremely beautiful despite the ordeal through which she had passed.

Vivian, always punctilious about such official matters, had ordered that wine should be distributed amongst the staff with which a toast should be drunk to his newly-born daughter.

The toast was drunk with relish, and relief that her ladyship was out of danger. Only one indoor servant of the old staff remained; Perkins, the head coachman, who had served Vivian's father, and blinded his eyes to the young man's failings.

Vivian could rely on Perkins' loyalty. He was not likely to open his mouth on the subject of Charlotte's lowly birth. He was too afraid of incurring Vivian's wrath. With the same callous unconcern for his inferiors that Vivian had shown the Forbes, he had dismissed the rest of the staff after the funeral of the Dowager. It was his wish that not one single servant should know about Charlotte.

Old Hannah, whom he had never forgiven for the part she had played in bringing his mother's notice to his seduction of Charlotte, left the house of her own accord as soon as her lady was laid to rest. She refused to accept Charlotte as her new mistress. Her boxes were packed and the old servant had gone long before Vivian could give her notice, for which he was devoutly thankful. He had always disliked her waspish tongue.

There was a new housekeeper now—a religious and goodly Scotswoman named Mrs. MacDougal, fresh from the service of a widowed Marchioness who had recently died in the district. Mrs. MacDougal brought several of the Marchioness' former staff with her.

Hester who had accompanied her upon her unhappy honeymoon, had been replaced by a girl called Suzanne. She had been brought over from Paris by his lordship. Suzanne was the perfect lady's maid, but Charlotte did not like her—from the start. She suspected that the pretty blonde French maid had been specially selected by Vivian. He forbade her to dismiss Suzanne on any pretext whatsoever.

"You may know your history dates and your Shakespeare, my dear Charlotte," he sneered, "but you are still too much the country bumpkin to suit me. You could assimilate some ideas of *chic* from a Parisienne who was once in the service of a great French lady."

In bitterness Charlotte had to accept this fresh humiliation. That Vivian should expect her to learn from a servant was an insult. However, Suzanne was punctiliously polite and attentive. But Charlotte always fancied there was derision, sometimes even pity, in the sparkling almond eyes of the *Mademoiselle*, when they regarded her.

The rest of the staff consisted of Mrs. Snook, an excellent cook; Williams, who had replaced the family butler, (the old one had followed Hannah), and Lucy, the head parlourmaid. There were a number of underlings, housemaids, tweenies, and others, whom Charlotte saw rarely, if ever. But there was one more whom she disliked as much as Suzanne and that was the valet who had replaced Browning. This young man was called Volpo. He was of Portuguese extraction but spoke perfect English. He was excellent at his job, had suave manners, and prided himself on his extreme tact. He had a slightly humped back, for which deformity Charlotte did not blame him—she was far too kind-hearted—but somehow she felt it was akin to the twist in his nature. She was positive that he was a sly, deceitful fellow. She disliked his hooded eyelids, and a way he had of creeping around soundlessly and appearing where one least expected him. She half suspected that he spied upon her at Vivian's behest, which was in fact the case. Vivian, in his mean fashion, was always hoping to discover some wrong action of which he could accuse his wife. From this point of view, Volpo was perfect; his loyalty was undoubted and he was ever partial to the bribes flung at him to keep his mouth shut on the subject of his master's nocturnal wanderings. Volpo was a vicious fellow and happy to serve a young gentleman whom he found equally so. No matter at what hour of the morning Vivian returned from his orgies, Volpo was up waiting, ready to undress his intoxicated master and put him to bed; impervious when Vivian snarled at him in a rage, enormously helpful and bound to secrecy when required. But the Portuguese returned her ladyship's dislike. He was a spiteful man and he was aware that the young Lady Chase would have got rid of him if she could. He was the first to voice an unfavourable comment on the birth of the daughter.

"Pity his lordship did not choose a lady who could bear a son," he said, and described, spitefully to the staff, how ill my lord had taken the news when they had told him the sex of the child.

Suzanne agreed. She had no liking for the humped

backed valet, but she was madly infatuated with his lordship.

The others spoke kindly of Lady Chase. They were in full agreement with Miss Dickson and loved my lady. Whenever they saw her she was sweet and gentle and interested in their private lives, which many ladies were not. Only the other day she had given a sovereign to Mrs. MacDougal for a humble tweeny whose family had fallen on bad times. Besides, nobody in the household was unaware of the fashion in which his lordship privately behaved towards his wife. Among themselves they wondered why, and their sympathies were entirely with my lady.

"God bless her and the wee girl," said Mrs. MacDougal with her rich Scots burr.

That same evening, the little Eleanora's father spent in London, whence he had betaken himself on the excuse that his godfather was seriously ill and had sent for him. It did, in fact, happen that Sir Harry Cawder conveniently chose that very night to give up the ghost;—so Vivian had a real cause of celebration—Sir Harry's death had freed him of the last shred of tiresome control.

He used the birth of his unwanted daughter as an excuse for carousing all night with one or two young "Bloods" who had been his friends at the University. It was one of the wild kind of nights that Vivian enjoyed, starting with champagne in the house of a musical comedy actress, (mistress of a well-known peer), continuing at a music hall, and ending in a private house for a session of gambling and licentiousness which lasted until dawn.

He woke with a thick head and a vile temper. He would have preferred to have stayed in London, for it was a pouring wet day. Clunes, in such weather, bored him to death. But for appearance sake, he must stay near his wife during her lying-in.

An accident befell Vivian on the way home. One accompanied by a strange psychic experience which had some real effect upon him. It was greatly to Charlotte's benefit and lasted for the next two or three months.

He was returning to the country by brougham. He was nodding in a corner, arms folded, snoring a little, exhausted by the night's excesses, when they passed through Harling. The rain had stopped, but there was a high wind and the horses were sliding all over the road. The coachman could hardly hold them. They had just reached the graveyard belonging to the little Norman church. The coachman had to pull hard on the horses to avoid a farm cart. One of the animals slipped and went down. The brougham skidded, rolled on drunkenly and turned over. Vivian was pitched violently out and passed from his inebriated slumber into unconsciousness.

He half recovered to find himself inside the church into which he had been carried by passers-by and the curate. A funeral service was being solemnized. The coffin of the deceased (an old lady of the parish) stood on trestles before the altar, covered with purple velvet. The young gentleman, who was wrapped in a cloak and bleeding from a gash in the forehead, was soon recognized as Lord Chase. One of the female mourners gave little cries of pity and concern as she saw the handsome boy lying there, white and bleeding from his ugly wound. She rushed forward and, kneeling down, lifted his head on to her lap and began staunching the blood with a voluminous handkerchief.

Another offered smelling salts. One of the wardens hastily ran to send an urgent message to Clunes. The coachman had been killed and his body was lying on the porch.

Vivian Chase, semi-concussed, and badly shocked, received in that moment a strange psychic impression. It was not, in his mind, a strange lady who ministered to him, but his mother. He groaned piteously:

"Mama!"

The lady who supported him looked tearfully up at the curate.

"His lordship is wandering; he calls for his mother," she whispered.

An hysterical young girl, peering down at Vivian from one of the pews, cried in a loud voice:

"Oh, alas! he is dying. *Lord Chase is dying!*"

It was those sinister words which penetrated through the mists whirling around Vivian's brain. Struggling to sit up, he now caught sight of the draped coffin in the flickering candlelight. He believed that he was about to die and that this coffin waited for *him*. He could see his mother's face, pale and accusing. He was, he presumed, about to enter the flames of hell; condemned for his sins to eternal damnation. A spectral voice spoke to him in a stern and hollow voice.

"Heir to Clunes, you shall inherit all, and nothing—for you have lost your soul. Die! You are no longer son of mine. You are a monster of iniquity, a vile seducer, a heartless father!"

Vivian gave a gurgle of pure terror, and dropped back into the arms of the strange lady, senseless.

Chapter Sixteen

Charlotte never rightly understood what happened to Vivian that January day. She only knew that, once she recovered from the shock of hearing that Vivian had been carried senseless into the house, a sudden blessed peace descended upon her and Clunes.

Miss Dickson told her the news, trying not to distress the young nursing mother too greatly.

"His lordship is safely in bed. Volpo appears to have knowledge of nursing. Dr. Castleby has left him in Volpo's care until the specialist arrives. Meanwhile I hear that the injuries are to his head and one leg, which was broken—the femur is fractured. It appears that, as the carriage swayed, the door swung open, being loose in the lock, so his lordship was pitched out. The poor coachman has expired."

Charlotte gave a gasp, her cheeks flushed with emotion. "Oh, alas, the poor man! We must compensate his family. And poor Vivian!" she whispered, "ought I not go to him?"

"Certainly not, your ladyship cannot be moved," said the nurse tartly. She added: "There is nothing to fear. His lordship is not as bad as they first thought. He is in no way critically ill, though naturally he suffers some pain. You might like to know, my lady, that he repeatedly calls upon your name as though it were a talisman."

Charlotte, her heart beating faster, was inclined to utter a cynical reply to this, but said:

"Indeed!"

She could hardly think that Vivian would call upon her name—he, who had left the house on the very day that their child had been born. And she was quite unprepared for a note which was brought to her an hour later by

Suzanne. The pretty French girl looked sullen, and as though she had been weeping. Bobbing a curtsy, she handed the envelope to Charlotte.

"His lordship has written this to you, my lady."

"Written to me?" repeated Charlotte, forgetful of her dignity.

"Yes," sniffed Suzanne and, curtsying again, retired. Her nose was out of joint. His lordship had sent for her and when she had begun to commiserate with him in a familiar fashion he had pointed a shaking finger at her, looking, as she thought, wild-eyed and haggard.

"Leave my sight, girl!" he ejaculated. "Go, kneel down by your bed and say your prayers, as I intend to say mine. My mother's ghost has visited me. I have seen my coffin waiting. I am doomed to the eternal flames unless I repent me of my sins. Look you to yours."

Suzanne had stared, goggling, then fled. Meeting Volpo on the landing, she complained to him. He spoke to her with a sardonic grin.

"Tush," he had said, "no need for tears, my girl. His lordship is raving. He does not know what he is saying. He will recover."

But the letter written to Charlotte was clear enough. The writing was uneven and the paper blotched by ink from the quill which he had used. But the contents made sense.

My beloved wife,

I have so much reason to ask your pardon that I hardly dare begin. The terrible injuries I have sustained from my accident are nothing compared with the wounds I now realize I have dealt your sensitive soul. As I recovered my senses after my accident, my mother appeared to me in Harling Church. She showed me my own coffin waiting. She renounced me as her son. Oh, Charlotte, help me to escape Almighty God's vengeance, and my mother's scorn. Forgive me my sins. Take me back to your loving arms. Redeem me. Henceforth I will be a model husband to you and a loving father to our little Eleanora. Henceforth this shall become a truly Christian household. You shall have no cause to fear or despise me. As soon as I am well enough to rejoin you, my Love, I shall be the

Vivian who once spoke to you with the voice of the poet Meredith, in our enchanted woods.

I cannot rest until I have heard you utter the words of forgiveness. I demanded to be carried to your room, but the old fossil, Castleby, fears for my leg. I am now waiting for Mr. Thistlebirt, the surgeon from London, who is driving down immediately to set the fracture which tortures me. Oh, Charlotte, do not let the flames engulf me. You are my guardian angel. You alone can guide me back to the path of virtue. Then, my mother will see and hear, and add her forgiveness to yours.

This extraordinary epistle was signed with a flourish, *"Your true Husband and Lover, Vivian."*

Hardly able to credit her sight, Charlotte read all this again then fell back on her pillows, her cheeks red, her mouth open.

What, in Heaven's name, had happened to bring about such a change of front, she wondered? Had the fall affected Vivian's mind? Was he deranged?

Her natural gentleness and generosity of heart, however, led her to send at once the reply he had asked for. The nurse brought her paper and ink. She penned the following:

My poor Vivian,

I grieve that you have had this terrible accident and that I cannot come to console you. I would have nursed you myself so gladly, were it not for my own poor state of health. But pray do not harbour fears of my feelings towards you. I am most ready and willing to forgive and forget. The moment I am permitted, I shall come to your bedside and embrace you.

Believe me, my Husband, I want nothing more than to live in love and peace with you and so wipe out the past. Let us never refer to it, for it has all been too sad and gloomy.

This shall be the beginning of a new, sweet life for us, I do earnestly pray.

Our little daughter smiles in her sleep and I am sure that smile is one of tenderness for her suffering Father.

This note, sent to Lord Chase's suite, brought another outburst from him of a similar nature. This time it was accompanied by a magnificent diamond star pendant hanging on a fine gold chain. Charlotte recognized it instantly. She had seen the Dowager Lady Chase wearing it, and the latter had told her that it was a wedding gift from Vivian's father. Since her death it had been locked among the family jewels in Vivian's sanctum. He allowed her to wear one or two of these only on special occasions when visitors came, and he wished his wife to show herself off, in all her glory. Vivian wrote:

> This star is now for you. Accept it as a token of my sincerity. I, better than any, know the purity of your intent and your innocence, which, alas, I have not until now respected. Wear the star—my mother's favourite—on your matchless bosom, beloved, and let me kiss it there when I see you again.

The astonished and bewildered Charlotte read this—the first real love-letter she had ever received—and dangled the pendant while Miss Dickson *"Oohed"* and *"Aahed"* as the firelight caught the fine stones. They glittered like a prism. Charlotte could only think, indeed, that Vivian was not in his right mind. For not so long ago he had told her spitefully that he would never allow her to wear Eleanor Chase's famous diamond star.

"A low-born creature like yourself is not worthy of it," he had said in one of his more insulting moods.

Now he addressed her as *"beloved"* and wrote in these penitent, almost maudlin, terms of affection. The young girl was stupefied.

Before she slept that night, she sent for Dr. Castleby and questioned him. Miss Dickson begged him to calm the young mother who was running a temperature through sheer overexcitement. The old doctor prescribed a sedative and gave Charlotte various explanations of Vivian's hysteria. It was the wound on the head, he said, coupled with a strange fantasy which Lord Chase had described to the doctor, in a high fever, after Mr. Thistlebirt had set the fractured leg. Groaning with pain, and in tears, the young man had alternated between cowardly moaning to Dr.

Castleby over his physical torments, and an apparently sincere repentance for his boyish follies.

"It seems that he saw an apparition while lying in the church," the doctor told Charlotte. He repeated Vivian's story which she already knew. She sighed and shook her head.

"How long do you think this condition will last?" she asked.

The physician spread out his hands. Who was to know, he said, what Lord Chase would be like as time went on? At the moment he could not be called *mad*, but he was somewhat mentally disturbed by the shock of the accident and this melancholy ghost that he imagined he had seen. Also, the sight of the coffin seemed to have frightened him considerably. Nothing Dr. Castleby said could make Lord Chase believe that it was not waiting for him. He felt he was doomed, unless he changed his way of life.

"But do not disturb yourself unduly, Lady Chase," ended the kindly doctor. "Do not be disturbed," he repeated, "for no matter what has caused his lordship to crave for a more Christian way of life, it is all to the good, if I may humbly say so."

With this Charlotte heartily agreed.

During the month that followed, Lord Chase's passionate wish to make up to his young wife for past wrongs and so save his own soul, persisted.

Charlotte now became the light of his eyes. He wrote notes continually. Each morning he sent special flowers to her from the greenhouses, with tender messages attached. Finally, he convinced her that whatever the cause, some supernatural visitation from his dead mother had brought about the metamorphosis. She even deceived herself into believing that the new Vivian had come to stay.

She wrote a letter to her friend, Mrs. Marsh, first thanking her for the present she had sent to her babe, then commenting upon her present bliss:

> Nobody, dearest Fleur, can be happier than I am today. I, who, when you saw me last, was so sad and disillusioned. Vivian's accident has reformed him. Peace reigns in my house.

(Here she told Fleur all about the gifts, the diamonds, the flowers, the letters exchanged.)

Today, St. Valentine's Day, is fine and sunny. The snows are melting. My baby is four weeks old and a most beautiful child. Her hair is beginning to curl. Her eyes are already turning darker and I trust that the little Eleanora will resemble her noble grandmother, whose name she bears. I asked Vivian if he would approve of your becoming her godmother, and to my delight he at once agreed. Anything for my happiness, he said.

Oh, Fleur, you cannot believe how he has changed. He has ordered the roasting of a whole ox which is to be cut up and delivered to all who work upon the estate at Clunes, on the day our daughter is christened, and a gold piece to be given the entire staff, indoors and out. (This will be on the 1st of March.) The first day I was permitted to walk on nurse's arm to Vivian's bedside, we had a touching reconciliation. He looks ill and thin and is much wasted by his suffering. The fracture has caused him frequent pain and has sorely tried his patience. Yet never has he appeared more patient, nor looked more handsome, nor been more kind. He held out both arms and said: "Come to my heart, my Charlotte, for you will feel it beating with a new desire to cherish you." He kissed me and took our infant in his arms and added: "Forgive your father for his past sins. He shall become the splendid parent to you that your noble grandfather was to him."

Mrs. Marsh wrote back from Pillars in tender terms, expressing her pleasure that her dearest Charlotte had found this happiness. She would drive with Peveril to see her goddaughter as soon as the snows melted and made the roads passable.

But to Peveril, Fleur spoke less optimistically after reading Charlotte's long letter.

"I do not trust this change. It is too sudden and violent," she said. "I can never forget how closely Lord Chase's character resembles St. Cheviot's. The leopard cannot change his spots. I fear that the greater part of this repentant state is due merely to Vivian's cowardly fear of Hell. Perhaps he *did* receive a visitation from his mother in his delirium, and it has unnerved him. But I mistrust his ability to keep up such a virtuous pose."

The artist nodded thoughtfully.

"Ay, 'when the Devil is sick, the Devil a saint would be!' " he quoted.

"Oh, Peveril, I pray that fresh misery does not face our dear little Charlotte in the future."

Peveril put an arm around his wife and looked with a tender smile into the soft violet eyes which, for him, had never lost their appeal. She was still the idol of his boyhood, the Madonna he had worshipped at Cadlington long, long ago.

"You are too tender-hearted, my love," he said. "Do not let your fears for Charlotte overcloud your spirit, for they may be groundless."

Meanwhile, at Clunes, Charlotte's happiness continued. Vivian even went so far as to say she might dismiss Suzanne from her service and, to her joy, the French girl was sent back to Paris and replaced by an older woman. The new maid was in her thirties, by name Gertrude. She was altogether different from Suzanne, and far more trustworthy, if not smart and calculated to amuse the master of the House. But Vivian meekly observed that if Gertrude suited Charlotte, that was all that he wanted. Charlotte would like to have got rid of the Portuguese valet too, but hesitated to ask this because Vivian had grown to rely on Volpo. She had to admit that he was a splendid nurse and seemed utterly devoted to his master. On the surface, he was deferential to her too. Volpo was a clever fellow. He did not for a moment suppose that Lord Chase's *volte-face* would endure. It was a period which the servant abhorred, and the wily Portuguese could not bear the pious, honest woman who had replaced Suzanne. But he was content to bide his time. He felt that the devil would not remain saint much longer. Meanwhile he did everything that he could to impress on milady, as well as milord, that his sole desire was to be a loyal servant.

Now Charlotte was up and about again, she quickly regained health and strength. Miss Dickson, with whom she was sad to part, was replaced by a woman they called "Nanna" and a nursery maid, both of whom had been engaged to take over the full care of little Eleanora. The beautiful nurseries in the sunny west wing that had once belonged to Vivian, had been re-papered and painted a soft blue, furnished with pretty white-painted furniture and filled with toys. Eleanora started her new life with these two attendants to see to her daily and nightly needs. Her mother coninued to feed her and although Charlotte would like to have seen more of the baby daughter, she was quite glad, in those early days, of the experienced help. The Nanna turned out to be a strict disciplinarian and often made my lady fear to enter the nurseries. But, as Vivian made more and more demands upon Charlotte's time, she *had* to be free for him. She could see little Eleanora only when feeding her, or for a short time while the infant was bathed.

The day of the christening came, Vivian was carried to a couch in the drawing-room for this. He impressed all the guests by his charm and geniality. Nobody seemed to doubt that Lord Chase had matured, and developed into a model husband and father. As for Charlotte, she looked radiant. A fine March day allowed her to wear a new and splendid dress of palest azure blue silk with frothy white lace collar and cuffs, and a handsome bustle. She wore a blue velvet bow in her chestnut hair. Her cheeks had become rounded and pink. Her eyes were brilliant. She sat by the couch, her hand clasped in her husband's, the picture of proud young motherhood, whilst the nurse, in blue linen, with starched cap and apron, walked around, exhibiting the infant, dressed in a magnificent silk and lace christening robe, to a circle of admiring ladies.

Little Eleanora cooed and gurgled her way through the christening at Harling church, held in the arms of her godmother, Mrs. Marsh. Fleur's painter husband had done a lightning sketch of the infant and presented it to the fond parents.

Fleur declared that she had never seen such a lovely child as Eleanora, who had also been given her own name of Fleur.

"Eleanora, the Flower, we will call her," Peveril declared.

But the sensitive Charlotte detected a hint of sadness in Fleur's violet eyes as she looked at the infant during the baptism. She cradled her closely. Her delicate lips quivered, and Charlotte thought, rightly:

"She thinks of the tragedy of her own infant's birth and death. I am lucky."

And for the first time since her association with Vivian, Charlotte knew what it was to feel fortunate. Vivian gave no sign of returning to his former, heartless conduct. Good had certainly come out of evil.

There had been difficulty about the choice of a godfather for little Eleanora. Vivian had admitted that few of his personal friends would rightly fill the position of religious guardian to his daughter. The choice fell finally upon Lord Marchmond in whose yacht Vivian had been cruising just before his marriage.

Marchmond, only son and heir of the Marquess of Englesby, a Gloucestershire nobleman, was a gay youth two years older than Vivian, but of more temperate habits. When he returned to England to find young Chase married to a girl about whom he had never even spoken, after swearing that he would remain a bachelor for as long as he could, Cecil Marchmond had been much surprised. But any curiosity he had shown about Charlotte's origin had received a terse reply, so he had inquired no further. At his first meeting with Charlotte, he thought her remarkably good-looking. Her child-like charm appealed to him. He was willing and happy to accept the honour of being a god-parent for the first time in his life. He came to stay at Clunes and brought for Eleanora an immense silver gilt christening mug. This was displayed with Eleanora's other gifts.

Charlotte liked Lord Marchmond. He was not handsome, but had a roguish twinkle and a shock of red hair which made him look homely, she thought, despite his illustrious birth. Mischievous he might be, and with an eye to a pretty girl, but she did not think he would have a bad influence upon Vivian. His great wealth had been the attraction for Vivian when he first met him at Oxford. Cecil came to the couch and chatted with his friend.

"When shall we see you on your feet again, Viv?" he asked.

"Old Castleby tells me that the specialist will not hear of my walking, even with crutches, until the end of this month," answered Vivian.

"You must be mightily sick of it."

Vivian stretched out a hand to Charlotte and gave her a languishing look.

"I have been sustained throughout by the devotion of my wife," he said, somewhat unctuously.

Lord Marchmond raised his brows. He wondered how long Vivian's pious attitude would last. But as he glanced at the young girl in her blue silk dress, he found her enchanting. He was not surprised that Vivian should be in love with his wife. Then Vivian added:

"On the first day that I am able to use my crutches, I declare that I shall give a grand ball. We have not held a ball at Clunes for many years."

"But my dearest, you could not dance—" began Charlotte.

"That is of no account," he broke in, "I can watch. And you shall open the ball with Cecil."

Feeling quite light-hearted, full of effervescing spirits, Charlotte responded:

"Oh, that will be *wonderful*, will it not, Cecil?"

"Yes, indeed," he nodded.

"Then it is as good as done," said Vivian and leaned back on his satin cushions languidly.

He did not feel quite so benevolent as he appeared.

For the greater part of the day he was exalted by his own excessive show of virtue. When he embraced Charlotte, it was with the old ardour with which he had wooed her nearly a year ago. But under this desire to be a model of righteousness, lay a feeling of irritation. This was becoming irksome—like his injured leg. The memory of his experience in the church had begun to fade. His love-life was not as exciting as his true nature required. He could not long be content with one woman. He found that he had had more than enough of his young wife since their reconciliation. When he saw the maid, Gertrude, these days, he thought how plain she was. He missed Suzanne and was sorry now that he had permitted her to be dismissed.

For the moment, however, he was content to lie low—indeed his injury forced him to do so.

But he must have some fresh amusement, so he set to work that next week or two to plan the grand ball in celebration of his recovery to health. And why not a costume ball, he suddenly suggested to Charlotte? The dresses of the ladies would give him something to look at.

"I will attend as a beggar on crutches, and look villainous, with a black patch over one of my eyes," he said.

Charlotte protested that she did not want her handsome husband to turn himself into a scurvy beggar, but he decided that it would amuse him to do so. She however, he said, must order a fancy dress to suit her present glowing charms. Why not a Pompadour, which would suit her well; the white curls, with those big honey-coloured eyes of hers, and black patches—would be delightful. Cecil also must wear a wig and costume of the eighteenth century. They two should lead the others in an opening minuet.

Charlotte fell in with all Vivian's suggestions and shared his somewhat childish mood, with pleasure. Money was to be no object. There would be a splendid buffet of wine and rich food, and an orchestra sent down from London. They would issue the invitations immediately.

The house would be filled with glorious flowers, and lights would be hung in Japanese lanterns, in the trees if it was a warm night, so that the dancers could stroll out on to the lawns.

"Oh, I am really looking forward to this!" exclaimed Charlotte, "and there can be yet another cause for celebration. Peveril Marsh has finished your portrait, Vivian. It shall be hung in the hall, do you not think, to replace that rather gloomy one of your great-uncle? Then everyone will see and admire it."

"Excellent," said Vivian, with a yawn.

But there were moments during those next few weeks when Vivian began to doubt if he had sufficient will to maintain his pose of saint; and when Charlotte, to her consternation, recognized the fact. The old symptoms were there, creeping back, now and again. Little fits of irritability, moods of depression and sulks caused not only, Charlotte feared, because the leg did not seem to be going on as well as Castleby liked.

It was nearly the end of the ninth week after his accident before Vivian was allowed to use his brand-new crutches. Then, once he began to hop around on the good leg, supported by Volpo and Charlotte, he snarled at them both. Once again he was rude to his wife in front of his valet.

Vivian made various attempts to overcome his rising impatience. Alone with Charlotte again, he kissed her hand and apologized for his boorishness, while she wiped the sweat from his forehead.

"I understand, my dearest, do not worry," she said.

But she could not forget the dreaded expression in the cold turquoise eyes. This was no longer the Vivian who had become her adoring spouse. She could only pray that once he was able to manage his crutches alone, he would settle down again.

He did so—but only up to a point. A fresh cause for ill-temper manifested itself when he found that the leg injury would leave him with a permanent limp. Castleby had been afraid to tell him until now. The young man, pale and haggard, ranted and raved over this misfortune.

"A limp—Vivian Chase with a limp—it is abominable!" he shouted.

He was with Charlotte in the library and Castleby had beat a hasty retreat. Vivian had just managed to walk, in a rather crab-like fashion, across the room, to a chair by the windows. At one point he nearly slipped on the polished floor. Charlotte took the full weight and supported him, but it strained her back and made her cry out. Whereupon he snapped at her:

"Anyone would think *you* had the injury, not I. Have the goodness to fetch me a glass of sherry, feeble creature that you are!"

Charlotte's heart jolted. Her cheeks burned. With down-cast lids she turned to ring for a servant. But Vivian shouted at her: "Fetch the wine yourself, lazy girl. Are you so much the fine Lady Chase these days that you cannot wait on your husband?"

Her spirits sank to zero. She paled. *Oh, dear heaven*, she thought, *do not let this be true, do not let the old Vivian come to life! I could not endure it.*

She had been so happy with the man he had appeared to be since his accident. She had grown to love such a generous, attentive husband. Willingly, she had sat by him, read to him, played her piano for him, done everything to prove herself a loving wife. Was there, in fact, some mental trouble causing his sudden and violent change of mood? She was in tears when she returned to his side with the wine. But *he* sat brooding over the thought of the limp which must henceforth spoil his gait. He used to be proud of the graceful agility with which he moved.

As he saw Charlotte's depression and wet eyelashes, he made an effort to control himself. The time was not yet ripe when he wished to recreate the old atmosphere of hatred and bitterness.

"Come, come, I did not mean to be so nasty. Give me a kiss, foolish child," he said.

At once her face brightened. She lifted her lips to his.

"Dearest Vivian, do not grieve too much over this trouble with your foot. Lord Byron won all feminine hearts and was a splendid success, and he limped far worse than you will ever do, did he not?"

Vivian shrugged. He sipped the wine she gave him. They talked again of the ball. Everybody had accepted. Preparations were nearly completed. All the guest chambers at Clunes would be full. The Marshes were going to stay the night because Peveril must be here to receive his share of praise after the unveiling of Vivian's portrait. One or two other married couples who were driving down with their daughters must also stay a night at Clunes. And now a footman had just brought Vivian a letter from Gloucestershire, bringing a request for rooms, from Cecil.

"Tell Mrs. MacDougal that two bachelor rooms must be prepared for Marchmond and a relative whom he is bringing with him," Vivian told his wife.

Charlotte, trying to tell herself not to worry and that Vivian's ugly mood had been of short duration, sat at his feet and stroked one of his hands.

"Who, then, is Cecil bringing, dear Vivian?"

Vivian tossed her the letter. She read it. Cecil wrote that he would esteem if a favour if Vivian would allow him to include Dominic in the list of guests. Dominic Unwin—was his adopted brother. It would be more pleasant, Cecil wrote, if he might make the long journey from Gloucestershire in Dominic's company.

Mr. Unwin was a man in the middle thirties, and a passionate disciple of Disraeli. A year ago Mr. Gladstone had been defeated and Disraeli had taken office as Prime Minister. Dominic had at that election again been returned as Member for a constituency in Gloucester. He was unmarried and Cecil wrote with his usual humour: *This should be of advantage to the young ladies.*

Charlotte looked up from the letter.

"Did you know Cecil had a brother by adoption? You never told me of him."

"I did not think of it. He has mentioned the fact from time to time," said Vivian carelessly. "But Dominic Unwin is considerably older than Cecil and rarely at Englesby. I remember now the Marchioness, herself, telling me when I was aboard the yacht, some story of how they had adopted this boy because no children had been born to them, and how, five years later, Cecil made his appearance."

"He may be an elderly bore," said Charlotte.

"But if he is talented, no doubt *you* will find him entertaining. Is it not one of your complaints, my love, that so few of my friends care for books or art," said Vivian yawning.

"I have not had much time lately for either books or art," she laughed. "But I admit I always welcome a discursive hour with a man of learning."

Vivian gave another prodigious yawn and told her to ring for Volpo. He was tired.

Before she went to carry out his wishes, she suddenly put her arms round Vivian's neck and looked up at the handsome sulky face.

"Do you not love you Charlotte today as much as yesterday?" she murmured, smiling at him with charming coquetry.

In better mood, he gave a little laugh and kissed her silken lashes.

"Of course. Little book-worm, you are still damned handsome. No one would think you the mother of that fat baby."

"I do love you, Vivian. Pray go on loving me," she said with deep emotion.

He was about to reply when a shadow fell between them. The shadow of the hump-backed valet in his dark suit. His thin, foxy face looked small and meaner than usual, half sunk in his collar. He bowed low:

"I came, my Lord, to see if you would like me to help you to bed for a rest before the evening meal."

"Clever fellow, you anticipate my wishes," said Vivian.

"Let me help too," began Charlotte.

"Volpo can manage alone," said Vivian abruptly. "Go and feed your infant, my dear."

Biting her lower lip a little, she watched the valet assist his master out of the library. She fancied that she saw a pleased expression playing round the lips of the Portuguese. And indeed, the latter was pleased, if not surprised, to find that my lord was once again in need of *him* rather than my lady. He, too, had noticed unmistakable signs in Vivian of the master who had first engaged him.

Despite the warmth of the sunny day and a big fire burning in the grate, Charlotte felt cold once she was alone.

The chill of doubt was creeping into her mind. She wished somehow that Vivian had not dismissed her so peremptorily. She loathed Volpo; she could not help it. She loathed and mistrusted him.

Slowly she picked up Cecil Marchmond's letter and began to read it again.

The name *Dominic* fell pleasantly on her ears. A man of law and of learning—well, she would look forward to some conversation with him.

"Dominic," she repeated the name aloud again. "It has a grave sound. I have never heard it before, but I like it."

Chapter Seventeen

It seemed that, as far as the weather was concerned, fortune smiled on Clunes, for the April evening of the ball followed the warmest day of the season. It developed into a sparkling evening of full moon and glittering stars. In between the dances most of the guests walked in the garden. It was a lovely scene upon which Dominic Unwin looked as he stood on the terrace alone, smoking a cigar after supper.

Behind him, Clunes glittered like the chateau that it resembled—a miniature castle from a French fairy tale. A flag waved from one of the turrets. Japanese lanterns gleamed rosily from the branches of the budding trees. There were lights along the elm avenue and throughout the spacious grounds. The long windows of the ballroom opened to the terrace. Behind Dominic, the glitter and pomp of the flower-filled ballroom, the sigh of violins playing a waltz. In front, a crowd of guests in their fancy costume, wandering in and out of the trees, a motley gathering. Kings and Queens of former centuries, Egyptians, Greeks, dancing girls, nymphs. Each fresh costume made a vivid splash of colour against the dark green of yew hedges and the velvet of the lawns. It was eleven o'clock. It looked as though the ball might go on until the early hours of the morning. Nothing like it had ever been seen before at Clunes.

Dominic Unwin, however, cared little for dancing, drank only sparingly, and enjoyed solitude. He liked to stand back here alone in the shadows, and smoke the excellent cigar which Vivian offered him. All his adult life he had enjoyed contemplation of others. He was very partial to intelligent conversation, but he had little use for the frivolous exchange of words with empty-headed people.

Neither did he care about paying compliments to pretty young women. In fact, as he had told his foster-brother on their journey here from Cirencester, he was going to feel the odd man out at this party. He was too old for it, he said. At which Cecil had laughed.

"My dear fellow, there will be many grey heads at Clunes tonight, and you have not a single grey hair yet, nor will have for several years."

Nevertheless Dominic felt his age as he watched the youthful couples dancing and circling before him, laughing or whispering amorously as they strolled with clasped hands.

Dominic looked up at the moon a trifle cynically. It was a night for love. A night to stir a man's senses. Yet he was a trifle suspicious of the obvious, and all this was so artificial. It could only breed artificial emotion, he thought. He had, of course, been made very welcome at Clunes, but he had not taken to his host. When Dominic had first arrived, Vivian had been charming. He had looked his best, too—dressed impeccably—every inch a gentleman of distinction, yet Dominic had been repelled by that cold blue eye; by the arrogance which lay under the surface charm. He had been still more repelled once they had all gathered in the hall to laugh and criticize each other's costumes. Vivian then wore his sinister disguise of beggar on crutches; a patch over one eye, a stooping back. Somehow, he produced an atmosphere of malevolence which Dominic found strangely abhorrent.

He had not really wanted to pay this visit. He was working hard in the House these days. He needed rest and would much have preferred to stay at Englesby, which was one of the most gracious and peaceful houses in Gloucestershire—nay, in England. But Cecil had begged so hard that at last Dominic had given in. He was very attached to Cecil; as, indeed, he was to the whole Englesby family. He owed everything to them and he never forgot it. So, good humouredly, he agreed to make the journey. But as for fancy dress, Dominic refused to do more than attire himself as a barrister, in a black gown with a wig. Cecil, on the contrary, appeared as his host had wished as a splendid eighteenth-century gallant.

Now, suddenly, Dominic moved a little out of the shadows, pitched the stump of his cigar into some syringa bushes and looked intently at a young girl who was hurrying across the lawn. It was his hostess. Dominic was surprised to see Lady Chase unescorted. Until he came out here he had watched her dancing and found her adorable. In these days, it took a very fascinating woman to appeal to Dominic, who had long since turned his back upon the love of women. Tragedy in love had touched him too closely. But even *he* had to admit that Lady Chase was all and more than Cecil had described her.

"There is a mystery attached to her ladyship," his foster-brother had told him, when describing the family at Clunes. "As you know, Viv and I were friends at Oxford. He was more than a little crazy then, and sometimes unscrupulous, but an entertaining fellow. The trouble was that his father died when Viv was young and he was brought up by his mother, who was a saint. It had the cynical result of turning Viv into a devil. But he and I got on famously. I expected him to make a fine match, not yet, perhaps—later on. Instead of which, I returned from that cruise with Mama and Papa to find him married, to this unknown girl, and before getting his degree."

Cecil then informed Dominic of the many rumours and conjectures concerning Charlotte. All that was known for certain, however, was that she had once been a Miss Goff who lived at the Lodge; and that she was a protégée and pupil of the late Lady Chase. Presumably, Cecil ended, she and Vivian had fallen madly in love and had married hastily—and in private, on account of his mother's fatal malady.

All this, Dominic found of much interest. When he finally met Charlotte he was surprised by her extreme youthfulness, a touch of childish simplicity which greatly appealed to him. Then, when he looked down into the breathtaking beauty of her eyes, he realized that any man might well wish to snatch her for his own, no matter what she was, or whence she came. It was not just a case of mere physical beauty with Charlotte but of singular charm. A promise of passion, of sensuality, coupled with that child-like purity.

He and Charlotte had talked alone before the other guests joined them, and it had not taken Dominic long to understand why old Lady Chase had wanted to educate her. Dominic, too, probed and enjoyed her fine quick mind. He, who was himself a lover of literature, history and music, touched on all these subjects with her and found her learning matched his own. Charlotte could be gay as well as grave, but she did not seem to share with other girls of her age the perpetual thirst for flattery and frivolous entertainment. Of course, she was already a wife and mother; Dominic thought it delightful when she showed her infant to him with fond pride. Everything outwardly seemed to be well at Clunes at first glance. Later, a passage between husband and wife opened Dominic's eyes to the fact that there was decay under the glitter. Charlotte had accidentally brushed into her husband, and his crutch slipped. She caught and steadied him, with a laughing apology, but in that fleeting second, Dominic caught sight of Vivian's face. He was disturbed to see the look of fury that had altered its whole appearance. He heard the whispered oath:

"Damn you, Charlotte!"

It gave Dominic a sense of shock. Neither did Charlotte's reaction to this remain unnoticed by the observant Dominic. Her smile changed to concern. Her cheeks reddened with mortification. Then she passed on to welcome a newly-arrived guest. For the rest of the evening, whenever Dominic saw Vivian he found him a charming host. But the older man was quite unable to forget that naked fury that had, for a moment, been unleashed, and loosed on his young wife.

Now Dominic watched Charlotte approach. Her dress was dazzling; of rich powder-blue brocade, shot with silver. The full skirt was hooped at the sides and showed a cascade of silver lace. The low-cut neck revealed a curve of snow-white bosom. She looked older than she really was, with her hair powdered, dressed high, ornamented with blue and silver flowers; white curls gracefully falling on either side of her long neck around which sparkled a necklace of sapphires and diamonds. Her face was painted for the occasion. It gave her an artificial glow, for she was, in fact, feeling pale and tired. Even Dominic could see the faint mauve shadows under those huge eyes. But as she tripped on tiny silver shoes up the steps and on to the terrace, he felt a sudden wish to speak to her.

"Lady Chase!" he called.

Charlotte paused, her hand to her bosom. Then as she saw who spoke, her look of tension eased; a smile curved her lips. She came toward Dominic, and curtsied after the fashion of the ladies who used to wear such wide-hooped dresses.

"*Monsieur,*" she murmured.

"*Chère Madame*, you should not be without an escort," he smiled, "allow me to afford myself the privilege of taking you into the dance. You look disturbed."

She drew a quick breath.

"I was just—just—running away from somebody," she stammered.

"Then I feel pity for the 'somebody,' " he said, with a lightness that he rarely exhibited, but he wanted to see her smile. His wish was granted. She even laughed.

"Oh, do not; he was so—so hateful."

"Then I withdraw my pity and shall hate him," said Dominic.

Charlotte bit her lip. Mr. Unwin was not likely to know that the hateful "somebody" was her own husband. Vivian had come across his wife standing by an Italian statue with a gay young man who was dressed as a Greek. A boy no older than herself. The two had assumed a dramatic pose and were declaiming together to the moon. For Charlotte it had been a moment of fun, such as she rarely had. Then had fallen the shadow of the beggar in his rags. It had not taken her long to see that Vivian had drunk too much. For the first time since his accident he was so inflamed with wine that he did not mind his guests seeing him thus. Pointing at his wife with his crutch, he snarled:

"No more of this ridiculous play-acting. You forget, Madam, that you are Lady Chase, and the hostess at our party. Kindly return to your guests. And you, sir—" He had addressed the embarrassed Greek, "Choose yourself a young unmarried girl to join you in your idiotic gambolling."

At this, in an agony of shame, Charlotte picked up her skirts and ran back through the garden to the house.

She stayed talking with Cecil's adopted brother. He could see that she was not at ease. She kept throwing darting glances to the right and the left as though she feared the approach of this man whom she had called "hateful." No doubt Dominic thought, some not-quite-sober gallant had been paying her overbearing attentions. So the little Lady Chase was a prude, he thought. All to the good. Dominic liked women to be prudish.

"It was good of you to allow me to come to Clunes," he murmured, "I feel an interloper."

She told him with sincerity that she was glad he had accompanied Cecil. She knew herself to be strongly attracted to this man who, in comparison with her seventeen years, might almost be called "elderly." But he was charming. He had tremendous personality. To look at he was not, perhaps, a young girl's ideal. He had none of the sparkling golden beauty of Vivian Chase when first she grew to love him. But she was to learn for the first time the subtle power of a strong, fine nature. Dominic Unwin was an *individual*, with strength and fire behind his quiet presence. A hint of sadness, too, which intrigued her.

She examined him now with shy gravity as they stood there. She felt that they were quite alone in the crowd—on a mysterious island where they could not be reached. She had never before experienced this sense of *aloneness* with anybody. She talked with him as with an old friend.

Dominic was taller than Vivian, so slightly built that he gave one the impression of great height. He was so dark, too, that he might have been mistaken for a Spaniard. Charlotte presumed from that deep tan that he had spent much time abroad in the hot sun. His hair, under the barrister's wig, worn for tonight's entertainment, was black as a raven's wing springing back vitally from a broad forehead. His face was lean, a little hatchet-faced, lips repressed, even stern; yet, when he smiled, he looked youthful. But it was his eyes which interested Charlotte. For they were not dark, as one might expect with such colouring, but of a profound purplish blue. Whose eyes had she seen like these before? She asked herself the question but could not answer it. They were very beautiful eyes for a man and full of deep melancholy. What was his history? she wondered.

Suddenly Dominic said:

"You look at me very questioningly, Lady Chase." She blushed. He found enchantment in the way she touched one burning cheek with a lace-mittened hand and apologized.

"It was discourteous of me to stare."

"You were not staring, but I wondered what question you wished to ask me."

"N-nothing," she stammered with a laugh.

"I know," he said, nodding, "you have heard something—but not everything—about my relationship with the Englesbys. You would like to know more? Or do I flatter myself?"

"Indeed, you are exactly right, Mr. Unwin."

"A great many people have been intrigued by the position I hold at Englesby Castle."

"Oh!" exclaimed Charlotte, "it would seem most discourteous to wish to pry into the private life of my guest. I do assure you—"

But Dominic broke in.

"Somehow I feel I should like to talk about myself. A desire," he added, "that very rarely moves me."

"I am honoured."

"Walk with me a little," he said suddenly, "unless you wish to dance."

"No, I would rather walk with you."

"You will not be cold? The night grows cooler."

"I am not at all cold," she said breathlessly.

She took Dominic's arm and strolled with him across the moon-silvered lawn, toward the lake. Other couples walked by them, laughing and chattering. Charlotte felt a strange inner glow for which she could not account. She only knew that she wanted to go on talking to Dominic Unwin, and to hear him talk. What a voice he had! It was the rich golden voice of the born orator.

She remembered hearing Cecil tell her husband of the enormous impression Dominic had made in the House with his maiden speech. Charlotte could feel that warm humanity of which Lord Marchmond had also told her. Dominic gave her a feeling of confidence which, she could believe, must have led many thousands to return him as their Member.

"Is it a fact that you have never visited Clunes before?" she asked him. "Vivian tells me that in the past your family came here, but you—?"

"Not I, because there is such a difference of age between Cecil and myself," he said. "He and I seldom have the same friends. You forget that I am getting on for forty."

"I wish *I* were," sighed Charlotte.

"Why?" he asked, smiling down at the beautiful face.

"Because, when one is young, one is always making mistakes," she said before she could restrain herself.

"I find you full of good sense already and, possessed of more learning than most of your contemporaries."

"Thank you," she said, conscious of deep pleasure.

"And before I tell you a little more about myself," he went on, "I would like to know something more about my charming hostess—or would that be insolent?"

"Heavens! You could never be insolent, Mr. Unwin."

"Then tell me. Cecil seems as untutored as myself on the subject, though he has spoken often of your husband and the boyish escapades they shared at Oxford. But never of you."

Charlotte bit her lip.

"I—I have been much in the background," she said, and was conscious of Vivian's constant pressure upon her to say nothing to anybody about her past. But somehow to this grave man with his penetrating gaze she did not wish to lie.

Quietly Dominic said:

"Once I, too, was much in the background, Lady Chase."

They had come to the edge of the large lake which was fringed with delicate birches. The water was like a sheet of silver in the luminous night. Dominic stood still a moment, barely noticing the feather-like pressure of the girl's hand through the curve of his arm, yet feeling her to be very near in spirit. He was disturbed by his own reaction to that light touch. She was a child, but ageless. He could talk to her as he could not talk to many an older woman.

Abruptly, he said:

"I was adopted when a child of ten by the Englesby family, you know."

Even Vivian's threat which hung over her so constantly could not keep her from exclaiming:

"And I, too, was adopted. For my late mother-in-law took me from London to live at Clunes, in the Lodge, when I was twelve."

"I went to Cirencester to become the privileged son by adoption of the kindest of all great people, the Marquess and Marchioness of Englesby," said Dominic.

She looked with fresh interest at the sensitive face of this intriguing man.

"Pray, tell me more," she begged.

"Your history, first," he smiled.

She glanced at the lake. They heard the sudden mournful cry of a half-awakened heron nesting somewhere in the rushes. Charlotte's fingers played with the magnificent necklace about her slender throat.

She whispered, "I never speak of myself. Please keep what I tell you a secret."

"Your confidence shall be very safe with me, as I hope my own will be with you," he said gravely.

So he learned of that night of fog upon the Embankment when the Chase carriage had so nearly run over little Charlotte Goff, and of all that had followed at Clunes. All, that was, save the personal story of her love affair with Vivian. Dominic was no inquisitive boy to probe too deeply into a young girl's secrets. He kept quiet but guessed without being told what had really happened between those two. He said:

"We both have much to be thankful for. I was born in obscurity and might have been nothing. You started in poverty and have become an exalted wife and mother, and mistress of one of the most beautiful homes in England."

"My little daughter is adorable," she admitted.

He noted that she did not include her husband in her rhapsodies. Poor child, he thought, she was not very good at concealing things; but Dominic had drawn his own conclusions about Lord Chase. Little though he had seen, in recent years, of Cecil, he had often heard his adoptive parents begging him to give up this friendship with Vivian, rumours of whose bad reputation had drifted even as far as Cirencester.

"And now for your story," she said.

He told her briefly all that he knew about himself. What delighted her most was to see that he had no snobbery in his nature, none of Vivian's hateful arrogance and pride. Pride, Dominic Unwin might have, but of the right kind. And he loved all people, both of high and low degree. He was unashamed of his beginning, just as she in the depths of her heart had never felt embarrassed by knowledge of hers. Perhaps, she thought, it was his early experiences that had made him so sensitive. Loneliness and pain can enrich as well as embitter a man.

He did not actually know the secret of his parentage for he could remember little except an existence even more poverty-stricken than her own with Aunt Jem—a harsh life in a Charity school. He made light of this but admitted that he had suffered years in this school of bullying, intense cold, and even hunger. But he had soon risen above the heads of the other small boys, being possessed of a remarkable memory and many talents. One of his teachers had taken a strong interest in him (following the pattern of Charlotte's education). He had shown a brilliance of mind and wit, which amazed his teachers and finally caught the attention of the Marquess of Englesby who had, at the time, been a patron of the Charity school. The Marquess was a kindly gentleman, most interested in child welfare and his wife had had no children. So impressed was the Marquess by the intellectual powers of the orphan who knew no name save "Dick Smith" that he had taken him down to Englesby. Lady Englesby was immediately attracted by his raven hair and sad blue eyes, and she kept him at the Castle. There, he was given a tutor and at the age of fifteen he went to Charterhouse.

His name had been changed to Dominic Unwin. "Dominic," because it came from the Latin for *"Sunday"* and it was on the Sabbath that the boy first visited Englesby. *"Unwin"* was a family name on the Marchioness's side, and belonged to her favourite brother who had died young.

Dominic had been profoundly happy and it was a happiness that had not been lessened by the totally unexpected birth, at long last, of an heir to the Englesbys. The fifteen-year-old boy became a devoted brother to little Cecil, who, in turn, looked up to and admired his brother by adoption. Dominic had all the brains. Poor Cecil Marchmond possessed few.

Later on, the two boys saw less and less of one another. The young Earl of Marchmond was still at Preparatory school when Dominic got a double first at Oxford where he read Classics and Philosophy. There he became seriously interested for the first time, in politics. His adoptive parents were delighted.

Dominic gave Charlotte this history of himself with but faint, modest emphasis on much that he could have added about his talents. He ended by telling Charlotte that now, as a Member of Parliament, he was fulfilling his chief ambition.

"That is," he added, drily, "as far as worldly desires go. There are times when I feel that they go no way at all, and that true happiness and contentment lie in a man's soul alone."

"Oh, with that I agree!" exclaimed the young girl earnestly. "I, too, discovered that fact."

"You, who are so young, should still be brimming with the joy of life," he said, smiling.

She made no reply. Once again he was struck by the belief that this lovely young girl was not happy; and by an uncomfortable fear that Vivian Chase deserved his reputation as a libertine. Did she love him? She could not. She must already be disillusioned.

He tried to speak lightly.

"*La Jeunesse dorée,*" he said. "Golden youth. You have it. Would that it were also mine."

"But you have a wisdom and experience which I envy," she said with a deep sigh.

"I am not to be envied for experience. It has, in my case, been a tragic tutor," he said abruptly.

"You have never married," she said.

"No, never, and never shall do."

"Forgive me."

"Good heavens—for what?" he asked.

"For touching on a subject obviously painful to you."

Her sensibility, her sweetness suddenly broke through a crust in Dominic Unwin which had not been penetrated for many a long year. He stood a moment, hands clasped behind his back, staring across the romantic lake. His eyes held pain and sadness.

"I *was* to have married, when I was barely thirty," he said in a low tone. "She—died."

Quick to sympathize with suffering in any form, Charlotte murmured:

"I am so *very* sorry."

He turned to her.

"I have not spoken of this since it happened, not even to my dearest Lady Englesby, whom I regard as my mother. But—somehow you draw my story from me. Perhaps by virtue of the fact that you remind me of *her*. She, too, was only seventeen, very lovely and passionately attached to her books. She spoke somewhat with your voice. When I first heard it, I could have sworn that my poor little Dorothea lived again."

Charlotte stayed silent, intensely aware of what he was saying. After a moment he continued his story.

Eight years ago, he had met Dorothea Palmerston. She was distantly related to the famous statesman of that name. For the first time, Dominic had fallen in love. He had never been one to fritter his time away with pretty girls. When he loved it was deeply, and with his whole being. He described Dorothea as "an angel of purity and goodness." Charlotte felt her cheeks grow hot. The bitter thought leaped to her mind:

"He likens her to me but what would he think if he knew how far I fell from grace before my marriage?"

Dorothea returned Dominic's love. After a year's engagement they were to be married. Her parents were distinguished people. A grand wedding had been arranged in London. The Englesbys were, at the time, in their London house in Porchester Square. Dominic was with them, the happiest of men. Not only did a fine Parliamentary career stretch before him, but he would have a lovely talented young woman for a bride. Their home was prepared—a house in Richmond, for Dorothea was particularly fond of riding and Richmond Park was a favourite place with her.

The rest of that story was melancholy. On the very eve of the wedding, Dorothea went riding with her sisters in Richmond Park. Her horse was startled by something white which lay on the verge of the road. The animal took the bit between its teeth and bolted. Dorothea was thrown, her back was broken and she died instantly.

"She was buried," said Dominic in a low voice, "in the bridal gown she should have worn for me. Something of me was buried with her on the dreadful day of her funeral. Life continues, Lady Chase, but one never really recovers from such a catastrophe."

They had reached the terrace of Clunes. The gay sounds of a quadrille drifted through the French windows. Once again they had returned to the glittering atmosphere of the ballroom. The brief interlude of close companionship which they had exchanged was ended. Dominic knew a strange regret. Having unveiled some of the pain in a heart so long concealed from the world, he could not but feel a yearning towards the one who had inspired such confidence.

As for Charlotte, she stood a moment, hands clasped, looking up at him with eyes that were full of tears.

Hastily Dominic said:

"Oh, confound it, I have distressed you and on the night of your ball—how thoughtless of me."

"No, I am deeply honoured because you have told me about Dorothea. I think it is the saddest story I have ever heard, but I am glad you related it. I shall never forget it."

"No, no, you must forget," he said. "It is all so long ago now, and as I have just said—life must go on. Once more —forgive me for striking at your tender heart. I have made you sad."

"I was already sad," she said, and sighed. The sound was torn from the very depths of her being.

"Lady Chase—" began Dominic. But she had gone; run away from him. He watched the hooped, brocaded gown with the ruffled laces vanish in the crowd. He was left with only the faint odour of Charlotte's fragrance, and a memory of those honey-coloured eyes brimming with tears. And most of all a memory of those words:

"I was already sad."

They had shocked him. Poor Charlotte Chase, poor child. He would have given a lot to be able to help and comfort her; whatever her sorrow. Yet, he was still little more than a stranger to her.

Dominic walked into the ballroom. It was hot and full of the perfume of a thousand dying flowers. He looked for

Charlotte but could not see her. When finally he did catch sight of her she was accompanied by her husband. She threw Dominic a half smile but turned away at once, almost as though frightened to acknowledge him. He wondered why.

Vivian was drunk, slithering on his crutches, but he had thrown off his gait of beggar and discarded the patch over his eye. His face was inflamed, his fine features blurred by the wine he had been consuming. He looked horrible, Dominic thought, but Charlotte was gallantly trying to hide his condition from the guests, keeping one arm about him, smiling and bowing to their friends, pretending that it was the highly polished floor that caused Vivian to stagger so foolishly.

Dominic looked intently at the couple for a moment, then, with a feeling of acute depression, turned and left the room. He went up to his own chamber, from which he did not emerge again that night.

Chapter Eighteen

Twenty-four hours later, Dominic Unwin, with his brother Lord Marchmond, left Clunes. The young mistress of the house speeded the parting guests. Vivian was not well the morning after the Ball. He stayed in his rooms. No one had seen him but Volpo, who had, in his sardonic fashion, informed Charlotte that his lordship wished to remain undisturbed while his indisposition lasted.

Charlotte was none too happy about that message. Either it meant that Vivian was secretly drinking (aided and abetted by the vicious Portuguese who valeted him) or that he was genuinely sick.

But she had had one glorious morning of golden sunshine, with the brave sight of yellow-trumpeted daffodils as far as the eye could see, colouring the borders along the drive. A morning when she had much to do, starting with the attention she had to give to little Eleanora, then her duties to the guests. But finally, a memorable hour alone with Dominic Unwin. This, while Cecil Marchmond and the other men took horses from Vivian's stables and went riding. The ladies stayed in their rooms.

Dominic did not wish to ride. He lingered in the library with Charlotte who showed him many of the books collected by the late Lady Chase, some of which Charlotte had read and studied.

To Charlotte this was the most precious hour she had ever spent with any human being. So deeply impressed was she by the fine mind of this unusual man twenty years or so older than herself, that she had no consciousness of the difference in their ages. She only knew that she had found the perfect companion. One to whom she could talk and by whom she could be understood. They were agreed on so many matters. She sat down at her piano and played Bach for him. He listened gravely; then came to the piano and complimented her upon her talent. He himself then played for her, while she sat with hands folded in her lap, listening, watching him, and feeling deep peace; a joy which she had seldom experienced in the past except in a milder form when she used to study in this very room with Eleanor Chase.

Dominic was a finer pianist than Charlotte, and she was quick to comment on the fact. As he finished and turned on the stool to face her, he smiled at her youthful flattery.

"Maybe my technique exceeds yours, but of the two of us you would have made the better pianist. And remember that I have made music my hobby and practised for many years. I started before you were born."

Laughing at this, he rose and sauntered across the library. He picked up a slim volume of Keats which she had just shown him. He, too, was a great lover of that sensitive young poet. Charlotte's gaze followed him. She liked him dressed like this, in his grey travelling suit, sombre yet elegant. As he turned the pages of his book she looked at the fine stern profile, the dark springing hair. Was there a hint of grey over the ears? Maybe the sun showed up the silver threads. Remorseless time had already laid a finger upon Dominic Unwin. But she was filled with an emotion tantamount to hero-worship. He was, she thought, a man whom any woman, young or old, might adore. Little wonder the young Dorothea had loved him. And now she knew to her bitterness and cost the utter emptiness of a love based upon the senses alone, a sensuality rooted in dishonour. Now she knew that she had never really loved Vivian Chase at all. The shadow of fatality chilled her very being as she remembered the man who lay upstairs sleeping off the effects of a debauchery. Her little dream of regenerating Vivian, of growing to care for him again, was fast dying; if not already dead. She closed her left hand convulsively, hating the sight of her wedding ring. She thought of the babe which she had just fed and fondled; her own spirit was crushed.

"Alas, my poor babe," she thought, "and alas, for the folly of my passion which has burnt out, and left me only the ashes of despair."

Dominic raised his head. He glanced toward her as he closed the volume of poems.

He, too, had found this morning more than agreeable. It had been a pleasure shared unreservedly with this intelligent, sensitive young girl. Difficult for him this morning to believe her a wife and mother. The showy brocaded dress, the valuable jewels of the Pompadour, had been laid aside. Today Charlotte was a child, her chestnut hair looped simply back, tied with a velvet bow. A child, in her simple lilac-coloured gown with only a gold cross hanging from a chain at her throat.

She looked so defenceless, so sad; the sight pained him. Then she glanced in his direction. He could see unshed tears in her eyes. Something terrible weighed her mind and spirit down, he thought.

Involuntarily he stepped to her side.

"Lady Chase—Charlotte—let me call you that, for I am old enough to be your father—" he began.

She broke in, struggling for calm.

"Hardly so, Mr. Unwin."

"Nevertheless, much older than you. Could you not think of me as an elder brother, and call me '*Dominic*'?"

"I would like to," she whispered.

"I can think of you as a dear young sister," he went on, "for we seem to have shared much in our beginnings. We are, perhaps, two people set apart from the rest of the world."

She liked to be thus linked with him but her head drooped. Her slender fingers twined nervously in her lap.

"I know that I am set apart in a way that I could never explain to you," she said in a choked voice.

His sense of anxiety for her increased.

"Do you need a friend? Is it detestable of me even to suggest that you, Lady Chase, are friendless?"

Now she raised her face. He read such naked pain in her eyes that it struck him to the very quick.

"Good God, I am right!" he exclaimed. "You *have* some secret grief to endure. My poor child, can I not aid you?"

"I know grief, but no one in this world can help me," she said in a strangled voice.

"Are you so sure? Remember I am a Member of Parliament, a man who speaks to persons of both high and low degree; who sees life not only as it is at Clunes or Englesby, but in the raw among the sick and needy. Frequently I must touch below the surface. I am capable of understanding trouble. Who should be more so than I, who have suffered much myself," he added in a low tone. "If it would help to give me your confidence, I would be more than happy. I might even find some solution."

A moment's silence. Charlotte struggled with herself. She had never felt a greater inclination to tell any man all that had happened with Vivian, all that was happening now. But dearly though she wished to talk to Dominic Unwin, she was too loyal. Vivian was her husband and the father of her child. Sometimes she blamed her own existence for the very deterioration in Vivian's character. Whatever it was, she must not complain to a stranger; least of all to a man who appealed so vastly to her as this one. After a moment she whispered:

"Dear Mr. Unwin—Dominic—I have never before encountered any man in whom I would more gladly confide. I thank you for your interest in me, but my sorrows are not my own. To expose them could serve no useful purpose. What has been—has been. What is to be—must be. I pray only for greater strength of will; for a philosophic mind."

Dominic knit his brows. She was so very young, yet so tragic. He longed to pick her up in his arms and comfort her. It did not enter his head at this moment to regard her as a woman to be loved in a sensual way. But he felt an inexpressible tenderness towards her, such tenderness as he had experienced for no human being since Dorothea died.

"Then," at length he said, "I can only trust that you will remember my existence if you should ever have need of me."

Now her face cleared. She gave him a swift smile which he found ravishing. He was sure that the real Charlotte had a sunny disposition and could be capable of brilliance and humour. It was not natural for her to be so depressed.

"Thank you, thank you very much, Mr. Unwin," she said. "Indeed, I shall never forget what you say."

He took a leather wallet from his pocket, drew a card from it and handed it to her.

"This is my address, my Chambers are in London," he said. "I go only occasionally to Englesby. The greater part of my time is spent in the House; but should you ever need me, you will find me there—" he pointed to the address on the card.

She looked at it:

"Mr. Dominic Unwin, M.P., Albany, W. 1."

Somehow that little piece of pasteboard became in a single moment her dearest possession, her talisman against danger—and future grief. She clasped it between her hands and in that child-like fashion which he found so touching, smiled at him again.

"I thank you from the bottom of my heart."

"And I reassure you from mine that you will find me a ready listener to any woe which may in the future overwhelm you. I thank you also for our splendid morning together. It is a rare treat being able to exchange ideas and artistic delights as we have done."

"Yes, it was truly wonderful," sighed Charlotte.

As he put his wallet back in his pocket, he thought:

"God knows what is troubling this poor child, who is herself the mother of a child. But I feel that one day she may want to call upon my help. I do not like or trust the man whose name she bears. It is a thousand pities she was ever permitted to marry him."

At that moment the study door broke open. Cecil Marchmond came in, dressed in his riding clothes, his happy countenance reddened by the wind and the sun.

"So there you are, Dom—poring over books with Charlotte. You two melancholy scholars! You should have been riding with me. It is splendid in Vivian's park this morning."

The older man smiled.

"I have spent a far more pleasant morning with my hostess, whose taste in literature and music matches my own," he said.

"Indeed yes," echoed Charlotte, rising.

She felt an inner glow, a sensation that she was no longer quite alone in this bitter world. Her hands still clung lovingly to the card that bore Dominic's name and address.

She could not see the slightest possibility that she could ever make use of it, of the friendship he had offered her.

They lived in different worlds. He, engrossed in his career, she, in her own circle. Yet this morning, the confidences they had exchanged had forged a link between her and this unusual man which nothing on earth could break.

"He is utterly to be trusted," she thought.

She did not see him alone again. Luncheon was a formal affair in the big dining-room, after which all the guests departed and she had to go to her infant. But she slipped the little card into her *corsage* and kept it there. With it she kept the memory of Dominic's deep blue eyes looking with such kindness, such piercing sweetness, down into hers as he bade her good-bye.

"All my thanks for this visit," he said as he bowed low over her hand, "and pray, convey my thanks to my host."

Then the Chase carriage had driven Dominic and the young Earl to Harling Station. From a nursery window Charlotte watched that carriage disappear round a bend in the drive. A little cloud of dust followed.

She thought, with emotion:

"Now the dust settles over my life again! He is gone. He has gone and—*I could have loved him.* I *do* love him, as my one and only true friend, and, though I may never see him again, I shall always remember him."

As the nurse handed Charlotte the infant, the tiny creature put out a hand and clutched her breast. She bent low over the babe, her eyes smarting with the tears that scalded her lids. Desolately she performed her duties as a mother. Then, feeling strangely tired, she walked out of the nursery. She was about to enter her own room, when she heard a voice coming from her husband's wing.

"Charlotte! Charlotte! where the devil are you? Come here at once."

Her heart sank. She hurried towards Vivian's bedchamber. Volpo was not there. The curtains were still drawn, keeping out the sunlight. The handsome room, for all its spaciousness, was stuffy and offensive to Charlotte's nostrils. In his big, four-poster bed with the red damask curtains half drawn, Vivian Chase lay in one of his satin bed jackets; gold hair rumpled, face puffed and putty coloured, eyes inflamed. He presented an unattractive spectacle. A carafe of wine, half empty, stood on the table beside him. There were wine stains on the embroidered sheets.

Stains on the red satin eiderdown. Beside him, on the bed table, stood a pile of uncut yellow-backed French novels.

It seemed to the young girl that after the calm heaven of the morning in the sunlit library, conversing with a man like Dominic Unwin, this was like a sudden plunge into hell. And Vivian had the devil in his eyes as he growled at her:

"Where have you been?"

"Feeding our child," she said gently.

"Have her weaned," he said, "she takes up too much of your time. You pay less and less attention to me."

"But Vivian," she said, shocked. "It is a mother's duty to nurse her infant."

"Duty, *duty*," he broke in, "you are always the little saint. What an unlucky fellow I am! I had to listen for the first part of my life to a psalm-singing mother; now I must listen to a pious wife. But it does not become you to be so, my dear Charlotte. You amused me better when you were more accommodating."

Her heart sank very low indeed. With the departure of their guests it looked as though Vivian had made up his mind to put an end to all pretence of making a fresh start with her.

"I am sorry," she said, "that you think it necessary to be on these poor terms with me again. I thought we had begun to find true happiness once more."

He lowered his lids. His mouth was loose and cruel.

"Lying up with this damned leg made me fanciful. I gave too much time to thoughts of Heaven. But I am not dead yet, nor do I intend to die. To the devil with superstition. I have at last recovered from the hallucinations from which I suffered after my accident. You should be the first to congratulate me on my recovery, my dear wife."

She stood silent, one hand clutching the cross at her throat. He looked her up and down.

"Where did that unbecoming garment come from?"

"You mean my dress," said Charlotte. "It is one made for my trousseau."

"I thought I told you not to wear any more dresses made by that local idiot. I bought you handsome gowns in Monte Carlo. Where are they?"

"In my wardrobe—" she began.

"Then wear them," he broke in, "and your jewellery. You annoy me by your efforts to remain that little *ingénue* imbecile from the Lodge. God knows why I ever married her."

She made no answer. She thought:

"Indeed, God knows."

"Where is everybody?" snapped Vivian.

"Our guests have gone. They sent you farewell messages, Vivian."

"Good riddance," he said, "they bored me, except perhaps Cecil who is not a bad fellow. But as for that solemn dark-faced foster-brother of his, I could not tolerate him."

Charlotte clenched her hands.

"You saw little of Mr. Unwin."

"Enough to convince me that he is an intolerable bore."

She remained silent. She found that with her whole heart she resented the contempt with which he spoke of Dominic.

Vivian continued:

"I'd like to know the history behind that pious prig from Englesby. His hair and skin are as dark as a Spaniard's."

"Maybe he has Spanish blood. He was, like myself, adopted."

Vivian gave a loud, ugly yawn and stretched his arms.

"Confound this leg," he said between his teeth, "Castleby says it will be another five weeks before I walk without crutches, but when I do—" he gave a laugh and looked at her in a manner that drew a blush from Charlotte's cheek; it was so full of licentiousness.

"May I now go, please," she said, "I was very late last night and I want to rest."

"Late doing what—learning politics from the mouth of Cecil's upstart brother."

"He is no upstart," Charlotte was fired to answer. "Birth and breeding do not necessarily make princes of men, Vivian. No matter where Dominic Unwin originally sprang from, he is a gentleman with the finest instincts and character."

"So!" said Vivian in a drawling voice, and shut one eye as he looked at her. "How eloquently you speak of our Member of Parliament. Has he touched a cord in your romantic heart, my dear?"

She felt the blood rush to her cheeks and recede again; try as she would she could not keep herself from trembling.

"Please, Vivian, may I go now. Since you choose to be so discourteous to me, I would rather not stay."

She turned abruptly as though to leave the room but he shouted at her so violently that she turned back to him, afraid that the servants would hear.

"Vivian, pray do not shout."

"I will not have you speak to me in such a saucy fashion," he snarled. "This damned leg of mine, and your babe, have kept us too long apart. I think it is time you showed your husband a little love and attention. Do you hear? Come to me—"

Every drop of blood in Charlotte's body revolted from what she knew to be at the back of his poisonous mood. Reluctantly she advanced to the bedside, her nose wrinkling with disgust. She longed to throw back the curtains and let the fresh air of the April day into this stuffy room. She said:

"For the love of God, Vivian, let us not start *this* kind of association again. I implore you to return to your other self. The self that permitted you to treat me with the respect due to your wife."

He laughed and snatched at her, pulling her down upon him.

"I am myself now, in this moment. You smell delicious," he said. "You little hypocrite. Let us see the fire and enthusiasm that led to the conception of our daughter. No more of your prudery, Lady Chase. And I would find you more attractive with fewer clothes."

Praying for patience, she shut her eyes. He wrenched at the fastening of her pretty lilac gown and bared the smooth marble of her shoulders. As he did this, Dominic's card dropped out upon the bed. Charlotte had no time to recover it. Vivian's fingers seized upon it. He held it up to the light of the bedside table, scowling, then gave a long, low laugh. Such a laugh as struck chill at her.

"Well, w-e-l-l," he said, "*Mr. Dominic Unwin, M.P., Albany, W.1*. Your new hero. How singularly entertaining."

She choked.

"Mr. Unwin thought—if—if we returned to Eaton Square—we might like his address," she stammered.

Vivian tore the pasteboard into tiny pieces and flung them over the bed.

"That much for Dominic Unwin's address. I have no wish whatsoever to visit the gentleman, neither is it a friendship which I shall encourage for my wife. In any case, Cecil's foster-brother is middle-aged. Let him seek the companionship of women older than you. And if he has developed a slight fancy for my beauteous young wife, he will have to forget it."

She had no words. She looked with despair at the scattered pieces of card. It was symbolic, she thought, for in just such a way had Vivian torn her life to pieces and scattered it to the four winds.

"Oh, you are contemptible," she broke out in her misery, while he tugged at her curls and her clothes.

He laughed and closed her mouth with a violent kiss.

All the passion and pride in her nature rebelled to such an extent that she tried to pull away from him. He fought her and she was bruised in the contest. His arms were strong with desire and she could not escape. But she sobbed wildly.

"Mr. Unwin is a fine man and I know his address by heart. I don't need the card. I know, I tell you, just where to call upon him if I need his friendship."

"You *wanton*!" he said, "you with a babe scarce three months old. You are disgusting."

"I have done no wrong. Mr. Unwin is a stranger who has become a friend," she cried.

"This ends the friendship," said Vivian and struck her across the mouth.

After that she cried no more, and she lost all hope of future happiness with Vivian. While she lay in his hateful embrace, in dreadful bitterness, she thought:

"It is all over. He will see to it that I never set eyes upon Mr. Unwin again."

Yet even in that hell and through the black clouds that swirled around her, she could still see the shining tenderness in Dominic's eyes and heard his voice saying, *"My poor child, can I not aid you?"*

He could not. She was beyond aid, she told herself—bound for ever to this unspeakable man who had fathered her child.

In that hour, overwhelmed by Vivian, she touched the lowest depths of a woman's degradation and despair.

PART II

Chapter Nineteen

Nine years later.

Charlotte had already been awake for an hour, when Gertrude knocked on the door and carried in the tray with her early morning tea. Gertrude was astonished to see the lamp on the table beside the bed alight and my lady sitting up, reading what must be one of yesterday's newspapers.

It was bitterly cold this November morning. Gertrude clicked her tongue with disapproval as she saw that her young mistress had not even bothered to put a shawl over her shoulders.

"My lady!" she protested. "You will get a chill. Emily must come up at once and light your fire."

Charlotte smiled and a trifle guiltily laid aside the paper which she had been studying so earnestly.

"I am all right, thank you, Gertrude. But it *is* a raw morning. I must admit."

"It was snowing in the early hours, my lady," the maid informed her. She drew the heavy blue damask curtains, revealing to Charlotte a dismal, yellowish-looking morning. Charlotte caught only a glimpse of leafless branches of the trees in Eaton Square. But she could see that they were powdered with snow. She was glad when Gertrude hastened to wrap a fleecy pale blue shawl about her. Dear Gertrude—always so tender, so careful of her health. Charlotte had been suffering from a cough that had persisted all winter. She preferred to live at Clunes and lead a country life, even in this bitter weather. But Vivian liked to be in Town during the winter. So here she was. Clunes was shut and would only be reopened for Christmas week.

For a moment, Charlotte lay watching the maid move quietly around the big room, folding one or two articles of clothing, tidying the big walnut dressing table with its triple mirror, re-arranging the towels on the washstand. Her efficiency never failed to impress Charlotte. She had grown, too, to feel quite an attachment for this woman during the nine long years that Gertrude had been her personal maid.

Although always formal, and respectful, she had a human side which Charlotte found soothing. She could rely on Gertrude being behind her in all ways—more especially when Vivian chose to be difficult. And Gertrude felt that the excellent woman was in sympathy with her in her dislike of Volpo. He was their mutual enemy. Charlotte knew that Gertrude tried to save her from his continual spying and many other unpleasant moments. So, although in most things Charlotte had to submit to the will of her husband she had, throughout these years, refused to allow him to dismiss Gertrude.

"She is the one being in my household whom I trust and whom I know is attached to *me* and not only to her job. I will not have her taken from me," Charlotte declared, when Vivian, complaining that Gertrude was a "sour creature," and ugly, suggested getting rid of her. And Vivian shrugged his shoulders and said no more, being only faintly interested.

True, Gertrude had aged and grown scrawny and angular now that she was in her forties. The frizzed hair under the white cap with its long streamers, was turning grey. She looked down her long thin nose at most people in a derisive fashion. But all the kindliness of which she was capable shone in her small beady eyes when she glanced in Charlotte's direction. To her, my Lady Chase was one of the kindest, sweetest, and most considerate ladies she had ever served. Gertrude said:

"Will you have your breakfast earlier, since you are awake, my lady?"

"When it is ready, thank you, Gertrude."

"Afterwards, shall Mrs. MacDougal come and see you about tonight's meal, my lady?"

"No, Gertrude. I am dining out. Do you not remember?"

"Oh, yes, I beg your pardon, my lady."

Charlotte added:

"Tomorrow his lordship returns. Ask Volpo to make sure his rooms are well cleaned and prepared."

"I will tell him and Mrs. Mac, my lady."

Gertrude withdrew, closing the door quietly behind her. Outside, she sniffed and tossed her head. Oh, yes, my Lord Chase would be returning tomorrow from his trip to India. And there had been peace and quiet in the house for the last three months. Her ladyship had looked altogether different. A pity he had to come home, the servant reflected as she went downstairs. After tomorrow, there would be noise again, with his lordship strutting around, swearing at everybody in one of his vile tempers, or making my lady cry. No one knew better than Gertrude how often my lady shed tears behind closed doors; what a martyrdom her life was with his lordship.

Gertrude called the tweeny, Emily, sent her hurrying for stick and coal, and told Lucy to follow and light my lady's fire.

In her big double bed, Charlotte watched the two young maids clean the grate and set a fire ablaze. It was growing lighter outside. There was a rift in the clouds. It might be a nice day, after all. And it was certainly going to be a pleasant one for Charlotte. Fleur Marsh, her great friend, was in Town, and lunching with her, and tonight Charlotte was to accompany the Marshes to a Ball held by Lady Farringale, whose husband was in the Foreign Office. The Farringales had a particularly beautiful house in Piccadilly. Algernon Farringale was a nephew of old General Sir Harry Cawder, one-time guardian to Vivian; and although the two men had nothing much in common, the Chases were naturally on the Farringales' visiting list. So, in her husband's absence, Lady Chase had been invited to the Ball. Fleur's father, Sir Harry Roddney, had known the Farringales for years. So Charlotte was to have the rare pleasure of attending a dance with her dearest friends, and without the sinister shadow of Vivian to spoil it.

Nine years of marriage, following Eleanora's birth, had done nothing to improve matters for Charlotte. All the wealth, and the dazzling position which Charlotte now held, could not compensate her for the lack of love, of true companionship, with her husband. Deep down in her heart she was alone, and comfortless.

It was a loneliness that even motherhood had not been able to alleviate.

Two more children had been born to Charlotte, both

girls. With each birth, Charlotte had suffered agonizingly and received little from Vivian save reproaches, because she had not managed to give him a son. The joy of bringing a new babe into the world had been sadly quenched by the unnatural father's sour reception of each addition to his family. He was never done taunting and blaming Charlotte, as though it was her fault, alone.

Two years after Eleanora's birth, the second daughter arrived and was christened Beatrice, the name of Vivian's grandmother. A gap of three years, then Charlotte tried once more, dutifully, to give Lord Chase the son and heir he wanted. Once more, it was a tiny girl, and this time his lordship got into a drunken rage, stormed out of the house and did not return for three days. The poor unwanted infant was christened Victoria, after the Queen. Charlotte yearned over it, hoping to feed it and give it the love denied by its father, for it seemed particularly small and sickly. But she was not even allowed this pleasure. Little Victoria had been born in 1880. Vivian was bored at Clunes. He wished to go aboard the yacht he had recently purchased. He dragged Charlotte away with him, forcing her to wean the infant, and demanding, as he always did nowadays, her complete attention.

However, the third daughter lived and thrived. All three little girls grew up to be strong and healthy. Charlotte loved them devotedly. But she was not allowed to spend as much time in the nursery as she would have wished. She must ever accompany Vivian on his ceaseless round of social engagements. Even though he did not love her, he was proud of her beauty. It was a beauty that had matured with the years. Now, in her twenty-seventh year she was lovelier than she had been as a young girl. And because of her great intelligence and sympathetic nature, she was a favourite with many people who had little liking for young Lord Chase.

Vivian's character had not improved with age, and once he came into complete control of his father's fortune, he tried to dissipate it in the maddest fashion. He could not bear that any banquet or ball given by their friends should be on a more magnificent scale than those given at Clunes, or in his Eaton Square residence. In consequence, Charlotte was plunged into a ceaseless and wearisome effort to join Vivian in snobbish displays of grandeur. Always she must be at her tailors, her dressmakers, her *modiste* or in the hands of hairdressers and beauty experts. After the birth of each child, she must be massaged and groomed, so that her figure and her face should retain their perfection. Her jewels must outshine all others.

At Ascot and at the Opera, Lady Chase must be talked of as the most dazzling of the young matrons. Once Vivian settled down to his marriage, this had become an obsession with him. But for Charlotte it was a nightmare.

So time went on.

This morning, Charlotte looked back on the years and wondered if she could recognize herself as that shy, warm-hearted girl who once sat at the feet of Eleanor, Lady Chase, and lived at the Lodge in such innocent happiness.

Now she was no longer shy or diffident about fulfilling public engagements, or presiding over her grand household. She was complete mistress of herself and of any situation. She was known in London, and in the country, as a brilliant hostess, a provocative conversationalist. She had acquired polish and tact enough to please any husband. Outwardly she was what Vivian had made her. Even he, who did not love her, congratulated her when she achieved some new triumph. At least in this respect, he admitted that his mother had been right; Charlotte made him a dazzling wife.

But in private life, the pair meant nothing to each other. She suffered his embraces when he demanded them, but she could not love him. She knew that he had mistresses and said nothing. She presented a cool, haughty façade to the world in which he forced her to move. Under it, however, she remained the tender-hearted young girl who had once loved him, and whose love had been dragged through the mud.

As time went on, she felt an increasing resentment against the meaningless life she was forced to lead—its utter sterility. She longed to take her three little girls and flee from the gilded prison of the home Vivian provided. But she could not. She was left with her hopeless yearning for affection denied her, except when she was allowed in the nursery, or on the few occasions when she saw her friend, Fleur Marsh.

Vivian suddenly decided to go to India as the guest of a Maharajah who was at Oxford with him. It was a fascinating invitation to shoot tiger and stay in the Maharajah's magnificent palace. For once, he went away for a long time leaving Charlotte behind him. He also left strict instructions as to the way she was to conduct herself.

"You will adhere to your duties as a mother, madam, and no casting of languishing glances at gentlemen in my absence," he had said.

"Vivian, have I ever behaved in any way other than as a loyal wife?" she had begun, hotly protesting. He broke in, fixing her with his cold, stone-blue gaze, and with sneering lips.

"I seem to remember the day when you placed the address of a certain Member of Parliament in your fair bosom, my dear," he said. "Did you not languish in *that* direction—and as many years ago as when Eleanora was born?"

She had blushed crimson and turned away, her heart beating fast with indignation. But she could also attribute that burning colour to a slight sensation of guilt. Dear God, yes, she remembered *him*—his dear memory had remained with her throughout the years, although she had encountered him but once since their first meeting.

Chapter Twenty

She had met Dominic for the second time soon after she had discovered that she was to bear Vivian a third child. It was June. Beatrice was still only a baby. Charlotte had accompanied her husband to the Opera. He did not care for music, but he liked people to think he did, and besides, it was "the thing" to go to Covent Garden in the season. On such occasions Charlotte was happy and excited. She adored opera and particularly Wagner.

On this occasion they were hearing *Tristan und Isolda.* While Vivian yawned and nodded behind his wife, the young Lady Chase sat in their box, kid-gloved hands clasped around the posy she carried, rapt gaze on the stage, her ears ravished by the glorious sound of swelling orchestra, and the voices of tenor and prima donna. Now and again Charlotte's great eyes filled with tears. Her heart throbbed with deep emotion—the desire to love and be loved, to know the ecstasy that Wagner's great love-duet suggested, and of which she knew herself to be capable. But a little snore from behind her reminded her of the grossly physical young man whose wife she was, and who gave her only a repulsive passion as love's counterfeit.

She was then only twenty-two; the mother of two children and a new life just beginning in her womb. She was the unhappiest woman among this glittering crowd of bejewelled and befeathered ladies. Yet many glanced at her box and envied her the priceless emeralds around her throat and wrists. She was cynically aware of the fact. From time to time some infatuated girl also betrayed an envy of Charlotte because she was Vivian's wife. *If they only knew—!*

Suddenly she turned her head and looked across at the opposite box, conscious that someone was gazing in her direction. She saw a man, wearing formal "white tie and tails," and with a white carnation in his buttonhole, staring at her through his raised opera-glasses.

Just for a second she felt this to be insulting and drew back into the shadows. Then suddenly her heart leaped and she leaned forward again, this time raising her own small mother-of-pearl glasses. She focused them on the face of the man. At once she recognized him. It was Dominic Unwin. That same thin, brown face with the large expressive eyes, the air of distinction.

All the emotion already conjured up in her by the highly emotional opera overflowed now, as she saw Dominic Unwin again. She went burning red, then very pale. Lowering her glasses, she sat there, tingling from head to foot. The man in the opposite box continued to look at her.

His companion was a stranger to Charlotte. A woman of some beauty, with a touch of silver in her hair, and wearing a black lace dress with a bunch of violets. She was, perhaps, a year or two younger than Dominic who must, Charlotte ruminated, now be in his early forties. She was conscious of an altogether ridiculous pang of jealousy, a wild envy of the beautiful woman.

In any case, what should it matter to her? she asked herself, drearily. What was she to Dominic Unwin, or he to her?

They met, during the *entracte*, in the foyer. When at last she came face to face with him she wished passionately that this were not the Covent Garden Opera House, but the quiet library at Clunes, where she could talk to him alone, shut away from the rest of the world.

She wished, too, that she were not *enceinte*, did not feel so ill and tired, and wondered if she looked it. But her lips smiled brilliantly at him as he bent over her small hand and greeted her.

"This is an unexpected pleasure, Lady Chase," he murmured.

So close to him now she could see the marks of time on his face. A few more lines; a silvering of the dark, springing hair. But it suited him. He looked very handsome, she thought. His eyes smiled down at her with the old tremendous kindliness. It was as though the sweetness in those marvellous eyes poured over her soul's wounds and soothed them with a strange, magic balm.

"How are you, Unwin," put in Vivian, in a bored voice. "And where is old Cecil these days?"

"I believe he is at the moment in Paris," said Dominic, and thought that Charlotte's husband looked much older and had put on a lot of weight. The handsome, golden youth had become a flabby, unhealthy-looking man. Then Dominic introduced his companion.

"Mrs. Lyttleton, a cousin of Cecil's and mine, I think you may know her," he said. "Mercia, incidentally, is a harpist of no mean ability. We occasionally go to concerts or opera together. Her husband is often away in America on business."

Charlotte felt a relief almost more absurd than her jealousy when she first saw Dominic's companion. Of course, she knew now, she had heard Cecil Marchmond and Vivian speak of Mercia Lyttleton. A charming woman, a Marchmond by birth, and devoted to her husband, who was an American. Certainly there was not likely to be a sentimental attachment between her and Dominic.

Dominic stood by, inhaling his cigar, and listening to Charlotte talk with Mercia. When Charlotte had come down the staircase just now on her husband's arm, he had felt the tempo of his own heartbeats increase; a deep, real pleasure at the unexpected meeting. He had thought much about Charlotte Chase during the last five years. He had never been able to forget the pain in her wonderful eyes, the unspoken regret when she looked at him, and his own unusual emotion at leaving her. He knew, of course, that she had had another daughter; Cecil had called his attention to the fact. And going around London in the season, he often heard her name but had never once run into the Chases. He had, however, felt dismayed by the rumours that Vivian Chase was drinking too much and spending his fortune like water; also that everybody seemed to feel sorry for his young wife. It hurt Dominic profoundly to visualize the unhappiness of that young girl who must remain tied to an indifferent brute for the rest of her life.

Now he found her more beautiful than ever; older, a little graver, more self-possessed. She had, he thought, learned to cover up her personal feelings.

For one moment he managed to draw near enough to speak to her in an undertone.

"How is it with you?" he asked her, bending down his head.

Charlotte remembered for long afterwards the wild thrill that shot through her as he asked the question, the upward surge of joy she had never before experienced in her sad, disciplined life.

Her answer came in a low voice.

"I am tolerably well, thank you."

"And your children?"

She raised her eyes now that were glowing with pride in her motherhood, dispelling the intense sadness.

"Eleanora is beautiful and has grown darker, more like my mother-in-law. Beatrice is her father all over again, golden-haired, blue-eyed, and—"

"Difficult," Dominic might have broken in, but dared not. The word was left unsaid.

Once again, his heart ached for her. She read the message in his eyes and quickly raised her posy to her face, hiding it in case he should see that she recognized his pity and responded to it with all her soul.

After that, the conversation became general. Dominic moved away with Mrs. Lyttleton. Vivian and Charlotte strolled in the opposite direction, bowing and smiling to friends who recognized them. In a cold, sneering voice, Vivian said:

"So! Once again we have met your wonderful politician. Come, why are you not simpering with pleasure, my love?"

Her face crimsoned but she threw back her head proudly.

"I do not simper, Vivian. And there is no necessity for you to sneer at Mr. Unwin. He is publicly accepted as a coming man."

"Splendid," Vivian had sniggered, "I am impressed."

But on this cold November morning, as she sipped her morning tea and took up her newspaper again, she was able to luxuriate in the thought of Dominic Unwin and his triumphs. Only on occasions had she heard personal news of him through Cecil, whom she and Vivian met sometimes during the Season when they stayed in Eaton Square. She knew, for instance, that Dominic had remained unmarried. But she could and did, as now, re-reading the account of a brilliant speech he had made in the House, follow his career in the papers and rejoice that he was fulfilling his ambitions as a politician.

Charlotte felt a strange personal pride in his success. He had made a profound impact on her life. He remained enshrined in her heart as a being of infinite importance.

After breakfast the nurse brought the three little girls in to say "Good morning" to their Mama. The woman stood by, primly watching while her charges climbed on to the big bed, and Charlotte covered their fresh pink faces with kisses. Charlotte looked towards the nurse.

"You may leave them with me, Nanna."

"For only a short time then, my lady," said the woman. She had a cold, hard voice and a cold eye. "Eleanora has to start her lessons. Miss Tuft arrives at nine o'clock. Then I shall be taking the younger ones into the park."

"Why did you not bring them to me sooner?" Charlotte asked reproachfully.

"Eleanora was naughty; she would not eat her egg."

"I do not care for eggs, Mama, they make me feel sick," put in the little girl and nestled her cheek against her mother's hand.

Charlotte looked fondly into the big dark eyes that were so like her grandmother's.

"Then perhaps we could find you something that you do like," she said tenderly.

The nurse broke in.

"His lordship has particularly stated that he does not wish Eleanora to be spoiled. She is far too much of a 'madam' about her food."

Charlotte bit her lip. She felt Eleanora grip her fingers and hold them tightly as if for support. She longed to give it. If only she were allowed to bring up her daughters with tolerance, with humour, as she believed children should be reared. Not with this over-strict discipline, this starched attention to detail which the nurses enforced. But Charlotte dared not defy Vivian's wishes. She knew that he and Nanna had an understanding. Vivian saw to it that his daughters had all that money could buy. He spared no expense in their education. But the children seldom had what Charlotte called "real fun."

Little Victoria, of course, was still too young for lessons.

Towards her, the nurse softened on occasions; that was obvious. And she favoured Beatrice. But she did not like Eleanora and Charlotte knew it and disliked the woman in return. No, not even as a mother was Charlotte allowed happiness. When she had asked permission to dismiss the machine-like nurse, Vivian replied:

"Certainly not. She is most excellent and controls your daughters, which is what they need. Eleanora is very disobedient and far too fanciful."

This morning, looking at her eldest child, Charlotte brooded over the thought that Eleanora was not difficult, only misunderstood. She was imaginative and highly strung, and she was afraid of her father which annoyed him.

Charlotte's delicate fingers played with the little girl's hair. It had grown much darker and was cut with a fringe. She had a solemn beauty. She looked up at her mother beseechingly:

"Could I not stay with you for a treat, instead of going to Miss Tuft this morning, Mama?"

"It would be nice, my darling," murmured Charlotte.

Immediately the nurse intervened.

"His lordship returns tomorrow and he will ask Eleanora to repeat her lessons and show some progress."

"That is so," said Charlotte reluctantly.

Eleanora suddenly burst into tears.

"Oh, Mama, if only Papa were not coming back and I could stay alone with you, my own dear Mama!" she sobbed.

Beatrice, who was standing by the dressing table examining her mother's tortoiseshell and gold toilet set, joined in:

"You are a nasty horrid thing not to want Papa back. *I* want him."

"I want him," echoed Victoria, who sat on top of Charlotte's bed cuddling a huge flaxen-haired doll rather like herself.

Charlotte was silent. She hugged the weeping Eleanora with a sad passion, and looked over her head at the nurse. The woman was, she thought, as cold and hard as her starched white apron and cap, her stiff collar and cuffs, her voluminous blue linen skirts. Charlotte fancied that she dropped her eyes and smiled in a secret, malevolent way.

"I shall have to tell his lordship how Eleanora feels," she said.

Fiercely protective, Charlotte exclaimed:

"Nothing of the kind, Nanna. Eleanora meant no harm. She meant only that she wishes to see a little more of me. Is it not natural?"

The nurse continued to smile in her frozen fashion.

"Oh yes, my lady, but unnatural that she should not wish her dear, kind Papa to come home. Maybe she has heard a grown-up express this same sentiment. I must question her."

Charlotte's throat and face flamed.

Cruel, wicked woman. What was she insinuating? Was she going to whisper that she, Lady Chase, had tried to influence her small daughter against Vivian?

A feeling of confidence which she did not always have when Vivian was in the house made Charlotte defy the nurse this morning.

"Take Beatrice and Victoria back to the nursery. I will speak to Eleanora alone," she said.

The woman pursed her lips.

"Miss Tuft will be here, my lady."

"You heard my order!" exclaimed Charlotte.

The nurse hesitated, then took the two young children by the hand and led them out of their mother's bedroom.

Left alone with her eldest and dearest child, Charlotte hugged and kissed her.

"Do not cry, my love, you shall stay with me a moment longer. Look—on my table by the window is a box of bonbons. Untie the ribbon and choose one for yourself and take two for your sisters."

But Eleanora clung to her.

"I do not wish for chocolates, Mama. I wish to stay with you."

"Do you love your Mama so much?" questioned Charlotte.

"Oh, very much indeed," said the little girl, nodding, and she looked with adoration at her pretty young mother and touched one of the long silken curls escaping from the little linen embroidered cap which Charlotte wore in bed. Then she added with a sigh:

"But Nanna says that it is wicked to adore anybody except God."

"This is so, my darling," said Charlotte with difficulty.

"And Nanna says I must love Papa even more than you, Mama."

Charlotte had a tart reply ready on her lips but restrained it, colouring angrily. She had to force herself to say:

"Of course, you should love your Papa deeply, of course, darling."

"But he does not like me as much as he likes Beatrice and Vicky. And he is cruel to you."

Now Charlotte went quite white.

"Hush, Eleanora. You must not say such things. Who put such an idea into your head?"

"I heard it," said Eleanora, "and I know, for I have seen you crying and heard Papa's voice shouting at you."

Charlotte shut her eyes. She opened them again and tried to smile, even to laugh.

"My little darling has too much imagination. She speaks a lot of nonsense."

"Oh, *Mama*, can we not go away together, you and I?"

Charlotte could barely find words now, for her eyelids were smarting. How deeply she would love to go away with little Eleanora, the one being in the house who gave her true affection and sympathy.

Charlotte was forced now to send the poor child along to the schoolroom where Miss Tuft awaited her. If she did not, Eleanora would be the one to suffer. For, of course, that heartless nurse would tell tales to his lordship, and receive his praise and thanks (and, no doubt, a sovereign) for her pains.

After the little girl had gone, Charlotte lay still, no longer feeling as bright as she had done earlier. Not even Dominic's photo or the account of him in the paper could console her. Nor, really, had she much heart left for the Farringale Ball tonight, even though she would be with her best friends. She had a sinking sensation that accompanied the knowledge that tomorrow Vivian would be back. What kind of reunion would it be? she wondered. Certainly not an agreeable one. He would not come as a friend, or as a lover, anxious to be once more at the side of a beloved wife. His last letter had merely contained a list of the things he wished done for him in London; the appointments she was to make for him. She knew that once he was back, she would never have another moment to herself.

Charlotte thought of little Eleanora who wanted so much for her mama to take her away.

"Oh, God, if only I could," thought Charlotte, "If only I *could*—never to return!"

She turned her face to the pillow. But her eyes were dry. She had wept too long and too often. It was as though there were no more tears to shed.

Chapter Twenty-one

The Farringale Ball opened. Lady Farringale, a handsome woman of forty-five, had finished receiving her guests. She stood at the foot of the famous carved rosewood staircase, talking a moment to her tall, bearded husband.

Dominic Unwin was the last guest to arrive. He hastened into the hall, smoothing back his hair, and bowed over his hostess's hand. He murmured an apology.

Lady Farringale smiled graciously and begged him not to feel disturbed.

"We all know how hard you work, Mr. Unwin, and that the House has been sitting late," she said. "The rest of your party are, I think, already here. Cecil certainly is. He, as you know, is an indefatigable dancer and a great stand-by for any hostess."

Lord Farringale now said a few words to the late arrival. He, too, had a kindly smile for the tall, dark politician who had recently distinguished himself on so many occasions.

Dominic was here tonight because the Farringales were distantly related to the Englesbys and at this precise moment there were rumours of an attachment between the young Earl of Marchmond and Lydia, the Farringales' youngest daughter. But it had not entered Dominic's head that tonight would mark his third and most important meeting with the one woman in England who held the slightest interest for him.

He was waltzing with his hostess, threading a way in and out of the crowded ballroom in which there were many beautiful women when he suddenly saw *her*. Charlotte's gaze met Dominic's fully. It was as though an electric shock passed through him. He could feel the blood coursing more quickly through his whole body. Mechanically, he continued to guide Lady Farringale, but his gaze focused on that vision of loveliness in the circle of Cecil's arms.

Charlotte wore a dress of pearl grey gauzy material looped at the back into a high bustle and decorated with diamond drops, which also festooned the embroidered edge of her low *décolletage*. Her hair fell in graceful chestnut curls caught behind her neck. She wore a sparkling diamond tiara. As she came closer to him now, guided by Cecil, who had seen his brother, Dominic noted how well Charlotte was looking tonight. Her lips were actually parted in a happy smile which he had never before seen on that usually sad mouth. This was no child now, but a matron and a mother, he reflected.

He had seen the announcement of her third daughter. It had given him a pang; he knew not why. It was, however, a pang that he had swiftly suppressed, just as he had always tried to drive away from him the very memory of Charlotte Chase. He had no right to the sentiments it evoked. Only when he was very tired and alone, he allowed that image to return—first to bewitch—then to frustrate and to sadden him. He knew that he could have no part in her life, nor she in his. But as soon as she entered his world again, as she had done at the Opera four years ago, he became aware once more that she had a vital message for him, a strong subtle, irresistible fascination.

Lady Farringale had seen the approaching pair. She said to Dominic:

"Here comes Cecil with Lady Chase. Do you know her?"

"Yes, we have met."

"She is charming and unusually lovely," said Lady Farringale, and added in a quick, low note, "but I cannot abide her husband. I was delighted when the Peveril Marshes said that they would bring her alone. Chase is on his way home from India."

Dominic felt a surge of excitement. So Vivian had been abroad, and had not yet come home. He could well echo his hostess's words. How little was *he*, indeed, able to "abide" Lord Chase.

The music stopped. The dancers began to saunter through the ballroom, either to sit out in one of the conservatories, stroll through the portrait gallery, or seek refreshment in the supper room.

Face to face with Charlotte, Dominic spoke calmly:

"How do you do, Lady Chase? I trust I find you very well."

"Very well," she echoed, and gave him a hand, gloved in white kid, which he pressed almost imperceptibly. But as his eyes looked deeply down into hers she felt the colour drain from her face. She knew an intense emotion at seeing him again. It was a delight she had not expected. She reproached herself because she felt so deeply about him. She must not do so—she who was a wife, mother to three little girls. But it was truly wonderful to look up at that dark, strong face again and hear the rich, low voice which had haunted her dreams throughout the years.

Cecil was talking animatedly with Lady Farringale. Inevitably, Dominic offered Charlotte his arm. Her heart beat quite crazily as she walked with him across the polished dance floor towards one of the conservatories at the back of the house.

The violins were beginning to play again; a throbbing waltz. The big crystal chandelier gleamed with hundreds of candles. The great house, full of *objets d'art*, was warm with firelight, filled with a dazzling company of some of the most distinguished men and beautifully gowned women in England. But as Dominic Unwin and Charlotte Chase moved together into a quiet, dimly-lit conservatory which was perfumed with flowers and moist with green exotic plants, they had eyes and ears only for each other.

"Are you sure you do not wish to dance?" he asked her.

"Sure," she said, seating herself on one of the crimson plush sofas. Her eyes looked up at him with brilliance and feeling. "I would prefer to talk to you, Mr. Unwin."

"Was it not to be 'Dominic'?" he smiled down into those lovely eyes that innocently forced him to betray a life-time of self-control.

"Dominic," she repeated, with a rise of colour that made her look like a young girl again—it was difficult, he thought, to believe her any older than when they had met last time, at the Opera.

"Tell me what these years have done for you, Charlotte," he said. "Have they been kind?"

Her lids drooped. She toyed with the carved ivory handle of an exquisite painted fan which she carried.

"Let us talk of you, and your work," she parried.

"Oh, I am tired of myself."

"But you have done great things. I read of you frequently. I saw your photograph in *The Times* only yesterday. They speak of you as a politician who, given the opportunity, could do much for our Queen and country," she said.

He was flattered. His own colour rose a trifle. But he laughed.

"Not so."

"But I hear it from all sides," she insisted. "You work hard and long. I would I could hear you speak in the House. They say you are becoming such an orator that you are a shining light in your Party."

"You are more than kind to me," he murmured, bowing low.

She looked up at the strong, dark face.

"You still live in Albany?"

"Still, except when I go abroad for holidays. My adoptive mother, the Marchioness, has been very ill, as perhaps you have heard. I spent last summer at Englesby with her."

"She is better, I hope."

"But still a very sick woman, alas."

"I grieve for you. I know how attached you and Cecil both are to her. Incidentally, Vivian and I have not seen much of Cecil these last few years."

"Oh, he is here, there and everywhere. He does not settle down as our parents would wish."

"He has neither the brain-power nor the character of his elder brother," smiled Charlotte.

"You are bent on flattering me," said Dominic. He seated himself at her side, one arm resting on the back of the sofa, while his blue strange eyes examined her critically. She knew it and enjoyed being the focus of his criticism.

They discussed their families; she told him of her three little daughters. He listened, interested, but saddened as he had been at their former meeting, by the sure instinct that she had found neither the peace nor happiness she needed to make her a contented woman. She laughed; she talked brilliantly; she looked bewitching. But the shadow of bitterness, of a desperate distaste for the life she led, weighed her down. He was aware of it. She talked only briefly of her husband. Dominic knew of course that Vivian was the real cause of her unhappiness. But her whole face changed and her eyes sparkled as she described her small daughters, especially the eldest.

"She resembles you?" murmured Dominic.

"Her grandmother, the late Lady Chase."

"And the other two?"

"Beatrice is exactly like her father. Little Victoria too."

Silence fell between them then. The constraint was lifted only when Charlotte made an effort to talk about him again rather than about her affairs.

"How do you view our present political position, Dominic?"

"Has the young scholar grown into a thinking and erudite woman who likes to probe into subjects more usually reserved for men?" he asked, smiling.

"I follow my country's politics, I admit—" she said, but she could not add that it was mainly on account of *his* participation in them.

He told her a little of his present work, his hopes and fears.

"It is a bad business. There have been many serious riots this year."

"What is the cure for such festering sores, Dominic?"

"I hesitate to say," was Dominic's answer, his brows knitted. "Like my Leader, I sympathize deeply with the poor and oppressed. I would like to see us adopt a policy that would extend some kind of national service to the wretched people."

Her heart kindled.

"I agree. I am distressed to see and hear of those who have to beg a crust of bread for their starving families, while women like myself are decked with such as this—" she touched the diamond collar about her throat, then the tiara that scintillated in the chestnut masses of her high-piled hair.

Dominic was charmed by her words and the movement of her long slim fingers. He smiled tolerantly.

"Nay—you have a right to your jewels—they become you. And the problems of the starving unemployed in our country cannot, alas, be solved by the sale of a handful of diamonds—even were you to give your trinkets to the poor and needy."

"Nevertheless, I often feel undeserving of my position."

"It is rare to meet a woman who troubles to philosophize, to probe under the surface, Charlotte."

"I spend a great deal of time in thinking, Dominic."

"You always did—as a child. Although you are still a child to me," he smiled.

"With children of my own," she smiled back and sighed.

"Whatever has befallen you, it has left you curiously untouched," he said.

Now a fresh constraint fell upon them. In silence they regarded one another. Charlotte felt as though a great tidal wave of feeling surged across her very soul and drowned her, rending her unconscious of all human beings on earth save this one who sat at her side. His eyes held remarkable fire, she thought. All England knew of that fire in Dominic Unwin. The House had felt the heat of it—the magnetism of his personality as well as the mastery of his subjects. He possessed logic, and a shrewd common sense which had gained him the respect of his fellow Members. Yet he could be pungent, bitter, even merciless in his attack upon those who openly opposed his ideas, his idealism.

Charlotte found herself wondering what it would have been like to have loved and been loved by such a man; to be his wife, mother of his children. The sudden comparison with Vivian was so much to the detriment of the man to whom she was, in fact, joined by the bonds of matrimony, that Charlotte felt a spiritual sickness settle upon her. She turned pale and talked no more.

He felt her change of mood. He tried to recapture the light spirit of friendliness and exchange more views with her but failed. He, too, was conscious of a wild regret—that Charlotte must forever remain forbidden to him as a woman to be wooed and won. For the first time since his own dear Dorothea had died and left him alone and unconsolable, he knew the urgent need of a woman's affection; of the home and family which he had long since replaced by the sterner demands of a politician's career. But it was all to no purpose. Dominic told himself to return speedily to a sphere in which Charlotte Chase did not move—could not touch his sentiments.

"Come, you think too much of dull and weighty matters," he said with a gaiety he was far from feeling. "Let us return to the ballroom. I will do my best to show you that I *can* dance, after all. Will you grant me the opportunity?"

She gained her feet, trying to smile.

"If you wish," she said.

He did not wish it; he would rather have stayed here alone with her and delved further into her quick, delicate mind; listened to her, watched the varying expressions across her beautiful, mobile face. But he no longer trusted himself and that was a knowledge that frightened the man who prided himself on being afraid of nothing.

As they emerged from the quiet perfumed conservatory into the noise and crowd of the great ballroom, he put an arm round Charlotte and with a faint pressure of his hand against the small waist, guided her into the circle of waltzers. Then he knew a thrill that must essentially be dangerous, because it was so vastly exciting.

She experienced the same wild thrill, supported by his arm and with one of his hands clasping hers.

She looked up at him as they danced. She had never known a greater urgency. Neither could Dominic tear his fascinated glance from hers. They might have been alone in that crowd of dancers. She seemed to him without shallow coquetry, or false pride; human enough to be incapable of withholding from him, even if she wished, the fact that she was as greatly drawn to him as he to her.

He yielded to a passionate impulse to allow himself an increase of the pressure of his fingers upon hers. A long look passed between them, enriching a moment that was swiftly lost. They went on dancing sedately as dignity and decorum demanded. When the waltz ended, Charlotte was trembling. Dominic passed a cambric handkerchief over a forehead that had grown moist.

They moved away from the ballroom. As they went, a tall, fair, florid-looking man wearing impeccable evening dress, made his way through the crowd and approached them. Dominic stared, then his muscles tightened. He at once recognized Vivian Chase, despite the amount of fat he had put on, and the innovation of long, fair curled moustaches and side-whiskers which were fashionable.

"Lord Chase!" he exclaimed.

Charlotte stood still. Dominic saw every drop of blood drain from her cheeks. Obviously, Vivian's appearance was a complete surprise to her, and a disagreeable one. Her widened gaze turned from Vivian back to Dominic. He read the touch of fear as well as anguish in that glance, a glance that was almost an appeal for help, help which he could not give and which she must not ask.

Vivian stood before them. He gave an unpleasant smile as he greeted Dominic.

"Good evening, Unwin. I did not think to find our busy Member of Parliament at a dance," he said, with a sarcasm that Dominic found irritating, but he bowed courteously.

"How are you, Lord Chase? I thought you were on your voyage home from India."

"Yes, how come you to be home, Vivian?" put in Charlotte, trying to speak lightly, although her whole heart had sunk at the unexpected sight of her husband.

"We docked early this morning," he said. "I found I could get back to London this evening instead of tomorrow. I was told that you were at the Farringale Ball, my dear, so I followed on. You are, I am sure, pleased to include my name in your dance-programme, are you not?"

His voice retained its biting, sarcastic edge. His cold blue eyes ran up and down Charlotte's beautiful form, taking in every detail, from her tiara to the tips of her small, embroidered shoes.

"Your dress is charming," he added and crooked his arm. As she placed her gloved hand through it, Dominic intercepted the crushing look of misery in her eyes. It made him feel desperately sad for her. But he was impotent to afford her the slightest sympathy. He only knew that Charlotte hated the man who was her husband and the father of her children, and the fact was singularly distressing to him. Poor lovely, warm-hearted young thing; she deserved a better fate than this.

Vivian spoke again, stroking his moustache, narrowing his gaze as he turned it on Dominic.

"Do you not pity me, Unwin? Coming home unexpectedly to find, instead of a sorrowing wife, a truant who wears my diamonds and dances blithely with her admirers in my absence?"

"Really, Viv—" began Charlotte.

Dominic, flushing angrily, broke in:

"I see no cause to pity you, Lord Chase. You have a very beautiful and gracious wife and an engaging family."

"Do you find Charlotte gracious?" drawled Vivian. "You are to be congratulated. I cannot say that I ever see that side of her. She has only surly looks for me."

"Vivian!" protested Charlotte again.

Scarlet with shame, she did not meet Dominic's gaze now. This was too sudden a metamorphosis—the arrival of Vivian to spoil her wonderful evening, and in one of his unpleasant moods. He was not drunk, but obviously in a bad temper. She could guess that he was annoyed because he had reached home to find her out, enjoying herself. He begrudged her any pleasures which he did not himself arrange.

Poor Charlotte was all too soon made aware that Vivian's absence from her while he was in India had done nothing to improve their relationship. True, she expected little from him nowadays; yet one sign of genuine emotion, one ray of warmth might have softened her towards him, so starved was she of affection. But she felt that her very soul was being murdered by his insistent efforts to master her.

She was anxious to get him away from Dominic before he could say anything further to humiliate her and embarrass the politician.

"Come, Vivian," she said lightly. "Let us go through to the supper room. I feel sure you would like some refreshment."

The base cruelty that was never long absent in Vivian Chase made him take her hand now and press it to his lips with a kiss of simulated passion, while his eyes leered over those delicate gloved fingers at the other man. Dominic's face was rigidly set.

"How thoughtful of you, my love," said Vivian in an oily voice. "Is it not delightful for me to be granted one glimpse of the graciousness you just mentioned, Mr. Unwin?"

Dominic could not bring himself to reply. His hands locked behind his back. Never before had he felt a more impassioned dislike of any human being than for Charlotte's husband.

Great heavens, he thought, what an appalling character! And what a nightmare life must be for the young and tender-hearted woman married to him. He could see clearly now how she suffered. The light, the laughter, the joy of living, which had made her look so beautiful to-night, had been blighted for her by Vivian's return. He pitied and loved her, both, as he watched her walk away on Vivian's arm. The diamonds sparkled on her hair. She moved with grace and distinction. Yet every line of that beautiful form suggested pain to him, pain and the rigid necessity to act her part and conceal her feelings.

It would have been better, Dominic Unwin thought, that they had never met and talked again, never experienced the mutual ecstasy of that dance. For, though held apart from him at arm's length as a conventional waltz demanded, his hand had clasped her fingers and touched her waist; and he had breathed in the fragrance of her glorious hair, felt her silent trembling response to his admiration.

This is madness, he thought as he firmly strode through the hall to ask for his hat and cloak. *I must put her out of my mind. She is married to a monster but she has her children. Her life is set apart from mine. My love can do nothing but hurt her.*

That was the hardest knowledge of all for Dominic to bear—that in her tenderness, her grace, her vibrant need of love and warmth she was *doomed.*

Chapter Twenty-two

Dominic did not notice where he was going and brushed into a couple who were coming towards him. He stopped to utter his profound apologies.

He was almost too overwrought to see clearly, but the lady to whom he apologized seemed interested in him.

"It is Mr. Unwin, is it not?" she asked. "I think we met at the Chases' ball in Hertfordshire, some years ago. Mr. Unwin, this is my husband, Peveril Marsh."

Dominic bowed, and forcing a smile, murmured the conventional words expected of him.

Then suddenly he became conscious of interest awakening in him; a queer almost psychic intimation that he knew Fleur Marsh very well. With something of a shock he looked down into her large eyes, eyes as deeply blue as his own, and full of ineffable sweetness. Fleur Marsh! Yes, he had heard Charlotte Chase speak of her as her dearest friend.

Mrs. Marsh was growing old. Her delicate face was deeply lined. Hair, which had once been golden red, fell in silver curls on either side of her lovely face. She wore a black satin ball gown with white camellias on the *corsage* and a black Mantilla over her head. Like the charming-looking man beside her, she stooped a little, leaning on a silver and ebony stick. For the last five years Fleur had shared with her famous painter-husband this painful scourge of rheumatism that was gradually crippling them both.

Dominic knew of Mr. Marsh's work. He particularly admired, and had frequently gone to see, the portrait Peveril had painted of Charlotte, which had been hung in the Academy before the birth of her second daughter.

But it was more than these things which captured

Dominic's attention now. It was the extraordinary feeling that he had known Mrs. Marsh not for a year or two, but all his life.

What *was* it? he asked himself, mystified; and continued to stare at the beautiful old lady. Then he pulled himself together.

"I—I am just on my way home. It has been a wonderful party, has it not? May I bid you 'good night,' Mrs. Marsh, and you, sir," Dominic bowed to the old painter.

"Wait—" began Fleur Marsh in a strange voice.

But Dominic had gone and was lost to sight among the other guests who thronged the hall. Peveril Marsh took his wife's hand. He looked anxiously at her.

"What is it, my dearest? Are you ill?"

She passed a hand over her forehead.

"No, no. It is just that—"

"Just what?" he asked.

She was usually so calm; he had not seen her as *emotionée* as this for many years.

She shook her head as a swimmer does, who emerges suddenly from deep water in which he has been drowning.

"I don't know what came over me just now, Peveril; but Dominic Unwin has such an extraordinary face and compelling personality, and when he looked down at me I felt—"

"Felt what, my love?"

"That I knew him, had always known him well."

"He is Mr. Unwin who has lately impressed the House by so many of his fine speeches. And he is a friend of Charlotte's, too, is he not?"

"More than that, perhaps," said Fleur in a low voice. "For many years he has been her *beau ideal.* But what can account for my strange sensation that Mr. Unwin and I have met? Was it perhaps in another life?"

The portrait painter pressed his wife's fragile hand fondly and smiled.

"It is just a fancy of yours, my darling."

"Of course, I realize the fascination he must have for Charlotte," Fleur said almost inaudibly. "His gaze seems to go straight through one."

"Am I to lose my lovely wife even now that she is an old lady?" asked Peveril on a gay note.

"How can you say such a thing?" she exclaimed, her cheeks pink. "No, Peveril, it is something inexplicable that moved me to the depths of my being. Who *is* Dominic Unwin?"

"Related to the Englesbys, is he not?"

"Yes, now it returns to me," nodded Fleur. "He was adopted by the Marquess and was given one of the family names of the Marcioness."

"Really, my dear, you are quite struck by the handsome politician who so unceremoniously bumped into us," smiled Peveril.

Mrs. Marsh did not return his smile. She seemed in truth to be as her husband suggested—quite "struck."

She could not stop thinking about Dominic Unwin. His memory remained with her, worrying her strangely, for a long time.

But now she was given something else to think about, for she saw Charlotte hurrying towards her, looking pale and upset.

"I will not be going back with you, dearest Fleur," the girl said as she reached her friend. "Vivian returned twenty-four hours before expected. He has only just arrived, but he wishes to take me back to Eaton Square immediately. I am going to fetch my cloak."

Fleur looked with pity at the young woman whose private unhappiness was all too well known to her.

"I am sorry, my dear," she said, "can we not persuade Vivian to let you remain longer?"

Charlotte gave a twisted smile.

"No. He has already picked a quarrel with me and is in a rage."

"But why?"

"Because he found me dancing with Dominic Unwin," said Charlotte in a low voice.

Mrs. Marsh bit her lip.

"There can be no reason why you should not dance with Mr. Unwin," she murmured.

"Vivian is wildly jealous, Fleur," said Charlotte in a voice intended for her friend's ear alone.

Mr. Marsh moved discreetly away and left the two women alone.

"For what reason?" asked Fleur.

"Oh, do not ask. I do not understand Vivian, save that he is the same tonight, even after our long separation, as he has been since the day we married—happy only when tormenting me. The fact that I admire Dominic is enough to account for his spiteful attitude."

"I saw and spoke to Mr. Unwin just now," said Mrs. Marsh slowly.

"Oh, Fleur, is he not wonderful?" burst out Charlotte, and then turned away, her face working and added: *"I wish I were dead.* Oh, Fleur, I wish that my heart had stopped beating there, in the ballroom tonight, while he danced with me. I am so unhappy!"

The tears sprang to Mrs. Marsh's eyes.

"Would God I could help you, Charlotte. Sometimes I think Lord Chase is out of his mind."

"I have often thought that," said Charlotte.

She drove home with Vivian, listening to the clip-clop of the horses' hooves as they moved along Piccadilly and she looked out at the quiet dark streets. It was very cold at this midnight hour. She shivered, but not only with the raw cold; with exhaustion. This was the effect that Vivian always had upon her—to tear her nerves to pieces, to wear her out. She was not yet thirty but she felt that if she lived much longer with Vivian she would soon be an old spent woman.

She dare not even allow herself the comfort of remembering Dominic's face, and the touch of his hand. In one respect she deserved condemnation from her husband—in that she loved Dominic Unwin. But it was a love as pure and innocent as it was hopeless.

A yawning footman let them into their house. Volpo appeared out of the shadows to greet his master and inform him that he had unpacked the luggage, and that all was ready in his lordship's rooms.

"Excellent," said Vivian. "You need wait up for me no longer, my good Volpo."

"Thank you, my lord. Good night, my lord. Good night, my lady," said Volpo and cast a derisive look at Lady Chase out of the corners of his eyes. She moved up the staircase, her face set into rigid lines. It was indeed the end of freedom—coming back here to find not only Vivian in control but the hated valet back again. How she hated the slimy Portuguese spy!

Vivian followed his wife into their bedroom and told her to dismiss Gertrude who was also waiting up. The maid left the room with a pitying glance at her mistress. Charlotte caught the expression and writhed. It was so humiliating being the object of pity to her own servants.

As she sat down in front of her dressing table, Vivian came up behind her, picked up the diamond ear-rings which she had just taken from her ears and tossed them on the palm of his hand. He leered at her reflection in the mirror.

"You wear my jewels with stunning effect, my dear, and your figure is still magnificent, despite your child-bearing. But I would like to remind you that your smile should be reserved for your husband. I am no fool. I watched while you waltzed with Unwin. I saw how you looked at him."

She shut her eyes.

"Did you?"

"Yes I did!" Vivian's voice rose angrily, "and I will not have it. If I see you look at another man like that I will thrash you *and* the man you favour. *Do you hear me?*"

She turned and gave him a long bitter look from her weary eyes.

Every drop of blood in her body cried out against the wrongs, the injustice of her marriage. In hopeless misery she sat listening to Vivian's taunts and reproaches and then, worse—his demands for passion. But there came a sudden interruption—a repeated knock on the door which sent Vivian, in a violent temper, to unlock it. He shouted:

"Who is it? What the devil do you want?"

Charlotte drew a dressing gown over her shoulders. She was trembling from head to foot. Vivian flung open the door. The children's nurse stood there, her hair in curl papers, her face less stony and self-confident than usual.

"Oh, I beg your pardon, my lord—my lady," she stammered.

"Well, what is it, woman?" demanded Vivian, his puffy face crimson.

"It's Eleanora—" began the nurse.

Charlotte sprang to her feet.

"What's the matter with Eleanora?"

The nurse gave her a slightly resentful look.

"She was not well earlier in the day. I feared she was sickening for something, and sure enough now she has a high temperature and is delirious. I think we should send for the doctor."

"Oh, heavens!" cried Charlotte; "I must go to her at once."

But Vivian's hand shot out and gripped Charlotte's wrist, detaining her.

"Wait," he turned to the nurse. "What is wrong with the child? Is it not some minor ailment that can soon be put right?"

"I think it more serious, your lordship. I cannot quieten her. She keeps calling for her Mama," the woman added in a sulky tone.

Charlotte tried to get away from Vivian's steely fingers.

"Let me go to her, Vivian."

His eyes narrowed. That cruel look which she knew so well came into his eyes.

"No," he said, "you are far too emotional, my dear. If Eleanora is ill she will need a calming influence or perhaps a little discipline from her Papa. *I* will go to her."

"She calls for *me*, Nanna said so."

"Nevertheless, you will do as I say and stay here," said Vivian in a low venomous voice.

"I am sure his lordship would be of help, and I suggest we send for the doctor at once," put in the nurse. She then hastened away, but not before Charlotte had seen the satisfied smile that curved her lips.

"Let me go to Eleanora, please Vivian, *please*."

"When I say so and not before," said Vivian. He went out, shutting the door noisily behind him.

For a moment, Charlotte stood breathing fast, her eyes smarting with tears of frustration. This was the final cruelty. Vivian knew exactly what pain he was inflicting upon her by keeping her from her best loved child when she was ill.

In despair, Charlotte sat down on the edge of the bed and waited for her husband to come back. At least he would tell her how the child fared.

He did not come for a long time. Then, after a long wait, she heard footsteps and voices. Later, Charlotte gathered up enough courage to open the door and go out into the corridor. If Vivian had sent for a physician, it must mean that Eleanora was very ill indeed.

Charlotte caught sight of her husband and the doctor as they were coming out of Eleanora's night-nursery. Vivian looked at his wife in a disagreeable way.

"Pray, return to your bedroom, madam," he said. "Dr. Featherstone agrees with me that in these cases a sick child is better with her nurse."

Charlotte, her face drained of colour, caught at the doctor's arm:

"I must go to her. She has been calling for me, Dr. Featherstone. How is she? What is wrong?"

The doctor coughed and glanced somewhat uneasily at Lady Chase. The poor thing looked distraught. Lord Chase had whispered to him when he arrived that she was hysterical and had to be treated firmly, especially where the children were concerned. He said:

"I am not certain, Lady Chase, but I rather think our little patient has typhoid."

"Typhoid!" repeated Charlotte in a shocked voice. "But that is serious."

"It can be, but with care and good nursing I am sure that we will get her well again."

"Dr. Featherstone is sending a day and a night nurse at once, my dear," put in Vivian. "Eleanora will, of course, have to be segregated from the others. In fact, she is to be left here in the care of two hospital nurses. I will remain a day or two to make sure that all is well. You must take Beatrice and Victoria down to Clunes first thing in the morning and keep them out of the way."

"An excellent plan," said Dr. Featherstone.

But after the physician had gone, Charlotte turned to Vivian, the tears running down her face.

"It is her Mama whom Eleanora needs now that she is ill," she pleaded. "You go with the others to Clunes. Permit me to stay here."

"That would be very agreeable for you, my dear, I am sure. You would be able to see your charming politician and—"

"Vivian, you have no right to suggest any such thing!" she broke in with indignation. "I want only to be with my poor little girl; typhoid can be most serious for one of such tender years."

"Precisely. That is why Eleanora is to be left in the hands of expert nurses. You will do as you are told, madam, and leave London with your other children directly after breakfast."

"But if Ellie asks for me—" began Charlotte, choking.

"If the doctor thinks it necessary, you can be sent for. Meanwhile I do not wish you to expose yourself to the infection."

She gave him a long look of misery and hatred combined.

"If I ask nothing of you ever again, I ask now to be allowed to stay with Eleanora," she sobbed.

But she was defeated. He would not humour her and she knew it. All thoughts of Dominic Unwin were wrenched from her in this new cruel crisis. She was beyond fighting when Vivian's mood swung from anger to desire and dragged her into his arms. Her agony of mind was such that her reason almost forsook her. She lay in that loathed embrace in a state of semi-consciousness.

When morning came, Eleanora was already shut away from Charlotte in the care of the hospital nurses and Vivian saw to it that she did not go near the child's room. Anguished, Charlotte left the house with Nanna and the two younger children. She was driven in the brougham through the bleak foggy London streets towards the station. Away from her sick child. Away from Dominic Unwin. From everything, everybody, poor Charlotte told herself, that she cared for, or who cared for her.

Chapter Twenty-three

Charlotte did not see her beloved child again until Christmas Eve.

For five weeks, the unhappy mother ate her heart out in the country house to which she had been literally banished. For five weeks little Eleanora was seriously ill; too ill, in fact, to know or care who sat at her bedside. Dr. Featherstone's diagnosis of the typhoid turned out to be incorrect. Eleanora had developed some strange fever with symptoms understood by none of the specialists called in by Lord Chase. They hummed and hawed. They ordered various treatments and medicines. Perhaps through luck rather than through their ministrations the little girl did not die. She suffered aches and pains and was often in a delirium, during which she called for her mother; but the sadist who was her father, was determined that Charlotte's longing to answer those calls was not to be appeased. He had scene after scene with her, each resulting in her final defeat. It was her duty, he maintained, to stay at Clunes with Beatrice and little Victoria. He would not have her, or the younger children, exposed to whatever infection it was that had attacked Eleanora.

Fortunately for the little invalid, the two hospital nurses in charge of her in the London house were kindly, motherly women who lavished tender care upon her. They found Lord Chase charming and generous, and never had he been more amiable or tolerant with his eldest daughter than while she lay in her sick-bed. He seemed to one and all a devoted father. It was Charlotte whom the nurses criticized. It was hinted by his lordship that my lady was too afraid of infection to come near the place. They thought her a selfish cowardly young woman and pitied the handsome husband.

Vivian, meanwhile, enjoyed himself in London and finally joined his wretched wife and added to her misery by his overbearing presence in the home; his continued taunts because she could not seem to bear him a son. She had conceived as a result of that unhappy night of reunion when he returned from India. She lost much of her sparkling beauty and grew pale and listless with scarcely any spirit left with which to fight her husband.

When appearances forced Vivian to bring Eleanora home, that cold afternoon on Christmas Eve, he continued his persecution of the unhappy mother and the little girl.

"Eleanora is still not well and must be kept quiet. No disruption of nursery rules. Nanna will be in charge," Lord Chase announced the moment he came into the house, carrying his eldest daughter in his arms.

Charlotte, who had been awaiting this moment, wild with excitement and relief, held out her arms to Eleanora, her eyes shining at the sight of the beloved little face, the sight of which had been denied her for so many weary weeks.

"Oh, my darling, welcome home!" she exclaimed.

"Mama! Dearest Mama!" cried Eleanora and struggled to get down and go to her mother.

Vivian called to the nurse who came running down the stairs.

"Take Eleanora up to her schoolroom," he said. "Doctor's orders are that she should have plenty of rest and few lessons for the next month or so. And no excitement *downstairs*," he added, with a meaning glance at Charlotte.

The nurse flung my lady one of her withering glances. As Vivian set Eleanora on her feet, she took her by the hand.

"Come, dear—" she began.

But Eleanora broke away and threw herself into her mother's arms.

"I want to stay with Mama. I have not seen my Mama for ages and ages!" she cried.

Charlotte hugged her daughter convulsively, the tears in her eyes. Critically she examined the small pale face, the pretty little figure in the cherry velvet pelisse and bonnet trimmed with fur. She used to love choosing dainty clothes for her daughters, and Eleanora had worn this outfit last winter. Now the pelisse was too short, she reflected, the child had grown thin and lanky, quite an inch taller since her illness.

"We must fatten you up, my darling—" Charlotte began, covering the small face with kisses and looking fondly down into the big dark eyes which looked back at her with her grandmother's sympathy and sweetness.

But Vivian pulled Eleanora away from her.

"Come! Doctor's orders, Eleanora. None of this emotion and excitement. Go quietly upstairs with Nanna and see your sisters."

Charlotte stood by, nervously agitated, but she said no more. She did not wish to have a humiliating scene in front of the servants. She was blinded by tears of frustration and misery as she preceded Vivian into the library where tea had been laid in front of a blazing log fire. It looked so handsome, so cosy in here; for outside it was bitterly cold, and snowing again. All through Clunes, holly and mistletoe festooned the pillars and pictures and there was a festive Christmas atmosphere. But to Charlotte it was like all the other Christmas Eves: a hollow mockery, a mere reminder of the homely happy celebrations that were allowed to take place in other, happier, homes than this one.

This was the unhappiest Christmas of them all. Once a day only, the mother was allowed to see her eldest child. Eleanora got slowly better but fretted against the continual separation from her mother. She was kept virtually a prisoner in her schoolroom, on the pretext that she must be guarded from all possible excitement.

Charlotte waited for the moment when she was allowed to visit Eleanora for her brief half-hour, as allotted by Vivian. She rarely tried to see more of her because, if she did, Vivian curtailed further visits, and Eleanora always looked forward so passionately to seeing her beloved mama.

Charlotte looked long and sadly at the little girl this particular evening. It was a bleak January day. All Christmas decorations had long since been removed from Clunes. This being a Friday, Vivian was expecting some of his particular friends down from London for a shooting house party. None of them appealed to Charlotte. The men drank too much, like Vivian, and the wives were pretty silly creatures who had little in common with their hostess.

At this precise moment, Vivian was asleep. Charlotte sat with Eleanora on her lap, the child's thin arms around her neck while the sour-faced Nanna looked on; spying for Vivian, of course, the mother reflected bitterly.

Charlotte did not speak for a few moments. She just sat in silence, hugging Eleanora to her, her face puckered with misery while she stroked the little girl's silky brown hair, hair that had grown a trifle scanty since her illness.

"Dearest Mama, why can't you come and see me more often?" Eleanora whispered in her ear, her small hands tightly clenched about her mother's neck. Charlotte answered in a low voice:

"You must stay up here quietly, my darling, until—until the doctor thinks you well enough to come downstairs again."

Eleanora's eyes filled with tears.

"It is Papa who says I must stay with Nanna, is it not? Is it because I have been naughty? Will you not tell him that I try hard to be good. I have learned my French lessons well this week. Mlle St. Claire, when she was here on Monday, said that I had greatly improved."

Charlotte swallowed hard. There were a thousand loving things she wanted to say to comfort the perplexed and unhappy child but she dared not. Oh, how she hated that stiff, starched woman in her cap and apron who sat there by the window, sewing, listening with both ears to the conversation, enjoying her mistress's embarrassment. Oh, how she wished that she could take Eleanora and fly from this house, never to return, away from Vivian's abominable tyranny and even from her two younger daughters who teased and taunted Eleanora, even as she, Charlotte, was teased and taunted by their father.

This evening Charlotte felt more ill than usual. She was nearly two and a half months advanced in her pregnancy now and never able to enjoy her food, or sleep well, with Vivian snoring off a drunken orgy at her side. She had to force herself to sit at the head of his table during the interminable, over-rich dinners, listening to his noisy joking friends and trying to pretend that she enjoyed it all.

After her half-hour with Eleanora ended, Charlotte left the child trying not to cry and annoy her nurse. Charlotte's own feelings were unspeakable.

"It is killing me. I can bear my own pain but I cannot live and watch my little Eleanora suffer," she thought. "Oh, God, help me!"

She walked unsteadily down the staircase and stopped before a portrait of the late Lady Chase. She looked up at it with hot bitter eyes.

"You whom I loved and who loved me, your devoted pupil, *you* condemned me to this life with your son. Can you not see from your heaven and pity me the hell in which I exist?" she asked aloud.

When, later on, Vivian joined Charlotte in the library, she approached him with a courage that was rooted in sheer desperation.

"Vivian, I must speak to you. I must tell you. I cannot go on like this," she said.

He was standing before the fireplace in the act of lighting a cigar, and as he puffed at it he glanced malevolently at her. She looked less attractive than usual he thought; that dark blue velvet tea gown made her seem dull. She was sallow and there were dark circles under her eyes. No doubt she was suffering from the effects of this new life that was soon to quicken within her. It had better be a son this time, he thought gloomily.

"For heaven's sake, go change your gown for something of a more charming colour, and apply some cosmetic, if you have any, to your greasy face," he said in a loud rude voice. "Your looks are becoming deplorable."

Nervously Charlotte pulled at her lace-edged handkerchief.

"I do not care how my looks strike you, Vivian. I have no wish to be attractive to you. But I do say, here and now, I will not stand for your mean, cruel efforts to keep me apart from Eleanora."

He smiled and glanced at the end of his cigar.

"I shall not argue with you. My orders must be obeyed."

Her face flushed crimson.

"Will you not listen, will you not relent, Vivian, and allow me free access to my child, and her to me? It is so abominable—throwing me your outrageous orders before that nurse who hates me and is glad to see me humiliated. Or before Volpo, whom you know I dislike. Vivian, I am not well. I am *enceinte*. You have a crowd coming to Clunes that I must entertain. I am physically and mentally unable to stand this state of affairs any longer. You *must* listen to me, and treat me, and Eleanora who loves me, with more kindness."

Silence. Charlotte was weeping. The man in the chair stroked his fair, curled moustache, pretended to be bored, although inwardly he was alert, watching her every movement, listening to her every word. He liked it when Charlotte was reduced to tears.

At length he said:

"My dear, you are overwrought. It is, of course, the result of your condition. I am an understanding man and shall excuse you from the party tonight. You may retire and go to your bed which is what you need."

She strove for composure.

"I warn you," she repeated, shaking, "you go too far."

"Do not dare to issue warnings to me. Indeed, what do you think you can do?" He laughed in the way which so often made her believe that he was smitten with insanity.

"I will go to Eleanora, and I will stay with her, or—" she began, then broke off swallowing.

"Or what," Vivian put in.

"*Or I will leave you*," she said in a choked voice.

His eyes widened. He burst out laughing.

"Leave me? *Oh ho!* That is interesting, very interesting, madam. So you have the money to keep yourself? You came to me penniless, a nobody."

"I never forget that, nor do I cease to regret our union," she said wildly. "But that is old history. You know all too well how young, how ill-advised I was ever to be persuaded into tying myself up to you."

"Come, come, would you have had your precious Eleanora born in shame, a bastard?" he taunted her.

The crude word brought the hot colour to Charlotte's face. She retorted:

"Yes, *yes*, I would. If I could go back, I would rather have borne my poor child in sin and shame, than find myself living under the roof of a man as monstrous as yourself."

She stopped, breathing hard, her face ashen, her eyes wild with despair. Vivian flung away his cigar, stood up and came near her.

"Have you finished?" he said, his eyes flaming.

"No, I say more. That even though I starve, I shall leave this house, work for my living as a menial, anything, rather than subject myself any longer to your brutalities." She broke off and hid her face in her hands, sobbing. She had not dared say so much to him ever before. But now it was out, torn from the depths of her suffering heart.

Vivian turned to the mantelpiece. There stood upon it an exquisite Sèvres clock. He found a key and began to wind the clock, as though in complete disregard of what his wife had said. He even whistled under his breath.

Charlotte stared at his unrelenting back. For a moment, her breath coming unevenly, she watched him while he toyed with the clock. His indifference to her sufferings roused her to sudden madness. She went up to him and beat upon his chest with clenched hands.

"Brute, monster, *devil!*" she sobbed. "Did you not hear what I said to you?"

"I heard; and you bore me," he drawled.

The usually gentle and submissive Charlotte became demented. In her blind passion of resentment she seized the valuable clock from his fingers and dashed it on to the fireplace. It shattered into fragments. There came from it a discordance of broken chimes, a whirring; then silence.

Vivian's face went red. He looked first at the broken clock then at Charlotte's frenzied face. He slapped her cheek with his open hand.

"You bitch," he said.

"You will never strike me or call me by such a vile name again!" she said on a high hysterical note. "I have done with you and with enduring your abominable conduct. I shall leave the house."

"So you have threatened. Go—and be damned."

Outside the door, a young footman with his ear to the keyhole grimaced, moved away and motioned to her ladyship's maid, Gertrude, who was passing through the hall.

"Jimmeney—they're at it, the pair of 'em," he sniggered.

Suddenly the drawing-room doors were flung open.

Charlotte, her hair dishevelled, her face ghastly, rushed out, crying as she went:

"You shall not take Eleanora from me. *You shall not.* She goes with me, you inhuman creature!"

Gertrude and the footman hastened away and vanished into the shadows at the back of the hall where they cowered, listening, regarding each other in horrified excitement.

Lord Chase came blustering after his wife.

"If you leave my house, Eleanora stays here!" he shouted. "Do you hear me? I shall teach you who is the master at Clunes."

Charlotte was, however, beyond fear of such threats.

The last thread of her patience had snapped. She picked up her long flowing skirt and ran up the stairs, panting, followed by Vivian who snarled imprecations at her back. She called despairingly:

"Eleanora, Eleanora. Come, come to Mama—!"

Gertrude, faithful, devoted and deeply sorry for her lady, rushed to the foot of the staircase. She, better than anyone in this tragic household, knew what Charlotte put up with. She also knew how ill my lady was at the moment, how unfit to bear such a terrible emotional scene. Gertrude held her breath for fear as she saw his lordship catch up with my lady and clutch her, by one arm.

"You shall not go near your daughter!" he snarled.

"Let me go," said Charlotte, wildly struggling.

He fought with her, finding her grown suddenly strong in this mad rebellious mood. For a moment the maid watched. She saw Charlotte release one hand and beat at his lordship's face, a face ugly and inflamed. She saw Vivian try to imprison that fluttering hand again. In so doing, he swung Charlotte round so that she stood with her back to the stairs, poised perilously near to the edge.

Then it happened. Charlotte turned her ankle and slipped. With a final made effort she released herself from Vivian, but only to totter backwards and fall. She slid, rolling down the stairs. Had they not been so well carpeted, she might have struck her head on the marble and that fall might have proved fatal. As it was, the thick pile saved her. She reached the final stair and lay across it, arms outstretched, like a bird shot in flight.

Chapter Twenty-four

Vivian came running down the staircase. Gertrude rushed to her mistress and knelt beside her.

"My lady—oh, my lady!" she gasped.

Vivian stood staring at Charlotte's prostrate form. Her hair had loosened and tumbled across her shoulders. A trickle of blood came from the corner of her mouth where he had so cruelly struck her, in the library. For a moment conscience awakened. Memory took him back to an early morning hour in this very house, when he had attacked his young wife, and his mother had seen, and fallen *dead*.

Ashen-faced, he stared at Charlotte. He could not speak, but only breathed heavily.

Gertrude looked up at him.

"My lady is hurt, perhaps dying, your lordship," she stuttered and began to cry.

"No, no—she moves; she opens her eyes; she is not dead," answered Vivian. He knelt beside his wife and lifted one of her cold inert hands in his. "Charlotte, you have had a dreadful accident. You have fallen. My poor dear wife, speak to me!" he said in a loud voice, so that all could hear, for by now the hall was filling rapidly with members of the staff. The children's nurse had also come running out of the nursery and leaned over the banisters, looking in a frightened way at her ladyship's figure spread-eagled across the stairs.

Charlotte's dazed eyes moved from her husband's face to Gertrude's. She shuddered, conscious suddenly of a searing pain.

"Get—Dr. Castleby—" she whispered. "I—think—the baby—I am—" She got no further, for her eyes closed and she moaned in a way that made Gertrude's blood turn cold.

During the next few minutes all was chaos. The carriage had just brought four of Vivian's guests up to the front door. They arrived to witness this dreadful scene. Servants running hither and thither, Lord Chase carrying his wife's unconscious body up to her bedroom; while a footman was sent posthaste for the Harling physician.

There was to be no weekend party, no long drawn out dinner for Lady Chase that night. And no possibility of a son and heir for this house.

Charlotte, caught in the throes of a physical agony that temporarily superseded her mental misery, fought for her life until dawn. A London specialist was sent for, and arrived in the early hours to aid the local physician who was quite out of his depth in such a serious case. Lady Chase's life was at stake; not so much on account of her miscarriage as her general lowness of health and spirits. Both doctors agreed on that. She did not seem to want to recover.

Two hospital nurses joined the gathering. At dawn in her big bed, Charlotte lay like one from whom all colour, all animation had been drained. Her face was pinched and sharpened. Her chestnut curls were caught up in an embroidered white linen cap. She looked without apparent recognition at any of the people who bent over her. To Vivian's incessant appeals to her to forgive him, she remained impervious. The visiting physician, his finger on the feeble pulse, sat by the bedside in the dimly-lit, magnificent bedroom full of the scent of hot-house flowers, and looked sternly at Lord Chase.

"Your wife's condition is poor, sir," he said abruptly.

"But surely she is not to die," whimpered Vivian.

"No. She will live; but it will be many weeks before she recovers. I do not wish to intrude, sir, but I must ask you on account of my patient's extreme weakness and the misery that seems to overwhelm her, if you know of anything in particular that is troubling her inner spirit. Dr. Castleby and I are of the opinion, sir, that it is this, rather than the accident, the loss of the coming child, which has brought her so low."

Vivian looked away. Several times during the night, whenever, in fact, he had leaned over his semi-conscious wife and spoken her name, she had shrieked to him to go away. She called him "brute" and "monster." He knew that the eminent London doctor, as well as Castleby, had heard it. Sullenly, he reflected that there were limits to what he could do if he were to retain his place in respectable Society; that if he did not conduct himself more as a loving husband should, he would earn himself an unattractive reputation.

He answered the doctor as pleasantly as he could, mumbling excuses for Charlotte's state of mind; she was highly strung and difficult; he had had a poor time with her. But he would, of course, he said, take greatest care of her now, and induce her as soon as possible to accompany him with the children to some mild climate like Madeira, where the sunshine would revive her.

The physician interrupted. He did not believe a word, for he held privately a poor opinion of Lord Chase and felt the deepest pity for this beautiful wife; sentiments obviously shared by their own medical man.

"Lady Chase asks repeatedly that she should see the child who goes by the name of *Eleanora*," he said. "I would suggest to you, Lord Chase, that the little girl be brought to see her mother, and at once."

Vivian began to excuse himself again, mumbling that Eleanora had recently contracted an infectious illness and that he had considered it unwise to expose an expectant mother to any risk. Of course, he added, he would give way immediately to the distinguished gentleman's suggestion. Little Eleanora, wrapped in a shawl, was brought to her Mama's bed and placed beside her. Sleepy, but excited, the child flung herself on the still, pale figure.

"Mama, dearest, *sweetest* Mama!" she cried.

Now the men at the foot of the bed saw Charlotte's eyes open. Glazed with fever and pain, they rested on her eldest child's face. At once, Charlotte flushed pink and embraced the little form passionately.

"Mama, my own dear Mama!" repeated Eleanora and laid her dark curly head beside her mother's on the big embroidered pillow.

A happy smile replaced the tormented expression on Charlotte's mouth. She gave a long sigh of satisfaction.

Within a few moments, mother and daughter, locked in their embrace, were both sleeping peacefully, side by side.

The nurse in charge sat by the fire, watching and wondering what had been going on in this grand house. She was soon to be treated to all the gossip and rumours current in the servants' hall.

When another bleak day of wind and snow, that turned to sleet, broke over Clunes, there were many noticeable changes in that house.

Charlotte was still gravely ill and ordered absolute quiet and care. No visitors came to disturb the peace of the house. Vivian gave orders to the servants that her ladyship's merest whims were to be gratified. Eleanora's little bed was moved into her Mama's bedroom, for the invalid could not seem to feel at ease unless she could see the beloved little daughter from whom she had been separated for so long.

The nurse in charge of Beatrice and Victoria took her charges up to the Eaton Square mansion. His lordship followed. This, too, was Charlotte's wish. She could not bear to look at Vivian's florid, deceitful face or hear his hypocritical voice praising her, inquiring after her health, giving her promises that she knew he would not keep, once things settled down again.

Charlotte asked that Fleur should come to her. Mrs. Marsh travelled immediately to Clunes, accompanied by her husband. She was shocked by the sight of the poor young woman who looked so thin, so lifeless, so waxen pale. But from the moment that Fleur came to take charge of her, and with Eleanora at her side, Charlotte soon improved. There followed a period of blissful peace for Charlotte. There came a time when she knew even the comfort and happiness of hearing Dominic Unwin's forbidden name spoken in this house. Vivian was still in London, killing time among his card-playing, dice-throwing, hard-drinking friends.

One morning in March, Charlotte who was well again, was sitting by the fireside with her eldest daughter and her friend. They had been playing a game. Charlotte had regained some weight and a hint of colour, and was looking almost her beautiful self again. Once more there had been music and time for books and laughter in her life. It almost seemed as though her late beloved mother-in-law was back at Clunes and she, the radiant girl, seeking knowledge and gaining it. For Peveril was philosopher as well as artist.

Fleur sent the child out of the room on a small trifling errand, then handed Charlotte a morning paper. She had marked a photograph of Mr. Unwin talking to a friend.

Charlotte dropped the paper, looked round her drawing-room, then out at the garden. Rain veiled trees and bushes. The weather was still cold and bleak. March so far had been severe.

"I would like to go to London and perhaps meet and talk to Dominic Unwin again," she said in a low voice.

"He is a fine man and I do not see why you should not enjoy his friendship, my dear."

Charlotte bit her lip, remembering Vivian's insane jealousy and dislike of Cecil's adopted brother. She told Fleur, frankly, why the friendship could never be.

"It is sad," sighed Fleur.

"For me it is more than that," admitted Charlotte in a low yearning voice.

"My poor dear friend," said Mrs. Marsh pityingly.

Charlotte's eyes filled with tears.

"I have been so happy here, with you and Peveril," she said. "I have enjoyed friendship, and freedom of thought and speech, and the joy of watching my darling devoted little daughter grow happy and strong again. But it must all come to an end. I have received a letter from Vivian by this morning's post. He wishes us all to travel abroad the first week in April."

"Are you not to be permitted to live apart from that insensate bully?" demanded Fleur ever hot in her championship of Charlotte.

Charlotte smiled at the beautiful ageless face of her grey-haired friend.

"Nay, it is not possible. I have suggested a separation but he will not hear of it. He makes things difficult by declaring once again that he will make amends, turn over a new leaf and so on. But it is only because he was frightened by my accident and subsequent illness," she added in a low tone. "Once back with me, he will revert to his former self."

"I know, for Denzil St. Cheviot was just such another,"

nodded Mrs. Marsh, shuddering at the memory of her former husband.

"I must try, too, to love my other two children more," said Charlotte, her brows puckered. "But somehow they do not seem my own; only *his*. They are such cold, unloving little things, and have been turned against me by that unspeakable woman, their nurse."

"Surely you will insist upon her dismissal," said Fleur indignantly.

Charlotte nodded.

"Yes, when she brings Beatrice and Victoria home, she shall be sent away. I shall make Vivian see that this is essential to my well-being."

"And Volpo?" Fleur looked questioningly at her friend. She knew how acutely poor Charlotte disliked the wily Portuguese.

Charlotte shook her head. Even now, she was sure her husband, though wishing to behave tolerably well, would never dismiss his valet. Volpo was too well trained and useful to him, be it as servant, spy or right-hand man. She would have to accept his presence for as long as Volpo continued to serve Vivian without putting the wrong foot forward.

Eleanora came dancing back into the drawing-room, a tiny bunch of blue scillas in her hand. Her cheeks were red, her eyes shining.

"Mama, Mama, look! The first of the year! Soon it will be spring!"

Charlotte took the tiny bouquet and tucked it in her belt. Mother and daughter smiled into each other's eyes. Charlotte thought:

"She is really happy now. God grant that when Vivian and poor little Beatrice and Victoria return they will not seek to destroy that innocent happiness."

But, alas for Charlotte, that appeal to her Maker was not destined to be granted.

For Vivian was about to spring an iniquitous surprise upon the wife who was seeking to resign herself to a fresh reconciliation, for her children's sake. A surprise suggested by that very man whom Charlotte distrusted and abhorred. It was Volpo, himself, up in Eaton Square, in attendance upon his master after an amusing evening spent by his lordship in the company of his less moral and respectable friends, who whispered in his ear that it was regrettable that after this my lord would be forced to settle down and lead a godly and sober life with his family.

"It will not suit your lordship," Volpo said sadly while he folded Vivian's clothes. "Would my master not prefer his freedom once again?"

"Fool, how can I get it, tagged and nagged at by a lawful wedded wife?" muttered Vivian sourly.

The valet's thin lips smiled.

"I have an idea, but fear to present it to your lordship in case he might think me monstrously impudent."

Vivian blinked at his valet and kicked off a shoe.

"You *are* a monstrously impudent fellow, but you are a loyal servant and know what I like and do not like. What is your idea? Come, tell me before I fall asleep."

"A divorce, my lord, surely would set you free again."

"Divorce?" Vivian echoed the word crossly then snapped: "Fool, how can I divorce a faithful wife? If you cannot think of a better plan than that, shut your mouth."

"But I know more than you think, my lord," Volpo continued, kneeling before Vivian, and starting to remove his master's other shoe. "I fancy I know how her ladyship feels about a certain gentleman as I have taken the liberty, on your lordship's behalf of course, of watching and listening. I know how she preserves certain newspapers which contain this gentleman's photograph and—"

"Hold your peace," interrupted Vivian, his face scarlet. "I, too, know of such things, but I can assure you her ladyship is as pure as a lily—" He laughed coarsely, "And I could find no reason whatsoever to defile her name and rid myself of my domestic chains."

Volpo remained silent. That silence was pregnant. Suddenly a host of ideas swarmed in Lord Chase's ugly mind, inflaming him further to the idea of release from Charlotte. Since the night of her accident he had been forced to give way to her; but he hated her more than ever for that very fact. To find her out in a falsehood, put her in the wrong, be able to cast her out, and remain righteous in the eyes of Society, that would be a triumph indeed.

He prodded the kneeling valet with his toe. "What plan can you suggest, fool?" he asked. "Spit out your idiot suggestions."

Volpo did not take offence. He knew my Lord Chase too well. He knew, too, that if he could help him to rid himself of a wife who had, from the very start, been a burden to him, he, Volpo, would be remembered—and rewarded.

He stood up and began to talk—

Chapter Twenty-five

Twenty-four hours later the Marshes reluctantly bade farewell to Charlotte and left Clunes. It had to be, greatly though Fleur disliked having to leave her friend. She and Peveril must return to Pillars and, in any case, Charlotte expected her husband to return to Clunes with the two younger children this week-end.

Somewhat to Charlotte's astonishment, Volpo came down to the country house alone on the Thursday. His lordship had sent him in advance, he explained, as he handed her ladyship a note from his master. This was couched in affectionate terms and asked Charlotte if she would spare her personal maid to go up to London and fetch Beatrice and Victoria:

> Knowing your dislike of Nanna, I have dismissed her. You can choose a new nurse whom you will prefer and meanwhile you will not be distressed by the presence in the house of one to whom you are hostile. Volpo comes to open up my suite at Clunes and I shall be with you, my love, in the morning. Pray accept this bouquet as a token of my sincere desire to start life afresh as your loving and faithful husband.

Charlotte read his note with astonishment. It seemed so unlike Vivian. But she accepted it for what it was worth and was only too pleased to send Gertrude to fetch the other children. It was a relief to know she need not look again on the face of that woman who had helped so sadistically to keep her away from Eleanora.

For once, Charlotte tried to smile upon the valet who brought her a magnificent bunch of hothouse carnations from his master. She also tried to reassure herself that his smile was genuine, not the treacherous smirk which sent such shivers of repugnance through her.

She sent Gertrude to the station to catch the afternoon train to London, then drove into Harling to a toy shop to choose two new dolls for Beatrice and Victoria. Eleanora went with her.

"We must give your darling sisters a real welcome," Charlotte said gaily.

Eleanora tried not to be downcast, but in her tender young heart she wished profoundly that Papa and her sisters need never return to Clunes.

That night, Charlotte dined early. After playing her piano awhile, she took herself off to bed.

How quiet it was in the big house; without Vivian and with none of the usual quota of friends whom he liked to invite here. A delicious quiet. Charlotte was even thankful not to have Gertrude fussing over her but to be alone in her bedroom and look after herself.

She was beginning to feel quite strong again. She glanced at her reflection in the cheval mirror. In her long peignoir of white cashmere with its lace collar and cuffs, she looked tall and thin. Her face was thinner than usual; she no longer seemed so young, but old for her twenty-seven years, with a sad maturity, a gravity of eyes and lips. She had, however, regained much of her beauty and an added dignity born of excessive suffering nobly endured.

Her large eyes gazed back at her; they seemed to her, stranger's eyes. She could hardly believe that she had ever been that Charlotte Goff who had learned so much at Eleanora Chase's knee, and who had once worshipped Vivian as a young god.

She was in bed and half asleep when she heard carriage wheels on the drive and a dog barking.

She was a light sleeper and sat up at once, struck a match and lit the candle in the silver stick beside her. She listened, her pulses racing.

Again the barking dog—then men's voices—then a knock on the front door.

Charlotte frowned. Who could the caller be at such an hour? Her jewelled clock on the mantelpiece showed her that it was nearly eleven.

She got up and put on her peignoir. Tying the girdle, she

walked to the door and opened it. She saw a gleam of light and heard voices below. She moved quickly along the corridor. Could it be that Vivian had chosen to return unexpectedly? It would not be unlike him to choose such an unorthodox and inconvenient hour.

Then she heard a voice that sent the blood surging to her face and throat. A man's deep rich voice. It said:

"I wish to see Lady Chase—"

Charlotte gasped under her breath.

"Dominic—Dominic Unwin!"

What in heaven's name was *he* doing at Clunes and at such an hour? The last train had reached Harling station at nine o'clock. He asked for *her*. What could have occurred?

Charlotte was thunderstruck. But whatever the explanation of this extraordinary visit, the knowledge that Dominic was here, down in the hall, shook her to the core. She forgot that she was only wearing night-attire and dressing-gown. She ran down the wide staircase and stopped midway as she saw Dominic. He was wearing a cloak, and hat in hand, stood at the foot of the stairs. He was talking to Volpo who had, it seemed, opened the front door to him. Volpo was apologizing for his own night-attire over which he had thrown a coat.

Dominic did not listen to Volpo now. He looked upward at Charlotte, watching her as she came down the stairs. He had never seen her thus; with the glory of her unbound hair curling to her shoulders, she was slender and inexpressibly graceful, he thought, in her white *déshabillé*.

Volpo also looked up at his mistress. He bowed.

"If I have your permission, my lady, I will retire."

She did not answer. She seemed to be incapable of speaking, of looking in any direction save Dominic's. Volpo smiled and slunk away. He left a lamp burning, then closed the baize-covered door that led into the butler's pantry. But once outside, he rubbed his hands together gleefully and stood pondering. So far, so good; his plan was working out. Now for the rest. He must just listen, and wait.

Charlotte reached the bottom stair. She stood before the man whose face was ever before her mind's eye, no matter where she was or what she was doing. She said:

"Mr. Unwin—Dominic—you are always welcome but

why have you come here at this strange hour? I do not understand—"

He pulled a piece of paper from his pocket.

"I received this, brought to me at the House by messenger this afternoon," he said.

She stared, noting how tired he looked, almost careworn, as though the terrific work, which he had been doing recently in the House of Commons, had sapped his strength, both mental and physical. But his eyes were still young, as brilliant as ever, and his personality as vital. He made her feel as he always did—that his presence filled the entire house, not merely a small space.

She said:

"What has your note to do with me?"

He stared back at her.

"It was *from* you—" he said.

"From me?" she repeated. "It cannot possibly be. I have not written to you, Dominic."

"But—I do not comprehend. Read it, Charlotte," he said, and his cheeks flushed. He added: "I must confess, it confounded me, but I came when and how you requested. I could not do otherwise."

So warm, so vibrant was his tone, so full of strange meaning his handsome eyes, Charlotte felt as though she was being caught in a whirlpool of mysterious excitement and flung right off her feet.

She was beginning to shiver for it was cold in the big hall at this late hour. She turned from Dominic, the note still unread in her hand.

"Follow me," she said in a low voice, "We cannot stand here. It is too draughty. Let us go into the library. Perhaps the fire will still be burning in there."

He followed her, drawing off his cloak.

"Have you a match?" Charlotte asked him.

"I regret I have not."

She bit her lip and glanced into the library. The curtains were still drawn together and all was darkness save for a red gleam from the grate which showed that the fire still smouldered. She said:

"Then will you bring the lamp from the hall and from that we will light the others."

He went back and fetched the lamp. She bade him set it on the mantelpiece. As he did so, she bent and poked the fire and set up a little blaze.

"I will put on more wood," she began.

"Allow me," he said, and bent to find logs in a copper urn which he saw beside the fireplace. Charlotte, too, bent down. Almost the two heads touched, the dark, silver-streaked one of the man and the bright head of the young woman. Simultaneously, still kneeling, they turned and looked into each other's eyes. Each now felt the rapid warmth of each other's breathing; they were so close together in that dim roseate glow of the awakening fire. It was as though they looked into each other's very heart and soul and, magnetized, were unable to look away again.

There was silence now in the great house of Clunes. A warm rich pregnant silence. For Charlotte the world stood still. For the man, the moment was as a revelation of an emotional storm as wild and impossible as a dream. Usually so reserved, he had believed himself capable of only the lightest, most transient appreciation of a woman's charm and beauty. Because of Dorothea's death, he had thought that his heart had died—at least to *that* kind of emotion.

Yet now tonight, in this crazy moment, so close to Charlotte Chase, alone, not yet knowing who or what had brought him here, he temporarily lost his iron mastery of self. He uttered her name in a shaken whisper:

"Charlotte!"

She answered, her gaze still held by his, one hand pressed to her bare throat.

"Dominic," she answered in a strangled voice.

He caught at her and pulled her on to her feet. For a single instant she was no longer Lady Chase, another man's wife, but his own dear Charlotte, all his, melting to his touch. Wordlessly he kissed her on the mouth. Her senses swam. It was a moment full of poignant impassioned feeling for Charlotte. She knew now that she loved him with a love that was born of a new, mad hope, and of an old, anguished despair.

It was her first real kiss of pure awakening love. She was once more the Charlotte of years ago, the ardent girl who had had so much to give, but who had lost even the desire to give after her terrible marriage. Dominic with her sweetness crushed to him, her lips opening under the pressure of his, was deeply aware that this was the last, most significant passion of his life.

Only a moment could that sweet yet bitter kiss endure. Then, with a gasp, Charlotte broke from him, her hands pressed to her burning cheeks.

"Merciful God, what are we doing?" she whispered.

He put a hand to his head.

"Forgive me, Charlotte, beloved. I had no right."

"But I love you, Dominic."

"I love you, Charlotte."

His simple and direct assertion brought her but brief joy. She gave a low cry and buried her face in her hands.

"It can never be."

"No, never. It is my unhappy fate to have to say so. But I care for you with all my body, heart and soul. I did not really know it until tonight."

"I have loved you from the first day I looked on your face," she said, and, uncovering hers, gazed up at him, her eyes half blinded by tears.

"I knew it *almost* for a fact when I received your letter, for I laid everything aside—my most important work—to come to you."

Now the fire was burning brightly. But the great library was full of shadows for there was still only one small lamp alight. Charlotte shivered. Her hands were cold as ice. She said:

"The letter. Yes. What about this letter that I was supposed to have written?"

"Supposed?" he echoed. He looked down at her with a questioning expression. "Where is it? Please read it, Charlotte, I do not know your writing, so I could not judge. Read it and tell me what it means."

In a daze, she looked down. She saw the white notepaper on the crimson carpet. It must have dropped from her fingers when Dominic swept her into his arms. She picked it up and, taking it to the lamp, scanned it. As she did so, her features froze into a look of sheer amazement and fear.

This was what she was supposed to have written:

Dominic,

I believe you to be my dearest, my only man friend. I need your help. I need it urgently and can only ask for you to give it—in secret. It is essential nobody in our circle of friends should know about this. I am alone at Clunes. Vivian is still in London and will be till tomorrow. Please come to me tonight. Take the last train to Harling. It will get you there by nine, but go to an inn—anywhere—only do not approach Clunes until after half past ten. Then drive here—you can get a carriage from the Station Livery Stables—and knock on the front door. One of my servants will admit you. I deplore the fact that I must ask your visit to be so clandestine. Only do not fail me. I will explain all when I see you. Oh, Dominic, do not fail me. Come, I implore you.

Charlotte.

Twice she read this amazing missive—the second time aloud. Dominic, his dark face half in shadow from her, his brow furrowed, his eyes watching her, said:

"*Vivian*, I knew that meant—your husband. You see the terms in which this appeal is couched? Coming from you, how could I disregard it? I was flabbergasted—I admit. I could not think what plight had placed you in the position of having to make such an appeal to me. At first I was doubtful whether or not I should do as you asked. Then because of my deep regard for you, I knew I *had* to agree. I was sure you would, as you said, explain all when I got here."

Charlotte shook her head like one utterly confused.

"But I cannot, for I did not write this letter, Dominic."

"You did not?"

"I swear it."

She pointed to the signature.

"*That* is not mine," she went on, "I write my *'C'* with more of a flourish and two *t*'s I cross together, not separately, like this. I tell you, this was not sent by me, nor would I ever have appealed to you in such a manner."

"I must have been off my head to do—as I did just now," he said under his breath.

She did not hear. She was examining the note again.

"I am frightened," she said. "I do not recognize this writing but I am beginning to see that the letter must have been written by someone who *wished* you to come to Clunes tonight."

"But *who?*" he exclaimed.

"Yes, '*who*'?" she muttered. Biting her lip, she stared again at the signature purporting to be hers. *Who*, indeed, could have done such an iniquitous thing—appealed to Dominic Unwin's chivalry and thus brought him down to Clunes at dead of night?

"I am frightened," she said for the second time.

Tenderness welled up in Dominic. He came nearer her.

"My dear, my dearest, do not be afraid. No harm is done. I must just go away again, at once."

Her eyes burned up at him.

"No—wait—this mystery must be solved. It is a dangerous situation. Maybe a trick," she added.

"But who would play such a trick?"

She was silent. Her mind whirled with a dozen crazy ideas. None seemed sensible. The person who had written to Dominic in her name could only be one who knew of her secret friendship with him; and of his feeling toward her. It was no kind friend who had arranged this nocturnal *rendezvous*. It must be an enemy—someone wishing to hurt Dominic and put *her* in the wrong. Now Charlotte's face went deadly white. A sickness stole over her. There could only be one being who would wish to do either of these things. His name leapt before her sight in letters of scarlet. *Vivian*.

It was not Vivian's writing, but he could have induced someone to pen the note for him, and sent it to the House of Commons this morning.

She swayed.

"It may be Vivian himself, who has tricked you here," she said hoarsely.

Dominic stared down at the lovely, blanched face.

"Calm yourself, my dearest; it cannot possibly be."

"It can. You do not know Vivian Chase. He is a fiend, a devil incarnate. This may well be some devilish plot on his part."

"It cannot be," repeated Dominic incredulously.

"I tell you it can. And now I am beginning to understand many things. My personal maid, Gertrude—he has made me send *her* away for the night and Volpo is here!" Her teeth began to chatter. "Volpo is the Portuguese valet who let you in. He is viler than all others. *He* was sent down here in Gertrude's place—to spy on me. No doubt he was up and waiting for you. I tell you, Dominic, this is beginning to manifest itself as a vile and outrageous plot."

"But to do what?" demanded the astonished Dominic.

"To get rid of me and ruin you," she said.

Dominic stared down into her wild beautiful eyes, then gave a short laugh.

"You are distraught, my dearest Charlotte. It is impossible. Why should Vivian Chase behave so despicably towards you, his wife and the mother of his children? Or to me, whom he scarcely knows, and who has done him no harm?"

"You do not know Vivian—or what my life with him has been—or how jealous he is."

"Do not tell me. I could not bear to hear it," said Dominic, his brown rich skin flushing. "Your face—the thought of you has been before me all these long months and years. I have never forgotten you. On the few occasions when we have met and talked, I have felt that strange but imperative sensation that we were very close, that we must have met, and perhaps loved, in another life. I have many times wished with all my soul that you were free, free for me to approach honourably—in love—in marriage."

She gave a deep sigh. Her eyes looked up into his, less strained, softening.

"Praise God that I have at least heard you say those words. The memory of them will comfort me all the rest of my days."

"Oh, my darling, how can it be possible that you love me thus—you who are so young?" he broke out. "I am nearly twice your age, an old, tired man. It is ridiculous."

"To me you are neither old nor tired, but my heart's ideal," she said, clasping her hands.

He seized those hands and pressed long ardent kisses on them.

"Charlotte, Charlotte my love—would to God I had the

right to put an end to the tortures at which you hint, and to take care of you for ever."

She withdrew her fingers and looked with frightened gaze towards the hall. She had heard the silver chimes of a clock. It was close on midnight now.

"You must go—at once, Dominic. I am mad to let you stay here, and I only in my night attire. Go—please—immediately."

He picked up his cloak.

"Yes, but matters cannot rest like this. I will not be the recipient of fraudulent letters which are harmful to *you*. The mystery must be solved. We must discover who has done this thing. I still can scarcely believe that your own husband, Lord Chase, could perform an act so base, so dishonourable," he added, frowning.

"Vivian knows no honour," said Charlotte.

It was at that precise moment that Volpo stole soundlessly into the hall, in answer to a peculiar whistle, as from a night bird, and opened the front door to admit his master.

Chapter Twenty-six

"Everything has gone according to plan, my lord," Volpo whispered in Vivian's ear outside the library door, beneath which a crack of light was showing in the darkness. "*He* has answered in person the letter which I penned for your lordship. He came hot-haste. I took the liberty of sending his carriage back to the stables in Harling, so he can not get away, save on foot."

"Excellent," Vivian whispered back.

He was sober tonight. He had kept away from the brandy for he was bent on business, and unpleasant business at that. But he was in a good humour. He considered Volpo's plan the scheme of a genius. It looked to Vivian as though he had Charlotte on a hook, at last. Whether or not he wrecked an innocent man's reputation—a famous, much respected man into the bargain—he did not care. He only knew that he wanted his freedom from Charlotte, from his marriage. He was no longer going to be hounded into playing the amiable husband.

Now the fun was about to begin. It had all been arranged, in detail, between Vivian and his confidential servant. He was about to revenge himself upon Charlotte for the last ten years of bondage, *and* upon his mother's memory, he reflected with fiendish glee. In addition, his vengeance would extend to the unfortunate eldest daughter whom he would remove from Charlotte once and for all.

Suddenly, with a bold stroke, Vivian flung open the library door.

He had chosen an excellent moment, Dominic had just taken both Charlotte's hands in his and was kissing them in farewell.

"A farewell that must be for ever, else there is no honour in the world," he was murmuring to her. She stood, mute, tearless, looking with anguished passion at the bent head of the man who was so dear to her. A man nearly old enough to be her father. But she loved him and would go on doing so until the grave.

Vivian achieved the full theatrical effect he desired. The pair, discovered by the fireplace in that tender attitude, swung round as they heard the door open and stared open-mouthed at the man who stood on the threshold.

In horror Charlotte regarded her husband.

As Vivian moved towards Charlotte and Dominic, he bowed, first to his wife, then to the astounded Dominic, smiling evilly.

"My compliments," he drawled. "The tenderness of your attitude makes a touching tableau. It is, I presume, the *finale* to a stolen hour of a more than tender passion."

Silence. Then Charlotte gave a low cry:

"God in heaven! My fears were justified. This has been a loathly trick. It was *you*, Vivian, who arranged the whole thing."

He pretended surprise, letting his monocle drop. He began to dangle it on its black ribbon.

"My dear Charlotte! *Arranged* for you to receive your lover in my absence? Come, come, what sort of a husband do you think I am?"

"Wait," Dominic rapped out. He came forward and confronted Vivian. His face was ashen, his large fine eyes narrowed. "I will deal with this."

Vivian bowed again.

"You will be forced to deal with it, my dear fellow, as the co-respondent in the divorce suit which I intend to bring against you and my faithless wife."

"Vivian!" Charlotte cried the name aloud, her hands pressed to her scarlet cheeks.

Dominic rapped out:

"I fail to understand, sir. You are making a grave mistake and one which requires complete explanation."

"No explanation from *me* is necessary," said Vivian.

"On the contrary, sir, you have just made an outrageous accusation which has no basis whatsoever—" began Dominic.

Charlotte interrupted:

"For heaven's sake, Dominic, do not demean yourself by

engaging in a dispute with my husband. *He is out of his mind.*"

Vivian turned his gaze on her. She was convinced, now, of his madness, so red a light gleamed in those usually stony blue eyes. It was a glance of murderous hatred coupled with triumph.

"Adulteress," he hissed. "*You* will soon be out of my house—with your paramour."

She shrank back, the tips of her shaking hands pressed against her white lips. Dominic restrained himself from striking Vivian across the mouth only by a supreme effort. He realized that it was essential for him to keep his temper. When Vivian had first entered the room, Dominic had been slightly taken aback, not only by his appearance, but by the realization that Charlotte's suspicions of foul play were justified. Now, in control of himself, he stepped neatly in between husband and wife, and brought his dark, forceful face close to the other man's.

"You will take back that word with which you have just defiled the ears of the purest woman on earth, or I shall make you answer to me, Lord Chase."

"To you, her partner in guilt?" Vivian stepped back with a sneering laugh, and his hand went into his pocket and closed over the small neat revolver without which he rarely travelled. One never knew when it might be useful.

Dominic said:

"There is no question of guilt, Lord Chase. That you should say so is an outrage and I insist upon an explanation."

"I have the greater right to demand one from *you*, sir; stealing down to my house, believing me to be in London, in order to spend a forbidden night with my wife. Look at her in her *déshabillé*," he added with a wicked glance at Charlotte. She was as white as the gown she wore, and trembled violently.

"This is all too well contrived a scheme. I see it now," said Dominic tersely. "I have been victimized."

"Oh, great God, do not suppose that I am to blame!" cried Charlotte.

"Never! I know full well that this can never be laid at your door," Dominic said gently. "Do not concern yourself. It is now between Lord Chase and me."

"Between the three of us, sir," said Vivian. "Once again, I ask what you are doing in my house?"

"What are *you* doing here, Vivian?" broke in Charlotte hysterically. "How is it possible that chance alone brought you here at this precise hour, when you were not due to come home until morning with our children."

"I was warned of your intention to receive a nocturnal visitor, madam," he said.

"Impossible. I had no such intention."

"A loyal servant will bear witness that such is not the case."

"Of course, that reptile Volpo—" began Charlotte in despair, under her breath.

"You took advantage of the fact that your personal maid was out of the house, and out of your way," went on Vivian.

"It was you who told me to send Gertrude up to London."

"Innocent enough; in order that she should take care of our daughters."

"It is all contrived, I tell you—" she began.

Dominic interrupted.

"I beg of you to let me deal with Lord Chase. He must, indeed, be out of his mind," he added in a low voice.

Vivian stuck the monocle in his eye again and regarded the politician.

"I understand, Mr. Unwin, that you have always been considered a pillar of the Church, a primrose of respectability, as well as a successful Member of Parliament," he sneered. "It will be an astonishment and, no doubt, a disappointment to your constituency to learn that you have stooped to become the lover of another man's wife."

"That is a lie, sir," thundered Dominic. "I have known your wife for many years, as I have done you, yourself. I have seen her but rarely. I have the greatest respect for her. I value her friendship. But to suggest a forbidden intimacy is infamous and unwarranted. I have never even communicated with Lady Chase by letter."

"Never. He was tricked down to Clunes tonight by *you*!" put in Charlotte.

"Who is to believe that?" drawled Vivian.

"You have got to believe it," Charlotte said in a desperate voice.

"I shall leave a judge of the Divorce Court to decide," said Vivian.

Charlotte gasped.

"You cannot do this thing. It is insane."

"Bah," said Vivian. "Do not waste my time with idle abuse. Faithless creature that you are! Devoted, loving in public, and in secret—well, I shall not bother now to ask what you have done. Enough for me to find you in this incriminating position tonight—alone with your lover."

"He has never been my lover—" began Charlotte frenziedly.

"Hush," said Dominic sternly. "I cannot have you dragged into such an abominable *mêlée*. *I*, and I alone, must answer to Lord Chase."

"You will have every chance of doing so. Charlotte will give you the name of my solicitors. Good night, sir," said Vivian and turned on his heel.

"Wait," said Dominic, the colour leaving his cheeks, for he thought of what a public scandal might mean to Charlotte. "The matter cannot be left like this. You have no proof—"

Vivian turned.

"Every proof. My own valet has just informed me that you and my wife spent an hour together up in her bedroom and that Lady Chase asked for champagne to be sent up, in celebration. He was offered a bribe but he rejected it. He refused to serve the drink, being loyal to his master."

Charlotte gave a choking cry.

"Unspeakable lies!"

Dominic drew a sharp breath. The muscles on his cheeks were working. His patience was strained to the uttermost. He said:

"Great God, that any husband should stoop so to defile his wife and the mother of his children!"

Charlotte held out the letter she was supposed to have written to Dominic.

"*You* composed this and sent it to Mr. Unwin. *You!*—"

Vivian, pretending not to understand, took the letter, read it, then put it in his pocket.

"You are condemned by your own folly, madam. This epistle proves that you did, indeed, send for Mr. Unwin—No doubt to complain of your lot with me."

"I did not write it; it is not in my hand."

"On the contrary, I recognize the small print which you frequently use for diaries and verse," said Vivian with superb impudence.

She gave another gasp but remained speechless. Then Dominic said:

"Lord Chase, I give you my word of honour as a gentleman that I came here tonight because I was asked to come, but only as a friend—to give any help that was needed. But never have I been into your wife's bedchamber; nor, sir, dishonoured this house or you."

Vivian laughed harshly.

"You may tell that to a judge, sir."

"I admit now that I was indiscreet in coming to Clunes so late at night," added Dominic, frowning. "But I was asked to wait until half past ten, and since I imagined it to be a matter of urgency, I did as I *imagined* Lady Chase, herself, had requested."

Vivian, throwing back his head, laughed again.

"Surely a matter for amusement? You stand condemned by your own conduct. And even as I walked into this room, you were caught in a highly suspicious attitude."

"Such suspicion shall not be allowed to fall on your wife who is pure and undefiled, sir," said Dominic furiously, "I was bidding her good-bye, a permanent good-bye rather than do *you* an injury."

"Then you admit that what you feel for her is more than a passing regard?" said Vivian triumphantly.

Dominic looked at Charlotte, but answered Vivian with quiet dignity:

"I have no wish to lie to you, sir. I admit that had things been different, I might have expressed more than ordinary affection toward Lady Chase. But when I came here it was not to keep a stolen *rendezvous*. I came out of chivalry—as any gentleman might have done—in answer to a letter full of distress, asking for secrecy."

"A letter that I would never have dreamed of sending," put in Charlotte hotly.

"I do not believe either of you," said Vivian.

Charlotte covered her face with her hands and moaned: "Alas—that this should happen to you, Dominic—through me—through my insane husband—oh, God, why did I not die before this night!"

Even in the singularly disagreeable position in which he found himself, Dominic Unwin felt not the slightest sense of anger against Charlotte whom he loved. He could see how he had been snared.

"Do not distress yourself, Lady Chase," he said gently. "I, also, shall consult my legal advisers. This vile plot shall be brought to light, and Lord Chase shall be made to retract his calumnies."

"The public interest in such an affair will do you both such a lot of good," said Vivian with another fiendish laugh. "I shall greatly enjoy the sight of you squirming on the hook, my dear Unwin."

Dominic, taunted beyond endurance, sprang towards the younger man, fist upraised.

At once Vivian levelled the automatic upon him.

"Move a step nearer me, and I fire in self defence," he snarled. "My valet waits outside the door, and will witness that—if I shoot—it is because my wife's paramour has attacked me."

Dominic hesitated. Charlotte had time to throw herself between him and her husband.

"Do not dare," she said to Vivian, her eyes flashing. "Do not dare use that weapon."

But Dominic put her aside.

"This has gone far enough," he said quietly. "Put your revolver away, Lord Chase. You must be out of your mind."

"He is—*he is*," Charlotte moaned the words to herself.

Vivian turned on her.

"Get out of this house; and take your lover with you," he said.

"Use that word again, Lord Chase, and I shall fight with you whether you try to shoot me or not," said Dominic, his temper rising.

"He is not—and never has been—my lover!" Charlotte screamed the words at Vivian.

Suddenly Dominic changed his attitude. He had an idea that Charlotte's husband was, indeed, demented; not to be reasoned with. A sickness descended on him; a horror of this depraved monster to whom an innocent and long-suffering woman was tied. All thoughts of himself, the danger to his reputation, his social position, receded into the background. He thought now only of the trembling unhappy girl whom he loved. There was no passion, only the deepest tenderness and pity in his heart as he turned from Vivian and took Charlotte by one arm.

"Come," he said. "No good can come of us seeking to impress the truth upon Lord Chase. If I leave this house, you had better leave with me."

"Never—" began Charlotte, but Vivian interrupted. He flung his head back, bellowing with laughter.

"Now you see sense; and doubtless, my dear Unwin, you have no desire to be shot by an outraged husband."

Charlotte moaned:

"Do not heed him, Dominic. Go. Go quickly—out of his way."

"Yes, go quickly, Mr. Unwin," echoed Vivian, "and take my erring wife with you."

Charlotte was trembling so violently that Dominic had to hold her arm in order to support her. She broke out, desperately:

"My children! *Eleanora!*"

"The children stay with me," Vivian said with a sly smirk at her. "You do not expect, do you, madam, that I will hand my innocent daughters over to the mother who has dishonoured them? And her poor husband," he added with a hypocritical sigh.

"You know it is false," panted Charlotte.

"Hush! Do not upset yourself further," Dominic said under his breath and tightened his grip of her. He kept a watchful eye on Vivian who had moved away, but Dominic could see that he still handled the revolver. Dominic was no coward. He deplored the fact that Charlotte was here beside him and that he could not do as every instinct in him urged—throw himself, unarmed, upon Vivian and strike that sneering face. But his hands were tied. He dared not risk the bullet entering *Charlotte's* heart; neither was it of any use trying to reason with a maniac. For the moment, Vivian's vile plan had succeeded.

"Every allegation you have levelled against your wife

and myself has been deliberately concocted, and has not one grain of truth in it," Dominic addressed the madman. "Your valet is obviously in your pay. But my lawyers will communicate with yours, sir, I do assure you."

Vivian gave a sweeping bow. He was enjoying not only the discomfiture of the proud politician but the sight of Charlotte's ghastly face. He said:

"And mine will reply, sir. It will make an entertaining case."

"My poor Eleanora—" began Charlotte, but stopped, choking. The mere thought of her little girl so happily sleeping upstairs, ignorant of the hideous menace that hung over her head, reduced her to an anguish she could hardly control. Tears poured down her cheeks. She gasped:

"Let me take Eleanora with me, Vivian, I beseech you."

"Pray leave this house," he said. "You are no longer entitled to stay under my roof; nor shall you ever see your daughters again."

The malice in his voice appalled Dominic. He was filled with apprehension for Charlotte. He knew what motherhood meant to her.

She was crazy with pain at the thought of Eleanora's horror and despair tomorrow when she would wake and ask for Mama and be told by her spiteful father that her mother had deserted her. Charlotte continued to sob out her appeals to Vivian. Dominic saw the sadistic joy in the other man's eyes and it made him shudder. If he had ever had the smallest doubt that Charlotte's private life was a nightmare, he had none now. He said:

"Charlotte, my poor child, come with me now, I will protect you. I swear it."

"*Oh, God,*" she said in a voice of despair and looked wildly at him. She loved him; but now it was only of Eleanora that she was thinking.

Vivian, leaning an arm on the mantelpiece, lit a cigar. He was enjoying himself hugely. He knew perfectly well that he had not one shred of genuine evidence against either of these two. But Volpo's evil plan had been so successful, it intoxicated him. He saw that he could reasonably expect now to rid himself legally of Charlotte and so be free of domestic ties. As for the children—a good nurse and governess could take care of *them* down here at

Clunes, whilst he, Vivian, roamed the Continent, the world, as he wished. Not a word would Society be able to breathe against him in the future. But Charlotte and Dominic Unwin would stand condemned forever, ostracized.

The sight of the terrible pain on Charlotte's wet white face, as she walked unsteadily out of the library on Dominic's arm, compensated Vivian for every moment of annoyance that he had suffered on account of his marriage.

He called after Dominic.

"Mr. Unwin, have you forgotten that you dismissed your carriage, thinking no doubt that you could spend the rest of the night here, whilst I was so conveniently away?"

Dominic turned back.

"Sir, I did *not* dismiss my carriage."

"Nevertheless it has gone," said Vivian smiling.

Dominic set his teeth. This was fresh evidence of Lord Chase's vile plot to harm his unhappy wife.

"I do confess," added Vivian, "on account of my outraged feelings, I am disinclined to offer you the use of my own vehicles. You can count yourself lucky, Mr. Unwin, that I have so far controlled my temper as not to put a bullet through the head of the man who betrayed me."

"Oh, Dominic, Dominic, things go from bad to worse," groaned Charlotte.

"It is worse only because you must leave this warm house to walk, on a cold night, which you are not fit for," said Dominic briefly.

Vivian was so pleased now with the turn events had taken, he decided to be magnanimous.

"Let it not be said that I have forced a woman, even so abased as my wife, to take a country stroll in poor weather," he said, chuckling. "Besides, Charlotte has never been much of a walker. I will allow my coachman to drive you both to Harling."

Dominic whispered to the half-fainting Charlotte.

"You understand why I am not engaging in a fight now, this moment, with your husband, do you not, Charlotte? It would be to no purpose. He is mad and, if he shoots, you may be the victim. I cannot see you harmed."

She turned her agonized eyes to him.

"I would gladly die," she said, "but I agree with you—to fight tonight is useless. He is capable of killing you and telling the world that it was a *crime passionel*—in defence of his honour."

"Nevertheless it takes all my strength of will to keep my hands off him," muttered Dominic.

Vivian had pulled the bell. Volpo appeared. For a moment the Portuguese valet's narrow eyes turned to Lady Chase's ghastly face, and gloated an instant. He had been listening outside those doors; he was as delighted as his master at the result of tonight's duplicity. It would be a pleasure, he thought, to confront that ugly bitch Gertrude in the morning and inform her that her precious lady had eloped with her paramour.

Vivian told his valet to waken the coachman and order the brougham.

Charlotte said faintly:

"It is bitterly cold. I would like a wrap—"

"You shall have one, or I will see that every man and woman in this country hears of your husband's unnatural behaviour," said Dominic in a loud clear voice and turned his gaze full upon Lord Chase.

Vivian's eyelids drooped. He shrugged his shoulders and looked at Charlotte.

"You may fetch your coat and a night-bag," he said indifferently. "But do not awaken Eleanora or it will be worst for you and *her*," he added malevolently.

Chapter Twenty-seven

When Charlotte drove away with Dominic from Clunes that terrible March night, she was in a fainting condition; beyond speech or thought.

Once alone in the cold and darkness, Dominic put an arm about her. She leaned her head against his shoulder. She wore a warm dress, bonnet and cloak—velvet, fur-trimmed, luxurious—but in the small bag by the coachman's side there was only a change of under-linen and a few requisites for the night. She had taken nothing else. Terrified of Vivian, she had fled from the house that had been her home for ten long years. From her abhorred husband who had taken his revenge upon her; and perforce from Eleanora for whom her heart was breaking.

She could no longer weep. She lay with her face pressed against Dominic's coat. He stroked her hand gently. Whatever the turbulence of his thoughts—and all this had been a shock to him—he showed no sign of it. He remained calm and inexpressibly gentle. He tried all manner of arguments, first to reassure her that justice would be done and that she would soon see her children again, then to promise her his support.

But she would not be comforted. When she was able to speak, she did so with complete despair.

"Vivian is ruthless," she said, "without scruple. And he hates me. He will lie under oath in order to ruin me and take Eleanora from me for ever."

"He shall not," repeated Dominic sternly. Then with sudden curiosity, he added: "Why, though, has he also made *me* the object of vengeance? What harm have I done him?"

"Nothing, save that he must have suspected my admiration for you. You are the only man whose friendship I have ever dared to want—no matter how innocently."

Dominic tightened his hold of her.

"My poor child, to what an appalling end has your sweet friendliness towards me brought you."

"I do not mind for myself. But you are a famous man—in the public eye. Scandal must not be allowed to touch you."

"Lord Chase intends that it shall," said Dominic grimly.

Convulsively, she squeezed his gloved hand in hers.

"The idea terrifies me. Oh, forgive me, I implore you, for being instrumental in this. I did not know. I swear I had no knowledge of the letter that brought you to my side."

"I believe you implicitly. I have only myself to blame, because I came hot-haste, believing you needed me, not pausing to act more prudently. I should have realized how strange it was that you of all pure women should seek a meeting of clandestine nature."

"Oh, Dominic, I am more thankful than you will ever know to have you at my side tonight. I have endured too much pain, alone. To have your hand in mine, to hear your voice, gives me new faith and courage."

The carriage moved on slowly through the cold black night. Dominic thrilled to the haunting quality, the rich promise of love in Charlotte's voice. Once again he realized how dear she was to him, how completely he was enslaved by her, body, heart and soul. Fears for the future, regrets for the past, were swept away on a rising tide of emotions. He gathered her in a close embrace and pressed his lips to her cold, tear-stained cheek.

"My beloved child, alas, that I am so much too old for you! You are young, much too young to have to bear such anguish. But believe that I love you! I told you so earlier tonight, before we agreed to bid each other farewell. I tell you again. I love you, my darling Charlotte. I shall not leave you while you need me, no matter what befalls us."

The words were spoken, clearly and proudly, and hearing them, Charlotte's flagging spirits revived. The rich colour returned to her cheek and the light to her eyes. She flung her arms around his neck.

"You are not too old for me, dear, *dearest* Dominic, I love you better than life itself. I always have, from the first moment we met, and I always shall."

Dominic was suddenly, strangely at peace in this little world of their own making. He remembered neither his great work nor his previous unhampered, bachelor existence. He knew only that he would never be alone again, but must always belong to this lovely tender-hearted woman who to him was still a child, in years.

At last he said:

"Come what may of tonight's frightfulness, something beautiful and sacred has arisen out of it. We have become dear and necessary to each other."

"I like to hear you say that, but how can I allow you to give me your love or protection?" she said sadly. "I cannot, I shall not Let Vivian divorce me and—cite *you*!"

Cite him! How strangely those sinister words fell on his ears. A short while ago they would have made him shudder. Now he only bent his lips to Charlotte's cheek and brushed away the tears.

"Do not let us think too much about *that* just now," he said. "First we must consider what is to be done tonight. It is bitterly cold—" He leaned closer to the window and frowned as he saw the rain pouring down. The coachman was shouting to the horses and obviously finding it increasingly difficult to keep them from slipping. "God forgive that madman for turning you out on such a night," Dominic muttered.

"Where can we go until we can catch the first train to London?" she asked.

"You have no one around here, no friend to whom you could tell your story, and with whom I could leave you?"

"No one," she answered shaking her head, "they are all Vivian's friends. Even if they wished to be kindly disposed toward me, they would not want me with a possible scandal hanging over my head. Most of the families in the district have known the Chases for several generations. Remember that I was but Charlotte Goff and they will be only too ready to sneer."

She drew away from him.

"You must see for yourself, it is imperative that you, too, should have nothing to do with me. You must at least prove to the world that we are not an eloping couple."

The next words he spoke were stirring enough to warm her frightened heart.

"In a moment I shall convince myself that we are. I shall resign my seat in Parliament and take you away and make it my life's business to ensure that you never suffer again."

For a moment she could not speak but sat with her slender fingers laced together, and her throat working convulsively. Then she whispered:

"To hear you say it has wiped out years of pain. But it is out of the question."

"My poor child," he said, "and even my love cannot alleviate your fears for your eldest child. I know that."

She shut her eyes. She dared not allow herself to visualize Eleanora's misery tomorrow.

Now the carriage jolted to a standstill. A footman who sat beside the driver opened the carriage door letting a shower of rain on them.

"Harling Station, sir," he said, crossly, for he had been pulled out of his sleep to make this journey.

"Are the doors of the station open?" inquired Dominic.

"Nay, sir, shut," said the man and stared at his mistress who covered her face against the cold and rain with a fold of her mantle.

Dominic racked his brains. Impossible to allow a delicate woman to be exposed to these grim weather conditions, so late at night. Harling was wrapped in silence. The inhabitants slept. This carriage would not take them further. The driver had Lord Chase's orders. Even if Dominic woke the livery stables and tried to bribe the owner to get out hired horses and vehicle, where could they go? No hired coachman would risk a long drive. Charlotte's great friends, the Marshes, were twenty miles away. Tomorrow she could go to them, but not now.

Dominic said tersely:

"I have no option, Charlotte, but to take you to the local inn, rouse them and ask them to give you a bed."

"I know them at The Bell," she nodded. "Mr. Swain is the landlord. Vivian has in the past spent money drinking there with some of his friends. I would hate to go to The Bell. The Swains will gossip and everybody in the district will know."

"Lord Chase will, in any case, see that everybody knows. By this time tomorrow there will be little hope of keeping the thing a secret," said Dominic grimly.

The night-wind tore at Charlotte. She shivered with exhaustion and cold. After a moment, she agreed to Dominic's plan. They drove to the Bell Tavern, a sixteenth-century inn not far from Harling Church. The idea of entering the place was repugnant to her but she was helpless. Only, when Dominic said that he could not remain at The Bell, also, she uttered a protest.

"You cannot stay outside in this bitter cold. It is unthinkable."

"I am not young but I am strong and shall not faint by the wayside," said Dominic with a smile, "I can walk to a neighbouring village, be it five or ten miles, and there seek a room for the night. I shall not further embarrass you by remaining in this district."

She longed to say: *"Oh, my love, do not abandon me,"* but remained silent. She would have died rather than embarrass him further. She had been responsible enough already, although unwittingly, for the load of trouble that had fallen on his innocent shoulders.

Dominic roused the landlord and his wife.

Both the Swains came in answer to the repeated knocking. He, with a rough robe over his nightshirt, his nightcap still on his head; she in similar attire, hair done up in curl papers. They were a scraggy, bad-tempered-looking pair. When they recognized the fine lady who stood clinging to the gentleman's arm, they exchanged astonished glances, then smirks.

Of course, they said, bowing low, they would give her ladyship a bedroom, and the gentleman too, if he so wished. But Dominic refused the hospitality and reluctantly left Charlotte in the care of the unattractive couple.

"I will come for you in the morning and escort you to your friends' home," he told Charlotte.

She refused this.

"It must not be. *I* will hire a carriage and go alone to Pillars. You must stay away from me until our position is clarified," she said.

"It touches me that you should think of my good name in the midst of your own terrible plight," he said.

They were alone, for a moment, in the bar parlour of The Bell. In the dim light of the oil lamp which Mr. Swain had placed on one of the tables, Charlotte's face looked to Dominic so pinched and wan that he hesitated to leave her. She had become, this unforgettable night, dearer than life to him. He caught and held her a moment to his heart.

"Try to sleep, Charlotte. I shall be thankful to hear tomorrow that you are with your friends. I have ever been drawn to Mrs. Marsh who is as wise as she is a most beautiful old lady."

"At least *they* will not scorn me," said Charlotte in a strangled voice.

"Nobody shall scorn you," said Dominic and kissed her hands each in turn. "I will love and serve you to the best of my ability," he added huskily. "I shall see Mr. Glover, my solicitor, tomorrow, and we must act upon his judgment. If, as I fear, he says we ought not to meet again, I will obey, because my only desire is that you should have your children restored to you."

She trembled and clung to him.

"I thank you from the bottom of my heart, but oh, Dominic, *Dominic!*" she broke off and burst into a flood of anguished weeping.

Not for long. She steadied herself and, smiling through her tears, bade him leave her. She was positive the Swains would be waiting, gloating, watching how long they remained together. Five minutes more and Dominic left The Bell and started his uncomfortable walk through the wild stormy night.

Mrs. Swain showed her ladyship to the best room, where she had already lit a small fire. She had also placed a foot warmer in the big tester bed.

"I would have done more had I expected you, my lady," she began, looking at Charlotte in a sly way which Charlotte found offensive.

"It is no matter," Charlotte made herself reply with as much pride as she could muster. "Thank you—for your services."

Mrs. Swain bobbed and departed. Charlotte sat weakly on the edge of the bed. How cold and uninviting was this shabby room. With low ceilings and poor furniture, it had a musty odour and looked hideous after Charlotte's own beautiful bedroom at Clunes. Nevertheless she did not despise it, for at least she could be alone here. Her terrible husband could not disturb her rest—if there was to be any rest for her.

She covered her face with her hands, trying to control her shuddering. She felt dazed by all that she had been through since Dominic's unexpected arrival at Clunes. On the one hand all seemed lost and desperate; on the other lay the memory of Dominic's embrace and the knowledge that he returned her love. But she was assailed by a dozen fears for Eleanora's well-being.

She unclasped her mantle and let the bonnet fall from her weary head. Then she knelt down by the bed and clasping her hands, uttered a wild prayer for help.

"Do not let this thing happen—oh, God in heaven—do not permit it—for my children's sake, and for Dominic Unwin's," she said the words aloud.

In their room next door, the Swains whispered together.

"We'll have a nice story to tell in the morning," said Mr. Swain, "her ladyship arriving with a strange gentleman at this hour. Well, *well*—!" he smothered a ribald laugh.

"Did you note the languishing glances they gave each other?" said Mrs. Swain. "Who'd have dreamed *she* was that sort. His lordship has turned her out—that's plain to see."

"And her with three children," added Mr. Swain.

But Charlotte did not hear. After her prayers, she seated herself by the fire, and leaning back, fell into an uneasy slumber from which she woke stiff and cold and scarcely able to face the day that lay before her.

With one of those swift changes of mood for which the English climate is famous, the March morning that followed was warm, humid and full of the lush golden promise of spring.

Charlotte (who had reluctantly accepted money from Dominic—she had no choice, for Vivian never gave her a penny of her own), washed and tidied herself and soon after eight o'clock left the Bell Tavern in a hired vehicle. She was terrified that Vivian would get to hear that she had stayed the night in Harling, and was anxious to get away from the district as fast as possible.

She was conscious of Mr. and Mrs. Swain's leering glances which added a touch of insolence to their gushing civility but she hardly spoke to them. When at length she found herself well out of Harling she felt better.

But her agony of mind was terrible to bear. Try as she would, she could not stop imagining what would be going on at this very moment. Eleanora would run into Mama's bedroom and find Papa there, instead. God grant that Vivian would not be too harsh with his little daughter, thought the poor mother. Gertrude, of course, would return to Clunes this morning with the other two children. She would be not only astonished but deeply upset to find her lady missing. Oh, what would Vivian do? Dismiss Gertrude and bring back that terrible nurse whom Eleanora disliked? And would he really carry out his threat of implicating an innocent man in a trumped-up divorce case? It was a Charlotte in a sorry state who arrived many hours later at Pillars. They had stopped midway to rest the horses and take some refreshment and reached the Marshes' home by midday.

A bemused and half-fainting Charlotte was helped from the carriage by Fleur and Peveril, who were astonished and alarmed to see her.

"Good heavens, my child, what is wrong?" asked Fleur looking with dismay at her young friend's deathly face.

Charlotte had to be given coffee and brandy before she could tell the dreadful story. Once told, she broke down and wept piteously.

"What will happen to Eleanora?" she kept moaning. "And how can we save Mr. Unwin?"

Fleur and Peveril exchanged horrified glances. Peveril said:

"Of course Vivian Chase cannot be responsible. Our poor Charlotte must defend this case on the grounds that he is insane."

"Insanity has to be proved," sighed Fleur, who was sitting beside the couch stroking Charlotte's hair. "It is a monstrous thing but he seems to hold the trump cards. Not many would be willing to come forward and swear that he is a lunatic. But how terrible that Dominic Unwin should be involved!"

Charlotte turned a wild wet face to her.

"I love him with all my heart, Fleur," she said in a

choked voice, "and he loves me. Yet we are innocent and almost strangers. Is it not ironic?"

"It is pitiable for you both," said Fleur and her large violet eyes filled with tears.

The old painter adopted a man's practical attitude.

"Come, my dearest," he said, touching Fleur on the shoulder, "let us see that a room is prepared for our guest, and try to take a more cheerful view. At any rate, our home is hers for as long as she needs it."

Charlotte lifted a handkerchief to her lips and shook her head.

"You are kind, sir, but I came to you in desperation. I ought not to stay. The whole of England may soon ring with this story. My name will be dragged in the mud and it will be wrong for me to allow the world to criticize you two for befriending me."

They assured her, at once, that they feared no criticism. Charlotte Chase and Dominic Unwin were innocent people, victims of a vile and lunatic hatred. Why should they be ostracized?

"You are too good and only what I expected, but Vivian has done enough harm. I would not wish that harm extended to you," persisted Charlotte.

"Be comforted, dear child, and reassured that we can take care of ourselves," said Peveril gently, and smiled at her.

So Charlotte came to the peace, the beauty, the tranquillity of Pillars, and her kind friends.

Meanwhile, in London, Dominic Unwin forsook his usual routine of work and drove to Holborn to visit the offices of his solicitors. There he told Mr. Glover his story.

"The whole thing was an abominable trick," he ended, striding up and down the office, his hands locked behind his back, his face pale and stern. "Lord Chase must not be allowed to succeed."

Mr. Glover who had listened in shocked silence, looked at his distinguished client with dismay.

"Indeed he must not. I have *never* listened to a more terrible story."

Dominic came to a standstill before the desk and leaned a clenched fist upon it.

"I ask you to make it your sacred duty to prevent this fearful slur from falling upon a pure and innocent lady."

Mr. Glover, who was an elderly man, coughed and lowered his lids. A little red in the cheeks, he said:

"Forgive me, Mr. Unwin, if I seem impertinent, but I must ask you a few questions."

"Ask what you will," said Dominic, and passed a hand across his brow with an impatient gesture. He had returned to London by an early train this morning after a sleepless night in a small inn little better than The Bell in Harling. After that trudge through a wet stormy night he was exhausted. He had breakfasted in his rooms at Albany in a state of mind that could rightfully be called chaotic.

He answered Mr. Glover's questions; but when that gentleman suggested, apologetically of course, that his client might have been the dupe of the wife as well as the husband, Dominic became a lion in her defence.

"Do not dare suggest any such thing, Glover!" he said indignantly, "I tell you, Lady Chase is first and foremost a mother. She would not have sent that letter for one reason above all others—that it would risk her losing her children."

Mr. Glover looked uncomfortable and added:

"Your pardon, Mr. Unwin, it is my duty to probe into this case in detail. I—I—there was a chance—ahem—that Lady Chase might have wished for a divorce and used *you*—"

Dominic interrupted again, his face burning.

"Such is not the case and can be ruled out immediately."

Mr. Glover nodded and cleared his throat.

"If you will pardon me saying so, sir, was it not a little unwise of you to have adhered so strictly to the detailed instructions in her letter? Did it not seem to you peculiar that Lady Chase should demand a clandestine meeting in the country, late at night?"

Dominic walked to the window. Hands in his pockets he stared down at the traffic in High Holborn. Vans and carriages, horses and costermongers' barrows, vied with each other for space. He could hear their shouts, the clatter of hooves, the rolling of wheels on the cobbles as he stood up there by the half open dusty window. At length he said:

"I admit that I acted on a foolish impulse. I will also

confess to you, in confidence, Glover, that Lady Chase is one of my dearest friends. I have the highest regard for her and I felt that it would be unchivalrous to ignore the appeal that I *presumed* she, herself, made to me."

Mr. Glover made various notes and drew his private conjectures. What a position, he reflected, for the distinguished politician to find himself linked in what the world would call "an adulterous union" with Lady Chase. It was the last shadow that Mr. Glover had dreamed could ever fall across the brightness of Dominic Unwin's life and threaten his reputation.

When Dominic left his solicitor's office, it was in an unhappy frame of mind. Mr. Glover had somewhat bluntly let him know that if Chase persisted in swearing that the note was in his wife's handwriting and the valet swore under oath that he had actually found Mr. Unwin and her ladyship in *flagrante delicto,* it would be a hard case to defend. But it was suggested that counsel's opinion must be taken and an appointment should be made immediately with Sir Travis Emmerton, Q.C. He was one of the finest barristers in England today.

After that, things moved swiftly. Vivian lost no time in instructing his own lawyers and presenting his case. They, in turn, let it be known to Mr. Glover that Lord Chase intended to cite Mr. Unwin as a co-respondent in his divorce.

That night, every Club and nearly every house belonging to friends and associates of either the Englesbys or the Chases hummed with the news.

It was whispered from one to the other; spoken of in shocked whispers over dinner-tables; smirked at by ladies in their drawing-rooms.

The beautiful Lady Chase had left her husband and children and run away with Mr. Dominic Unwin, M.P., adopted son of the Englesbys.

Cecil was abroad at the time so the story had yet to reach his ears. But the Marquis of Englesby heard it and sent post-haste for his adopted son, from whom he demanded an explanation.

"The great lady who has been a mother to you since you were a boy lies at death's door. How could you have done such a thing? If it reaches her ears it will kill her," the Marquis said furiously.

Dominic answered him.

"I am not guilty and neither is the lady concerned. I have never lied to you, sir. I beg you to believe me now. This story is a vile fabrication on the part of a madman."

Later, when Dominic left Englesby Castle, his heart was heavy, but he did at least know that his adopted father accepted his word. A worse moment arrived. That next morning, he was sent for by his Leader. The great man, himself, demanded an explanation.

"I am amazed and disappointed in you, Unwin. That *you* should be so indiscreet and with a married woman who has children! Good God, what has come over you, man? I would never have believed it."

Now indeed Dominic Unwin knew what it was for the first time in his life to feel the cold breath of scorn upon him, the knife-edge of a vile suspicion. Yet remembering Charlotte's defencelessness and the love that she bore him, he faced the full blast and stood up to it calmly, reiterating that Lady Chase was blameless.

"Lord Chase is out of his mind. I shall defend the case, sir," he told Lord Salisbury, "and Lady Chase is with friends, not at my side. She and I are not lovers, nor have ever been. I ask you to take my word on this."

Salisbury looked troubled. He had always admired Unwin and marked him down for something big.

He put a hand on Dominic's shoulder.

"I shall try to take your word and pray that it is the truth, for you know what Her Majesty feels about divorce," he added.

Dominic left him with those words echoing in his ears. By the time that week came to an end he felt as though he had been through a hurricane. He could not put his mind to his work. In the Members' room, he knew that he was being looked at curiously by his colleagues, and in his own Club, one evening, he was cut dead by a certain peer of the realm who happened to have been at Oxford with Vivian Chase.

That slight had a curious effect upon Dominic. If he had not truly cared for Charlotte it might have made him dislike her. For it was a stinging blow to his pride, his sense of what was right and proper. Then it roused a bitter determination to fight this thing to the end, no matter what it cost him—for Charlotte's sake.

He could no longer restrain his impulse to see her, the woman whose name was linked with his and who had become inadvertently the cause of *his* disaster.

He had not heard from her, but a short note from Fleur Marsh had acquainted him with the fact that she was safely at Pillars. To this, Fleur had added an invitation to Dominic to go down to Pillars and see Charlotte when he wished.

Mr. Glover would of course, thought Dominic, say that it would be unwise of him to go near Charlotte at this stage of events. But Dominic was conscious now of something stronger than mere wounded vanity or fears for his own name. He experienced a deep longing for Charlotte. His love had become like a fire burning brighter and brighter in his heart and soul.

He decided to travel down to Epping and see Charlotte on the morrow.

Chapter Twenty-eight

Fleur Marsh was busy arranging her flowers when her butler announced: "Mr. Dominic Unwin."

Fleur walked toward the door with outstretched hands. She did not know that Dominic was coming but was not surprised to see him here. She had felt that nothing now would keep him away from Charlotte.

It was another lovely spring day. The gardens were a golden shimmer of daffodils. Fleur had just received a basket of flowers from the head gardener, and was about to decorate her morning room. Peveril was in his studio, painting. Charlotte was in her own room. She was busy with Fleur's dressmaker. The poor girl had come away from Clunes with no clothes and Fleur had insisted that one or two dresses must be made for her immediately. Both the women knew well that Vivian would not show Charlotte the courtesy of sending her even a portion of her wardrobe.

Fleur began:

"I am delighted to see you, Mr. Unwin—"

But she stopped and let her hands fall to her sides. Mr. Unwin, she knew, would be distressed by what had recently taken place, but she could not understand why he looked at *her* so strangely. He stared with a mixture of wonder and amazement, and with a pallor that showed under the warm brown of his skin. Fleur's welcoming smile faded.

"Mr. Unwin! Are you ill?" she began again.

He shook his head but remained dumb. His deeply blue eyes seemed to be drinking in the sight of her. Indeed, he could not stop staring at the delicate, lined face of this beautiful old lady who wore an enchanting dress of forget-me-not blue, with muslin frills at the throat, and a fringed blue lace shawl over her narrow shoulders. At length he managed to speak:

"Mrs. Marsh—I—I—" he stopped, shaking his head as though unable to find further words. He began to move into the sun-lit morning room which was, he thought, like the mistress of the house, dainty, beautiful, dignified. She motioned him to a winged arm-chair. He sat down gratefully.

"You must think me mad," he said in a low husky voice. "Indeed I feel that I *am*."

"Oh, dear," said Fleur anxiously. "It is an indisposition, Mr. Unwin."

"To you I must be Dominic," he said in a queer voice.

"My dear Dominic, has this terrible trouble afflicted you so sorely?"

"You mean Vivian Chase's abominations?"

"Yes."

"No," Dominic shook his head. "I can stand up to them well enough. Up till yesterday evening my thoughts were concerned only with *her*, poor sweet Charlotte."

"And hers have been with you," said Fleur gently, "with you and the children from whom she has been so cruelly wrenched. Shall I call her and let the sight of her face revive you?"

Dominic shook his head. He took a handkerchief from his pocket and wiped his brow. He was obviously labouring under some strong emotion. Fleur wondered for an instant if she should send for her husband—that dear man who for forty-six long years had been her staunch defender from all anxieties.

But Dominic said:

"No—let us remain alone. Dear Mrs. Marsh, I have much to say which may come as a fearful shock to you."

"To me?" The old lady's exquisite face coloured. She flickered lashes that were still long and silken. "How can that be?"

"Pray be seated and let me talk to you," he said.

Fleur hesitated.

"Shall I not send for Charlotte, then?"

"Not for a moment. I want to speak to you alone. You are strong enough to stand what I am going to tell you?" he asked.

"Come!" she protested, "you are too mysterious, Mr. Un—I mean Dominic. What can this thing be which is of such significance to *me?*"

"I grieve to have to take your mind back to a time which must have been singularly distasteful to you," he said, "but I think I am right in recalling that you were married to Lord St. Cheviot in London on the 15th September, 1838."

Now Fleur's Dresden-china figure stiffened. With one hand she caught at the cameo brooch at her throat.

"That is so—but *why*—?"

"I beg you to let me continue," broke in Dominic.

Her brows drew together.

"I am vastly perplexed, but go ahead."

"In the June following you—gave birth to a son."

Now Fleur changed colour. Both her hands gripped at the arms of the chair in which she was seated.

"Mr. Unwin—Dominic—why are you bringing to light these facts relating to my past? It is my husband's and my wish that that period of my life should remain a closed book. I know that you and Charlotte are going through much pain and difficulty, but it cannot compare with the pain to which I was once subjected. It is too terrible for me to dwell upon."

Dominic leaned towards her. His face was as pale as hers.

"I do assure you I would not wish to cause you an instant's distress. The words I speak are wrung from me, but *must* be spoken."

"Tell me what you have to say. Do not delay a moment longer," she begged.

Then Dominic with an immense effort and lowering his head, said:

"That miserable infant did not die as you believed. *He lived. He lived and I am he.*"

Silence followed these words. It was as though Fleur had been struck by lightning. Rooted to her chair, she sat staring at Dominic Unwin. For an instant she thought he must be insane and then knew that he was not. Without further questioning, she believed him. Those eyes, of that particular shade of violet which she, and Harry Roddney, her father had possessed, were set also in *his* head. They could be only the eyes of a Roddney that regarded her now.

He spoke:

"Is this too much for you? I know it must be a terrible shock. Shall I call Mr. Marsh?"

She was losing some of her frozen immobility but she answered faintly. "No—*wait*—tell me more. In God's name how do you *know* this thing?"

Then he told her.

The astounding revelation had come following the serious events concerning Charlotte Chase. Yesterday, while he was still in the House he received a message that his presence was urgently required at the hospital for old soldiers in Chelsea. There, an old Corporal of the Guards, named William Smith, lay dying and had expressed a wish to see Mr. Unwin. He had something of infinite importance to reveal to him.

Dominic knew this man and went at once to the hospital. He had thought William Smith dead. He had lived for the first few years of his life with Mr. Smith and his wife. At that time, William was a lamplighter. Later he went to the Crimea, was wounded and must now be well over seventy. He had not communicated with Dominic for over thirty years.

"But I must not confuse you by telling you the story in this order. I must begin from the beginning," said

"Yes, pray do," said Fleur trembling with agitation, her gaze riveted on Dominic's face.

He referred to the hour of his birth. Dominic had all the facts. He knew now that he had been born with a brown skin and that in consequence Lord St. Cheviot, his own father, had in demoniac fury disowned him. The midwife, terrified of St. Cheviot, announced that the baby had never breathed, and carried it out of the house. She had intended to dispose of the tiny body but, realizing that it was alive, took it with her to her cottage in Monks Risborough. There she put it to the breast of a niece who had just given birth to a still-born child. This woman (Mrs. Smith) fed the little boy and became attached to him. She was not repulsed by his colour. Indeed, as he revived, he seemed to grow lighter in hue, and the Smiths admired the beauty of his strange blue eyes, his delicately fashioned limbs. The midwife was too terrified to utter the name of the infant's real parents. So her niece took the babe with her to London where her husband had secured a new job as lamplighter. Only on her death-bed did the nurse reveal to William Smith, the true identity of the child. By that time the Baron of Cadlington was dead and Lady St. Cheviot had married again.

"I stayed with these kindly people, the Smiths, until I was ten," Dominic went on. "After which, as I think you already know, I was sent to a Charity school, from which the Englesbys adopted me. But it appears always to have been on William Smith's conscience that I was the rightful heir to Cadlington, and that my name was not Unwin but—St. Cheviot. So troubled was he, that in his dying hours he felt he must reveal the facts. Thus he sent that message to me at the House. He handed me this—"

Now Dominic gave Fleur a fine gold chain which had attached to it a tiny enamel heart bearing the initial *"C,"* in diamonds. Fleur took it on the palm of her hand. Her fingers shook so that they could scarcely hold the trinket. Her face turned from white to crimson. She stammered:

"Great God in heaven, *then it is true*. For while I was in labour, I handed the midwife this chain with the little heart (the initial was "C" for Cadlington, as you might imagine). I said that when my child was born, the chain was to be placed around his neck to bring him good luck. It was a mother's whim—no more."

"I was surprised," said Dominic, "that the midwife did not steal it. She must have been an honest woman, in her way. And Smith was a decent fellow and did not sell it despite his poverty."

"The one who was supposed to have buried the infant was the best of my two nurses," said Fleur hoarsely. "She was no murderess and would not want a living child to die. I can see it all now. She knew that the Baron would have tried to exterminate the infant had he dreamed it still drew breath. Oh, heavens. And you are here, today, *my son*, my child—a grown, mature man, Dominic Unwin!"

She broke off. Outside in the garden, she could hear the sound of birds singing, and of a bell ringing from Epping Church. She turned her gaze again to the face of this man, this politician, whom she had once thought little more than a stranger. Terrible, wonderful, *incredible* fact. *He was her son*. Her babe, who forty-six years ago had not died but lived to become a distinguished Member of Parliament.

Now she knew why she had been so curiously drawn to Dominic. She understood many things. She realized why he had shown unusual brilliance when a child, a mere schoolboy. For had not Hélène Roddney, his grandmother, been one of the most erudite and brilliant women of her time? She could see why his manner held so much charm; for just such another splendid and charming person had been his grandfather, Harry Roddney. Thank God, Fleur reflected, he resembled his father not at all. The brutality, the coarseness, the cruelty of St. Cheviot had passed him by. He belonged wholly to *her* side of the family. There was nothing of St. Cheviot about him except, perhaps, the blackness of his hair.

So he had come to Pillars, his mother's old home. It was the most fantastic, satisfying thing that could ever have happened to any woman in the world, she thought. What did the hue of his skin matter? He was not, by any means the native that St. Cheviot had feared. Dominic's skin was a light brown such as could be seen on thousands of men in the Latin countries. The delicate lips, the straight nose, eyes, were *hers*. And now Fleur began to trace a dozen other endearing resemblances. The chin was her father's, the smile Hélène's. Yes, he was Lady Roddney's grandson with that strange magnetism that would make a woman love him (as Charlotte did) without hope of reward, for love's sake alone.

All the starved years of her repressed motherhood seemed to fall away from Fleur Marsh. It was with a sob of complete fulfilment that she held her arms out to Dominic.

"My son," she said, her voice breaking, "My dear boy—"

Speechlessly he fell at her feet and laid his head against her knee. The strong man was not ashamed of his tears. He kissed one of Fleur's frail delicate hands repeatedly. For the first time uttered that sacred name:

"My mother!"

It was a long time before either of them became calm or practical. There was so much to be said. After a while, Dominic sat beside the beautiful old lady and drank in every word she said. He knew nothing of his father or his inheritance. He wanted to hear everything. It was a staggering revelation—the history of Cadlington, with its great Tower, which had been burned down on the day that his grandfather ran Denzil St. Cheviot through the heart, the poignant story of Fleur's own marriage, the dramatic events that had led up to his—Dominic's birth.

After a moment Dominic said:

"You have endured more than most human beings could bear, my poor little mother. You must have had immense courage."

"It was Peveril who helped me through it. It is to him I owe everything."

"Then I, too, am beholden to him, and could want for no finer stepfather."

"How strange that sounds," sighed Fleur. "Only the other day when he heard me sigh, he guessed that it was because I had always missed the little child whom I thought had perished. It is strange, Dominic, but I seem to feel no ill will towards you because you are St. Cheviot's son."

"I pray not," said Dominic and raised his mother's hand to his lips, "for you will from now onward, in unison with Charlotte Chase, become the light of my life. I shall always be fond of the mother who adopted me; ever grateful, also to the Marquess who gave me my chances in life. But blood is thicker than water, and you are truly *mine*."

"My darling," whispered Fleur, her eyes brimming with tears.

Dominic stood up. Walking to the window, he looked out at the grounds. He felt dazed. He had felt so ever since seeing William Smith yesterday. He went on talking to Fleur.

"In time to come, there is much more that I must know. This native blood of mine, I am curious about it. I had always imagined myself Spanish or Italian, perhaps, but *African*—no!"

"Let it not displease you, my dear," said Fleur gently, "your African great-great-grandfather was, so I was told, a fine and noble man. There is no disgrace in your ancestry."

"And my grandmother—Lady Roddney—showed no sign of it?"

"None. Like me she was white-skinned and red-haired, except that she had very dark eyes."

"Strange," muttered Dominic. "So it was I, alone, who reverted to type, after three generations."

Fleur stretched out her hand.

"Do not let that disturb you, Dominic. I remember the poor old doctor who delivered me, telling me one day when we were discussing this question of black blood, that it was not likely ever to happen again. The time is past. *Your* children when you marry should be one hundred per cent European. And, dear Dominic, you do not *look* native—but Spanish, or Italian, or Greek perhaps. With those intensely blue eyes you might be truly an Englishman who has been much in the East."

"If I resemble *you*, it is enough," he said. "I am the most fortunate man on earth to have found such a beautiful, gentle mother."

"Your father—" she began and stopped.

"My father seems to have been an unpleasant fellow," said Dominic with a grim smile.

"In some way he resembled Vivian Chase," she sighed. "Yet Denzil *had* noble blood in him. He was a fine sportsman and a man of tremendous courage. There was only one swordsman in Europe to match him and that was my father, Harry Roddney."

Fleur's heart thrilled. Old and frail though she was, even today the indomitable spirit of Hélène Roddney burned in her blood. She was proud, proud to look at this splendid serious-minded man whom Charlotte loved and know that he was her son.

"Dominic," she said as though she found the word sweet, "*Dominic*—I like that name. *Unwin*, too, has served you well. But you must, in future, bear your rightful title. You will take this story to my family solicitors. The Cadlington estates must be returned to you, as well as the immense fortune which Denzil left and which I as his widow refused to touch. But *you* are Dominic St. Cheviot. Thus the full circle comes around! By some strange chance, yours are the same initials as his. *'D. St. C.'* Once more there is a Baron of Cadlington. The best and noblest of them all," Fleur added softly.

It was at this juncture that Charlotte and Peveril came into the room. They had met in the hall, each on their way to join Fleur for tea.

When Charlotte saw the tall man in grey her heart jolted. All the misery and anxiety of the past few days dropped from her shoulders.

"Dominic," she said in a strangled voice.

He took her hand, looking at her wan sweet face with great tenderness. Now that he saw her again, he knew how much he had wanted this reunion. It did not seem to matter what evil Vivian Chase was scheming, what devil's brew he had in store for them.

Silently they regarded each other. Heart and soul were in that gaze.

Peveril walked to his wife's side. Shocked, he saw that her lashes were wet.

"My dearest, something has happened to upset you—" he began.

She squeezed his hand and interrupted.

"No, but listen, my beloved, for I have astounding news for you—news, that will, I think, thrill you, for my sake. Dominic—" she turned to address her new-found son—"take Charlotte into the garden. It is fine and warm. Walk with her awhile and tell her what you have just told me. I will repeat it all to Peveril."

Still holding hands, Charlotte and Dominic walked out into the sunlight.

Chapter Twenty-nine

The story that Dominic related to Charlotte left her amazed and delighted.

"How *wonderful!*" she exclaimed, "to know you are the son of one who has been such a dear friend to me."

Dominic and Charlotte were sitting in the arbour that faced the ornamental lake; that same arbour in which Dominic's grand-parents had sat hand in hand, fifty years ago.

Dominic played with one of Charlotte's fine long hands. He looked at it thoughtfully.

"Do you find it repellent that four generations back there was African blood in my family?"

"Of course not," she said indignantly, "why should I?"

"There are those who would be put off."

"Not I. We are all God's children—black or white—and, dear Dominic, there are thousands of people who must be ignorant about their origin. Who amongst us can boast of pure unbroken lineage? Besides—I like you as you are. I love the essential man in you. I respected you as Dominic Unwin. I revere you neither more nor less because you have become the Baron of Cadlington."

He kissed her hand fervently.

"That title falls strangely on my ear. I have yet to get accustomed to it."

"In a way it takes you further from me," she said on a sudden note of sadness. For up till now she had been excited and happy, concentrating on his personal news.

"Why so," he asked, "on the contrary you should feel nearer because I am Mrs. Marsh's son."

She bit her lip and did not reply. He saw her shiver as she turned and gazed with melancholy across the sun-gilded lake.

"You are thinking of our invidious position, and of your children," he asked gently.

"Yes," she nodded, "all day, ever since I last saw you, I have been worrying about Eleanora. The days have seemed like years because I have no notion of what is going on at Clunes."

"Poor little Charlotte?"

"Do not pity me," she said with a strangled sob, "for I have repeatedly blamed myself that you are tied up with me in this beastliness. Vivian has already made the news public. Yes, we have heard echoes of it down here. London is, I am sure, buzzing with the disgraceful scandal."

"It is," said Dominic grimly.

Charlotte looked at him with eyes full of love and a profound humility.

"Whatever happens, do not hold this against me," she begged. "*I* would have died rather than allow a shadow to fall upon *your* name."

"Hush, child," he said, "I have repeatedly told you that I never blame you; that I am happy to stand by your side in your tribulation."

"But Dominic—" began Charlotte.

"No," he interrupted, "say no more, beloved, for I tell you here and now that if Lord Chase is instrumental in ruining my good name—I shall not let it eat into my heart like a festering sore. That heart is too full now of the thought of you—and my mother. Let it be remembered that I am Baron of Cadlington—a St. Cheviot—and a Roddney. These are powerful names, and I have a new birthright, a proud heritage that will enable me to defeat Vivian Chase. Yes, no matter what he does to me. There remains not only my unflinching desire to retrieve the good reputation of the St. Cheviots that my father lost but my wish to protect you and restore you to your children."

He covered one of her hands between two of his. Tenderly he regarded her. She wore a fringed cashmere shawl borrowed from Fleur, and the tobacco-coloured travelling dress which she had put on before she left Clunes. Sorrow was engraved on her features. The cheek bones jutted out a little. The eyes were enormous and heavily shadowed. Yet there sat upon her still, he thought, that air of innocence, of unworldiness, that made her look so young despite her harrowing experiences.

"My dearest," he said, "the more that I am with you, the more do I feel that I would like you to drop your defence of the case and let your husband do his worst. Then, when the case is over, we could be married."

The burning colour swept her face.

"You have said that before but I must always answer in the same way. Never, never, can I be instrumental in taking you from the work you love."

"But child, I have grown to love *you* more—far more—than my work."

She bent her head and passionately kissed the firm strong hands imprisoning her own.

"I love you, Dominic, dear, *dear* Dominic. I worship you, but I must be strong and so must you. Emotion might lead you in this crisis to feel that you would gladly abandon your career for me. But there would come a day when you would regret it. It can never be."

The touch of her fresh young lips against his fingers thrilled him and filled him with a strange humility. He took her head between those hands which she kissed and raised it. He looked deeply into her eyes.

"My beloved Charlotte—unselfish to the end. You cannot love me more than I do you. That love has become an integral part of my existence. And ever a wonder and amazement," he added, "for I am an old man compared with you."

"I want no more of other men," she said. "And to me you are young and all that my heart desires. But, oh, Dominic, I can see nothing but separation ahead of us."

"My darling child, how can I ever let you go back to that hell on earth at Clunes?" he muttered, rising to his feet. She too, rose and stood beside him. His arm gathered her close. In silence they looked across the lake and beyond to the fringe of silver birches, so delicately green, bearing the first buds of spring. She said:

"At this moment, I, too, feel that I could not bear to go back. But for my children's sake, particularly for Eleanora's, I must. I have no choice. Besides I do not feel I ought to leave poor little Beatrice and Victoria to grow up with *him*. For he will train them to be as he is—selfish, cold, worldly—"

"If he loses the case, I have no doubt you could plead and prove cruelty, and get a judicial separation."

"Gertrude, my personal maid, would certainly witness what I have been through," she nodded.

"On Monday I shall see my lawyer again and ask him to travel down here and talk with you and hear your side of things," said Dominic. Then he took her into his arms. "Meanwhile, my dearest, know that I love you above all things," he said and kissed her on the mouth.

Her hungry heart responded to that kiss. Her lips clung to his while her two hands clasped his neck. This was the fulfillment of all her dreams. This was love as she had always wanted it; far, far removed from Vivian's gross appetite. But that warm generous heart of hers was near to breaking as she walked with Dominic back to the house. They must not meet in the future, except before the stern eye of their legal adviser. And Dominic must not come down to Pillars again until the case was heard.

"There is, of course, a chance that Lord Chase will drop it," Dominic said finally.

"I do not think so," said Charlotte in a low voice, "not while he thinks that there is a chance of perpetrating a final act of injustice upon me."

"We shall see," said Dominic gruffly, "little more and I shall seek him and fight it out with him in person, for my blood grows hot at the mere thought of all that he has done to you."

But Charlotte paused and looked up at him with eyes full of fear.

"I implore you not to go near Vivian," she breathed. "There would be a fight. He would try to kill you, as he threatened to do at Clunes, then present himself to the world as the outraged husband. Oh, *no*, Dominic, do not risk that for my sake—or for your *mother's*."

"What must he not do for my sake?" came from Fleur Marsh gaily. She had heard Charlotte's last words as the couple entered the hall, for she, herself, was coming to look for them and tell them that tea was served.

She looked radiant, and wore a posy of yellow primroses

pinned to her dress. Peveril had just picked them for her in the woods where they had walked and talked together of this new and wonderful thing that had come about.

"That word '*mother*' falls very muscially upon my ear," she said looking almost shyly at her tall strong son.

Dominic took one of her hands and bending over it, kissed it.

"My dear little mother, you have all my homage," he said huskily.

The old artist, who had joined the group, put his hands in his pockets and stared with some astonishment and curiosity at Dominic Unwin. The even tenor of existence at Pillars had indeed been disturbed by the news that had been brought here this morning. Peveril could scarcely believe it. Yet he, too, could not doubt that this was Fleur's son. For now he saw that it was with her violet-blue eyes that Dominic looked at him. The eyes that Peveril had admired so greatly when, as a youth, he had first grown to love Fleur St. Cheviot.

When she had first broken the shattering news to him, he had reflected how vastly interesting it was to know that her unfortunate babe had not after all perished at birth. A relief to know that Dominic had grown into this fine and noble man. For Peveril could not recall one thing that he had liked about the late Baron of Cadlington. Strange, *strange*, to look now at Dominic's darkly tanned face, the fine resolute features, and even mark the resemblance—(yes it was there)—to Denzil St. Cheviot himself. What a mad fool Denzil had been to disown such a son. As for the hue of his skin, he was by no means negroid—far from it. And had not Lord Salisbury, himself, said that Dominic was "a shining light in the House"?

Peveril, artist and dreamer, was not one to concern himself with worldly affairs. But he knew well enough the gravity of the present situation. He knew that it would not be good for Dominic's future if Lord Chase was granted his divorce. No matter how much they loved each other, the "guilty" pair would be outlawed by society. And that would hurt Fleur who was Dominic's mother as well as Charlotte's friend.

Well, it was no good jumping the fence before coming to

it, Peveril decided, and held out a hand to Dominic, who grasped it warmly.

"I welcome you as a stepson," said Peveril with his delightful smile, "and I must now be permitted to use these old eyes of mine and paint your portrait, before they fail. Incidentally one of the finest full length portraits I painted in my life was of your own father at Cadlington. I remember well the black St. Cheviots. The hair and brows of your ancestors are yours. A pity my painting was burnt with the rest of the treasures."

Dominic smiled and smoothed his greying hair.

"I thank you, sir, for your kindly welcome and for all that you have ever done for my mother."

"She is utterly happy to have her son restored to her so miraculously," said Peveril.

From that hour onward the two men were destined to be great friends. Charlotte's heart was full as she walked beside Fleur into the drawing-room. That night there was a festive dinner party at Pillars. Mother and son appeared radiantly happy in their discovery of each other, and could not stop talking. Peveril had ordered his choicest wine to be served. Toasts were drunk and speeches made. And from the walls of the beautiful, panelled room there smiled the painted faces of Sir Harry Roddney as a boy in hunting attire, and of Fleur's lovely mother in her radiant youth. Looking now at Hélène Roddney's face, Charlotte could trace a very strong resemblance to *"La Belle Hélène's"* grandson.

There was much talk about Cadlington and the old title and estates and how Dominic would at once visit his mother's lawyers and set about proving his identity and attending to the legal side of the matter.

It should all have been so splendid, so perfect, Charlotte thought as she listened and, now and again, exchanged long significant glances with Dominic. But, alas, the shadow of the unpredictable future remained to chill the warmth of her own gay spirit. Was she, she wondered, destined never to know peace of mind or respite from suffering?

To her sad question there could be no answer on that unforgettable day.

Chapter Thirty

A dark shadow hung over Clunes.

In the great kitchen, sitting at the long scrubbed wooden table which was the pride of her life, Mrs. Snook, the cook, discussed matters in a sombre way with her friend the housekeeper, Mrs. MacDougal. The other servants were busy at their work, for the master was expected home to dinner tonight.

A plump duck was roasting. Vegetables were now being prepared in the adjoining scullery. Volpo, who usually arrived before his master, had just been down to tell the staff to put the best foot forward. His lordship had weighty matters on his mind and needed a good dinner. Tomorrow he would be entertaining a large house party, but tonight he was alone. "Not very well, and going to bed early," Volpo had observed with a sly wink at Mrs. Snook.

The cook sat with her arms crossed, gossiping.

"*Not very well!* H'm! *that* means the drink again," she said with pursed lips.

"Aye, it's been a turrible time since her ladyship flitted," agreed Mrs. MacDougal.

They had discussed Charlotte's disappearance from Clunes *ad nauseam*. All the servants here felt pity for her ladyship. Those who served her had received nothing but kindness from Lady Chase. His lordship's charm was less frequently displayed and then, as a rule, only for the younger and prettier maid servants. He had many times stormed abuse at Mrs. Snook if the meal was not to his liking.

Volpo had told them that her ladyship was a wanton and had gone off with a fine gentleman in politics and that she would never be seen at Clunes again.

The two senior members of the female staff could not

believe this possible. But Volpo assured them that he had both *seen* and *heard*, and would be giving evidence for his lordship. Neither Mrs. Snook nor Mrs. MacDougal were happy about it. They were both righteous, God-fearing women who could not approve of infidelity. But her ladyship was angelic. She could *not* be guilty. They would hand in their notice. They intended to follow Gertrude—poor Gertrude who had already gone—dismissed at a moment's notice.

"I don't like what's going on here," announced Mrs. Snook with a nod and a compression of her lips, "and one person I cannot abide is that hoity-toity Nanna who has come back to torment poor Miss Eleanora."

"Aye," said the Scotswoman and sighed heavily. "That puir wee lassie. I saw her face this morning, all puffed up with crying for her Mam. It isn't Christian to treat her as his lordship is doing. They say he yelled at her and slapped her because she kept grieving for my lady. It's only natural for the bairn to do so."

"I'd like to know the ins and outs of it," said the cook. Leaning forward she whispered over her tea-cup, "Take it from me, Mrs. Mac, that slimy valet knows more than he tells *us*. But you know Emmy, that girl we had as under housemaid—the one who was fetched away by her mother because of her condition?—"

"Aye," said Mrs. MacDougal in a shocked voice. "The puir creature, Emmy, and she only sixteen."

"I warrant from what Volpo said that it was the *master!*" declared Mrs. Snook, sniffing.

"I shall be glad to get away from this place and back to ma native Scotland where there are no such carryings-on," said Mrs. MacDougal.

It was a warm spring evening, with a slight drizzle casting a veil across the beautiful gardens of Clunes. Shortly after six o'clock Vivian Chase, driven from Harling station in his brougham, entered the house. He was in a foul temper, having had several nights of drinking and gambling in London where he would have preferred to remain; but convention ruled that he must return home and be with his children. After all, he was supposed to be the sorrowing husband, left to console the abandoned little ones. He would be judged accordingly if he, too, deserted them.

Until the divorce was over and Charlotte ruined once and for all, he must, he suppose, retain an air of respectability. But he had arranged for several of his more amusing friends to come down this weekend and liven up what he called "this tombstone of a house." As soon as he was free of Charlotte, he intended to shut the place up and go abroad for a long while.

Everything got on his nerves down at Clunes. When Nanna brought the three little girls to bid him good night, he stood in front of the library fireplace, fingers locked behind his back, and looked at them with complete lack of humour or paternal warmth. He was irritated even by his pets, the golden-haired Beatrice and Victoria who kissed him prettily and prattled about their games. His brooding gaze rested on his eldest child. Heavens, what a little sight she had grown since her mother left! According to the nurse, the wretched brat never stopped weeping. Her eyes were swollen, her face was pinched and she had a furtive hang-dog look that destroyed her natural childish charm. She trembled when he spoke to her. In consequence, he bellowed and frightened her still more.

"Smile, damn you! What the devil is the matter with you? Anybody would think you were ill-treated in this house where you have everything you want, and for which mark you, miss, I pay handsomely."

The nurse stood by looking at his lordship under her drooping lids. She, herself, had lost all patience with Eleanora. At first she had tried to be kind to her because she was sorry for the child, and had stretched a point and allowed her to talk, upstairs, about her mother, which his lordship had strictly forbidden. All Eleanora could do was to beg to be allowed to go to Mama. Gradually the woman lost patience and a great deal of slapping and bullying went on.

Eleanora pressed her fingers to her lips. Her huge weary eyes scrutinized her father with a mixture of terror and defiance. She was so confused by what had happened that she could not attain any degree of peace or understanding. All her security had gone. She had been so happy with Mama. It had given her a hideous jolt when she had run gaily along to the bedroom that fatal morning and found Papa, alone.

Vivian glared at her. Now that he could no longer vent his spite on Charlotte, his ill-temper, inflamed with constant drinking and debauchery, was directed against Charlotte's best-loved daughter.

"Answer me!" he snarled at her, "Why do you not smile at me?"

She shrank back but dared to utter the words that were ever foremost in her bemused little mind.

"I want to see my Mama. When is my Mama coming home?"

The ugly colour rushed to Vivian's flabby face. He raised a hand as though to strike the innocent little girl, then let it fall.

"You will never see your Mama again! Get that into your stubborn mind and learn, also, to be agreeable to your Papa," he said in a furious voice.

Eleanora buried her face in her hands and began to sob in a terrified way. The nurse hustled the three little girls out of the library, and up the stairs.

Vivian pulled the tapestried bell. When the butler appeared, he snapped:

"Bring brandy, then send Volpo to me."

"Yes, my lord. What time would your lordship like to dine?"

"I shall not be dining at home. It depresses me," said Vivian who had in that moment decided that he would go down to Roma Gresham's house and try to find some amusement. He was beginning to pity himself and even foster a belief that he was, indeed, an outraged husband deserving sympathy and consolation. That *bitch*, Charlotte, he thought venomously, no doubt she was with her friends Fleur and Peveril Marsh, if not with her lover. As for *him* Vivian had received through his lawyers an ice-cold but telling missive from Dominic Unwin, suggesting that he intended to fight this case to the bitter end and prove both his own and Charlotte's innocence. He had added that once that was done, he would be glad to meet Lord Chase in person, and fight a duel with whatever weapons Lord Chase cared to choose.

Duel, indeed, Vivian had snorted when he read this letter. He had no intention whatsoever of indulging in a hand to hand combat with Mr. Unwin. A shot in the back was one thing, but a duel in which he, Vivian, might be the loser, was another.

That was last week. Whilst in London and at the Clubs or walking down Piccadilly, Vivian had raised his hat to several distinguished ladies and gentlemen and been put out when they looked the other way. It would seem that a great deal of sympathy was directed towards Charlotte and Mr. Unwin, which was displeasing to Vivian; it was no part of his scheme that *he* should be ostracised, rather than Charlotte and Dominic. And now had come this new excitement over Dominic's real identity—an unpleasant shock for Vivian. Dominic had made inquiries and proved to the hilt the fact that he was no foundling adopted by the Englesbys, risen to fame only through brains and wit. He was lawful son and heir of the late Baron of Cadlington and of *Fleur Marsh*, formerly widow of the Baron. As Dominic St. Cheviot, he owned a great title and vast estates all of which he was claiming.

Whichever way the wind blew, it seemed to Vivian that Charlotte might get the best of it. He had hoped to make an outcast, a divorcée, of her and ruin Mr. Unwin's career. But the career would be of secondary importance now to a gentleman possessed of an older title and bigger fortune than Vivian's own.

These facts had only been disclosed to Vivian last night and so accounted for his ugly humour this evening.

When Volpo came into the library in his stealthy way, Vivian, who had started to drink brandy, snarled at him:

"I wish to get out of my travelling attire. Have the hip bath taken to my dressing-room," he snapped. "And my dinner clothes laid out. I intend to call on an old friend."

Volpo put his tongue in his cheek. So long had he served my Lord Chase now that he knew perfectly well who the "old friend" was likely to be.

Cook was ranting and carrying on in her kitchen because the splendid meal she had prepared for his lordship was no longer wanted. Volpo, at this moment, felt scarcely more agreeable than Vivian. He had had a "few words" with his master in London yesterday, for the first time since he had entered his service. Volpo had served his master well by arranging that evening with Mr. Unwin and so helping to get rid of my lady. No other servant would have thought of such a scheme or carried it out with such cunning. And what had been his reward? Nothing so far but a miserly present of five sovereigns. Last night Volpo had suggested that he would like a little more and Vivian had told him to go to the devil.

At this moment Volpo looked moodily at his lordship. Vivian, stretched in a chair, glowered back at his valet.

"Well—what is it—what are you gaping at me for?"

Volpo cleared his throat.

"Just a slight matter of finance, my lord."

"Finance!" echoed Vivian and then flung back his head and laughed. "I see! Another request for money. You insolent fellow, are you stooping to blackmail? Is that it? Do I not pay you handsomely enough for your meagre services? Get out—run to your duties. I want my bath."

But Volpo stood his ground. He was not afraid of his master. *He knew too much.* His hot Portuguese temper could be aroused as easily as Vivian's.

"Your lordship fails to recall that without my services which he dubs 'meagre,' her ladyship would still be here to nag and annoy him. Also that—"

"Get out!" interrupted Vivian, showing his teeth.

"But my lord, I have a right to demand payment for what I have done," began Volpo indignantly. "It was a dangerous action. It still has danger attached to it. Everyone in London says Mr. Unwin is very angry and I shall be called upon to commit perjury on behalf of your lordship when the case is heard."

On normal occasions, Vivian would have seen the truth in this and behaved with more discretion; for after all Volpo was his confederate. But things were not going as he wanted, and, when Vivian was crossed, he lost all powers of reasoning. In maniacal rage he flung the glass of brandy straight at the valet's face. The hunchback ducked but not quite in time. The glass hit his forehead and shattered. The brandy splashed half blinding him. He gave a cry of pain and clapped his hands to his face.

"Get out, reptile!" shouted Vivian. "Do not let me see you again tonight or hear you mention what you have done for me. Remember only what *I* have done for *you*, you insolent Portuguese cripple!"

Silence. Volpo cowered back, whimpering, trying to

wipe his eyes with his handkerchief and to staunch a trickle of blood on his forehead. He was hurt but not badly. The true hurt was in his mind. He swung from a servile devotion to his master to burning and implacable hatred. He could see that he was not to be rewarded as he had anticipated, for services rendered to Lord Chase. Very well. Let his lordship rave, and insult him. He would live to regret it.

Vivian had not bargained with the spirited blood that ran in Volpo's veins. The hot blood of a Latin who knows the real meaning of the word *vendetta.*

The hunchback turned on his heel and walked quietly out of the library, the handkerchief held to his face. Vivian did not see him again before he left Clunes and was on his way to Roma Gresham's establishment.

The early drizzle of the day had cleared up and a glorious night followed with a full moon. After his bath, Vivian felt in a better humour. Seeing that it was so fine, he went on foot to Roma Gresham's house, walking through the grounds of his home, through the orchard and out of the little gate into those very woods wherein he had seduced young Charlotte Goff more than ten years ago.

His mind was far removed from her, however, and concentrating upon the anticipation of an amusing evening *chez* Roma; a new love, a new thrill to while away the night. He did not like to be alone, or to think too much. What little conscience he possessed had a habit of waking when he was by himself. The memory of his dead mother and his living wife returned to trouble and upbraid him. He knew himself infinitely guilty towards both.

In the moonlight, impeccably dressed in the latest fashion, a diamond pin flashing in his cravat, a cigar between his fingers, golden hair pomaded, fair moustache curled, he looked handsome and attractive. Vivian Chase at his best. Almost the romantic boy to whom little Charlotte Goff had given her heart.

He reached the gates of Mrs. Gresham's house and strolled through, unaware of the fact that he had been followed all the way from Clunes by the deformed figure of his man, Volpo. Volpo walked stealthily and silently like a cat. He kept in the shadows until the very moment that Lord Chase reached the front door of Mrs. Gresham's discreet establishment which was heavily shuttered and curtained for the night. Then the hand of vengeance struck. Under cover of the portico, Vivian reached out towards the knocker, but never touched it.

He felt a sharp and terrifying pain between his shoulder blades. He uttered a cry of pain and fear that was stifled in its birth. The cigar dropped from his fingers. He crumpled up in a heap, passing from full pulsating life into an impenetrable blackness, the anguish of sudden and violent death.

Without a backward look at the figure of the man who had called him an insolent Portuguese cripple, Volpo turned and ran out of sight. He made his way back to Clunes as quickly as he had come. Within the next few moments, wearing an apron, he was in the pantry, cleaning his lordship's shoes; making a noise, talking to the other sleepy servants so that they should notice him and be ready to swear if necessary that he had never left the house.

It was Mrs. Gresham herself who found Vivian. She had a Siamese cat which she wished to let out. As she walked out of the house she stumbled over something. With a cry of horror, she saw a man wearing evening dress and an opera cloak lying across the steps. Roma let the cat fly from her arms and set up a scream which brought her servants hurrying out to her. They turned the body over. As Roma Gresham saw the bloodless face, the dishevelled fair hair, the clenched teeth grinning hideously in the moonlight, she shrieked again.

"Oh, God, *it is Lord Chase!*"

She could see that he was dead. This was the last time he would ever come to her house to dine and wine with her "friends" (and pay handsomely for the pleasure of it!).

How he had died, she knew only when one of the servants lifted his hand and she saw that it was covered with blood. The butler muttered:

"There is a wound in his back. It looks like murder, madam."

At that, Roma Gresham foresaw appalling scandal and herself and her hideaway implicated. She would be ruined. One of the gentlemen who had been dining with her came out to see what was afoot, and was just in time to catch his hostess as she fainted dead away.

Chapter Thirty-one

Soon after nine o'clock next morning, a man on horseback galloped up to the front door of Pillars. He slid from his sweating animal and knocked loudly on the door.

Charlotte heard the knocking. She had been awake for a long time, tormented by her longings both for Eleanora and for Dominic. She, like Mrs. Marsh, usually breakfasted in bed. But on this particular day the countryside looked so beautiful, with an amber sun breaking through the mists, that Charlotte rose and dressed.

She was halfway down the staircase when Fleur's maid waylaid her and told her that Jameson, a stable boy from Clunes, had come with an urgent note for her.

Charlotte's golden eyes widened with astonishment. Her colour heightened.

"I will see him at once," she said.

She had written three days ago to Mrs. MacDougal—a short piteous note begging for news of the children.

> Now that Gertrude has left, I must rely on you to help me and to believe me that I am innocent of the accusations directed against me. Pity a mother's torn heart and send me news of my daughters. If you have the opportunity, tell Eleanora that her Mama did not desert her. With all my heart I implore you not to betray this confidence to his lordship.

There was a wild hope in Charlotte's heart that Mrs. Mac had taken pity on her and sent Jameson with a reply.

The tow-headed stable boy looked curiously at his one-time mistress, touched his forehead, and handed her the note. Charlotte's heart began to knock even before she slit open the envelope which was addressed to her in a somewhat illiterate hand.

"Mrs. Mac sent me with this," said Jameson, "I would have come earlier, my lady, but Firefly lost a shoe and I had to stop at the smithy at Epping."

Charlotte did not reply. Scanning Mrs. Mac's letter, her face went ashen. The terrible news made her feel sick. Two lines only:

> Come home at once, my lady. His lordship has been murdered.
>
> Flora MacDougal.

Charlotte, shaking from head to foot, stared at the stable boy.

"Do you know the contents of this letter?" she gasped.

"Yes, my lady, 'tis a turrible thing."

"But what happened? Tell me all you know."

"I don't know nothing, my lady, save his lordship was found wi' a knife wound in his back."

"A knife wound in his back," repeated Charlotte.

She swayed and had to catch at the lintel of the door by which she was standing.

"Merciful heavens!" she whispered.

The boy went on to say that first thing this morning, Mrs. Mac had sent a pantry-boy to rouse him, and bidden him ride his fastest to Epping. Mrs. Mac had received her ladyship's note. She knew where to find her. Last night his lordship had gone out to dine, Jameson volunteered, and the police had brought his dead body back to Clunes just before midnight. When Charlotte questioned him further, she presumed that Dr. Castleby had seen Vivian. He said that the knife had gone straight through the heart. Most of the maid servants were in hysterics. Mr. Volpo, the valet, refused to leave his master's body and had been weeping over it ever since.

Charlotte bade Jameson go through to the servants' quarters and get a meal and a glass of ale. She then rushed upstairs to Mrs. Marsh's bedroom. She threw herself beside Fleur's bed.

"Vivian is dead. He is *dead,*" she cried, breathing fast, Mrs. Mac's letter crumpled in her hands.

When Fleur discovered what had happened, she turned as pale as her friend, but in her practical way called for

Peveril to fetch brandy, for Charlotte looked ghastly. It had been a terrible shock to her.

"Keep calm, my dearest," begged Mrs. Marsh, "do not give way. Yes, Vivian is dead. Someone whom he has injured, has taken his revenge."

"But who—who could have hated him as much as that?"

"It remains to be seen."

"*I* hated him, but *murder*—the very word fills my soul with horror."

"You must go at once to Clunes, to your children," said Fleur. "I will send a message to my coachman. He shall take you."

Charlotte stood up. Some of the colour returned to her cheeks.

"Yes, I must go to my children," she breathed.

Mingling with the sense of shock and dismay came a sense of overwhelming relief. *Vivian was dead.* She was free. Without divorce, or any act of law, she had been set free from the tyrant who had tried so monstrously to destroy her life's happiness.

She could go back to Clunes—*to Eleanora.* There would be no one to stop her. Unhampered, she could deliver her poor daughter from that dreadful nurse and restore her childish faith. Unhampered, she could seek to control Beatrice and Victoria, too; and, with God's help, mould their little characters into a rightful way of life, as Vivian would never have done. She was free—*free to love Dominic.*

The reaction was almost too much for Charlotte. She flung herself into her friend's arms, and the two women wept together.

Stroking Charlotte's head, Fleur whispered:

"I will write at once to my son and bid him come here to see you. Do what has to be done at Clunes, and after the funeral return to Pillars. Bring your little girls with you. I know a nurse in the village who is kind and devoted and who will look after them."

Charlotte kissed one of Fleur's frail hands. She loved Fleur Marsh more than ever, for was she not Dominic's own mother?

"You can be sure I shall come back as soon as I can for

this is more truly my home than Clunes has ever been," she said.

But there was much to be gone through before a new day could obliterate the black night of Charlotte Chase's long martyrdom.

She reached her house on this ironically lovely morning and found the beautiful house that Eleanor, Lady Chase, had loved so much under a sinister shadow. The master of Clunes was laid out in his bedroom, still and rigid under a white sheet. The blinds were down at all the windows. Except for the sound of weeping and whispering as the staff tip-toed around, there was silence. The silence of death.

Charlotte's first action was to fling off her bonnet and coat and run straight upstairs to the nurseries.

"Eleanora," she whispered, "*Eleanora!*"

Nurse had gone. According to Mrs. Mac who had taken charge here in her sensible Scots fashion, the woman as soon as she knew his lordship was dead, had abandoned her charges and taken the first train from Harling. A young nursery maid remained in charge of the three little girls.

Eleanora was in bed with a slight fever. Beatrice and Victoria had gone out with the nursemaid to pick wild flowers.

"Best to get them away from the house, your ladyship," Mrs. Mac observed.

"Thank you," said Charlotte in a strangled voice, "and thank you for all you have done for me. You shall be rewarded."

Mrs. Mac bobbed.

"I am sure we are all pleased to see your ladyship back," she said and dabbed at her eyes.

A cry rose from Eleanora's little bed as she saw the beautiful, pale-faced woman who ran across the big bedroom towards her.

"Mama! Mama!" the child cried in a frenzied voice and held out her arms.

"My darling! Oh, Ellie, my *darling!*" said Charlotte, and gathered the slight white-robed body to her heart. For a long time mother and daughter wept together. At last Eleanora said:

"I have been so miserable. Please, please, dearest Mama, never leave me again."

"Pray God I shall never have to," sighed Charlotte and laid a cool hand on the little girl's hot forehead.

Eleanora echoed the sigh.

"Now I will eat my dinner," she said. "My food kept sticking in my throat at mealtimes, Mama, and made me sick, and Nanna and Papa were cross. But today I will eat lots and lots because my own dear Mama is home again."

Mrs. Mac wiped a corner of her eye again with her frilly apron and went downstairs to tell Mrs. Snook that she had never witnessed a more affecting scene.

"And if my lady is guilty as a wife and mother, I'll eat my hat!" she exclaimed.

The two servants fell to gossiping in their usual way. Rumours were already spreading through the district that his lordship had met his death in a house of ill repute actually down *here*, in Harling.

"Serve him right," they said, "it was what he deserved." "Poor Mr. Volpo," they said. "Nobody liked him, but he seems in a bad way, so upset about his master."

Poor Mr. Volpo, had they but known it, was not so much upset as frightened. He had killed Lord Chase in a mad fit of rage. When the local police first questioned him, he had felt that he carried things off quite smoothly, and that nobody suspected that it was he who had stabbed his master. But there were gentlemen from Scotland Yard on their way down from London to investigate, and of them Volpo was a little more apprehensive.

He had buried the knife with which he had stabbed Vivian in the woods between here and Mrs. Gresham's house. He did not think it possible that he could be convicted but the Portuguese was at heart a coward. He swung from hatred to remorse. Some of the tears which he had shed in his lordship's bedroom by the side of the poor corpse had been genuine. For the most part he remained locked in his bedroom. Servants passing by, heard him alternately moaning and uttering prayers in his native Portuguese.

Came the moment when Charlotte had to stand beside Vivian's bed, which she did, leaning heavily on the arm of Dr. Castleby.

"He is at peace," muttered the old doctor.

At peace, thought Charlotte; yes, he who wrecked the peace in this house for me and for our first child. And God alone knows how many others he hurt.

At peace, foully murdered, yet now, how strangely young he looked! It was almost the Vivian whom she had first married. Thinned and spiritualized by death were those bloated features. The eyes were closed. The lips bore a slightly ironic smile as though Vivian Chase had found at last the answer to the riddle of the universe. He looked handsome and proud in death as a Chase should, Charlotte brooded. One of the women who had laid him out had put a posy of flowers between his folded hands. "*He makes a beautiful corpse*," they said. But Charlotte saw no beauty in him, neither did his dead body soften her heart or draw from her a single tear. She knew only bitterness and that loathing for him in death that his terrible cruelties had aroused in her while he was alive. She could not forgive him—*yet*. She had put on the black garments and weeds of widowhood. The sunlight was shut out from this house; but Charlotte was no hypocrite. She could not mourn such a husband's passing. Her own torments she might have forgiven, but not Eleanora's.

As Dr. Castleby led her out of the death chamber, he said:

"It is to be hoped that Scotland Yard will find the murderer. It must have been somebody after money, although Lord Chase's wallet was found untouched, which is curious. Presumably the assassin was disturbed at his deed and fled."

Charlotte passed a handkerchief over her lips. She and the doctor were in the library now. On the desk were all the documents which she must hand over and sign, once the family solicitors arrived. She could see that there was much to be done. The doctor inquired anxiously after her health and suggested that she should go to bed; but Charlotte answered that she was well and able to perform her duties. Soon there would be an inspection by the London police who would take over the criminal investigations. Later, the funeral arrangements. No one of Vivian's relatives was left to mourn him except one of his old great aunts who was well over ninety-five and senile.

Dr. Castleby who had seen Charlotte through the births of all her daughters and the many illnesses in this house marvelled now at her coolness and composure.

He said nothing, but in his heart the old doctor was profoundly glad that my Lord Chase had died—even in so violent a manner. Lady Chase, poor pretty young thing, had had more than her share of suffering—and well Castleby knew it.

Late that afternoon Charlotte faced the Chief Inspector from the Criminal Investigation Department of Scotland Yard. He was soon satisfied that Lady Chase had nothing to do with the crime and had been staying at Epping at the time.

"We offer our deepest respect and sympathy, my lady," the chief inspector told her.

Charlotte moved into another wing of the house, taking her three daughters and the nursemaid with her. The little girls were too young to know what had taken place. They played happily in their room, or out in the gardens.

Over Eleanora had come a marked and rapid change. Her temperature fell. She lost her expression of strain and fear, but could scarcely bear to let her darling Mama out of her sight.

Charlotte bade her be good and read her books, or play card-games with her sisters who were behaving with greater friendliness now that Papa was not here to influence them against Eleanora.

Charlotte looked at the faces of the little girls and then away again. Beatrice's eyes were the turquoise blue of *his*. Charlotte reflected, *"I will have to train myself to forget the resemblance, and to love poor Beatrice and Victoria, as I do Eleanora."*

It was some time before suspicion turned upon Vivian's personal servant. Volpo tried to answer the Chief Inspector's repeated questions with nonchalance, and failed. Finally he began to tremble and cry and dropped down in a kind of seizure. They carried him to his room. The detectives, discussing the matter with Lady Chase, suggested that it might well be the hand of a Latin rather than an Englishman that had plunged the fatal knife between his lordship's shoulder blades. When the *post morten* was carried out, it became obvious that he wound was caused by a long sharp kind of blade resembling a *stiletto*. The weapon was missing but the police were out with the dogs, continually and carefully examining every step of the pathway that led between Clunes and Mrs. Gresham's house.

Investigations were carried out at Roma Gresham's establishment, but it was decided that nobody there was guilty of the crime. The crime, in the Inspector's opinion, had been committed by one at Clunes who knew his lordship's intentions to visit that house, and had followed him. *Who else but his personal valet*, whose answers were so wild and unsatisfactory?

"Volpo was devoted to my husband—" began Charlotte.

The Inspector interrupted her.

True, Mr. Volpo was devoted but it must also be remembered that her ladyship had, in confidence, told the detectives that Mr. Volpo had plotted with his lordship to give false evidence about her own conduct. Was it not possible if this was a fact, that his lordship and Mr. Volpo might have fallen out over the question of money? Unsuccessful blackmail might, indeed, be the cause of the crime.

Before darkness fell upon Clunes, the Inspector had proved his point.

Charlotte had gone to lie down in a room shared with her beloved eldest child. Exhausted and overcome by the horror of the whole proceedings she tried to sleep and failed.

Vivian's body had been removed from Clunes. That had been a relief to her. This evening the former master of the house lay in a coffin covered with purple velvet drapes in the little church at Harling. She could not stop thinking about it. Of the horror of sudden and violent death. Somehow her mind would keep reverting to that day, years ago, when Vivian had been taken into the same church with a wound in his head, and imagined that he saw his own coffin there. Strange that it should have come to pass just as he visualized it.

Between her hands, Charlotte held a letter which she had received earlier in the day from the man who was now Lord St. Cheviot.

Beloved Charlotte,

Tomorrow, I travel to Pillars in order to be near you if you need me. At last a ray of light shines through the darkness. The hope that when these fearful days are over, you will come to me and allow me to take care of you for ever.

I love and revere you. I am with you in my heart and spirit during your present ordeal.

With my most tender affection,

Your Dominic.

Charlotte kissed this letter and mused about Dominic and his future. She was still too dazed to think clearly about her own. But it was good to know that Dominic with all his chivalry, his idealistic love, awaited her. And, whereas at one time she would have been shocked by the thought of his abandoning his political career as he now firmly declared he would do, she realized that now, as the Baron of Cadlington, there would be other important work for him to do—his own estates in Buckinghamshire to be put in order and a new house to be built out of the ruins of Cadlington Hall, once his ancestral home.

It was six o'clock in the evening when one of the maids knocked on Lady Chase's door and told her that the Chief Inspector wished urgently to see her in the morning-room.

Very pale and spent, she went downstairs where the Inspector stood talking to two policemen in plain clothes. Then Charlotte saw the familiar hunch-backed figure of Vivian's valet. He was crouched in a chair, his head in his hands. His wrists were manacled.

Charlotte uttered a cry. Volpo raised his head. His face was ghastly, yellowish in hue, sweating. His black eyes rolled at her. He fell upon the floor, and grovelled at her feet.

"My lady, my lady, forgive me, intercede for me, do not let them hang me!" he babbled, obviously in a state of wild terror.

Charlotte recoiled as he caught at her black skirts.

"What is this?" she demanded.

The Chief Inspector informed her that they had just arrested Volpo for the murder of her husband. Right from the start, after his first investigation, the detective had suspected the Portuguese. Volpo had not been very clever in his efforts to conceal his crime. Two glaring clues led to his final arrest. A pair of shoes belonging to him, and found in his room, were still damp; with wet leaves similar to those strewing the pathway through the woods, clinging to the soles.

Then, an hour ago, one of the police dogs had picked up the scent and led them to the dagger which the Portuguese had buried in those same woods. On the blade they had found not only traces of blood, but Volpo's initials. It was an Italian-type stiletto. It had been identified as belonging to him. Several of the other manservants at Clunes had often seen it in Volpo's possession.

All was easy after that. At first the valet attempted to make denials, but finally broke down and confessed to the crime.

While the Inspector took down notes, Volpo croaked out the whole story, adding his personal reasons for the murder.

So at last, Charlotte, white and silent, heard of the infamous pact he had made with Vivian to ruin her. The note that Charlotte was supposed to have sent, had been written by *Volpo* himself. She was told the whole sordid story.

"I will confess it to the judge," babbled Volpo, "but do not let them hang me, my lady. You are good and kind. His lordship was out of his mind—stark raving mad. He tortured you, I will swear to it, if you will only ask them to spare my life."

But Charlotte hid her face in her hands and could not answer. It was all too terrible. They took Volpo away. She was left alone and soon a great calm seemed to descend upon her—and Clunes. A sense of thankfulness. The full circle had come round. Not only was she free from Vivian, but Dominic's good name—and her own—would be cleared.

Tomorrow, Volpo would be charged in court with the murder of his master. His confession would be read. The newspapers would blazen forth the facts, and not a soul in London but would soon know that Lord St. Cheviot and Charlotte Chase were guiltless, victims of a madman's desire for revenge and a servant's treachery.

For a long time after the detectives had left Clunes, Charlotte sat alone in the morning-room, thinking—trying to reorientate her emotions—to believe that she was indeed freed from evil, liberated from pain.

Beside the fireplace there hung a miniature of Vivian's mother as a girl, with curls falling upon a snowy bosom and large eyes shining. Charlotte gazed at it. Involuntarily, she thought: *"Eleanora will look like that when she is sixteen—"* And she whispered:

"Dearest Lady Chase, the only mother I ever knew, maybe in your spirit world you have already received the soul of your erring son. Maybe your tears, your prayers, will save him from eternal damnation. Who is to know? But this I promise you—that the Clunes which you love shall not be allowed to go to rack and ruin. That your grandchildren shall learn to laugh and dance here. The old title is extinct but *your* graciousness, *your* tenderness, we will all remember. Vivian, poor madman, we must learn to forget!—"

Somebody knocked on the door. As Charlotte said, "Come in," a little crowd of her servants, headed by Mrs. MacDougal, filed in. They stood there. Mrs. Snook, the cook, looking red and anxious. The butler—Lucy the housemaid—and other familiar faces. They formed a little circle around her. One by one they bowed or bobbed. Then Mrs. MacDougal, with her soft Scots burr, said:

"Begging your pardon, my lady, we have all come to offer our sincere condolences in your ladyship's grief and —*ahem*"—she coughed—"we know now about Mr. Volpo's confession, my lady. We want, one and all, to state our righteous indignation at the undeserved misery which his wickedness caused our kind and gentle mistress."

Mrs. Mac broke off with another cough. The servants nodded at each other and smiled at Charlotte. She sat before them looking very white and shadowy-eyed and a little dazed. All strength, all buoyancy, seemed to have left her. She was obviously so deeply moved that she could not speak for a moment. Two tears gathered in her eyes. In a strangled voice she said:

"I thank you all—from the bottom of my heart."

They tip-toed out of the morning-room again, as though they wished to leave her undisturbed.

"That is one of the nicest things that has ever happened to me," Charlotte whispered to herself.

But that apology from the staff, the awkward but kindly suggestion that all was now understood, and that her name had been completely cleared, was only the beginning of others. Letters of understanding, of condolence, couched in conventional terms and hinting secret sympathy, poured into Clunes from all parts of England. The hand of friendship was rapidly extended to Lord Chase's widow and to the new Lord St. Cheviot. In itself, the discovery of the Baron was one of the most romantic and dramatic events that had taken place for a long time. The full story of the boy whom the Englesbys had adopted, swept like wild-fire through the country.

Within a few short weeks, Dominic St. Cheviot and Charlotte Chase became hero and heroine of a tremendously stirring drama. Those who had not bothered before hastened to call at Clunes, to send flowers, and drop cards, and issue invitations. But Charlotte's one wish was to get away—to hide from the world. There were only a few letters of sympathy and friendship which she really valued. One was from Dominic's adoptive mother, the fine old lady who had not long to live. She wrote to Charlotte immediately after Vivian Chase had been laid to rest in the family crypt at Harling.

> I know all from Dominic, and of his high regard for you. You must have suffered very greatly, my poor child. There is not much time left to me—but perhaps if I last awhile longer Dominic will bring you down to Englesby Castle. I know that he loves you and I would like to look upon your face before I die.
>
> Dominic has been as dear to me in this life as my own son. The affection between us is not changed by the knowledge that his own mother still lives. But the Marquess and I both are glad that his true name and rightful heritage have been restored to him.

Charlotte showed that letter to Dominic about a month after Vivian's funeral. They were sitting together in the drawing-room at Pillars.

Clunes was shut. Charlotte and her children had come to

stay with Dominic's mother. Later they intended to take a house at Trouville where the children would get sea-air, and Charlotte a complete change. Fleur and Peveril were going with them—their first holiday away from their beloved Pillars for many long years. Fleur's physician had said that it would do neither of them any harm. They both suffered from a rheumatic condition and it would be beneficial for them to get away from the low-lying Essex country.

Dominic would, of course, go over to France to see them. But most of his time must be spent in Buckinghamshire. There was a number of legal formalities to go through connected with the late Baron's possessions. Dominic was engrossed now in the business side of his inheritance. He had put politics completely behind him.

"All I want," he said, "is to make the new Cadlington a home worthy of you and the three little girls who are to be my stepdaughters."

This morning, as Dominic read his adoptive mother's letter to Charlotte, he felt a pleasurable thrill. The shadows were, indeed, lifting. There seemed no barrier now to the greatest joy of all—his marriage with Charlotte. She stood by one of the tall windows with the sunlight falling upon her, looking a little thinner and older in her black dress which was relieved only by a white frill at her throat and wrists. But there was peace in her eyes, those lovely eyes in which, far too often, he had read fathomless sorrow.

"Shall you come with me to Englesby before you go to Trouville?" he asked her.

She looked up at the fine face of the man whom she worshipped.

"I would like to, Dom."

She often used this foreshortening of his name now. It reminded him, he told her laughingly, of his boyhood. They always called him "Dom" at Englesby.

She held out both hands to him. He took them fast.

"Sometimes I wake up and ask myself if it is true that life can have changed for me so blissfully," she said. "Am I really that same Charlotte who dared not speak your name—who hardly dared think of you?"

He put his lips against the slender fingers, kissing each one in turn.

"My dearest, try to feel as I do that your past life was a

nightmare, and that like all nightmares, it has vanished upon awakening, and will never return."

They stood a moment with their arms about each other. Through the window Charlotte could see her three little girls playing croquet with Gertrude—dear devoted Gertrude who had rushed most willingly back to serve her mistress.

Since Vivian's death, Eleanora had put on weight. How well she looked, thought the mother. And it was a great joy to her to see, also, that her two younger children were gradually thawing in the sunshine and warmth of the love she extended to them. They were learning not to snap and quarrel or look at life in the cold, self-seeking fashion their Papa and former nurse had encouraged. Today, it was not only Eleanora, but also Beatrice and Victoria who called eagerly for "Mama" and ran to her loving arms.

Dominic said:

"It is a beautiful day, my dearest. Shall I drive you and the children to the forest for a picnic. Would you like that?"

Charlotte laughed. He liked to hear Charlotte laugh—it was a new and delightful habit she was forming.

"I haven't had a picnic for so very long. I think it's a charming idea," she said.

Fleur opened the drawing-room door and put in her pretty head.

"My dears, Peveril is taking me for a turn down by the lake. Is there anything you want?"

Dominic, still holding Charlotte's hand, turned to her.

"Nothing, Mother, we are planning a picnic with the children because the sun is so warm and it will do them all good to be out."

"Splendid," said Fleur. "I will call Gertrude and tell her."

And the beautiful little old lady went out smiling, well satisfied. She felt that she had never seen a happier and more handsome couple than her wonderful son and his future wife.

Yet again, she thought, fortune was smiling upon Pillars. Here, her own parents Hélène and Harry Roddney had lived and loved. Here, she, Fleur, with her dear Peveril had reached the fulfilment of her dreams. And now the third generation—Dominic, her son—and Charlotte Chase were soon to solve the problem of life together.

"God is good," said Fleur Marsh as she walked slowly out upon the velvety lawn to join the children. They rushed eagerly towards her. Already they were beginning to feel that she was, virtually, their grandmother.

Once Fleur had thought she needed no happiness save that which she had gained with her husband. But now she had her son. And she could see into the not too distant future when she would also have a lovely and devoted daughter-in-law.

"God is good," said Fleur Marsh again, and opened her arms to receive Charlotte's three little girls.

She was all things to two men.

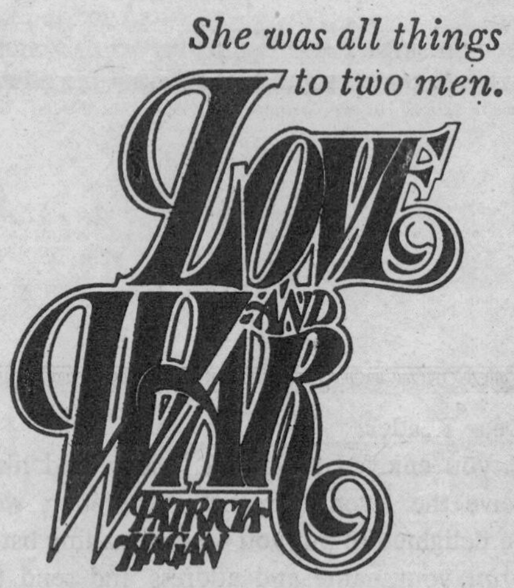

Across a landscape consumed by the scorching emotions of Civil War, comes an epic tale of love and conflict, desire and hate, of beautiful, rebellious Katherine Wright who was abducted, ravished, and torn between two men:

Nathan Collins, the Rebel, who dreamed of making Katherine his wife, but would never accept her craving for a life of her own.

Travis Coltrane, the Yankee, who made her wild with fury one moment, and delirious with passion the next.

Two loyalties. Two loves. One triumphant saga that rips across war-torn lands and the embattled terrains of the heart!

Avon 37960 $2.25 LW 6-78